Orbitsvill

Racing from the certain vengeance of Earth's tyrant ruler, space captain Vance Garamond flees the Solar System. And discovers the almost unimaginably vast spherical structure soon to become famous as 'Orbitsville' – a new home for Earth's huddled masses.

A Wreath of Stars

Thornton's Planet is an anti-neutrino planet detected on its approach to Earth. It can be seen only through the newly developed magniluct lenses and its arrival causes a wave of panic. When its course carries it past the Earth, interest in Thornton's Planet wanes. But the visit of Thornton's Planet has had effects on Earth further-ranging than anyone could have imagined.

The Ragged Astronauts

Land and Overland – twin worlds a few thousand miles apart. On Land, humanity faces a threat to its very survival – an airborne species, the ptertha, has declared war on humankind, and is actively hunting for victims. The only hope lies in migration. Through space to Overland. By balloon.

Also by Bob Shaw

Orbitsville
Orbitsville (1975)
Orbitsville Departure (1983)
Orbitsville Judgement (1990)

Warren Peace
Who Goes Here? (1977)
Warren Peace: Dimensions (1993)

Land and Overland
The Ragged Astronauts (1986)
The Wooden Spaceships (1987)
The Fugitive Worlds (1989)

Other Novels
Night Walk (1967)
The Two-Timers (1968)
The Palace Of Eternity (1969)
One Million Tomorrows (1970)
The Shadow of Heaven (1970, rev 1991))
The Peace Machine (aka Ground Zero Man) (1971)
Other Days, Other Eyes (1972)
A Wreath of Stars (1976)
Medusa's Children (1977)
Ship of Strangers (1978)
Vertigo (aka Terminal Velocity) (1978)
Dagger of the Mind (1979)
The Ceres Solution (1981)
Fire Pattern (1984)
Killer Planet (1989)

Collections
Tomorrow Lies In Ambush (1973)
Cosmic Kaleidoscope (1976)
A Better Mantrap (1982)

Bob Shaw
SF GATEWAY OMNIBUS

ORBITSVILLE
A WREATH OF STARS
THE RAGGED ASTRONAUTS

GOLLANCZ
LONDON

First published in Great Britain in 2013 by Gollancz
An imprint of the Orion Publishing Group
Orion House, 5 Upper St Martin's Lane,
London WC2H 9EA

An Hachette UK Company

A CIP catalogue record for this book is available
from the British Library

ISBN 978 0 575 11120 2

1 3 5 7 9 10 8 6 4 2

Typeset by Input Data Services Ltd, Bridgwater, Somerset

Printed and bound by CPI Group (UK) Ltd, Croydon, CR0 4YY

The Orion Publishing Group's policy is to use papers
that are natural, renewable and recyclable products and
made from wood grown in sustainable forests. The logging
and manufacturing processes are expected to conform to
the environmental regulations of the country of origin.

www.orionbooks.co.uk
www.gollancz.co.uk

CONTENTS

ENTER THE SF GATEWAY . . .

Towards the end of 2011, in conjunction with the celebration of fifty years of coherent, continuous science fiction and fantasy publishing, Gollancz launched the SF Gateway.

Over a decade after launching the landmark SF Masterworks series, we realised that the realities of commercial publishing are such that even the Masterworks could only ever scratch the surface of an author's career. Vast troves of classic SF & Fantasy were almost certainly destined never again to see print. Until very recently, this meant that anyone interested in reading any of those books would have been confined to scouring second-hand bookshops. The advent of digital publishing changed that paradigm for ever.

Embracing the future even as we honour the past, Gollancz launched the SF Gateway with a view to utilising the technology that now exists to make available, for the first time, the entire backlists of an incredibly wide range of classic and modern SF and fantasy authors. Our plan, at its simplest, was – and still is! – to use this technology to build on the success of the SF and Fantasy Masterworks series and to go even further.

The SF Gateway was designed to be the new home of classic Science Fiction & Fantasy – the most comprehensive electronic library of classic SFF titles ever assembled. The programme has been extremely well received and we've been very happy with the results. So happy, in fact, that we've decided to complete the circle and return a selection of our titles to print, in these omnibus editions.

We hope you enjoy this selection. And we hope that you'll want to explore more of the classic SF and fantasy we have available. These are wonderful books you're holding in your hand, but you'll find much, much more . . . through the SF Gateway.

www.sfgateway.com

INTRODUCTION

from The Encyclopedia of Science Fiction

Bob Shaw was the working name of Northern Irish writer Robert Shaw (1931–1996). He worked in structural engineering until the age of twenty-seven, then aircraft design, then industrial public relations and journalism, becoming a full-time author in 1975. Shaw was early involved in sf FANDOM, his first book being *The Enchanted Duplicator* (**1954**) with Walt WILLIS, an allegory of fan and FANZINE activities, and he received HUGOS in 1979 and 1980 for his fan writing. Shaw published his first professional story, 'Aspect', with NEBULA SCIENCE FICTION in August 1954; during the mid-1950s he contributed several more stories to that magazine and one to AUTHENTIC SCIENCE FICTION before ceasing to write for some years. After a strong 'come-back' tale – '… And Isles Where Good Men Lie' (1965 NEW WORLDS) – he published 'Light of Other Days' (1966 ANALOG), which established his reputation as a writer of remarkable ingenuity. Built around the intriguing concept of SLOW GLASS, a kind of TIME VIEWER through which light can take years to travel – thus allowing people to view scenes from the past – this story remains his best known. He later incorporated it, together with two thematically-related examinations of the theme, into *Other Days, Other Eyes* (**1974**).

Shaw's first novel was *Night Walk* (**1967**), a fast-moving chase story. A man who has been blinded and condemned to a penal colony on a far planet invents a device that enables him to see through other people's and even animals' eyes, and thus manages to escape. *The Two-Timers* (**1968**), a well written tale of PARALLEL WORLDS, DOPPELGANGERS and murder, demonstrates Shaw's ability to handle characterization and, in particular, his talent for realistic dialogue. In *The Palace of Eternity* (**1969**) he still more impressively controls a wide canvas featuring interstellar warfare, the environmental degradation of an Edenic planet, and human TRANSCENDENCE; the central section of the novel, where the hero finds himself reincarnated as an 'Egon' or soul-like entity, displeased some critics, though it is in fact an effective handling of a traditional sf displacement of ideas from METAPHYSICS or RELIGION. This intelligent reworking of well worn sf topoi was from the first Shaw's forte, as was demonstrated in his next novel, *One Million Tomorrows* (**1970**), an IMMORTALITY tale whose twist lies in the fact that the option of eternal youth entails sexual impotence.

All Shaw's early books – which include also *Shadow of Heaven* (**1969**), involving ANTIGRAVITY, and *Ground Zero Man* (**1971**; revised as *The Peace Machine* **1985**) – were published first (and sometimes solely) in the USA; and their efficient anonymity of venue may result from a highly competent attempt to appeal to a transatlantic audience. Only slowly did Shaw come to write tales whose placement and protagonists were distinctly UK in feel; and it could be argued, sadly, that his best work was his most impersonal. The fine first volume of the **Orbitsville** sequence – comprising *Orbitsville* (**1975**), *Orbitsville Departure* (**1983**) and *Orbitsville Judgement* (**1990**) – can almost certainly stand, after *Other Days, Other Eyes,* as his finest inspiration. Like Larry NIVEN'S *Ringworld* (**1970**) and Arthur C. CLARKE'S *Rendezvous with Rama* (**1973**), the **Orbitsville** books centre on the discovery of – and later developments within – a vast alien artefact in space, in this case a DYSON SPHERE. Within the living-space provided by the inner surface of this artificial shell – billions of times the surface area of the Earth – Shaw spins an exciting story of political intrigue and exploration, which in later volumes develops, perhaps revealing an undue impatience with the venue he had invented, into a heavily plotted move into another universe entirely. *Orbitsville* gained a 1976 BSFA AWARD.

A Wreath of Stars (**1976**) may be Shaw's most original, and perhaps his finest, singleton. A rogue planet, composed entirely of antineutrino matter approaches the Earth. It passes nearby with no immediately discernible effect. However, it is soon discovered that an antineutrino 'Earth' exists within our planet whose orbit has been seriously perturbed by the passage of the interloper. This is an ingenious, almost a poetic, idea, to which the plot only just fails to do full justice. Other books followed quickly: the overcomplicated *Medusa's Children* (**1977**); the **Warren Peace** sequence – comprising the successfully comic *Who Goes Here?* (**1977**) and its disappointing sequel *Warren Peace* (**1993**) – both being *jeux d'esprit* akin to Harry HARRISON'S *Bill, the Galactic Hero* (**1965**), and suffering, as did Harrison's sequence, from rapidly diminishing inspiration; *Ship of Strangers* (**1978**), an homage to A. E. VAN VOGT in which the crew of the Stellar Survey Ship *Sarafand,* after some routine adventures, confront a striking COSMOLOGICAL issue; *Vertigo* (**1978**), an effective *policier* set in a world transformed by ANTIGRAVITY devices allowing personal flight; plus *Dagger of the Mind* (**1979**) and *The Ceres Solution* (**1981**), in both of which Shaw's ingenuity declined, for a period, into something close to jumble. He had meanwhile been writing short stories – his collections include *Tomorrow Lies in Ambush* (**1973**), *Cosmic Kaleidoscope* (**1976**), *A Better Mantrap* (**1982**), *Between Two Worlds* (**1986**) and *Dark Night in Toyland*

(1989) – which again demonstrate his professional skills but tend to lack a sense of commitment, to the point that some later stories seemed strained, frivolous, anecdotal.

However, with the **Ragged Astronauts** sequence – *The Ragged Astronauts* **(1986)**, *The Wooden Spaceships* **(1988)** and *The Fugitive Worlds* **(1989)** – Shaw returned to his very best and most inventive form, creating an ALTERNATE COSMOS which allowed him to describe with joyful exactness the sensation of emigrating, via hot-air Balloon, up the hourglass funnel of atmosphere that connects two planets which orbit each other. After his pattern, later volumes lose some of the freshness and elation of the first, but the series as a whole emphasizes Shaw's genuine stature in the genre as an entertainer who rarely failed to thrill the mind's eye with a new prospect. At his best, Shaw was an ingenious fabricator and lover of the worlds of sf.

For a more detailed version of the above, see Bob Shaw's author entry in *The Encyclopedia of Science Fiction*: http://sf-encyclopedia.com/entry/shaw_bob

Some terms above are capitalised when they would not normally be so rendered; this indicates that the terms represent discrete entries in *The Encyclopedia of Science Fiction*.

ORBITSVILLE

CHAPTER ONE

The President was called Elizabeth, and it was thought by some that the mere coincidence of name had had a profound influence on her life-style. Certainly, she had – since the death of her father – made Starflight House into something which more resembled an historic royal court than the headquarters of a business enterprise. There was a suggestion of neo-Elizabethan ritual, of palace intrigue, of privilege and precedence about the way she ran her trillion-dollar empire. And the touch of antiquity which annoyed Garamond the most – although probably only because it was the one which affected him most – was her insistence on personal interviews with ship commanders before their exploratory missions.

He leaned on a carved stone balustrade and stared, with non-committal grey eyes, at the tiers of descending heated gardens which reached to the Atlantic Ocean four kilometres away. Starflight House capped what had once been a moderate-sized Icelandic hill; now the original contours were completely hidden under a frosting of loggias, terraces and pavilions. From the air it reminded Garamond of a gigantic, vulgar cake. He had been waiting almost two hours, time he would have preferred to spend with his wife and child, and there had been nothing to do but sip pale green drinks and fight to control his dangerous impatience with Elizabeth.

As a successful flickerwing captain he had been in her presence several times, and so his distaste for her was personified, physical. It influenced his attitude more pervasively than did his intellectual unease over the fact that she was the richest person who had ever lived, and so far above the law that she had been known to kill out of sheer petulance. Was it, he had often wondered, because she had the mind of a man that she chose to be an unattractive woman in an age when cosmetic surgery could correct all but the most gross physical defects? Were her splayed, imperfect teeth and pallid skin the insignia of total authority?

And as he watched the coloured fountains glitter in the stepped perspectives below, Garamond remembered his first visit to Starflight House. He had been about to undertake his third mission command and was still young enough to be self-conscious about the theatrical black uniform. The knowledge that he was entering the special relationship reputed to exist between President Lindstrom and her captains had made him taut and apprehensive, keyed up to meet any demand on his resourcefulness. But nobody in Fleet Command, nor in Admincom, had warned him in advance that Elizabeth gave off a sweet, soupy odour which closed the throat when one was most anxious to speak clearly.

None of his advisers on Starflight House protocol had given him a single clue which would have helped a young man, who had never seen anything but perfection in a female, to conceal his natural reaction to the President. Among his confused impressions, the predominant one had been of an abnormally curved spine at the lower end of which was slung a round, puffy abdomen like that of an insect. Garamond, frozen to attention, had avoided her eyes when she nuzzled the satin cushion of gut against his knuckles during her prolonged formal inspection of his appearance.

As he leaned on the artificially weathered balustrade, he could recall emerging from that first interview with a cool resentment towards the older captains who had told him none of the things which really mattered in personal dealings with the President; and yet – when his own turn came – he had allowed other raw Starflight commanders to go unprepared to the same inauguration. It had been easy to justify his inaction when he considered the possible consequences of explaining to a new captain that the coveted special relationship would involve him in exchanging looks of secret appreciation with Liz Lindstrom when – in the middle of a crowded Admincom flight briefing – she handed him a scrap of paper upon which she, the richest and most powerful human being in the universe, had printed a childish dirty joke. If the time for suicide ever came, Garamond decided, he would choose an easier and pleasanter way ...

'Captain Garamond,' a man's voice said from close behind him. 'The President sends her compliments.'

Garamond turned and saw the tall, stooped figure of Vice-President Humboldt crossing the terrace towards him. Holding Humboldt's hand was a child of about nine, a sturdy silver-haired boy dressed in pearlized cords. Garamond recognized him as the President's son, Harald, and he nodded silently. The boy nodded in return, his eyes flickering over Garamond's badges and service ribbons.

'I'm sorry you have been kept waiting so long, Captain.' Humboldt cleared his throat delicately to indicate that this was as far as he could go towards expressing views which were not those of Elizabeth. 'Unfortunately, the President cannot disengage from her present commitment for another two hours. She requests you to wait.'

'Then I'll have to wait.' Garamond shrugged and smiled to mask his impatience, even though the tachyonic reports from the weather stations beyond Pluto had predicted that the favourable, ion-rich tide which was sweeping through the Solar System would shortly ebb. He had planned to sail on that tide and boost his ship to lightspeed in the shortest possible time. Now it looked as though he would have to labour up the long gravity slope from Sol with his ship's electromagnetic wings sweeping the vacuum for a meagre harvest of reaction mass.

'Yes. You'll have to wait.'

'Of course, I could always leave – and see the President when I get back.'

Humboldt smiled faintly in appreciation of the joke and glanced down at Harald, making sure the boy's attention was elsewhere before he replied. 'That would never do. I am sure Liz would be so disappointed that she would send a fast ship to bring you back for a special interview.'

'Then I won't put her to that inconvenience,' Garamond said. He knew they had both been referring to a certain Captain Witsch, a headstrong youngster who had grown restless after waiting two days in Starflight House and had taken off quietly at night without Elizabeth's blessing. He had been brought back in a high-speed interceptor, and his interview with the President must have been a very special one, because no trace of his body had ever been found. Garamond had no way of knowing how apocryphal the story might be – the Starflight fleet which siphoned off Earth's excess population was so huge that one captain could never know all the others – but it was illustrative of certain realities.

'There is a compensation for you, Captain.' Humboldt placed one of his pink-scrubbed hands on Harald's silver head. 'Harald has been showing a renewed interest in the flickerwing fleet lately and has been asking questions on subjects which loosely come under the heading of spaceflight theory and practice. Liz wants you to talk to him about it.'

Garamond looked doubtfully at the boy whose attention seemed absorbed by a group of metal statues further along the terrace. 'Has he any flair for mathematics?'

'He isn't expected to qualify for a master's papers this afternoon.' Humboldt laughed drily. 'Simply encourage his interest, Captain. I know admirals who would give their right arms for such a public token of the President's trust. Now I must return to the board-room.'

'You're leaving me alone with him?'

'Yes – Liz has a high regard for you, Captain Garamond. Is it the responsibility ...?'

'No. I've looked after children before now.' Garamond thought of his own six-year-old son who had shaken his fist rather than wave goodbye, expressing his sense of loss and resentment over having a father who left him in answer to greater demands. This extra delay the President had announced meant that he had left home four hours too early, time in which he might have been able to heal the boy's tear-bruised eyes. On top of that, there were the reports of the ion wind failing, fading away to the level of spatial background activity, while he stood uselessly on an ornate terrace and played nursemaid to a child who might be as neurosis-ridden as his mother. Garamond tried to smile as the Vice-President withdrew, but he had a feeling he had not made a convincing job of it.

'Well, Harald,' he said, turning to the silver-and-pearl boy, 'you want to ride a flickerwing, do you?'

Harald examined him coolly. 'Starflight employees of less than Board status usually address me as Master Lindstrom.'

Garamond raised his eyebrows. 'I'll tell you something about space-flying, Harald. Up there the most minor technician is more important than all your Admincom executives put together. Do you understand that, Harald? Harry?' *I'm more of a child than he is,* he thought in amazement.

Unexpectedly, Harald smiled. 'I'm not interested in space-flying.'

'But I thought ...'

'I told them that because they wanted to hear it, but I don't have to pretend with you, do I?'

'No, you don't have to pretend with me, son. What are we going to do for the next two hours, though?'

'I'd like to run,' Harald said with a sudden eagerness which – in Garamond's mind – restored him to full membership of the brotherhood of small boys.

'You want to *run*?' Garamond managed a genuine smile. 'That's a modest ambition.'

'I'm not allowed to run or climb in case I hurt myself. My mother has forbidden it, and everybody else around here is so afraid of her that they hardly let me blink, but ...' Harald looked up at Garamond, triumphantly ingenuous, '... you're a flickerwing commander.'

Garamond realized belatedly that the boy had been manoeuvring him into a corner from the second they met, but he felt no annoyance. 'That's right – I am. Now let's see how quickly you can make it from here to those statues and back.'

'Right!'

'Well, don't stand around. *Go!*' Garamond watched with a mixture of amusement and concern as Harald set off in a lopsided, clopping run, elbows pumping rapidly. He rounded the bronze statues and returned to Garamond at the same pace, with his eyes shining like lamps.

'Again?'

'As many times as you want.' As Harald resumed his inefficient expenditure of energy Garamond went back to the stone balustrade of the terrace and stared down across the gardens. In spite of the late afternoon sunshine, the Atlantic was charcoal grey and tendrils of mist from it were wreathing the belvederes and waterfalls in sadness. A lone gull twinkled like a star in its distant flight.

I don't want to go, he thought. *It's as simple as that.*

In the early days he had been sustained by the conviction that he, Vance Garamond, would be the one who would find the third world. But interstellar flight was almost a century old now and Man's empire still included only one habitable planet apart from Earth, and all of Garamond's enthusiasm and certitude had achieved nothing. If he could accept that he would never reach a habitable new planet then he would be far better to do as Aileen wanted, to take a commission on the shuttle run and be sure of some time at home every month. Ferrying shiploads of colonists to Terranova would be dull, but safe and convenient. The ion winds were fairly predictable along that route and the well-established chain of weather stations had eliminated any possibility of being becalmed ...

'Look at me!'

Garamond turned, for an instant was unable to locate Harald, then saw him perched dangerously high on the shoulders of one of the statues. The boy waved eagerly.

'You'd better come down from there.' Garamond tried to find a diplomatic way to hide his concern over the way in which Harald had increased his demands – emotional blackmailers used the same techniques as ordinary criminals – from permission to run on the terrace to the right to make risky climbs, thus putting Garamond in a difficult position with the President. Difficult? It occurred to Garamond that his career would be ended if Harald were to so much as sprain an ankle.

'But I'm a *good* climber. Watch.' Harald threw his leg across a patient bronze face as he reached for the statue's upraised arm.

'I know you can climb, but don't go any higher till I get there.' Garamond began to walk towards the statues, moving casually but adding inches to each stride by thrusting from the back foot. His alarm increased. Elizabeth Lindstrom, whose title of President was derived from her inherited ownership of the greatest financial and industrial empire ever known, was the most important person alive. Her son was destined to inherit Starflight from her, to control all construction of starships and all movement between Earth and the one other world available to Man. And he, Vance Garamond, an insignificant flickerwing captain, had put himself in a position where he was almost certain to incur the anger of one or the other.

'Up we go,' Harald called.

'Don't!' Garamond broke into an undisguised run. 'Please, don't.'

He surged forward through maliciously thick air which seemed to congeal around him like resin. Harald laughed delightedly and scrambled towards the upright column of metal which was the statue's arm, but he lost his grip and tilted backwards.

One of his feet lodged momentarily in the sculpted collar, acting as a pivot, turning him upside down. Garamond, trapped in a different continuum, saw the event on a leisurely timescale, like the slow blossoming of a spiral nebula. He saw the first fatal millimetre of daylight open up between Harald's fingers and the metal construction. He saw the boy seemingly hanging in the air, then gathering speed in the fall. He saw and heard the brutal impact with which Harald's head struck the base of the statuary group.

Garamond dropped to his knees beside the small body and knew, on the instant, that Harald was dead. His skull was crushed, driven inwards on the brain.

'You're not a good climber,' Garamond whispered numbly, accusingly, to the immobile face which was still dewed with perspiration. 'You've killed us both. And my family as well.'

He stood up and looked towards the entrance of the main building, preparing to face the officials and domestics who would come running. The terrace remained quiet but for the murmur of its fountains. High in the stratosphere an invisible aircraft drew a slow, silent wake across the sky. Each passing second was a massive hammer-blow on the anvil of Garamond's mind, and he had been standing perfectly still for perhaps a minute before accepting that the accident had not been noticed by others.

Breaking out of the stasis, he gathered up Harald's body, marvelling at its lightness, and carried it to a clump of flowering shrubs. The dark green foliage clattered like metal foil as he lowered the dead child into a place of concealment.

Garamond turned his back on Starflight House, and began to run.

CHAPTER TWO

He had, if he was very lucky, about one hundred minutes.

The figure was arrived at by assuming the President had been precise when she told Garamond to wait an extra two hours. There was a further proviso – that it had been her intention to leave her son alone with him all that time. With the full span of a hundred minutes at his disposal, Garamond decided, he had a chance; but any one of a dozen personal servants had only to go looking for Harald, any one of a thousand visitors had only to notice a bloodstain ...

The numbers in the game of death were trembling and tumbling behind his eyes as he stepped off the outward bound slideway where it reached the main reception area. His official transport was waiting to take him straight to the shuttle terminal at North Field, and – in spite of the risks associated with the driver being in radio contact with Starflight House – that still seemed the quickest and most certain way of reaching his ship. The vast ice-green hall of the concourse was crowded with men and women coming off their afternoon shifts in the surrounding administrative buildings. They seemed relaxed and happy, bemused by the generosity of the lingering sunlight. Garamond swore inwardly as he shouldered through conflicting currents and eddies of people, doing his best to move quickly without attracting attention.

I'm a dead man, he kept thinking in detached wonderment. *No matter what I do, no matter how my luck holds out in the next couple of hours ... I'm a dead man. And my wife is a dead woman. And my son is a dead child. Even if the ion tide holds strong and fills my wings, we're all dead – because there's no place to hide. There's only one other world, and Elizabeth's ships will be waiting there ...*

A face turned towards him from the crowd, curiously, and Garamond realized he had made a sound. He smiled – recreating himself in his own image of a successful flickerwing captain, clothed in the black-and-silver which was symbolic of star oceans – and the face slid away, satisfied that it had made a mistake in locating the source of the despairing murmur. Garamond gnawed his lip while he covered the remaining distance to his transport which was stacked in one of the reserved magazines near the concourse. The sharp-eyed middle-aged driver saw him approaching, and had the vehicle brought up to ground level by the time Garamond reached the silo.

'Thanks.' Garamond answered the man's salute, grateful for the small saving in time, and got inside the upholstered shell.

'I thought you'd be in a hurry, sir.' The driver's eyes stared knowingly at him from the rear view mirror.

'Oh?' Garamond controlled a spasm of unreasonable fear – this was not the way his arrest would come about. He eyed the back of the driver's neck which was ruddy, deeply creased and had a number of long-established blackheads.

'Yes, sir. All the Starflight commanders are in a hurry to reach the field today. The weather reports aren't good, I hear.'

Garamond nodded and tried to look at ease as the vehicle surged forward with a barely perceptible whine from its magnetic engines. 'I think I'll catch the tide,' he said evenly. 'At least, I hope so – my family are coming to see me off.'

The driver's narrow face showed some surprise. 'I thought you were going direct ...'

'A slight change of plan – we're calling for my wife and son. You remember the address?'

'Yes, sir. I have it here.'

'Good. Get there as quickly as you can.' With a casual movement Garamond broke the audio connection between the vehicle's two compartments and picked up the nearest communicator set. He punched in his home code and held the instrument steady with his knees while he waited for the screen to come to life and show that his call had been accepted. Supposing Aileen and Chris had gone out? The boy had been upset – again Garamond remembered him shaking his fist instead of waving goodbye, expressing in the slight change of gesture all the emotions which racked his small frame – and Aileen could have taken him away for an afternoon of distraction and appeasement. If that were the case ...

'Vance!' Aileen's face crystallized in miniature between his hands. 'I was sure you'd gone. Where are you?'

'I'm on my way back to the house, be there in ten minutes.'

'Back here? But ...'

'Something has happened, Aileen. I'm bringing you and Chris with me to the field. Is he there?'

'He's out on the patio. But, *Vance,* you never let us see you off.'

'I ...' Garamond hesitated, and decided it could be better all round if his wife were to be kept in ignorance at this stage. 'I've changed my mind about some things. Now, get Chris ready to leave the house as soon as I get there.'

Aileen raised her shoulders uncertainly. 'Vance, do you think it's the best thing for him? I mean you've been away from the house for three hours and he's just begun to get over his first reactions – now you're going to put him through it all again.'

'I told you something has come up.' *How many pet dogs,* Garamond asked himself, *did I see around the Presidential suite this afternoon? Five? Six?*

'What has come up?'

'I'll explain later.' *At what range can a dog scent a corpse? Liz's brood of pets could be the biggest threat of all.* 'Please get Chris ready.'

Aileen shook her head slightly. 'I'm sorry, Vance, but I don't ...'

'Aileen!' Garamond deliberately allowed an edge of panic to show in his voice, using it to penetrate the separate universe of normalcy in which his wife still existed. 'I can't explain it now, but you and Chris must be ready to come to the field with me within the next few minutes. Don't argue any more, just do what I'm asking.'

He broke the connection and forced himself to sit back, wondering if he had already said too much for the benefit of any communications snoops who could be monitoring the public band. The car was travelling west on the main Akranes auto-link, surging irregularly as it jockeyed for position in the traffic. It occurred to Garamond that the driver's performance was not as good as it had been on the way out to Starflight House, perhaps through lack of concentration. On an impulse he reconnected the vehicle's intercom.

'... at his home,' the driver was saying. 'Expect to reach North Field in about twenty minutes.'

Garamond cleared his throat. 'What are you doing?'

'Reporting in, sir.'

'Why?'

'Standing orders. All the fleet drivers keep Starflight Centra-data informed about their movements.'

'What did you tell them?'

'Sir?'

'What did you say about my movements?'

The driver's shoulders stirred uneasily, causing his Starflight sunburst emblems to blink redly with reflected light. 'I just said you decided to pick up your family on the way to North Field.'

'Don't make any further reports.'

'Sir?'

'As a captain in the Starflight Exploratory Arm I think I can make my way around this part of Iceland without a nursemaid.'

'I'm sorry, but ...'

'Just drive the car.' Garamond fought to control the unreasoning anger he felt against the man in front. 'And go faster.'

'Yes, sir.' The creases in the driver's weather-beaten neck deepened as he hunched over the wheel.

Garamond made himself sit quietly, with closed eyes, motionless except for a slight rubbing of his palms against his knees which failed completely to remove the perspiration. He tried to visualize what was happening back on the hill. Was the routine of Elizabeth's court proceeding as on any other afternoon, with the boards and committees and tribunals deliberating in the pillared halls, and the President moving among them, complacently deflecting and vibrating the webstrands of empire with her very presence? Or had someone begun to notice Harald's absence? And his own? He opened his eyes and gazed sombrely at the unrolling scenery outside the car. The umbra of commercial buildings which extended for several kilometres around Starflight House was giving way to the first of the company-owned residential developments. As an S.E.A. commander, Garamond had been entitled to one of the 'choice' locations, which in Starflight usage tended to mean closest to Elizabeth's elevated palace. At quiet moments on the bridge of his ship Garamond had often thought about how the sheer massiveness of her power had locally deformed the structure of language in exactly the same way as a giant sun was able to twist space around itself so that captive worlds, though believing themselves to be travelling in straight lines, were held in orbit. In the present instance, however, he was satisfied with the physics of Elizabeth's gravitation because it meant that his home was midway between Starflight House and the North Field, and he was losing the minimum of time in collecting his family.

Even before the vehicle had halted outside the pyramidical block of apartments, Garamond had the door open and was walking quickly to the elevator. He stepped out of it on the third floor, went to his own door and let himself in. The familiar, homely surroundings seemed to crowd in on him for an instant, creating a new sense of shock over the fact that life as he knew it had ended. For a moment he felt like a ghost, visiting scenes to which he was no longer relevant.

'What's the matter, Vance?' Aileen emerged from a bedroom, dressed as always in taut colourful silks. Her plump, brown-skinned face and dark eyes showed concern.

'I'll explain later.' He put his arms around her and held her for a second. 'Where's Chris?'

'Here I am, Daddy!' The boy came running and swarmed up Garamond like a small animal, clinging with all four limbs. 'You came back.'

'Come on, son – we're going to the field.' Garamond held Chris above his head and shook him, imitating a start-of-vacation gesture, then handed the child to his wife. It had been the second time within the hour that he had picked up a light, childish body. 'The car's waiting for us. You take Chris down to it and I'll follow in a second.'

'You still haven't told me what this is all about.'

'Later, *later!*' Garamond decided that if he were stopped before the shuttle got off the ground there might still be a faint chance for Aileen and the boy if she could truthfully swear she had no idea what had been going on. He pushed her out into the corridor, then strode back into the apartment's general storage area which was hidden by a free-floating screen of vari-coloured luminosity. It took him only a few seconds to open the box containing his old target pistol and to fill an ammunition clip. The long-barrelled, saw-handled pistol snagged the material of his uniform as he thrust it out of sight in his jacket. Acutely conscious of the weighty bulge under his left arm, he ran back through the living space. On an impulse he snatched an ornament – a solid gold snail with ruby eyes – from a shelf, and went out into the corridor. Aileen was holding the elevator door open with one hand and trying to control Chris with the other.

'Let's go,' Garamond said cheerfully, above the deafening ratchets and escapement of the clock behind his eyes. He closed the elevator door and pressed the 'DOWN' button. At ground level Chris darted ahead through the long entrance hall and scrambled into the waiting vehicle. There were few people about, and none that Garamond could identify as neighbours, but he dared not risk running and the act of walking normally brought a cool sheen to his forehead. The driver gave Aileen a grudging salute and held the car door open while she got in. Garamond sat down opposite his wife in the rear of the vehicle and, when it had moved off, manufactured a smile for her.

She shook her dark head impatiently. 'Now will you tell me what's happening?'

'You're coming to see me off, that's all.' Garamond glanced at Chris, who was kneeling at the rear window, apparently absorbed in the receding view. 'Chris should enjoy it.'

'But you said it was important.'

'It was important for me to spend a little extra time with you and Chris.'

Aileen looked baffled. 'What did you bring from the apartment?'

'Nothing.' Garamond moved his left shoulder slightly to conceal the bulge made by the pistol.

'But I can see it.' She leaned forward, caught his hand and opened his fingers, revealing the gold snail. It was a gift he had bought Aileen on their honeymoon and he realized belatedly that the reason he had snatched it was that the little ornament was the symbolical cornerstone of their home. Aileen's eyes widened briefly and she turned her head away, making an abrupt withdrawal. Garamond closed his eyes, wondering what his wife's intuition had told her, wondering how many minutes he had left.

At that moment, a minor official on the domestic staff of Starflight House was moving uncertainly through the contrived Italian Renaissance atmosphere of the carved hill. His name was Carlos Pennario and he was holding leads to which were attached two of the President's favourite spaniels. The doubts which plagued his mind were caused by the curious behaviour of the dogs, coupled with certain facts about his conditions of employment. Both animals, their long ears flapping audibly with excitement, were pulling him towards a section of the shady terrace which ringed the hill just at the executive and Presidential levels. Pennario, who was naturally inquisitive, had never seen the spaniels behave in this way before and he was tempted to give them their heads – but, as a Grade 4 employee, he was not permitted to ascend to the executive levels. In normal circumstances such considerations would not have held him back for long, but only two days earlier he had fallen foul of his immediate boss, a gnome-like Scot called Arthur Kemp, and had been promised demotion next time he put a foot wrong.

Pennario held on to the snuffling, straining dogs while he gazed towards a group of statues which shone like red gold in the dying sunlight. A tall, hard-looking man in the black uniform of a flickerwing captain had been leaning on the stone balustrade near the statues a little earlier in the afternoon. The moody captain seemed to have departed and there was nobody else visible on the terrace, yet the spaniels were going crazy trying to get up there. It was not a world-shaking mystery, but to Pennario it represented an intriguing diversion from the utter boredom of his job.

He hesitated, scanning the slopes above, then allowed the spaniels to pull him up the broad shallow steps to the terrace, their feet scrabbling on the smooth stone. Once on the upper level, the dogs headed straight for the base on which the bronze figures stood, then with low whines burrowed into the shrubbery behind.

Pennario leaned over them, parted the dark green leaves with his free arm, and looked down into the cave-like dimness.

They needed another thirty minutes, Garamond decided. If the discovery of Harald's body did not take place within that time he and his family would be clear of the atmosphere on one of the S.E.A. shuttles, before the alarm could be broadcast. They would not be out of immediate danger but the ship lying in polar orbit, the *Bissendorf,* was his own private territory, a small enclave in which the laws of the Elizabethan universe did not hold full sway. Up there she could still destroy him, and eventually would, but it would be more difficult than on Earth where at a word she could mobilize ten thousand men against him.

'I need to go to the toilet,' Chris announced, turning from the rear window with an apologetic expression on his round face. He pummelled his abdomen as if to punish it for the intervention.

'You can wait till we reach the field.' Aileen pulled him down on to her knee and enclosed him with smooth brown arms.

A sense of unreality stole over Garamond as he watched his wife and son. Both were wearing lightweight indoor clothing and, of course, had no other belongings with them. It was incredible, unthinkable that – dressed as they were and so unprepared – they should be snatched from their natural ambience of sunlight and warm breezes, sheltering walls and quiet gardens, and that they should be projected into the deadliness of the space between the stars. The air in the car seemed to thin down abruptly, forcing Garamond to take deep breaths. He gazed at the diorama of buildings and foliage beyond the car windows, trying to think about his movements for the next vital half-hour, but his mind refused to work constructively. His thoughts lapsed into a fugue, a recycling of images and shocked sensory fragments. He watched for the hundredth time as the fatal millimetres of daylight opened between Harald's silhouette and the uncomprehending metal of the statue. And the boy's body had been so *light*. Almost as light as Chris. How could a package contain all the bone and blood and muscle and organs necessary to support life, and yet be so light? So insubstantial that a fall of three or four metres ...

'Look, Dad!' Chris moved within the organic basketwork of his mother's arms. 'There's the field. Can we go on to your shuttle?'

'I'll try to arrange it.' Garamond stared through the wavering blur of the North Field's perimeter fence, wondering if he would see any signs of unusual activity.

Carlos Pennario allowed the shrubs to spring together again and, for the first time since his youth, he crossed himself.

He backed away from what he had seen, dragging the frantic dogs with him, and looked around for help. There was nobody in sight. He opened his mouth with the intention of shouting at the top of his voice, of unburdening his dismay on the sleepy air, then several thoughts occurred to him almost at once. Pennario had seen Elizabeth Lindstrom only a few times, and always at a distance, but he had heard many stories told in the nighttime quietness of the staff dormitory. He would have given a year's wages rather than be brought before her with the news that he had allowed one of her spaniels to choke on a chicken bone.

Now he was almost in the position of having to face Elizabeth in person and describe his part in the finding of her son's corpse.

Pennario tried to imagine what the President might do to the bringer of such news before she regained whatever slight measure of self-control she was supposed to have ...

Then there was the matter of his superior, Arthur Kemp. Pennario had no right to be on the terrace in the first place, and to a man like Kemp that one transgression would be suggestive, would be *proof*, of others. He had no idea what had happened to the dead boy, but he knew the way Kemp's mind worked. Assuming that Pennario lived long enough to undergo an investigation, Kemp would swear to anything to avoid any association with guilt.

The realization that he was in mortal danger stimulated Pennario into decisive action. He knelt, gathered the spaniels into his arms and walked quickly down the steps to the lower levels. Shocked and afraid though he was, his mind retained those qualities which had lifted him successfully from near-starvation in Mexico to one of the few places in the world where there was enough air for a man to breathe. Locked away in his memory was a comprehensive timetable of Kemp's daily movements in and around Starflight House, and according to that schedule the acidulous little Scot would shortly be making his final inspection tour of the afternoon. The tour usually took him along the circular terrace, past the shrubbery in which

Harald's body was hidden – and how much better it would have been if Domestic Supervisor Kemp had made the fearful discovery.

Pennario kept slanting downwards across the hill until he had reached the lowest point from which he could still see a sector of the upper terrace and gauge Kemp's progress along it. He moved into the shade of an ivy-covered loggia, set the dogs on the ground and pretended to be busy adjusting their silver collars. The excited animals fought to get free, but Pennario held them firmly in check.

It was important to him that they did not make their predictable dash to the terrace until Kemp was in exactly the right place to become involved with their discovery. Pennario glanced at his watch.

'Any minute now, my little friends,' he whispered. 'Any minute now.'

In contrast to what Garamond had feared, the field seemed quieter than usual, its broad expanses of ferrocrete mellowed to the semblance of sand by the fleeting sunlight. Low on the western horizon a complexity of small clouds was assembled like a fabulous army, their helmets and crests glowing with fire, and several vaporous banners reached towards the zenith in deepening pink. As the car drew to a halt outside the S.E.A. complex Garamond shielded his eyes, looked towards his assigned take-off point and saw the squat outline of the waiting shuttle. Its door was open and the boarding steps were in place. The sight filled him with a powerful urge to drive to the shuttle, get Aileen and Chris on board, and blast off towards safety. There were certain pre-flight formalities, however, and take off without observing them could lead to the wrong sort of radio message being beamed up to the *Bissendorf* ahead of him. He pushed a heavy lock of hair away from his forehead and smiled for the benefit of Aileen and the driver.

'Some papers to sign in here, then we'll take the slidewalk out to the shuttle,' he said easily as he opened the car door and got out.

'I thought Chris and I'd be going up to the observation floor,' Aileen replied, not moving from her seat.

'There's no fun in that, is there, Chris?' Garamond lifted the boy off Aileen's knee and set him down on the steps of the S.E.A. building. 'What's the point in having a Dad who's a flickerwing captain if you can't get a few extra privileges? You'd like to look right inside the shuttle, wouldn't you?'

'Yes, Dad.' Chris nodded, but with a curious reserve, as if he had sensed something of Aileen's unease.

'Of course, you would.' Garamond took Aileen's hand, drew her out of the car and slammed the door. 'That's all, driver – we can look after ourselves from here on.' The driver glanced back once, without speaking, and accelerated away towards the transport pool.

Aileen caught Garamond's arm. 'We're alone now, Vance. What's …?'

'Now you two stand right here on these steps and don't move till I come out. This won't take long.' Garamond sprinted up the steps, returned the salutes of the guards at the top, and hurried towards the S.E.A. Preflight Centre. The large square room looked unfamiliar when he entered, as though seen through the eyes of the young Vance Garamond who had been so impressed by it at the beginning of his first exploratory command. He ran to the long desk and slapped down his flight authorization documents.

'You're late, Captain Garamond,' commented a heavily built ex-quarter-master called Herschell, who habitually addressed outgoing captains with a note of rueful challenge which was meant to remind them he had not always held a desk job.

'I know – I couldn't get away from Liz.' Garamond seized a stylus and began scribbling his name on various papers as they were fed to him.

'Like that, was it? She couldn't let you go?'

'That's the way it was.'

'Pity. I'd say you've missed the tide.' Herschell's pink square face was sympathetic.

'Oh?'

'Yeah – look at the map.' Herschell pointed up at the vast solid-image chart of the Solar System and surrounding volume of interstellar space which floated below the domed ceiling. The solar wind, represented by yellow radiance, was as strong as ever and Garamond saw the healthy, bow-shaped shock wave on the sunward side of Earth, where the current impacted on the planet's geomagnetic field. Data on the inner spirals of the solar wind, however, were of interest only to interplanetary travellers – and his concern was with the ion count at the edge of the system and beyond. Garamond searched for the great arc of the shock front near the orbit of Uranus where the solar wind, attenuated by distance from Sol, built up pressure against the magnetic field of the galaxy. For a moment he saw nothing, then his eyes picked out an almost invisible amber halo, so faint that it could have represented nothing more than a tenth of an ion per cubic centimetre. He had rarely seen the front looking so feeble. It appeared that the sun was in a niggardly mood, unwilling to assist his ship far up the long gravity slope to interstellar space.

Garamond shifted his attention to the broad straggling bands of green, blue and red which plotted the galactic tides of fast-moving corpuscles as they swept across the entire region. These vagrant sprays of energetic particles and their movements meant as much to him as wind, wave and tide had to the skipper of a transoceanic sailing ship. All spacecraft built by Starflight – which meant all spacecraft built on Earth – employed intense magnetic fields to sweep up interstellar atomic debris for use as reaction mass. The system made it possible to conduct deep-space voyages in ships weighing as little as ten thousand tons, as against the million tons which would have been the minimum for a vessel which had to transport its own reaction mass.

Flickerwing ships had their own disadvantages in that their efficiency was subject to spatial 'weather'. The ideal mission profile was for a ship to accelerate steadily to the midpoint of its journey and decelerate at the same rate for the remainder of the trip, but where the harvest of charged particles was poor the rate of speed-change fell off. If that occurred in the first half of a voyage it meant that the vessel took longer than planned to reach destination; if it occurred in the second half the ship was deprived of the means to discard velocity and would storm through its target system at unmanageable speed, sometimes not coming to a halt until it had overshot by light-days. It was to minimize such uncertainties that Starflight maintained chains of automatic sensor stations whose reports, transmitted by low-energy tachyon beams, were continuously fed into weather charts.

And, as Garamond immediately saw, the conditions in which he hoped to achieve high-speed flight were freakishly, damnably bad.

More than half the volume of space covered by the map seemed entirely void of corpuscular flux, and such fronts as were visible in the remainder were fleeing away to the galactic south. Only one wisp of useful density – possibly the result of heavy particles entangling themselves in an irregularity in the interplanetary magnetic field – reached as far back as the orbit of Mars, and even that was withdrawing at speed.

'I've got to get out of here,' Garamond said simply.

Herschell handed him the traditional leather briefcase containing the flight authorization documents. 'Why don't you take off out of it, Captain? The *Bissendorf* is ready to travel, and I can sign the rest of this stuff by proxy.'

'Thanks.' Garamond took the briefcase and ran for the door.

'Don't let that ole bit of dust get away,' Herschell called after him, one flickerwing man to another. 'Scoop it up good.'

Garamond sprinted along the entrance hall, relieved at being able to respond openly to his growing sense of urgency. The sight of ships' commanders running for the slidewalks was quite a common one in the S.E.A. Centre when the weather was breaking. He found Aileen and Chris on the front steps, exactly where he had left them. Aileen was looking tired and worried, and holding the boy close to her side.

'All clear,' he said. He caught Aileen by the upper arm and urged her towards the slidewalk tunnel. She fell in step with him readily enough but he could sense her mounting unease. 'Let's go!'

'Where to, Vance?' She spoke quietly, but he understood she was asking him the big question, communicating on a treasured personal level which neither of them would ever willingly choose to disrespect. He glanced down at Chris. They were on the slidewalk now, slanting down into the tunnel and the boy seemed fascinated by the softly tremoring ride.

'When I was waiting to see the President this afternoon I was asked to take care of young Harald Lindstrom for an hour ...' The enormity of what he had to say stilled the words in his throat.

'What happened, Vance?'

'I ... I didn't take care of him very well. He fell and killed himself.'

'Oh!' The colour seeped away from beneath the tan of Aileen's face. 'But how did you get away from ...?'

'Nobody saw him fall. I hid the body in some bushes.'

'And now we're running?'

'As fast as we can go, sweet.'

Aileen put her hand on Chris's shoulder. 'Do you think Elizabeth would ...?'

'Automatically. Instinctively. There'd be no way for her *not* to do it.'

Aileen's chin puckered as she fought to control the muscles around her mouth. 'Oh, Vance! This is terrible. Chris and I can't go up there.'

'You can, and you're going to.' Garamond put his arm around Aileen and was alarmed when she sagged against him with her full weight. He put his mouth close to her ear. 'I can't do this alone. I need your help to get Chris away from here.'

She straightened with difficulty. 'I'll try. Lots of women go to Terranova, don't they?'

'That's better.' Garamond gave her arm an encouraging squeeze and wondered if she really believed they could go to the one other human-inhabited Starflight-dominated world in the universe. 'Now, we're almost at the end of the tunnel. When we get up the ramp, pick Chris up and walk straight on to the shuttle with him as if it was a school bus. I'll be right behind you blocking the view of anybody who happens to be watching from the tower.'

'What will the other people say?'

'There'll be nobody else on the shuttle apart from the pilots, and I'll talk to them.'

'But won't the pilots object when they see us on board?'

'The pilots won't say a word,' Garamond promised, slipping his hand inside his jacket.

At Starflight House, high on the sculpted hill, the first man had already died.

Domestic Supervisor Arthur Kemp had been planning his evening meal when the two spaniels bounded past him and darted into the shrubbery on the long terrace. He paused, eyed them curiously, then pushed the screen of foliage aside. The light was beginning to fail, and Kemp – who came from the comparatively uncrowded, unpolluted, unravaged north of Scotland – lacked Carlos Pennario's sure instinct concerning matters of violent and premature death. He dragged Harald's body into the open, stared for a long moment at the black deltas of blood which ran from nostrils and ears, and began to scream into his wrist communicator.

Elizabeth Lindstrom was on the terrace within two minutes.

She would not allow anybody to touch her son's remains and, as the staff could not simply walk away, there formed a dense knot of people at the centre of which Elizabeth set up her court of enquiry. Standing over the small body, satin-covered abdomen glowing like a giant pearl, she spoke in a controlled manner at first. Only the Council members who knew her well understood the implications of the steadily rising inflexions in her voice, or of the way she had begun to finger a certain ruby ring on her right hand. These men, obliged by rank to remain close to the President, nevertheless tried to alter their positions subtly so that they were shielded by the bodies of other men, who in turn sensed their peril and acted accordingly. The result was that the circle around Elizabeth grew steadily larger and its surface tension increased.

It was into this arena of fear that Domestic Supervisor Kemp was thrust to give his testimony. He answered several of her questions with something approaching composure, but his voice faltered when – after he too had confirmed Captain Garamond's abrupt departure from the terrace – Elizabeth began pulling out her own hair in slow, methodical handfuls. For an endless minute the soft ripping of her scalp was the only sound on the terrace.

Kemp endured it for as long as was humanly possible, then turned to run. Elizabeth exploded him with the laser burst from her ring, and was twisting blindly to hose the others with its fading energies when her senior physician, risking his own life, fired a cloud of sedative drugs into the distended veins of her neck. The President lost consciousness almost as once, but she had time to utter three words:

'Bring me Garamond.'

CHAPTER THREE

Garamond crowded on to the stubby shuttlecraft with Aileen and looked forward. The door between the crew and passenger compartments was open, revealing the environment of instrument arrays and controls in which the pilots worked. A shoulder of each man, decorated with the ubiquitous Starflight symbol, was visible on each side of the central aisle, and Garamond could hear the preflight checks being carried out. Neither of the pilots looked back.

'Sit there,' Garamond whispered, pointing at a seat which was screened from the pilots' view by the main bulkhead. He put his fingers to his lips and winked at Chris, making it into a game. The boy nodded tautly, undeceived. Garamond went back to the entrance door and stood in it, waving to imaginary figures in the slidewalk tunnel, then went forward to the crew compartment.

'Take it away, Captain,' he said with the greatest joviality he could muster.

'Yes, sir.' The dark-chinned senior pilot glanced over his shoulder. 'As soon as Mrs Garamond and your son disembark.'

Garamond looked around the flight deck and found a small television screen showing a picture of the passenger compartment, complete with miniature images of Aileen and Chris. He wondered if the pilots had been watching it closely and how much they might have deduced from his actions.

'My wife and son are coming with us,' he said. 'Just for the ride.'

'I'm sorry, sir – their names aren't on my list.'

'This is a special arrangement I've just made with the President.'

'I'll have to check that with the tower.' There was a stubborn set to the pilot's bluish jaw as he reached for the communications switch.

'I assure you it's all right.' Garamond slid the pistol out of his jacket and used its barrel to indicate the runway ahead. 'Now, I want you to get all the normal clearances in a perfectly normal way and then do a maximum-energy ascent to my ship. I'm very familiar with the whole routine and I can fly this bug myself if necessary, so don't do any clever stuff which would make me shoot you.'

'I'm not going to get myself shot.' The senior pilot shrugged and his younger companion nodded vigorously. 'But how far do you think you're going to get, Captain?'

'Far enough – now take us out of here.' Garamond remained standing between the two seats. There was a subdued thud from the passenger door as it sealed itself, and then the shuttle surged forward. While monitoring the cross talk between the pilots and the North Field tower, Garamond studied the computer screen which was displaying flight parameters. The *Bissendorf* was in Polar Band One, the great stream of Starflight spacecraft – mainly population transfer vessels, but with a sprinkling of Exploratory Arm ships – which girdled the Earth at a height of more than a hundred kilometres. Incoming ships were allocated parking slots in any of the thirty-degree sectors marked by twelve space stations, their exact placing being determined by the amount of maintenance or repair they needed. The *Bissendorf* had been scheduled for a major refitting lasting three months, and was close in to Station 8, which the computer showed to be swinging up over the Aleutian Islands. A maximum-energy rendezvous could be accomplished in about eleven minutes.

'I take it you want to catch the *Bissendorf* this time round,' the senior pilot said as the shuttle's drive tubes built up thrust and the white runway markers began to flicker under its nose like tracer fire.

Garamond nodded. 'You take it right.'

'It's going to be rough on your wife and boy.' There was an unspoken question in the comment.

'Not as rough as ...' Garamond decided to do the pilots a favour by telling them nothing – they too would be caught up in Elizabeth's enquiries.

'There's a metallizer aerosol in the locker beside you,' the co-pilot volunteered, speaking for the first time.

'Thanks.' Garamond found the aerosol container and passed it back to Aileen. 'Spray your clothes with this. Do Chris as well.'

'What's it for?' Aileen was trying to sound unconcerned, but her voice was small and cold.

'It won't do your clothes any harm, but it makes them react against the restraint field inside the ship when you move. It turns them into a kind of safety net and also stops you floating about when you're in free fall.' Garamond had forgotten how little Aileen knew about spaceflight or air travel. She had never even been in an ordinary jetliner, he recalled. The great age of air tourism was long past – if a person was lucky enough to live in an acceptable part of the Earth he tended to stay put.

'You can use it first,' Aileen said.

'I don't need it – all space fliers' uniforms are metallized when they're made.' Garamond smiled encouragingly. *The pilot didn't know how right he was,* he thought. *This is going to be rough on my wife and boy.* He returned his attention to the pilots as the shuttle lifted its nose and cleared the ground. As soon as the undercarriage had been retracted and the craft was aero-dynamically clean the drive tubes boosted it skywards on a pink flare of recombining ions. Garamond, standing behind the pilots, was pushed against the bulkhead and held there by the sustained acceleration. Behind him, Chris began to sob.

'Don't worry, son,' Garamond called. 'This won't last long. We'll soon be ...'

'North Field to shuttlecraft Sahara Tango 4299,' a voice crackled from the radio. 'This is Fleet Commodore Keegan calling. Come in, please.'

'Don't answer that,' Garamond ordered. The clock behind his eyes had come to an abrupt and sickening halt.

'But that was Keegan himself. Are you mixed up in something big, Captain?'

'Big enough.' Garamond hesitated as the radio repeated its message. 'Tune that out and get me Commander Napier on my bridge.' He gave the pilot a microwave frequency which would by-pass the *Bissendorf*'s main communications room.

'But …'

'Immediately.' He raised the pistol against multiple gravities. 'This is a hair trigger and there's a lot of G-force piling up on my finger.'

'I'm making the call now.' The pilot spun a small vernier on the armrest of his chair and in a few seconds had established contact.

'Commander Napier here.' Garamond felt a surge of relief as he recognized the cautious tones Napier always employed when he did not know who was on the other end of a channel.

'This is an urgent one, Cliff.' Garamond spoke steadily. 'Have you had any communications about me from Starflight House?'

'Ah … no. Was I supposed to?'

'That doesn't matter now. Here's a special instruction which I'm asking you to obey immediately and without question. Do you understand?'

'Okay, Vance,' Napier sounded puzzled, but not suspicious or alarmed.

'I'm on the shuttle and will rendezvous with you in a few minutes, but right now I want you to throw the ultimate master switch on the external communications system. *Right now, Cliff!*'

There was a slight pause, during which Napier must have been considering the facts that what he had been asked to do was illegal and that under Starflight Regulations he was not obliged to obey such an order – then the channel went dead.

Garamond closed his eyes for a second. He knew that Napier had also thought about their years together on the *Bissendorf*, all the light-years they had covered, all the alien suns, all the hostile useless planets, all the disappointments which had studded their quest for *lebensraum*, all the bottles of whisky they had killed while in orbit around lost, lonely points of light both to console themselves and to make the next leg of a mission seem bearable. If he and Aileen and Chris had any chance of life it lay in the fact that a spaceship was an island universe, a tiny enclave in which Elizabeth's power was less than absolute. While in Earth orbit the ship's officers would have been forced to obey any direct order from Starflight Admincom, but he had successfully blocked the communications channels … A warning chime from the shuttle's computer interrupted Garamond's thoughts.

'We have some pretty severe course and speed corrections coming up,' the younger pilot said. 'Do you want to advise your wife?'

Garamond nodded gratefully. The sky in the forward view panels had already turned from deep blue to black as the shuttle's tubes hurled it clear of the atmosphere. In a maximum-energy ballistic-style sortie it was understood that there was no time for niceties – the computer which was controlling the flight profile would subject passengers to as much stress, within programmed limits, as they could stand. Garamond edged backwards until he could see Aileen and Chris.

'Get ready for some rollercoaster stuff,' he told them. 'Don't try to fight the ship or you'll be sick. Just go with it and the restraint field will hold you in place.' They both nodded silently, in unison, eyes fixed on his face, and he felt a crushing sense of responsibility and guilt. He had barely finished speaking when a series of lateral corrections twisted space out of its normal shape, pulling him to the left and then upwards away from the floor. The fierce pressure of the bulkhead against his back prevented him from being thrown around but he guessed that his wife and son must have been lifted out of their seats. An involuntary gasp from Aileen confirmed her distress.

'It won't be long now,' he told her. Stars were shining in the blackness ahead of the shuttle, and superimposed on the random points of light was a strip of larger, brighter motes, most of which had visible irregularities of shape. Polar Band One glittered like a diamond bracelet, at the midpoint of which Sector Station 8 flared with a yellowish brilliance. The two distinct levels of luminosity, separating man-made objects from the background of distant suns, created a three-dimensional effect, an awareness of depth and cosmic scale which Garamond rarely experienced when far into a mission. He remained with the pilots, braced between their seats and the bulkhead, while the shuttle drew closer to the stream of orbiting spaceships and further corrections were applied to match speed and direction. By this time Starflight Admincom would have tried to contact the *Bissendorf* and would probably be taking other measures to prevent his escape.

'There's your ship,' the senior pilot commented, and the note of satisfaction in his voice put Garamond on his guard. 'It looks like you're a little late, Captain – there's another shuttle already drifting into its navel.'

Garamond, unused to orienting himself with the cluttered traffic of the Polar Band, had to search the sky for several seconds before he located the *Bissendorf* and was able to pick out the silvered bullet of a shuttle closing in on the big ship's transfer dock. He felt a cool prickling on his forehead. It was impossible for the other shuttle to have made better time on the haul up from Earth, but Admincom must have been able to divert one which was already in orbit and instruct it to block the *Bissendorf*'s single transfer dock.

'What do you want to do, Captain?' The blue-chinned senior pilot had begun to enjoy himself. 'Would you like to hand over that gun now?'

Garamond shook his head. 'The other shuttle's making a normal docking approach. Get in there before him.'

'It's too late.'

Garamond placed the muzzle of the pistol against the pilot's neck. 'Ram your nose into that dock, sonny.'

'You're crazy, but I'll try.' The pilot fixed his eyes on the expanding shape of the *Bissendorf*, then spun verniers to bring his sighting crosshairs on to the red-limned target of the dock which was already partially obscured by the other shuttle. As he did so the retro tubes began firing computer-controlled bursts which cut their forward speed. 'I told you it was too late.'

'Override the computer,' Garamond snapped. 'Kill those retros.'

'Do you want to commit suicide?'

'Do you?' Garamond pressed the pistol into the other man's spine and watched as he tripped out the auto control circuits. The image of the competing shuttle and the docking target expanded in the forward screen with frightening speed.

The pilot instinctively moved backwards in his seat. 'We're going to hit the other shuttle, for Christ's sake!'

'I know,' Garamond said calmly. 'And after we do you'll have about two seconds to get those crosshairs back on target. Now let's see how good you are.'

The other shuttle ballooned ahead of and slightly above them until they were looking right into its main driver tubes, there was a shuddering clang which Garamond felt in his bones, the shuttle vanished, and the vital docking target slewed away to one side. Events began to happen in slow motion for Garamond. He had time to monitor every move the pilot made as he fired emergency corrective jets which wrenched the ship's nose back on to something approximating its original bearing, time to brace himself as retros hammered on the craft's frame, even time to note and be grateful for the discovery that the pilot was good. Then the shuttle speared into the *Bissendorf*'s transfer dock at five times the maximum permitted speed and wedged itself into the interior arrester rings with a shrieking impact which deformed its hull.

Garamond, the only person on the shuttle not protected by a seat, was driven forward but was saved from injury by the restraint field's reaction against any violent movement of his clothing. He felt a surge of induced heat pass through the material, and at the same time became aware of a shrill whistling sound from the rear of the ship. A popping in his ears told him that air was escaping from the shuttle into the vacuum of the *Bissendorf*'s dock. A few seconds later Chris began to sob, quietly and steadily. Garamond went aft, knelt before the boy and tried to soothe him.

'What's happening, Vance?' The brightly-coloured silk of Aileen's dress was utterly incongruous.

'Rough docking, that's all. We're losing some air but they'll be pressurizing the dock and ...' He hesitated as a warbling note came from the shuttle's address system. 'They've done it – that's the equalization signal to say we can get out now. There's nothing to worry about.'

'But we're falling.'

'We aren't falling, honey. Well, we are – but not downwards …' It came to Garamond that he had no time at that moment to introduce his wife to celestial mechanics. 'I want you and Chris to sit right here for a few minutes. Okay?'

He stood up, opened the passenger door and looked out at a group of officers and engineering personnel who had gathered on the docking bay's main platform. Among them was the burly figure of Cliff Napier. Garamond launched himself upwards from the sill and allowed the slight drag of the ship's restraint field to curve his weightless flight downwards on to the steel platform where his boots took a firm grip. Napier caught his arm while the other men were saluting.

'Are you all right, Vance? That was the hairiest docking I ever saw.'

'I'm fine. Explain it all later, Cliff. Get through to the engine deck and tell them I want immediate full power.'

'Immediate?'

'Yes – there's a streamer of nova dust lagging behind the main weather front and we're going to catch it. I presume you've pre-set the course.'

'But what about the shuttle and its crew?'

'We'll have to take the shuttle with us, Cliff. The shuttle and everybody on it.'

'I see.' Napier raised his wrist communicator to his lips and ordered full power. He was a powerfully built bull-necked man with hands like the scoops of a mechanical digger, but there was a brooding intelligence in his eyes. 'Is this our last mission for Starflight?'

'It's my last, anyway.' Garamond looked around to make sure nobody was within earshot. 'I'm in deep, Cliff – and I've dragged you in with me.'

'It was my decision – I didn't have to pull the plug on the communications boys. Are they coming after you?'

'With every ship that Starflight owns.'

'They won't catch us,' Napier said confidently as the deck began to press up under their feet, signalling that the *Bissendorf* was accelerating out of orbit. 'We'll ride that wisp of dust up the hill to Uranus, and when we've caught the tide … Well, there's a year's supplies on board.'

'Thanks.' Garamond shook hands with Napier, yet – while comforted by the blunt human contact – he wondered how long it would be before either of them would refer openly to the bitter underlying reality of their situation. They were all dressed up with a superb ship. But a century of exploration by the vast Starflight armada had proved one thing.

There was nowhere to go.

CHAPTER FOUR

They were able to put off the decision for three days.

During that time there was only one direction in which the *Bissendorf* could logically go – towards the galactic south, in pursuit of the single vagrant wisp of particles which lingered behind the retreating weather fronts. They had caught it, barely, and the vast insubstantial ramjets formed by the ship's magnetic fields had begun to gather power, boosting it towards lightspeed and beyond. It was the prototypes of starships such as the *Bissendorf* which, a century earlier, had all but demolished Einsteinian physics. On the first tentative flights there had been something of the predicted increase in mass, but no time dilation effect, no impenetrable barrier at the speed of light. A new physics had been devised – based mainly on the work of the Canadian mathematician, Arthur Arthur – which took into account the lately observed fact that when a body of appreciable mass and gravitic field reached speeds approaching .2C it entered new frames of reference. Once a ship crossed the threshold velocity it created its own portable universe in which different rules applied, and it appeared that the great universal constant was not the speed of light. It was time itself.

On his earlier missions Garamond had been grateful that Einstein's work had its limitations and that time did not slow down for the space traveller – he would have had no stomach for finding his wife ageing ten years for his one, or having a son who quickly grew older than himself. But on this voyage, his last for Starflight, with Aileen and Christopher aboard, it would have resolved many difficulties had he been able to trace a vast circle across one part of the galaxy and return to Earth to find, as promised by Einstein, that Elizabeth Lindstrom was long dead. Arthurian physics had blocked that notional escape door, however, and he was faced with the question of where to go in his year of stolen time.

His thinking on the matter was influenced by two major considerations. The first was that he had no intention of condemning the 450-strong crew of the *Bissendorf* to a slow death in an unknown part of the galaxy in a year's time. The ship had to return to Earth and therefore his radius of action was limited to the distance it could cover in six months. Even supposing he travelled in a straight line to one preselected destination, the six-month limitation meant he would not reach far beyond the volume of space already totally explored by Starflight. Chances of this one desperate flight producing a habitable world on which to hide had been microscopic to begin with; when modified by the distance factor they vanished into realms of fantasy.

The other major consideration was a personal one. Garamond already knew where he wanted to go, but was having trouble justifying the decision.

'Cluster 803 is your best bet,' Clifford Napier said. He was leaning back in a simulated leather chair in Garamond's quarters, and in his hand was a glass of liqueur whisky which he had not yet tasted but was holding up to the light to appreciate its colour. His heavy-lidded brown eyes were inscrutable as he continued with his thesis.

'You can make it with time to spare. It's dense – average distance between suns half a light-year – so you'd be able to check a minimum of eight systems before having to pull out. And it's prime exploration territory, Vance. As you know, the S.E.A. Board recommended that 803 should be given high priority when the next wave is being planned.'

Garamond sipped his own whisky, with its warmth of forgotten summers. 'It makes sense, all right.' The two men sat without speaking for a time, listening to the faint hum of the ship's superconducting flux pumps which was always present even in the engineered solitude of the skipper's rooms.

'It makes sense,' Napier said finally, 'but you don't want to go there. Right?'

'Well, maybe it makes too much sense. Admincom could predict that we'd head for 803 and send a hundred ships into the region. A thousand ships.'

'Think they could catch us?'

'There's always that chance,' Garamond said. 'It's been proved that four flickerwings getting just ahead of another and matching velocities can control it better than its own skipper just by deciding how much reaction mass to let slip by.'

There was another silence, then Napier gave a heavy sigh. 'All right, Vance – where's your map?'

'Which map?'

'The one showing Pengelly's Star. That's where you want to go, isn't it?'

Garamond felt a surge of anger at having his innermost thoughts divined so accurately by the other man. 'My father actually met Rufus Pengelly once,' he said defensively. 'He told me he'd never known a man less capable of trickery – and if there was one thing my father could do it was judge character just by ...' He broke off as Napier began to laugh.

'Vance, you don't need to sell the idea to me. We're not going to find the third world, so it doesn't matter where we go, does it?'

Garamond's anger was replaced by a growing sense of relief. He went to his desk, opened a drawer and took out four large photoprints which appeared to be of greyish metallic or stone surfaces on which were arranged a number of darker spots in a manner suggestive of star maps. The fuzziness of the markings and the blotchy texture of the background were due to the fact that the prints were computer reconstructions of star charts which had been destroyed by fire.

A special kind of fire, Garamond thought. *The one which robbed us of a neighbour.*

Sagania had been discovered early in the exploratory phase. It was less than a hundred light-years from Sol, only a quarter of the separation the best statisticians had computed as the average for technical civilizations throughout the galaxy. Even more remarkable was the coincidence of time-scales. In the geological lifespans of Sagania and Earth the period in which intelligent life developed and flourished represented less than a second in the life of a man, yet the fantastic gamble had come off. Saganians and Men had coexisted, against all the odds, within interstellar hailing distance, each able to look into the night sky and see the other's parent sun without optical aid. Both had taken the machine-using philosophy as far as the tapping of nuclear energy. Both had shared the outward urge, planned the building of starships, and – with their sub-beacons trembling in the blackness like candles in far-off windows – it was inevitable that there would have been a union.

Except that one day on Sagania – at a time when the first civilizations were being formed in the Valley of the Two Rivers on Earth – somebody had made a mistake. It may have been a politician who overplayed his hand, or a scientist who dealt the wrong cards, but the result was that Sagania lost its atmosphere, and its life, in an uncontrolled nuclear reaction which surged around the planet like a tidal wave of white fire.

Archaeologists from Earth, arriving seven thousand years later, had been able to discover very little about the final phase of Saganian civilization. Ironically or justly, according to one's point of view, the beings who had represented the peak of the planet's culture were the ones who removed vir-tually all trace of their existence. It was the older, humbler Saganian culture which, protected by the crust of centuries, had been uncovered by the elec-tronic probes. Among the artifacts turned up were fragments of star maps which excited little comment, even though a few researchers had noticed that some of them showed a star which did not exist.

'This is the earliest fragment,' Garamond said, setting the photoprint on a table beside Napier. He pointed at a blurry speck. 'And that's the sun we've christened Pengelly's Star. Here's another map tentatively dated five hun-dred years later, and as you see – no Pengelly's Star. One explanation is that at some time between when these two maps were drawn the star vanished.'

'Maybe it got left out by mistake,' Napier prompted, aware that Garamond wanted to go over all the familiar arguments once more.

'That can't be – because we have two later maps, covering the same region but drawn several centuries apart, and they don't record the star either. And a visual check right now shows nothing in that region.'

'Which proves it died.'

'That's the obvious explanation. A quick but unspectacular flare-up – then extinction. Now here's the fourth map, the one found by Doctor Pengelly. As you can see, this map shows our star.'

'Which proves it's older than maps two and three.'

'Pengelly claims he excavated it at the highest level of all, that it's the youngest.'

'Which proves he was a liar. This sort of thing has happened before, Vance.' Napier flicked the glossy prints with blunt fingers. 'What about that affair in Crete a few hundred years ago? Archaeologists are always …'

'Trying to win acclaim for themselves. Pengelly had nothing to gain by lying about where he found the fragment. I personally believe it was drawn only a matter of decades before the Big Burn, well into the Saganians space-going era.' Garamond spoke with the flatness of utter conviction. 'You'll notice that on the fourth map the star isn't represented by a simple dot. There are traces of a circle around it.'

Napier shrugged and took the first sip of his whisky. 'It was a map showing the positions of extinct suns.'

'That's a possibility. Possibly even a probability, but I'm betting that Saganian space technology was more advanced than we suspect. I'm betting that Pengelly's Star was important to them in some way we don't understand. They might have found a habitable world there.'

'It wouldn't be habitable now. Not after its sun dying.'

'No – but there might be other maps, underground installations, anything.' Garamond suddenly heard his own words as though they were being spoken by a stranger, and he was appalled at the flimsiness of the logical structure which supported his family's hopes for a future. He glanced instinctively at the door leading to the bedroom where Aileen and Chris were asleep. Napier, perceptive as ever, did not reply and for a while they drank in silence. Blocks of coloured light, created for decorative purposes by the same process which produced solid-image weather maps, drifted through the air of the room in random patterns, mingling and merging. Their changing reflections seemed to animate the gold snail on Garamond's desk.

'We never found any Saganian starships,' Napier said.

'It doesn't mean they didn't have them. You'd find their ships anywhere *but* in the vicinity of a burnt-out home world.' There was another silence and the light-cubes continued to drift through the room like prisms of insubstantial gelatin.

Napier finished his drink and got up to refill his glass. 'You're almost making some kind of a case, but why did the Exploratory Arm never follow it up?'

'Let's level with each other,' Garamond said. 'How many years is it since you really believed that Starflight wants to find other worlds?'

'I ...'

'They've got Terranova, which they sell off in hectare lots as if it was a Long Island development property in the old days. They've got all the ships, too. Man's destiny is in the stars – just so long as he is prepared to sign half his life away to Starflight for the ride, and the other half for a plot of land. It's a smooth-running system, Cliff, and a few cheap new worlds showing up would spoil it. That's why there are so few ships, comparatively speaking, in the S.E.A.'

'But ...'

'They're more subtle than the railroad and mining companies in the States were when they set up their private towns, but the technique's the same. What are you trying to say?'

'I'm trying to agree with you.' Napier punched his fist through a cube of lime-green radiance which floated away unaffected. 'It doesn't matter a damn where we go in this year, so let's hunt down Pengelly's Star. Have you any idea where it ought to be?'

'Some. Have a look at this chart.' As they walked over to the universal machine in the corner Garamond felt a sense of relief that Napier had been so easy to convince – to his own mind it gave the project a semblance of sanity. When he was within voice-acceptance range of the machine he called up the map it had prepared for him. A three-dimensional star chart appeared in the air above the console. One star trailed a curving wake of glowing red dashes in contrast to the solid green lines which represented the galactic drift of the others.

'I had no direct data on how far Pengelly's Star was from Sagania,' Garamond said. 'But the fact that we're interested in it carries the implication that it was a Sol-type sun. This gives an approximate value for its intrinsic luminosity and, as the dot representing it on the earliest Saganian map was about equal in size to other existing stars of first magnitude, I was able to assign a distance from Sagania.'

'There's a lot of assuming and assigning going on there,' Napier said doubtfully.

'Not all that much. Now, the stars throughout the entire region share the same proper motion and speed so, although they've all travelled a long way in seven thousand years, we can locate Pengelly's Star on this line with a fair degree of certainty.'

'Certainty, he says. What's the computed journey time? About four months?'

'Less if there's the right sort of dust blowing around.'

'It'll be there,' Napier said in a neutral voice. 'It's an ill wind ...'

Later, when Napier had left to get some sleep, Garamond ordered the universal machine to convert an entire wall of the room into a forward-looking viewscreen. He sat for a long time in a deep chair, his drink untouched, staring at the stars and thinking about Napier's final remark. Part of the invisible galactic winds from which the *Bissendorf* drew its reaction mass had been very ill winds for somebody, sometime, somewhere. Heavy particles, driven across the galactic wheel by the forces of ancient novae, were the richest and most sought-after harvest of all. An experienced flickerwing man could tell when his engine intakes had begun to feed on such a cloud just by feeling the deck grow more insistent against his feet. But a sun going nova engulfed its planets, converting them and everything on them to incandescent gas, and at each barely perceptible surge of the ship Garamond wondered if his engines were feeding on the ghosts of dawn-time civilizations, obliterating all their dreams, giving the final answer to all their questions.

He fell asleep sitting at the viewscreen, on the dark edge of the abyss.

Aileen Garamond had been ill for almost a week.

Part of the trouble was due to shock and the subsequent stress of being catapulted into a difficult environment, but Garamond was surprised to discover that his wife was far more sensitive than he to minute changes in acceleration caused by the ship crossing weather zones. He explained to her that the *Bissendorf* relied largely on interstellar hydrogen for reaction mass, ionizing it by continuously firing electron beams ahead of the ship, then sweeping it up with electromagnetic fields which guided it through the engine intakes. As the distribution of hydrogen was constant the ship would have had constant acceleration, and its crew would have enjoyed an unchanging apparent gravity, had there been no other considerations. Space, however, was not the quiescent vacuum described by the old Earthbound astronomers. Vagrant clouds of charged particles from a dozen different kinds of sources swept through it like winds and tides, heavy and energetic, clashing, deflecting, creating silent storms where they met each other head-on.

'On available hydrogen alone our best acceleration would be half a gravity or less,' Garamond said. 'That's why we value the high-activity regions and, where possible, plot courses which take us through them. And that's why you feel occasional changes in your weight.'

Aileen thought for a moment. 'Couldn't you vary the efficiency of the engines to compensate for those changes?'

'Hey!' Garamond gave a pleased laugh. 'That's the normal practice on a passenger ship. They run at roughly nine tenths of full power and this is automatically stepped up or down as the ship enters poor or rich volumes of space, so that shipboard gravity remains constant. But Exploratory Arm ships normally keep going full blast, and on a trip like this one ...' Garamond fell silent.

'Go on, Vance.' Aileen sat up in the bed, revealing her familiar tawny torso. 'You can't take it easy when you're being hunted.'

'It isn't so much that we're being hunted, it's just that to make the best use of our time we ought to move as fast as possible.'

Aileen got out of the bed and came towards where he was seated, her nakedness incongruous in the functional surroundings of his quarters. 'There's no point in our going to Terranova, is there? Isn't that what you're telling me?'

He leaned his face against the warm cushion of her belly. 'The ship can keep going for about a year. After that ...'

'And we won't find a new planet. One we can live on, I mean.'

'There's always the chance.'

'How much of a chance?'

'It has taken the entire fleet a hundred years of searching to find one habitable planet. Work it out for yourself.'

'I see.' Aileen stood with him for a moment, almost abstractedly holding his face against herself, then she turned away with an air of purpose. 'It's about time for that guided tour of the ship you promised Christopher and me.'

'Are you sure you're feeling well enough?'

'I'll get well enough,' she assured him.

Garamond suddenly felt happier than he had expected to be ever again. He nodded and went into the main room where Chris was eating breakfast. As soon as the boy had got over his unfortunate introduction to spaceflight on board the shuttle, he had adapted quickly and easily to his new surroundings. Garamond had eased things as much as possible by putting in very little time in the *Bissendorf*'s control room, allowing Napier and the other senior officers to run the ship. He helped his son to dress and by the time he had finished Aileen had joined them, looking slightly self-conscious in the dove-grey nurse's coverall he had ordered for her from the quartermaster.

'You look fine,' he said before she could ask the age-old question.

Aileen examined herself critically. 'What was wrong with my dress?'

'Nothing, if you're on the recreation deck, but you must wear functional clothing when moving about the other sections of the ship. There aren't any other wives on board, and I don't like to rub it in.'

'But you told me a third of the crew were women.'

'That's right. We have a hundred-and-fifty female crew of varying ages and rank. On a long trip there's always a lot of short-term coupling going on, and occasionally there's a marriage, but no woman is taken on for purely biological reasons. Everybody has a job to do.'

'Don't sound so stuffy, Vance.' Aileen looked down at Christopher, then back at her husband. 'What about Christopher? Does everybody know why we're here?'

'No. I blocked the communications channels while we were on the shuttle. The one other person on board who knows the whole story is Cliff Napier – all the others can only guess I'm in some sort of a jam, but they won't be too concerned about it.' Garamond smiled as he remembered the old flicker-wingers' joke. 'It's a kind of relativity effect – the faster and farther you go, the smaller the President gets.'

'Couldn't they have heard about it on the radio since then?'

Garamond shook his head emphatically. 'It's impossible to communicate with a ship when it's under way. No signal can get through the fields. The crew will probably decide I walked out on Elizabeth the way a commander called Witsch once did. If anything, I'll go up in their estimation.'

It took more than an hour to tour the various sections and levels of the *Bissendorf,* starting with the command deck and moving 'downwards' through the various administrative, technical and workshop levels to the field generating stations, and the pods containing the flux pumps and hy-drogen fusion plant. At the end of the tour Garamond realized, with a dull sense of astonishment, that for a while he had managed to forget that he and his family were under sentence of death.

Boosted by the ion-rich tides of space, the ship maintained an average acceler-ation of 13 metres per second squared. Punishing though this was to the crew, whose weight had apparently increased by one third, it was a rate of speed-increase which would have required several months before the Bissendorf *could have reached the speed of light under Einsteinian laws. After only seven weeks, however, the ship had attained a speed of fifty million metres a second – the magical threshold figure above which Arthurian physics held sway – and new phenomena, inexplicable in terms of low-speed systems, were observed. To those on board acceleration remained constant, yet the* Bissendorf's *speed increased sharply until, at the mid-point of the voyage, only twelve days later, it was travelling at vast multiples of the speed of light.*

Retardation produced a mirror image of the distance-against-time graph, and in an elapsed time of four months the ship was in the computed vicinity of Pengelly's Star.

'I'm sorry, Vance.' Cliff Napier's heavy-boned face was sombre as he spoke. 'There's just no sign of it. Yamoto says that if we were within ten light-years of a black sun his instruments couldn't miss it.'

'Is he positive?'

'He's positive. In fact, according to him there's less spatial background activity than normal.'

I'm not going to let it happen, Garamond thought irrationally. Aloud he said, 'Let's go down to the observatory – I want to talk to Yamoto about this.'

'I'll put him on your viewer now.'

'No, I want to see him in person.' Garamond left the central command console and nodded to Gunther, the second exec, to take over. This was the moment he had been dreading since the *Bissendorf*'s engines had been shut down an hour earlier, making it possible – in the absence of the all-devouring intake fields – to carry out radiation checks of the surrounding space. The reason he was going to the observatory in person was that he had a sudden need to move his arms and legs, to respond to the crushing sense of urgency which had been absent while the ship was in flight and now was back with him again. He wanted some time away from the watchful eyes of the bridge personnel.

'I'm sorry, Vance.' Napier always had trouble adjusting to zero-gravity conditions and his massive figure swayed precariously as he walked in magnetic boots to the elevator shaft.

'You said that before.'

'I know, but I'd begun to believe we were on to something, and somehow I feel guilty over the way it has turned out.'

'That's crazy – we always knew it was a long shot,' Garamond said. *You liar,* he told himself. *You didn't believe it was a long shot at all. You had convinced yourself you'd find a signpost to the third world because you couldn't face the fact that you condemned your wife and son to death.*

As the elevator was taking him down he thought back, for perhaps the thousandth time, to that afternoon on the terrace at Starflight House. All he had had to do was keep an eye on Harald Lindstrom, to refuse when asked for permission to run, to do what anybody else would have done in the same circumstances. Instead, he had let the boy trick him into doing his hardened spacefarer bit, then he had allowed himself to be pressured, then he had turned his back and indulged in daydreams while Harald was climbing, then he had been too slow in reaching the statue while the first fatal millimetre of daylight opened up between the boy's fingers and the metal construction and he was falling ... and falling ... *falling.*

'Here we are.' Napier opened the elevator door, revealing a tunnel-like corridor at the end of which was the *Bissendorf*'s astronomical observatory.

'Thanks.' Garamond fought to suppress a sense of unreality as he walked out of the elevator. He saw, as in a dream, the white-clad figure of Sammy Yamoto standing at the far end of the corridor waving to him. His brain was trying in a numbed way to deal with the paradox that moments of truth, those instants when reality cannot be avoided, always seem unreal. And the truth was that his wife and child were going to die. *Because of him.*

'For a man who found nothing,' Napier commented, 'Sammy Yamoto's looking pretty excited.'

Garamond summoned his mind back from grey wanderings.

Yamoto came to meet him, plum-coloured lips trembling slightly. 'We've found something! After I spoke to Mister Napier I became curious over the fact that there was less matter per cubic centimetre than the galactic norm. It was as if the region had been swept by a passing sun, yet there was no sun around.'

'What did you find?'

'I'd already checked out the electro-magnetic spectrum and knew there couldn't *be* a sun nearby, but I got a crazy impulse and checked the gravitic spectrum anyway.' Yamoto was a fifty-year-old man who had looked on many worlds in his lifetime, yet his face was the face of a man in shock. Garamond felt the first stirrings of a powerful elation.

'Go on,' Napier said from behind him.

'I found a gravity source of stellar magnitude less than a tenth of a light-year away, so ...'

'I knew it!' Napier's voice was hoarse. 'We've found Pengelly's Star.'

Garamond's eyes were locked on the astronomer's. 'Let Mister Yamoto speak.'

'So I took some tachyonic readings to get an approximation of the object's size and surface composition, and ... You aren't going to believe this, Mister Garamond.'

'Try me,' Garamond said.

'As far as I can tell ...' Yamoto swallowed painfully. 'As far as I can tell, the object out there ... the thing we have discovered is a spaceship over three hundred million kilometres in diameter!'

CHAPTER FIVE

Like everyone else on board the *Bissendorf,* Garamond spent a lot of time at the forward viewscreens during the long days of the approach to the sphere.

He attended many meetings, accompanied by Yamoto who had become one of the busiest and most sought-after men on the ship. At first the Chief Astronomer had wanted to take advantage of the drive shut-down period to get a tachyonic signal announcing his discovery off to Earth. Garamond discreetly did not point out his own role as prime mover in the find. Instead he made Yamoto aware of the danger of letting fame-hungry professional rivals appear on the scene too early, and at the same time he insured against risks by ordering an immediate engine restart.

Yamoto went back to work, but the curious thing was that even after a full week of concentrated activity he knew little more about the sphere than had been gleaned in his first hurried scan. He confirmed that it had a diameter of some 320,000,000 kilometres, or just over two astronomical units; he confirmed that its surface was smooth to beyond the limits of resolution, certainly the equivalent of finely machined steel; he confirmed that the sphere emitted no radiation other than on the gravitic spectrum, and that analysis of this proved it to be hollow. In that week the only new data he produced were that the object's sphericity was perfect to within the possible margin of error, and that it rotated. On the question of whether it was a natural or an artificial object he would venture no professional opinion.

Garamond turned all these factors over in his mind, trying to gauge their relevance to his own situation. The sphere, whatever its nature, no matter what its origins might be, was a startling find – the fact that it had been indicated on an antique Saganian star chart radically altered the accepted views about the dead race's technological prowess. Possibly the whole science of astronomy would be affected, but not the pathetically short futures of his wife and child. What had he been hoping for? A fading sun which still emitted some life-giving warmth? An Earth-type planet with a vast network of underground caverns leading down into the heat of its core? A race of friendly humanoids who would say, 'Come and live with us and we'll protect your family from the President of Starflight'?

It was in the nature of hope that it could survive on such preposterous fantasies. But only when they were confined to the subconscious, where – as long as they existed at all – the emotions could equate them with genuine prospects of survival, enabling the man on the scaffold steps to retain his belief that something could still turn up to save him. Garamond and his wife and boy were on the scaffold steps, and the fantasies of hope were being dissipated by the awful presence of the sphere.

Garamond found that trying to comprehend its size produced an almost physical pain between his temples. The object was big enough by astronomical standards, so large that with Sol positioned at its centre the Earth's orbit would be within the shell, assuming that the outer surface was a shell. It was so huge that, from distances which would have reduced Sol to nothing more than a bright star, it was clearly visible to the unaided eye as a disc of blackness against the star clouds of the galactic lens. Garamond watched it grow and grow in his screens until it filled the entire field of view with its dark, inconceivable bulk – and yet it was still more than 150,000,000 kilometres away.

Something within him began to cringe from it. In the early stages of the approach he had nursed the idea that, because of the smoothness of its surface, the sphere had to be an artifact. The notion faded when exposed to the mind-punishing reality of the sphere's magnitude, because there was no way to visualize engineering on that scale, to conceive of a technology so far beyond anything mankind could dream of achieving. Then, in the final stages of the approach, the *Bissendorf*'s sensors became aware of a planet orbiting outside the sphere.

There was no optical evidence of the planet's existence, but a study of its gravitic emissions showed that it was of approximately the same diameter and mass as Earth, and that its almost-circular orbit lay some 80,000,000 kilometres outside the sphere's surface. Although the discovery of the planet was of value in itself, the real importance lay in what could now be deduced about the nature of the sphere.

Chief Astronomer Yamoto sent Garamond a report which stated, un-equivocally, that it was a thin shell enclosing an otherwise normal sun.

By the time the ship had matched velocities with the hidden star and slipped into an equatorial parking orbit, it was just over two thousand kilometres from the surface of the dark sphere. The range was inconvenient for the rocket-propelled buggy which would carry the exploration party, but the *Bissendorf* had never been intended for close manoeuvring, and Garamond decided against jockeying in closer with the rarely-used ion tubes. He sat in the central control area and watched the stereo image of the EVA group as they prepared themselves in the muster station. Garamond knew all the men and women of his crew by sight if not by name, but there was one blond fresh-complexioned youngster he was having trouble identifying. He pointed at the screen.

'Cliff, is that one of the shuttle crew we shanghaied?'

'That's right. Joe Braunek. He fitted in well,' Napier said. 'I think you did him a favour.'

'Did Tayman select him for this mission?'

'He volunteered. Tayman referred it back to me and I interviewed Braunek in person.' Napier broke off to contemplate a memory which appeared to amuse him.

'Well?'

'He says he's entitled to log the flying time because you wrecked his shuttle and dumped it near Saturn.'

Garamond nodded his approval. 'What about the other shuttle pilot? The one with the blue chin.'

'Shrapnel? Ah … he didn't fit in so well. In fact, he's pretty resentful. He wouldn't sign on the crew and I've had to keep him under surveillance.'

'Oh? I seem to remember sending him an apology.'

'You did. He's still resentful.'

'I wonder why?'

Napier gave a dry cough. 'He wasn't planning to be separated from his wife for this length of time.'

'I'm a self-centred bastard – is that it, Cliff?'

'Nothing like it.'

'Don't give me that – I recognize that Chopin cough you get every time I go off the rails.' Garamond visualized the shuttle pilot, tried to imagine the man in the context of a family like his own, but found the exercise strangely difficult. 'Shrapnel knows he'll only be away for a year. Why doesn't he try to make the best of it?'

Napier coughed once more. 'The EVA group are about ready to go.'

'Your TB is back again, Cliff. What did I say that time?' Garamond stared hard at his next-in-command.

Napier took a deep breath, altering the slopes of his massive chest and shoulders. 'You don't like Shrapnel, and he doesn't like you, and that amuses me – because you're both the same type. If you were in his shoes *you'd* be broody and resentful and looking for an opportunity to twist things back the way you wanted them. He even looks a bit like you, yet you sit there telling everybody he's weird.'

Garamond gave a smile he did not feel. Napier and he had long ago discarded all remnants of formal relationship, and he felt no resentment at the other man's words, but he found them disturbing. They had implications he did not want to examine. He selected the EVA group's intercom frequency and listened to the clamorous, overlapping voices of the men as the buggy was sealed and the dock evacuation procedure began. They were complaining in a good-natured way about the discomfort of the space-suits which they normally donned only twice a year in practice drills, or about the difficulty of carrying instruments and tool kits in gloved hands, but Garamond knew they were genuinely excited. Life on board an S.E.A. vessel consisted of routine outward journeys, brief pauses while it was established by long range instruments that the target suns had no planets or no usable planets, and equally dull returns to base. This was the first occasion in the *Bissendorf*'s entire span of service on which it had been necessary for men to leave its protective hull and venture into alien space with the object of making physical contact with something outside humanity's previous experience. It was a big moment for the little exploratory team and Garamond found himself wishing he could take part.

He watched as the outer doors of the dock slid aside to reveal a blackness which was unrelieved by stars. At a distance of two thousand kilometres the sphere not only filled one half of the sky, it *was* one half of the sky. The observed universe was cut into two hemispheres – one of them glowing with starclouds, the other filled with light-absorbent darkness. There was no sensation of being close to a huge object, rather one of being poised above infinite deeps.

The restraining rings opened and allowed the white-painted buggy to jet out clear of the mother ship. Its boxy, angular outline shrank to invisibility in a few seconds, but its interior and marker lights remained in view for quite a long time as the craft moved 'downwards' from the *Bissendorf.* Garamond stayed at central control while the buggy descended, watching several screens at once as its cameras sent back different types of information. At a height of three hundred metres the buggy's commander, Kraemer, switched on powerful searchlights and succeeded in creating a greyish patch of illumination on the sphere's surface.

'Instruments show zero gravity at surface,' he reported.

Garamond cut in on the circuit. 'Do you want to go on down?'

'Yes, sir. The surface looks metallic from here – I'd like to try a touchdown with magnetic clamps.'

'Go ahead.'

The indistinct greyness expanded on the screens until the clang of the buggy's landing gear was heard. 'It's no use,' Kraemer said. 'We just bounced off.'

'Are you going to let her float?'

'No, sir. I'm going to go in again and maintain some drive pressure. That should lock the buggy in place against the surface and give us a fixed point to work from.'

'Go ahead, Kraemer.' Garamond looked at Napier and nodded in satisfaction. The two men watched as the buggy was inched into contact with the surface and held there by the thrust of its tubes.

Kraemer's voice was heard again. 'Surface seems to have a reasonable index of friction – we aren't slipping around. I think it's safe to go out for samples.'

'Proceed.'

The buggy's door slid open, spacesuited figures drifted out and formed a small swarm around the splayed-out landing gear. Bracing themselves against the tubular legs, the figures went to work on the vaguely seen surface of the sphere with drills, cutters and chemicals. At the end of thirty minutes, by which time the team operating the valency cutter could have sliced through a house-sized block of chrome steel, nobody had managed even to mark the surface. The result was in accordance with Garamond's premonitions.

'This is a new one on me,' said Harmer, the chemist. 'We can't make a spectroscopic analysis because the stuff refuses to burn. At this stage I can't even say for sure that it's a metal. We're just wasting our time down here.'

'Tell Kraemer to bring them up,' Garamond said to Napier. 'Is there any point in firing the main ionizing gun against it?'

'None at all,' put in Denise Serra, the Chief Physicist. 'If a valency cutter at a range of one centimetre achieved nothing there's no point in hosing energy all over it from this distance.'

Garamond nodded. 'Okay. Let's pool our ideas. We've acquired a little more information, although most of it is negative, and I'd like to have your thoughts on whether the sphere is a natural object or an artifact.'

'It's an artifact,' Denise Serra said immediately, with characteristic firmness. 'Its sphericity is perfect and the surface is smooth to limits of below one micron. Nature doesn't operate that way – at least, not on the astronomical scale.' She glanced a challenge at Yamoto.

'I have to agree,' Yamoto said. 'I've been avoiding the idea, but I can't conceive of any natural mechanism which would produce that thing out there. However, that doesn't mean I can see how it was constructed by intelligent beings. It's just too much.' He shook his head dispiritedly. The haggardness of his face showed that he had been losing a lot of sleep.

O'Hagan, the Chief Science Officer, who was a stickler for protocol, cleared his throat and spoke for the first time. 'Our difficulties arise from the fact that the *Bissendorf* is an exploration vessel and very little more. The correct procedure now would be to send a tachyon signal back to Earth and get a properly equipped expedition out here.' His severe grey gaze held steadily on Garamond's face.

'That's outside the scope of the present discussion,' Napier said.

Garamond shook his head. 'No, it isn't. Gentlemen, and lady, Mister O'Hagan has put into words something which must have been on all your minds since the beginning of this mission. It can't have been difficult for you to work out for yourselves that I'm in trouble with Starflight House. In fact, it's personal trouble with Elizabeth Lindstrom – and I think you all know what that means. I'm not going to give you any more details, simply because I don't want you to be involved any more than you are at present.

'Perhaps it is enough to say that this has to be my last voyage as a Starflight commander, and I want this year in full.'

O'Hagan looked pained, but he held his ground doggedly. 'I'm sure I'm speaking for all the other section heads when I say that we feel the utmost personal loyalty to Captain Garamond, and that our feelings aren't affected by the circumstances surrounding the start of this voyage. Had it turned out to be a normal, uneventful mission I, for one, wouldn't have considered questioning its legality – but the fact remains that we have made the most important discovery since Terranova and Sagania, and I feel it should be reported to Earth without delay.'

'I disagree,' Napier said coldly. 'Starflight House didn't direct the *Bissendorf* to this point in space. The sphere was discovered because Captain Garamond acted independently to check out a personally-held theory. We'll hand it over to Starflight, as a bonus they didn't earn, at the end of the mission's scheduled span of one year.'

O'Hagan gave a humourless smile. 'I still feel ...'

Napier jumped to his feet. 'What do you mean when you say you *feel*, Mister O'Hagan? Don't you think with your brain like the rest of us? Does the fact that you *feel* these things turn them into something for which you have no personal responsibility?'

'That's enough,' Garamond said.

'I just want O'Hagan to stand over his words.'

'I said ...'

'Gentlemen, I withdraw my remarks,' O'Hagan interrupted, staring fixedly at his notepad. 'It wasn't my intention to divert the discussion away from the main topic. Now, we seem agreed that the sphere is of artificial origin – so what is its purpose?' He raised his eyes and scanned the assembled officers.

There was a lengthy silence.

'Defence?' Denise Serra's round face mirrored her doubts. 'Is there a planet inside?'

'There might be a planet on the far side of the sun which hasn't shown up much on our gravitic readings.' Yamoto said. 'But if we had the technology to produce that sphere, could there be an enemy so powerful that we would have to cower behind a shield?'

'Supposing it was a case of "Stop the galaxy, I want to get off"? Maybe the builders were pacifists and felt the need to hide. They made a pretty good job of concealing a star.'

'I hope that isn't the answer,' Yamoto said gloomily. 'If *they* needed to hide ...'

'This is getting too speculative,' Garamond put in. 'The immediate practical question is, does it have an entrance? Can we get inside? Let's have your thoughts on that.'

Yamoto stroked his wispy beard. 'If there is an entrance, it ought to be on the equator so that ships could hold their positions over it just by going into a parking orbit the way we did.'

'So you suggest doing a circuit of the sphere in the equatorial plane?'

'Yes – in the opposite direction to its rotation. That way we would get the advantage of its seventy thousand kilometres an hour equatorial rotation and cut down on our own G-forces.'

'That's decided then,' Garamond said. 'We'll turn around as soon as Kraemer and his team are on board. I hope we'll recognize an entrance if we find one.'

Three duty periods later he was asleep beside Aileen when his personal communicator buzzed him into wakefulness.

'Garamond here,' he said quietly, trying not to disturb his wife.

'Sorry to disturb you, Vance,' Napier said, 'but I think we're going to reach an entrance to the sphere in a couple of hours from now.'

'*What?*' Garamond sat upright, aware of deceleration forces. 'How could you tell?'

'Well, we can't be certain, but it's the most likely explanation for the echoes we're picking up on the long-range radar.'

'What sort of echoes?'

'A lot of them, Vance. There's a fleet of about three thousand ships in parking orbit, dead ahead of us.'

CHAPTER SIX

The ships were invisible to the naked eye, yet on the detector screens on board the *Bissendorf* they appeared as a glowing swarm, numerous as stars in a dense cluster. High-resolution radar, aided by other forms of sensory apparatus, revealed them to be of many different sizes and shapes, a vast and variegated armada poised above one point on the enigmatic sphere.

'You could have told me they weren't Starflight ships,' Garamond said, easing himself into his seat in central control, his eyes fixed on the forward screens.

'Sorry, Vance – it didn't occur to me.' Napier handed Garamond a bulb of hot coffee. 'As soon as I saw the lack of standard formations I knew they couldn't be Starflight vessels. The silhouettes and estimated masses produced by the computers confirmed it – none of the ships in that bunch can be identified by type.'

Second Officer Gunther gave a quiet laugh. 'That was a pretty nervy moment up here.'

Garamond smiled in sympathy. 'I guess it was.'

'Then we realized we were looking at a collection of hulks.'

'You're positive?'

'There's no radiation of any kind. Those are dead ships, and they've been that way for a long time.' Napier shook his head. 'This is turning out to be one hell of a trip, Vance. First there was the sphere itself, and now ... We always wondered why no Saganian starships had ever been found.'

One hell of a trip, Garamond repeated to himself, his mind trying to deal with the magnitude of the new discovery and at the same time cope with the shocking and unexpected presence of something akin to hope. He had fled from the Earth as an obscure flickerwing commander, but now had the prospect of returning as the most celebrated explorer since Laker had founded Terranova and Molyneaux had found Sagania. It was bound to make things more difficult for Elizabeth. In practice she was outside the law, but even for the President of Starflight Incorporated there were limits to how far she could go in full view of the mass television audience – and Garamond was going to be a public figure. A rigged trial, with witnesses primed to swear Harald's death had been the result of wilful action, would destroy Garamond. It would, however, focus the world's attention on him even more firmly and help deny Elizabeth the personal revenge she had never been known to forgo. If he and his family were to die it would probably have to appear accidental. And even the most carefully planned accidents could be prevented, if not indefinitely, at least for a reasonable length of time. The future still looked dangerous, but its uncompromising blackness had been alleviated to some extent.

Maintaining its height above the surface of the sphere, the *Bissendorf* – which had been closing with the immense fleet at a combined speed of almost two hundred thousand kilometres an hour – swung out of the equatorial plane. It described a wide semicircle around the ships and approached them from the opposite direction, carefully matching velocities until it shared approximately the same parking orbit. In the latter stages of the manoeuvre, telescopic observations by Chief Astronomer Yamoto revealed that several of the vessels at the centre of the swarm were shining by reflected light. He deduced that there was a beam of sunlight being emitted from an aperture in the surface of the sphere, and reported to Garamond accordingly. Shortly afterwards the aperture revealed itself in the telescopes as a thin line of faint light which gradually opened to a narrow ellipse as the *Bissendorf* crept closer.

The big ship's central command gallery took on a crowded appearance as officers who were not on duty found reasons to stay near the curving array of consoles. They were waiting for the first transmissions from the surveillance torpedo which had been dispatched towards the spaceships illuminated by the column of light escaping from Pengelly's Star. There was an atmosphere of tension which made everyone on board the *Bissendorf* aware of how uneventful all their previous wanderings in the galaxy had been.

'I'm not used to this excitement,' Napier whispered. 'Round about this stage on a trip I'm usually tucked away quietly with a bottle of ninety-proof consolation, and I almost think I liked it better that way.'

'I didn't,' Garamond said firmly. 'This is changing things for all of us.'

'I know – I was kidding. Have you tried to work out what the prize money ought to be if it turns out that all these ships can still be flown?'

'No.' Garamond had finished his third bulb of coffee and was bending over to put it in the disposal chute.

'Forget it,' Napier said, with a new note in his voice. 'Look at that, Vance!'

There was a murmur of shock from the central gallery as Garamond was raising his head to look at the first images coming back from the distant torpedo. They were of a large grey ship which had been ripped open along its length like a gutted fish. Twisted sections of infrastructure were visible inside the wound, like entrails. Lesser scars which had not penetrated the hull criss-crossed the remainder of the great ovoid's sunlit side.

'Something really chopped her up.'

'Not as much as the next one.'

The images were changing rapidly as the surveillance torpedo, unhampered by any considerations of the effects of G-force on human tissue, darted towards a second ship, which proved to be only half a ship. It had been sliced in two, laterally, by some unimaginable weapon, sculpted ripples of metal flowing back from the sheared edges. A small vessel, corresponding in size to a lifeboat, hung in space near the open cross-section, joined to the mother ship by cables.

After the first startled comments a silence fell over the control gallery as the images of destruction were multiplied. An hour passed as the torpedo examined all the ships in the single shaft of sunlight and spiralled outwards into the darkness to scan others by the light of its own flares. It became evident that every vessel in the huge swarm had died violently, cataclysmically. Garamond found that the ships illuminated dimly by the flares were the most hideous – their ruptured hulls, silent, brooding over gashes filled with the black blood of shadow, could have been organic remains, preserved by the chill of space, contorted by ancient agonies.

'A signal has just come up from telemetry,' Napier said. 'There's a malfunctioning developing in the torpedo's flare circuits. Do you want another one sent out?'

'No. I think we've seen enough for the present. Have the torpedo come round and take a look through the aperture. I'm sure Mister Yamoto would like some readings on the sun in there.' Garamond leaned back in his seat and looked at Napier. 'Has it ever struck you as odd that we, as representatives of a warlike race, don't carry any armament?'

'It has never come up – the Lindstroms wouldn't want their own ships destroyed by each other. Besides, the main ionizing beam would make a pretty effective weapon.'

'Not in that class.' Garamond nodded at the viewscreens. 'We couldn't even aim it without turning the whole ship.'

'You think those hulls prove Serra's theory about the sphere being a defence?'

'Perhaps.' Garamond's voice was thoughtful. 'We won't know for sure until we have a look inside the sphere and see if there was anything worth defending.'

'What makes you think you would see anything?'

'That.' Garamond pointed at the screen which had just begun to show the new images being transmitted back from the torpedo. The aperture in the dark surface of the sphere was circular and almost a kilometre in diameter. A yellow Sol-type sun hung within it, perfectly centred by the torpedo's aiming mechanisms, and the remarkable thing was that the space inside the sphere did not appear black, as the watchers on board the *Bissendorf* knew it ought to do. It was as blue as the summer skies of Earth.

Two hours later, and against all the regulations concerning the safety of Starflight commanders, Garamond was at the head of a small expedition which entered the sphere. The buggy was positioned almost on the edge of the aperture, held in place against the surface by the thrust of its tubes. Garamond was able to grip the strut of a landing leg with one hand and slide the other over the edge of the aperture. Its hard rim was only a few centimetres thick. There was a spongy resistance to the passage of his hand, which told of a force field spanning the aperture like a diaphragm, then his gloved fingers gripped something which felt like grass. He pulled himself through to the inside of the sphere and stood up.

And there – on the edge of a circular black lake of stars, suited and armoured to withstand the lethal vacuum of interplanetary space – Garamond had his first look at the green and infinite meadows of Orbitsville.

CHAPTER SEVEN

Garamond's sense of dislocation was almost complete.

He received an impression of grasslands and low hills running on for ever – and, although his mind was numbed, his thoughts contained an element of immediate acceptance, as if an event for which he had been preparing all his life had finally occurred. Garamond felt as though he had been born again. In that first moment, when his vision was swamped by the brilliance of the impossible landscape, he was able to look at the circular lake of blackness from which he had emerged and see it through alien eyes. The grass – the tall, lush grass grew right to the rim! – shimmered green and it was difficult to accept that there were stars down in that pool. It was impossible to comprehend that were he to lie at its edge and look downwards he would see sunken ships drifting in the black crystal waters ...

Something was emerging from the lake. Something white, groping blindly upwards.

Garamond's identity returned to him abruptly as he recognized the spacesuited figure of Lieutenant Kraemer struggling to an upright position. He moved to help the other man and became aware of yet another 'impossibility' – there was gravity sufficient to give him almost his normal Earth weight. Kraemer and he leaned against each other like drunk men, bemused, stunned, helpless because there were blue skies where there should have been only the hostile blackness of space, because they had stepped through the looking glass into a secret garden. The grass moved gently, reminding Garamond of perhaps the greatest miracle of all, of the presence of an atmosphere. He felt an insane but powerful urge to open his helmet, and was fighting it when his tear-blurred eyes focused on the buildings.

They were visible at several points around the rim of the aperture, ancient buildings, low and ruinous. The reason they had not registered immediately with Garamond was that time had robbed them of the appearance of artifacts, clothing the shattered walls with moss and climbing grasses. As he began to orient himself within the new reality, and the images being transmitted from eyes to brain became capable of interpretation, he saw amid the ruins the skeletons of what had once been great machines.

'Look over there,' he said. 'What do you think?'

There was no reply from Kraemer. Garamond glanced at his companion, saw his lips moving silently behind his faceplate and remembered they were still on radio communication. Both men switched to the audio circuits which used small microphones and speakers on the chest panels.

'The suit radios seem to have packed up,' Kraemer said casually, then his professional composure cracked. 'Is it a dream? Is it? Is it a dream?' His voice was hoarse.

'If it is, we're all in it together. What do you think of the ruins over there?'

Kraemer shielded his eyes and studied the buildings, apparently seeing them for the first time. 'They remind me of fortifications.'

'Me too.' Garamond's mind made an intuitive leap. 'It wasn't always possible to stroll in here the way we just did.'

'All those dead ships?'

'I'd say a lot of people once tried to come through that opening, and other people tried to keep them out.'

'But why should they? I mean, if the whole inside of the sphere is like this …' Kraemer gestured at the sea of grass. 'Oh, Christ! If it's all like this there's as much living room as you'd get on a million Earths.'

'More,' Garamond told him. 'I've already done the sums. This sphere has a surface area equivalent to 625,000,000 times the total surface of Earth. If we allow for the fact that only a quarter of the Earth's surface is land and perhaps only half of that is usable, it means the sphere is equivalent to five billion Earths.'

'That's one each for every man, woman and child in existence.'

'Provided one thing.'

'What's that?'

'That we can breathe the air.'

'We'll find that out right now.' Garamond felt a momentary dizziness. When he had been playing around with comparisons of the size of Earth and the sphere he had treated it as a purely mathematical exercise, his mind solely on the figures, but Kraemer had gone ahead of him to think in terms of people actually living on the sphere, arriving at the aperture in fleets sent from crowded and worn-out Earth, spreading outward across those prairies which promised to go on for ever. Trying to accommodate the vision along with his other speculations about the origins and purpose of the sphere brought Garamond an almost-physical pain behind his eyes. And superimposed on all his swirling thoughts, overriding every other consideration, a new concept of his personal status was struggling to be born. If he, Vance Garamond, gave humanity five billion Earths … then *he*, and not Elizabeth Lindstrom, would be the most important human being alive … then his wife and child would be safe.

'There's an analyser kit in the buggy,' Kraemer said. 'Shall I go for it?'

'Of course.' Garamond was surprised by the lieutenant's question, then with a flash of insight he understood that it had taken only a few minutes of exposure to the unbounded *lebensraunt of* the sphere to alter a relationship which was part of the tight, closed society of the Two Worlds. Kraemer was actually reluctant to leave the secret garden by climbing down into the circular black lake, and – as the potential owner of a super-continent – he saw no reason why Garamond should not go instead. *So quickly,* Garamond thought. *We'll all be changed so quickly.*

Aloud he said, 'While you're getting the kit you can break the news to the others – they'll want to see for themselves.'

'Right.' Kraemer looked pleased at the idea of being first with the most sensational story of all time. He went to the edge of the aperture, lay down and lowered his head into the blackness, obviously straining to force the helmet through the membrane field which retained the sphere's atmosphere. After wriggling sideways a little to obtain his grip on the buggy's leg, Kraemer slid out of sight into the darkness. Garamond again felt a sense of dislocation. The fact that he had weight, that there was a natural-seeming gravity pulling him 'downwards' against the grassy soil created an illusion that he was standing on the surface of a planet. His instincts rebelled against the idea that he was standing on a thin shell of unknown metal, that below him was the hard vacuum of space, that the buggy was close underneath his feet, upside down, clinging to the sphere by the force of its drive.

Garamond moved away from the aperture a short distance, shocked by the incongruity of the heavy spacesuit which shut him off from what surely must be his natural element. He knelt for a closer look at the grass. It grew thickly, in mixed varieties which to his inexperienced eye had stems and laminae very similar to those of Earth. He parted the grass, pushed his gloved fingers into the matted roots and scooped up a handful of brown soil. Small crumbs of it clung to the material of his gloves, making moist smears. Garamond looked upwards and for the first time noticed the lacy white streamers of cloud. With the small sun positioned vertically overhead it was difficult to study the sky, but beyond the cloud he thought he could distinguish narrow bands of a lighter blue which created a delicate ribbed effect curving from horizon to horizon. He made a mental note to point it out to Chief Science Officer O'Hagan for early investigation, and returned his attention to the soil. Digging down into it a short distance he came to the ubiquitous grey metal of the shell, its surface unmarked by the damp earth. Garamond placed his hand against the metal and tried to imagine the building of the sphere, to visualize the creation of a seamless globe of metal with a circumference of a billion kilometres.

There could be only one source for such an inconceivable quantity of shell material, and that was in the sun itself. Matter is energy, and energy is matter. Every active star hurls the equivalent of millions of tons a day of its own substance into space in the form of light and other radiations. But in the case of Pengelly's Star someone had set up a boundary, turned that energy back on itself, manipulating and modifying it, translating it into matter. With precise control over the most elemental forces of the universe they had created an impervious shell of exactly the sort of material they wanted – harder than diamond, immutable, eternal. When the sphere was complete, grown to the required thickness, they had again dipped their hands into the font of energy and wrought fresh miracles, coating the interior surface of the sphere with soil and water and air. Organic acids, even complete cells and seeds, had been constructed in the same way, because at the ultimate level of reality there is no difference between a blade of grass and one of steel . . .

'The air is good, sir.' Kraemer's voice came from close behind. Garamond stood up, turned and saw the lieutenant had opened his faceplate.

'What was the reading like?'

'A shade low in oxygen, but everything else is about right.' Kraemer was grinning like a schoolboy. 'You should try some.'

'I will.' Garamond opened his own helmet and took a deep breath. The air was soft and thick and pure. He discovered at that moment that he had never known truly fresh air before. Low shouts came from the direction of the aperture as other spacesuited figures emerged.

'I told the others they could come through,' Kraemer said. 'All except Braunek – he's holding the buggy in place. It's all right, isn't it?'

'It's all right, yes. I'll be setting up a rota system to let everybody on the ship have a look before we go back.' Again Garamond sensed a difference in Kraemer's attitude – before the lieutenant had seen the interior of the sphere he would not have cleared the buggy without obtaining permission.

'Before we go back? But as soon as we signal Earth the traffic's all going to be coming this way. Why go back?'

'No reason, I suppose.' Garamond had been thinking about Aileen's reluctance ever to travel more than a few kilometres from their apartment. He had been planning to return her to the old familiar surroundings as soon as possible, but perhaps there was no need. Standing on the interior surface of the sphere was as close as one could get to being on the infinite plane of the geometer, yet there was nothing in the experience to inspire agoraphobia. The line of sight did not tangent away from the downward curve of a planet and so the uniform density of the air set a limit to the distance a man could see. Garamond studied the horizon. It appeared to curve upwards slightly, in contrast to that of Earth, but it did not seem much further away. There was no sense of peering into immensities.

Kraemer put the toe of one boot down into the small hole Garamond had made and tapped the metal at the bottom. 'Did you find anything?'

'Such as?'

'Circuits. For this synthetic gravity.'

'No. I don't think we'll find any circuits in our sense of the word.'

'What then?'

'Atoms with their interiors rearranged or specially designed to do a job. Perfect machines.'

'It sounds incredible.'

'We've taken the first step in that direction ourselves with our magnetic resonance engines. Anyway, what could be more incredible than all this?' Some instinct prompted Garamond to push the soil back into the hole and tamp it down with his foot, repairing the damage he had done to the grassy surface. In the region close to the aperture the soil was thinly distributed, but there were hills in the distance which looked as though they could have been formed by drifting.

'As soon as your men have got over the shock tell them to gather vegetation and soil samples,' he said.

'I already have,' Kraemer replied carelessly. 'By the way – none of the suit radios is working, though mine was all right again when I went back out through the aperture.'

'There must be a damping effect – that's something else for O'Hagan to investigate when he gets here. Let's have a look at some of those ruins.'

They walked to the nearest of the indistinct mounds. Under the blanket of climbing grasses there was just enough remaining structure to suggest a floor plan of massive walls and simple square rooms. Here and there, close to the black lake of stars, were distorted metallic stumps which had once been parts of machines. They had a sagging, lava-flow appearance as though they had been destroyed by intense heat.

Kraemer gave a low whistle. 'Who do you think won? The people who were trying to get in, or the ones who were trying to keep them out?'

'I'd say the invaders won, Lieutenant. I've been thinking about all those dead ships hanging out there. They can't be in their battle stations because even if they had been stationary during the fight the forces used against them would have kicked them adrift and there would have been nothing for us to find. It looks as though they were rounded up and carefully parked just outside the aperture.'

'Why?'

'For salvage, perhaps. There may be no metals available within the sphere.'

'For beating into ploughshares? It's good farming country, all right – but where are the farmers?'

'Nomads? Perhaps you don't have to till the soil. Maybe you just keep moving for ever, following the seasons, with the grain always ripening just ahead of you.'

Kraemer laughed. 'What seasons? It must always be high summer here – and high noon, too. It can't even get dark with that sun right above your head.'

'But it *is* getting dark, Lieutenant.' Garamond spoke peacefully, all capacity for surprise exhausted. 'Look over there.'

He pointed at the horizon beyond the black ellipse of the aperture to where the shimmering blue-greens of the distance had begun to deepen. There was an unmistakable gathering of shade.

'That's impossible,' Kraemer protested. He looked up at the sun. 'Oh, no!'

Garamond looked up and saw that the sun was no longer circular. It had one straight side, like a gold coin from which somebody had clipped a generous segment. Shouts from the other men indicated that they had noticed the event. While they watched, the still-brilliant area of the sun's disc grew progressively smaller as though a shutter were being drawn across it. At the same time, keeping pace, the darkness increased on the corresponding horizon and a new phenomenon made itself apparent. The delicate ribbed effect which Garamond had noticed in the sky earlier became clearer, the alternating bands of lighter and darker blue now standing out vividly. In the space of a minute, as the sun began to disappear completely, the slim curving ribs became the dominant feature of the sky, swirling across it from two foci, sharply defined as the striations in polished agate. Near the horizon, where they dipped behind denser levels of air, the bands blurred and dispersed into a prismatic haze. The last searing sliver of sun vanished and Garamond glimpsed a wall of shadow rushing over the landscape towards him at orbital speed, then it was night, beneath a canopy of stratified sapphire.

Garamond stayed beside the lake of stars for an hour before returning to his ship and sending a tachyonic signal to Starflight House.

CHAPTER EIGHT

It was almost exactly four months later that Elizabeth Lindstrom's flagship took up its station outside the sphere's entrance.

Garamond had spent part of the time carrying out investigations into Orbitsville – the name for the sphere had originated with an unknown crew member – but, as it was primarily equipped for locate-and-report missions, the *Bissendorf* did not carry a large science team, and the studies were necessarily limited. The astronomy section, under Sammy Yamoto, made the most profound discovery of all – that there was yet another sphere surrounding Pengelly's Star.

It was smaller than Orbitsville, non-material in nature yet capable of reflecting or deflecting the sun's outpourings of light and heat. Yamoto described it as a 'globular filigree of force fields', a phrase of which he appeared inordinately proud, judging by the frequency with which it was used in his reports. Of the inner sphere's surface area, precisely half was made up of narrow strips, effectively opaque, curving in a general north-south direction. Their function was to cast great moving bars of shadow on the grasslands of Orbitsville, producing the alternating periods of light and darkness, day and night, without which plant life could not survive. Yamoto was not able to observe the inner sphere directly, but he could chart its structure by studying the bands of light and darkness as they moved across the far side of Orbitsville, 320 million kilometres away in the 'night' sky. And he was able to show that the shadow sphere not only created night and day but was also responsible for a progression of seasons. In one quarter of the sphere, corresponding to winter, the opaque night-producing strips were wider and therefore separated by narrower gaps of light; at the opposite side the strips were reduced in width to engender the shorter nights and longer days of summer.

To facilitate Yamoto's work a small plastic observatory was prefabricated in the *Bissendorf*'s workshops and transferred to a site within Orbitsville. Several more buildings were added as other sections found reason to prolong their work in the interior, and the nucleus of a scientific colony was formed.

A substantial portion of the effort was put into trying to solve the annoying riddle of why no radio communicator would work inside the sphere. At first it was anticipated that a simple solution and practical remedy would be found, but the weeks slipped by without any progress being made. It appeared that the equally inexplicable synthetic gravity field was responsible for damping out all electromagnetic radiation. In an effort to get new data on the possible mechanics of the phenomenon, O'Hagan's team took a photographic torpedo and gave it enough extra thrust to enable it to take off from the inner surface of Orbitsville. The purpose of the experiment was to measure the gravity gradient and to see if the radio guidance and telemetry systems would operate if the signals were travelling at right angles to the surface. After a flawless programmed start, the torpedo began tracing random patterns in the sky and made a programmed automatic landing several kilometres away from the aperture. Pessimists began to predict that the only long-range communication possible on Orbitsville would be by modulation of light beams.

Another discovery was that the utterly inert and incredibly hard shell of the sphere was impervious to all radiation except gravity waves. The latter were able to pass through, otherwise the star system's outer planet would have tangented off towards interstellar space, but not even the most energetic particles entered Orbitsville from the outer universe, except by means of the aperture. Certain peculiarities in the measurements of radiation levels from Pengelly's Star itself led O'Hagan to give Garamond a confidential report in which he suggested that flickerwing ships might not be able to operate within the sphere, due to lack of available reaction mass. The subject was earmarked for priority investigation by the fully equipped teams which would arrive later.

Garamond received an increasing number of requests from crewmen, especially those who were inactive when the main drive was not in use, for permission to stay on Orbitsville under canvas. At first he encouraged the idea, but Napier reported that the remaining personnel were becoming resentful of their relaxed and sunburned colleagues whose eyes held a new kind of contentment and surety when they returned to ship duties. Partly to combat the divisive forces, Garamond took the *Bissendorf* on a circuit of Orbitsville's equatorial plane and established that no other entrances were visible.

He also set teams of men to work on moving the swarm of dead ships to a position a thousand kilometres down orbit from the aperture. With the ships at their new station, photographic teams went inside as many as was practicable and made records of their findings. They confirmed Garamond's first guess that the hulls had been used as mines and sources of supply. The interiors were gutted, stripped to the bare metal of their hulls, and in some cases it turned out that what had first been thought of as the havoc of battle was actually the work of scavengers. An unfortunate by-product was that virtually nothing was found which would have let researchers deduce the appearance of the aliens who had built and flown the huge fleet. The most significant find was a section of metal staircase and handrailing which hinted that the aliens had been bipeds of about the same size as humans.

Where were they now?

The question came in for more discussion than did speculations on the whereabouts of the beings who had created Orbitsville. It was understood that the sphere-builders had possessed a technology of an entirely different order to that of the race which had produced the ships. The instinctive belief was that the sphere-builders were unknowable, that they had moved on to new adventures or new phases of their existence, because it would be impossible to be near them without their presence being felt. Orbitsville appeared to be and was accepted as a gift from the galactic past.

Garamond brought Aileen and Christopher into the sphere, through the newly constructed L-shaped entrance port, for a strangely peaceful vacation. Aileen was, as he had predicted, able to adjust to Orbitsville's up-curving horizons without any psychological upsets, and Chris took to it like a foal turned loose in spring pastures. In the daytime Garamond watched the boy's skin acquire the gold of the new-found sun, and at nights he sat outside with Aileen beneath the fabulous archways of the sky, their gratification all the more intense because of the period of despair which had preceded it.

Only in dreams, or in the half-world between consciousness and sleep, did Garamond feel any apprehension at the thought of Elizabeth advancing across the light-years which lay between Orbitsville and Earth.

To the unaided vision it would have appeared that her flagship came alone, but in fact it was at the head of a fleet of seventy vessels. An interstellar ramjet on main drive was surrounded by its intake field, a vast insubstantial maw with an area of up to half a million square kilometres, and for this reason the closest formation ever flown was in the form of a thousand-kilometre grid. The fleet was unwieldy even by Starflight standards. It spent two days in matching velocities with the galactic drift of Pengelly's Star and in deploying its individual units in parking orbit. When each ship had been accurately positioned and its electromagnetic wings furled, the flagship – *Starflier IV* – advanced slowly on ion drive until it was almost alongside the *Bissendorf.* Captain Vance Garamond received a formal invitation to go on board.

The very act of donning the black-and-silver dress uniform, for the first time ever in the course of a mission, made him aware that once again he was within Elizabeth's sphere of influence. He was not conscious of any fear – Orbitsville had had too profound an effect on the situation for that – yet he was filled with a vague distaste each time he thought of the forthcoming interview. For the past four months he had been certain of the fact that Elizabeth's consequence had been reduced to normal human dimensions, but her arrival at the head of an armada suggested that the old order was still a reality. For her, the only reality.

The sight of his dress uniform had disturbed Aileen, too. As the doors of the transit dock opened and the little buggy ventured out on to the black ocean of space, Garamond remembered the way his wife had kissed him before he left. She had been abstracted, almost cold, and had turned away quickly. It was as though she were suppressing all emotion, but in his final glimpse of her she had been holding their golden snail against her cheek. He stood behind the pilot of the buggy for the whole of the short trip, watching the flagship expand until it filled the forward screens. When the docking manoeuvre had been completed he stepped watchfully but confidently into the transit bay where a group of Starflight officials were waiting. Behind the officials were a number of men in civilian dress and carrying scene recorders. With a minimum of ceremony Garamond was escorted to the Presidential suite and ushered into the principal stateroom. Elizabeth must have given previous instructions, because his escorts withdrew immediately and in silence.

The President was standing with her back to the door. She was wearing a long close-fitting gown of white satin – her favourite style of dress – and three white spaniels floated drowsily in the air close to her feet. Garamond was shocked to see that Elizabeth had lost most of her hair. The thinning black strands clung to her scalp in patches, making her look old and diseased. She continued to stand with her back to him although she must have been aware Of his presence.

'My Lady ...' Garamond scuffed the floor with his magnetic-soled boots, and the President slowly turned around. The skin of her small-chinned face was pale and glistening.

'Why did you do it, Captain?' Her voice was low. 'Why did you run from me?'

'My Lady, I ...' Garamond, unprepared for a direct question, was lost for words.

'Why were you afraid of me?'

'I panicked. What happened to your son was a pure accident – he fell when I wasn't even near him – but I panicked. And I ran.' It occurred to Garamond that Elizabeth might have sound political and tactical reasons for choosing to meet him as a mother who had lost a child rather than as an empress in danger of being usurped, but it did not lessen her advantage.

Incredibly, Elizabeth smiled her asymmetrical, knowing smile. 'You thought I wouldn't understand, that I might lash out at you.'

'It would have been a natural reaction.'

'You shouldn't have been afraid of me, Captain.'

'I ... I'm glad.' *This is fantastic,* Garamond thought numbly. *She doesn't believe any of it. I don't believe any of it. So why go on with the charade?*

'... suffered, and you've suffered,' Elizabeth was saying. 'I think we always will, but I want you to know that I bear you no grudge.' She came closer to him, still smiling, and her soft satiny abdomen brushed his knuckles. Garamond thought of spiders.

'There isn't any way I can express how sorry I am that the accident occurred.'

'I know.' Elizabeth's voice was gentle, but suddenly the room was filled with her sweet, soupy odour and Garamond knew that, just for an instant, she had thought of killing him.

'My Lady, if this is too much for you ...'

Her face hardened instantly. 'What makes you think so?'

'Nothing.'

'Very well, then. We have important business matters to discuss, Captain.

Did you know that the Council, with my consent, has authorized the payment to you of ten million monits?'

Garamond shook his head. 'Ten million?'

'Yes. Does that seem a lot of money to you?'

'It seems all the money there is.'

Elizabeth laughed and turned away from him, disturbing the spaniels in their airborne slumbers. 'It's nothing, Captain. *Nothing!* You will, of course, be appointed to the council I'm setting up to advise on the development and exploitation of Lindstromland, and your salary from that alone will be two million monits a year. Then there's ...' Elizabeth paused.

'What's the matter, Captain? You look surprised.'

'I am.'

'At the size of your salary? Or the fact that the sphere has been officially named after my family?'

'The name of the sphere is unimportant,' Garamond said stonily, too disturbed by what Elizabeth had said to think about exhibiting the proper degree of deference. 'What is important is that it can't be controlled and exploited. You sounded as if you were planning to parcel up the land and sell it in the same way that Terranova is handled.'

'We don't sell plots on Terranova – they are given freely, through Government-controlled agencies.'

'To anybody who can pay the Starflight transportation Charge. It's the same thing.'

'Really?' Elizabeth examined Garamond through narrowed eyes. 'You're an expert on such matters, are you?'

'I don't need to be. The facts are easily understood.' Garamond felt he was rushing towards a dangerous precipice, but he had no desire to hold back.

'In that case you'll make an excellent council member – all the others regard the Starflight operation as being extremely complex.'

'In practice,' Garamond said doggedly. 'But not in principle.'

Elizabeth gave her second unexpected smile of the interview. 'In principle, then, why can't Lindstromland be developed in the normal way?'

'For the same reason that water-sellers can make a living only in the desert.'

'You mean where there's a lot of water freely available nobody will pay for it.'

'No doubt that sounds childishly simple to you, My Lady, but it's what I meant.'

'I'm intrigued by your thought processes, Captain.' Elizabeth was giving no sign of being angered by Garamond's attitude. 'How can you compare selling water and opening up a new world?'

Garamond gave a short laugh. 'Yours are the intriguing thought processes if you're comparing Orbitsville to an ordinary planet.'

'Orbitsville?'

'Lindstromland. It isn't like an ordinary planet.'

'I'm aware of the difference in size.'

'You aren't.'

Elizabeth's tolerance began to fade. 'Be careful about what you say, Captain.'

'With respect, My Lady, you aren't aware of the difference in size. Nobody is, and nobody ever will be. *I'm* not aware of it, and I've flown right round Orbitsville.'

'Surely the fact that you were able to …'

'I was travelling at a hundred thousand kilometres an hour,' Garamond said in a steady voice. 'At that speed I could have orbited Earth in twenty-five minutes. Do you know how long it took to get round Orbitsville? *Forty-two days!*'

'I grant you we're dealing with a new order of magnitude.'

'And that's only a linear comparison. Don't you see there's just no way you can handle the amount of living space involved?'

Elizabeth shrugged. 'I've already told you that Starflight doesn't concern itself with the apportionment of land, so the exact area of Lindstromland is of no concern to us. We will, of course, continue to make a fair profit from our transportation services.'

'But that's the whole point,' Garamond said angrily. 'Even if it wasn't a disguised land charge, the transportation fee should be abolished.'

'Why?'

'Because we now have all the land we can use. In those circumstances it is intolerable that there should be any kind of economic brake on the natural and instinctive flow of people towards the new land.'

'You, of all people, should know that there's nothing natural or instinctive about building and sailing a flickerwing ship.' A rare tinge of colour was appearing in Elizabeth's waxy cheeks. 'It can't be done without money.'

Garamond shook his head. 'It can't be done without *people*. A culture which had never developed the concept of money, or property, could cross space just as well as we do.'

'At last!' Elizabeth took two quick steps towards Garamond, then stopped, swaying in magnetic shoes. 'At last I know you, Captain. If money is so distasteful to you, I take it you are refusing a place on the development council?'

'I am.'

'And your bounty? Ten million monits taken from the pockets of the people of the Two Worlds. You're refusing that, too?'

'I'm refusing that, too.'

'You're too late,' Elizabeth snapped, savouring a triumph which only she understood. 'It has already been credited to your account.'

'I'll return it to you.'

Elizabeth shook her head decisively. 'No, Captain. You're a very famous man back on the Two Worlds – and I must be seen to give you everything you deserve. Now, return to your ship.'

On the way back to the *Bissendorf,* Garamond's mind was filled with the President's admission that he had become too important to be disposed of like any other human being. *And yet,* came the disturbing thought, *there had been that look of satisfaction in her eyes.*

CHAPTER NINE

The new house allocated for Garamond's use was a rectangular, single-storey affair. It was one of several dozen built from plastic panels which had been prefabricated in a Starflight workshop on board one of Elizabeth's ships.

The compact structure was situated less than two kilometres from the aperture to the outside universe, where the coating of soil was still thin, and so was held in place by suction pads which gripped the underlying metal of the shell. After a matter of days living in it Garamond found that he could forget about the hard vacuum of space beginning only a few centimetres below his living-room floor. The furnishings were sparse but comfortable, and a full range of colour projectors and entertainment machines – plus an electronic tutor for Christopher – gave it something of the atmosphere of a luxury week-end lodge.

There was an efficient kitchen supplied with provisions from shipboard stores in the early stages, but the expectation was that the colonists would become self-supporting as regards food within a year. It was late summer in that part of Orbitsville and the edible grasses were approaching a tawny ripeness. Even before a systemized agriculture could be established to produce grain harvests, the grass would be fully utilized – part of it synthetically digested to create protein foods, the rest yielding cellulose for the production of a range of acetate plastics.

Garamond was technically still in command of the *Bissendorf,* but he spent much of his time in the house, telling himself he was helping his family to put down roots. In reality he was trying to cope with the sense of having been cut adrift. He acquired the habit of standing at a window which faced the aperture and watching the ever-increasing tempo of activity at the Starflight outpost. Machinery, vehicles, supplies of all kinds came through the L-shaped entry tubes in a continuous stream; new buildings were erected every day amid moraines of displaced soil; a skein of dirt roads wound around and through the complex, with in loose ends straggling off into the grasslands. Earth's beachhead was becoming well established, and as it did so Garamond felt more and more redundant.

'The weirdest thing about it is that I feel possessive,' he said to his wife. 'I keep lecturing people about the inconceivable size of Orbitsville, telling them it couldn't be controlled by a thousand Starflight corporations – yet I have a gut-feeling it's my personal property. I guess that in a way I'm as much out of touch with reality as Liz Lindstrom.'

Aileen shook her head. 'You're angry at the way she's proposing to handle things.'

'Angry at myself.'

'Why?'

'What made me think Starflight House would quietly bow out of existence to make way for a publicly-funded transportation system? From what I hear, Liz's public relations teams are plugging the notion that Starflight already *is* a semi-governmental concern. That was a hard one to put over when there was just Terranova and the amount of land a settler got was determined by how much he paid for his passage, but now it's different.'

'In what way?' Aileen looked up from the boy's shirt she was hand-stitching. Her deeply tanned face was sympathetic but unconcerned – since arriving on Orbitsville she had developed a peaceful optimism. It seemed that the principal element of his wife's personality, her unremarkable pleasantness, was standing her in good stead in the alien environment.

'There's to be a standard transportation charge and no limitation to the amount of land a settler can occupy. That will make the operation seem pretty altruistic to most people. The trouble is it's easy to see how they would get that impression.'

Since turning down membership of Elizabeth's development council Garamond had found it difficult to keep himself informed of her activities, but he could visualize the approach she was using to sell Orbitsville on overcrowded Earth. The newly-established fact that the volume of space within the sphere was totally free of hydrogen or other matter, ruling out the use of flickerwing ships, could even be turned to Starflight's advantage. It was likely that a very long time would elapse before the unwieldy and inefficient type of ship which carried its own reaction mass could be redeveloped sufficiently to make any impression on the five billion Earth-areas available within the sphere. Orbitsville, then, was truly the ultimate frontier, a place where a man and his family could load up a solar-powered vehicle with supplies, plus an 'iron cow' to convert grass into food, and drive off into a green infinity. The life offered would be simple, and perhaps hard – in many ways similar to that of a pioneer in the American West – but in the coast-to-coast *urbs* of Earth there was a great yearning for just that kind of escape. The risk of dying of overwork or simple appendicitis on a lonely farm hundreds of light-years from Earth was infinitely preferable to the prospect of going down in a food riot in Paris or Melbourne. No matter how much Star-flight charged for passage to Orbitsville, there would always be more than enough people to fill the big ships.

'Does the President have to be altruistic?' Aileen said, and Garamond knew that she was drawing comparisons between Liz Lindstrom and herself, between a woman who had unexpectedly lost a son and one whose husband and child had been reprieved. 'What's wrong with making a reasonable percentage on services rendered?'

'In this case – everything.' Garamond suppressed a pang of annoyance. 'Don't you see that? Look, Earth has been raped and polluted and choked to death, but right here on Orbitsville there's room for every human being there is to lose himself for ever. We've made all the mistakes and learned all the lessons back on Earth, and now we've been given this chance to start off from scratch again. The whole situation demands an almost complete transfer of population – and it could be done, Aileen. At our level of technology it could be done, but the entire Star-flight operation is based on it *not* being done!

'In order for Elizabeth to go on making her quote reasonable percentage unquote there has to be a potential, a high population pressure on Earth and a low one elsewhere. I wouldn't be surprised if it turned out that the Lindstroms are behind the failure of all the main population control programmes.'

'That's ridiculous, Vance.' Aileen began to laugh.

'Is it?' Garamond turned away from the window, mollified by his wife's evident happiness. 'Maybe so, but you don't hear them complaining much about the birth rate.'

'Talking about birth rates – our own has been pretty static for a long time.' Aileen caught his hand and held it against her cheek. 'Wouldn't you like to be the father of the first child born on Orbitsville?'

'I'm not sure, but it's impossible anyway. The first shiploads of settlers are on their way, and – from what I've heard about the Terranova run – a lot of the women always arrive pregnant. It's something to do with the lack of recreational facilities on the journey.'

'How about the first one conceived on Orbitsville then?'

'That's more like it.' Garamond knelt beside his wife's chair, took her in his arms and they kissed.

Aileen drew back from him after a few seconds. 'You'll have to do better than that.'

'I'm sorry. I keep thinking about the people, beings or gods – whatever you want to call them – who built Orbitsville.'

'Who doesn't?'

'I don't understand them.'

'Who does?'

'You know, there's enough living space in Orbitsville to support every intelligent being in the galaxy. For all we know, that's why it was created, and yet ...'

Garamond allowed his voice to die away. He suspected Aileen would accuse him of paranoia if he speculated aloud about why the sphere-builders had created a hostel for an entire galaxy's homeless – and then played into Elizabeth Lindstrom's hands by providing only one entrance.

Chick Truman was one of a breed of human beings who had come into existence with the development of interstellar travel. He was a frontiersman-technician. His father and grandfather had helped with the opening up of Terranova and with the initial surveying of a dozen other planets which, although unsuitable for colonization, had some commercial or scientific potential. He had received little in the way of formal technical training but, like all other members of the fraternity of gypsy-engineers, seemed to have an inborn knowledge of the entire range of mechanical skills. It was as though the accumulated experience *of* generations had begun to produce men for whom the analysis of an electrical circuit or the tuning of an engine was a matter of instinct.

One attribute which distinguished Truman from most of his fellows was a strong, if undisciplined, interest in philosophy. And it was this which had fired his mind as he set up camp on the lower slopes of the hills which ringed Orbitsville's single aperture at a distance of about sixty kilometres. He was half of a two-man team which had been sent out to erect a bank of laser reflectors as part of an experimental communications system. They had reached their target minutes before the wall of darkness had come rushing from the east, and now Truman's partner, Peter Krogt, was busy preparing food and laying out their sleeping bags. Truman himself was concerned with less prosaic matters. He had lit a pipe of tobacco, was comfortably seated with his back to the transporter and was staring into the incredible ribbed archways of the sky at night.

'The Assumption of Mediocrity is a useful philosophical weapon,' he was saying, 'but it can backfire on the guy who uses it. I know that some of the greatest advances in human thought were achieved by assuming there's nothing odd or freakish about our own little patch – that's what set Albert Einstein off.'

'Help me open these containers,' Krogt said.

Without moving, Truman released a cloud of aromatic smoke. 'But consider the case of, say, two beetles living at the bottom of a hole on a golf course. These bugs have never been out of that hole, but if they have a philosophical turn of mind they can describe the rest of the universe just by using available evidence. What would their universe be like, Pete?'

'Who cares?'

'Nice attitude, Pete. Their projected universe would be an infinite series of round holes with big white balls dropping into them during daylight hours.'

Krogt had opened the food containers unaided and he handed one to Truman. 'What are you talking about, Chick?'

'I'm telling you what's wrong with the management back at base. Listen … We've been on Orbitsville for months, right?'

'Right.'

'Now take this little jaunt you and I are on right now. These hills are three hundred metres high. Our orders are to set up the reflectors at an elevation of two hundred and fifty metres. We've been told where to set them, where to aim them, what deviation will be acceptable, how long to take with the assignment – but there's one thing we *haven't* been told to do. And I find it a pretty astonishing omission, Pete.'

'Your yeasteak's getting cold.'

'Why did nobody tell us to climb the extra fifty metres to the top of the hill and have a look at the other side?'

'Because there's no need,' Krogt said heavily. 'There's nothing there but grass and scrub. The whole inside of this ball is nothing but prairie.'

'There you go! The Assumption of Mediocrity.'

'It isn't an assumption.' Krogt gestured with his fork towards the shimmering watered-silk canopy of the sky. 'They've had a look around with telescopes.'

'Telescopes!' Truman sneered to cover up the fact that he had forgotten about telescopic examination of the far side of Orbitsville, then his talent for rapid mental calculation came to his aid. 'We're talking about a distance of more than two astronomical units, sonny. If you were standing on Earth, what would one of those spyglasses tell you about life on Mars?'

'More'n I want to know. Are you going to eat this yeasteak or will I?'

'You eat it.'

Truman got to his feet, slightly dismayed at the way in which a discussion on philosophy had led him to renounce his meal, and marched away up the slope. He was breathing heavily by the time he reached the rounded summit and paused to re-light his pipe. The yellow flame from the lighter dazzled his eyes and almost a minute had passed before Truman appreciated that, spread out on the plain below him, dim and peaceful, were the lights of an alien civilization.

CHAPTER TEN

The arrival of the first wave of ships had surprised Garamond in two ways – by its timing, which could have been achieved only if it had set out within days of Elizabeth's own arrival on Orbitsville; and by its size. There were eighty Type G2 vessels, each of which carried more than four thousand people. A third of a million settlers, who originally must have been destined for the relatively well-prepared territories of Terranova, had been diverted to a new destination where there was not even a shed to give them shelter for their first night.

'It beats me,' Cliff Napier said, sipping his first coffee of the day. He was off duty and had spent the night in Garamond's house. 'All right, so Terranova has only one usable continent and it's filling up fast, but the situation isn't *that* urgent. No matter how you look at it, these people are going to have a rough time at first. They haven't even got proper transportation.'

'You're wondering why they agreed to come?' Garamond asked, finishing his own coffee.

Napier nodded. 'The average colonist is a family man who doesn't want to expose his wife and kids to more unknown risks than necessary. How did Starflight get them to come here?'

'I'll tell you.' Aileen came into the room with a pot of fresh coffee and began refilling the cups. 'Chris and I were down at the store this morning while you two were still in your beds, and I talked to people who saw the first families disembarking before dawn. You know, you don't learn much by lying around snoring.'

'All right, Aileen, we both think you're wonderful. Now, what are you talking about?'

'They were given free passages,' Aileen said, obviously pleased at being able to impart the news.

Garamond shook his head. 'I don't believe it.'

'It's true, Vance. They say Starflight House is giving free travel to anybody who signs on for Lindstromland within the first six months.'

'It's a trick.'

'Oh, Vance!' Aileen's eyes were reproachful. 'Why don't you admit you were wrong about Elizabeth? Besides, what sort of a trick could it be? What could she hope to gain?'

'It's a trick,' Garamond said stubbornly. 'What she's done isn't even legal – the teams from the Government land agencies haven't got here yet.'

'But you always say the law doesn't mean anything to the Lindstroms.'

'Not when they want to take something. This is different.'

'Now you're being childish,' Aileen snapped.

'He isn't,' Napier said. 'Take our word for it, Aileen – Liz Lindstrom never acts out of character.'

Aileen's face had lost some of its natural colour. 'Oh, you know it all, of course. You know all about how it feels for a woman to lose her only ...' She stopped speaking abruptly.

'Child,' Garamond finished for her. 'Don't hold anything back for my benefit.'

'I'm sorry. It's just ...' Lenses of tears magnified Aileen's eyes as she walked out of the room.

The two men finished their coffee in silence, each dwelling on his own thoughts. Garamond wondered if the sense of pointlessness which was silting through his mind was due to his having to stand by helplessly while the President imposed her will on Orbitsville, or if it sprang from the slow realization that he was out of a job. The entire Stellar Exploration Arm had become superfluous because there was no need for the big ships to search the star fields ever again. *Could it be,* he wondered, *that I existed only for the search?*

With an obvious effort at diplomacy, Napier began discussing the work being carried out by the Starflight research teams. Despite the use of more sophisticated and more powerful cutting tools than had been available on board the *Bissendorf* nobody had even managed to scratch the shell material. At the same time, studies of the inner shell were indicating that its movement was not a simple east-west rotation, but that subtle geometries were involved with the object of producing a normal progression of day and night close to the polar areas.

Another team had been working continuously on the diaphragm field which prevented the atmosphere from rushing into space through the kilometre-wide aperture in the outer shell. No significant progress had been made there, either. The force field employed was unlike anything ever generated by human engineers in that it reacted equally against the passage of metallic and non-metallic objects. Observations of the field showed that it was lenticular in shape, being several metres thick at the centre. Unlike the shell material, it was transparent to cosmic rays and actually appeared to refract them – a discovery which had led to the suggestion that, as well as being a sealing device, it was intended to disperse cosmic rays in such a way as to produce a small degree of mutation in Orbitsville's flora and fauna – if the latter existed. In general, the field seemed more amenable than the shell material to investigation because it had proved possible to cause small local alterations in its structure, and to produce temporary leaks by firing beams of electrons through it.

'Interesting stuff, isn't it?' Napier concluded.

'Fascinating,' Garamond said automatically.

'You don't sound convinced. I'm going to have a look at the new arrivals.'

Garamond smiled. 'Okay, Cliff. We'll see you for lunch.'

He got to his feet and was walking to the door with Napier when the communicator set, which had been connected to the central exchange by a landline pending a solution of the radio transmission problem, chimed to announce an incoming call. Garamond pressed the ACCEPT button and the solid image of a heavy-shouldered and prematurely grey young man appeared at the projection focus. He was wearing civilian clothing and his face was unknown to Garamond.

'Good morning, Captain,' the stranger said in a slightly breathless voice. 'I'm Colbert Mason of the Two Worlds News Agency. Have any other reporters been in touch with you?'

'Other reporters? No.'

'Thank God for that – I'm the first,' Mason said fervently.

'The first? I didn't know Starflight had authorized transportation for newsmen.'

'They haven't.' Mason gave a shaky laugh. 'I had to emigrate to this place with my wife more or less permanently, and I know other reporters have done the same thing. I'm just lucky my ship disembarked first. If you'll give me an interview, that is.'

'Have you been off-world before?'

'No, sir. First time, but I'd have gone right round the galaxy for this chance.'

Garamond recognized the flattery but also found himself genuinely impressed by the young newsman. 'What did you want to talk to me about?'

'What did I …?' Mason spread his hands helplessly. 'The lot! Anything and everything. Do you know, sir, that back on Earth you're regarded as the most famous man ever? Even if you'd answered the tachygrams we sent you we'd still have considered it worthwhile to try for a face-to-face interview.'

'Tachygrams? I got no signals from Earth. Hold on a minute.' Garamond killed the audio channel and turned to Napier. 'Elizabeth?'

Napier's heavy-lidded eyes were alert. 'I'd say so. She didn't like your views on how Orbitsville should be handled. In fact, I'm surprised this reporter got through the net. He must have been very smart, or lucky.'

'Let's make him luckier.' Garamond opened the audio circuit again. 'I've got a good story for you, Mason. Are you prepared to run it exactly as I tell it?'

'Of course.'

'Okay. Come straight out to my place.'

'I can't, sir. I called you because I think I'm being watched, and there may not be much time.'

'All right, then. You can report that in my opinion the potential of Orbitsville is ...'

'Orbitsville?'

'The local name for Lindstromland ...' Garamond stopped speaking as the image of the reporter broke up into motes of coloured light which swarmed in the air for a second before abruptly vanishing. He waited for the image to re-establish itself but nothing happened.

'I thought it was too good to be true,' Napier commented. 'Somebody pulled out the plug on you.'

'I know. Where do you think Mason was speaking from?'

'Must have been from one of the depot stores. Those are the only places where he'd have any access to a communicator set.'

'Let's get down there right now.' Garamond pulled on a lightweight jacket and, without waiting to explain to Aileen, hurried from the house into Orbitsville's changeless noon. Christopher looked up from the solitary game he was playing in the grass but did not speak. Garamond waved to the boy and strode out in the direction of the clustered buildings around the aperture.

'It's bloody hot,' Napier grumbled at his side. 'I'm going to buy a parasol for walking about outdoors.'

Garamond was in no mood to respond to small talk. 'It's getting too much like Earth and Terranova.'

'You won't be able to prove the call was blocked.'

'I'm not even going to try.'

They walked quickly along the brown dirt road which threaded through the scattering of residences and reached the belt of small administrative buildings, research laboratories and windowless storehouses which surrounded the aperture. The black ellipse began to be disjointedly visible through a clutter of docking machinery and L-shaped entry ports. Garamond was no longer able to think of it as a lake of stars – now it was simply a hole in the ground. As they were passing an unusually large anonymous building his attention was caught by sunlight glinting on a moving vehicle – one of the few yet to be seen on Orbitsville. It stopped at the entrance to the building, four men got out and hurried inside. One of them had a youthful build which contrasted with his greying hair.

Napier caught Garamond's arm. 'That looked like our man.'

'We'll see.' They sprinted across a patch of grass and into the dense shade of the foyer, just in time to see an interior door closing. A doorman wearing Starflight emblems came out of a kiosk and tried to bar their way, but Garamond and Napier went by on each side of him and burst through to the inner room. Garamond's first glance confirmed that he had found Colbert Mason. The reporter was between two men who were gripping his arms, and three others – one of whom Garamond identified as Silvio Laker, a member of Elizabeth Lindstrom's personal staff – were standing close by. Mason's face had a dazed, drugged expression.

'Hands off him,' Garamond commanded.

'Out of here,' Laker said. 'You're outside your territory, Captain.'

'I'm taking Mason with me.'

'Like hell you are,' said one of the men holding Mason, stepping forward confidently.

Garamond gave him a bored look. 'I can cripple you ten different ways.' He was lying, never having been interested in even the recreational forms of personal combat, but the man suddenly looked less confident. While he was hesitating, his partner released Mason and tried to snatch something from his pocket, but was dissuaded by Napier who simply moved his three-hundred-pound bulk in a little closer and looked expectant. A ringing silence descended on the sparsely furnished room.

'Are you all right?' Garamond said to Mason.

'My neck,' the reporter said uncertainly, fingering a pink blotch just above his collar. 'They used a hypodermic spray on me.'

'It was probably just a sedative to keep you quiet.' Garamond fixed his gaze on Laker. 'For your sake, I hope that's right.'

'I warned you to stay out of this,' Laker said in a hoarse voice, his short round body quivering with anger. He extended his right fist, on which was a large gold ring set with a ruby.

'Lasers are messy,' Garamond said.

'I don't mind cleaning up.'

'You're getting in over your head, Laker. Have you thought about what Elizabeth would do to you for involving her in my murder?'

'I've an idea she'd like to see you put away.'

'In secret, yes – but not like this.' Garamond nodded to Napier. 'Let's go.' They turned the compliant, stupefied reporter around and walked him towards the door.

'I warn you, Garamond,' Laker whispered. 'I'm prepared to take the chance.'

'Don't be foolish.' Garamond spoke without looking back. The door was only a few paces away now and he could feel an intense tingling between his shoulder blades. He put out his hand to grasp the handle, but in the instant of his touching it the door was flung open and three more men exploded into the room. Garamond tensed to withstand an onslaught but the newcomers, two of whom were wearing field technician uniforms, brushed past with unseeing eyes.

'Mr Laker,' shouted the third man, who was wearing the blue uniform of a Starflight engineering officer. 'You've got to hear this! You'll never ...'

Laker's voice was ragged with fury. 'Get out, Gordino. What the hell's the idea of bursting in here like ...?'

'But you don't understand! We've made contact with outsiders ! Two of my technicians went over the hills to the west of here last night and they found an alien community – one that's still in use!'

Laker's jaw and threatening fist sagged in unison. 'What are you saying, Gordino? What kind of a story is this?'

'These are the two men, Mr Laker. They'll tell you about it themselves.'

'Two of your drunken gypsies.'

'Please.' The taller of the technicians raised his hand and spoke in an incongruous and strangely dignified voice. 'I anticipated a certain degree of scepticism, so instead of returning to base immediately I waited till daylight and took a number of photographs. Here they are.' He produced a sheaf of coloured rectangles and offered them to Laker. Garamond pushed Napier and the still-dazed Mason out through the door and, forgetting all notion of fleeing, strode back to Laker and snatched the photographs. Other hands were going for them as well, but he emerged from the free-for-all with two pictures. The background in each was the limitless prairie of Orbitsville and ranged across the middle distance were pale blue rectangles which could be nothing other than artificial structures. Near the base of some of the buildings were multi-coloured specks, so small as to be represented only by pinpricks of pigment beneath the glaze of the photographs.

'These coloured dots,' Garamond said to the tall technician. 'Are they ...?'

'All I can say is that they moved. From the distance they look like flowers, but they move around.'

Garamond returned his attention to the pictures, trying to drive his mind down a converging beam at the focus of which were the bright-hued molecules – as if he could reach an atomic level where alien forms would become visible, and beyond it a nuclear level on which he could look into the faces and eyes of the first companions Man had found in all his years of star-searching. The reaction was a natural one, conditioned by centuries during which the sole prospect of contacting others lay in close examination of marks on photographic plates, but it was swept aside almost at once by forces of instinct. Garamond found himself walking towards the door and was out in the sunlight before understanding that he was heading for the Starflight vehicle parked near the entrance. The figures of Napier and

Mason were visible a short distance along the road, apparently on their way to Garamond's house. He got into the crimson vehicle and examined the controls. The car was brand-new, having been manufactured on board one of the spaceships specifically for use on Orbitsville, and no keys were needed to energize the pulse-magnet engine. Garamond pressed the starter button and accelerated away in a cloud of dust as Laker and the others were coming out of the building.

He ignored their shouts, gunned the engine for the few seconds it took to catch up on Napier, brought his heel down on the single control pedal and skidded the car to a halt. He threw open a door. Napier glanced back at the Starflight men who were now in pursuit and, without needing to be told, bundled Mason into the vehicle and climbed in after him. The engine gave a barely perceptible whine as Garamond switched from heel to toe pressure on the pedal, sending the car snaking along the packed earth of the road as the excess of power forced its drive wheels to slide from side to side.

In less than a minute they had cleared the perimeter of the township and were speeding towards the sunlit hills.

The alien settlement came in view as soon as the car reached the crest of the circular range of hills. It was composed of pale blue rectangles shining in the distance like chips of ceramic. His brief study of the photographs had given Garamond the impression that the buildings were in a single cluster, but in actuality they spanned the entire field of view and extended out across the plain for several kilometres. Garamond realized he was looking at a substantial city. It was a city which appeared to lack a definite centre – but nevertheless large enough to sustain a population of a million or more, judging by human standards. Garamond eased back on the throttle, slowing the car's descent. He had just picked out the colourful moving specks which he believed were the first contemporaries mankind had ever encountered beyond the biosphere of his birth planet.

'Cliff, didn't I hear something about the Starflight science teams duplicating our experiment with a reconnaissance torpedo?' Garamond frowned as he spoke, his eyes fixed on the glittering city.

'I think so.'

'I wonder if the cameras were activated?'

'I doubt it. They could hardly have missed seeing this.'

Mason, who had recovered from his shot of sedative, stirred excitedly in the rear seat, panning with his scene recorder. 'What are you going to say to these beings, Captain?'

'It doesn't matter what any of us say – they won't understand it.'

'They mightn't even hear it,' Napier said. 'Maybe they don't have ears.'

Garamond felt his mouth go dry. He had visualized this moment many times, with a strength of yearning which could not be comprehended by anyone who had not looked into the blind orbs of a thousand lifeless worlds, but the prospect of coming face to face with a totally alien life form was upsetting his body chemistry. His heart began a slow, powerful pounding as the pale blue city rose higher beyond the nose of the car. Without conscious bidding, his foot eased further back on the throttle and the hum of the engine became completely inaudible at the lower speed. For a long moment there was no sound but that of the tough grasses of Orbitsville whipping at the vehicle's bodywork.

'What's the trouble, Vance?' Napier's eyes were watchful and sympathetic. 'Arachnid reaction?'

'I guess so.'

'Don't worry – I can feel it too.'

'Arachnid reaction?' Mason leaned forward eagerly. 'What's that?'

'Ask us some other time.'

'No, it's all right,' Garamond said, glad of the opportunity to talk. 'Do you like spiders?'

'I can't stand them,' Mason replied.

'That's fairly universal. The revulsion that most people get when they see spiders – arachnids – is so strong and widespread it has led to the theory that arachnids are not native to Earth. We have a sense of kinship, no matter how slight, with all creatures which originated on our own world, and this makes them acceptable to us even when they're as ugly as sin. But if the arachnid reaction is what some people think it is – loathing for something instinctively identified as of extra-terrestrial origin – then we might be in trouble when we make the first contact with an alien race.

'The worry is that they might be intelligent and friendly, even beauti-ful, and yet might trigger off hate-and-kill reactions in us simply because their shape isn't already registered in a kind of checklist we inherit with our genes.'

'It's just an idea, of course.'

'Just an idea,' Garamond agreed.

'What's the probability of it being right?'

'Virtually zero, in my estimation. I wouldn't …' Garamond stopped speaking as the car lifted over a slight rise and he saw two bright-hued beings only a few hundred paces ahead. The aliens were a long way out from the perimeter of their city, isolated. He brought the car to a gradual halt.

'I guess … I have a feeling we ought to get out and walk the rest of the way.'

Napier nodded and swung open his door. They got out, paused for a moment in the heat of Orbitsville's constant noon, and began walking towards the two man-sized but unearthly figures. Mason followed with his scene recorder.

As the distance between them narrowed, Garamond began to discern the shape of the aliens and was relieved to discover he was not afraid of them in spite of the fact that they were unlike anything he had ever imagined. The creatures seemed, at first, to be humanoids wrapped in garments which were covered with large patches of pink, yellow and brown. At closer range, however, the garments proved to be varicoloured fronds which partly concealed complex, asymmetrical bodies. The aliens did not have clearly defined heads – merely regions of greater complexity at the tops of their blunt, forward-leaning trunks. From a wealth of tendrils, cavities and protuberances, the only organs Garamond was able to identify with any certainty were the eyes, which resembled twin cabochons of green bloodstone.

'What are they like?' Napier whispered.

'I don't know.' Garamond felt a similar need to relate the aliens to something from his past experience. 'Painted shrimps?'

He became aware that the reporter had fallen behind, and that he and Napier were now only a few paces from the aliens. Both men stopped walking and stood facing the fantastic creatures, which had not moved nor given any indication of being aware of their approach. Silence descended over the tableau like liquid glass, solidifying around them. The plain became a sun-filled lens and they were at the centre of it, immobilized and voiceless. Psychic pressures built up and became intolerable, and yet there was nothing to do or say.

Garamond's mind escaped into irrelevancy. *It doesn't matter that I wasn't able to think of anything to say for the benefit of posterity – there's no way to communicate. No way.*

A minute endured like an age, and then another.

'We've done our bit,' Napier announced finally. 'Let's go, Vance.'

Garamond turned thankfully and they walked towards Mason, who backed away from them, still holorecording all that was happening. Not until he had reached the car did Garamond look in the direction of the aliens. One of them was moving away towards its city with a complicated ungainly gait; the other was standing exactly where they had left it.

'I'll drive back,' Napier said, climbing into the car first and experimenting with the simplified controls while the others were taking their seats. He got the vehicle moving, swung it round and set off up the hill at an oblique angle. 'We'll go the long way round in case we run into a crowd following our tracks out.'

Garamond nodded, his thoughts still wholly absorbed by the two creatures on the plain. 'There was no arachnid reaction – I suppose that's something we can feel good about – but I felt totally inadequate. There was no point to it at all. I can't see us and them ever relating or interacting.'

'I don't know about relating, Vance, but there's going to be plenty of interacting.' Napier pointed out through the windshield to the left, where the curve of the hill was falling away to reveal new expanses of prairie. The pale blue buildings of the alien city, instead of thinning out, were spread across the fresh vistas of grassland like flowers in a meadow, seemingly going on for ever.

Mason whistled and raised his recorder. 'Do you think it makes a circle outside the hills? Right round our base?'

'It looks that way to me. They must have been here a long time ...' Napier allowed his words to tail off, but Garamond knew at once what he was thinking.

Liz Lindstrom had brought a third of a million settlers with her on the very first load, and the big ships would soon be bringing land-hungry humans in batches of a full million or more. Interaction between the two races was bound to take place in the near future, and on a very large scale.

CHAPTER ELEVEN

Rumours of massacre came within a month.

There had been a short-term lull while the shallow circular basin centred on Beachhead City absorbed the first waves of settlers. During this brief respite a handful of External Affairs representatives arrived, aware of their inadequacy, and ruled that no humans were to go within five kilometres of the alien community until negotiations had been completed for a corridor through to the free territory beyond. A number of factors combined against their efficacy, however. The Government men had been late on the scene, no broadcasting media were available to them, and – most important – there was a widespread feeling among the settlers that attempting diplomatic communication with the Clowns, as they had been unofficially named, would be an exercise in futility.

At first the bright-hued aliens had been approached with caution and respect, then it was learned that they possessed no machines beyond the simplest farming implements. Even their houses were woven from a kind of cellulose rope extruded from their own bodies in roughly the same way that a spider produces its web. When it was further discovered that the Clowns were mute, the assumption of their intelligence was called into question by many of the human settlers. One theory advanced was that they were degenerate descendants of the race which had built the fortifications around the Beachhead City aperture; another that they were little more than domestic animals which had outlived their masters and developed a quasiculture of their own.

Garamond was disturbed by the attitude implicit in the theories, partly because it was a catalyst for certain changes which were taking place in the Earth settlers. The subtle loosening of discipline he had noticed among his own men within minutes of their setting foot on Orbitsville had its counterpart among the immigrants in the form of a growing disregard for authority. Men whose lives had been closely controlled in the tight, compacted society of Earth now regarded themselves as potential owners of continents and were impatient for their new status. All they had to do to transform themselves from clerks to kings was to load up the vehicles provided by the Starflight workshops and set out on their golden journeys. The only directive was that they should travel far, because it was obvious that the further a man went when fanning out from Beachhead City the more land would be available to him.

As the mood took hold of the settlers even the earliest arrivals, who had staked out their plots of land within the circular hills, became uneasily aware of the incoming hordes at their heels and decided to move onwards and outwards.

In a normal planetary situation the population pressures would not have been concentrated so fiercely on one point, but Earth technology was geared to the Assumption of Mediocrity. During the development of the total transport system of flicker-wing ships and shuttles it had never occurred to anyone to make provision for an environment in which, for example, it would not be possible for a ship to gather its own reaction mass. It would have been completely illogical to do so, in the universe as it was then understood – but in the context of Orbitsville a deadly mistake had been made.

Territories of astronomical dimensions were available, but no means of claiming them quickly enough to satisfy the ambitions of men who had crossed space like gods and then found themselves reduced to wheeled transportation. Given time to build or import fleets of wing-borne aircraft, the difficulties could have been lessened but not removed completely. Each family unit or commune had to become self-supporting in the shortest possible time and, even with advanced farming methods and the use of iron cows, this meant claiming possession of large areas without delay.

It was a situation which, classically, had always resulted in man fighting man. Garamond was not surprised therefore when reports began to reach him that the outermost settlers had forced their way through the Clown city in a number of places and were pouring into the prairie beyond. He did not try to visit any of the trouble spots in person, but had no difficulty in visualizing the course of events at each. Still haunted by the sense of having lost his purpose, he devoted most of his time to his family, making only occasional visits to the *Bissendorf* in his capacity of chief executive. He deliberately avoided watching the newscasts which were piped into his home along the landlines, but other channels were open.

One morning, while he was sleeping off the effects of a prolonged drinking session, he was awakened by the sound of a child's scream. The sound triggered off a synergistic vision of Harald Lindstrom falling away from the blind face of a statue and, almost in the same instant, came the crushing awareness that he had not been sufficiently on his guard against Elizabeth. Garamond sat up in bed, gasping for air, and lurched to the living-room. Aileen had got there before him and was kneeling with her arms around Christopher. The boy was now sobbing gently, his face buried in her shoulder.

'What happened?' Garamond's fear was subsiding but his heart was pounding unevenly.

'It was the projector,' Aileen said. 'One of those *things* appeared on it. I turned it off.'

'What things?' Garamond glanced at the projection area of the solid-image television where the faint ghost of a tutor in one of the educational programmes was still dissolving into the air.

Christopher raised a streaked, solemn face. 'It was a Crown.'

'He means a Clown.' Aileen's eyes were slaty with anger.

'A Clown? But ... I told you to keep the images fairly diffuse when Chris is watching so that he won't get confused between what's real and what isn't.'

'The image was diffused. The thing still scared him, that's all.'

Garamond stared helplessly at his wife. 'I don't get it. Why should he be afraid of a Clown?' He turned his attention to Christopher. 'What's the matter, son? Why were you afraid?'

'I thought the Crown was coming to get me too.'

'That was a silly thing to think – they never harmed anybody.'

The boy's gaze was steady and reproachful. 'What about all the people they froze? All the dead people?'

Garamond was taken aback. 'What do you mean?'

'Don't confuse him,' Aileen said quietly. 'You know perfectly well what's been in the newscasts for the last couple of days.'

'But I *don't!* What did they say?'

'About the outer planet. When they built Lindstromland they shut off all the light and heat to the outer planet and froze it over.'

'They? Who were they?'

'The Clowns, of course. '

'But that's wonderful!' Garamond began to smile. 'The Clowns created Orbitsville!'

'Their ancestors.'

'I see. And there were people on the outer planet? People who got frozen to death?'

'They showed photographs of them.' A stubborn note had crept into Aileen's voice.

'Where did they get these photographs?'

'A Starflight ship must have gone there, of course.'

'But, honey, if the planet is frozen over how could anybody take photographs of its surface or anything on it? Just try thinking it over for a while.'

'I don't know how they did it – I'm only telling you what Chris and I and everybody else have seen.'

Garamond sighed and walked to the communicator and called Cliff Napier on board the *Bissendorf*. The familiar head appeared almost immediately at the projection focus and nodded a greeting.

'Cliff, I need some information about ship movements within the Pengelly's Star system.' Garamond spoke quickly, without preamble. 'Has there been an expedition to the outer planet?'

'No.'

'You're positive?'

Napier glanced downwards, looking at an information display. 'Absolutely.'

'Thanks, Cliff. That's all.' Garamond broke the connection and Napier's apparently solid features faded into the air just as an expression of puzzlement was appearing on them. 'There you are, Aileen – a direct, clear statement of fact. Now, where are the photographs supposed to have come from?'

'Well, perhaps they weren't actual photographs. They might have been ...'

'Artists' impressions? Reconstructions?'

'What difference does it make? They were shown ...'

What difference?' Garamond gave a shaky laugh as the mental chasm opened between himself and his wife, but he felt no annoyance with her. Their marriage had always been simple and harmonious, and he knew it was based on deeper attachments than could be achieved through mere similarity in interests or outlook. One of the first things he had learned to accept was the certainty of lasting incompleteness on some levels of their relationship, and usually he knew how to accommodate it.

'It makes all the difference in the world,' he said softly, almost as if speaking to a child. 'Don't you see how your attitude towards the Clowns has been affected by what you've seen or think you've seen on the viewers? That's the way people are manipulated. It used to be more difficult, or at least they had to be more subtle when literacy was considered vital to education ...' Even to his own ears the words sounded dry and irrelevant, and he stopped speaking as he noticed Aileen's predictable loss of interest. His wife absorbed most of her information semi-instinctively, through images, and he had no picture to show her. Garamond felt an obscure sadness.

'I'm not stupid, Vance.' Aileen touched his hand, her intuition in sure control.

'I know.'

'What did you want to tell me?'

'I just want you to remember the Starflight Corporation is like ...' he strove for a suitably vivid image, '... like a snowball rolling down a hill. It keeps getting bigger and bigger, and it keeps going faster, and it can't slow down. It can't afford to stop, even when somebody gets in the way ... and that's why it's going to roll right on over the Clowns.'

'You always seem so certain about things.'

'The signs are all there. The first step is to implant in people's minds the idea that the Clowns *ought* to be rolled over. Once that's been done the rest is easy.'

'I don't like the Crowns,' Christopher said, breaking a long silence. His grain-gold face was determined.

'I'm not asking you to like them, son. Just don't believe that everything you see on the viewer is real and true. Why, if I went to the outer planet myself I could ...' Garamond stopped speaking for a moment as the idea took hold of his mind.

'Why not? After all, that's the sort of work the S.E.A. ships were designed to do,' Elizabeth had said, reasonably, and at that point she had smiled. 'You're on indefinite leave, Captain, but if you would prefer to return to active service and visit the outer world I have no objections.'

'Thank you, My Lady,' Garamond had replied, concealing his surprise.

Elizabeth's imperfect smile had grown more secretive, more triumphant. 'We will find it very useful to possess some hard data about the planet – in place of all the speculations which are filling the air.'

Garamond reviewed the brief conversation many times during the period in which the *Bissendorf* was extending its invisible wings and disengaging from fleet formation. It came to him that he had proposed the exploratory flight partly as a challenge to the President, hoping that a duel with her would ease the growing tensions in his mind. Her ready agreement to the mission was the last thing he had expected and, as well as drawing a few pointed comments from Aileen, it had left him feeling both disappointed and uneasy.

He sat in the control gallery for hours, watching the bright images of the other Starflight ships perform the patient manoeuvres which would bring each one in turn to the entrance of Orbitsville where it could discharge its load of human beings or supplies. When the *Bissendorf*'s own progression had taken it out through the regulated swarm, and nothing but stars lay in front, Garamond remained on station watching the irregular stabs of the main electron gun, the ghostly blade of energy which flickered through space ahead of the ship. The harvest of reaction mass was not plentiful in the immediate vicinity of Pengelles Star and in the early stages of the flight it was necessary to ionize the cosmic dust to help the intake fields do their work. Gradually, however, as the ship spiralled outwards, the night-black plain of Orbitsville's shell ceased to blank off an entire half of the visible universe. The conditions of space became more normal and speed began to build up. Once again Garamond had difficulty in setting his perceptions to the correct scale. Everything in his past experience conspired to make him think he was in a tiny ship which was painfully struggling to a height of a few hundred kilometres above a normal-sized planet, whereas at a hundred million kilometres out it was still necessary to turn one's head through ninety degrees to take in both edges of Orbitsville's disc.

The size of the sphere was, in a way, painful to Garamond, causing familiar questions to seethe again in his mind. Was the fact that it was large enough to accommodate every intelligent being in the home galaxy a clue to its purpose? Why was there only one entrance to such a huge edifice? Did the physics of the sphere's existence dictate of necessity that neither flicker-wing ship nor radio communicator could operate inside it? Or were those features designed in by the Creators to preserve the sphere's effective size, and to prevent ingenious technicians turning it into a global village with their FTL ships and television networks? And where were the Creators now?

Napier appeared with two bulbs of coffee, one of which he handed to Garamond. 'The weather section reports that the local average density of space is increasing according to their predictions. That means we should be able to pick up enough speed to reach the outer planet in not much more than a hundred hours.'

Garamond nodded his approval. 'The probe torpedo should be fitted out by then.'

'Sammy Yamoto wants to lead a manned descent to the surface.'

'That could be dangerous – we'll have to get a better report on the surface conditions before authorizing anything like that.' Garamond began to sip his coffee, then frowned. 'Why should our Chief Astronomer want to risk his neck out there? I thought he was still wrapped up in his globular filigree of force fields.'

'He is, but he reckons he can deduce a few things about how Orbitsville was built by examining the outer planet.'

'Tell him to keep me posted.' Garamond looked at Napier over the mouth-piece of his coffee bulb and saw an uncharacteristic look of hesitancy on the big man's face. 'Anything else coming to the boil?'

'Shrapnel seems to have gone AWOL.'

'Shrapnel? The shuttle pilot?'

'That's right.'

'So he took off. Isn't that what we expected?'

'I expected him to do it once, but not twice. He disappeared for the best part of a day soon after the Starflight crowd got here. It was during the time he was on ground detachment so I decided he had gone back to Starflight with a hard luck story, and I wrote him off – but he was back on duty again that night.'

'That surprised you?'

'It did, especially as he came back without the chip on his shoulder. His whole attitude seemed to have changed for the better, and since then he's been working like a beaver.'

'Maybe he discovered he didn't like the Starflight HQ staff.'

Napier looked unconvinced. 'He didn't object or try to cry off when orders were posted for this flight, but he isn't on board.'

'I'd just forget about him.'

'I'm trying to,' Napier said, 'but the *Bissendorf* isn't a sailing ship tied up in a harbour. A man who is able to come and go unofficially must have some organization behind him. It makes me think Shrapnel had contacts in Starflight.'

'Let's have some whisky,' Garamond suggested. 'We're both getting too old for this type of work.'

Even before it was denied the light and heat of its own sun, the outer planet of the Pengelly's Star system had been a bleak, sterile place.

Less than half the size of Earth, and completely devoid of atmosphere, it was a ball of rock and dust which patrolled a lonely orbit so far out that its parent sun appeared as little more than a bright star casting barely perceptible shadows in an inert landscape. And when that sun vanished it made very little difference to the planet. Its surface became a little colder and a little darker, but the cooling stresses were not great enough to cause anything as spectacular as movements of the crust. Nothing stirred in the blackness, except for infrequent puffs of dust from meteor strikes, and the uneventful millennia continued to drag by as they had always done.

Using its radar fans like the feelers of a giant insect, the *Bissendorf* groped its way into orbit around the invisible sphere which was the dead world.

The ship was in the form of three equal cylinders joined together, with the central one projecting forward from the other two by almost half its length. The command deck, administrative and technical levels, living quarters and workshops were contained in the central cylinder. This exposed position meant the inhabited regions of the vessel could have been subjected to an intense bombardment during high speed flight, when – due to the ship's own velocity – even stationary motes of interstellar dust registered as fantastically energetic particles. The problem had been solved by using the same magnetic deflection techniques which guided the particles into the ramjet's thermonuclear reactors. Both the *Bissendorf*'s flux pumps shaped their magnetic lines of force into the form of a protective shield around which the charged particles flowed harmlessly into the engines.

An inherent disadvantage of the system was that a starship could never coast at high speed – with the flux pumps closed down the crew would quickly have been fried in self-induced radiation. Communications with a ship which was under way were also precluded, and under these conditions even radar sensing could not be employed. The approach to the dark planet had been made at modest interplanetary speeds, however, and the *Bissendorf* was able to proceed by using its main drive in short bursts, between which it was possible to run position checks. Because it was designed for exploration work in unknown planetary systems, the vessel was further equipped with conventional nuclear thrusters and a limited amount of stored reaction mass which gave it extra capability for close manoeuvring. The task of slipping into stable orbit was therefore accomplished quickly and efficiently, even though the target planet remained invisible to the *Bissendorf*'s crew.

It took only one pass to enable the long-range sensors and recording banks to answer all of Garamond's questions.

'This is pretty disappointing,' Sammy Yamoto said as he examined the glowing numerals and symbols of the preliminary analysis. 'The planet has no atmosphere now and appears never to have had one at any time in its past. Its surface is completely barren. I was hoping for the remains of some kind of plant life which would have told us whether the radiation from the primary was cut off suddenly or over a period of years.'

Chief Science Officer O'Hagan said, 'We can still do a lot with samples of dust and rock from the surface.'

Yamoto nodded without enthusiasm. 'I guess so, but botanical evidence would have been so precise. So *nice*. With nothing but inorganic evidence we're going to have margins of error of what? A thousand years or more?'

'On an astronomical timescale that's not bad.'

'It's not bad, but it's not …'

'Is it the opinion of the group,' Garamond put in, 'that a manned descent is still worthwhile?'

O'Hagan glanced around the other science officers who were anchored close to the information display, then shook his head. 'At this stage it would be enough to drop a robolander and take three or four cores. Somebody can always come back if the cores prove to be of exceptional interest, but I don't hold out much hope.'

'Right – it's decided we send down one probe.' Garamond used his end-of-meeting voice. 'Get it down there and back again as quickly as possible, and include flares and holorecording gear in the package – I want to be able to present certain people with visible evidence.'

Denise Serra, the physicist, raised her eyebrows. 'I heard the Starflight Information Bureau was propagating some fantasy about a beautiful civilization being snuffed out in its prime, but I didn't believe it. I mean, who would swallow an idea like that?'

'You'd be surprised,' Garamond told her ruefully. 'I've been learning that there are different kinds of naivety. We're subject to one kind – it's an occupational hazard associated with spending half your life cut off from the big scene – but there are others just as dangerous.'

'That may be so, but to believe that the Clowns created Orbitsville!'

'Genuine belief isn't required – the story is only a formula which allows certain manipulations to be carried out. We all know the square root of minus one is an unreal quantity, and yet we've all used it when it suited us to do so. Same thing.'

Denise's eyes twinkled. 'It isn't the same.'

'I know, but my statement was an example of the general class of thing we were talking about.'

'Neat footwork.' Denise laughed outright and, for no reason which was immediately apparent to him, Garamond suddenly became aware of how much he enjoyed simply looking at her. He had accepted the phrase 'easy on the eyes' as pure metaphor but now was surprised to discover that letting his gaze rest on the physicist's pale sensitive face actually produced a soothing sensation in his eyes. The phenomenon entranced and then disturbed him.

When the meeting broke up he went to his own quarters and devoted several hours to his principal spare-time occupation of recording television interviews for Colbert Mason. The reporter, after his initial difficulties on Orbitsville, had established himself in a position of relative strength, and had obtained an office in Beachhead City from which he sent back a prolific stream of news stories for syndication on the Two Worlds. Garamond co-operated with him as much as he could, mainly because in his estimation his personal fame was still his family's best protection against Elizabeth Lindstrom.

There were times when he was almost persuaded by Aileen that he was wrong in his suspicions of the President, but against that there were persistent rumours that she had slain a member of her domestic staff who had found her son's body. Garamond continued to maintain his defences. The system was that Mason supplied him with tridi tapes of recorded questions and when it was convenient Garamond used his own equipment to fill in his answers and comments. On a number of occasions Mason had confessed that he was making a fortune from the arrangement and had proposed sharing the profits but Garamond had refused to accept any money, stipulating only that Mason obtain for him the widest possible exposure. It appeared that this objective was being achieved because there was a growing clamour for the discoverer of Lindstromland to make a personal return to Earth.

Garamond spent most of the current session giving suitable reasons for not being able to return and in describing, in precise details, what had been learned about the invisible planet. Assuming the material would be safely relayed to the Two Worlds by Mason and broadcast on the planet-wide networks, he had gone a long way towards killing any suggestion that the Clowns or any other beings connected with Orbitsville had obliterated an entire civilization.

He stored the tapes away carefully, again wondering at the great latitude Elizabeth was permitting him, and fastened himself into his bed with the intention of catching up on his sleep. The slow-drifting cubes of coloured radiance merged and shimmered in the air above him, creating hypnotic patterns. Once more there came the idea that he might be completely wrong about Elizabeth Lindstrom, and he found himself wishing it were possible to discuss the subject emotionlessly and intellectually with his wife. There would be, he decided sleepily, no communications problem with a woman like Denise Serra who shared his background and his interests, and who produced the curiously pleasant sensation in his eyes when he ...

Garamond slept.

He awoke two hours later with an unaccountable sense of unease and decided to put a call through to Aileen and Christopher before going out on to the control gallery. The communications room made the necessary connection and in less than a minute Garamond was looking at the image of his wife, but a winking sphere of amber told him he was viewing and hearing a recording. It said:

'I was hoping you would call, Vance. I know you are only making a short trip, but Chris and I have got so used to having you with us lately that we are spoiled and the time is passing very slowly. Something very exciting has happened, though. You'll never guess.' The unreal Aileen paused for a moment, smiling, to demonstrate to Garamond his inability to divine what was coming next.

'I had a personal call from the President – yes, Elizabeth Lindstrom herself – inviting Chris and me to stay with her in the new Lindstrom Centre for a few days …'

'Don't go!' Garamond was unable to restrain the words.

'… knew I'd be feeling lonely while you were away,' the image was saying contentedly, 'but what really decided me was that she said she was the one who would benefit most from the visit. She didn't actually put it into words, but I think she is looking forward to seeing a child about the place again. Anyway, Vance, I must go now – the President's car is calling for us in a few minutes. By the time you hear this I'll be wallowing in luxury and high living at the Octagon, but don't worry – I'll be at home to cook you a meal when you arrive. Love you, darling. Bye.'

The image dissolved into a cloud of fading stars, leaving Garamond cold, shaken, and angry at his wife. 'You silly bitch,' he whispered to the fleeting points of light. 'Why do you never ever, *never ever,* listen to anything I tell you?'

The last handful of stars vanished in silence.

The probe torpedo worked its way up the gravity hill from the dead planet, carrying its samples of dust and rock, and homed in on the *Bissendorf.* Although there was a sun only three astronomical units away, its light was screened off and the torpedo was moving through a blackness equivalent to that of deep interstellar space. In that darkness the mother ship appeared to some of the probe's sensors as a faint cluster of lights, but to other sensors concerned with different sections of the electromagnetic spectrum the ship registered as a brilliant beacon whose radiation embodied many voices commanding, guiding, coaxing it homewards. Responding with greater and greater precision as the electronic voices grew louder, the torpedo approached the ship with the familiarity of a parasite fish flittering about a whale. At last it made physical contact and was taken on board.

During the final manoeuvres Garamond had waited on the *Bissendorf*'s control gallery with growing impatience. As soon as the signal announcing closure of the docking bay was received he gave the order for the main drive to be activated. Initial impetus was given to the ship by the relatively feeble ion thrusters, but that propulsion system was shut down when the ramjet intake field had been fanned out to its maximum area of half a million square kilometres and reaction mass was being scavenged from the surrounding space. As the scooped-up hydrogen and other matter were fed into the fusion reactors the ship wheeled away sunwards, and the acceleration restored close-to-normal gravity throughout the inhabited levels of the central cylinder.

The feeling of the deck pressing firmly on the underside of his feet helped Garamond to regain his composure. He assured himself that if Elizabeth were to move against his family it would be done anywhere but in the crystal cloisters of her new residence. Into the bargain, Elizabeth knew that Garamond would be back from the dark planet in only a few days, imbued with an even greater amount – if that were possible – of the power called fame. The hours and the duty periods went by and, as Orbitsville filled the forward view panels with its unrelieved blackness, Garamond was able to satisfy himself that he had panicked for no good reason.

The *Bissendorf* had accomplished turnover at mid-point on the return journey, and was two days into the retardation phase, when explosions occurred simultaneously in both field generators, robbing the vessel of its means of coming to a halt before it would smash into the impregnable outer shell of Orbitsville.

CHAPTER TWELVE

'The starboard explosion was the worst,' Commander Napier reported to the emergency meeting of the *Bissendorf*'s executive staff. 'It actually breached the pressure hull in the vicinity of Frame S.203. The pressure-activated doors functioned properly and sealed off the section between Frames S.190 and 210, but there were five technicians in there at the time, and they were killed.'

O'Hagan raised his grey head. 'Blast or decompression?'

'We don't know – the bodies were exhausted into space.'

'I see.' O'Hagan made a note on his pad, speaking aloud at the same time. 'Five missing, presumed dead.'

Napier stared at his old antagonist with open dislike. 'If you know how we can turn the ship to recover the bodies this would be a good time to tell us about it.'

'I merely ...'

'Gentlemen!' Garamond slapped the table as loudly as was possible in conditions of almost zero gravity. 'May I remind you that we are scheduled to be killed in about eight hours? That doesn't leave much time for bickering.'

O'Hagan gave a ghastly smile. 'It gives us eight hours for bickering, Captain – there's nothing else we can do.'

'That's for this meeting to decide.'

'So be it.' Chief Science Officer O'Hagan shrugged and spread his dry knobbly hands in resignation.

Garamond felt a reluctant admiration for the older man who seemed determined to remain egotistical and cantankerous right to the end. O'Hagan also had a habit of being right in everything he said, and in that respect too it seemed he was going to preserve his record. Although reaction mass was not plentiful in the region of Pengelly's Star, the *Bissendorf* had been aided in its return journey by the pull of the primary and had achieved a mean acceleration of close on one gravity. Modest though the acceleration and distances were, the ship had been travelling at 1,500 kilometres a second at turn-over point and, although it had been slowing down steadily for two days when the explosions occurred, its residual velocity was still above a hundred kilometres in each second. At that speed it was due to impact with Orbitsville in only eight hours, and it appeared to Garamond that there was nothing he or anybody else on board could do about it. The knowledge boomed and pounded beneath all other thoughts, and yet he felt a surprising absence of fear or any related emotion. It was, he decided, a psychological by-product of having eight hours in hand. The delay created the illusion that something might still be done, that there was a chance to influence the course of events in their favour, and – miraculously – this held good even for an experienced flicker-wing man who understood only too well the deadly parameters of his situation.

'I understand that both auxiliary drive systems are still functional,' Administrative Officer Mertz was saying, his round face glowing like pink plastic. 'Surely that makes a difference.'

Napier shook his head. 'The ion tubes are in action right now – which accounts for the very slight weight you can feel – but they were intended only to give the ship a close-manoeuvring capability, and they won't affect our speed very much. I guess the only difference they'll make is that we'll vaporize against Orbitsville a minute or two later than we would otherwise.'

'Well, how about the secondary nuclears? I thought they were for collision avoidance.'

'They are. Maximum endurance twenty minutes. By applying full thrust at right angles to our present course we could easily avoid an object as large as Jupiter – but we're dealing with *that*.' Napier pointed at the forward view panels, which were uniformly black. Orbitsville was spanning the universe.

'I see.' Mertz's face lost some of its pinkness. 'Thank you.'

The operations room filled with a silence which was broken only by faint irregular clangs transmitted through the ship's structure. Far aft, a repair crew was at work replacing the damaged hull sections. Garamond stared into the darkness ahead and tried to assimilate the idea that it represented a wall across the sky, a wall which was rushing towards him at a hundred kilometres a second, a wall so wide and high that there was no way to avoid hitting it.

Yamoto cleared his throat. 'There's no point in speculating about why the ship was sabotaged, but do we know how the bombs got on board?'

'I personally believe it was done by Pilot Officer Shrapnel,' Napier said. 'There isn't much evidence, but what there is points to him. We gave all the information in our emergency call to Fleet Control.'

'What did they say?'

'They promised he would be investigated.' Napier's voice had a flinty edge of bitterness. 'We are assured that all necessary steps will be taken.'

'That's good to know. Isn't that good to know?' Yamoto pressed the back of a hand to his forehead. 'I had so much work still to do. There was so much to learn about Orbitsville.'

They're going to learn at least one thing as a result of this mission, Garamond thought. *They're going to find out how the shell material stands up to the impact of fifteen thousand tons of metal travelling at a hundred kilometres a second. And they won't even have to go far from the aperture to see the big bang* ... Garamond felt an icy convulsion in his stomach as he half-glimpsed an idea. He sat perfectly still for a moment as the incredible thought began to form, to crystallize to the point at which it could be put into words. His brow grew chill with sweat.

'Has anybody,' Denise Serra asked in a calm, clear voice, 'considered the possibility of adjusting our course in such a way that we would pass through the aperture at Beachhead City?'

Again the room filled with silence. Garamond felt a curious secondary shock on hearing the words he was still formulating being uttered by another person. The silence lasted for perhaps ten seconds, then was broken by a dry laugh from O'Hagan.

'You realize that, at our speed, running into a wall of air would be just like hitting solid rock? I'm afraid your idea doesn't change anything.'

'We don't have to run into a wall of air – not if we turn the ship over again and go in nose first with the electron gun operating at full power.'

'Nonsense,' O'Hagan shouted. He cocked his head to one side as if listening to an inner voice and his fingers moved briefly on the computer terminal before him. 'It isn't nonsense, though.' He corrected himself without embarrassment, nodding his apologies to Denise Serra, and others at the conference table began to address the central computer through their own terminals.

'Overload power on the gun should give us enough voltage for the few seconds we would need it. It should be enough to blast a tunnel through the atmosphere.'

'At this stage we have enough lateral control over our flight path to bring it through the aperture.'

'But remember we haven't got the full area of the aperture as a target. We'd be going in at an angle of about seventy degrees.'

'It's still good enough – as long as no other ships get in the way.'

'There's still time to do some structural strengthening on the longitudinal axis.'

'We'll shed enough kinetic energy …'

'Hold it a minute,' Garamond commanded, raising his voice above the suddenly optimistic clamour, 'We have to look at it from all angles. If we did go through the aperture, what would be the effect on Beachhead City?'

'Severe,' O'Hagan said reflectively. 'Imagine one purple hell of a lightning bolt coming up through the aperture immediately followed by an explosion equivalent to a tactical nuclear weapon.'

'There'd be destruction?'

'Undoubtedly. But there's plenty of time to evacuate the area – nobody would have to die.'

'Somebody mentioned colliding with another ship.'

'That's a minor problem, Vance.' O'Hagan looked momentarily surprised at having used Garamond's given name for the first time in his life. 'We can advise Fleet Control of our exact course and they'll just have to make certain the way is clear.'

Garamond tried to weigh the considerations, but he could see only the faces of his wife and child. 'Right! We do it. I want to see a copy of the decision network plan, but start taking action right away. In the meantime I'll talk to Fleet Control.'

The ten science-oriented and engineering officers at the table instantly launched into a polygonal discussion and the noise level in the room shot up as communications channels were opened to other parts of the ship. Within a minute perhaps thirty other men and women were taking part, many of them vicariously present in the form of miniaturized, but nonetheless solid and real-looking, images of their heads, which transformed the long room into a montage of crazy perspectives.

Garamond could almost feel the wavecrest of hope surging through all the levels of the disabled vessel. He told Napier to make an announcement about the situation on the general address system, then went into his private suite and put a call through to Fleet Control. It was taken not by the Fleet Movements Controller, as Garamond had expected, but by a Star-flight admin man, Senior Secretary Lord Nettleton. The Senior Secretary was a handsome silver-haired man who had a reputation for his devotion to the Lindstrom hierarchy. He was of a type that Elizabeth liked to have around, capable of presenting a benign fatherly image, while keeping himself remote from the inner workings of the system.

'I was expecting somebody on the operations side,' Garamond said, dispensing with the standard formal mode of address.

'The President has taken the matter under her personal control. She is very much concerned.'

'I'll bet she is.'

'I beg your pardon?' Nettleton's resonant voice betrayed a degree of puzzlement which was an open challenge to Garamond to speak his mind.

Again Garamond thought about his wife and child. 'The President's concern for the welfare of her employees is well known.'

Nettleton inclined his head graciously. 'I'm aware of how futile words are under the circumstances, Captain Garamond, but I would like to express my personal sympathy for you and your crew in this ...'

'The reason I called is to inform Starflight that the *Bissendorf* has enough lateral control to enable it to pass through the aperture into the interior of Orbits ... Lindstromland, and that is what I intend to do.'

'I don't quite understand.' Nettleton's image underwent several minute but abrupt changes of size which told Garamond other viewers were switching into the circuit. 'I am informed that you are travelling at a hundred kilometres a second and have no means of slowing down.'

'That's correct. The *Bissendorf* is going to hit Beachhead City like a bomb. You will have to evacuate the area around the aperture. My science staff can help with the estimates of how wide-spread the damage will be, but in any case I strongly recommend that you issue warnings immediately. You have less than eight hours.' Garamond went on to explain the proposed action in detail, while continued perturbations of the image showed that his unseen audience was increasing every second.

'Captain, what happens if your ship misses the aperture and strikes the shell material below the city itself?'

'We are confident of passing through the aperture.'

'All you're saying is that the probability is high, but supposing you *do* miss?'

'It is our opinion that the shell would be undamaged.'

'But the shell is one of the greatest scientific enigmas ever known – on what do you base your predictions about its behaviour under that sort of impact?'

Garamond allowed himself a smile. 'In the last hour or so our instinct about these things has become highly developed.'

'This is hardly a time for jokes.' Nettleton looked away for a moment, nodded to someone off screen, and when he turned back to Garamond his eyes were sombre. 'Captain, have you thought about the possibility that Starflight may not be able to grant you permission to aim for the aperture?'

Garamond considered the question. 'No – but I've thought about the fact that there is absolutely nothing Starflight can do to stop me.'

Nettleton shook his head with regal sadness. 'Captain, I'm going to put you through to the President on a direct connection.'

'I haven't the time to speak to her,' Garamond told him. 'Just send a message to my wife that I'll be back with her as soon as I can.' He broke the connection and returned to the operations room, hoping he had sounded more confident than he felt.

Lindstrom Centre was austere compared to its equivalent on Earth, but it was the largest and most palatial building on Orbitsville. It was octagonal in plan and had been built on a slight eminence some twenty kilometres east from Beachhead City, to which it was joined by power and communication cables stretched on low pylons. No attempt had yet been made to sculpt the hill according to the President's ideas of what it ought to be, so the glass-and-acrylic edifice was incongruously lapped by a sea of grass. Its first three floors housed those elements of the Starflight administration which the supreme executive had transported from the Two Worlds, and the top floor was her private residence.

On this evening, the guards who patrolled the perimeter fence were distinctly uneasy. They had heard that a maniac of a flickerwing captain was going to try to crash his vessel through the aperture at interplanetary speed, and the rumour had even quoted an exact minute for the event to occur – 20.06 Compatible Local Time. As the moment grew nearer each man felt a powerful urge to fix his gaze on the distant scattering of buildings, just below the upcurved horizon, which was Beachhead City. They had been told that most of the city had been hastily evacuated to escape the promised pyrotechnics, and nobody wanted to miss the spectacle.

At the same time, however, their eyes were frequently drawn upwards to the transparent west wall of the Presidential suite. Elizabeth Lindstrom herself could be glimpsed up there, screened only by sky reflections, her silk-sheathed abdomen glowing like a pearl – and it was well known that she sometimes kept watch on her guards through a magnifying screen. None of the men relished the idea of being dismissed from Starflight service and sent back to the crowded tower blocks of Earth, and yet the compulsion to stare into the west grew greater with each passing minute.

The suspense was also making itself felt on the top floor of the Octagon, but in the case of Elizabeth Lindstrom it was a pleasurable sensation, heady and stimulating, akin to pre-orgasmic tension.

'My dear,' she said warmly to Aileen Garamond, 'do you think you are wise to watch this?'

'Quite sure, My Lady.'

'But the boy ...'

'I'm positive my husband knows what he is doing.' Aileen's voice was firm and unemotional as she laid her hands on her son's shoulders, forcing him to face the west. 'Nothing will go wrong.'

'I admire your courage, especially when the chances are so ...' Elizabeth checked herself just in time. The common, characterless woman beside her appeared genuinely to believe that a ship could run into a solid wall of air at a speed of a hundred kilometres a second and not be destroyed on the instant. Elizabeth was girded with the mathematics which showed how incredible the idea was, but she knew the equations would mean nothing to her guest. In any case, she had no desire to break the news in advance – she wanted to watch Mrs Garamond's face as she saw her husband's funeral pyre blossom on the horizon. Only then would she receive the first payment against the incalculable debt which the Garamond family owed her.

The concept of grief cancelling grief, of pain atoning for pain, was one which few people could properly understand, Elizabeth had often told herself. Even she had not appreciated the logic of it until days after Harald's small body had been cast in sun-coloured resin and stood in its place in the Lindstrom chapel. But it was so *true!*

There were no flaws in the system of double entries – anguish against anguish, love against love – and this realization had given Elizabeth the strength to go on, even when it appeared that the Garamonds had chosen to die in the black deeps of space. That episode had been nothing more and nothing less than God's way of telling her that he was simply building up the Garamonds' credit to the point at which it could be used to wipe out all their debts. In retrospect, it had been fortunate that she had not been able to extract payment immediately, because there would still have been an imbalance and she would never have found her heart's ease. A child is a focus, a repository of love which is added to in each year of its life, and it was crystal-clear that the death of a boy of nine could never be compensated for by the death of a boy of ...

'I have the latest computations for you, My Lady.' The projected voice of Lord Nettleton broke in on Elizabeth's thoughts. 'The impact will occur in exactly three minutes from ... now.'

'Three minutes,' Elizabeth said aloud, knowing that the accurately beamed sound would not have reached the other woman's ears. Without giving any sign that she had heard, Aileen picked her son up and her face was screened by the boy's body. Elizabeth moved quietly to the other side, as was her due, and waited.

She waited through eons and eternities.

And the ribbed canopy of the sky ceased to turn.

Time was dead ...

The lightning bolt came first. An arrow-straight line of hell, searing upwards at an angle into the heavens, isolated for the first perceptible instant, then joined by writhing offshoots, tributaries and deltas of violet fire which flickered and froze on the retina. Faint shadows fled across the sky as the air above Beachhead City was hurled outwards by the fountain of energy. Appalling though the general display was, there existed at its core – on the threshold of vision – a sense of even greater forces in the shock of opposition. There was a feeling of cataclysmic upward movement, then a bright star burned briefly and dwindled in the south-west. The day returned to normalcy, but seemingly darker than it had been before.

Elizabeth drew a deep quavering breath – no other death she had ever witnessed had been so final. She turned her gaze on to Aileen Garamond's face, and was shocked to see there a look of serenity.

'It was to be expected,' she said.

'I know.' Aileen nodded contentedly, and hugged her child. 'I told you.'

Elizabeth gaped at her. 'You *fool!* You don't think he's still alive after what you've just ...' She was forced to stop speaking as the waves of thunder rolling out from Beachhead City, slow moving in the low-pressure air of Orbitsville, engulfed the building. Reflections of lights stretched and shrank and stretched again as the transparent walls absorbed energy, and small objects throughout the room stirred uneasily in their places. Christopher buried his face in his mother's hair.

'Your husband is dead,' Elizabeth announced when silence was restored to the room. 'but because you are the widow of the most distinguished of all my S.E.A. captains, you will remain here as my guest. No other arrangement would be acceptable.'

Aileen faced her, pale but immovable. 'My Lady, you are mistaken. You see – I *know.*'

Elizabeth shook her head incredulously and a little sadly. She had been planning to spend perhaps a year in a game of subtleties and suggestions, watching the other woman's slow progression from doubt to certainty about her son's eventual fate. But it was obvious now – in view of Aileen Garamond's mentality, or lack of it – that such strategies would be ineffective. If the full payment were to be extracted, as God had decreed it should be, she would have to speak plainly, in words a child could understand. Elizabeth touched a beautiful micro-engineered ring on her left hand, ensuring that no listening devices could remain in operation nearby, and then explained the accountancy of retribution which demanded that Christopher Garamond should be allowed another three years. He was to have the same lifespan as Harald Lindstrom – but not a day longer.

When she had finished she summoned her physician. 'Captain Gara-mond's death has left Mrs. Garamond in a state of hysteria. Give her suit-able sedation.'

Aileen opened her mouth to scream but the physician, an experienced man, touched her wrist in a quick movement which did not even disturb the boy she was holding in her arms. As the cloud of instant-acting drug sighed through her skin Aileen relaxed and allowed herself to be led away.

Alone again, Elizabeth Lindstrom stood looking out across the western grasslands and was aware – for the first time in over a year – of something approaching happiness. She began to smile.

CHAPTER THIRTEEN

The integrity of the *Bissendorf*'s design was so great, and the on-board preparation had been so thorough, that less than a tenth of the crew died as a result of the passage through the eye of the needle.

Every available man and woman had been co-opted on to the teams which had welded into place a new computer-designed structure, creating load paths which actually utilized the forces of the impact to give the shell enough strength to survive. Until only a matter of minutes before the hellish transit, other gangs had swarmed on the outside of the ship, adding hun-dreds of sacrificial anodes to those which were already in place serving as focal points for the ion exchange which would otherwise have eaten away the hull during normal flight. The new anodes, massive slabs of pure metal, withstood the brief but incredibly fierce attrition of the lightning which wreathed the ship as it passed along the atmospheric tunnel created by its electron gun. On emerging from its ordeal the *Bissendorf*'s principal di-mensions had altered, in some cases by several metres, but it had gone in with all pressure doors sealed – in effect it had been converted into dozens of separate, self-contained spaceships – and there was no loss of life due to decompression.

The entire crew had donned spacesuits for primary protection. Each person had been injected with metallic salts and the ship's restraint fields stepped up to overload intensity, creating an environment in which any sudden movement of human tissue would be resisted by a pervasive jelly-like pressure from all sides. This measure, while undoubtedly a major factor in crew survival, also caused an unavoidable number of deaths. In the few sections where severe structural failure occurred some of the occupants had 'fallen' varying distances under multiple gravities, and the heat induced by electromotive interaction had caused their blood to boil. But, for the vast majority, the internal bracing of their organs against immense G-shocks had meant the difference between life and death.

And yet, all the preparation, all the frenzied activity, would have amounted to nothing more than a temporary stay of execution had it not been for the exotic nature of Orbitsville itself.

The synthetic gravity of the shell material attenuated much more rapidly than that of a solid mass. Although the *Bissendorf*'s slanting course was drawn into the shape of a parabola the curve remained flat, and the crew had sufficient time to control their re-entry into the atmosphere from the inner vacuum of Orbitsville. The vessel's ion tubes and short-term reaction motors were effective against the weak pull of the shell, and it was possible for the *Bissendorf* to skip along the upper fringes of the air shield, gradually shedding velocity. It was even possible, using the fading reserves of reaction mass, to bring the ship down in one piece, with no further loss of life.

What was manifestly impossible, however, was to make the ship fly again.

All its external sensors had been seared cleanly from the hull, and many of the internal position-fixing devices had been destroyed or confused by the unnatural physics of Orbitsville. But the clocks were still in operation – and they had recorded a time lapse of five days. Five days from the passage through the Beachhead City aperture to the final touchdown on a hillside far into the interior. Starting from that basic fact, and using only a pocket calculator, it took just a few seconds for those on board to realize that they had travelled a distance of more than fifteen million kilometres.

In terms of the overall size of Orbitsville the journey was infinitesimal. A short hop, a stone's throw, a stroll across sunlit grass and woodlands – but in human terms the distance itself was more of a barrier than mountains or torrents. It was known, for instance, that back on Earth many a country postman had in his lifetime walked a total distance equal to a trip to the Moon, but that was only 385,000 kilometres. Walking back to Beachhead City would have been a task to be carried out by successive generations over a period of a thousand years.

Using the vast resources of the *Bissendorf*'s workshops it would have been possible to build a fleet of vehicles which might have cut the journey time down to a mere century – except that wheels and other automobile components wear out in a matter of months. It would not be possible to transport the maintenance and manufacturing facilities which might have enabled the caravan to complete its golden journey.

There was also the difficulty that no man or machine knew the exact direction in which to travel. It would have been possible to get a rough bearing from the angle of the day and night ribs across the sky, but a rough bearing would be of no value. At the distances involved, a deviation of only one degree would have caused the train to miss Beachhead City by hundreds of thousands of sun-gleaming kilometres.

By the time the dead had been buried, the day was well advanced, and the remaining men and women of the *Bissendorf*'s crew were ceasing to be citizens of Earth. They were experiencing the infinity-change, the wistful, still contentment which poured down from the motionless sun of Orbitsville.

> *... that calm Sunday that goes on and on;*
> *When even lovers find their peace at last,*
> *And Earth is but a star, that once had shone.*

CHAPTER FOURTEEN

'We're going back,' Garamond announced flatly.

He studied the faces of his executive staff, noting how they were reacting. Some looked at him with open amusement, others stared downwards into the grass, seemingly embarrassed. Behind them, further along the hillside, the great scarred hulk of the *Bissendorf* shocked the eye with its incongruity, and beyond it microscopic figures moved on the plain in the rituals of a ball game. The sun was directly overhead, as always, creating only an occasional flicker of diamond-fire on the dark blue waters of the lakes which banded the middle distance. Garamond began to feel that his words had been absorbed by Orbitsville's green infinities, sucked up cleanly before they reached the edge of the irregular ring in which the group was sitting, but he resisted the urge to repeat himself.

'It's a hell of a long way,' Napier said, finally breaking the heavy silence. His statement of the obvious, Garamond knew, constituted a question.

'We'll build aircraft.'

O'Hagan cleared his throat. 'I've already thought of that, Vance. We have enough workshop facilities still intact to manufacture a reasonable subsonic aircraft, and the micropedia can give us all the design data, but the distance is just too great. You run into exactly the same problem as with wheeled vehicles. Your aircraft might do the trip in three or four years – except that we haven't the resources to build a plane which can fly continuously for that length of time. And we couldn't transport major repair facilities.' O'Hagan glanced solemnly around the rest of the group, reproving them for having left it to him to deal with a wayward non-scientist.

Garamond shook his head. 'When I said we are going back, I didn't mean all of us, in a body. I meant that *I* am going back, together with any of the crew who are sufficiently determined to make it – even if that means only half-a-dozen of us.'

'But ...'

'We're going to build a fleet of perhaps ten aircraft. We're going to incorporate as much redundancy as is compatible with good aerodynamics. We're going to fly our ten machines towards Beachhead City, and each time one of them breaks down we're going to take the best components out of it and put them in the other machines, and we're going to fly on.'

'There's no guarantee you'll get there, even with the last aircraft.'

'There's no guarantee I won't.'

'I'm afraid there is.' O'Hagan's pained expression had become even more pronounced. 'There's this problem of direction which we have already discussed. Unless you've got a really accurate bearing on Beachhead City there's no point in setting out.'

'I'm not worried about getting a precise bearing,' Garamond said, making a conscious decision to be enigmatic. He was aware that in the very special circumstances of the *Bissendorf*'s final flight the whole concept of command structure, of the captain-and-crew relationship, could easily lose its validity. It was necessary at this stage to re-establish himself in office without the aid of insignia or outside authority.

'How do you propose to get one?'

'I propose instructing my science staff to attend to that chore for me. There's an old saying about the pointlessness of owning a dog and doing your own barking.' Garamond fixed a steady challenging gaze on O'Hagan, Sammy Yamoto, Morrison, Schneider and Denise Serra. He noted with satisfaction that they were responding, as he had hoped – already there were signs of abstraction, of withdrawal to a plateau of thought upon which they became hunters casting nets for a quarry they had never seen but would recognize at first sight.

'While they're sorting that one out,' Garamond continued, speaking to Napier before any of the science staff could voice objections, 'we'll convene a separate meeting of the engineering committee. The ship has to be cut up to get the workshop floors level, but in the meantime I want the design definition drawn up for the aircraft and the first production tapes prepared.' He got to his feet and walked towards the improvised plastic hut he was using as an office. Napier, walking beside him, gave a dry cough which was out of place issuing from the barrel of his chest.

'TB again?' Garamond said with mock sympathy.

'I think you're going too fast, Vance. Concentrating too much on the nuts and bolts, and not thinking enough about the human element.'

'Be more specific, Cliff.'

'A lot of the crew have got the Orbitsville syndrome already. They don't see any prospect of getting back to Beachhead City, and many of them don't even want to get back. They see no reason why they shouldn't set up a community right here, using the *Bissendorf* as a mine for essential materials.'

Garamond stopped, shielded his eyes and looked beyond the ship towards the plot of land, marked with a silver cross, where forty men and women had been buried. 'I can understand their feelings, and I'm not proposing to ride herd on those who want to stay. We'll use volunteers only.'

'There could be less than you expect.'

'Surely some of them, a lot of them, have reasons for getting back.'

'The point is that you aren't proposing to take them back, Vance. The planes won't make it all the way, so you're asking them to choose between staying here in a strong sizeable community with resources of power, materials and food – or being dropped somewhere between here and Beachhead City in groups of ten or less with very little to get them started as independent communities.'

'Each plane will have to carry an iron cow and a small plastics plant.'

'It's still a hell of a lot to ask.'

'I'll also guarantee that a rescue mission will set out as soon as I get back.'

'If you get back.'

A dark thought crossed Garamond's mind. 'How about you, Cliff? Are you coming with me?'

'I'm coming with you. All I'm trying to do is make you realize there's more to this than finding the right engineering approach.'

'I realize that already, but right now I've got all the human problems I can handle.'

'Others have wives and families they want to get back to.'

'That's the point – I haven't.'

'But ...'

'How long do you think Aileen and Chris will survive after I'm presumed dead? A week? A day?' Garamond forced himself to speak steadily, despite the grief which kept up a steady thundering inside his head. 'The only reason I'm going back is that I have to kill Liz Lindstrom.'

Although it had been equipped and powered to carry out one emergency landing on the surface of a planet, the *Bissendorf* was in a supremely unnatural condition when beached with its longitudinal axis at right angles to the pull of gravity. The interior layout was based on the assumption that, except during short spells of weightlessness, there would be acceleration or retardation which would enable the crew to regard the prow as pointing 'upwards' and to walk normally on all its levels. Now the multitudinous floors of the vessel had become vertical walls to which were attached, in surrealistic attitudes, clusters of consoles, pedestals, desks, chairs, lockers, beds, tables and several hundred machines of varying types and capabilities. Because design allowance had been made for periods of free-fall – most small items, including paperwork, were magnetically or physically clamped in position – very little material had fallen to the lowermost side of the hull, but many of the ship's resources could not be tapped until key areas were properly orientated to the ground.

Teams of forcemasters using valency cutters and custom-built derricks began slicing the *Bissendorf*'s structure into manageable sections and rotating them to horizontal positions. The work was slowed down by the need to sever and reconnect power channels, but within a week the cylinder of the central hull had been largely converted into a cluster of low circular or wedge-shaped buildings. Each was roofed with a plastic diaphragm and linked by cable to power sources on the ground or within the butchered ship. The entire complex was surrounded by an umbra of tents and extemporized plastic sheds which gave it the appearance of an army encampment.

Garamond had placed maximum priority on the design and workshop facilities which were to create his aircraft, and the work was advancing with a speed which would have been impossible even a century earlier. The assembly line was already visible as nine sets of landing skids surmounted by the sketchy cruciforms of the basic airframes.

After weighing all considerations, the computers from the spaceship had decreed that the stressed-skin principle of aircraft construction, universal to aviation, should be abandoned in favour of the frame-and-fabric techniques employed in the Wright Brothers era. This permitted most of the high technology and engineering subtlety to be concentrated in a dozen pieces of alloy per ship, and the tape-controlled radiation millers hewed these from fresh billets in less than a day. The plastic skinning could then be carried out to the standards of a good quality furniture shop, and the engines – standard magnetic pulse prime movers – fitted straight from the shelf. It was the availability of engines, of which there were twenty-one in the *Bissendorf*'s inventory, which had been the main parameter in deciding upon a fleet of nine twin-engined ships which would set out upon the journey with three powerplants in reserve.

Garamond, sitting alone in the prismatic twilight at the entrance to his tent, was halfway through a bottle of whisky when he heard someone approaching. The nights never became truly dark under the striped canopy of

Orbitsville's sky, and he was able to recognize the compact figure of Denise Serra while she was still some distance away. His annoyance at being disturbed faded somewhat but he sat perfectly still, making no sign of welcome. The whisky was his guarantee of sleep and to bring about the desired effect it had to be taken in precise rhythmic doses, with no interruptions to the ritual. Denise reached the tent, stood without speaking for a moment while she assessed his mood, then sat in the grass at the opposite side of the entrance. Appreciating her silence, Garamond waited till his instincts prompted him to take another measure of the spirit's cool fire. He raised the bottle to his lips.

'Drinking that can't be good for you,' Denise said.

'On the contrary – it's very good for me.'

'I never got to like whisky. Especially the stuff Burton makes.'

Garamond took his slightly delayed drink. 'It's all right if you know how to use it.'

'Use it? Aren't you supposed to enjoy it?'

'It's more important to me to know how to use it.'

She sighed. 'I'm sorry. I've heard about your wife being ...'

'What did you want, Denise?'

'A child, I think.'

Garamond knew himself to have been rendered emotionally sterile by despair for his family, but he still retained enough contact with the mainstream of humanity to feel obliged to cap his bottle and set it aside.

'It's a bad time,' he said.

'I know, but that's the way I feel. It must be this place. It must be the Orbitsville syndrome that Cliff keeps talking about. We're here, and it's all around us, for ever, and things I used to think important now seem trivial. And, for the first time in my life, I want a child.'

Garamond stared at the girl through the veils of soft blue air, and a part of his mind – despite the pounding chaos of the rest – was intensely aware of her. It was difficult to pick out a single special attribute of Denise Serra, but the overall effect was right. She was a neat, complete package of femininity, intelligence and warmth, and he felt ashamed of having nothing to offer her.

'It's still a bad time,' he repeated.

'I know. We all know that, but some of the other women are drinking untreated water. It's only a matter of time till they become pregnant.' Her eyes watched him steadily and he remembered how, in that previous existence, it had given him pleasure to look at her.

'Haven't you already got a partner, Denise?'

'You know I haven't.'

That's it into the open, he thought. *For me to know that Denise Serra, among all the other female crew members, had no liaisons I would have to have been taking a special interest in her.*

'I guess I did know.' Garamond hesitated. 'Denise, I feel ...'

'Honoured?'

'I think that's the word I would have used.'

'Say no more, Vance. I know what it means when somebody starts off by feeling honoured. I've done it myself.' She stood up in one easy movement.

Garamond tried for something less abrupt, and knew he was being clumsy. 'Perhaps in a year, a few months ...'

"The special unrepeatable offer will be closed before then,' Denise said with an uncharacteristic harshness in her voice. 'Have you thought about what you're going to do if we can't get a bearing on Beachhead City, if your flight never gets off the ground?'

'I'm counting on your getting that bearing.'

'Don't!' She turned quickly, walked away for a few paces, then came back and knelt close to him. 'I'm sorry, Vance.'

'You haven't done anything to apologize for.'

'I think I have. You see, we've pretty well solved the problem. Dennis O'Hagan didn't want to say anything to you till he'd made a check on the math.'

'But ...' Garamond's attention was fully captured. 'How is it going to be done?'

'Mike Moncaster, our particles man, came up with the idea. You know about delta particles?'

'I've heard of delta rays.'

'No, that's historic stuff. Delta particles – deltons – are a component of cosmic rays discovered only a few years ago. During his last leave Mike got himself seconded on to the team investigating cosmic ray refraction by the force field which seals Beachhead City aperture. They were glad to have him because he's pretty good on the Conservation of Strangeness and ...'

'Denise! You started to tell me how you were going to get a bearing.'

'That's what I'm doing. Deltons don't interact much. That's why it took so long to find them, but it also means they could travel ten or fifteen million kilometres through the air. Mike is fairly certain they get refracted by the force lens, just like other components of cosmic rays, so we're going to build a big delton detector. Two of them, in fact. One behind the other to give us co-ordinates. All we need then is to pick up a delton, just one, and going back the way it came will give us a straight line home.'

'Do you think it'll work?'

'I think so.' Denise's voice was kind. 'What we still have to determine is how long we're likely to wait before a particle comes this way. It could be quite a while if things aren't in our favour, but we can swing the odds by making the detectors as big as possible, or by erecting a whole bank of them.'

Garamond felt the distance between himself and Elizabeth Lindstrom shrink a little and the joyful sickness spurted within him. 'This ... is good news.'

'I know,' Denise said. 'My dowry.'

'You'll have to explain that one.'

'The first time you ever noticed me was on board ship, when I gave the news you wanted to hear about going through the aperture,' she laughed ruefully. 'Being a pragmatist, I must have decided that if it worked once it would work again.'

Garamond moved his hand uncertainly in the dimness and touched her cheek. 'Denise, I ...'

'Let's not play games, Vance.' She pushed his hand away and stood up. 'I was childish, that's all.'

Later, while waiting for sleep to relieve him of the burden of identity, Garamond was acutely aware – for the first time in months – that the hard, angry vacuum of space began only a short distance beneath his cot. The feeling persisted into surrealistic dreams in which he had a sense of being poised, dangerously, on the rim of a precipice, with a kind of moral vertigo drawing him over the edge.

CHAPTER FIFTEEN

On his way to the airstrip Garamond was surprised to notice one of his crewmen wearing what could only be described as a coolie hat. He eyed the young man curiously, received a half-hearted salute, and decided the unusual headgear must be a personal souvenir of a tourist trip to the Orient. A minute later, while passing the workshop area, he saw two more men wearing similar hats, which he now realized were woven from fresh silver-green straw. The ancient peasant-styling, with all that it symbolized in Earth's history, was repugnant to Garamond and he hoped it would not become a full-blown fad such as occasionally swept through the crew levels. When he reached the test site, the glinting of flat green triangles in the distance told him that coolie hats were being worn by at least half the men who were clearing grass at the far end of the airstrip.

Cliff Napier was waiting for him at the door to the operations shed, his shoulder-heavy bulk filling the entrance. 'Morning, Vance. We're nearly ready to fly.'

'Good.' Garamond eyed the first aircraft appraisingly then turned his gaze back along the strip. 'It looks like a paddy field down there – why are the men wearing those sunhats?'

'Would you believe,' Napier said impassively, 'to protect them from the sun?'

'But why that sort of hat?' Garamond ignored the sarcasm.

'I guess it's because they're light and easy to make. And it's a good shape if the sun's directly above you and you're working in the dirt all day.'

'I still don't like them.'

'You're not working in the dirt all day.' This time there was no mistaking the coldness in the big man's manner.

Garamond locked eyes with Napier and was shaken to feel a momentary surge of anger and dislike. *This can't be,* he thought. Aloud he said, 'Do you expect me to? Do you think I'm not making the most efficient use of human resources?'

'From your point of view, you are.'

'And from their point of view?'

'The cold season's coming down soon. Most of the crew are staying here, remember. They'd rather be building houses and processing grass into protein cakes.'

Garamond decided against answering immediately in case he damaged a working relationship. He glanced up at the sky and saw that, behind the shield of brilliance, the broadest ribs of light blue were well in the ascendant in the west. They signified that summer was approaching the diametrically opposite point on Orbitsville's shell, that Autumn was ending on the near side.

'This Orbitsville syndrome of yours,' he said after a pause. 'An early symptom is that a man develops an aversion to taking orders, right?'

'That seems to come into it.'

'Then let's sit down together and agree a common set of goals. That way ...'

'That way we'd do everything you want and you wouldn't even have to give the orders,' Napier said sharply, but this time he was smiling.

Garamond smiled in return. 'Why do you think I suggested it?' Although the little crisis had passed, he had a feeling it carried significance for the future and he was determined to take appropriate action. 'We'll open a bottle tonight and get our ideas straightened out.'

'I thought we were out of whisky.'

'No. There's plenty.'

'You're on the stuff that Burton makes?'

'Why not?'

An incongruous primness appeared briefly on Napier's dark features.

'Maybe we can fix something up later. How about looking at this airplane?'

'Certainly.' They walked out towards the waiting machine which was the biscuit colour of unpainted plastic. It was a high-wing monoplane, sitting nose-high on its skids and looking like something from a museum of aeronautics, but Garamond had no doubts about its capabilities. The ungainly ship would carry a crew of five at a maximum cruise of five hundred kilometres an hour for fifty days at a stretch, landing after that time to replenish food and water. Even this limitation was forced on it by the fact that more than two-thirds of the payload would be taken up by spares, an iron cow and other supplies.

Garamond glanced from the newly completed machine to the others of its kind further back on the open-air production line, and from them up to the black rectangular screen of the delton detector on the hillside. He felt a vague spasm of alarm over the extent to which his future was dependent on complex artifacts, but this was obliterated by the yearning hunger which kept him alive and was the motive force behind all his actions. It was ironic, he had often thought in the hours before sleep, how – in depriving him of all that was worth living for in his previous life – Elizabeth Lindstrom had provided, in herself, the single goal of his new existence. She had also given him the means of escaping from it, for he could foresee no way of long surviving the act of pulling the President's ribcage apart with his bare hands and gripping the heaving redness within and ...

'I know what you're thinking, Vance.'

'Do you?' Garamond stared into the face of the stranger who had spoken to him, and he made the effort which allowed him to associate it with Cliff Napier. There was a psychic wrench and once again he was back into the sane world, walking towards the aircraft with his senior officer.

'Well, don't keep me in suspense,' he heard himself saying.

'I think you're secretly pleased the electronics lab isn't able to build autopilots. If we're going to fly that distance we want to *fly* it. We want to be able to tell people we did it with our hands.'

Garamond nodded. *With our hands,* he thought. One of the group standing at the plane was wearing a coolie hat and when its owner turned to greet him Garamond was startled to see the sweat-beaded features of Troy Litman, the senior production executive. Litman was a short pudgy man who had always compensated for the natural untidiness of his physique by paying strict attention to his uniform and off-duty dress, and he was one of the last Garamond would have expected to favour a badly-woven grass hat. Garamond began to doubt his earlier conviction that the design of the grass headgear was symbolic rather than utilitarian.

'The ship looks good,' Garamond said. 'Is she ready to fly?'

'As near as she'll ever be.'

Like the hat, the answer was not what Garamond would have expected of Litman. 'How near is that?'

'Relax, Vance.' Litman grinned within the column of shadow projected by the brim of his hat. 'That ship will take you as far as you want to go.'

'I'm ready to take her up now, sir,' Braunek said opportunely, from the opposite side of the group.

'You're happy enough about it?'

'If the computer's happy I'm happy, sir. Anyway I did a few fast taxis yesterday and she felt fine.'

'Go ahead, then.' Garamond watched the young man climb into the plane's glasshouse and strap himself into his seat. A few seconds later the propellers started to turn, silently driven by the magnetic resonance engines, and the control surfaces flicked in anticipation. As the propeller revolutions built up the group moved out of the backwash and a similar scattering took place among the work gangs at the far end of the runway. The plane began to move and several excited shouts went up, signifying that, despite the computer predictions and tape-controlled machines, there had remained some areas of human participation.

In its unloaded condition the aircraft used very little of the runway before lifting cleanly into the air. It continued in a straight line for about a kilometre, rising steadily, shadow flitting over the grass directly below, then banked into a lazy turn and circled the encampment. The soundless flight seemed effortless, like that of a gull riding on a fresh breeze, but on the third pass Garamond thought he saw a small object detach itself from the aircraft and go fluttering to the ground.

'What was that?' Napier said, screening his eyes. 'I saw something fall,'

'Nothing fell,' Litman asserted very quickly.

'I saw something too,' Garamond put in. 'You'd better get a medic on to the truck, just in case.'

'It wouldn't do any good – we had to pull the transmission out.'

'What?' Garamond stared in disbelief at Litman's uneasy but defiant face. 'One of the first basic procedures we agreed was that the truck would be kept at readiness during flight testing.'

'I guess I forgot.'

Garamond flicked a hand upwards, sending Litman's hat tumbling behind him. 'You are not a peasant,' he said harshly. 'You are not a coolie. You are a Starflight executive officer and I'm going to see that you ...'

'Braunek's coming back,' someone said and Garamond returned his attention to the aircraft. The pilot had not tried, or had been unable, to line up on the runway but was coming in parallel to it, his ship rising and sinking noticeably as it breasted the wind. Garamond estimated the touchdown point and relaxed slightly as he saw it would be well to the north of the buildings and tents which were clustered around the hulk of the *Bissendorf*. The plane continued its descent, side-slipping a little but holding fairly well to its course.

'I told you there was nothing to worry about,' Litman said in a reproachful voice.

'You'd better be right.' Garamond kept his eyes on Braunek's ship. The side-slipping was more noticeable now, but each skid brought the plane a little closer to the centreline of the cleared strip and Garamond hoped that Braunek was good enough at his trade to be doing it on purpose. He knew, however, that there had to come a moment, a precise moment, in every air crash when the spectator on the ground was forced to accept that the pilot had lost his struggle against the law of aerial physics, that a disaster had to occur. For Garamond, the moment came when he saw that the starboard propeller was ceasing to spin. The plane pulled to the right, as though the wing on that side had hit an invisible pylon, and it staggered down the perilous sky towards the hillside. Towards, Garamond suddenly realized, the black rectangle of the delton detector. He was unable to breathe during the final few seconds of flight as the doomed ship, see-sawing its wings, became silhouetted against land instead of sky and then flailed its way through the delton screen. And it was not until the sound of the crash reached him that he was freed from his stasis and began to run.

Braunek's life was saved by the fact that the lightweight frames of the detector screens served as efficient absorbers of kinetic energy. They had accepted the impact, folding almost gently around the ship, stretching and twisting, and then trailing out behind it like vines. By the time Garamond reached the location of the crash Braunek had been helped out of the wreckage and was sitting on the grass. He was surrounded by technicians who had been working in and had run out of the small hut linked to the screens, and one of them was spraying tissue sealant over a gash on his leg.

'I'm glad you made it,' Garamond said, feeling inadequate. 'How do you feel?'

Braunek shook his head. *'I'm* all right, but everything else is screwed up.' He tried to raise himself from the ground.

Garamond pushed him back. 'Don't move. I want the medics to have a proper look at you. What happened anyway?'

'Starboard wing centre panel dropped off.'

'It just *dropped* off?'

Braunek nodded. 'It took the engine control runs with it, otherwise I could have brought the ship in okay.'

Garamond jumped to his feet. 'Litman! Find that panel and bring it here. *Fast!*'

Litman, who was just arriving on the scene, looked exasperated but he turned without a word and ran back down the hillside. Garamond stayed talking with Braunek until a medic arrived to check him over, then he surveyed the ruins of the delton screen. Somewhere in the middle of the wreckage a damaged aircraft engine was still releasing gyromagnetic impulses which sent harmless flickers of detuned energy racing over the metalwork like St Elmo's fire. Where accidental resonances occurred a feeble motive force was conjured up and the broken struts of the framework twitched like the legs of a dying insect. The destruction looked final to Garamond but he checked with O'Hagan and confirmed that the screen had been rendered useless except as a source of raw materials.

'How long till you have another one operational?'

'A week perhaps,' O'Hagan said. 'We'll go for modular construction this time. That means we could have small areas operational in a couple of days, and we could build up to a useful size before your airplanes are ready to take off.'

'Do that.' Garamond left his Chief Science Officer staring gloomily into the wreckage and went down the hillside to meet the group which had retrieved the lost wing section. The men set the plastic panel down in front of him and stood back without speaking. Garamond ran his gaze over it and saw at once that the two longitudinal edges which should have been ridged with welding overlays were square and clean except for small positioning welds which had broken.

Garamond turned to face Litman. 'All right – who was responsible for the welding of this panel, and who was supposed to inspect?'

'It's hard to say,' Litman replied.

'Hard to say?'

'That's what I said.'

'Then check it out on the work cards.' Garamond spoke with insulting gentleness.

'What work cards?' Litman, suddenly tired of being pushed, turned a red, resentful face up to Garamond's. 'Where have you been, Mister Garamond? Did nobody tell you we've only got bits of a workshop left? Did nobody tell you that winter's coming and we just can't *afford* all the time and material that's going into these flying toys of yours?'

'That isn't in your area of competence.'

'Of course not!' The redness had spread into Litman's eyes as he glanced around the gathering crowd. 'I'm only a production man. I'm just one of the slobs who has to meet your airy-fairy target dates with no bloody equipment. But there's something you seem to forget, Mister Garamond. Out here a man who knows how to use his hands is worth twenty Starflight commanders who have nothing left to command.'

'What'll you do if we decide not to finish your planes?' A low, interested murmur arose from the men behind Litman.

Cliff Napier stepped into the arena. 'For a so-called production man,' he said, 'you seem to do a lot of work with your mouth, Litman. I suggest that you …'

'It's all right,' Garamond cut in, placing a restraining hand on Napier's arm. He raised his voice so that he could be heard by everybody in the vicinity. 'I know how most of you feel about settling down here and making the best of things. And I know you want to get on with survival work before the weather turns. Furthermore, I can sympathize with your point of view about obsolescent Starflight commanders – but let me assure you of one thing. I'm leaving here with a fleet of airplanes, and the airplanes are going to be built properly, to the very highest standards of which we are capable. If I find they don't work as well as they ought to I'll simply turn them around and fly them right back to you.

'So the only way – the *only* way – you'll get me out of your hair permanently is by building good airplanes. And don't come sniffling to me about target dates or shortage of equipment. Don't forget – I've seen how you can work when you feel like it. What sort of a target date did we have when we were getting ready to punch a hole right through the middle of Beachhead City?' Garamond paused and out-stared the man nearest to him.

'A nice finishing touch,' Napier whispered. 'If they still have pride.'

'Ah, hell,' somebody growled from several rows back. 'We might as well finish the job now we've done most of the work.' There was a general rumble of assent and the crowd, after a moment's hesitation, began to disperse. The response was not as wholehearted as Garamond could have wished for, but he felt a sense of relief at having secured any kind of decision over Litman. The production executive, his face expressionless, was turning away with the others.

'Troy,' Garamond said to him, 'we could have talked that one out in private.'

Litman shrugged. 'I'm satisfied with the way things went.'

'Are you? You used to be known as the best production controller in the S.E.A. fleet.'

'That's all in the past, Vance. I've got bigger things on my mind now.'

'Bigger than a man's life? Braunek could have been killed over that sloppy workmanship.'

'I'm sorry about young Braunek getting hurt, and I'm glad he's all right.' Litman paused and retraced his steps towards Garamond. 'The reason the men went along with you a moment ago is that you gave them Orbitsville –

and that's important to them. They're going to spread out through Orbitsville, Vance. This camp won't hold together more than a year or two, and then most likely it will be left empty.'

'We were talking about the plane crash.'

'We don't stand united any more. Any man who trusts his life to a machine he hasn't made by himself and personally checked out by himself is a fool. You should remember that.' Litman turned and plodded away down the hillside, probably intent on retrieving his coolie hat. Garamond stared after the compact figure, filled with the uneasy dislike that a man always feels for another who seems in closer touch with the realities of a situation. He thought hard about Litman's words during the midday meal and as a result decided to turn himself into a one-man inspection and quality assurance team, with entire responsibility for the airworthiness of his aircraft.

The self-imposed task – with its round of visual and physical checking of every aspect of the fleet production – occupied nine-tenths of Garamond's working hours, and brought the discovery that he still retained the ability to sleep without stunning his system with alcohol.

Garamond was spread-eagled across the tailplane of the seventh aircraft, examining the elevator hinges, when he felt a tap on his shoulder. It was late in the day and therefore hot – temperatures on Orbitsville built up steadily throughout each daylight period, before dropping abruptly at nightfall – and he had been hoping to finish the particular job without interruption. He kept his head inside the resinous darkness of the inspection hatch, hoping the interloper would take the hint and go away, but there came another and more insistent tap. Garamond twisted into a sitting position and found himself looking into the creased dry face of O'Hagan. The scientist had never been a happy-looking man but on this occasion his expression was more bleak than usual, and Garamond felt a stab of concern.

He switched off his inspection light and slid to the ground. 'Has anything happened, Dennis?'

O'Hagan gave a reluctant nod. 'We've recorded a delta particle.'

'You've recorded a ...' Garamond pressed the back of his hand to his forehead and fought to control his elation. 'Isn't that what we've been trying to do? What's your worry?'

'We've only got about eighty per cent of the original screen rebuilt.'

'So?'

'It's too soon, Vance. I've been through Mike Moncaster's math a couple of times and I can't fault him. With two complete screens – which is what we planned for – giving a receiving area of five hundred square metres, we should have had to wait eighty or ninety days even to ...'

'We were lucky,' Garamond interrupted, laughing and astonished to realize he still remembered how. 'It just shows that the laws of probability are bound to give you a break eventually. Come on, Dennis, admit it.'

O'Hagan shook his head with sombre conviction. 'The laws of probability are not bound to give you anything, my friend.'

The eight aircraft took off at first light, while the air was cool and thick, and climbed steadily against the seriate blue archways of the Orbitsville sky. At the agreed cruising height of five hundred metres the ungainly, stiff-winged birds levelled off, exchanging brief communications through pulses of modulated light. They assumed a V-formation, and circled once around the base camp, their shadows falling vertically on to the remains of the *Bissendorf*, the metallic egg which had brought about their slow and painful birth. And then, without lingering further, they set course towards the prismatic mists which lay to the east.

CHAPTER SIXTEEN

Day 8. Estimated range: 94,350 kilometres

For a start, I am determined to avoid the abbreviations traditionally used by diarists – their function is that of shortening a necessary task, whereas my aim is to prolong a superfluous one. (The term 'ship's log' might be more appropriate than 'diary'; but, again, the log is a record of the events of a voyage, whereas the daily entries in my book are likely to be the only pseudo-events in a continuum of pure monotony.) (If I go on splitting hairs like this about the precise meanings of words in the opening sentence, I'll never get beyond it; but the reference to abbreviations isn't quite right, either. I intend to use the symbol 'O' instead of writing out 'Orbitsville' in full each time. O is much shorter than Orbitsville, but that is coincidental – it is also more expressive of the reality.)

Cliff Napier was right when he guessed I was glad the job of manufacturing autopilots was beyond our resources. My reasoning was that flying the ship by hand would keep us occupied and help to reduce the boredom. It isn't working out that way, though. There are five of us on board and we spell each other at the controls on a rota which is arranged so that the two most experienced pilots – Braunek and myself – are in the cockpit at daybreak and nightfall. These are the only times when flying the ship becomes more difficult than driving an automobile. Because day and night are caused by bands of light and darkness sweeping over the land at orbital speed, there is no proper dawn and no proper dusk, and some fairly violent meteorological processes take place.

In the 'morning' a sector of cold air which has been sinking steadily for hours suddenly finds itself warming up again and rising, causing anything from clear air turbulence to heavy rain. At nightfall the situation is reversed but can be even more tricky because the air which cools and begins to descend conflicts with currents rising from the still-warm ground.

All it amounts to, however, is that there are two half-hour periods when the control column comes to life. Not enough to occupy us for the next three to four years, I'm afraid, although we in the lead ship are a little luckier than the others in having a little extra work to do. There is the inertial course reference to be monitored, for instance. It is a simple-looking black box, created by O'Hagan and his team, and inside it is a monomaniac electronic brain which thinks of nothing but the bearing they fed into it. Any time we begin to wander off course a digital counter instructs us to go left or right till we're back on line again, and the rest of the squadron follows suit.

Linked to the black box there is a one-metre-square delton detector which in a year or two, as we get considerably closer to Beachhead City, should begin to pick up other delta particles and provide course confirmation. Sometimes I watch it, just in case, or just to pass the time, but there isn't really any need. It would feed a fresh bearing into the course reference automatically, and is also fitted with an audio attention-getter. I still watch it, though ... and dream about EL. No abbreviations – Elizabeth Lindstrom.

Day 23. Estimated range: 278,050 kilometres

We've completed perhaps a fortieth of the journey, having flown a distance roughly equivalent to going round the Earth seven times. Without stopping. Another way to reckon it is that, after 23 days, we've gone nearly as far as a ray of light would have travelled in one second, but that's a depressing thought to anyone who has been accustomed to Arthurian flight at multiples of light-speed. A more positive thought is that we've learned quite a lot about O.

Somehow, I'd always thought of it as being composed entirely of featureless prairie, but I was wrong. Perhaps it started off that way, eons ago, and the subsequent action of wind led to the formation of the mountains we've seen. None of them was very high, not more than a couple of thousand metres, but with the land area of five billion Earths not yet explored who's to say what will be found? The mountains are there, anyway, and some of them are capped with snow because our flight is taking us into the winter sector, and there are rivers and small seas. Our formation passes over them in a dead straight line, quietly and steadily, and sometimes the telescopes pick up herds of grazing animals. Perhaps settlers will not have to rely exclusively on vegetable protein, after all.

The unexpected variegation of the terrain is making the journey a little easier to endure, but after a time all seas are the same, all hills look alike . . .

When I wrote in an earlier entry that the five of us in the lead ship were luckier than the others in having more to do, I was not thinking about the members of the science staff. Sammy Yamoto in No 4 seems to be fully occupied with astronomical readings, including precise measurements of the width of the day and night bands as we cross them, or as they cross us. He now says that, even with improvised equipment, he could probably take a bearing on Beachhead City which would be accurate to within a degree or so. I suspect he is passing up his turn at the flying controls so that he can carry on with his work. I hope this is not the case, because he is one of the least expert pilots and needs the practice. Although five per ship is ample crew strength, this could be cut down, by illness, for example, and I'm making no provision for unscheduled stops. Any ships which have to go down for long periods will be stripped and left behind. With their crews.

Cliff Napier in No 2 is filling in free time by helping Denise Serra in a series of experiments connected with recording radiation and gravity fluctuations.

Sometimes – in fact, quite often – I find myself wishing Denise was on my ship. I could have arranged it at the start, of course, but I wanted to play fair with her. Having turned her down that night, I felt the least I could do was avoid obstructing the field. But now . . . Now when I dream about Aileen and Chris I dream they are dead, which means I'm beginning to accept it, and with the acceptance my pragmatic, faithless body seems to be nominating Aileen's successor. I feel ashamed about this, but perhaps it is not as purely physical as I was supposing. Delia Liggett, who was a catering supervisor on the Bissendorf, is on my ship and two of the other men have a good practical relationship with her – but I can't work up much interest in a hot bunking system. I'm positive this isn't a ridiculous remnant of a captain-to-crew attitude, a notion that I ought to have her exclusively because I had the most silver braid on my uniform.

Outside the agreed goals of this mission I have, probably with some assistance from the pervading influence of the Big O, completely discarded the old command structure. I do remember, though, feeling some surprise at the make-up of the thirty-nine volunteers who came with me. My first supposition was that they would all be of executive rank and above, career-oriented men and women who were determined to take the *Bissendorf* incident in their stride. Instead, I found that over half of the seventy original volunteers were ordinary crewmen. Those who remained, after the selection procedure which cut the number down to the precise requirement, I regard and treat as exact equals.

O makes us equal.

In comparison to it we are reduced to the ultimate, human electrons, too small to admit of any disparity in size.

Day 54. Estimated range: 620,000 kilometres

We have completed our first scheduled landing and are in flight again. After fifty days in the air, the prospect of three days on the ground was exhilarating. We landed in formation on a level plain, the eight fully qualified pilots at the controls, and spent practically all the down-time in gathering grass and loading it into the processing machines. This is what passes for winter on O. The sun is still directly overhead, naturally enough, but with the days being shorter the temperature does not build up as high and has a much longer time to bleed away at night. It results in nothing more than a certain briskness in the air during the day, although the: nights are a lot colder. (It makes me wonder why the designers of O bothered to build in a mechanism to provide seasons. If the hostel-for-the-galaxy notion is correct, presumably the designers carried out a survey of intelligent life-forms in their region of space to see what the environmental requirements were. And if that is the case, the majority of life-bearing worlds must closely resemble Earth, even to the extent of having a moderately tilted axis and a procession of seasons. Could this, for some reason I don't fathom, be a universal pre-requisite for the evolution of intelligence?)

It seems that weather isn't going to be any problem during future stops, but our physical condition might. The simple task of cutting and gathering grass pretty well exhausted a lot of people, and now we are instituting programmes of exercises which can be performed on board ship.

Day 86. Estimated range: 1,038,000 kilometres

With more than a million kilometres behind us, it was beginning to look as though our journey time would be better than predicted, but the first hint of mechanical difficulties has shown up. The starboard propeller bearing on ship No 7 has started to show some wear. This is causing vibration at maximum cruise and we have had to reduce fleet speed by twelve kilometres per hour. The loss of speed is not very significant in itself, because it could be compensated for by extended engine life, but the alarming thing is that the propeller shaft bearings on all the ships are supposed to have been made in Magnelube Alloy Grade E. It is inconceivable that a bearing made to that specification could begin to show wear after only 83 days of continuous running – and the suspicion crosses my mind that Litman may have substituted Magnelube D, or even C. (I do not believe he would have done this out of pure malice, but if there was a shortage of blocks of the top grade metal and

I had discovered it I would have ordered a redesign or would have stripped some of the *Bissendorf*'s main machinery to get the bearings. Either way, Litman would have had a lot of extra work on his hands, and the person he has become would not take kindly to that.) We must now keep a careful watch on all propeller shaft bearings because we carry no stocks of Magnelube Alloy and, in any case, barely retain the ability to machine it to the required tolerances. Like archaeologists burrowing deeper into the past, we are retrogressing through various levels of technical competence.

In the meantime, the flight continues uninterrupted. Over prairies, lakes, mountains, seas, forests – and then over more and more of the same. A million kilometres is an invisible fraction of O's circumference, and yet seeing it like this has stunned one part of my mind. I was taught at school that a man's brain is unable to comprehend what is meant by a light-year – now I know we cannot comprehend as much as a light-second. So far in this journey we have, in effect, encircled twenty-five Earths; but my heart and mind are suspended, like netted birds, some-where above the third or fourth range of mountains. They have run into the comprehension barrier, while my body has travelled onwards, heedless of what penalties may fall due.

Day 93. Estimated range: 1,080,000 kilometres

Like Litman, like the others, I am becoming a different person.

I sometimes go for a whole day without thinking about Elizabeth Lindstrom. And now I can think about Aileen and Chris without experiencing much pain. It is as if they are in a mental jewel box. I can take them out of it, examine them, receive pleasure – then put them back into it and close the lid. The thought has occurred to me that the life of a loved one must be considered algebraically – setting the positive total of happiness and contentment against the negative quantity represented by pain and death. This process, even for a very short life, results in a positive expression. I wish I could discuss this idea with someone who might understand, but Denise is on another ship.

Day 109. Estimated range: 1,207,000 kilometres

We have lost Tayman's ship, No 6. It happened while we were landing for our second scheduled stop, putting down in formation on an ideal-looking plain. There was a hidden spar of rock which wrecked one of Tayman's skids, causing the plane to dip a wing. Nobody was hurt, but No 6 had to be written off. (In future we will land in sequence on the lead aircraft's skid marks to reduce the risk of similar incidents.) Tayman and his crew – which includes two women – took the mishap philosophically and we spent an extra day on the ground getting them set up for a prolonged stay. Among the parts we took from No 6 were the propeller shaft bearings, one of which was immediately installed in No 7's starboard engine.

I suppose the latter has to be regarded as a kind of bonus – fleet speed is back to maximum cruise – but the loss of Jack Tayman's steady optimism is hard to accept. Strangely, I find myself missing his aircraft most at night. We have no radio altimeters or equivalents because the conditions on O will not permit electromagnetic transmission, and the environment also makes barometric pressure readings too unreliable, so we use the ancient device of two inclined spotlights on each aircraft, one at each end of the fuselage. The forward laser ray is coloured red, the aft one white, and they intersect at five hundred metres, which means that a machine flying at the chosen height projects a single pink spot. Looking downwards through the darkness we can see our V-formation slipping across the ground, hour after hour, a squadron of silent moons, and the disappearance of one of those luminous followers is all too apparent.

Day 140. Estimated range: 1,597,000 kilometres

Within the space of ten days propeller shaft bearing trouble has developed on five ships, and fleet speed has been reduced by fifty kilometres an hour. Prognosis is that there will be continued deterioration, with progressive cuts in flying speed. Everybody is properly dismayed, but I think I can detect an undercurrent of relief at the possibility of so many aircraft having to drop out at the same time, thus providing for the setting up of a larger and stronger community. I have discussed the situation with Cliff Napier over the lightphone and even he seems to be losing heart.

The only aspect of the matter which looks at all 'hopeful' is that the ships which have experienced the trouble are No 3 through to No 8, which reflects the order in which they came off the production line. The first and second ships – mine and Napier's – are all right, and it may be that Litman had enough Grade E metal available for our propeller bearings. I put the word hopeful in quotes in this context because, on reflection, it simply is not appropriate. Being reduced to two airplanes at this stage of the mission would be disastrous, and it would take fairly comprehensive technical resources to restore us to strength. Resources which are not available.

I am writing this at night, mainly because I can't sleep, and I find it difficult to fight off a sense of defeat. The Big O is too …

Garamond set his stylus aside as Joe Braunek, who had been in the cockpit serving as stand-by pilot, appeared in the gangway beside his bunk. The young man's face was deeply shadowed by the single overhead light tube but his eyes, within their panda-patches of darkness, were showing an abnormal amount of white.

'What is it, Joe?' Garamond closed his diary.

'Well, sir …'

'Vance.'

'Sorry, I keep … Do you want to come up front a minute, Vance?'

'This gets us back to square one – is there anything wrong? I'm trying to rest and I don't want to get up without a good reason.'

'There are some lights we can't explain.'

'Which panel?'

Braunek shook his head. 'Not that sort of light. Outside the ship – near the horizon. It looks like there's a city of some kind ahead of us.'

CHAPTER SEVENTEEN

At first sight, the lights were disappointing. Because the fleet was travelling roughly eastwards, the blue and darker blue bands which represented day and night on other parts of Orbitsville were arcing across the sky from side to side. The lower one looked in the eastern sky the narrower and closer together the bands appeared to grow, until they merged in the opalescent haze above the upcurving black horizon. Even when Braunek had shown him where to look Garamond had to scan the darkness for several seconds before he picked out a thin line of yellowish radiance, like a razor cut just below the edge of a cardboard silhouette.

Delia Liggett, who was at the controls, raised her face to him. 'Is there any chance that…?'

'It isn't Beachhead City,' Garamond said. 'Let's get that clear.'

'I thought there might have been a mistake over distances.'

'Sorry, Delia. We're working on a very rough estimate of how far the *Bissendorf* travelled, but not that rough. You can start looking out for Beachhead City in earnest a couple of years from now.' There was silence in the cockpit except for the insistent rush of air against the sides of the ship.

Then what is that?'

Garamond perversely refused to admit excitement. 'It looks like sky reflections on a lake.'

'Wrong colour,' Braunek said, handing Garamond a pair of binoculars. 'Try these.'

'It has to be an alien settlement,' Garamond admitted as the glasses revealed the beaded brightness of a distant city. 'And it's so far from the entrance to the sphere.'

At that moment Cliff Napier's voice came through on the lightphone. 'Number Two speaking – is that Vance I can see in the cockpit?'

'I hear you, Cliff.'

'Have you seen what we've seen?'

'Yeah – and are you wondering what I'm wondering?'

Napier hesitated. 'You mean, what's an alien city doing way out here? I guess they got to Orbitsville a very long time before we did. It might have taken them hundreds or thousands of years to drift out this far.'

'But why did they bother? You've seen what Orbitsville's like – one part is as good as another.'

'To us, Vance. Aliens could see things a different way.'

'I don't know,' Garamond said dubiously. 'You always say things like that.' He dropped into one of the supernumerary seats and fixed his eyes on the horizon, waiting for the wall of daylight to rush towards him from the east. When it came, about an hour later, sweeping over the ground with thought-paralysing speed, the alien settlement abruptly became an even less noticeable feature of the landscape. Although it was now within a hundred kilometres, the 'city' was reduced in the binoculars to a mere dusting of variegated dots almost lost in greenery. During the lightphone conversations between the aircraft there had been voiced the idea that it might be possible to obtain new propeller bearings or have the existing ones modified. Garamond, without expressing any quick opinions on a subject so important to him, had been quietly hopeful about the aliens' level of technology – but his optimism began to fade. The community which hovered beyond the prow of his ship reminded him of a Nineteenth Century town in the American West.

'Looks pretty rustic to me.' Ralston, the telegeologist, had borrowed the glasses and was peering through them.

'Mark Twain land?'

'That's it.'

Garamond nodded. 'This is completely illogical, of course. We can't measure other cultures with our own yardstick, but I have a feeling that that's a low-technology agricultural community up there. Maybe it's because I believe that any race which settles on Orbitsville will turn into farmers. There's no need for them to do anything else.'

'Hold on a minute, Vance.' Ralston's voice was taut. 'Maybe you're going to get those bearings, after all. I think I see an airplane.'

Numb with surprise, Garamond took the offered binoculars and aimed them where Ralston directed. After a moment's search he found a complicated white speck hanging purposefully in the lower levels of the air. The absence of any lateral movement suggested the other plane was flying directly away from or directly towards his own, and his intuition told him the latter was the case. He kept watching through the powerful, gyro-stabilized glasses and presently saw other motes of coloured brightness rising, swarming uncertainly, and then settling into the apparently motionless state which meant they were flying to meet him head-on. Ralston gave the alert to the six other ships of the fleet.

'It's a welcoming party, all right,' he said as the unknown planes became visible to the naked eye, 'and we've no weapons. What do we do if they attack us?'

'We have to assume they're friendly, or at least not hostile.' Garamond adjusted the fine focus on the binoculars. 'Besides – I know I'm judging them by our standards again – but that doesn't look like an air force to me. The planes are all different colours.'

'Like ancient knights going out to do battle.'

'Could be, but I don't think so. The planes seem to be pretty small, and all different types.' A stray thought crossed Garamond's mind. He turned his attention back to the city from which the planes had arisen, and was still scanning it with growing puzzlement when the two fleets of aircraft met and coalesced.

A green-and-yellow low-wing monoplane took up station beside Garamond's ship and wiggled its wings in what, thanks to the strictures of aerial dynamics, had to be the universal greeting of airmen. The alien craft had a small blister-type canopy through which could be seen a humanoid form. Braunek, now at the controls, laughed delightedly and repeated the signal. The tiny plane near their wingtip followed suit, as did a blue biplane beyond it.

'Communication!' Braunek shouted. 'They aren't like the Clowns, Vance – we'll be able to talk to these people.'

'Good. See if you can get their permission to land,' Garamond said drily.

'Right.' Braunek, unaware of the irony, became absorbed in making an elaborate series of gestures while Garamond twisted around in his seat to observe as many of the alien ships as he could. He had noted earlier that no two were painted alike; now he was able to confirm that they all differed radically in design. Most were propeller-driven, but at least two were powered by gas turbines and one racy-looking job had the appearance of a home-made rocket ship. In general the alien planes were of conventional/universal cruciform configuration, although he glimpsed at least one canard and a twin-fuselage craft.

'A bit of a mixture,' Ralston commented, and added with a note of disappointment in his voice. 'I see a lot of internal combustion engines out there. If that's the level they're at they won't be much use to us.'

'How about supplies of fossil fuel?'

'There could be some about – depends on the age of Orbitsville.' Ralston surveyed the ground below with professional disgust. 'My training isn't worth a damn out here. The ordinary rules don't apply.'

'I think it's okay to go down,' Braunek said. 'Our friend has dipped his nose a couple of times.'

'Right. Pass the word along.'

As the fringes of the alien settlement began to slide below the nose of the aircraft Braunek sat higher in his seat and turned his head rapidly from side to side. 'I can't see their airfield. We'll have to circle around.'

Garamond tapped the pilot's shoulder. 'I think you'll find they haven't got a centralized airfield.'

The aircraft banked into a turn, giving a good view of the ground. The city wheeling below the wing was at least twenty kilometres across but had no distinguishable roads, factories or other buildings larger than average-sized dwellings. Garamond's impression was of thousands of hunting lodges scattered in an area of woodland. Here and there, randomly distributed, were irregular cleared areas about the size of football pitches. The brightly coloured alien planes dispersed towards these, crossing flight paths at low altitude in an uncontrolled manner which brought audible gasps from Braunek. They landed unceremoniously, one to a field, leaving the humans' ships still aloft in the circuit.

'This is crazy – I'm not going to try putting us down in somebody's back yard,' Braunek announced.

'Find a good strip outside of town and we'll land in sequence the way we'd already planned,' Garamond told him. He sat back in his seat and buckled his safety straps. The plane lost altitude, completed two low-level orbits and landed, with a short jolting run on its skids, in an expanse of meadow. Braunek steered it off to one side and they watched as the six other ships of the fleet touched down on the same tracks and formed an untidy line. Their propellers gradually stopped turning and canopies were pushed upwards like the wing casings of insects.

Green-scented air flooded in around Garamond and he relaxed for a moment, enjoying the sensation of being at rest. The luxuriousness of his body's response to the silence awakened memories of what it had been like arriving home for a brief after a long mission. Ecstasy-living was a phenomenon well known to S.E.A. personnel, as were its attendant dangers. Rigid self-control was always required during home leave, to prevent the ecstasy getting out of control and causing a fierce negative reaction at the beginning of the next mission. But in this instance, as he breathed the cool heavy air, Garamond realized he had been tricked into lowering his guard ...

I can't possibly take another two years of flying night and day, the thought came. *Nobody could.*

'Come on, Vance – stretch the legs,' Braunek called as he leapt down on to the grass. He was followed in close succession by Delia Liggett, Ralston and Pierre Tarque, the young medic who completed the crew of No 1. Garamond waved to them and made himself busy with his straps.

Two whole years to go – at least! – and what would it achieve?

The sound of laughter and cheerful voices came from outside as the crews of the seven aircraft met and mingled. He could hear friendly punches being swapped, and derisive whoops which probably signified an overlong kiss being exchanged.

Even if I get near enough to the President to kill her, which is most unlikely, what would that achieve? It's too late to do anything for Aileen and Chris. Would they want me to get myself executed?

Garamond stood up, filled with guilty excitement, and climbed out of the glasshouse. From the slight elevation, the alien settlement looked like a dreamy garden village. He glanced around, taking in all the lime-green immensities, and dropped to the ground where Cliff Napier and Denise Serra were waiting for him. Denise greeted him with a warm, direct gaze. She was wearing regulation-issue black trousers, but topped with a tangerine blouse in place of a tunic, and he suddenly appreciated that she was beautiful. They were joined almost at once by O'Hagan and Sammy Yamoto, both of whom looked greyer and older than Garamond had expected. O'Hagan wasted no time on pleasantries.

'We're at a big decision point, Vance,' he began. 'Five of our ships have sub-standard propeller bearings and if we can't get them upgraded there's no point in continuing with the flight.' He tilted his head and assumed the set expression with which he always heard arguments.

'I have to agree.' Garamond nodded, rediscovering the fact that looking at Denise produced a genuine sensation of pleasure in his eyes.

O'Hagan twitched his brows in surprise. 'All right, then. The first thing we have to do when we meet these aliens is to assess their engineering capabilities.'

'They can't be at the level of gyromagnetic power or magnetic bearings – you saw their aircraft.'

'That's true, but I think I'm right in saying a magnelube bearing can be considerably upgraded by enclosing it within another bearing, even one as primitive as a ball race. All we would have to do is commission the aliens to manufacture twenty or so large conventional bearings which we can wrap around our magnelubes.'

'They'd need to be of a standard size.'

O'Hagan sniffed loudly. 'That goes without saying.'

'I think you'll find ...' Garamond broke off as an abrupt silence fell over the assembled crews. He turned and saw a fantastic cavalcade approaching the aircraft from the direction of the city. The aliens were humanoid – from a distance surprisingly so – and shared the human predilection for covering their bodies with clothes. Predominant hues were yellows and browns which toned in with sand-coloured skin, making it difficult to determine precise details of their anatomies. Some of the aliens were on foot, some on bicycles, some on tricycles, some on motor-cycles, some in a variety of open cars and saloons including a two-wheeled gyro car, some were perched on the outside of an erratic air-cushion vehicle. They approached to within twenty metres of the parked aircraft and came to a halt. As the heterogeneous mixture of engines associated with their transport coughed, clanked and spluttered into silence, Garamond became aware that the aliens were producing a soft humming noise of their own. It was a blend of many different notes, continuously inflecting, and he tentatively concluded that it was their mode of speech. The aliens were hairless but had identifiable equivalents of eyes, ears and mouths agreeably positioned on their heads. Garamond was unable to decide what anatomical features their flimsy garments were meant to cover, or to see any evidence of sexual differentiation. He felt curiously indifferent to the aliens in spite of the fact that this first contact looked infinitely more propitious than the wordless futility of his encounter with the Clowns. No adventure in the outside universe held much significance compared to the voyage of discovery he was making within himself.

'Do you want to try speaking with them?' O'Hagan said.

Garamond shook his head. 'It's your turn to get your name in the history books, Dennis. Be my guest.'

O'Hagan looked gratified. 'If it were done when 'tis done, then 'twere well it were done scientifically.' He advanced on the nearest of the aliens, who seemed to regard him with interest, and the movement of his shoulders showed he was trying to communicate with his hands.

'There's no *need*,' Garamond said in a low voice.

Yamoto turned his head. 'What did you say?'

'Nothing, Sammy. I was talking to myself.'

'You should be careful who you're seen speaking to.'

Garamond nodded abstractedly. *The thing Dennis O'Hagan doesn't realize about these people is that they'll never do what he wants. He has missed all the signs.*

All right – assuming we can't get them to make the bearings, is there any point in continuing with the flight? Answer: no. This isn't just a personal reaction. The computers agreed that two airplanes of the type available would not constitute a sufficiently flexible and resourceful transport system. Therefore, I simply can't get back to Beachhead City. It's as clear-cut as that. It always was too late to do anything for Aileen and Chris, and now there's nothing I can even attempt to do.

I've been born again.

The aliens stayed for more than an hour and then, gradually but without stragglers, moved away in the direction of their city. They reminded

Garamond of children who had been enjoying an afternoon at a funfair and had become so hungry they could not bear to miss the meal waiting at home. When the last brightly painted vehicle disappeared behind the trees there was a moment of utter silence in the meadow, followed by an explosive release of tension among the plane crews. Bottles of synthetic liqueur were produced and a party set off to swim in a nearby lake.

'That was weird,' Joe Braunek said, shaking his head. 'We stood in two lines and looked, at each other like farm boys and girls at a village dance on Terranova.'

'It went all right,' Garamond assured him. 'There's no protocol – what are you supposed to do?'

'It still was weird.'

'I know, but just think what it would have been like if there'd been any diplomats or military around. We met them, and stared at them, and they stared at us, and nobody tried to take anything that belonged to the others, and nobody got hurt. Things could have been worse, believe me.'

'I guess so. Did you see the way they kept counting our ships?'

'I did notice that.' Garamond recalled the repeated gesture among the onlookers, long golden fingers indicating, stepping their way along the line of aircraft.

'Seemed important to them, somehow. It was as if they'd never seen ...'

'We've made genuine progress, Vance.' O'Hagan approached with a sheaf of hand-written notes and a recorder. 'I've identified at least six nouns or noun-sounds in their speech and I believe I'd have done better if I'd had musical training.'

'Can't you get somebody to help?'

'I have. I'm taking Paskuda and Shelley and going into the city. We won't stay long.'

'Take as long as you need,' Garamond said casually.

'All right, Vance.' O'Hagan gave him a searching stare. 'I want to see something of their machine capability as soon as possible. I think that would be a good idea, don't you?'

'Excellent.' Garamond had seen a flash of tangerine further down the line of aircraft and was unable to take his eyes away from it. He quickly disengaged from O'Hagan, walked towards Denise Serra but hesitated on seeing that she was involved in a discussion with the six other women of the flight crews. He was turning away when she noticed him and signalled that he was to wait. A minute later she came to him, looking warm, competent, desirable and everything else he expected a woman to be. The thought of lying with her caused a painful stab in his lower abdomen as glandular mechanisms, too long suppressed, found themselves reactivated. Denise glanced around her, frowned at the proximity of other people, and led the way towards an unspoiled area of tall grass. The quasi-intimacy of her actions pleased Garamond.

'It's good to see you again,' he said.

'It's good to see you, Vance. How do you feel now?'

'Better. I'm coming to life again.'

'I'm glad.' Denise gave him a speculative look. 'That was an official meeting of Orbitsville Women's League, detached chapter.'

'Oh? Carry on, Sister Denise.'

She smiled briefly. 'Vance, they've voted to drop out of the flight.'

'Unanimously?'

'Yes. Five airplanes are going to have to give up eventually, and we might as well pick the spot. The Hummers seem friendly and making a study of their culture will give us something to do. Apart from bringing up babies, that is.'

'Do you know how many men will want to stay?'

'Most of them. I'm sorry, Vance.'

'Nobody has to apologize for the operation of simple logic.'

'But that leaves you only two aircraft, and it isn't enough.'

'It's all right.' Garamond wondered how long he could go on with the role of martyr before telling Denise he had already come to terms with himself.

She caught his hand. 'I know how disappointed you must be.'

'You're making it easy to take,' he said. Denise released his hand on the instant and he knew he had said something wrong. He waited impassively.

'Has Cliff not told you I'm having a baby?' Denise's eyes were intent on his. 'His baby?'

Garamond forced himself to compose a suitable reply. 'He didn't need to.'

'You mean he *hasn't*? Just wait till I get my hands on the big ...'

'I'm not completely blind, Denise.' Garamond produced a smile for her. 'I knew as soon as I saw both of you together this morning. I just haven't got around to congratulating him yet.'

'Thanks, Vance. Out here we'll need all the godfathers we can get.'

'Can't help you there, I'm afraid – I'll be a few million kilometres east of here by that time.'

'Oh!' Denise looked away from him. 'I thought ...'

'That I was quitting? Not until I'm forced – and you know better than I do that the computers didn't say two aircraft *couldn't* reach Beachhead City. It's just a question of odds, isn't it?'

'So is Russian Roulette.'

'I'll see you around, Denise.' Garamond turned away, but she caught his arm.

'I shouldn't have said that. I'm sorry.'

'Please forget it.' He squeezed her hand before removing it from his arm.

'I really am glad that you and Cliff have got something good. Now, please excuse me – I have a lot of work to do.'

Garamond had been occupied for several hours on the load distribution plans for his two remaining aircraft when darkness came. He switched on the fuselage interior lights and continued working with cold concentration, ignoring the sounds of revelry which drifted into the cabin on the evening breeze. His fingers moved continually over the calculator keyboard as he laboured through dozens of load permutations, striving to decide the best uses for his payload capability. The brief penumbral twilight had fled when he felt vibrations which told him someone was coming on board. He looked up and saw O'Hagan squeezing his way towards the small chart-covered table.

'I've just discovered how much I used to rely on computers,' Garamond said.

O'Hagan shook his head impatiently. 'I've just spent the most fantastic day of my life, and I need a drink to get over it. Where's the supply?' He sat quietly while Garamond found a plastic bottle and handed it to him, then he took a short careful swallow. 'This stuff hasn't been aged much.'

'The man who made it has.'

'Like the rest of us.' O'Hagan took another drink and apparently decided he had devoted too much time to preamble. 'We haven't got a hope in hell of getting the bearings we need from these people. Know why?'

'Because they've no machine tools?'

'Because they make everything by hand. You knew?'

'I guessed. They've got some airplanes, but no airplane factory or airport. They've got some cars, but no car factory or roads.'

'Good work, Vance – you were way ahead on that one.' O'Hagan drummed his fingers on the table, the sound filling the narrow confines of the cabin, and his voice lost some of its usual incisiveness. 'They picked an entirely different road to ours. No specialization of labour, no mass production, no standardization. Anybody who wants a car or a cake-mixer builds it from scratch, if he has the time and the talent. You noticed their planes and cars were all different?'

'Yes. I noticed them counting our ships, too.'

'So did I, but I didn't know what was going on in their minds. They must have been astonished at seeing seven identical models.'

'Not astonished,' Garamond said. 'Mildly surprised, perhaps. I've a feeling these people haven't much curiosity in their make-up. If you allow only one alien per house that city out there must have a population of twenty thousand or more, but I doubt if as many as two hundred came out to look at us today – and practically all those who came had their own transport.'

'You mean we got the lunatic fringe.'

'Gadgeteers anyway – probably more interested in our aircraft than in us. They could be a frustrating bunch to have as next door neighbours.'

O'Hagan stared significantly at the paperwork scattered on the table. 'So you intend to press on?'

'Yes.' Garamond decided to let the single word do the work of the hundreds he might have used.

'Have you got a crew?'

'I don't know yet.'

O'Hagan sighed heavily. 'I'm sick to death of flying, Vance. It's killing me. But I'd go crazy if I had to live beside somebody who kept inventing the steam engine every couple of years. I'll fly with you.'

'Thanks, Dennis.' Garamond felt a warm prickling in his eyes. 'I …'

'Never mind the gratitude,' O'Hagan said briskly. 'Let's see what sort of mess you've been making of these load distributions.'

Against Garamond's expectations, he was able to raise two crews of four to continue the flight. Again making use of the extra lift to be gained from cold air, the two machines took off at dawn and, without circling or giving any aerial signal of goodbye, they flew quietly into the east.

CHAPTER EIGHTEEN

Day 193. Estimated range: 2,160,000 kilometres

This may be my last journal entry. Words seem to be losing their meaning, the act of writing them is losing all significance, and I notice that we have virtually stopped speaking to each other. The silence does not imply or induce separateness – the eight of us have compacted into one. It is simply that there is something embarrassing about watching a man go through the whole pointless performance of shaping his lips and activating his tongue in order to push sound vibrations out on the air. It is peculiar, too, how a spoken word resolves itself into meaningless syllables, and how a single syllable can hang resonating in the air, in your mind, long after the speaker has turned away.

I fancy, sometimes, that the same phenomenon takes place with images. We have steered our ships above a thousand seas, ten thousand mountain ranges, all of which have promised to be different – but which are all becoming the same. A distinctive peak or river bend, a curious group of islands, the coloration of a wooded valley – geographical features appear before us with the promise of something new and, having cheated us, fall behind. Were it not for the certainty of the inertial guidance system I might imagine we were flying in circles. No, that isn't correct, for we have learned to steer a constant course against the stripings of the sky. We seem to exist, embedded, in a huge crystal paperweight and one of the advantages, perhaps the only one, is that we can tell where we are going by reference to its millefiori design. If I hold the milk-blue curvatures in a certain precise relationship, crossing windshield and prow just so, I can fly for as long as thirty minutes before the black box chimes and edges me to left or right. The other black box, the portable delton detector, remains inert even after all this time. (Dennis was right when he said we were lucky to find that first particle so soon.) The up-curving horizon provides a constant reference for level flying. It occurred to me recently that Orbitsville is so big that we should not be able to detect any upward curvature in the horizon. As usual, Dennis was able to explain that it was an optical illusion – the horizon is straight but, through a trick of perception, appears to sag in the middle. He told me that the ancient Greeks compensated for this when building their temples.

The two aircraft are behaving as well as can be expected within their design limits. Each is carrying a reserve power-plant which takes up a high proportion of its payload, but this is unavoidable. A gyromagnetic engine is little more than a block of metal in which most of the atoms have been orchestrated to resonate in tune. It is without doubt one of the best general-purpose medium-sized power-plants ever conceived, but it has a fault in that – without warning and for no apparent reason – the orchestra can fall into discord and the power output drops to zero. When that happens there is no option than to install a new engine, so we can afford it to happen only twice. We have also had minor mechanical troubles. As yet there has been nothing serious enough to cause an unscheduled landing, but the potential is always there and grows daily.

The biggest cause for concern, however, is the biological machinery on board – our own bodies. Everybody, except for young Braunek, is subject to headaches, constipation, dizziness and nausea. Many of the symptoms are probably due to prolonged stress but, with increasingly unreliable aircraft to fly, we dare not resort to tranquillizers. Dennis, in particular, is causing me alarm and an equal amount of guilt over having brought him along. He gets greyer and more tired every day, and less and less able to do his stint at the controls. The protein and yeast cakes on which we live are not appetizing at the best of times, but Dennis is finding it almost impossible to keep them down and his weight is decreasing rapidly.

I am reaching the conclusion that the mission should be abandoned, and this time there are no emotional undertones in my thinking. I know it is not worth the expenditure of human lives.

A short time ago I could not have made such an admission – but that was before we had fully begun to pay for our mistake of challenging the Big O. The journey we attempted was perhaps only a hundredth of O's circumference, and of that tiny fraction we have completed only a fraction. My personal punishment for this presumption is that O has scoured out my soul. I can think of my dead wife and child; I can think of Denise Serra; I can think of Elizabeth Lindstrom ... and nothing happens.

I feel nothing.

This is my last diary entry.

There is nothing more to write.

There is nothing more to say.

Kneeling on the thrumming floor beside O'Hagan's bunk, Garamond said, 'It's summertime down there, Dennis. We've flown right into summer.'

'I don't care.' Beneath its covering of sheets, the scientist's body seemed as frail and fleshless as that of a mummified woman.

'I'm positive we could find fruit trees.'

O'Hagan gave a skeletal grin. 'You know what you can do with your fruit trees.'

'But if you could eat something you'd be all right.'

'I'm just fine – all I need is a rest.' O'Hagan caught Garamond's wrist. 'Vance, you're not going to call off the flight on my account. Promise me that.'

'I promise.' Garamond disengaged the white, too-clean fingers one by one and stood up. The decision, now that it had come, was strangely easy to make. 'I'm calling it off on my own account.'

He ignored the other man's protests and went forward along the narrow aisle to the blinding arena of the cockpit. Braunek was at the controls and Sammy Yamoto was beside him in the second pilot's seat. He had removed a cover from the delton detector and was probing inside it. Garamond tapped him on the shoulder.

'Why aren't you asleep, Sammy? You were on duty most of the night.'

Yamoto adjusted his dark glasses. 'I'm going to kip down in a minute – as soon as I put my mind at rest about this pile of junk.'

'Junk?'

'Yes. I don't think it's working.'

Garamond glanced at the detector's control panel. 'According to the operating light it's working.'

'I know, but look at this.' Yamoto clicked the switch of the main power supply to the detector box up and down several times in succession. The orange letters which spelled, SYSTEM FUNCTIONING, continued to glow steadily in their dark recess.

'What a botch,' Yamoto said bitterly. 'You know, I might never have caught on if a generator hadn't cut itself out during the night. I was sitting here about two hours later when, all of a sudden, it hit me – the lights on the detector panel hadn't blinked with all the others.'

'Does that prove it isn't working?'

'Not necessarily – but it makes me doubt the quality of the whole assembly. Litman deserves to be shot.'

'Don't worry about it.' Garamond lowered himself into the supernumerary seat. 'Not at this stage anyway – we have to call off the flight.'

'Dennis?'

'Yes. It's killing him.'

'I don't want to seem callous, but ...' Yamoto paused to force a multi-connector into place, '... don't you think he could die anyway?'

'I can't take that chance.'

'Now I *have* to sound callous. There are seven other men on this ...' Yamoto stopped speaking as the delton detector emitted a sharp tap, like a steel ball dropped on to a metal plate. He instinctively jerked his hand away from the exposed wiring.

Garamond raised his eyebrows. 'What have you done to it?'

'All I've done is fix it.' Yamoto gave a quivering, triumphant grin as two more tapping sounds were heard almost simultaneously.

'Then what are those noises?'

'Those, my friend, are delta particles going through our screen.' The astronomer's words were punctuated by further noises from the machine. 'And their frequency indicates that we are close to their source.'

'Close? How close?'

Yamoto took out a calculator and his fingers flickered over it. 'I'd say about twenty or thirty thousand kilometres.'

A cool breeze from nowhere played on Garamond's forehead. 'You don't mean from Beachhead City.'

'Beachhead City is the only source we know. That's what it's all about.'

'But ...' A fresh staccato outburst came from the detector as Garamond, knowing he should have been excited, looked out through the front windshield of the aircraft at a range of low mountains perhaps an hour's flying time ahead. They seemed no more and no less familiar than all the others he had seen.

'Is this possible?' he said. 'Could we have overestimated the flight time by two years?'

Yamoto turned an adjusting screw on the delton detector, decreasing the sound level of its irregular tattoo. 'Anything is possible on Orbitsville.'

It was late on the following day when the two stiff-winged, ungainly birds began to gain altitude to cross the final green ridges. All crew members, including a fever-eyed O'Hagan, were gathered to watch as the mountain crests began to sink in submission to their combined wills. Changing parallaxes made the high ground below them appear to shift like sand.

Yamoto switched off the detector's incessant roar with a flourish. 'The instrument is no longer of any use to us. Astronomically speaking, we have reached our destination.'

'How far would you say it is, Sammy?'

'A hundred kilometres. Perhaps less.'

Joe Braunek squirmed in his seat, but his hands and feet were steady on the flying controls. 'Then we have to see Beachhead City as soon as we clear this range.'

Garamond felt the conviction which had been growing in him achieve a leaden solidity. 'It won't be there,' he announced. 'I don't remember seeing a mountain range this close to the city.'

'It's a pretty low range,' Yamoto said uncertainly. 'You wouldn't have noticed it unless you had a specific ...'

His voice faded as the ground tilted and sloped away beneath them to reveal one of Orbitsville's mind-stilling prairies. In the hard clean light of the sun they could see to the edges of infinity, across oceans of grass and scrub, and there was no sign of Beachhead City.

'What do we do now?' Braunek spoke with a curious timidity as he looked back at the other three men. The resilience which all the months of flight had not been able to sap now seemed to have left him. 'Do we just fly on?'

Garamond, unable to feel shock or disappointment, turned to Yamoto. 'Switch the detector on again.'

'Right.' The astronomer reactivated the black box and the cabin immediately filled with its roar. 'But we can't change what it says – we're right on target.'

'Is it directional?'

'Yes.' Yamoto glanced at O'Hagan, who nodded tiredly in confirmation.

'Swing to the left,' Garamond told Braunek. 'Not too quickly.' The plane banked slowly to the north and, as it did so, the sound from the delton detector steadily decreased until it faded out altogether.

'Hold it there! We're now flying at right angles to the precise source of the particle bombardment. Right, Sammy?'

Yamoto raised the binoculars and looked in the direction indicated by the aircraft's starboard wing. 'It's no use, Vance. There's nothing there.'

'There has to be something. We've got an hour of daylight left – take a new bearing and we'll follow it till nightfall.'

While Yamoto used the lightphone to bring the second crew up to date on what was happening, Joe Braunek steered the aircraft on to its new heading and shed height until they were at cruise altitude. The two machines flew onwards for another hour, occasionally swinging off course to make an up-dated check on their direction. Towards the end of the hour O'Hagan's strength gave out and he had to be helped back to his bunk.

'We messed it up,' he said to Garamond, easing himself down.

Garamond shook his head as he covered the older man's thin body. 'It wasn't your fault.'

'Our basic premise was wrong, and that's unforgivable.'

'Forget it, Dennis. Besides, you were the one who warned me we had no right to pick up that first particle so soon. As usual, you were right.'

'Don't try to butter me. I'm too ...' O'Hagan closed his eyes and seemed to fall asleep at once. Garamond made his way back to the cockpit and sat down to weigh up the various factors involved in the ending of the mission. He sensed that the resistance of the other men, which had surprised him earlier, would no longer be a consideration. They had allowed themselves to hope too soon, and Orbitsville had punished them for it. What remained now was the decision on where to make the final landing. His own preference was for the foothills of a mountain chain which would provide them with rivers, variety of vegetation and the psychologically important richness of scenery. It might be best to turn back to the range they had just crossed rather than fly onwards over what seemed to be the greatest plain they had encountered so far. There was the possibility that something could go wrong with one of the aircraft when they were part way across that eternity of grass; and there was the certainty that what they would find on the far side would be no different to what they had left behind. Unless they came to a sea, Garamond reminded himself. A sea would add even more ...

'I think we've arrived,' Braunek called over his shoulder. 'I see something in front of us.'

Garamond moved up behind the pilot and peered through the forward canopy at the flat prairie. It stretched ahead, unbroken, for hundreds of kilometres. 'I don't see anything,' he said.

'Straight ahead of us. About ten kilometres.'

'Is it something small?'

'Small? It's huge! Look, Vance, right there!'

Garamond followed the exact line of Braunek's pointing finger and a cold unease crept over him as he confirmed his belief that they were looking at featureless flatlands.

Yamoto shouldered his way into the cockpit. 'What's going on?'

'Straight ahead of us,' Braunek said. 'What do you think that is?'

The astronomer shielded his eyes to see better and gave a low whistle. 'I don't know, but it would be worth landing for a closer look. But before we go down I want to get an infrared photograph of it.'

Garamond examined the sand-smooth plain once more, and was opening his mouth to protest when he saw the apparition. He had been looking for an object which distinguished itself from its surroundings by verticality and texture, but this was a vast area of grass which differed from the rest only in that it was slightly darker in colour. It could have been taken for a natural variation in the grass, perhaps caused by soil composition, except for the fact that it was perfectly circular. From the approaching aircraft it appeared as a ghostly ellipse of green on green, like a design in an experimental painting. Yamoto opened his personal locker, took out a camera and photographed the slowly expanding circle. He reeled the print out, glanced at it briefly and passed it round for the others to see. On it the area of grass stood out darkly against an orange background.

'It's quite a few degrees colder,' Yamoto said. 'I would say that the entire area seems to be losing heat into space.'

'What does it mean?'

'Well, the grass there is of a slightly different colour to the rest – which could mean the soil is absorbing some mineral or other. And there's the heat loss. *Plus* the fact that radiation from the outside universe is being admitted ... It adds up to just one thing.'

'Which is?'

'We've found another entrance to Orbitsville.'

'How can that be?' Garamond felt a slow unexpected quickening of his spirit. 'We did a survey of the equatorial region from the outside, and besides ... there's no hole in the shell.'

'There is a hole,' Yamoto said calmly. 'But – a very long time ago – somebody sealed it up.'

They landed close to the edge of the circle and, although darkness came flooding in from the east only a few minutes later, began to dig an exploratory trench. The soil was several metres thick in the area, but in less than an hour an invisible resistance to their spades told them they had encountered the lenticular field. A short time later a massive diaphragm of rusting metal was uncovered. They sliced through it with the invisible lance of a valency cutter.

Two men levered a square section upwards and then, without speaking the others took it in turn to look downwards at the stars.

CHAPTER NINETEEN

'This is North Ten, the most advanced of our forward distribution centres,' Elizabeth Lindstrom said, with a warm note of pride in her voice. 'You can see at once the amount of effort and organization that has been put into it.'

Charles Devereaux walked across to the parapet of the roof of the administration building and looked out across the plain. Four hundred kilometres to the south lay Beachhead City, and the arrow-straight highway to it was alive with the small wheeled transports of settlers. Here and there on the road, before it faded into the shimmering distance, could be seen the larger shapes of bulk carriers bringing supplies. The highway ended at North Ten, from which point a series of dirt tracks fanned out into the encircling sweep of prairie. For the first few kilometres the tracks made their way through an industrial area where reaping machines gathered the grass which was used as a source of cellulose to produce plastics for building purposes. Immediately beyond the acetate factories the homesteads began, with widely spaced buildings sparkling whitely in the sun.

'I'm impressed with everything Starflight has done here, My Lady,' Devereaux said, choosing his words with professional care. 'Please understand that when I put questions to you I do so solely in my capacity as a representative of the Two Worlds Government.'

Do you think I would waste time answering them otherwise? Elizabeth suppressed the thought and bent her mind to the unfamiliar task of self-control. 'I do understand,' she assured the dapper grey man, smiling. 'It's your duty to make sure that all that can possibly be done to open up Lindstromland is in fact being done.'

'That's precisely it, My Lady. You see, the people on Earth and Terranova have heard about the fantastic size of Lindstromland and they can't understand why it is that, if there is unlimited living space available, the Government doesn't simply set up a programme of shipbuilding on a global scale and bring them here.'

'A perfectly understandable point of view, but ...' Elizabeth spread her hands to the horizons, fingers flashing with jewel-fire, '... this land I have given to humanity makes its own rules and we have no option but to abide by them. Lindstromland is unthinkably large, but by providing only one entrance – and placing restrictions on interior travel and communications – its builders have effectively made it small. My own belief is that they decided to enforce a selection procedure, or its equivalent. As long as Lindstromland can accept immigrants only in regulated quantities the quality of the stock which arrives will be higher.'

'Do you think the concept of stock and breeding would have been familiar to them?'

'Perhaps not.' Elizabeth realized she had used an unfortunate trigger-word, one to which the upstart of a civil servant reacted unfavourably. It struck her that things had already gone too far when she, President of Starflight, was being forced to placate an obscure official in the weakest government in human history. The circumstances surrounding the discovery of Lindstromland, she was beginning to appreciate, had been ill omens.

Devereaux apparently was not satisfied. 'It would be a tragedy if Earth were to export attitudes such as nationalism and ...'

'What I'm saying,' Elizabeth cut in, 'is that it would be an even bigger tragedy if we were to empty every slum and gutter on Earth into this green land.'

'Why?' Devereaux met her eyes squarely and she made the discovery that his greyness had a steely quality. 'Because the transportation task would be too great to be handled by a private concern?'

Elizabeth felt her mouth go dry as she fought to restrain herself. Nobody had ever been allowed to speak to her in this manner before, with the possible exception of Captain Garamond – and he had paid. It was infuriating how these small men, nonentities, tended to lapse into insolence the moment they felt secure.

'Of course not,' she said, marvelling at the calmness of her voice. 'There are many sound reasons for regulating population flow. Look at the squalid difficulties there were when the first settlers here encountered those creatures they call Clowns.'

'Yes, but those difficulties could have been avoided. In fact, we think they may have been engineered.'

For one heady moment Elizabeth considered burning Devereaux in two where he stood, even if it led to a major incident, even if it meant turning Lindstromland into a fortress. Then it came to her that Devereaux – in abandoning all the rules of normal diplomacy – was laying his cards on the table. She regarded him closely for a moment, trying to decide if he was offering himself for sale. The approach, in greatly modified form, was a familiar one among government employees – show yourself to be dangerous and therefore valuable in proportion. She smiled and moved closer to Devereaux, deliberately stepping inside his proximity rejection zone, a psychological manoeuvre she had learned at an early age. His face stiffened momentarily, as she had known it would, and she was about to touch him when Secretary Robard appeared on the edge of the stair-well. He was carrying a headset and feeding wire out of a reel as he walked.

Elizabeth frowned at him. 'What is this, Robard?'

'Priority One, My Lady, Your flagship is picking up a radio message which you must hear.'

'Wait there.' She moved away from Devereaux. The brusqueness of her man's voice, so out of keeping with his normal manner, told her something important had happened. She silently cursed the obtuse physics of Lindstromland which had denied her easy radio contact with the outside universe. A voice was already speaking when she put on the headset. It was unemotional, with an inhuman steadiness, and the recognition of it drained the strength from her legs. Elizabeth Lindstrom sank to her knees, and listened.

'... using the resources of the *Bissendorf*'s workshops we built a number of aircraft with which it was planned to fly back to Beachhead City. The ships proved inadequate for the distance involved, but they got eight of us to the point from which I am making this broadcast, the point where we have discovered a second entrance to the sphere.

'The entrance was not discovered during the equatorial survey because it is sealed with a metal diaphragm. The metal employed has nothing in common with the material of the Orbitsville shell. I believe it is the product of a civilization no further advanced than our own. This belief is strengthened by the fact that we had no difficulty in cutting a hole in it to let us extend a radio antenna.'

There was a crackling pause, then the voice emerged strongly in its relentless measured tones. 'The fact that we were able to find a second entrance so quickly, with such limited resources, can only mean that there must be many others. Many hundreds. Many thousands. It is logical to assume that all the others have been similarly blocked, and it is equally logical to assume that it was not done by the builders of the sphere.

'This raises questions about the identity and motivation of those who sealed the entrances. The evidence suggests that the work was carried out by a race of beings who found Orbitsville long before we did. We may never know what these beings looked like, but we can tell that they shared some of the faults of our own race. They, or some of them, decided to monopolize Orbitsville, to control it, to exploit it; and the method they chose was to limit access to the interior of the sphere.

'The evidence also shows that they succeeded – and that, eventually, they failed.

'Perhaps they were destroyed in the battle we know to have taken place at the Beachhead City entrance. Perhaps in the end they lost out to Orbitsville itself. By being absorbed and changed, just as we are going to be absorbed and changed. The lesson for us now is that the entire Starflight organization – with its vested interest in curbing humanity's natural expansion – must be set aside. All of Orbitsville is open to us. It is available as I speak ...'

Elizabeth removed the headset, cutting herself off from the dreadful didactic voice. She put her hands on the smooth surface of the roof and sank down until she was lying prone, her open mouth pressed against the foot-printed plastic.

Vance Garamond, she thought, her mind sinking through successive levels of cryogenic coldness. *I have to love you ... because you are the only one ever to have given me real pain, ever to hurt me, and hurt me.* She moved her hips from side to side, grinding against the roof with her pubis. *Now that all else is ending ... it is my turn ... to make love ... to you ...*

'My Lady, are you ill?' The voice reached her across bleak infinities. Elizabeth raised her head and, with effort, identified the grey anxious face of Charles Devereaux. She got to her feet.

'How dare you!' she said coldly. 'What are you suggesting?'

'Nothing. I ...'

'Why did you let this ... *object* enter my quarters?' Elizabeth turned and stared accusingly at Robard who had quietly retrieved the headset and was reeling in the attached wire. 'Get him out of here!'

'I'm going – I've seen enough.' Devereaux hurried towards the stairwell. Elizabeth watched him go, twisting a ruby ring on her finger as she did so. It turned easily on bearings of perspiration.

Robard bowed nervously. 'If you will excuse me ...'

'Not yet,' Elizabeth snapped. 'Get me Doctor Killops on that thing.'

'Yes, My Lady.' Robard murmured into the instrument, listened for a moment, and then handed it to her. He began to withdraw but she pointed at a spot nearby, silently ordering him to stay.

Elizabeth raised the communicator to her lips. 'Tell me, Doctor Killops, has Mrs Garamond had her sedative today yet? No? Then don't give it to her. Captain Garamond is returning, alive, and we want his wife to be fully conscious and alert for the reunion.' She threw the instrument down and Robard stooped to pick it up.

'Never mind that,' Elizabeth said quietly. 'Get my car ready to leave in five minutes. I have urgent business in Beachhead City.'

The shock of hearing by radio that his wife and son were still alive had stormed through Garamond's system like a nuclear fireball. In its wake had come relief, joy, gratitude, bafflement, renewal of optimism – and finally, as a consequence of emotional overload, an intense physical reaction. There was a period of several hours during which he experienced cold sweats, irregular heartbeat and dizziness; and the symptoms were at their height when the little transit boat from fleet headquarters arrived underfoot.

As had happened once before, he felt disoriented and afraid on seeing a spacesuited figure clamber upwards through a black hole in the ground. The figure was followed by others who were carrying empty spacesuits, and – even when the faceplates had been removed and the two parties were mingling – they still looked strange to him. At some time in the preceding months he had come to accept the thin-shouldered shabbiness of his own crew as the norm, and now the members of the rescue party seemed too sleek and shiny, too alien.

'Captain Garamond?' A youthful Starflight officer approached him and saluted, beardless face glowing with pleasure and health. 'I'm Lieutenant Kenny of the *Westmorland*. This is a great honour for me, sir.'

'Thank you.' The action of returning the salute felt awkward to Garamond.

Kenny's gaze strayed to the sloping, stiff-winged outlines of the two aircraft and his jaw sagged. 'I'm told you managed to fly a couple of million kilometres in those makeshifts. That must have been *fantastic*.'

Garamond suppressed an illogical resentment. 'You might call it that. The *Westmorland*? Isn't that Hugo Schilling's command?'

'Captain Schilling insisted on coming with us. He's waiting for you aboard the transit boat now. I'll have to photograph those airplanes, sir – they're just too …'

'Not now, Lieutenant. My Chief Science Officer is very ill and he must be hospitalized at once. The rest of us aren't in great shape, either.' Garamond tried to keep his voice firm even though a numbness had enveloped his body, creating a sensation that his head was floating in the air like a balloon.

Kenny, with a flexibility of response which further dismayed Garamond, was instantly solicitous. He began shouting orders and within a few minutes the eight members of the *Bissendorf*'s crew had been suited up for transfer to the waiting boat. Garamond's mind was brimming with thoughts of Aileen and Chris as he negotiated the short spacewalk, with its swaying vistas of star rivers and its constrained breathing of rubber-smelling air. As soon as he had passed through the airlock he made his way to the forward compartment, which seemed impossibly roomy after his months in the aircraft's narrow fuselage. Another spacesuited figure rose to greet him.

'It's good to see you, Vance,' Hugo Schilling said. He was a blue-eyed, silver-haired man who had been in the Exploration Arm for twenty years and treated his job of wandering unknown space as if he was the pilot of a local ferry.

'Thanks, Hugo. It's good to …' Garamond shook his head to show he had run out of words.

Schilling inspected him severely. 'You don't look well, Vance. Rough trip?'

'Rough trip.'

'Enough said, skipper. We're keeping the suits on, but strap yourself in and relax – we'll have you home in no time. Try to get some sleep.'

Garamond nodded gratefully. 'Have you seen my wife and boy?'

'No. Unlike you, I'm just a working flickerwing man and I don't get invited out to the Octagon.'

'The Octagon! What are they doing out there?'

'They've been staying with the President ever since you … ah … disappeared. They're celebrities too, you know – even if there is some reflection of glory involved.'

'But …' A new centre of coldness began to form within Garamond's body. 'Tell me, Hugo, did the President send you out here to pick us up?'

'No. It was an automatic reaction on the part of Fleet Command. The President is out at North Ten – that's one of the forward supply depots we've built.'

'Will she have heard my first message yet?'

'Probably,' Schilling pointed a gloved finger at Garamond. 'Starting to sweat over some of those things you said about Starflight? Don't worry about it – we all know you've been under a strain. You can say you got a bit carried away with the sense of occasion.'

Garamond took a deep breath. 'Are there any airplanes or other rapid transport systems in use around Beachhead City?'

'Not yet. All the production has been concentrated on ground cars and housing.'

'How long will it take the President to get back to the Octagon?'

'It's hard to say – the cars they produce aren't built for speed. Eight hours, maybe.'

'How long till we get back?'

'Well, I'm allowing five hours in view of Mister O'Hagan's condition.'

'Speed it up, Hugo,' Garamond said. 'I have to be back before the President, and she's had a few hours' start.'

Schilling glanced at the information panel on which changing colour configurations showed that the ship was sealed and almost ready for flight. 'That would mean fairly high G-forces. For a sick man …'

'He won't mind – go ask him.'

'I don't see…'

'Supposing I said it was a matter of life or death?'

'I wouldn't believe you, but …' Schilling winked reassuringly, opened an audio channel to the flight deck and instructed the pilot to make the return journey in the shortest possible time consistent with O'Hagan's health. Garamond thanked him and tried to relax into the G-chair, wishing he had been able to take the other man into his confidence. Schilling was kindly and uncomplicated, with a high regard for authority. It would have been difficult, possibly disastrous, for Garamond to try telling him he believed

Elizabeth Lindstrom was a psychopath who would enjoy murdering an innocent woman and child. Schilling might counter by asking why Elizabeth had not done it as soon as she had had the chance, and Garamond would not have been able to answer. It would not have been enough to say that he felt it in his bones. He closed his eyes as the acceleration forces clamped down, but his growing conviction of danger made it impossible for him to rest. Thirty minutes into the flight he got an idea.

'Do you think there'll be a reception when we get back? A public one?'

'Bound to be,' Schilling said. 'You keep hogging the news. Even while you were away a reporter called Mason, I think, ran a campaign to persuade somebody to go looking for your ship. The betting was fifty-to-one you were dead, though, so he didn't have much success.'

Garamond had forgotten about the reporter from Earth. 'You said my wife and boy are well known, too. I want them to meet me at the Beachhead City transit tube. Can you arrange that?'

'I don't see why not – there's a direct communications link to the Octagon from the President's flagship.' Schilling spoke into the command microphone of his spacesuit, waited, spoke again, and then settled into a lengthy conversation. Only occasional whispers of sound came through his open faceplate, but Garamond could hear the exchange becoming heated. When it had finished Schilling sat perfectly still for a moment before turning to speak.

'Sorry, Vance.'

'What happened?'

'Apparently the President has sent instructions from North Ten that your family are to wait in the Octagon until you get there. She's on her way there now, and they can't contact her, so nobody would authorize transportation into the City for your wife. I don't understand it.'

'I think I do,' Garamond replied quietly, his eyes fixed on the forward view plate and its image of a universe which was divided in two by the cosmic hugeness of Orbitsville, one half in light, the other in total darkness.

The effort of moving under multiple gravities was almost too much for Garamond, but he was standing in the cramped airlock – sealed up and breathing suit air – before the transit boat reached the docking clamps. He cracked the outer seal on the instant the green disembarkation light came on, went through the boat's outer door and found himself in a lighted L-shaped tube. It was equipped with handrails and at the rounded corner, where the sphere's gravitation came into effect, there was the beginning of a non-skid walkway.

Garamond pulled himself along the weightless section with his hands, forced his way through the invisible syrup of the lenticular field, achieved an upright position and strode into the arrival hall. He was immediately walled in by faces and bodies and, as soon as he had opened his helmet, battered by the sound of shouting and cheering. People surged around him, reaching for his hands, slapping his back, pulling hoses and connectors from his suit for souvenirs.

At the rear of the crowd were men with scene recorders and, as he scanned their faces, an uncontrollable impulse caused Garamond to raise his arm like a Twentieth Century astronaut returning from an orbital mission. He cursed the autonomous limb, appalled at its behaviour, and concentrated on finding the right face in the bewildering seething mass, aware of how much he had always depended on Cliff Napier in similar circumstances. There was a high proportion of men in the uniforms of top-ranking Starflight officials, any of whom could have arranged transport to the Octagon, but he had no way of knowing which were members of Elizabeth's inner cadre and therefore hostile. After a blurred moment he saw a heavy-shouldered young man with prematurely greying hair working his way towards him and recognized Colbert Mason. He caught the outstretched hand between both of his gloves.

'Captain Garamond,' Mason shouted above the background noise, 'I can't tell you how much …'

Garamond shook his head. 'We'll talk later. Have you a car?'

'It's outside.'

'I've got to get out of here right now.'

Mason hesitated. 'There's official Starflight transportation laid on.'

'Remember the first day we met, Colbert? You needed wheels in a hurry and I …'

'Come on.' Mason lowered his head and went through the crowd like an ice-breaking ship with Garamond, hampered by the bulk of the suit, struggling in his wake. In a matter of seconds they had reached a white vehicle which had 'TWO WORLDS NEWS AGENCY' blazoned on its side in orange letters. The two men got in, watched by the retinue which had followed them from the hall, and Mason got the vehicle moving.

'Where to?' he said.

'The Octagon – as fast as this thing will go.'

'Okay, but I'm not welcome out there. The guards won't let this car in.'

'I'm not welcome either, but we're going in just the same.' Garamond began working on the zips of the spacesuit.

That was a good line to hand the Press, he thought as the yammerings of panic began to build up. *That was an authentic general-purpose man of action speaking. Why do I do these things? Why don't I let him know I'm scared shitless? It might make things easier …*

Mason hunched over the wheel as he sped them through the industrial environs of the city. 'This is the part you flattened, but they rebuilt it just as ugly as ever.'

'They would.'

'Can you tell me what's going on?'

Garamond hesitated. 'Sorry, Colbert – not yet.'

'I just wondered.'

'Either way, you're going to get another big story.'

'Hell, I know that much already. I just wondered ... as a friend.'

'I appreciate the friendship, but I can't talk till I'm sure.'

'It's all right,' Mason said. 'We'll be there in less than ten minutes.'

For the rest of the short drive Garamond concentrated on removing the spacesuit. In the confines of the car it was an exhausting, frustrating task which he welcomed because it enabled his mind to hold back the tides of fear. By the time he had finally worked himself free the octagonal building which housed the Starflight Centre was looming on a hilltop straight ahead, and he could see the perimeter fence with its strolling guards. As the car gained height, and greater stretches of the surrounding grasslands came into view, Garamond saw that there was also a northern approach road to the Octagon. Another vehicle, still several kilometres away, was speeding down it, trailing a plume of saffron dust. It was too far away for him to distinguish the black-and-silver Starflight livery, but on the instant a steel band seemed to clamp around his chest, denying him air. He stared wordlessly at the massive gate of the west entrance which was beginning to fill the car's windshield. The car slowed down as guards emerged from their kiosk.

'Go straight through it,' Garamond urged. 'Don't slow down.'

'It's no use,' Mason said. 'It would take a tank to batter down that gate – we'd both be killed. We'll just have to talk our way in.'

'Talk?' Garamond looked north and saw that the other vehicle seemed to be approaching with the speed of an aircraft.

'There's no time for talking.'

He leaped from the car as soon as it had slid to a halt and ran to the kiosk at the side of the: gate. A sunvisored guard emerged, carrying a rifle, and stared warily at Garamond's stained travesty of a Starflight uniform.

'State your business,' he said, at the same time making a signal to the other two guards who were seated inside.

'I'm Captain Garamond of the Stellar Exploration Arm. Open the gate immediately.'

'I don't know if I can do that, Captain.'

'You've heard of me, haven't you? You know who I am?'

'I know who you are, Captain, but that doesn't mean I should let you in. Have you an authorization?'

'Authorization?' Garamond considered putting on a display of righteous indignation, but decided it would not work coming from a man who looked like a hobo. He smiled and pointed at the dust-devil which was now within a kilometre of the northern gate. 'There's my authorization. President Lindstrom is in that car, coming here specially to meet me.'

'How do I know that's true?'

'You'll know when she finds out you wouldn't let me through. I think I'll go back to my car and watch what happens.' Garamond turned away.

'Just a minute.' The guard gave Garamond a perplexed look. 'You can come in, but that other guy stays where he is.'

Garamond shrugged and walked straight at the gate. It rolled out of his way just in time, then he was inside the perimeter and heading for the Octagon's west entrance door, not more than a hundred paces away. A second before it was lost to view behind the flank of the building, he glimpsed the other car arriving at the north gate. It was black and silver, and he was able to see a pale feminine figure in the shaded interior. The certainty of being too late made his heart lapse into an unsteady, lumping rhythm. He was breaking into a run, regardless of what the watchful patrolmen might think, when his attention was caught by a flicker of movement as a window opened in the transparent wall of the uppermost floor. Again he picked out a womanly figure, but this time it was that of his wife. And she was looking down at him.

He cupped his hands to his mouth and shouted. '*Aileen!* Can you hear me?'

'Vance!' Her voice was faint and tremulous, almost lost in the updraft at the sheer wall.

'Pick up Christopher and bring him down to this door as fast as you can.' He indicated the nearby entrance. 'Did you get that?'

'Yes – I'm coming down.'

Aileen vanished from the window. Garamond went to the door, held it open and saw a short deserted corridor with four openings on each side. He debated trying to find stairs or elevator shaft, then decided that if he tried to meet Aileen part way he might miss her. Elizabeth was bound to be in the building by this time and on her way up to the private suite. Aileen and Christopher should be on their way down – but supposing there was only one central stairwell and they met Elizabeth head on? Garamond entered a chill dimension of time in which entire galaxies were created and destroyed between each thunderous beat of his heart. He tried to think constructively, but all that was left to him was the ability to be afraid, to feel pain and terror and ...

One of the corridor doors burst open. He caught a flash of brown skin and multi-coloured silks, then Aileen was in his arms. *We've made it,* Garamond exulted. *We're all going to live.*

'Is it really you?' Aileen's face was cool and tear-wet against his own. 'Is it really you, Vance?'

'Of course, darling. There's no time to talk now. We've got to get ...' Garamond's voice was stilled as he made the discovery. 'Where's Christopher?'

Aileen looked at him blankly. 'He's upstairs in his bed. He was asleep ...'

'But I told you to bring him!'

'Did you? I can't think ...' Aileen's eyes widened. 'What's wrong?'

'She's gone up there to get Chris. I *told* you to ...' Voices sounded behind him and Garamond's hunting eyes saw that two guards had followed him almost to the entrance. They had stopped and were looking upwards at the building. Holding Aileen by the wrist, Garamond ran to them and turned. High up within the transparent wall, where Aileen had been a minute earlier, Elizabeth Lindstrom was standing, pearly abdomen pressed against the clear plastic. She stared downwards, screened by reflected clouds, and raised one arm in languorous triumph.

Garamond rounded on the nearest guard and, with a single convulsive movement, snatched the rifle from his shoulder and sent him sprawling. He thumbed the safety catch off, selected maximum power and raised the weapon, just in time to see Elizabeth step backwards away from the wall, into shelter. Garamond's eyes triangulated on his wife's ashen face.

'Is Christopher's room on this side of the building?'

'Yes. I ...'

'Where is it? Show me the exact place?'

Aileen pointed at a wall section two to the left of where Elizabeth had been standing. The fallen guard got to his feet and came forward with outstretched hands, while his companion stood by uncertainly. Garamond pointed at the power setting on the rifle, showing it to be at the lethal maximum. The guard backed off shaking his head. Garamond raised the weapon again, aimed carefully and squeezed the trigger. The needle-fine laser ray pierced the transparent plastic and, as he swung the rifle, took out an irregular smoking area which tumbled flashing to the ground. A second later, as Garamond had prayed it would, a small pyjama-clad figure appeared at the opening. Christopher Garamond rubbed his eyes, peering sleepily into space. Garamond dropped the rifle and ran forward, waving his arms.

'Jump, Christopher, *jump!*' The sound of his hoarse, frightened voice almost obliterated the thought: *He won't do it; nobody would do it.* 'Come on, son – I'll catch you.'

Christopher drew back his shoulders. A pale shape appeared behind him, grasping. Christopher jumped cleanly through the opening, into sunlit air.

As had happened once before, on a quiet terrace on Earth, Garamond saw the childish figure falling and turning, falling and turning, faster and faster. As had happened once before, he found himself running in a slow-motion nightmare, wading, struggling through molasses-thick tides of air. He sobbed his despair as he lunged forward.

Something solid and incredibly weighty hit him on the upper chest, tried to smash his arms from their sockets. He went down into dusty grass rolling with the priceless burden locked against his body. From a corner of his eye he saw a flash of laser fire stab downwards and expire harmlessly. Garamond stood up, treasuring the feel of the boy's arms locked around his neck.

'All right, son?' he whispered. 'All right?'

Christopher nodded and pressed his face into Garamond's shoulder, clinging like a baby. Garamond estimated he was beyond the effective range of Elizabeth's ring weapons and ran towards the gate without looking back at the Lindstrom Centre. Aileen, who had been standing with her hands over her mouth, ran with him until they had reached the perimeter. The guards, frozen within their kiosk, watched them with uncomprehending eyes. Colbert Mason was standing beside his car holding up a scene recorder. He glanced at a dial on the side of the machine.

'That took two minutes all but fifteen seconds,' he said admiringly, then kissed the recorder ecstatically. 'And it was all good stuff.'

'The best is yet to come,' Garamond assured him, as they crowded into the car.

Garamond, made sensitive to the nature of the benevolent trap, never again went far into the interior of Orbitsville.

Not even when Elizabeth Lindstrom had been deposed and removed from all contact with society; not even when the Starflight enterprise had made way for communal transport schemes as natural and all-embracing as the yearly migration of birds to warmer climes; not even when geodesic networks of commerce were stretched across the outer surface of Orbitsville.

He chose to live with his family on the edges of space, from which viewpoint he could best observe, and also forget, that time was drawing to a close for the rest of humanity.

Time is a measurement of change, evolution is a product of competition – concepts which were without meaning or relevance in the context of the Big O. Absolved of the need to fight or flee, to feel hunger or fear, to build or destroy, to hope or to dream, humanity had to cease being human – even though metamorphosis could not take place within a single season.

During Garamond's lifetime there was a last flare-up of that special kind of organized activity which, had Man not been drawn like a wasp into the honeypot, might have enabled his descendants to straddle the universe. There was a magical period when, centred on a thousand star-pools, a thousand new nations were born. All of them felt free to develop and flower in their own separate ways, but all were destined to become as one under the influence of Orbitsville's changeless savannahs.

In time even the flickerwing ships ceased to ply the trade lanes between the entrance portals, because there can be no reward for the traveller when departure point cannot be distinguished from destination.

The quietness of the last long Sunday fell over an entire region of space.

Orbitsville had achieved its purpose.

A WREATH OF STARS

CHAPTER ONE

Gilbert Snook sometimes thought of himself as being the exact social equivalent of a neutrino.

He was an aircraft engineer, and therefore not formally schooled in nuclear physics, but he knew the neutrino to be an elusive particle, one which interacted so faintly with the normal hadronic matter of the universe that it could flit straight through the Earth without hitting or disturbing one other particle. Snook was determined to do much the same thing on his linear course from birth towards death, and – at the age of forty – was well on the way to achieving his aim.

His parents were faded and friendless individuals, with insular tendencies, who had died when he was a child, leaving him little money and no family bonds of any kind. The only type of education made available to Snook by the local authority was of a technical nature, presumably because it was a quick and well-proven way of converting community liabilities into assets, but it had matched his aptitudes quite well. He had worked hard, easily holding his place in the classroom, always leading his group in benchwork. After collecting an adequate sheaf of certificates he had chosen to be an aircraft engineer, mainly because it was a trade which involved extensive foreign travel. He had inherited his parents' liking for solitude and had made full use of his professional mobility to avoid concentrations of people. For almost two decades he had shuttled through the Near and Middle East, impartially selling his skills to anyone – oil company, airline or military organisation – who was straining aircraft to the limits and was prepared to pay well to keep them flying.

Those years had seen the painful splintering of Africa and Arabia into smaller and smaller statelets, and there had been times when he had found himself in danger of becoming associated or identified with one upflung political entity or another. The involvement might have resulted in anything from having to accept a permanent job to facing an executioner's machine gun while it counted its lethal rosary of brass and lead. But in each case – neutrino-like – he had slipped away, unscathed, before the trap of circumstance could close on him. When necessary, he had changed his name for short periods or had accepted different types of work. He had kept moving, and nothing had touched him.

In the microcosms of nuclear physics, the only particle which could threaten the existence of a neutrino would be an anti-neutrino; and it was ironic, therefore, that it was a cloud of those very particles which – in the summer of 1993 – interacted so violently with the life of the human neutrino, Gil Snook.

The cloud of anti-neutrinos was first observed crossing the orbit of Jupiter on the third day of January, 1993 – and, because of the extreme difficulty of detecting its existence at all, the astronomers were quite content to use the term 'cloud' in their early reports. It was not until a month had passed that they dropped the word and inserted in its place the more accurate, though highly emotive, phrase 'rogue planet'.

This closer definition of the phenomenon was made possible by improvements in the newly invented magniluct viewing equipment, which – as so often has happened in the history of scientific discovery – had come along at the precise moment it was required.

Magniluct was a material which looked like ordinary blue glass, but in fact it was a sophisticated form of quantum amplifier which acted like a low-light camera, without the latter's complex electronics. Goggles or glasses with magniluct lenses made it possible to see clearly at night, giving the wearer the impression that his surroundings were illuminated by blue floodlights. Military applications, such as the use of magniluct spectacles in night-fighting, had come first – providing the inventor/manufacturers with handsome dividends – but an astute marketing team had promoted the new material in many other fields. Miners, photographic darkroom staff, speleologists, night watchmen and police, theatre ushers, taxi and train drivers – anybody who had to work in darkness was a prospective customer. Staff in astronomical observatories found magniluct spectacles particularly useful because, thus equipped, they could work efficiently without splashing unwanted light over colleagues and instruments.

Also in the classic tradition of scientific discovery was the circumstance that it was an amateur astronomer, working in a home-made dome in North Carolina, who became the first man to see the rogue planet as it drew nearer to the sun.

Clyde Thornton was a good astronomer, not in the modern usage of the word – which might have implied that he was a competent mathematician or stellar physicist – but good in the sense that he loved looking at the heavens and knew his way around them better than he knew the district of Asheville in which he had grown up. He also could locate every item in his small observation dome in pitch darkness, and therefore had bought his pair of magniluct glasses a week previously as much out of curiosity as for any practical reason. Thornton liked and appreciated technical novelties, and the idea of an inert transparency which turned night into day intrigued him.

He had set up his telescope to record the nebula on a thirty-minute exposure and was contentedly pottering about, wearing his new glasses, while the photographic plate absorbed light which had begun its journey to Earth before man's ancestors had discovered the use of the club. A stray impulse caused him to glance into the auxiliary sighting scope to check that the main instrument was exactly following its target, and – momentarily forgetful – he did so without removing his low-light spectacles.

Thornton was a modest man in his early sixties, soft-spoken and free of commercial ambition, yet like all other quiet watchers of the skies he had a hankering for the discreet immortality which is granted to the discoverers of new stars and planets. He experienced a moment of heart-lurching giddiness as he saw the first-magnitude object perched on the horizontal crosshair of his scope, like a diamond where no diamond had any right to be. Thornton stared at the bright speck for a long time, assuring himself it was not a man-made satellite, then became aware of an annoying blue fuzziness in his vision. He tried to rub his eye and his knuckles encountered the frame of the magniluct spectacles. Clucking with impatience, he threw the glasses aside and looked into the sighting scope again.

The bright object was gone.

An insupportable weight of disappointment bore down on Thornton as he checked the luminous settings of the telescope to make sure he had not accidentally jarred the mounting. It was just as he had positioned it except for the minute creeping of the clockwork slow-motion drive. Unable to relinquish hope, he detached the camera from the main telescope, slipped in a low-power eyepiece and looked through it. The nebula he had been photographing was centred in his field of view – further proof that the telescope had not been jolted – and there was no sign of Thornton's Star, as the object might later have been listed in the catalogues.

Thornton's shoulders drooped as he sat in the darkness and deliberated on his own foolishness. He had allowed himself to get worked up, as other astronomers had done before, over an errant reflection in his equipment. The night air whispering through the open sector of the dome suddenly seemed colder, and he recalled that it was past two in the morning. It was an hour at which a man of his age should have been warmly bedded down for the night. He looked around for his magniluct glasses, put them on and – in the blue radiance they seemed to create – began gathering up his notebooks and pens.

It was a whim, a brief refusal to accept the dictates of common sense, which caused him to turn back to the telescope. Still wearing the glasses, he put his eye to the sighting scope. The new star glittered on the cross-hair as before.

Thornton crouched at the sighting scope for a full minute, alternately

viewing with the glasses and without them, before fully accepting the phenomenon of a star which could be seen only through a magniluct screen.
He took the glasses off and held them in unsteady fingers, feeling the em-
bossed lettering of the trade name – AMPLITE – on the plastic frame, then
came the urge to have a fresh, and clearer, look at his discovery. He manoeuvred himself on to the low stool and looked through the eyepiece of
the big refractor. There was the unavoidable lack of definition associated
with a magniluct transparency, but the object was plainly visible, looking
exactly as it had done in the low-powered finder scope. Strangely, it was no
brighter.

Thornton's brow creased as he considered the implications of what he was
seeing. He had expected the object to appear much more brilliant, due to the
light-gathering power of the main telescope's twenty-centimetre lens. The
fact that the object looked just the same meant … Thornton's mind wres-
tled with the unfamiliar data … that it was emitting no light, that he was
seeing it by means of some other type of radiation detected by his Amplite
spectacles.

Anxious to make a further check, he struggled to his feet, twisting past
the telescope's mounting, and stepped out of the dome on to the pliant turf
of his back lawn. The winter night stabbed through his clothing with dag-
gers of black glass. He looked up at the sky and – aided only by the spectacles
– selected the region in which he was interested. Coma Berenices was an
inconspicuous constellation, but it was one which Thornton had known well
since his childhood, and he saw at once the brand-new jewel tangled in the
maiden's hair. When he took the glasses off the new star vanished.

At that point Thornton did something which, for him, was very uncharacteristic – he ran towards his house at top speed, careless of the possibility
of a twisted ankle, determined to reach his telephone without wasting another second. Many thousands of people throughout the world owned and
wore magniluct nightglasses. Any one of them could glance upwards at any
time and notice the unfamiliar new object in the heavens – and Thornton
had a fierce yearning for it to bear his name.

The past few minutes had been the most exciting in his forty years of
practical astronomy, but the night held one more surprise for him. In the
utter darkness of the house he put the glasses on again, rather than switch
on a light, and made his way to the telephone in the hall. He picked up the
handset and punched in the number of an old friend, Matt Collins, who was
professor of astronomy at the University of North Carolina. While waiting
for the connection to be made, Thornton glanced upwards in a reflex action
which aimed his gaze in roughly the same direction as he had been pointing
his telescope.

And there, glittering like a blue diamond, was his special star, as clearly visible as if the upper part of his house, with its beams and rafters and tiles, consisted of nothing more substantial than shadows. As long as he wore the magniluct glasses, the new star could be clearly seen – shining through solid matter with undiminished brilliance.

Doctor Boyce Ambrose was doing his best to salvage a bad day.

He had awakened early in the morning with, as sometimes happened, a gloomy sense of failure. One annoying aspect of these moods was that he had no way of predicting their arrival, or even of knowing what caused them. On most days he felt reasonably pleased with his post as director of the Karlsen planetarium, with its superb new equipment and constant stream of visitors, some of them VIPs, some of them attractive young fe-males anxious to hear everything he knew about the heavens, even to the extent of encouraging his discourses to continue through to breakfast the following morning. On most days he enjoyed the leisurely administrative routine, the opportunities constantly afforded by local newsmen to pontifi-cate on every event which took place between the limits of the stratosphere and the boundaries of the observable universe, the round of social functions and cocktail parties at which it was rare for cameras not to record his pres-ence as he went about his business of being tall, young, handsome, learned and rich.

Occasionally, however, there came the other days, the ones on which he saw himself as that most despicable of creatures – the trendy astronomer. These were the days when he recalled that his doctorate had been awarded by a university known to be susceptible to private financial grants, that his thesis had been prepared with the aid of two needy but scientifically quali-fied 'personal secretaries' engaged by his father, that his job at the planetar-ium had been up for grabs by anyone whose family was prepared to sink the greatest amount of money into buying the projection equipment. In his ex-treme youth he had been taken with the idea of proving he could carve out a career with no assistance from the Ambrose fortune, then had come the dis-covery that he lacked the necessary application. Had he been poor it would have been much easier for him to put in the long hours of solitary study, he eventually reasoned, but he was handicapped by being able to afford every possible distraction. Under the circumstances, the only logical thing to do was to use the money to counteract its effect on his academic career, to buy the things it prevented him from winning.

Ambrose was able to live happily with this piece of rationalisation im-planted beneath his skin – except on the bad days when, for example, an incautious glance at one of the scientific journals would confront him with equations he should have been able to comprehend. On those occasions he often resolved to bring his work at the planetarium up to a new level of ef-ficiency and creativity, and that was why he had made an early three-hour drive to see Matt Collins in person instead of simply contacting him by televiewer.

'I'm not an expert on this thing,' Collins told him as they sipped coffee in the professor's comfortable tan-coloured office. 'It was a pure coincidence that Thornton and I were old friends and that he rang me first. In fact, I doubt if there is such an animal as an expert on Thornton's Planet.'

'Thornton's Planet.' Ambrose repeated the words as he felt a pang of jealousy towards the small-town amateur whose name was going into astronomical history merely because he had nothing better to do than spend most of his nights in a tin shed on his back lawn. 'We know for sure that it is a planet?'

Collins shook his massive head. 'Not really – the word doesn't have much relevance in this case. Now that it has begun to exhibit a disk we've been able to estimate its diameter at about 12,000 kilometres, so it's of planetary size, all right. But, for all we know, in its own frame of reference it might be a dwarf star or a comet or … anything.'

'What about surface features?'

'Don't know if it has any.' Collins sounded perversely happy with his lack of knowledge. He was a giant of a man who seemed impervious to worries which might beset normal-sized individuals.

'My problem is that I have to find some way to represent it at the planetarium,' Ambrose said. 'What about a magniluct telescope? Can't they make lenses with that stuff?'

'There's no problem with making lens *shapes* out of magniluct material. They would serve pretty well if they were used as nothing more than light amplifiers – but they won't work if you try to obtain a magnified image of Thornton's Planet.'

'I don't get it,' Ambrose said despairingly, deciding to admit his ignorance. 'I'm the director of a planetarium, and I'm supposed to be an instant expert on everything that happens up there, and I don't know what the hell this is all about. Reporters have begun to call me every day and I don't know what to say to them.'

'Don't worry about it – there are a lot of so-called experts in the same boat.' Collins gave a smile which softened his rough-hewn features. He took two cigars from the pocket of his white shirt and flipped one across the desk to Ambrose. 'If you've got time, I'll give you a quick run-down on what little I know.'

Grateful for the other man's diplomacy, Ambrose nodded his head as he unwrapped the cigar which he did not really want. 'I've got lots of time.'

'Okay.' Collins ignited both cigars and leaned back, causing his chair to creak loudly. 'First of all, I wasn't giving you double-talk about magniluct lenses.'

'I didn't think you …'

Collins raised a large pink hand, commanding silence. 'I've got to get the physics over in one burst because it's all new to me and I only know it up here and not down here.' He tapped his forehead and chest in succession, and began to recite.

'Magniluct is a transparent material with a high density of hydrogen atoms in it. There were reports some time ago that it might be useful as a kind of super scintillator to detect neutrinos, but as far as I know nobody took much interest in that aspect until Thornton's Planet came blundering into the Solar System. The planet isn't radiating on any of the known energy spectra – that's why you can't see it in the ordinary way – but it's pumping out neutrinos in four-pi space. When a neutrino enters a lens of your magniluct glasses, it interacts with protons and produces neutrons and beta-plus particles which excite other atoms in the material and in turn produce emissions in the visible region.

'That's why you can't focus the radiation and get a magnified image – the neutrinos go through in a straight line. In fact, it's only because of forward scattering of particles that you're able to see that slightly blurry image of the planet at all. How did I do?' Collins looked like a schoolboy seeking praise.

'Very well,' Ambrose said, 'especially if particle physics isn't your field.'

'It isn't.'

Ambrose decided against mentioning that nucleonics had been his own field in case it became apparent that he knew less than might reasonably have been expected. He tapped the first striated section of ash from his cigar and thought hard about what he had just been told.

'This emission of nothing but neutrinos,' he said slowly. 'I take it that was the basis for deciding that Thornton's Planet is composed of anti-neutrino matter?'

'So I'm told.'

'Which means it's a kind of a ghost world. As far as we're concerned, it almost doesn't exist.'

'Correct.'

'Just my luck,' Ambrose said with a wry smile. 'How am I going to show it in the planetarium?'

'That, I'm pleased to say, is your problem and not mine.' Collins spoke in sympathetic tones which contrasted with the form of words he had chosen. 'Would you like to see where the intruder is at present?'

'Please.'

Ambrose sucked gently on his cigar while Collins tapped an instruction into the computer terminal on his desk, calling up an astronomical diagram on the wall screen. As the picture appeared he became aware that the big man was watching him with covert interest, as though hoping for some kind of reaction on Ambrose's part. Ambrose studied the screen which showed two dotted green lines, designated as the orbits of Jupiter and Mars, sliced across by a solid red line representing the path of Thornton's Planet. The diagram was pretty well what he had expected to see, and yet there was a wrongness about it ... something connected with the mass of data which had just been presented to him ...

'This is a corrected plan view, normal to the plane of the ecliptic,' Collins said, his eyes intent on Ambrose's face. 'We've been getting positional fixes on the planet by triangulation and they're fairly accurate because we've been using the Moon colony as the other end of our baseline. The effective length keeps changing, of course, but ...'

'Hold on,' Ambrose snapped, abruptly realising what was wrong with the computer chart. 'The red line is curved!'

'So?'

'Well, an anti-neutrino world wouldn't be affected by the sun's gravity. It should sail right through the Solar System in a dead straight line.'

'You picked up on that one rather quickly,' Collins said. 'Congratulations.'

Ambrose derived no pleasure from the compliment. 'But what does it mean? The diagram suggests that Thornton's Planet is being captured by the sun, but – from what we know about the planet – there's no way that could happen. Are they sure it is an anti-neutrino world?'

Collins hesitated. 'If there are any doubts on that score, they'll be resolved in a few months' time.'

'You sound pretty sure about that,' Ambrose said. 'How can you be so certain?'

'It's quite simple,' Collins said soberly. 'As far as we can determine at this stage, there's every chance that Thornton's Planet is going to pass right through the Earth.'

CHAPTER TWO

On the morning of March 25, 1993, Gilbert Snook – the human neutrino – was sitting in a bar, quietly enjoying a cigarette and a suitably chill gin-and-water. He was a lean man of medium height, with black crew-cut hair and neat, hard features. The unusually crisp definition of his muscles, even those around his mouth, suggested physical power, but otherwise his appearance was unremarkable.

His sense of contentment derived from a combination of factors, one of them being that he was having his first day of idleness in two weeks. In the daytime temperatures of the lower Arabian Peninsula the maintenance of light aircraft was an occupation which induced a fine appreciation of luxuries such as merely being cool. Inside the metal shell of a plane the heat was unbearable – metal surfaces had to be covered with rags to stop them inflicting burns, and engine oil thinned out so much that experienced mechanics threw away manufacturers' viscosity recommendations and chose lubricants which would have behaved like treacle in normal circumstances.

The working conditions in Malaq discouraged most foreign technicians from staying long, but they suited Snook's temperament. It was one of several statelets which had been formed after the break-up of the ancient Sultanate of Oman, and the principal attraction to Snook was that it contained only about two people per square kilometre. The mental pressures he disliked in densely populated areas were virtually absent in Malaq. It was even possible for him to avoid newspapers, fax sheets and broadcasts. All that was required of him was his assistance in keeping the ruler's small fleet of military transports and ageing jet fighters in an airworthy condition, in return for which he was accommodated in the country's only hotel and given a generous tax-free salary. Habitually, he sent most of the money to a bank in his native Ontario.

The day had begun well for Snook. He had awakened fresh from a long sleep, enjoyed a western-style breakfast, drifted in the swimming pool for a couple of hours, and now was having a pre-lunch drink. The airfield and native township, five kilometres away, were hidden behind a low headland, making it easy for Snook to convince himself there was nothing in the whole world but the hotel, the broad blue ocean, and the scimitars of white sand curving away on each side of the bay. From time to time he thought about the date he had that evening with Eva, an interpreter with a German engineering consultancy in the town, but for the moment he was concentrating on becoming mildly and happily drunk.

He was puzzled, therefore, to discover a sense of unease growing within himself as the sun passed its zenith. Snook had learned to trust his premonitions – he sometimes suspected he was slightly prescient – but as he looked around the spacious and almost empty lounge he could think of nothing which might have triggered subconscious alarms. From his seat at the window, Snook could see into a small storeroom behind the bar and he was surprised to notice the white-coated barman going into it and putting on what appeared to be a pair of magniluct low-light spectacles. The barman, a suave young Arab, stood perfectly still for a moment, staring upwards, then put the glasses away and returned to the counter where he whispered something to the black-skinned floor waiter. The waiter's eyes flared whitely in his African face as he glanced apprehensively at the ceiling.

Snook took a ruminative sip from his drink. Now that he thought of it, he had noticed a group of European visitors carrying magniluct glasses at the swimming pool and had wondered briefly why they wanted low-light spectacles amid such searing brilliance. At the time it had seemed just another example of the peculiarities which afflicted over-civilised human beings, but other thoughts were beginning to stir.

This was close to the end of May, Snook recalled with effort, and some important astronomical event was almost due. He had no interest in astronomy and, from overhearing conversations among the pilots, had gleaned only a vague notion about the approach of some large but tenuous object, less substantial than the gaseous tail of a comet. When he had learned that the object could not even be seen, except through some tricky property of magniluct glasses, Snook had classed it as little more than an optical illusion and had dismissed it from his mind altogether. It seemed, however, that other people were intensely interested, and this was yet another proof that he was out of step with the rest of humanity.

He took a long swallow from the misted crystal of his drink, but found that his feeling of unease had not been dispelled – there was nothing new in the realisation that he marched to the sound of a different drum. The midday intoxication he had been savouring abruptly vanished, much to his annoyance. He got to his feet and stood at the long window, narrowing his eyes against the influx of light from sand, sea and sky. The European party were still grouped at the screened pool. For a moment he considered going to them and asking if there had been a recent development he should know about, but that would involve him with unnecessary human contacts and he decided against it. He was turning away from the window when he noticed the dust cloud of a vehicle approaching at speed from the north, the direction in which lay the town and airfield. In less than a minute he was able to discern that it was a jeep painted with the desert camouflage of the Sultan's armed forces.

That's it, he thought, oddly satisfied. *That one's for me.*

He returned to his seat, lit a fresh cigarette and tried to guess what had happened. From vast experience, it could be anything from one of the jet engines having swallowed a bird, wrecking its metallic digestion in the process, to a faulty warning light on the Sultan's private Boeing. Snook settled down further into the upholstery and made up his mind that he would refuse to respond to any so-called emergency unless it was a matter of life or death. He had just finished his cigarette when Lieutenant Charlton, a pilot in the Skywhip flight, strode into the lounge, red-faced and bristling in his wheat-coloured uniform. Charlton was an Australian of about thirty, who was on a three-year contract to fly fighter planes, and who had less feel or regard for machinery than any other man Snook had ever met. He came straight to Snook's table and stood with his bare gold-haired knees pressed against the white plastic. His eyes were pink-stained with rage.

'Why are you sitting here drinking, Snook?' he demanded.

Snook considered the question calmly. 'I prefer it to standing drinking.'

'Don't be ...' Charlton took a deep breath, apparently deciding on a change of approach. 'Didn't the desk clerk give you my message?'

'He knows better,' Snook said. 'This is my first day off in two weeks.'

Charlton stared helplessly at Snook, then lowered himself into a chair and looked cautiously around the bar before he spoke. 'We need you out at the field, Gil.'

Snook noted the use of his first name and said, 'What's the trouble, Chuck?'

Charlton, who always insisted on ground crew addressing him formally, closed his eyes for a second. 'There's a riot brewing up. There's a chance of some of the planes being wrecked and the CO has decided to move them up country until things calm down a bit.'

'A riot?' Snook was mystified. 'Everything was quiet when I left the field yesterday.'

'It sprang up overnight – you should know what the Malaqi are like by this time.'

'Well, what about the Sultan's militia? What about the *firquat*? Can't they control it?'

'It's the bloody *firquat* who are stirring things up.' Charlton wiped his brow. 'Gil, are you coming or are you not? If we don't get those aircraft out of there in one hell of a hurry there aren't going to *be* any aircraft.'

'If you put it like that ...' Snook stood up at the same time as Charlton. 'It won't take me a minute to change.'

Charlton caught his arm and urged him towards the door. 'There's no time. This is a come-as-you-are party.'

Thirty seconds later Snook found himself in the passenger seat of the jeep and hanging on tightly as it took off in a spurting shower of gravel. Charlton brought the vehicle out on to the coast road in a barely-controlled power drift and drove northwards at top speed, accelerating to the limit in each gear. A hot wind, so different to the air-conditioned coolness of the hotel, roared under the tilted windscreen and made Snook's breathing difficult, while the barren ramparts of the *jebel* shimmered beyond the plain to his left. It came to Snook that he had allowed himself to be bulldozed into giving up a well-earned rest period, and into taking a ride with a dangerously reckless driver, without actually learning the reason for it all.

He tugged Charlton's sleeve. 'Is this thing worth getting killed for?'

'Not in the slightest – I always drive like this.' Charton's spirits appeared to have picked up now that he was accomplishing his mission.

'What's the riot all about?'

'Don't you ever listen to the news?' Charlton took his eyes off the road to scan his passenger's face and the jeep wandered close to the encroaching sand and boulders.

'No. I've got other ways of making myself miserable.'

'Perhaps you're wise. Anyway, it's Thornton's Planet that's causing all the fuss. Not just here – there's trouble flaring up everywhere.'

'Why should there be trouble? I mean, the planet doesn't really exist, does it?'

'Would you like to try explaining that to the average Australian bushman? Or even to the average Italian housewife? The way a lot of people figure it out is that ... *whoops!*' Charlton broke off to swing the jeep back into the centre of the road, then resumed shouting above the rush of air. 'People like that reckon that if you can see it coming, you'll feel it when it gets here.'

'I thought you couldn't see it without Amplite glasses.'

'Those things are *everywhere* now, sport. Biggest growth industry since they invented sex. In poorer areas the importers snap them in half and sell them off as monocles.'

'I still don't get it.' Snook contemplated the jouncing horizon for a few seconds. 'How can they get worked up over a kind of optical illusion?'

'Have you had a look at it yourself recently?'

'No.'

'Here.' Charlton felt in his breast pocket, took out a pair of blue-tinted glasses and handed them to Snook. 'Have a look up there ... about due east.'

Snook shrugged and put the glasses on. As he had expected, the sunlit sea appeared intolerably brilliant through the special lenses, but the sky was somewhat darker. He tilted his face upwards – and his heart seemed to lurch to a standstill. Thornton's Planet glared down on him, a vast hurtling ball, somehow frozen in its deadly descent, dominating the whole sky with its baleful blue radiance. An ageless and superstitious dread gripped Snook, paralysing his reason, warning him that all the old orders were about to be swept away. He snatched the glasses off and returned to a world of reassuring normalcy.

'Well?' Charlton looked maliciously amused. 'What did you think of our optical illusion?'

'I ...' Snook searched the sky again, overjoyed at its emptiness, striving to cope with the idea of two separate realities. He half-raised the glasses, with the intention of putting them back on, then changed his mind and handed them to Charlton. 'It looked real.'

'It's just as real as the Earth, but at the same time it's less real than a rainbow.' Charlton bounced in his seat like a horseman calling for more speed. 'You've got to be a physicist to understand it. *I* don't understand it, but I'm not worried because I trust anybody with letters after his name. These people don't think the same way, though. They think it's going to destroy the world.' He gestured towards the wooden huts at the outskirts of the township which was coming into view beyond the diagonal line of a hill. Black-hooded women and small children could be seen among the patchwork buildings.

Snook nodded, filled with a new understanding now that he had looked into an alien sky. 'They're bound to blame us, of course. We made the thing visible, therefore we made it exist.'

'All I know,' Charlton bellowed, 'is that we've got to move some aeroplanes and we haven't enough pilots. You could handle one of the old Skyvans, couldn't you?'

'I haven't got a licence.'

'Nobody'll give a tinker's about that. This is your chance for a medal, sport.'

'Great,' Snook said gloomily. He tightened his hold on the jeep's handgrips as Charlton turned off the coast road on to a track which bore west of the town and ran directly to the airfield. Charlton made no concession to the poorer driving conditions and Snook found it difficult to avoid being thrown from the vehicle as it hammered its course among stones and potholes. He was glad when the airfield's perimeter fence came into view, and relieved to see that only a handful of men in Malaqi costume had gathered at the entrance gate, although most of them were carrying modern rifles which denoted they were members of the Sultan's militia. As the jeep approached the gate he saw there were other Malaqi in the uniform of regular soldiers positioned inside the fence with their rifles at the ready. His hopes that the situation was less urgent than Charlton had said began to fade. Charlton sounded a long blast on the horn and waved one arm furiously to clear the way ahead.

'You'd better slow down,' Snook shouted to him.

Charlton shook his head. 'If we slow down too much we won't get through.'

He kept going at high speed until they were close to the entrance and white-robed figures leapt to each side with angry cries. Charlton braked hard at the last possible moment and swung the jeep in between two scrapped aircraft tail fins which served as gateposts. It was looking as though his tactics had proved completely successful when an elderly Arab, who had been standing on top of a large oil drum, jumped down in front of the vehicle with upraised arms. There was no time for Charlton to react. A pulpy impact shook the jeep and the old man disappeared beneath its front end. Charlton skidded to a halt beyond the protective line of soldiers and looked at Snook with indignant eyes.

'Did you see that?' he breathed, his face losing its colour. 'The stupid old bastard!'

'I think we killed him,' Snook said. He twisted in the seat, saw that a knot of men had gathered around the fallen body, and began to descend from the jeep. A bearded sergeant appeared from nowhere and roughly pushed him back into the vehicle.

'Don't go back there,' the sergeant warned. 'They will kill you.'

'We can't just …' Snook's words were lost as Charlton gunned the engine and the jeep, snaking its rear end, accelerated towards the line of hangars on the south side of the runway. 'What are you doing?'

'The sergeant wasn't joking,' Charlton told him grimly, and as if to punctuate his words there came an irregular burst of small arms fire. Sand fountained briefly in several places close to the jeep.

Snook sank down in his seat, trying to make himself into a smaller target, while reluctantly conceding that Charlton – although wrong-headed in many other things – was right in this respect. There were so few cars in Malaq that its people had never come to accept the inevitability of road fatalities. The relatives of an accident victim always treated his death as a case of wilful murder and, even in normal times, set out to gain revenge. Snook knew one aircraft fitter who had accidentally run over a child the previous year and who had been smuggled out of the country by air the same day to preserve his life.

He sat up straight again as the jeep passed into the shelter of a line of revetments and finally came to a halt outside the single-storey building which housed the operations room. Squadron Leader Gross, an ex-RAF man who was deputy commander of the Sultan's Air Force, came running out to meet them. He paused, wordlessly, while three Skywhip jet fighters took off in formation from the nearby strip. His clean-shaven face was streaked with dust.

'I heard some firing,' he said, as soon as the thunder of the jets had receded. 'What happened?'

Charlton shifted uneasily and stared at his hands which were clenched on the steering wheel. 'They were shooting at us, sir. One of the locals … ah … got in the way as I was coming in through the gate.'

'Dead?'

'He was pretty old.'

'Trust you, Charlton,' Gross said bitterly. 'Christ Almighty! As if things weren't bad enough!'

Charlton cleared his throat. 'I managed to find Snook, sir. He's agreed to fly a Skyvan out.'

'There are only two Skyvans still here – and they're not going anywhere.' Gross pointed into the shade of the nearest hangar where two of the boxy old aircraft were sitting. The starboard propeller of one had chewed through a wingtip of the other, apparently as a consequence of inept taxiing at close quarters.

Snook jumped down on to the hot concrete. 'I'll have a look at the damage.'

'No, I'm moving all civilian personnel up north till this blows over. You'd better go with Charlton in his Skywhip.' Gross fixed Charlton with an unfriendly stare. 'I wish you a safe journey.'

'Thank you.' Snook turned and ran behind Charlton who was already halfway to the waiting jet. He climbed into the rear seat and put on the intercom headset while Charlton spun up the engine. The aircraft surged forward almost at once, jolting solidly on its undercarriage, and wheeled on to the runway. Snook was still struggling with his safety straps when the rumbling shocks coming up through the airframe abruptly ceased, letting him know they were airborne. He examined his clothing – dark blue silk shirt, pale blue shorts and lightweight sandals – shocked at its incongruity amid the functional machinery of the cockpit. His watch showed the time to be 01.06, which meant that only nine minutes earlier he had been sitting in the hotel with his watered gin.

Even for Gil Snook, the human neutrino, the uncommitted particle of humanity, the pace of events had been bewildering. He tightened the last buckle, raised his head and saw at once that they were flying south. Not wanting to jump to conclusions, he waited until the aircraft had levelled off at 7,000 metres without changing course before he spoke to the pilot.

'What's the idea, Chuck?' he said coldly.

Charlton's voice was crisp and unabashed in the headphones. 'Look at it this way, sport – we're both finished in Malaq. That old scarecrow who jumped out in front of us probably had thirty or forty sons and nephews, and no matter where you go they'll be potting at you with their Martinis and Lee-Enfields. Most of them are lousy shots, but they'll get in close enough some day and it won't do you any good to explain you were just a passenger. Believe me, I know about these things.'

'So where are we going?'

'I've finished flying for Gross anyway. We're supposed to be a strike force and all we do is ...'

'I asked you where we're going.'

Charlton's hand appeared above the rim of his ejector seat, the index finger pointing straight ahead in the direction of flight. 'There's the whole of Africa to choose from.'

Snook shook his head in disbelief. 'My passport is back in my hotel room. Where's yours?'

'Back in my quarters.' Charlton sounded supremely confident. 'But don't worry about a thing – we're within range of at least six brand-new republics where they'll be glad to give us asylum. In exchange for the aircraft, of course.'

'Of course.' Snook glanced upwards into the eastern sky, frowning. Thornton's Planet was invisible and unreal, but – like any other spectre in the heavens – it had been an omen of ill luck.

CHAPTER THREE

By the Spring of 1996 the passage of Thornton's Planet was fading from the memories of those peoples who had been most alarmed at the time of its close approach to Earth. It had actually passed through the cosmic needle's eye which was the space between the Earth and the Moon, but – as various authorities had predicted – the physical effects had been zero as far as the man in the street was concerned. As the object had dwindled in size to that of any other planet, so had its significance shrunk for the average human being who continued to be faced with the task of remaining alive in an increasingly hungry and factious world. Thornton's Planet could still be seen by anybody who chose to put on magniluct glasses to search for it, but the novelty of sometimes being able to look downwards and observe a blue star shining up through the entire bulk of the Earth remained just a novelty. It provided neither food nor warmth, and was of no other practical value – therefore it was relegated to the same category of astronomical curiosities as auroras and falling stars.

The situation was different in the world's scientific community. The very nature of the celestial intruder hampered its observation and study, but long before Thornton's Planet swept past the Earth it had become obvious that it was being captured by the sun. Angling down through the plane of the ecliptic, it had plunged inside the orbit of Mercury, gaining speed all the while, swung around the sun, then had retreated back through the dim outer limits of the Solar System. Its behaviour was not quite compatible with that of a planet made of normal hadronic matter, but calculations showed that it had adopted a highly elliptical precessing orbit with a period of little more than twenty-four years. The elements of the orbit were such that the planet was expected to revisit the Earth when it had completed four revolutions, that is, in slightly less than a century after its first pass.

This information had a mixed reception among scientific workers of many disciplines, all of whom – given the available data as a theoretical exercise – would have predicted that an anti-neutrino body should pass on through the Solar System in a straight line, completely unaffected by the sun's gravitic pull. Most were appalled at seeing the entire citadel of human science threatened by a casual, heedless visitor from infinity; others were uplifted by the new challenge to man's intellect. And a few totally rejected the interpretation of the data, denying that Thornton's Planet could have any objective reality whatsoever.

For his part, Gilbert Snook knew beyond any shadow of doubt that Thornton's Planet genuinely existed. He had looked into its livid, blind face, and he had experienced the devastation of his whole way of life.

There were a number of things which Snook disliked about his new career in the nine-years-old republic of Barandi, although – he was compelled to admit – many of the problems had been of his own making. The first of these had arisen within one minute of the Skywhip rolling to a standstill on Barandi's principal military airfield on the northern shore of Lake Victoria.

Lieutenant Charlton, after some fast talking on the local communications band, had managed to arrange a sympathetic reception for himself. And when it was realised he was making Barandi the gift of a well-maintained counter-insurgency aircraft, plus his own services as a pilot, the reception was elevated to a state ceremony in miniature, with several high-ranking officers and their ladies present.

The belated discovery of diamonds in western Kenya had caused local acceleration of a world-wide process – the breaking up of countries into smaller and smaller political units as strong centralised government became impossible. Barandi was one of several new statelets in the region which were poised on the brink of legality, and it was hungry for defence equipment which would consolidate its position. Consequently there had been a distinct atmosphere of self-congratulation, almost of gaiety, among the resplendent group which assembled to greet the benefactors who were swooping down out of the northern skies.

Unfortunately, Snook had marred the occasion by turning to Charlton as soon as they were both on the ground and felling him with the hardest single punch he had ever thrown. Had it been his intention simply to induce unconsciousness he would have gone for Charlton's solar plexus or chin, but he had been gripped by an overwhelming desire to mess up the pilot's face, and therefore had hit him squarely between the eyes. The result had been two black panda-patches and an enormously swollen nose which had gone a long way towards spoiling Charlton's public image of a clean-cut young airman.

That had been almost three years earlier, but – on days when his spirits were at a low ebb – Snook could still get a boost from remembering how Charlton's social activities had been curtailed by his grotesque appearance during the first week in his adopted country.

His own life had been even more restricted, of course. There had been two days in prison while Charlton was making up his mind not to bear a grudge; a day of interrogation about his political attitudes; and a further month of confinement after he had made it clear that he was not going to service the Skywhip or any other Barandian aircraft. Finally he had been released, warned against trying to leave the country, and – in view of his engineering qualifications – given a job teaching illiterate tribesmen who worked the deep mines west of Kisumu.

Snook believed his post was something of a fiction, created as part of a scheme to give Barandi status in the eyes of UNESCO, but he had devised a workable routine and had even discovered certain aspects of the life which he could enjoy. One of them was that there was a plentiful supply of a superb Arabic coffee, and he made a practice of drinking four large cups of it every morning before thinking about work.

This was the part of the day, just at dawn, during which he most enjoyed being alone, so when the noise of a disturbance at the mine head reached him he doggedly continued with his fourth cup. The trouble, whatever it was, did not seem too serious. Against a background hubbub of voices there was a single high-pitched yammer which sounded like one man in-dulging in hysterics. Snook guessed that somebody had contracted a fever or had been drinking too much. Either way it was not his concern – pick-ing up bugs and falling down drunk were almost national pastimes in Barandi.

The thought of alcohol reminded Snook of his solitary excesses of the pre-vious night. He left the bungalow's small kitchen, went into the living room and retrieved two empty gin bottles and a glass. The sight of the second bottle brought a momentary pang of dismay – he was fairly certain both had not been full on the day before, but the fact that there was a lingering doubt was proof enough that he was drinking far too much. It was coming near the time for him to move on to another part of the world, regardless of passport or other difficulties.

Snook went out to the back and was ceremoniously smashing the green bottles into the other glittering fragments in his rubbish bin when he real-ised he could still hear the lone voice in the distance, and for the first time he sensed the fear in it. Once again he felt the familiar yet ever-strange stir-rings of prescience. There was the sound of footsteps at the side of the house and George Murphy, a superintendent at the mine, came hurrying into view. Murphy was a black man, a former Kenyan, but the new Barandian nationalism scorned the use of Swahili names as a relic of the past, on a level with performing tribal dances and carving wooden souvenirs for tourists, and every citizen had an Anglican name for official and general use.

'Good morning, Gil.' Murphy's greeting seemed relaxed, but the heaving of his chest beneath the silvercord shirt showed he had been running. His breath smelled of mint chewing gum.

'*Jambo,* George. What's the problem?' Snook replaced the lid of the bin, covering his trove of artificial emeralds.

'It's Harold Harper.'

'Is he the one who's making all the fuss?'

'Yes.'

'What is it? A touch of the horrors?'

Murphy looked uneasy. 'I'm not sure, Gil.'

'What do you mean?'

'Harper doesn't drink much – but he says he saw a ghost.' Murphy was a mature, intelligent man and it was clear that he was embarrassed by what he was saying, yet was determined to see it through.

'A ghost!' Snook gave a short laugh. 'It's amazing what you can see through the bottom of a glass.'

'I don't think he was drinking. The shift foreman would have noticed.'

Snook's interest quickened. 'You mean he was in the mine when it happened?'

'Yes. Coming off night shift on the bottom level.'

'What did this ... ghost look like?'

'Well, it's hard to get much sense out of Harper the way he is at the moment ...'

'You must have some idea. Are we talking about a lady in a long white dress? Something like that?'

Murphy shoved his hands deep into his trouser pockets, hunched his shoulders and rocked on the balls of his feet. 'Harper says a head came up out of the rock floor then sank back into it again.'

'That's a new one on me.' Snook was unable to resist being callous. 'I knew a guy once who used to see long-necked geese walking out from under his bed.'

'I told you Harper wasn't drinking.'

'You don't have to be swigging right up to the minute the DTs start.'

'I wouldn't know about that.' Murphy was beginning to lose his patience. 'Will you come and talk to him? He's badly shaken up and the doctor's away at Number Four.'

'What good would I do? I'm not a medic.'

'For some reason Harper looks up to you. For some reason he thinks you're his friend.'

Snook could see the superintendent was growing angry, but his own reluctance to become involved was just as strong as ever. Harper was a member of several of his classes and on a few occasions had stayed behind to discuss points of special interest to him. He was a willing student, but many of the miners were hungry for knowledge and Snook failed to see that he should therefore be put on stand-by, ready to go running each time one of them bloodied his nose.

'Harper and I get on all right,' Snook said, digging in. 'I just don't think I can help him in a case like this.'

'I don't think so, either.' Murphy's voice, as he turned to leave, showed his disgust at Snook's attitude. 'Perhaps Harper is just a crazy man. Or maybe there's something wrong with his Amplites.'

Snook suddenly felt cold. 'Wait a minute. Was Harper wearing Amplites when he saw this ... thing?'

'What difference does it make?'

'I don't know – it seems odd, that's all. How can anything go wrong with magniluct glasses?'

Murphy hesitated. He obviously realised he had caught Snook's interest and was taking revenge by being meagre with his information. 'I don't know what can go wrong with them. Flaws in the material, maybe. Funny reflections.'

'George, what are you talking about?'

'This isn't the first incident we've had this week. On Tuesday morning a couple of men coming off the night shift said they saw some kind of a bird flying around on the bottom level. If you ask me, they *had* been on the bottle.' Murphy began to move away. 'I won't take up any more of your time.'

Snook thought about the unmanning dread he had felt during the one moment, almost three years earlier, when he had looked on the blotched, glowering face of Thornton's Planet at its closest to Earth. An instinct prompted him to wonder if Harold Harper, similarly unready, had made contact with the unknown.

'If you wait till I get my boots on,' he said to Murphy, 'I'll go down to the mine with you.'

Barandi National Mine No. 3 was one of the most modern in the world, and had few of the trappings associated with traditional-style diggings. The main shaft was perfectly circular in cross-section, having been sunk by a track-mounted parasonic projector which converted the clay and rock within its beam to monomolecular dust. Apart from the various hoist mechanisms, the dominant feature of the mine head was the snaking cluster of vacuum tubes which drew away the dust created by hand-held projectors on the working levels. It was then piped off to a nearby processing plant where, as a by-product, it formed the basis of high-quality cement.

One thing the mine had in common with all others yielding the same precious material was a very strict security system. His work as a teacher allowed Snook to move freely in the outer circle of administrative buildings and stores, but he had never before been through the single gate in the fence which surrounded the mine head itself. He looked about him with interest as the armed guards examined his identification. A military jeep bearing the star-and-sword emblem of the Barandian government was parked at the miner check-out shed.

Snook pointed the vehicle out to Murphy. 'Royal visit?'

'Colonel Freeborn is here. He visits us about once a month to check the security procedures in person.' Murphy slapped his own jaw lightly in annoyance. 'We could have done without this trouble today of all days.'

'Is he a big man with a dent in the side of his skull?'

'That's right.' Murphy looked curiously at Snook. 'Have you met him?'

'Just once – quite a while ago.'

Snook had been interviewed by several army officers during his one day of interrogation after arriving in Barandi, but he remembered Colonel Freeborn most clearly. Freeborn had questioned him in detail about his reasons for refusing to work on Barandian aircraft, and had nodded thoughtfully each time Snook had given a deliberately obtuse answer. In the end Freeborn had said, with perfect candour, 'I'm an important man in this country, a friend of the President, and I have no time to waste on white foreigners, least of all you. If you don't start giving plain answers to my questions, you'll leave this office with a skull like mine.' He had reinforced his meaning by picking up his cane and fitting the gold ball at its top neatly into the cup-shaped depression on his shaven head. The little demonstration had persuaded Snook that his wisest course would be one of co-operation, and it still rankled with him that he had been cowed so thoroughly within the space of ten seconds. He thrust the memory aside as being unproductive.

'I don't hear Harper now,' he said. 'Perhaps he's calming down.'

'I hope so,' Murphy replied. He led the way across rutted hard clay to a mobile building which had a red cross on its side … They went up the wooden steps and into a reception room which was bare except for some utility chairs and World Health Organisation posters. Harold Harper, a broad-shouldered but very thin man in his mid-twenties, was slouched in one of the chairs, and two seats away – maintaining his professional detachment – was a black male nurse with watchful eyes. Harper gave a lopsided smile when he saw Snook, but did not speak or move.

'I had to give him a shot, Mister Murphy,' the nurse said.

'Without the doctor being here?'

'It was Colonel Freeborn's order.'

Murphy sighed. 'The Colonel's authority doesn't extend to medical situations.'

'Are you kidding?' The nurse's face was a caricature of indignation. 'I don't want no dent in my head.'

'Perhaps the shot was a good idea,' Snook said, going forward and kneeling in front of Harper. 'Hey, Harold, what's been going on? What's all this about a ghost?'

Harper's smile faded. 'I saw a ghost, Gil.'

'You were in luck – I've never seen one of those things in my whole life.'

'Luck?' Harper's gaze slid away, seeming to focus on something far beyond the confines of the small room.

'What exactly did you see, Harold?'

Harper spoke in a dreamy voice, occasionally lapsing into Swahili. 'I was down on Level Eight … far end of the south pipe … started to run out of yellow clay, kept hitting rock … needed to reset my projector, but I knew it was near the end of the shift … turned back and saw something on the floor … a little dome, like the top of a coconut … shining, but I could see through it … tried to touch it – nothing there … took off my Amplites for a better look, you know how you do it, automatic like, but there's hardly any light down there … without the glasses I couldn't see a thing … so I put them on again … and … and …' Harper stopped speaking and began to take heavy, measured breaths. His feet moved slightly, as though a signal to flee was not being fully suppressed.

'What did you see, Harold?'

'There was a head … my hand was inside the head.'

'What sort of head?'

'Not human … not like an animal … about this size …' Harper crooked his fingers as though holding a football. 'Three eyes … all together near the top … mouth near the bottom … my hand was inside the head, Gil. Right inside it.'

'Did you feel anything?'

'No. I just got back from it. I was up against the end of the pipe. I couldn't get away … so I just sat there.'

'Then what happened?'

'The head turned round a bit … the mouth moved, but there was no sound … then it sank down into the rock. It was gone.'

'Was there a hole in the rock?'

'There was no hole in the rock.' Harper looked mildly reproachful. 'I saw a *ghost,* Gil.'

'Could you show me the exact spot?'

'I could.' Harper closed his eyes, and his head rolled slightly. 'But I sure as hell won't. I'm not going back down there again. Not ever ...' He leaned back in the chair and began to snore.

'You! Florence Nightingale!' Murphy jabbed the nurse's shoulder with a broad forefinger. 'How much stuff did you shoot into this man?'

'He'll be all right,' the nurse said defensively. 'I've sedated men before.'

'He'd better be all right, man. I'll be back every hour or so to check – so you'd better bed him down and look after him.' The superintendent, big and competent in his expensive silvercords, was genuinely concerned about Harper, and – uncharacteristically for him – Snook felt the sudden warmth of liking and respect.

'Listen,' he said, as soon as they got outside. 'I'm sorry I was so slow off the mark up at my place. I didn't realise what Harper was up against.'

Murphy smiled, completing the human link. 'Okay, Gil. You believed what he told you?'

'It sounds crazy, but I think I do. It was the bit about the glasses that did it. When he took them off he couldn't see the head, or whatever it was.'

'That made me think there was something wrong with the glasses.'

'It made me think that what Harper saw is very real, though I can't explain it. Do all the miners wear Amplites?'

'They're standard issue. They cut lighting bills by ninety per cent – and you know the energy situation now that they're giving up the nuclear power plant.'

'I know.' Snook narrowed his eyes, watching the sun begin its vertical climb from behind the mountains due east. One of the things he disliked about living on the equator was that there was so little variation in the sun's daily path. He imagined it wearing a groove in the firmament, getting into a rut. A line of men had formed at the entrance to the hoist, on their way to go on shift, and Snook became aware that a number of them were grinning and waving at him. One proffered his yellow safety helmet and pointed at the mine entrance, and others near him burst out laughing as Snook gave an exaggerated shake of his head.

'They seem in good form,' Snook said. 'Most of them aren't so chirpy in class.'

'They're scared,' Murphy told him. 'Rumours spread fast in a mining camp and the two men who thought they saw birds on Tuesday morning have been talking their heads off. This story of Harper's has gone round the camp already, and when he gets into the bar tonight and has a few drinks ...'

'What are they scared of?'

'Ten years ago most of these men were herders and farmers. President Ogilvie rounded them up like their own cattle, gave them all Anglo names, banned the Bantu languages in favour of English, dressed them up in shirts and pants – but he hasn't changed them in any way. They never liked going down the mines, and they never will.'

'You'd think that after ten years ...'

'As far as they're concerned, it's another world down there. A world they've no business to enter. All they need is a hint, just one hint, that the rightful inhabitants of that world are objecting to their presence and they'll refuse to go back into it.'

'What would happen then?'

Murphy took a pack of cigarettes from his shirt pocket and gave one to Snook. They both lit up and gazed at each other through complex traceries of smoke.

'This single mine,' Murphy said, 'produced more than forty thousand metric carats last year. What do you think would happen?'

'Colonel Freeborn?'

'That's right – Colonel Freeborn would happen. Right now the government pays the men a living wage ... and provides facilities like medical aid, even though there's only one qualified doctor serving four mines ... and free education, even though the teacher is an out-of-work aircraft mechanic ...' Murphy's eyes twinkled as Snook performed a stiff bow.

'The system doesn't cost much, and the President's advisers get what propaganda value they can out of it,' Murphy continued, 'but if the miners tried refusing to work, Colonel Freeborn would introduce another system. This has always been good slave country, you know.'

Snook studied his loosely-packed aromatic cigarette for a moment. 'Aren't you taking a bit of a risk by talking to me like this?'

'I don't think so. I take care to know the man I speak to.'

'It's nice of you to say that,' Snook replied warily, 'but would you be insulted if I went on thinking you must have a reason?'

'Not insulted – disappointed, perhaps.' Murphy gave a high-pitched chuckle which seemed incompatible with his solid torso, and the minty smell of his breath reached Snook. 'The men like you because you're honest. And because you're nobody's fool.'

'You're still being nice to me, George.'

Murphy spread his hands. 'What I've been saying is relevant. Look, if you will investigate this ghost thing and come up with some reassuring explanation the men will accept it. And you'll be doing them a big favour.'

'Anything that teacher says must be true.'

Murphy nodded. 'In this case, yes.'

'I'm interested.' Snook turned to face the steel-framed structures which covered the entrance to the three-kilometre vertical shaft. 'But I thought visitors weren't allowed down there.'

'You're a privileged case. I talked to Alain Cartier, the mine manager, a while ago and he has already signed the special authorisation.'

CHAPTER FOUR

Snook had requested that lighting should be kept to a minimum, and as a result the darkness at the end of the south pipe on Level Eight was almost complete. He felt as though he was standing in a well of black ink which not only robbed him of light but drained all the warmth from his body. There was a flashlight attached to his belt, but the only relief he permitted himself from the pressure of night was occasionally to touch the display stud on his wristwatch. The fleeting appearance of the angular red numerals, telling him that dawn was approaching the world above, also created an illusion of heat. He felt a gentle touch on his arm.

'What'll we do if nothing happens?' Murphy's voice, although he was standing only two paces away, was almost inaudible.

Snook grinned in the blackness. 'There's no need to whisper, George.'

'Damn you, Snook.' There was a pause, then Murphy repeated his question in a voice which was very slightly louder than at first.

'We come back tomorrow, of course.'

'Then I'm bringing a hot water bottle and a flask of soup.'

'Sorry,' Snook said. 'No heat sources – one of the cameras has infrared film in and I don't want to chance spoiling the results. Photography isn't one of my fields.'

'But you think a magniluct filter will work on a camera?'

'I don't see why it shouldn't. Do you?'

'I see bugger all,' Murphy whispered gloomily. 'Even with my Amplites on.'

'Keep them on – just before dawn seems to be the most likely time for an appearance, if there's going to be one.'

Snook was wearing his own low-light glasses and, like Murphy, could see almost nothing. The magniluct lenses were designed to amplify meagre scatterings of light to a level at which the wearer's surroundings became visible, but where there was less than a threshold level their performance was uncertain. He leaned against the end wall of the pipe, constantly moving his eyes, determined not to miss the slightest manifestation of anything unusual, and occasionally took the Amplites off for a second to compare the two forms of vision. Perhaps ten minutes had passed when Snook began to think he could sense a slight difference – it seemed to him that the blackness was less intense while he was looking through the glasses. No shapes were visible, not even a localised variation in the near-luminance, and yet he became almost certain his field of view was infinitesimally brighter, as if a faintly luminous gas was seeping in to the tunnel.

He said, 'George, do you notice anything?'

'No.' The other man's reply was immediate.

Snook cursed his lack of proper equipment. He had no way of proving that the apparent increase in brightness was not due to the sensitivity of his eyes improving with the long stay in darkness. Suddenly a speck of light, faint as a minor star, appeared at his left and wandered lazily across his vision. Snook pushed the button which, by means of a device he had built during the day, operated the shutters of four cameras. The multiple clicks and the sound of the winding-on mechanisms were shockingly loud in the taut blackness. He checked the time by his watch and memorised it.

'Did you see that?' he said. 'A thing like a small firefly?'

There was a moment of silence, then Murphy said, 'Gil – look at the floor!'

A spot of dim light appeared on the floor and gradually became a disk. When the circle was as large as a man's hand, Snook became aware that he was in fact looking at a transparent luminous dome, tufted on top like a co-conut. He fought to control his breathing, and by an effort of will operated the cameras again. Within seconds the dome had risen and enlarged itself into a roughly spherical object resembling a head upon which travesties of human lineaments were barely visible. The body below it glowed *within* the rock.

There were two eyes near the top, and between them – only slightly lower down – was a third hole which might have been a nose, unadorned by nostrils. No ears were visible, and very close to the bottom was a slitted mouth, tremendously wide and mobile. Even as Snook watched, the mouth twitched and writhed, assuming compound curvatures and quirks which – on a man's face – would have indicated an interplay of feelings ranging from boredom to anger to amusement to impatience, plus others for which there were no human counterparts.

The sound of Murphy's harsh breathing reminded Snook that he still had a job to do. He took another set of photographs and, without conscious thought, kept on operating the cameras every few seconds as the apparition steadily rose higher, coming more completely into view.

The alien head was followed by narrow, sloping shoulders and strangely jointed arms which emerged from a complicated arrangement of robes, frills and straps, made more intricate by the fact that they were semi-transparent and thus could be glimpsed at the back of the figure as well as at the front. Shadowy organs slid and pulsed internally. The creature continued to rise through the floor at the same steady pace, in utter silence, until it was fully in view. It stood about the height of a small man, on two disproportionately thin legs which were hazily seen amid the hanging folds of its robes. The feet were triangular and flat, displaying radial arrays of bones among which wove the thongs of what appeared to be sandals.

When the creature had emerged fully into the tunnel it turned slightly and, in a curiously human gesture, raised one hand to its eyes as if shading them from a bright light. It gave no indication of being aware of the two men. Snook's powers of reasoning were all but obliterated by a pounding dread, yet he discovered he still had capacity for further surprise. Conditioned by the physical laws of his own existence, he had expected the glowing figure to cease its upward movement when it was on a level with himself, but it continued rising at the same unchanging rate until its head passed into the tunnel roof. The head was followed into the solid rock by the rest of the blue-sketched translucent body.

Spreading outwards horizontally from the plane of its feet, like an insubstantial floor, was a surface of radiance which also travelled upwards, creating the illusion that the tunnel was filling with glowing liquid. When its level passed above Snook's eyes he found himself blinded with cloudy luminescence and in sudden panic he snatched off the Amplite glasses.

The tunnel plunged into its former state of utter darkness, and for a moment Snook found himself trembling with relief at the sheer luxury of not being able to see anything. He stood perfectly still for a time, breathing heavily, then turned on his flashlight.

'How's it going, George?' he said tentatively.

'Not too well,' Murphy replied. 'I feel sick.'

Snook gripped Murphy's arm and urged him away from the end wall of the pipe. 'So do I, but we'd better save it for later.'

'Why?'

'I don't know how high our visitor intends to go, but I think you should get the men out of the level above this one. If they see what we just saw the mine will close down for ever.'

'I ... What do you think it was?' Murphy sounded as though he wanted Snook to produce an immediate scientific label for the apparition and render it harmless.

'It was a ghost, George. By most of the classical definitions it was a ghost.'

'It wasn't human.'

'Ghosts aren't.'

'I mean it wasn't the ghost of a human being.'

'There's no time to worry about that now.' Snook put his Amplite glasses on again and found his vision still filled with a cloudy radiance which partially obscured details of what he could see in the tunnel, even with the flashlight on. He took them off and checked the time on his watch. 'Let's see … this pipe is about two metres high and the thing we saw went up through it in about six minutes.'

'Was that only six minutes?'

'That's all it was. Is there a pipe directly above this one?'

'Only the whole Seven-C system, that's all.'

'How far?'

'Varies according to the shape of the clay deposits – could be only five or six metres in some places.' Murphy's voice was mechanical, remote. 'Did you notice its feet? They were like a bird's feet. A duck's feet.'

Snook shone his light directly into Murphy's eyes, trying to irritate him into coming to grips with the problem. 'George, if the thing keeps rising at the same speed it'll be on the next level in maybe less than ten minutes. You should get the men out of there before that happens.'

Murphy covered the light with his hand, fingers redly translucent. 'I haven't the authority to take the men out.'

'All right – just stand back and watch them take themselves out. I've got to look after these cameras.'

'There's going to be a panic.' Murphy was suddenly alert. 'I'd better get on the phone to the mine manager. Or even the Colonel.' He switched on his own handlight and began hurriedly picking his way over the vacuum pipes which curved along the floor.

'George,' Snook called after him, 'the first thing to do is get the men to take off their Amplites and make their way out by ordinary light. That way they won't see anything unusual.'

'I'll try.'

Murphy passed out of sight around a curve in the tunnel and Snook busied himself with the task of dismantling his improvised camera equipment. In the absence of proper tripods he had set the four cameras up on a small folding table. He was working as quickly as possible in the hope of transporting everything to a higher level in time to intercept the ghost again, but it was cold in the tunnel and his fingers refused to function properly. Minutes passed before he had loaded the cameras and the connecting servos into a cardboard carton, gathered up the table and set off in the direction of the main shaft. He had just reached the continuous elevator when the first panic-stricken shouts began to echo down from above.

The electric lighting was stronger on the Level Eight gallery which surrounded the shaft, but Snook was severely hampered by his load and almost missed his footing as he stepped into one of the ascending cages. He steadied himself against a steel mesh wall and made ready to get out at Level Seven-C. The shouting grew louder during the few seconds it took to reach the next gallery, and as Snook was leaving the cage he found his way blocked by three men who were pushing their way in. They jammed the exit momentarily, each clawing the other back. By the time Snook had forced his way out the cage had risen more than a metre above the rock floor and he made an awkward bone-jarring landing, dropping the table in the process.

Other miners, most of them wearing Amplites, had surged out of the south tunnel and were already fighting their way into the succeeding cage. Snook heard the lightweight table splintering beneath their boots.

Protecting his carton of photographic equipment, he breasted the tide of frightened men until he had reached a clear space at the entrance to a pipe which was not being worked. Breathing heavily, he felt in his pocket for his magniluct glasses and put them on. His picture of his surroundings instantly flared into brightness and he saw that he and the other men on the gallery were apparently waist-deep in a pool of radiance. Snook thought of it as a kind of floor on which the spectral visitor stood, and the sight of it confirmed what he already knew from the behaviour of the miners – that the creature had penetrated to Level Seven.

'Take off your Amplites,' he shouted to the men who were milling around the elevator, but his voice was lost in the aural flux of shouts and grunts. Snook decided against trying to make his way into the south tunnel in case his cameras got smashed. He stood with his back to the wall, waiting for the steadily-moving elevator to carry the miners up to the surface, then became aware of another facet of the ghostly phenomenon. The plane of bluish radiance, the phantom floor, was sinking towards the level of the rock floor. As he watched, the two levels merged and – coincidentally – the exodus of men from the south pipe abruptly ceased.

Snook darted into the tunnel and found that it veered quite sharply to the west. He swung around the first bend, ran along a lengthy straight section with its tangle of vacuum pipes and discarded projectors, and reached a second bend. When he got round it he stumbled to a halt.

Here, at least ten of the luminous figures were visible.

All were sinking into the floor at a noticeable rate, but in addition these beings had lateral movement. They were walking, with a curious turkey-like gait, some of them in pairs, emerging from one wall of the tunnel and fading into the other. The complex transparencies of their robes swirled around the thin legs as they moved; the eyes – too close to the tops of the tufted heads – rolled slowly; and the impossibly wide slits of mouths, alien in their degree of mobility, pursed and twisted and reshaped in silent parodies of speech.

Snook, paralysed with awe, had never seen anything so essentially alien, and yet he was reminded of textbook illustrations of ancient Roman senators strolling and conversing at their leisure about matters of empire. He watched for the several minutes that it took for the figures to sink down into the tunnel floor, until only the glowing heads were visible moving purposefully through the skeins of vacuum tubes, until finally there was nothing to be seen but the normal evidences of human existence.

When the last luminous mote disappeared it was as if a clamp had been released from about his chest. He took a deep breath and turned away, anxious to get back to the surface world and its familiar perspectives. On his way to the elevator it occurred to him that he had not tried to photograph the alien scene, and that the chance to do so would probably recur were he to go back down to Level Eight. He shook his head emphatically and kept walking at a steady pace to the elevator, clutching his box of cameras. The circular gallery was deserted when he got there, and he had no difficulty in stepping into an empty cage. At Level Four two young miners – one of whom was in Snook's English class – jumped into the cage with him. They were glancing at each other and smiling nervously.

'What been happen, Mister Snook?' said the boy who was in Snook's class. 'Somebody say we all go to a special meet up top. Others all go *pesi.*'

'Nothing much happened,' Snook told him in a matter-of-fact voice. 'Some people have been seeing things, that's all.'

Stepping out of the cage into a bright morning world of sunshine, colour and warmth gave Snook a powerful sense of reassurance. Life, it seemed, was continuing exactly as usual regardless of what terrors lurked beneath the ground. It took Snook a few seconds to appreciate that a tense and highly abnormal situation was developing within the mine head enclosure. Perhaps two hundred men were gathered outside the check-out building, from the steps of which Alain Cartier was addressing them in an angry mixture of English and Swahili, laced here and there with expletives in his native French. Some of the miners were giving their attention to Cartier, others were engaged in group arguments with various supervisors who moved among them. The management were putting across the message that it was the duty of the miners to return to work without further delay; while the latter – as Snook and Murphy had predicted – were refusing to go underground.

'Gil!' Murphy's voice came from close by. 'Where have you been?'

'Having another look at our transparent visitors.' Snook scanned the superintendent's face. 'Why?'

'The Colonel wants to see you. Right now. Let's go, Gil.' Murphy was almost dancing in his impatience and Snook began to feel an obscure anger at the men, and the power they wielded, which could affect other and better human beings in that way.

'Don't let Freeborn buffalo you, George,' he said with deliberate stolidity.

'You don't understand,' Murphy replied in a low, urgent voice. 'The Colonel has already sent to Kisumu for troops – I heard him on the radio.'

'And you think they'd fire on their own people?'

Murphy's gaze was direct. 'The Leopard Regiment is stationed at Kisumu. They'd massacre their own mothers if the Colonel gave the word.'

'I see. And what am I supposed to do?'

'You have to make Colonel Freeborn believe you can smooth things over and get the men back to work.'

Snook gave an incredulous laugh. 'George, you saw that thing down there as well as I did. It was *real*. There's no way anybody can convince those men it didn't exist.'

'I don't want any of them to get killed, Gil. There's got to be some way.' Murphy pressed the back of a hand to his mouth in a childlike gesture. Snook felt a pang of sympathy which surprised him with its intensity. *It's happening,* he thought. *This is the way you get involved.*

Aloud he said, 'I've got an idea I can put up to the Colonel. He might listen, I suppose.'

'Let's go and see him.' Murphy's eyes signalled gratitude.

'He's waiting in his office.'

'Okay,' Snook walked several paces with the superintendent, then stopped and clutched his lower abdomen. 'Bladder,' he whispered. 'Where's the lavatory?'

'That can wait.'

'Want to bet? Listen, George, I don't make a good advocate when I'm standing in a pool of urine.'

Murphy pointed at a low building which had red flowers growing in window boxes. 'That's the supers' rest room. Go in there. First door on the left. Here – I'll hold the cameras for you.'

'It's all right.' Snook walked quickly to the door of the building, went through to the toilets and was glad to find them empty – it appeared that the disorderly meeting was keeping the supervisors busy. He locked himself in a cubicle, set his carton on the toilet seat, picked up the camera which had been fitted with a magniluct filter and took out its spool of self-developing film. A quick glance at it showed him that the improvised technique had been successful – there were surprisingly clear images of the first appari- tion he had seen – and he dropped the spool into his pocket. Working as swiftly as he could, Snook put a fresh film in the camera, pressed the palm of his hand over the lens to block out all light, and pushed the shutter button twelve times, producing the same number of exposures as were in the other cameras. He put the camera back in the box, flushed the toilet and went outside to where Murphy was waiting.

'That took long enough,' Murphy grumbled, his composure fully recovered.

'It doesn't do to rush these things.' Snook handed the box of cameras and equipment to the superintendent, dissociating himself from it. 'Now where's Führer Freeborn?'

Murphy led the way to another prefabricated building which was partly screened by oleander bushes. They went into a reception room, where Murphy spoke quietly to an army sergeant who was seated at a desk, and then were ushered into a larger room which was given a vaguely military atmosphere by the presence of numerous maps on the walls. Colonel Freeborn was exactly as Snook had remembered him – tall, lean, hard as the polished teak of which he seemed to be carved, somehow managing to appear meticulously neat and rough-shod at the same time. The cup-shaped depression glistened at the side of his shaven skull. He looked up from the paperwork he had been studying and focused on Snook with intent brown eyes.

'All right,' he snapped, 'what have you found?'

'And a very good morning to you, too,' Snook said. 'Are you well?'

Freeborn gave a tired sigh. 'Oh, yes – I remember you. The aircraft engineer with principles.'

'I don't care about principles – I just don't like being shanghaied.'

'If you remember, it was your friend Charlton who brought you to Barandi. I simply offered you a job.'

'And refused me permission to leave.'

'Worse things have happened to men who entered this country illegally.'

'No doubt.' Snook eyed the cane with the spherical gold knob which lay on the desk.

Freeborn got to his feet, went to the window and stood looking out towards where the miners' meeting was still in progress. 'I have been informed that you have done valuable educational work among the labour force at this mine,' he said in a surprisingly mild voice. 'It is very important, at this stage, that the education of the miners should continue. In particular, it should be impressed on them that ghosts do not exist. Primitive beliefs can be harmful ... if you know what I mean.'

'I know what you mean.' Snook was about to announce that he preferred the Colonel not to try being subtle, when he intercepted a pleading glance from Murphy. 'But there's nothing I can do about it.'

'What do you mean?'

'I've just been down to the bottom levels. The ghosts do exist – I've seen them.'

Freeborn spun on his heel and pointed an accusing finger.

'Don't try it, Snook. Don't try to be clever.'

'I'm not being clever. You can see them for yourself.'

'Right! I'd be very much interested in that.' Freeborn picked up his cane. 'Take me to see the ghosts.'

Snook cleared his throat. 'The snag is that they only appear shortly before dawn. I don't know why it is, but they rise up into the bottom levels of the mine around dawn. Then they sink down out of sight again. They seem to be rising higher each day, though.'

'So you can't show me these ghosts?' Freeborn's lips twitched into a smile.

'Not now, but they'll probably appear tomorrow morning again – that seems to be the pattern. And you'd need to be wearing Amplite glasses.'

Aware of how incredible his story sounded, Snook went on to describe everything he had seen and done in the mine, with a full description of the ghosts and of his experimental camera equipment. When he had finished speaking he called upon Murphy to corroborate his statement. Freeborn gave Snook a speculative stare.

'I don't believe a word you've told me,' he said, 'but I love all the circumstantial detail. You say these day-trippers from Hades are only visible through low-light glasses?'

'Yes – and that's your solution to the whole problem. Issue instructions that every man has to turn in his Amplites and the ghosts won't be seen again.'

'But how would the men see to work?'

Snook shrugged. 'You'd have to install full-scale lighting the way they did before magniluct was invented. It would be expensive – but a lot cheaper than closing down the mine.'

Freeborn raised his cane, in an absent-minded gesture, and its gold head slid naturally into the depression on his skull. 'I've got news for you, Snook. There isn't the remotest possibility of the mine being closed down, but I'm still fascinated by this story you've dreamed up. Now, about those cameras – I presume you didn't think of using self-developing film?'

'As a matter of fact, I did.'

'Open them up and let me see what you got.'

'Suits me.' Snook began opening the cameras and removing the spools. 'I'm not too happy about the polarised or the infrared, but the one with the magniluct filter should show something if we're in luck.' Snook unrolled the spool in question, held it up to the light, and clucked with disappointment. 'It doesn't look like there's anything here.'

Freeborn tapped Murphy on the shoulder with his cane. 'You're a good man, Murphy,' he said evenly, 'and that's why I'm not going to have you punished for wasting my time today. Now get this lunatic and his cameras out of my office, and never bring him near me again. Have you got that?'

Murphy looked apprehensive, but stood his ground. 'I saw something down there, too.'

Freeborn flicked his cane. Its weighty head travelled only a short distance, but when it collided with the back of Murphy's hand there was a sound like that of a twig being snapped. Murphy drew breath sharply and gnawed his lower lip. He did not look down at his hand.

'You're dismissed,' Freeborn said. 'And, from now on, anybody who contributes to the mass hysteria that's been going on here will be regarded as a traitor to Barandi. You know what that means.'

Murphy nodded, turned quickly and walked to the door. Snook got to it first, turned the handle for him and they went outside together. The miners' meeting was still in progress and had grown even noisier than before. Murphy raised his right hand and Snook saw that it had already begun to swell.

He said, 'You'd better get that seen to – I think you've got a broken bone.'

'I *know* I've got a broken bone, but it can wait.' Murphy caught Snook's shoulder with his good hand and stopped him walking. 'What was all that meant to be about? I thought you had an idea you were going to try out on the Colonel.'

'I tried it. Full lighting in the mine … no magniluct glasses … no ghosts.'

'Is that all?' Murphy's face showed his disappointment. 'I thought you were going to prove to him that the ghosts were real. You and your bloody box of tricks!'

Snook paused thoughtfully. The more people who knew about his plan the greater the risks would be, and yet he had forged a rare link with Murphy and had no wish to endanger it. He decided to take the chance.

'Look, George.' Snook pressed his fingers against the side pocket of his jacket, outlining the film spool within. 'When I went into the toilets a while ago I took this film out of one of the cameras and put a new one in its place. This one shows our ghost.'

'*What?*' Murphy tightened his grip on Snook's shoulder. 'That's what we needed! Why didn't you show it to the Colonel?'

'Calm down.' Snook twisted free of the other man's grasp. 'You'll ball the whole thing up if you make too much fuss. Trust me, will you?'

'To do what?' Murphy's brown face was rigid with anger.

'To change the situation. That's your only hope. Freeborn's on top right now because this is his private little universe where he can order a massacre if he wants, and get away with it. If he had seen the evidence that ghosts really exist he would have buried it, and probably us too.

'You saw the interest he took in the cameras. He didn't believe what we told him, but he wanted to look at the film – just in case. It suits people like Freeborn to keep things the way they are, with nobody in the outside world giving a damn about Barandi or anything that happens in it.'

'What can you do about that?' Murphy said.

'If I can reach the Press Association man in Kisumu with this film, I promise you that by this time tomorrow the whole world will be looking over Freeborn's shoulder. He'll have to call off his Leopards – and there'll be a chance to find out what our ghosts really are.'

CHAPTER FIVE

The day began to go wrong while Boyce Ambrose was having breakfast.

His fiancée, Jody Ferrier, had stayed at his family home near Charleston all week-end, which had been fine with Ambrose except that – in deference to his mother's famous Puritanism – they had had separate bedrooms. The arrangement meant that he had spent more than two days in Jody's company without being able to indulge in any of the love games at which she was so naturally and deliciously good. Ambrose was not oversexed and had not been particularly disturbed by the two days and three nights of abstinence, but the experience had focused his attention on an alarming fact.

Jody Ferrier – the girl he had promised to marry – talked a great deal. Not only did she talk a great deal, but none of the subjects which engaged her attention was of the slightest interest to him. Furthermore, each time he had tried to divert the conversation towards more fruitful grounds, she – with masterly ease – had brought it back at once to fashion trends, local real estate values, and the genealogies of important Charleston families. These were the points at which, had they been alone in one of their apartments, he would have silenced her with a bout of old-fashioned physical grappling – and, during the week-end, Ambrose had come to suspect that what he had been regarding as a richly sexual relationship had, in fact, been a prolonged struggle to keep Jody quiet.

By Sunday night his forebodings about his planned marriage had reached the pitch at which he had become morose and withdrawn. He had gone to bed quite early, and in the morning had found himself actually looking forward to the day's work at the planetarium. There had, however, been an unexpected development. Jody was clever, as well as rich and beautiful, and it appeared that during the night she had correctly deduced his frame of mind. At breakfast she had announced, for the first time since they had met, that she had always possessed a burning curiosity about all things astronomical and was proposing to gratify it by spending the day at the planetarium. The idea, once it had germinated, seemed to blossom in her mind.

'Wouldn't it be wonderful,' she had said to Ambrose's mother, 'if there was some way I could help Boyce with his vocation? On a purely voluntary basis, of course – perhaps for two or three afternoons a week. Some tiny little job. I wouldn't care how unimportant it was as long as I was helping to make people aware of the wonders of the universe.'

Ambrose's mother had been impressed with the scheme and thought it was splendid that her son and her future daughter-in-law shared the same intellectual interests. She was certain Jody could find something useful to do at the planetarium, perhaps on the public relations side. For his part, Ambrose had been disappointed in Jody. He regarded himself as a leading expert on every aspect of pretence – after all, he had made a career of it – and he had previously felt a grudging respect for his fiancée's honesty in openly not giving a damn about his work. *All right,* he had thought, *I'll go along with this thing … provided she never says 'light years in the future'.*

He had remained quiet during the early part of the drive to the planetarium, preferring to listen to the radio, and this had given Jody the chance to demonstrate her cosmic awareness.

'If only people could be made to realise how insignificant the Earth is,' she was saying, 'if they would just understand that it's only a speck of dust in the universe, there'd be less war and less petty strife. Isn't that so?'

'I don't know,' Ambrose replied, determined to be unhelpful. 'It might work the other way round.'

'What do you mean, darling?'

'If they start thinking the Earth is insignificant, they could decide that nothing they do will make any difference to anything and start raping and pillaging even harder.'

'Oh, *Boyce!*' Jody laughed incredulously. 'You didn't mean that!'

'I do. Sometimes I worry in case the shows at the planetarium are encouraging the human race to snuff itself out.'

'That's nonsense.' Jody fell silent for a moment, gauging Ambrose's mood, and a shift took place in his hearing, bringing the words of a radio newscast to the forefront of his attention.

'*… claims that the ghosts are real beings, which can only be seen with the aid of magniluct low-light glasses. The diamond mine is in Barandi, one of the small African republics which have not yet been admitted to the United Nations. Real or not, the ghosts have caused …*'

'I've heard you say *dozens* of times that the only real justification for astronomy is …'

'Let me hear this,' Ambrose put in.

'*… science correspondent says that Thornton's Planet, which passed close to the Earth in the spring of 1993, is the only other known example of …*'

'That's another thing – your mother says the lectures you gave about Thornton's Planet were the best …'

'For God's sake, Jody, I'm trying to hear something.'

'Well, all right! There's no need to shout.'

'... *new theories about the atomic structure of the sun. South America. The dispute between Bolivia and Paraguay came one step closer to all-out war last night when ...*' Ambrose switched the radio off and concentrated on the mechanical tasks of driving. There had been a fall of snow during the night and the road, which had been cleared down to the tarmac, was like a swathe of India ink in a scraperboard landscape.

Jody put a hand on his thigh. 'Go ahead and listen to the radio – I'll be quiet.'

'No you go ahead and talk – I won't listen to the radio.' It occurred to Ambrose that he was being unfair. 'I'm sorry, Jo.'

'Are you always grouchy in the morning?'

'Not every morning. But the trouble with being a trendy astronomer is that I hate being reminded that other people are doing real work.'

'I don't understand you. Your work is important.'

Jody's hand moved higher on Ambrose's thigh, sending a tingle of sensation racing into his groin. He shook his head, but was grateful for the little intimacy, with its message that there were other values in life besides those of the laboratory. Forcing himself to relax, he tried to enjoy the remainder of the journey to the pleasant modern building in which he worked. The air was sharp and jewel-bright after the snowfall, and by the time they had got from his car to the office at the side of the dome Ambrose was feeling better. Jody was pink-cheeked and fresh, like a girl in a health foods advertisement, and he felt absurdly proud as he introduced her to his secretary and office manager, May Tate.

He left the two women together and went into his private suite to see what communications had filtered through the various systems to reach his desk. At the top of the heap was a fax sheet on which May had put a ring of dayglow ink around one of the main stories. Ambrose read the terse, tongue-in-cheek story of how a Canadian teacher, with the inelegant name of Gil Snook, had gone down a diamond mine in Barandi and taken a photograph of a grotesque 'ghost' – and, as he stood there in the warm luxury of his office, he began to feel ill.

Ambrose's sudden lack of well-being stemmed from a number of factors.

There was the guilt he felt about the betrayal of his own academic potential. In the past this guilt had manifested itself as jealousy towards the amateur astronomer who, as the reward of years of quiet diligence, had been privileged to attach his name to a star. And here, represented by a few lines of type, was another example of the same kind of thing. How had it come about, Ambrose demanded of himself, that an obscure teacher with a ridiculous name had been at the right place at the right time? And how had this man known to do all the right things, the things which would make him world-famous? There was no mention of Snook having any kind of scientific qualifications – so why had he, of all people in the world, been chosen to make an important discovery?

There was no doubt in Ambrose's mind that what had happened in the backwoods African republic was important, although it was as yet too early for him to say what the significance of the event actually was. The news story contained two items which clamoured in his thoughts – and one of these was that the ghostly sightings happened just before dawn. Ambrose was good at geography, and therefore he knew that Barandi straddled the Earth's equator.

As an astronomer, regardless of his trendiness, he also knew that the Earth was like a vast bead sliding along the unseen wire which was its orbit. The wire did not enter and leave the surface of the globe at fixed positions, as with an ordinary bead – these two points wove a lazy curve up and down the Earth's torrid zone as the planet completed a daily revolution on its axis. And at this time of the year, late winter in the northern hemisphere, when it was dawn in Barandi – and the ghosts were walking – the 'forward' orbital intersection point would be passing invisibly through the tiny republic. Every instinct Ambrose possessed told him there was no element of coincidence involved.

The second news item was that the apparitions were visible only with the aid of maniluct glasses, and in Ambrose's opinion this linked them in some way with the passage of Thornton's Planet almost three years earlier.

He sat down at his desk, filled with a sense of imminence, feeling cold and sick and yet curiously elated. Something was happening inside his head, right behind his eyes, a strange and rare event he had only read about in connection with a few other men. He folded his arms on the deep-glazed wood of the desk, lowered his forehead to rest on them, and remained absolutely still. For the first time in his life, Doctor Boyce Ambrose was encountering the phenomenon of inspiration. And when he raised his head he knew exactly why it was that apparitions had begun to appear in the lower levels of Barandi National Mine No. 3.

Jody Ferrier entered his office a minute later and found Ambrose whitefaced and chill behind his desk. 'Boyce, darling!' Her voice was taut with concern. 'Are you all right?'

He looked at her with bemused eyes. 'I'm all right, Jo,' he said slowly. 'The only thing is ... I think I have to go to Africa.'

The journey to Barandi was a difficult one for Ambrose, even with his money and extensive family connections.

He had originally planned to make an SST flight from Atlanta to Nairobi, and perhaps charter a light aircraft to cover the remaining three hundred kilometres to his destination. This scheme had been scrapped, on the advice of the travel agency, because relations between Kenya and the newly-formed Confederation of East African Socialist Republics were particularly bad at the time. Ambrose had accepted the situation philosophically, remembering that Kenya and other countries had lost valuable territory to the Confederation. He then had aimed for Addis Ababa, only to be told that Ethiopia was on the point of mounting a military operation against the Confederation – to re-establish her southern border – and that all commercial flights between the two were on the point of being suspended.

In the end he had flown in an uncomfortably crowded SST to Dar-es-Salaam in Tanzania, and had been forced to wait seven hours for a place on a shabby turboprop. The latter had taken him to the new 'city' of Matsa, in the republic of the same name, which was Barandi's neighbour to the west. Now he was waiting at the airport for a commuter flight to Kisumu, and was beginning to question the impulse which had driven him to leave the States in the first place.

With the advent of the dangerous Nineties, the great age of tourism had ended. Ambrose was a wealthy man and yet had rarely been abroad, and then only to recognised stable countries such as England and Iceland. As he stood in the searing brilliance of the concourse, with its dioramas of mountain ranges and shimmering ferrocrete runways, he could feel a growing xenophobia. Many of the waiting travellers appeared to be journalists or photographers, presumably being attracted to Barandi by the same magnet, but the faint sense of kinship they inspired was more than offset by the frequent sight of black soldiers wearing short-sleeved drills and carrying machine guns. Even the gleaming newness of the building disturbed Ambrose by reminding him that he was in a part of the world where institutions were not revered, where things which were not present yesterday could equally well have vanished by tomorrow.

He had lit a cigarette and was wandering in a lonely little circle, keeping within easy view of his luggage, when he noticed a tall blonde girl looking cool and composed in a white blouse and lime green tailored skirt. She seemed so out-of-place, so much like a fashion plate for expensive British clothes, that Ambrose glanced around half-expecting to see cameras and lighting equipment being set up in the vicinity. The girl was alone, however, and unperturbed by the stares of the heterogeneous males standing nearby. Ambrose, both captivated and filled with the desire to appoint himself protector of the fair lady, was unable to resist staring too. He was filling his eyes with the sight of her when she took out a cigarette, pouted her lips on to it and continued peering into her purse with traces of a frown. Ambrose stepped forward and offered her a light.

'I've seen this happen so many times on old TV movies,' he said, 'that I feel self-conscious about doing it in real life.'

She lit the cigarette, appraising him all the while with calm grey eyes, then smiled. 'It's all right – you do it very well. And I did need a smoke.' Her accent was English. Well-educated English, Ambrose thought.

Encouraged, he said, 'I know the feeling. Hanging around airports depresses me.'

'I do it so much that it has ceased to register.'

'Oh?' Unused to dealing with British girls, Ambrose tried in vain to assign a background to this one. Actress? Air hostess? Model? Jet setter? He stopped musing when she gave a delighted laugh, showing perfect teeth which had a very slight inward slope. His puzzlement increased.

'I'm sorry,' she said, 'but you looked so baffled. Perhaps you would like everybody to wear labels showing their occupations.'

'I'm sorry. It was just …' Ambrose turned away, but she stopped him by touching his arm.

'Actually; I do have a label. A badge, really, but I never wear it because it's a silly thing and the pin destroys my clothes.' Her voice had become warmer. 'I work for UNESCO.'

Ambrose made one of his best smiles. 'The badge makes you sound like an investigator.'

'You could say I'm a kind of investigator. Why are you going to Barandi?'

'I'm an investigator, too.' Ambrose debated with his conscience about claiming to be a physicist or an astronomer, and in the end he added one vague qualifier. 'Scientific.'

'How interesting! Are you ghost hunting?' The complete absence of mockery in her voice made Ambrose think of the incredulous scorn he had endured from both Jody and his mother when he had announced his plans to visit Barandi.

He nodded. 'But right now the only thing I'm hunting is a cold drink. How about you?'

'I'd love one.' The girl gave Ambrose a direct smile which modified all his opinions about Africa, foreign travel and the design of airports. The potential rewards for the globe-trotter, he decided, greatly outweighed the dangers and discomforts. Leaving his luggage to fend for itself, he escorted the girl to the mezzanine bar, feeling boyishly pleased at the resentful glances from men who had witnessed the entire meeting.

Over chilled Camparis with soda he learned that her name was Prudence Devonald. She had been born in London, read economics at Oxford, travelled extensively with her father who was in the Foreign Office, and joined UNESCO three years earlier. Currently she was on secondment to the Economic Commission for Africa, visiting the African states of recent origin who had applied for UN membership and checking that the money they received in the form of educational grants was being spent in an approved manner. Ambrose was intrigued to hear that her trip to Barandi was not a matter of routine, but had been occasioned by the sensational news stories concerning National Mine No. 3. Barandi was promoting itself as one of the most progressive members of the CEASR, with high educational standards for all its citizens. Prudence's office had been surprised, therefore, to hear that a man called Gilbert Snook – who had no listed teaching qualifications, and had been involved in the theft of a military aircraft from another country – apparently was head of the mine school. The affair was a delicate one because there had been pressure from some quarters to suspend educational grants to Barandi. Her brief was to investigate the situation, with special reference to Gilbert Snook, and make a confidential report.

'That's quite a big responsibility for somebody your age,' Ambrose commented. 'Can it be that, in secret, you're a hard-hearted woman?'

'There's no secret about it.' Prudence's finely-moulded features assumed an impersonal quality, like those of a beautiful but highly functional robot. 'Perhaps we should get it clear that it was I who picked you up a few minutes ago. It didn't happen the other way round.'

Ambrose blinked. 'Who said anybody got picked up?'

'What would you call it? What's the latest Americanism?'

'All right – why should you want to pick me up?'

'I need a male escort as far as Barandi – to save me the trouble of fending off various undesirables – and I picked you.' She took a sip of her drink, grey eyes unyielding above the glassy rim.

'Thanks.' Ambrose considered her remarks and found a crumb of comfort. 'It's good to know I'm not an undesirable.'

'Oh, you're very desirable – much more so than any ordinary scientist.'

Ambrose felt an impostor's guilt. 'Assuming there is such an animal as an ordinary scientist,' he said, 'what makes you think I'm not one?'

'In the first place, your wristwatch cost you at least three thousand dollars. Shall I go on?'

'Don't bother.' Ambrose was taken aback and unable to prevent himself being pompous. 'I'm interested in the value of things, not the price.'

'Wilde.'

Ambrose floundered for a moment – convinced she had used the word 'wild' like a mid-century hipster – then understanding came. 'Did Oscar Wilde say that?'

Prudence nodded. 'Something like it. In "Lady Windermere's Fan".'

'That's a pity – I've been going around for years passing it off as my own.'

He gave her a rueful smile. 'Christ knows how many people I've convinced that I'm semi-literate.'

'Don't worry about it – I'm sure you've got lots of other qualities.' Prudence leaned forward and, unnecessarily, touched the back of his hand. 'I like your sense of humour.'

Ambrose looked closely at her, made wary by his glimpse of the tough-minded, hard-edged person who inhabited such an essentially female body. Prudence's face had not altered, but he found he could now see it in two different ways, revealing two different characters, as with an op art picture in which shifts of perception changed heights into depths. He was intrigued, impressed and attracted all at once, and for this reason the idea of simply being picked up, used and discarded rankled more than ever.

'What would happen if I refused to chaperone you to Barandi?' he said.

'Why should you refuse?'

'Because you don't need me.'

'But I explained that I do need you – to fend off undesirables. That's what chaperones are for.'

'I know, but …'

'Would you abandon any other girl in the same situation?'

'No, but …'

'Then why me?'

'Because I …' Ambrose shook his head, lost for words.

'I'll tell you why, Doctor Ambrose.' Prudence's voice was low, but firm. 'It's because I don't play the old game. You know the one I mean. Every time a helpless female accepts courtesy from a gallant male there's the implication – even though it's rarely taken seriously – that, if everything develops favourably, she'll repay him by making herself available. Now, I like you, and it's possible that if we were in Barandi long enough, and you were keen, that we might go to bed together – but it wouldn't be because you held a door open for me or carried my case on to a plane. Do I make myself clear?'

'Gin clear.' Ambrose swallowed a large portion of his drink. 'That's a British expression, isn't it?'

'Yes, but feel free to use Americanisms as well. I've been around.' Prudence gave him another of her perfect, dizzying, ambiguous smiles.

Ambrose cleared his throat and surveyed the baking landscape outside. 'Nice weather we're having, isn't it?'

'All right – equality isn't fair.' Prudence took out another cigarette and accepted a light for it. 'Tell me what you're going to do about these ghosts. Are you going to exorcise them?'

'No exorcism is possible in this case,' Ambrose said soberly.

'Really? You've got a theory?'

'Yes – I'm here to check it out.'

Prudence shivered with an excitement Ambrose found gratifying. 'Does it explain why they can only be seen with those special glasses? And why they keep rising up and sinking back into the ground again?'

'Hey! You've really been paying attention to the news.'

'Of course! Come on – don't keep me in suspense.'

Ambrose cooled his fingertips on the dewy sides of his glass. 'This is a little awkward. You know how an artist doesn't like anybody to see a painting until it's finished? Well, scientists are like that with their pet theories. They don't like making them public until they've tied up every loose end.'

'I can understand that,' Prudence was unexpectedly docile. 'I'll look forward to hearing about it on the radio.'

'Ah, hell,' Ambrose said. 'What difference does it make? I know I'm right. It's a bit involved, but I'll try explaining it to you if you want.'

'Please.' Prudence moved forward on her chair until her knees were touching Ambrose's.

'You remember Thornton's Planet?' he said, trying to ignore the distraction. 'The so-called ghost world that came near the Earth about three years ago?'

'I remember the riots – I was in Ecuador at the time.'

'Everybody remembers the riots, but the thing that sticks in the average physicist's craw is that Thornton's Planet was captured by our sun. It's composed of anti-neutrino matter and therefore should have gone through the Solar System in a straight line and never been seen again. The fact that it went into orbit upset a lot of people and they're still trying to dream up whole new sets of interactions to account for it. But the simplest explanation is that inside our sun there's another one composed of the same kind of matter as Thornton's Planet. An anti-neutrino sun inside our hadronic sun.'

Prudence frowned. 'Underneath the big words, it sounds as though you're saying two things can occupy the same space at the same time. Is that possible?'

'In nuclear physics it is. If a field has a flock of sheep in it does that stop you driving in a herd of cows?'

'Please let's try it without the Will Rogers routine.'

'Sorry – it's hard to know how far to go with analogies. What I'm saying is that if there's an anti-neutrino planet centred on the Earth. Who is Will Rogers?'

'Before your time. Are you serious about this world within a world?'

'Absolutely. It's slightly smaller than the Earth and that's why, even if magniluct had been around a long time, we would not know about the inner world. Its surface would normally be many kilometres below our ground level.'

Prudence dropped her unsmoked cigarette into a pedestal ashtray. 'And this inner world is inhabited by ghosts.'

'Well, ghosts is a terribly unscientific word, but you've got the idea. To the inhabitants of that world *we* would be ghosts. The big difference is that, because the Earth is bigger, we inhabit their stratosphere – so it's unlikely they would ever have detected us.'

'So what happened? Was it something to do with …?'

Ambrose nodded. 'Thornton's Planet is composed of the same kind of matter as our inner world, and therefore would have had a strong effect on it. Strong enough to disturb it in its orbit. That's why the inner world has begun to emerge through the Earth's surface – the two worlds are steadily separating from each other.' He looked beyond Prudence's rapt, dreaming face and noticed the heat-wavering image of an aircraft on final approach. 'I think this is our plane.'

'There's no need to hurry – besides, you haven't told me everything.'

Prudence was gazing at him with what seemed to be open admiration. Ambrose found himself reluctant to break the spell of the moment, and yet his memory told him there was another Prudence Devonald, self-interested and pragmatic, who might be playing him along for reasons of her own.

'Are you interested in astronomy?' he said.

'Very much.'

He grinned. 'Do you ever say "light years in the future"?'

Prudence gave a good-natured sigh. 'Is that your own personal *pons asinorum*?'

'I guess so. I'm sorry if I …'

'Don't apologise, Doctor. Is it enough to say that a light year is a measurement of distance, or do I have to work it out in metres?'

'What else did you want to know?'

'Everything,' Prudence said. 'If there's an inner world coming out through the Earth, as you say, why do the ghosts keep rising up to where they can be seen and then sinking back down out of sight again?'

'I was hoping you wouldn't ask me that.'

'Why? Does it hurt your theory?'

'No – but it's hard to explain without diagrams. If you draw a circle, then draw another circle inside it and slightly off centre so that they touch at the left side, it will give you an idea of the current relative positions of the two worlds.'

'That seems simple enough.'

'It's simple because your diagram is static. The fact is that the Earth turns on its axis once every day – and apparently the inner world does the same – so both your circles should be rotating. If you put a mark at the point where they touch, and rotate both circles, you'll find the mark on the inner circle sinking below the same point on the outer circle. By the time you've given both circles a half turn the inner point will have sunk to its maximum distance below the outer point, then if you go on turning they'll gradually approach each other again. This is why the ghosts have only been sighted around dawn – there's a twenty-four hour wait for your points to coincide again.'

'I see.' Prudence spoke with the wondering voice of a small child.

'As well as rotating your circles, it's also necessary to keep moving the inner circle to the left. This means that, instead of coinciding once a day, your inner point will begin travelling further and further *outside* the outer point.'

'It's beautiful,' Prudence breathed. 'It all *fits*.'

'I know.' Again, Ambrose was gratified.

'Are you first with this theory?'

Ambrose laughed. 'Before I left home I wrote a couple of letters staking a claim to it, but it will soon be in the public domain. You see, the ghosts are going to spread. Before long they'll be visible on the surface – there'll be no need to go down a diamond mine – then the circle of emergence will grow quite rapidly. At first the sightings will be confined to the equatorial regions, places like Borneo and Peru, then they'll spread north and south through the tropics into the temperate zones.'

Prudence looked thoughtful. 'That's going to cause some excitement.'

'You,' Ambrose said, finishing his drink, 'are a master of the art of understatement.'

CHAPTER SIX

Snook's telephone began to ring and, at the same instant, somebody knocked loudly on the front door of his bungalow.

He went to the living-room window, parted two slats of the blind and peered out. Three black soldiers were standing on the veranda – a lieutenant, a corporal and a private – all wearing the black-and-tan spotted berets of the Leopard Regiment. The corporal and the private had the inevitable sub-machine guns slung on their shoulders, and they also wore expressions that Snook had seen many times before in other parts of the world. They were examining his house with the appraising, faintly proprietary looks of men who had been authorised to use any degree of force necessary to accomplish their mission. As he watched, the lieutenant pounded the door again and took one step backwards, waiting for it to be opened.

'Hold on a minute,' Snook shouted as he went to the telephone, picked it up and gave his name.

'This is Doctor Boyce Ambrose,' the caller said. 'I've just arrived in Barandi from the States. Has my secretary been in touch with you to explain why I'm here?'

'No. International communications don't operate too well in these parts.'

'Oh, well – I expect you can guess what brought me to Barandi, Mister Snook. May I come out to the mine to see you? I'm very much ...' Ambrose's words were lost in an even louder hammering on the front door. It sounded as though a gun butt was being used, and Snook guessed that the next step would be to burst the door open.

'Are you in Kisumu?' he snapped into the phone.

'Yes.'

'At the Commodore?'

'Yes.'

'Hang on there and I'll try to contact you – right now I've got some visitors at the door.'

Snook heard the beginnings of a protest as he set the phone down, but his principal concern was with the impatient group on his doorstep. He had been expecting some kind of reaction to his publicity campaign from Colonel Freeborn and it remained to be seen how violent the storm was going to be. He hurried to the door and flung it open, blinking in the midmorning sun.

'You are Gilbert Snook?' The lieutenant was a haughty young man with an angry stare.

'I am.'

'It took you a long time to come to the door.'

'Well – you were knocking at it for a long time,' Snook said with the tricky obtuseness he had been practising for years and which he knew to infuriate officials, especially those whose native tongue was not English.

'That's not the ...' The lieutenant paused, recognising the danger of involving himself in verbal exchanges. 'Come with us.'

'Where to?'

'I am not required to give that information.'

Snook smiled like a teacher disappointed by a child's lack of comprehension. 'Son, I have just required it of you.'

The lieutenant glanced at his two men, and his face showed he was reaching a difficult decision. 'My orders are to bring you to Kisumu to see President Ogilvie,' he said finally. 'We must leave at once.'

'You should have said so at the beginning,' Snook chided. He took a lightweight jacket from a hook, stepped out and closed the door behind him.

They went to a canvas-topped jeep, Snook was given a rear seat beside the corporal and the vehicle surged away immediately. Almost at once, Snook saw two Land-Rovers emblazoned with the sign 'Pan-African News Services'. As they passed the minehead enclosure he was interested to see that the four armoured cars which had been sitting at the fence the night before were now absent. A number of men were moving through the mine buildings, but the vacuum tubes which snaked away to the south were translucent – instead of opaque with speeding dust – which showed that no excavation was taking place below ground.

Snook knew the mine had never before ceased production for as much as a single day, and he guessed that economic pressures were building up somewhere. The conflict was between the new Africans and the old; between modern ambitions and ancient fears. President Paul Ogilvie and Colonel Freeborn were men of the same breed, adventurers whose nerve and lack of scruples had enabled them to hack a prime cut from the carcase of Africa. Ogilvie, in particular, promoted the notion that Barandi had a wide-based economy – with its exports of pyrethrum flowers and extract, coffee, soda ash and some electronic products – but the diamond mines were what had brought the country into being and were what kept it in existence. Snook could imagine the President's growing rage at the closure of National Mine No. 3.

The interesting thing, however, was that Ogilvie and Freeborn still had no true idea of what they were up against, of the strength of the miners' determination not to go underground again. It was one thing to dismiss the ghosts as a product of mass hysteria, without having seen them; but it was something else to stand in a dark tunnel, kilometres below the surface, and watch the procession of silent, glowing figures with their slow-turning heads and mouths which warped in response to unknown emotions. With the bright morning air flowing around him, and the ambience of a motor vehicle with its sounds and smells and chipped paintwork – the essence of human normalcy, even Snook found it difficult to believe in the ghosts.

He sat without speaking for the whole of the jolting ride into Kisumu and beyond it to the new complex of governmental offices which sprawled over eighty hectares of parkland. The cubist architecture was softened and modified by islands of jacarandas, palms and Cape chestnuts. Positioned near the centre of the complex was the presidential residence. It was surrounded by a small lake which was sufficiently ornamental to disguise the fact that it served the same function as a moat. The jeep passed across a bridge, stopped at the main entrance to the residence, and a minute later Snook was ushered into a room of high windows, oiled woods and Murano glass. President Ogilvie was standing at a desk near one of the windows. He was a man of about fifty, with a thin-lipped, narrow-nosed cast of features which, to Snook's eyes, made him look like a Caucasian in dark stage make-up. His clothing was exactly as in all the pictures Snook had seen of him – blue business suit, white stiff-collared shirt, narrow tie of blue silk. Snook, normally not susceptible to such things, abruptly became aware of the sloppiness of his own clothes.

'Sit down, Mister Snook,' Ogilvie said in a dry unaccented voice. 'I believe you have already met Colonel Freeborn.'

Snook turned and saw Freeborn standing in a shaded corner with his arms folded. 'Yes, I've met the Colonel,' Snook said, lowering himself on to a chair.

Freeborn uncrossed his arms, long-muscled beneath the half-sleeves of his drill shirt, and the gold head of his cane shone like a miniature sun. 'When you speak to the President use the correct form of address.'

Ogilvie raised a slim hand. 'Forget it, Tommy, we're here to talk business. Now, Mister Snook – Gilbert, isn't it? – you realise we have a problem here. A very expensive problem.'

Snook nodded. 'I can see that.'

'There's a school of thought which holds you responsible.'

'I'm not.' Snook glanced briefly at Freeborn. 'In fact, when I was talking to the school of thought in his office a couple of days ago, I gave him good advice on how to avoid the problem. He wasn't interested.'

'What was your advice?'

'The ghosts can be seen only through magniluct glasses. Take the miners' glasses away, install full lighting – no ghosts. It's too late now, of course.'

'You still insist that these ghosts really exist?'

'Mister President, I've seen them, and I've photographed them.' Snook, who had been leaning forward in his earnestness, sat back and wished he had avoided any reference to the pictures.

'That brings me to another point,' Ogilvie said, taking a thin cigar from a box and sitting on one corner of his desk to reach for a lighter. 'Colonel Freeborn tells me you took the film from the camera in his presence, and at that time it was blank. How do you explain that?'

'I can't,' Snook said simply. 'The only thing I can suggest is that the radiation by which we see the ghosts takes a long time to register on a negative.'

'That's crap,' Ogilvie stated unemotionally, examining Snook through smoke-narrowed eyes. Snook received a distinct impression that the preliminaries had ended and that the serious business of the interview was about to begin.

'I don't know much about these things,' he said, 'but now that scientific researchers have begun to arrive in Kisumu from the States maybe we'll get a better understanding of what's going on.'

'Have you spoken to any of these people?'

'Yes – I'm meeting a Doctor Ambrose later today.' Snook resisted the temptation to add that it would cause comment if he failed to keep the appointment. He knew that he and Ogilvie were communicating on two levels, one of which required no words.

'Doctor Ambrose.' Ogilvie moved behind his desk, sat down and made a note on a writing pad. 'As you know, it is my policy to encourage tourists to visit Barandi – but it would be very wrong to entice them to come here with exaggerated ideas of what the country has to offer. Tell me, Gilbert, did you fake those photographs?'

Snook looked shocked. 'I wouldn't know how, Mister President. But even if I did know how – why should I?'

'That's another thing I can't understand.' Ogilvie smiled his regret. 'If I could attribute a motive ...'

'How did the photographs get into the hands of the Press?' Freeborn put in from his place in the corner.

'Well, *that* was my fault,' Snook replied. 'I came into town that night for a drink and ran into Gene Helig, the Press Association man. We got to talking about the ghosts. Then I remembered I had shoved the film spools into my pocket and I took them out. You can imagine the surprise I got when Gene noticed the images on one film.'

Ogilvie gave a humourless laugh. 'I can imagine.'

Snook decided to get back on to firmer ground. 'The central issue, Mister President, is that these so-called ghosts do exist and the miners won't go anywhere near them.'

'That's what they think,' Freeborn said.

'I don't believe in supernatural phenomena,' Snook continued. 'I think there's bound to be a plain explanation for the things that have been seen, and I think the only efficient way to clear up the whole mess is to find out what the explanation is. The whole world's watching Barandi at this time and ...'

'Don't belabour the point.' Ogilvie had begun to sound bored. 'You've stuck your nose into a lot of things without any authority – are you prepared to act as official liaison man if I give permission for a full scientific investigation to be carried out at the mine?'

'I'd be glad to.' Snook fought to conceal his surprise.

'All right. Go and see your Doctor Ambrose, and tie in with Cartier, the mine manager. And keep Colonel Freeborn fully informed. That's all.' Ogilvie turned his swivel chair and sent a cloud of cigar smoke rolling in the direction of the nearest window.

'Thank you, Mister President.' Snook got to his feet and, without looking in the direction of Colonel Freeborn, hurried from the room. The interview with the President had gone better than he could have hoped for, and yet he had an uneasy feeling that he had been out-manoeuvred.

Freeborn waited a few seconds, ensuring that Snook had gone, before he moved forward into the light. 'Things are bad, Paul,' he said. 'Things are bad when a grease monkey like that can swagger in and out of here, laying down the law.'

'You think he should be shot?'

'Why waste a bullet? A plastic bag over the head is more satisfactory – it gives them lots of time to repent.'

'Yes, but unfortunately our grease monkey – by accident or design – has done all the right things to keep himself alive.' President Ogilvie stood up and paced the length of the room, marking his path with blue smoke clouds, and looking like a corporation executive discussing a sales plan. 'What do you know of his history?'

'Only that I should have ended it three years ago when I had the chance.' Freeborn, in a reflex action, raised his cane and slid its gold head into the dent in his skull.

'There's more to him than you think, Tommy. For instance, the suggestion he gave you about collecting all the miners' low-light glasses had a lot of merit.'

'It would have involved a complete new lighting system for the mine. Have you any idea how much that would cost these days? It isn't as if your nuclear power station had begun to work when it was supposed to.'

'New lighting would have been a trifle compared to the cost of a major shut-down – in any case, there's more than money involved.' Ogilvie wheeled and pointed at the bigger man with his cigar. 'Money means very little to me, Tommy. I've got more of it than I'll ever be able to spend. The only thing I really want now is for this country, Barandi, the country that I made, to be given its rightful membership of the United Nations. I want to walk into that building in New York and see my flag up there among all the others. That's why the diamond mines have to keep going. Because without them Barandi wouldn't last a year.'

Freeborn's eyes shuttled briefly as he sought the right words to use. He had been exposed to the President's megalomania in the past and had no sympathy with it. The idea of his country's leader dreaming of hoisting a scrap of cloth in a foreign city beyond the ocean – while there were hostile forces on the borders only a matter of kilometres distant – filled him with impatience and dismay, but he was accustomed to concealing his thoughts and biding his time. He had even learned to endure seeing the President take white and Asian whores to his bed, but a day was approaching when he would be in a position to give Barandi the firm military leadership it cried out for. In the meantime, he had to maintain and consolidate his own power.

'I share your dreams,' he said slowly, flooding his voice with sincerity, 'but that's all the more reason for us to take decisive steps right now, before the situation deteriorates any further.'

Ogilvie sighed. 'I haven't gone soft, Tommy. I have no objection to you turning your Leopards loose on the rabble at Number Three – but it can't be done when there are outside observers present. The logical first step is to get them out of the country.'

'But you've just given permission for them to go right into the mine.'

'What else could I do? Snook was right when he said the whole world is watching us.' Ogilvie suddenly relaxed and smiled. He took his cigar box from the desk and offered it to Freeborn. 'But the world soon grows tired of watching one part of Africa after another – you should know that as well as I do.'

Freeborn accepted a cigar. 'And in the meantime?'

'In the meantime I want you – unofficially, of course – to make life difficult for our little scientific community from abroad. Don't do anything obtrusive or newsworthy, just make life difficult for them.'

'I see.' Freeborn felt a resurgence of confidence in the President. 'How about the Press Association man, Helig? Is he to be put out of business?'

'Not now – it's too late to correct that particular mistake. Just watch him in future.'

'I'll look after things.'

'Do that. And there's something else – we'll have to refuse entry to any further foreign visitors. Find some valid reason to cancel all entry permits.'

Freeborn frowned in thought. 'Smallpox outbreak?'

'No, that could interfere with trade. It would be better if there was a military emergency. Say, an attack by one of our long-established neighbours. We'll discuss the details over lunch.'

Freeborn lit his cigar, inhaled deeply, then smiled with something approaching genuine pleasure. 'The Gleiwitz technique? I have a few awkward prisoners in reserve.'

President Ogilvie, the image of a corporation executive in his conservative blue suit, nodded his assent. 'Gleiwitz.'

Freeborn's smile developed into a chuckle. He had never been a student of European history, but the name of Gleiwitz, a speck on the map close to Germany's border with Poland, was familiar to him because it had been the scene of a Nazi operation which both Ogilvie and he had emulated more than once in their own careers. There, in the August of 1939, the SS Gestapo had staged a fake Polish attack on the German radio station and – as visible evidence of the crime by their neighbours – had strewn the area with the bodies of men whom they had dressed in Polish army uniforms and then shot. The incident had been used in propaganda as justification for the invasion of Poland.

Colonel Freeborn regarded it as an exemplary piece of military tactics.

Snook's mind was still seething with suspicion about President Ogilvie's reactions when he got out of the taxi at the Hotel Commodore. It was almost noon, and the sun was hanging directly overhead like an unshaded lamp. He plunged into the prism of shadow beneath the hotel canopy, went through the split-level foyer – ignoring a signal from the desk clerk – and straight into the bar. Ralph, the senior barman, saw him coming and without speaking took a quarter-litre glass, half filled it with Tanqueray's gin and topped it up with ice water.

'Thanks, Ralph.' Snook sat on a stool, cushioned his elbows on the puffy leather facing of the bar and took a long therapeutic drink from his glass. He felt its coolness travel all the way to his stomach.

'Rough morning, Mister Snook?' Ralph put on the look of rueful sympathy he always used with hangover sufferers.

'Grim.'

'You'll feel better after that.'

'I know.' Snook took another drink. He had enacted the same little tableau, with exactly the same dialogue, many times before and he drew comfort from the fact that Ralph had sufficient empathy never to vary the routine. It was about the only kind of communication Snook enjoyed.

Ralph leaned across the bar and lowered his voice. 'Two people over there waiting to see you.'

Snook turned in the indicated direction and saw a man and a woman regarding him with dubious expectancy, and the phrase 'the beautiful people' sprang into his mind. They were a well-matched couple – both young, immaculate and with finely chiselled, fair-skinned good looks – but it was the woman who held Snook's attention. She was slim, with intelligent grey eyes, full-lipped, cool and sensuous at the same time; and to Snook came a sudden fear that his entire way of life had been a mistake, that this was the sort of prize he might have won had he opted for life in the glittering cities of the occident. He lifted his glass and went towards their table, disturbed at the pang of jealousy he felt towards the man who rose to meet him.

'Mister Snook? I'm Boyce Ambrose,' the man said as they shook hands. 'We spoke on the telephone.'

Snook nodded. 'Call me Gil.'

'I'd like you to meet Prudence Devonald. Miss Devonald is with UNESCO. Actually, I think she wants to talk business with you, too.'

'This must be my lucky day.' Snook spoke the words automatically as he sat down, his mind busy with the realisation that the couple were not married, as he had somehow assumed. He saw that the girl was giving him a look of frank appraisal and, for the second time that day, became conscious of the fact that his clothing was barely passable and even then only because the material was indestructible.

'It isn't your lucky day,' Prudence said. 'In fact, it could be quite the reverse. One of the things I have to do in Barandi is check up on your teaching qualifications.'

'What qualifications?'

'That's what my office would like to know.' She spoke with a direct unfriendliness which saddened Snook and also goaded him into his standard pattern of reaction.

'You work for an inquisitive office?' He met her gaze squarely. 'Do you report to the desk or the filing cabinet?'

'In English,' she said, with insulting sweetness, 'the word "office" can also mean the staff who work there.'

Snook shrugged. 'It can also mean a lavatory.'

'I was just about to get us a couple more Homosexual Harolds,' Ambrose said quickly to Snook. 'You know ... Camp Harrys. Would you like another drink?'

'Thanks. Ralph knows my tipple.' While Ambrose went to the bar Snook leaned back comfortably, looked at Prudence and decided she was one of the most beautiful women he had ever met. If there was anything short of perfection in her face it was that her upper teeth had a very slight inwards slope, but for some reason this served to enhance the aristocratic impression she created in his mind. *I want you,* he thought. *You're a bitch, but I want you.*

'Perhaps we should start over again,' he said. 'We seem to have got off on the wrong something or other.'

Prudence almost smiled. 'It's probably my fault – I should have guessed you'd be embarrassed to answer my questions with a third party present.'

'I'm not embarrassed.' Snook allowed himself to sound mildly surprised at the notion. 'And, just for the record, I won't be answering any of your questions.'

Her grey eyes triangulated on him angrily, but at that moment Ambrose arrived back at the table with the Camparis and gin. He set them down and examined the accompanying sales slip with a puzzled expression.

'There seems to be a mistake here,' he said. 'This round cost three times as much as the last one.'

'That's my fault.' Snook raised his drink in salute. 'I order my gin by the beer glass to save trotting backwards and forwards to the bar.' He glanced at Prudence. 'I get embarrassed.'

Her lips tightened. 'I'd be interested to hear how you can drink like that and hold down a job as a teacher.'

'I'd be even more interested,' Ambrose put in heartily, 'to hear your first-hand account of ...'

Snook silenced him with an upraised hand. 'Hold on a moment, Boyd.'

'Boyce.'

'Sorry – Boyce. I'd be most interested of the lot to hear why this lady keeps quizzing me about my private business.'

'I'm with UNESCO.' Prudence took a silver badge from her purse. 'Which means that your salary comes ...'

'My salary,' Snook interrupted, 'consists largely of one crate of gin and one sack of coffee every two weeks. Any hard cash I get I earn by repairing automobile engines around the mine. In between times I teach English to miners on the nights when they've no money left for pleasures of the flesh. These clothes I'm wearing are the same ones they gave me when I came here three years ago. I often eat my dinner straight out of the can, and I brush my teeth with salt. I get drunk a lot, but otherwise I'm a model prisoner. Now, is there anything else you want to know about me?'

Prudence looked concerned, but gave no ground. 'You claim you're a prisoner here?'

'What else?'

'How about political refugee? I understand there's the question of a fighter plane which disappeared from Malaq.'

Snook shook his head emphatically. 'The pilot of that plane is a political refugee here. I was a passenger who thought it was going in the opposite direction, and I'm a prisoner here because I refused to service it for the Barandian Army.' Snook was alarmed to discover that he had discarded all his defences for a woman he had met only a few minutes earlier.

'I'll include this in my report.' Prudence held her silver badge closer to her mouth, revealing that it was also a recorder, and her lips developed an amused quirk. 'Do you spell your name just the way it sounds?'

'It is a funny name, isn't it?' Snook said, slipping back into character. 'How clever of you to decide to be born into a family called Devonald.'

The colour rose in Prudence's cheeks. 'I didn't mean ...'

Snook turned away from her. 'Boyce, what's going on here? Are you a UNESCO man, too? I came here because I thought you were interested in what we saw at the mine.'

'I'm a private researcher and I'm intensely interested in what you saw.' Ambrose gave Prudence a reproachful glance. 'It was pure coincidence that I met Miss Devonald – perhaps if we arranged separate appointments ...'

'There's no need – I'm going to shut up for a while,' Prudence said, and suddenly Snook saw in her the schoolgirl she had been not many years earlier. He began to feel like a veteran legionary who had chosen to sharpen his sword on a raw recruit.

'Gil, have you any idea of what you actually did see at the mine?' Ambrose tapped Snook's knee to regain his attention. 'Do you know what you discovered?'

'I saw some things which looked like ghosts.' Snook had just made the more immediate discovery that, in moody relaxation, Prudence Devonald's profile inspired in him an obscure anguish which had to do with the transience of beauty, of life itself. It was his first conscious experience of the kind, and it was not entirely welcome.

'What you saw,' Ambrose said, 'were the inhabitants of another universe.'

It took a few seconds for the words to come to a sharp focus in Snook's mind, then he began to ask questions. Twenty minutes later he leaned back in his chair, took a deep breath, and realised he had forgotten about his drink. He sipped from the glass again, trying to accustom himself to the idea that he was sitting at the crossroads of two worlds. Once more, within the space of a single hour, he was being forced to think in new categories, to make room in his life for new concepts.

'The way you put it,' he said to Ambrose, 'I have to believe you – but what happens next?'

Ambrose's voice developed a firmness which had not been there earlier. 'I should have thought the next step was quite obvious. We have to make contact with these beings – find a way of talking to them.'

CHAPTER SEVEN

The news that Ambrose wanted to begin observations that very night did not bother Snook – his own imagination had been fired by what he had heard – but he was irritated by the practical consequences.

Ambrose's theory confirmed that the ghostly appearances would not start until near dawn, although they would gradually start earlier and finish later each day. The road from Kisumu to the mine was long and difficult, especially for someone who was unfamiliar with it, and Snook had felt obliged to invite Ambrose to stay the night at his bungalow. This was going to involve Snook being in continuous proximity to the other man for the best part of a day and a night, and his nature rebelled against the imposition. The fact that Prudence had invited herself along, clad in a Paris designer's impression of a safari suit, had not made things any better.

After the friction of their initial meeting she had treated him with impersonal politeness, and he was responding in kind, but all the while he was intensely aware of her presence. It was an odd radar-like, three-dimensional kind of perception which meant that even when he was not looking at Prudence he knew exactly where she was and what she was doing. This invasion of his mind was troublesome and disturbing, and when he found that it extended to minutiae like the design of her jacket buttons and the pattern of stitching in her boots his sense of aggravation increased. He slumped in the spacious darkness of the rear seat of the car Ambrose had rented that afternoon and thought nostalgically about other girls he had known. There had, for instance, been Eva – the German interpreter in Malaq – who understood the principle of sexual *quid pro quo*. That had been less than three years earlier, but Snook was annoyed to find he could no longer remember Eva's face.

'… have to give the planet a name,' Ambrose was saying in the front seat. 'It has always been, literally, an underworld, but it doesn't seem right to call it Hades.'

'Gehenna would be worse,' Prudence replied. 'And there's Tartarus, but I think that was even further down than Hades.'

'It hardly fits, under the circumstances. From what Gil says about the levels in the mine, the anti-neutrino world will have completely emerged from the Earth in about seventy years.' Ambrose swerved to avoid a pothole and roadside trees were momentarily doused with light from the headlamps. 'That's if it continues separating at the same rate, of course. We don't know for sure that it will.'

'I've got it!' Prudence moved closer to Ambrose, and Snook – watchful in his dark isolation – knew she had clutched his arm. 'Avernus!'

'Avernus? Never heard of it.'

'All I know is that it was another one of those mythological underworlds, but it's much more euphonious than Hades. Don't you think it sounds quite pastoral?'

'Could be,' Ambrose said. 'Right! You've just christened your first planet.'

'Do I get to break a bottle of champagne over it? I've always wanted to do that.'

Ambrose laughed appreciatively and Snook's gloom deepened. The situation at the mine was tense and dangerous, one in which he felt the need to have the big battalions behind him, and he was heading back into it accompanied by what seemed to be the world's last example of the squire-scientist and his new girlfriend. There was also the possibility of having to listen to their small-talk right through the night, a prospect he found unbearable. Snook began to whistle, quite loudly, choosing an old standard he had always liked for its sadness, *Plaisir d'amour*. Prudence allowed him to complete only a few bars then leaned forward and switched on the radio. The strains of a heavily orchestrated version of the same song filled the car.

Ambrose half-turned in the driving seat. 'How did you do that?' he said over his shoulder.

'Do what?'

'You began to whistle a tune and then we got the same one on the radio.' Ambrose was obviously intrigued. 'Do you have an ear set?'

'No. I just started to whistle.' Snook failed to see why the other man should be so interested in a trivial occurrence which, while not common in his own experience, was not exceptionally rare either.

'Have you thought of the odds against that happening?'

'They can't be too high,' Snook said. 'It happens to me every now and again.'

'The odds are pretty fantastic – I know some people in ESP research who would love to get their hands on you.' Ambrose began to sound excited. 'Have you ever considered that you might be telepathic?'

'On radio frequencies?' Snook said sourly, wondering if he should revise his estimate of Ambrose's standing in the scientific world. He had gleaned that the man had a doctorate in nuclear physics and was director of a planetarium – qualifications which, Snook belatedly realised, were strangely incompatible and no guarantee that he was not dealing with a plausible crank.

'Not on radio frequencies – that wouldn't work,' Ambrose replied. 'But if thousands of people all around you were listening to a tune on their radios, you might pick it up directly from their brains.'

'I usually live where there's nobody around me.' Snook began to have doubts about Ambrose's whole concept of an anti-neutrino universe. Back in the hotel, with the gin glowing in his stomach, and in the verbal high tide of Ambrose's enthusiasm, it had all seemed perfectly logical and natural, but ...

'Do you get any other indications?' Ambrose was unabashed. 'Premonitions, for example. Do you ever get a feeling that something's going to happen before it actually does?'

'I ...' The question caused upheavals in Snook's subconscious.

Prudence came in, unexpectedly. 'I once read about a man who could hear radio broadcasts because he had metallic fillings in his teeth.'

Snook laughed gratefully. 'Some of my back teeth are like steel bollards,' he lied.

'All kinds of effects can crop up if somebody is close to a powerful radio transmitter,' Ambrose persisted, 'but that's got nothing to do with ...' He paused as the music on the radio was cut off by the strident chimes of a station announcement.

'*We interrupt this programme,*' an urgent male voice said, '*because reports are coming in of a serious incident on the border between Barandi and Kenya, near the main road from Kisumu to Nakuru. It is reported that fighting has flared up between the Barandian Defence Forces and a unit of the Kenyan Army which had crossed into Barandian territory. A communiqué from the Presidential office states that the intruders have been repulsed with heavy casualties, and there is no danger to Barandian civilians. This is the National Radio Corporation of Barandi serving all its citizens, everywhere.'* The chimes sounded again and the music returned.

'What does that mean, Gil?' Ambrose looked out through the side windows as though expecting to see bomb flashes. 'Are we going to be mixed up in a war?'

'No. It sounds like another exercise by Freeborn's Mounted Foot.' Snook went on to tell what he knew about Barandi's military organisations, ending with a brief character sketch of Colonel Tommy Freeborn.

'Oh well, you know what they say,' Ambrose commented. 'Inside every nut there's a colonel trying to get out.'

'I like that.' Prudence laughed and moved even closer to Ambrose. 'This trip is turning out to be more fun than I expected.'

Snook squirming in the rear seat, lit a cigarette and thought dismal thoughts about the difficulties of remaining in control of one's own life. In this case, he could pinpoint the exact moment at which things had begun to slip from his grasp – it was when he had yielded to moral pressure from George Murphy and agreed to see the hysterical miner. Since then he had become more and more entangled. It was high time for the human neutrino to slip away, to regain his remoteness in a new phase of life in a distant place, but the bonds had grown strong. He had allowed himself to interact with other human particles, and it now seemed likely that he had strayed inside the radius of capture ...

When they reached Snook's bungalow the car lights showed three men sitting on the front steps. Remembering his visit from the soldiers in the morning, Snook got out of the car first. He was relieved to see that one of the men was George Murphy, although the other two were strangers. They were boyish-looking Caucasians, both with sandy moustaches. Murphy came forward, smiling and handsome in his silver-cords, and waved a heavily bandaged hand.

'Gil,' he said happily, 'I'll never know how you did it.'

'Did what?'

'Got this scientific commission set up. Alain Cartier called me and said the mine was officially closed until an investigation had been completed. I've to co-operate with you and the team.'

'Oh, yes – the team.' Snook glanced at the car in which Ambrose and Prudence were busy gathering up possessions. 'We haven't exactly got a Manhattan Project going here.'

Murphy looked in the same direction. 'Is that all there is?'

'That's all, so far. As far as I can make out there was quite a bit of Press interest in our ghosts, but the way Helig's story was handled mustn't have impressed many scientific bodies. Who have you got here?'

'Two kids from the electronics plant – Benny and Des, they call themselves. They're so keen to see the ghosts that they came out from town on a motorbike this afternoon. It was right after I spoke to Cartier so I told them to hang around until you got back. Do you think they'll be able to help?'

'That's something for Doctor Ambrose to decide,' Snook said sombrely, 'but, if you ask me, we're going to need all the help we can get.'

As Snook would have predicted, Prudence Devonald avoided even setting foot in his kitchen, and so he spent the next few hours making coffee on an almost continuous basis. Between times, he watched carefully as Ambrose explained his theory to Murphy, Benny Culver and Des Quig. The young men, it turned out, were New Zealanders with good electronic engineering qualifications. They had been attracted to Barandi by the high salaries offered in the electronics plant which President Ogilvie had set up four years earlier in an attempt to broaden the country's economy. Snook got the impression that they were clever individuals and he was interested to note that, after a period of free-wheeling discussion, both completely accepted Ambrose's ideas and became feverishly enthusiastic.

George Murphy was no less convinced, and at Ambrose's request went off to his office to fetch layout charts of the mine workings. When he returned, Ambrose taped the charts to a wall, questioned Murphy closely about the exact positions of the sightings, and drew two horizontal lines across the sectional view. He measured the distance between the lines, then drew others above them at equal spacings. The eighth line lay just above ground level.

'The bottom line is approximately the level the Avernians rose to on the morning the first one was seen by the miner, Harper,' Ambrose said. 'The next one up shows roughly the level they reached on the following morning when Gil took his photographs, and the scale of the chart indicates there was an increase of just over five hundred metres. Assuming a constant rate of separation between Avernus and Earth, we can predict levels they will attain on successive days. Two days have passed since the last sighting, which means that around dawn this morning we can expect the Avernians to reach here.' Ambrose touched the fifth line from the bottom, one which ran through an area in which extensive tunnelling was indicated.

'We could wait for them at any of the lower levels, of course, but the geometry involved means that when they reach the highest point there is a period when they almost stop moving vertically with reference to us. I see from the chart that, luckily, there has been a lot of excavation around that level. What we have to do is spread out laterally as much as possible – probably just one person to a tunnel – and look for buildings materialising. We're not so much interested in the Avernians themselves at this stage, but we do want to find buildings.'

'I seem to have missed something,' Snook said, setting down a pot of coffee. 'Why are buildings so important?'

'They represent our best chance of establishing contact with the Avernians, and even then it may not work. The only reason we were able to detect them is that a mine is a pretty dark place, and so the conditions were good for seeing ghosts. In daylight they might never have been noticed.'

'We were able to see Thornton's Planet in daylight,' Culver said.

Ambrose nodded. 'True – but in its own universe. Thornton's Planet is a very dense assembly of anti-neutrinos and is emitting neutrinos in four-pi space at a very high rate. The planet Avernus is less dense, in its own universe, and therefore its surface appears to us as the milky luminance which Gil and George described. The *inhabitants* of Avernus are less dense again – just the way my hand is a lot less solid than a steel bar – so their neutrino flux is even more attenuated, and they are therefore much harder to see. Okay?'

'I think I get it, but does that explain the way the Avernians were seen gradually emerging bit by bit from the floor? If we see them by virtue of their neutrino emission shouldn't they be more or less visible all the time? Shouldn't we see them right through the solid rock?'

'No. Not to any important extent anyway. The neutrino flux decreases according to the inverse square law, and if you start off with a weak emitter, like an Avernian being, the flux soon attenuates to below the threshold level at which the Amplites will produce an image. The glasses aren't a very efficient way of seeing the Avernian universe – at best they leave us desperately short-sighted.'

'But they're super-efficient in this universe,' Quig put in. 'Even in the dark they would give you a good image of the floor and that could blot out faint images of what was below the floor.'

'Correct.' Ambrose nodded his agreement. 'It's a bit like not being able to see stars in the daytime sky, even though they're there just the same.'

'And the reason we're hoping to find structures,' he continued for Snook's benefit, 'is that it might be dark inside an Avernian building, and that would give them a better chance to see us. Don't forget that, as far as they're concerned, *we* are the ghosts. Right now, sitting in this room, we're sailing along in their atmosphere. The rotation of the two planets means that we're on a kind of glide path which will intersect with their equivalent of Barandi just before dawn.'

Prudence raised her head. 'Is it night time in Avernus?'

'In this hemisphere, yes.'

'Then maybe they know about us. Perhaps they can look up in the sky and see us.'

'No. If you look at the two circles again you'll notice that the Avernians are under the surface of the Earth, so all they would see, if they see anything, is a general radiance – as happened when Gil and George sank under their surface. The only time we can communicate with them is when the two surfaces are roughly coincident.'

'Hell! I've just thought of something which wrecks the whole plan,' Culver put in, slapping his forehead. 'We would never have detected the Avernians at all if our miners hadn't been wearing magniluct glasses. So the Avernians would need special viewing aids to see us, wouldn't they. And the chances that they'd just happen to be wearing them are bound to be millions to one against.'

'Good point.' Ambrose smiled at Culver, obviously pleased at the question having arisen. 'But, fortunately, the relationship between the two universes is not symmetrical, and the advantage is on our side. What it boils down to is that we are better emitters than they are. I've done a few sums and it looks to me that if we stand in an intermediate vector boson field it will have the effect of making us glow fairly strongly in their universe.'

'Bosons? That's a funny kind of radiation, isn't it?'

'Yes, but it should be the Avernian equivalent to a shower of photons.'

'Will you need a Moncaster machine? Des and I have a friend at the power station who uses one sometimes.'

'A lab model would be too big and heavy. I brought some portable equipment with me from the States – it creates a low-intensity field, but it should be good enough for our purpose. I only had room for one so we're going to need good communications in the mine. Anybody who finds what he thinks is an Avernian building will signal the others and we'll get the radiation equipment to him as fast as we can.'

Des Quig put up his hand, like a boy in class. 'If we need communicator sets I can rig up something at the plant.'

'Thanks, but we're too short of time. That's why I brought as much commercially available equipment as I could get in the few hours I had – pulse code modulation sets and ...'

'Hey! It sounds as if you're planning to talk to the ghosts.'

Ambrose looked surprised. 'Of course! It's technically feasible, isn't it? If they can see us and we can see them, that means light is being exchanged. All you have to do is modulate it to get sound communication.'

'That's assuming Avernians use speech among themselves, that they are a technical race at the same level as ourselves or more advanced, and that we can get the idea of light-to-sound conversion over to them. And all that's on top of assuming we will even manage to make them see us.'

'Correct. I know I'm rushing a lot of fences, and I know that being wrong in any one of the assumptions you mention will wreck the whole scheme, but we've got to make the effort – starting tonight.'

Quig burst out laughing. 'Where did I get the idea that astronomers were patient, slow-moving types? Why all the hurry?'

'We're hurrying because it was a stroke of pure luck that the Avernians were seen in a deep mine, and it has given us a few days' grace in which to try making contact.' Ambrose tapped the sectional chart again.

'Let me remind you of the geometry of the situation. We're dealing with two kinds of movement. One of them is the separation of the two worlds – Avernus is emerging from the Earth at a speed of just over five hundred metres a day. This creates a problem in itself because they rise that much higher each time we see them. At dawn this morning they'll get to about fifteen hundred metres from the surface, tomorrow morning it will be a thousand metres from the surface, the morning after five hundred, and the morning after that they'll be visible on the surface – right out there among the trees and mine buildings, or here in this room.' Ambrose paused and smiled as Prudence gave a theatrical shiver.

'That's the stage at which the surface of Avernus coincides with the surface of the Earth – from then on the Avernians will start rising into the sky above us, five hundred metres higher every day, as the planets begin to separate. That would be awkward enough, but the daily rotation of the two worlds complicates everything even further because it is translated into vertical movement between corresponding points on the surfaces of the two spheres.'

'That's the bit I'm having trouble with,' Murphy confessed, shaking his head.

'Well, you've seen it for yourself. We're standing on the surface of a rotating sphere, the Earth. Just below us is another and slightly smaller rotating sphere which has moved off centre until the surfaces are touching at one side. As the spheres turn, corresponding points will move closer together until they meet at the contact zone, but as the rotation continues they have to move apart again. Twelve hours later, half a day, they'll be at maximum separation, with the inner point far beneath the outer point.

'That's why the Avernians rise up through the floor and sink back down again. The best time to try making contact is when they're at the top of the curve and the downward motion hasn't yet begun. What do you call it when a piston reaches the top of its stroke?'

'Top dead centre,' Snook supplied.

'That's when we've got to try to make the first contact with the Avernians

– when they're at top dead centre – and that's why there's no time to waste. Tomorrow morning, and for three mornings after that, top dead centre will occur at fairly convenient positions for us – after that it will take place in the air, higher and higher above the mine.'

'Four chances,' Quig said. 'Being strictly realistic about it, Boyce, what can you hope to achieve even if you strike lucky the very first time? Four brief meetings would hardly give the Avernians time to react.'

'Oh, we wouldn't be limited to four meetings,' Ambrose said airily.

'But you just said …'

'I said I was hoping for first contact while top dead centre is in a convenient location, that is, either below ground or on it. After that, when top dead centre is in the air above the mine, we would be able to have quite long meetings.'

'For God's sake, how?'

'Think it out for yourself, Des. If you wanted to rise slowly into the air, hover for a while and sink vertically downwards again – what sort of machine would you use?'

Quig's eyes widened. 'A helicopter.'

'Exactly! I provisionally chartered one today.' Ambrose beamed at his audience, like a fond parent surprising his children with an extravagant gift. 'Now that we've got that out of the way, let's discuss the immediate problems for a while.'

Listening to the conversation, Snook once again began to revise his opinions of Boyce Ambrose. The category he had invented for him, playboy scientist, still seemed appropriate – but Ambrose was playing in earnest, like a man who had a definite goal in mind and was determined that nothing would prevent him from reaching it.

Although all work had stopped at the mine, the perimeter fence was still floodlit and the security patrols were in operation. Snook felt vulnerable and self-conscious as he approached the gate, accompanied by George Murphy and the other four members of the group, under the interested stares of the mine guards. He was carrying six squares of heavy cardboard, placards which Ambrose had insisted on making, and they were proving strangely difficult to handle. The night breezes were slight, but even the gentlest puff of air was enough to make the smooth cards twist and slither in his grasp. He began to swear over Cartier's ruling that they could not bring a vehicle into the enclosure.

Murphy, who was well known to the guards, was nevertheless stopped by them and had to produce a letter signed by Cartier before the group were admitted. They straggled through the gate with the various boxes of equipment Ambrose had produced. Prudence remained close to Ambrose, talking quietly to him all the while. This fact produced a fretful resentment in Snook. He explained it to himself by reasoning that she was, if not actually a hindrance, certainly the least useful member of the group and it was therefore inordinate for her to occupy so much of the leader's time. Another level of his mind, one which was immune to deception, regarded this explanation with contempt.

'I see they've taken your advice – too late.' Murphy nudged Snook and pointed at new notices, in red lettering, which stated that all below-ground workers were required to hand in their Amplite glasses pending the installation of improved lighting systems in the mine.

'It helps cover up for the closure,' Snook said, his attention elsewhere. He had just noticed that two army jeeps were parked in the darkness beyond the gatehouse, each of them containing four men of the Leopard Regiment. As soon as the soldiers saw Prudence they began whooping and jeering. The two drivers switched on spotlights and directed them at Prudence's legs, and one soldier – to the cheers of his comrades – left his vehicle and ran up to her for a close inspection. She walked on calmly, looking straight ahead, holding on to Ambrose's arm. Ambrose, too, ignored the soldier.

Snook took his Amplites from his breast pocket, put them on and looked towards the jeeps. In the blue pseudo-radiance he saw that a lieutenant, the same one who had been at his house in the morning, was sitting in one of the vehicles with his arms folded, unperturbed by the behaviour of his men.

'What do these bastards think they're doing?' Murphy whispered fiercely, starting towards the nearby soldier.

Snook restrained him. 'It isn't our problem, George.'

'But that ape needs a kick where it'll do him the most damage.'

'Boyce brought her here,' Snook said stolidly. 'Boyce will have to look after her.'

'What's the matter with you, Gil?' Murphy stared at Snook, then gave a low chuckle. 'I get it. I thought I saw you doing a bit of quiet mooning in that direction, but I wasn't sure.'

'You saw nothing.'

Murphy remained quiet for a moment as the soldier grew tired of the game and re-joined his comrades. 'Was there nothing doing, Gil? Sometimes those aristocratic types go for a bit of rough – just for a change, you know.'

Snook kept his voice steady. 'What's discipline like in the Leopard Regiment? I thought they were kept on a pretty tight rein.'

'They are.' Murphy became thoughtful. 'Was there an officer watching the show?'

'Yes.'

'That doesn't have to mean anything.'

'I know what it doesn't have to mean.'

They reached the mine head and Snook felt his concern about the be-haviour of the soldiers abruptly vanish as it came to him that, in all proba-bility, he was due for another encounter with the silent, translucent beings who walked in the depths of the mine. It was all right for Ambrose, who had never seen the apparitions, to talk knowledgeably about geometries and planetary movements – facing the reality of the blue ghosts was another matter entirely. Snook discovered in himself an intense reluctance to go un-derground, but he concealed it as the group assembled at the continuous hoist and Murphy set the machinery going. The Avernians' mouths were what he dreaded seeing most, the inhumanly wide, inhumanly mobile slits which at times seemed to express a sadness beyond his comprehension. It occurred to Snook that Avernus might be an unhappy world, well named after a mythological hell.

'I'll go down first because I know the level we want,' Murphy announced. 'The hoist moves continuously so you'll have to step off smartly when you see me, but don't worry – it's as easy as using an escalator. If you don't get out in time, stay on until you reach the gallery below, get off there, walk round to the ascending side and come up again. We haven't lost a visitor yet.'

The others laughed appreciatively, their spirits recovering from the un-easiness which had been inspired by the near-incident at the gate. They stepped into descending cages two by two, Snook going last with his awk-ward bundle of cards. His ears popped during the patient, rumbling descent. When he reached the circular landing at Level Three he found Ambrose already holding court, assigning people to the various radial tunnels. The radiation generator, which was the size of a small suitcase, was to be left at the hoist and carried to anyone who shouted that he had found an Avernian building.

'I want everybody to take one of the cards that Gil is holding,' Ambrose said. 'I know they're a bit of a long shot, but we're playing so many long shots that one more won't make any difference.' He took one of the placards and held it up. The design, heavily drawn in black, consisted of three elements – a close-pitched sine wave, and an arrow which pointed from it to another sine wave of much wider pitch.

'This banner with the strange device symbolises the conversion of light to sound.' He looked at Quig and Culver. 'I think its meaning is quite clear, don't you?'

Quig nodded doubtfully. 'Provided the Avernians have eyes and provided they know something about acoustics and provided they have developed a wave theory of light and provided they use electronics and provided ...'

'Don't go on, Des – I've already admitted that the chances aren't good. But there's so much at stake that I'm prepared to try anything.'

'Okay. I don't mind carrying a card,' Quig said, 'but I'm mainly interested in getting photographs. I think that's the most we can hope for.' He tapped the camera which was slung round his neck.

'That's all right – I appreciate any help I can get at this stage.' Ambrose glanced at his watch. 'There's only about a quarter of an hour to go – the Avernians must already be in the lower levels of the mine – so let's take up our stations. Sound carries well in these tunnels, but the acoustics aren't good, so don't go more than about a hundred metres from the central shaft. Keep wearing your Amplites, turn off all flashlights ten minutes from now, and don't forget to holler at the top of your voice if you find what we're looking for.'

There was another general laugh which filled Snook with a perverse malice – he wondered how many of the group would still be amused when, and if, the Avernians kept their appointment. He started for the south pipe, then noticed that Prudence was walking beside him on her way to an adjoining branch. She was carrying a card and a flashlight, but her slim figure and salon clothing were incongruous against the backdrop of rock surfaces and mine machinery. Snook felt an unwanted pang of concern.

'Are you going in there alone?' he said.

'Don't you think I should?' Her face was inscrutable behind the blue lenses of her Amplites.

'Frankly, no.'

The curvature of her lips altered. 'I didn't see you showing much concern for my safety when your friends were having their bit of fun at the gate.'

'*My* friends!' Snook was so taken aback by the unfairness of the remark that he was unable to frame a sentence before Prudence was flitting away along the tunnel. He stared after her, lips moving silently, then went on his separate way, swearing inwardly at his own foolishness for having spoken.

The deposits of diamond-bearing clay had been wide and deep here, and its removal had left the semblance of a natural underground cavern. Parasonic projectors turned rock and clay into dust, without affecting the harder material of diamonds, and they had another advantage in that they did not split or strain the rock structures, which meant that little shoring was required. Snook followed the curvature of the spacious tunnel until he estimated he had gone a hundred metres, then he stopped and lit a cigarette. A very small amount of illumination reached this far from the fluorescent tubes in the main shaft, but his Amplites transformed it into a visible wall of light which he felt might be strong enough to screen out any ghosts which appeared. Accordingly, he turned his back to the light and stood facing the darkest part of the tunnel. Even then, the glow of his cigarette was almost unbearably bright when seen through the magniluct glasses. Snook ground the cigarette out under his foot and stood perfectly still, waiting.

A few minutes went by, like so many hours, then – without warning – a large glowing bird emerged at speed from the wall beside his head, flashed silently across his field of view, and disappeared into the sculpted rock at the far side of the tunnel. Its image had been faint, but he had the impression that he had still been able to see it for a second after it entered the wall, as though the stone itself was becoming lacy and insubstantial.

Snatching for breath, he turned and looked back towards the main shaft. The wall of bluish light was there as before, but now it had several darker rectangles in it. Snook frowned, wondering why he had not noticed the angular patches before, then came the realisation that he was looking at the outline of windows.

'This way!' he shouted, sick with apprehension, yet unable to prevent himself running forward. 'South tunnel! There's something in the south tunnel!'

He headed straight for one of the dim rectangles, hesitated briefly, and plunged through the vertical barrier of radiance. An Avernian was standing before him, cradling an indistinct object in its arms, the complex folds of its robes fluttering slightly in a breeze which did not exist on Earth. Its eyes rotated slowly near the top of the tufted head, and the wide mouth was partially open.

'Hurry up,' Snook bellowed. 'I'm in a room with one of them!'

'Hold on, Gil,' came a reassuring, echoing reply from the distance.

The voice contact with another human being eased the churning in Snook's mind. He made a conscious effort to be observant, and saw that the Avernian seemed taller than the others. He glanced down at its feet and discovered that the horizontal plane of milky blue radiance which was the Avernian's floor was on a level with his own knees. As he watched, the level crept slowly up his thighs. At the rate of movement the ghostly floor would soon be above Snook's head. He looked around the room and picked out shapes that were recognisably furniture, a table and chairs of curious proportions. The Avernian swayed slightly, in a nameless dance, unaware that its privacy was being violated by a watcher from another universe.

'Hurry up, for Christ's sake,' Snook shouted. 'Where are you, Boyce?'

'Right here.' The voice came from close at hand, and Snook saw human figures moving. 'The machine was heavier than I thought. Stand still – I'm going to try to light you up for him. There! Now hold the card above your head and move it around.'

Snook had forgotten about his placard. The pool of faint luminance had reached his chest, but its rate of climb had decreased. He raised the card above his head, then moved to the side so that he was facing the alien figure.

His eyes looked into the Avernian's. The Avernian's eyes looked into his. And nothing happened.

I'm not real, Snook thought. *I don't exist.*

'This isn't working,' he called out to Ambrose. 'There's no reaction.'

'Don't give up – I'm increasing the field intensity.'

'Okay.' There was a clicking of cameras in the background.

Snook noticed that the floor level of the other room was beginning to sink down his body again, then it dawned on him that the Avernian had not moved for several seconds, that its eyes were still fixed on him. The wide slash of its mouth writhed.

'I think something might be happening,' Snook said.

'Could be.' Ambrose had moved until he was standing beside Snook in the extra-dimensional room.

The alien turned abruptly, the first rapid action Snook had seen any of its kind perform, and strode across the floor. It appeared to sit at the table and there were movements of the oddly jointed arms. The translucent floor level continued to fall until it had merged with the rock floor of the tunnel, then the Avernian's webbed feet began to sink into it.

'There isn't much time left,' Ambrose said. 'I think we were wrong to expect a reaction.'

Quig joined them, camera held to his eye. 'I'm getting as much as I can on film anyway.'

At that moment the Avernian stood up in a slow-flowing movement and turned to face them. Its arms were extended from the pleated robes and in its hands was a faintly visible square of thin material. Due to the translucency of the alien and everything about it, Snook had trouble in discerning that there were marks on the square sheet. He narrowed his eyes and picked out an almost invisible design: tightly-waved lines; an arrow; loosely-waved lines.

'That's our message,' Ambrose breathed. 'We got through to him. And so *fast!*'

'There's something else there,' Snook said. Further down on the faint square was another diagram – two slightly irregular circles almost fully superimposed.

'It's astronomical.' Ambrose was hoarse with excitement. 'They know what's happening!'

Snook kept staring at the second diagram, and deep in his guts there heaved the iciness of premonition. The symbols of the upper diagram were flawlessly drawn – the sine waves exactly regular, the lines of the arrow dead straight, which suggested the Avernian was a good draughtsman. And yet the two overlapping circles of the lower diagram – which Ambrose supposed to represent two well-nigh perfect spheres – had definite irregularities. They also had several internal markings ...

The Avernian was now sinking, with its world, below the rock floor of the tunnel.

It came towards Snook, apparently wading knee-deep in stone, and reached upwards with webbed translucent hands, the long trembling fingers circling to enclose Snook's head.

'No!' Snook backed off from the yearning hands, unable to prevent himself from shouting. 'I'm not doing it. Never!'

He turned and ran towards the main shaft.

CHAPTER EIGHT

'Gil, I don't see why you refuse to accept this thing,' Boyce Ambrose said impatiently.

He threw the sheaf of photographs down on the table. 'When we were driving out here – only hours after having met you – I suggested you were telepathic. That sort of thing is an established and respectable scientific phenomenon these days. Why won't you admit it?'

'Why do you want me to admit it?' Snook spoke in a sleepy voice, nursing his drink.

'I mean the fact that you understood the Avernian diagram, when I thought it was astronomical, *shows* that you have a telepathic faculty.'

'You still haven't said why you're so keen for me to claim this power,' Snook persisted.

'Because ...'

'Go on, Boyce.'

'I would do it,' Ambrose said, a hint of bitterness in his voice. 'I would do it if I had been chosen.'

Snook swirled the gin in his glass, creating a miniature vortex. 'That's because you've got the scientific spirit, Boyce. You're one of those people who would fly a kite in a thunderstorm, regardless of the danger, but I'm not going to let any blue monster shove its head inside mine.'

'The Avernians are people.' Prudence eyed Snook with disdain.

Snook shrugged. 'All right – I'm not going to let any blue people shove their heads inside mine.'

'The idea doesn't bother me.'

'That remark just cries out for an obscene reply, but I'm too tired.' Snook settled further down in the armchair and closed his eyes, but he had time to see Prudence tighten her lips in anger. *I owed you that one,* he thought, pleased at having scored a point, yet appalled at his own childishness.

'Too drunk, you mean.'

Without opening his eyes, Snook raised his glass in Prudence's direction and took another drink. He found he could still see the translucent blue face advancing on his own, and a hard knot formed in his stomach.

'I think,' Ambrose said anxiously, 'it might be a good idea if we all got some rest. We've been up all night and we're bound to be tired.'

'I've got to get back to the plant,' Culver said. He turned to Des Quig, who was still examining the pictures he had taken. 'How about you, Des? Want a ride back?'

'I'm not going back,' Quig replied, absently stroking his sandy moustache. 'This is too much fun.'

'How about your job?' Ambrose asked. 'I appreciate your help here, but ...'

'They can shove my job. Do you know what they've got me doing? Designing radios, that's what I'm doing.' He had been drinking neat gin, while exhausted and hungry, and his voice was beginning to slur. 'That would be bad enough, but I design them a *good* radio and they hand it over to the commercial people. You know what happens then? The commercial people start taking bits out of it ... and they keep doing that till the radio stops working ... then they put the last bit back in again – and *that's* the radio they put into production. It makes me sick. No, I'm not going back there. I'm damned if I'll ...'

Recognising a cry from the heart, Snook opened his eyes and saw Quig lay his head on his arms and promptly fall asleep.

'I'll go then,' Culver said. 'See you tonight.' He left Snook's living room and George Murphy went at the same time, saluting tiredly with his bandaged hand.

Snook got to his feet, waving the two men goodbye, and turned to Ambrose. 'What do you want to do?'

Ambrose hesitated. 'I've had about four hours' sleep in the last three days. I hate to impose, but the thought of driving back to Kisumu ...'

'You're welcome to stay here,' Snook said. 'I've got two bedrooms, with one bed in each. Des seems very comfortable at the table, so if I sleep on the couch in here, you and Prudence can have a bedroom each.'

Prudence stood up also. 'I wouldn't dream of keeping you out of your own bed. I'll go in with Boyce – I'm sure I won't come to much harm.'

Ambrose grinned and rubbed his eyes. 'The tragedy is that, the way I feel now, you probably won't come to *any* harm.' He put an arm around

Prudence's shoulders and they walked into the bedroom which was directly across the corridor from the living room. Prudence reappeared in the opening as she closed the door and, in the narrowing aperture, her eyes steadied on Snook's for the briefest instant. He tried to smile, but his lips refused to conform.

Snook went into the other bedroom. The early morning sun was blazing in from the east, so he closed the blind, creating a parchment-coloured dimness. He lay down on the bed without undressing, but the tiredness which had been so insistent a few minutes earlier seemed to have fled his system, and it was a long time before he was able to escape from his loneliness into sleep.

Snook was awakened in the late afternoon by the sound of a loud, unfamiliar voice filtering through from his living room. He got up, ran his fingers through his hair and went to see who the visitor was. He found Gene Helig, the Press Association representative, standing in the centre of the room and talking to Ambrose, Prudence and Quig. Helig, who was a lean, greying Englishman with drooping eyelids, gave Snook a critical glance.

'You look bloody awful, Gil,' he said heartily. 'I've never seen you look so bad.'

'Thanks.' Snook sought a parry to Helig's remarks but the pounding in his head made it difficult to think. 'I'm going to make some coffee.'

Des Quig sprang to his feet. 'I've already done it, Gil. Sit down here and I'll fetch you a cup.'

Snook nodded gratefully. 'Four cups, please. I always have four cups.' He dropped into the chair Quig had vacated and looked around the room. Ambrose was regarding him with concerned eyes; Prudence appeared not to have noticed his arrival. Though wearing the same clothes as on the previous day, she was as cream-smooth and immaculate as ever. Snook wondered if, at any time during their hours in bed, Ambrose had succeeded in disturbing that practised serenity.

'You've set the cat among the pigeons this time,' Helig boomed. 'Do you know a couple of Freeborn's men have been following me around since I filed that story of yours?'

'Please, Gene.' Snook pressed his temples. 'If you'll speak in normal conversational tones I'll hear you all right.'

Helig switched to a penetrating whisper. 'That convinced me there was something important in it. I wasn't too sure, you know, and I'm afraid it showed through in the way I wrote the piece.'

'Thanks, anyway.'

'That's all right.' Helig switched to his usual stentorian voice. 'It's all different now, of course, what with your ghosts having popped up in Brazil and Sumatra as well.'

'What?' Snook glanced at Ambrose for confirmation.

Ambrose nodded. 'I said this would happen. It was perhaps a little sooner than I expected, but it doesn't do to regard the Earth's equator as a perfect circle. The whole planet is deformed slightly by tidal forces and, of course, the Earth wobbles in its orbit as it swings around the Earth-Moon bary-centre. I don't know how closely Avernus follows that movement, and there could be all kinds of libration effects which ...' Ambrose stopped speaking as Prudence leaned across to him and pressed a hand to his mouth. The little public intimacy caused Snook to look quickly in another direction, racked with jealousy.

'Sorry,' Ambrose concluded. 'I tend to get carried away.'

'There's a hell of a lot of world interest now,' Helig said. 'I heard Doctor Ambrose's name mentioned a couple of times this morning on the main satellite networks.'

Prudence laughed delightedly, and gave Ambrose a playful push. 'Fame at last!'

Snook, still intensely aware of Prudence and everything in her ambit, saw an unreadable expression flicker across Ambrose's face, perhaps a mixture of wistfulness and triumph. It was gone on the instant, to be replaced by Ambrose's customary look of humorous alertness, but Snook felt he had gained an insight into the other man's character. The playboy scientist, it seemed, was hungry for fame. Or respect. The respect of his professional peers.

'Does that mean a lot more people will be coming here?' Quig said, arriving with Snook's coffee.

'I doubt it.' Helig spoke with the bored concern of a colonial who has watched the antics of the natives for too many years. 'The President's office has cancelled all new visas for an indefinite period because of this spot of bother with Kenya. Besides, all the scientist johnnies have other places to go now. A hell of a sight easier to pop down to Brazil from the States than to come here, eh? Less chance of getting a *panga* up your backside, too.' Helig gave a thunderous laugh which reverberated in the cup from which Snook was drinking. Snook closed his eyes, concentrated on the aromatic taste of sanity, and wished Helig would leave.

'How are you getting on here, anyway?' Helig continued, planted solidly in the centre of the room. 'If these ghosts really are inhabitants of another world, do you think we'll ever find a way to talk to them?'

Ambrose spoke cautiously. 'We were hoping we might have had a lead in that direction, but naturally it's a tricky problem.'

Snook looked over the rim of his cup and his eyes met those of Ambrose and Prudence.

Helig peered at the settings of his wrist recorder. 'Come on, Doctor – confession is good for the soul.'

'It's too soon,' Snook said, reaching a decision he was unable to explain to himself. 'Come back tomorrow or the day after, and we might have a good story for you.'

When Helig had gone, Ambrose followed Snook out to the kitchen where he was brewing more coffee.

'Did you mean what I thought you meant?' Ambrose said quietly.

'I guess so.' Snook busied himself with the rinsing out of cups in the sink.

'I'm grateful.' Ambrose picked up a cloth and began drying cups in an inexpert manner. 'Look, I don't want you to take this the wrong way, but scientific workers get paid like any other workers. Now, I know you had reasons of your own for getting involved in this thing, but I'd be happy to get it on to a proper business footing if you ...'

'There's one thing you could do for me,' Snook interrupted.

'Name it.'

'Somewhere in Malaq there's a Canadian passport belonging to me – and I'd like to have it back.'

'I think I can arrange that.'

'It could cost you quite a bit in what they call commission.'

'Don't worry about it. We'll get you out of Barandi somehow.' Ambrose, having dried two cups, apparently felt he had contributed enough in that direction and set his cloth aside. 'Actually, tomorrow morning's experiment will be nothing like the last one.'

'Why's that?'

'I've been looking at the plans and the vertical section through the mine – and where tomorrow's top dead centre occurs there hasn't been any excavation. We'll have to intercept the Avernian coming through exactly the same spot as last time. He'll be ascending fairly quickly at that stage but, if you feel like it, there'll be another chance when he's on the way down again.'

Snook began drying the remaining cups. 'We're assuming he'll be there, waiting for us ...'

'It's the smallest assumption we've made yet. That character was *fast* – no human could have responded so quickly and in such a positive manner. It's my guess that we're dealing with a race which is superior to our own in many ways.'

'That wouldn't surprise me, but do you really believe I'll get some kind of telepathic message when our brains are occupying the same space?'

Ambrose raised his shoulders. 'There's just no way to predict what will happen, Gil. The most probable result, according to our science – orthodox science, that is – is that nothing at all will happen. After all, your brain has occupied the same space as Avernian rock and you didn't get a headache.'

'You chose an unfortunate example.' Snook pressed two fingertips delicately against a throbbing vein in his temple, as if taking his pulse.

'Why do you drink so much?'

'It helps me to sleep.'

'You'd be better with a woman,' Ambrose said. 'Same result, but the side-effects are all good.'

Snook drove a painful vision from his mind, a vision of Prudence cradled in his left arm, her face turned to his. 'We were talking about the telepathy experiment – you think nothing will happen?'

'I didn't say that. The trouble is we know so little about the subject. I mean, telepathy between human beings wasn't proved until a few years ago when they finally got round to throwing out those stupid card-guessing routines. A lot of people would say the brain structure, thought processes and language structure of an extra-terrestrial race are bound to be so incompatible with ours that no communication at all could take place, telepathically or any other way.'

'But the Avernians aren't extra-terrestrial – they're just the opposite.' Snook wrought with unfamiliar concepts. 'If they've existed a few hundred kilometres under our feet for millions of years, and if telepathy really exists, the link might be already established. There might be something like resonance … you know, sympathetic resonance … the Avernians might be responsible for …'

'Common elements in religions? Plutonic mythologies? The universal idea that hell is under the ground?' Ambrose shook his head. 'You're going way beyond the scope of the investigation, Gill, and I wouldn't recommend it. Don't forget that, even though the Avernians do exist inside the Earth, in many respects they're further away from us than Sirius. The most distant star you can see in the sky is at least part of our own universe.'

'But you still think the experiment is worth trying?'

Ambrose nodded. 'It's got one thing going for it that I can't ignore.'

'What's that?' Snook paused in his chores to concentrate on Ambrose's answer.

'The Avernian himself seemed to think it would work.'

When the party set out for the mine in pre-dawn blackness, Snook noticed that Prudence had remained behind in his bungalow, and it intrigued him that neither she nor Ambrose had made reference to this fact. They had driven into Kisumu in the afternoon for a meal and a change of clothing at their hotel, and had returned looking like newly-weds. Since then there had been lots of time for discussion of the various arrangements, and yet Prudence's non-participation had not been mentioned, in Snook's presence anyway. It could have been a common sense decision to avoid possible trouble with the soldiers at the gate, but Snook suspected she had no wish to take part in an event where he was to be the central figure, especially as she had been openly scornful of his running away the previous time. Snook knew he was being reduced to childishness again, but he was perversely pleased at what was happening because it showed she had singled him out, that there was a continuing personal reaction – even if a negative one.

The four men – Snook, Ambrose, Quig and Culver – were met at the enclosure gate by George Murphy, who was already talking to the guards. Murphy came forward to meet the group.

'I don't want any more days like yesterday,' he said. 'I'm just about wrecked.'

'You look okay to me.' Snook had never seen Murphy look more assured and indomitable, and he drew comfort from the big man's presence. 'What's been happening to you?'

'Been sitting in on arguments. Carrier keeps telling the workface crews that the ghosts don't exist because they can't see them any more, and that they weren't ghosts anyway. The miners keep telling him they know a ghost when they see one, and even when they can't see them they can feel them. I think Colonel Freeborn is turning up the pressure on Cartier.'

Snook fell into step close beside Murphy as they were passing through the gate and spoke to him quietly. 'I think he's turning up the pressure on everybody. You know, this thing isn't working out the way we hoped it would.'

'I know that, Gil. But thanks for doing what you're doing.'

'Isn't there any way you could convince the miners that the Avernians can't do them any harm?'

Murphy remained silent for a moment. 'You're convinced, but ...'

'But I ran. Point taken, George.'

As they reached the dimness beyond the gatehouse Snook saw two fully-manned jeeps parked in the same place as before. He put on his Amplites, creating for himself a bluish radiance in which he was able to identify the same haughty young lieutenant he had already encountered. The lieutenant's eyes were hidden by his Amplites, standard issue for soldiers on night duties, but his sculpted ebony face gave an impression of fierce watchfulness. It was a look which caused the old stirrings far back in Snook's mind.

'The lieutenant over there,' he said. 'Is he related to the Colonel?'

Murphy slipped his own magniluct glasses on. 'Nephew. That's Curt Freeborn. Stay out of his way. If possible, never even speak to him.'

'Oh, Christ,' Snook sighed, 'not another one.'

At the same moment the jeeps' engines roared into life and the spotlight beams lanced through the group of walkers, streaming them with long shadows. The two vehicles rolled forward and began slowly circling the group, sometimes coming so close that one or more of the men had to give way. With the exception of the young lieutenant, the soldiers in the jeeps grinned hugely throughout the manoeuvres. None of them made any sound.

'Those are open vehicles,' Murphy said. 'You and I could easily yank the drivers out.'

'You and I could easily get shot. It isn't worth it, George.' Snook kept walking steadily towards the mine head and eventually the jeeps pulled back to their former positions. The group reached the sodium-lit hoist shed and Ambrose set his radiation generator down with a thud.

'First thing in the morning,' he said indignantly, 'I'm going to report that harassment to the authorities. I'm running out of patience with those bastards.'

'Let's get underground,' Snook said, exchanging glances with Murphy, 'to the devil we don't know.'

'And I told you that's the wrong sort of thinking.' Ambrose picked up his black box and led the way to the hoist.

The cavern-like tunnel of Level Three did not unnerve Snook as much as he had expected, mainly because he felt himself part of a group which was acting in concert. Ambrose stalked about purposefully, examining luminous crayon marks he had made on the rock floor, setting up his machine, and flicking his fingers over a pocket computer. Culver occupied himself with the pulse code modulator, and Quig with cameras and magniluct filters, while Murphy pottered about clearing small pieces of debris away from the scene of expected action. Snook began to feel unnecessary, helpless.

'About ten minutes to go,' Ambrose said to Snook, looking up from his computer. 'Now remember, Gill, you're not being pressurised in any way. This is actually just an auxiliary experiment – I'm pinning my faith on the pulse code modulator – so just take it as far as you feel you are able. Okay?'

'Okay.'

'Right. Keep on the look-out for some sort of roof structure coming up into view. From what you told us, you missed that yesterday, and it will give a good advance warning.' Ambrose raised his voice, beginning to sound happy again. 'If you have time, make sketches on the pads I gave you. The design of a roof will also tell us things about the Avernians themselves – say, whether they have rain or not – so everybody keep their eyes open for details.'

Leaning against the tunnel wall and watching the final preparations, Snook took out his cigarettes only to have Ambrose give a warning shake of his head. He put the pack away resignedly, wishing he was in another part of the world, doing something else. For instance, lying in a peaceful room, in parchment-coloured shade, with Prudence Devonald's head cradled in his arm, the left arm – as decreed in the Song of Solomon, Chapters Two and Eight, so that his right hand would be free to touch ...

A luminous blue line began to appear on the rock floor of the tunnel.

Within seconds it had risen to become a triangular ridge and Snook, chilled to the core, moved to his designated place. The floor was strangely transparent.

He was so intent on the materialisation that he scarcely noticed George Murphy at his side. Murphy's large dry hand sought his and slid into it a tiny whitish object which felt as though it was made of polished ivory.

'Take this,' Murphy whispered. 'It might help.'

Snook was baffled, mind-numbed. 'What is it? An amulet?'

'I'm not a bloody savage.' Murphy's voice was amiably aggrieved. 'It's chewing-gum!'

He retreated to the sidelines as a faintly glowing roof structure gradually emerged from the solid rock, looking surprisingly Earth-like in its arrangement of rafters and ties. Snook put the gum into his mouth and was grateful for its commonplace minty warmth as he found himself sinking into a vaguely seen square room where three Avernians waited for him, slit mouths curving and contorting. Two of the translucent beings carried oblong machines, and suddenly there were noises – sad, mewling, alien noises – coming from the direction of the corresponding machine held by Culver. A human voice sounded too, but Snook was unable to identify the speaker, nor to comprehend the words, because the third Avernian was coming towards him with its arms outstretched.

I can't take this, Snook thought in pure panic. *It's too much.*

The taste of the chicle grew strong in his mouth, a reminder that he was not alone in his ordeal, and – as the floor levels merged – he obediently stepped towards the Avernian.

The insubstantial face drew near his own, the mist-pools of the eyes growing larger. Snook inclined his head forward, yielding himself. There was a merging.

Snook grunted with surprise as his identity was ... lost.

Deep peace of the running wave.

I am Felleth. My function in society is that of Responder – which means that I give advice to others, tell them what to do or what should be done next. No, your concept of the oracle is incorrect, my function reversed. An oracle would give forewarning of events, and leave its audience to devise their own – perhaps incorrect – responses. As the concept of prediction is invalid when one goes beyond the causality of the growing seed reaching maturation or the falling stone reaching the ground, it is necessary only to appreciate the significance of what has already occurred and to give infallible advice on how to react ...

Oracle. Logic arrow pointing to related concept. The stars foretell. True as the stars above. Astra. Dis-astra.

Disaster!

Wait, wait, wait! I am in pain.

The stars in their courses. Planets? Plural? Cyclic? What is a year?

No! Your concept of time is incorrect. Time is a straight thread, tightly drawn between the Past Infinity and the Future Infinity, light and dark strands – night and day – appearing to alternate, but each is continuous. Continuous, but twisted …

Wait! The pain increases.

Sun, the provider of day. Planets, ellipses, axial spin. No cloud-roof. Clear skies, many suns. Logic arrow pointing to related concept. Particles, anti-particles. Correct – our relationship almost precisely defined – but there is something else. Anti-particle planet, seen beyond the cloud-roof. In the year 1993 …

Confusion concepts. It is not possible to measure time in any way other than minus-now or plus-now. And yet …

One thousand days ago the weight of our oceans decreased. The waters rose into the sky, until they touched the cloud-roof. Then they swept away the People. And the houses of the People …

You say I should have known. That I should have been able to predict.

You say …

NO!

The minty warmth on Snook's tongue became real again. He found himself kneeling on hard rock, in the midst of anxious faces, his body being steadied by several hands. His Amplites were gone and somebody had switched on a portable light, bringing the tool-marked contours of the tunnel walls into sharp relief and at the same time making them seem stagey and unreal.

'Are you all right, Gil?' Murphy's voice was noncommittal, an indication that he was really concerned.

Snook nodded and got to his feet. 'How long was I out?'

'You weren't out,' Ambrose said, sternly professorial. 'You fell down on your knees. That was when George switched on the light – against my instructions, I might add – and brought the experiment to a premature end by almost blinding us.' He turned to Murphy. 'You know, George, the instructions with magniluct glasses clearly warn you against switching on a bright light where people are wearing them.'

Murphy was unrepentant. 'I thought Gil was hurt.'

'How could he have been hurt?' Ambrose became business-like once more. 'Oh, well – there's no point in holding a post mortem. We can only hope the few seconds of recordings we did get are worth …'

'Just a minute,' Snook put in, floundering, still trying to orient himself in what should have been the familiar universe. 'How about Felleth? Did you see how he reacted?'

'Who's Felleth?'

'The Avernian. Felleth. Didn't you ...?'

'What are you talking about?' Ambrose's fingers clawed into Snook's shoulders. 'What are you saying?'

'I'm trying to find out how long the Avernian's head was ... you know ... inside mine.'

'Hardly any time at all,' Culver said, knuckling his eyes. 'I thought I saw him jumping back from you, then George nearly burned my retinas out with his ...'

'*Quiet!*' Ambrose's voice was almost frantic. 'Did it work, Gil? Did you get an impression of the Avernian's name?'

'An impression?' Snook smiled tiredly. 'More than that. I was part of his life for a while. That's why I wanted to know how long the contact had been – it seemed like minutes. Perhaps hours.'

'What can you remember?'

'It isn't a good place, Boyce. Something went wrong. It's funny, but before we came down here this time I got a kind of idea ...'

'Gil, I'm going to give you a de-briefing right now and get it on tape while it's still fresh in your memory. Do you feel up to it? Are there any ill effects?'

'I'm a bit shagged out, but it's all right.'

'Good.' Ambrose held his wrist recorder close to Snook's mouth. 'You've already said his name was Felleth – did you get a name for their planet?'

'No. They don't seem to have given it a name. It's the only world they know about, so maybe it doesn't need a name. Anyway, the contact wasn't like that – we didn't have a conversation.' Snook began to feel doubts about his ability to give a proper description of the experience, and at the same time something of its enormousness began to dawn on him. An inhabitant of another universe, a ghost, had touched his mind. Lives had mingled ...

'All right – try going back to the beginning. What is the first thing you remember?'

Snook closed his eyes and said, 'Deep peace of the running wave.'

'Was that a greeting?'

'I think so – but it seemed more important to him. Their world seems to be mostly water. The wind could take a wave right ... Oh, I don't know.'

'Okay. Skip the greeting – what came next?'

'Felleth calls himself a Responder. That's something like a leader, but he doesn't think of himself as leading. Then there was a kind of argument about oracles and predictions, with him doing all the arguing. He said prediction was impossible.'

'An argument? I thought you said you didn't have a conversation.'

'We didn't – but he must have had access to my ideas.'

'This is important, Gil,' Ambrose said briskly. 'Do you think he got as much information from you as you got from him?'

'I can't say. It must have been a two-way process, but how could I tell who got the most?'

'Did you get any sense of being pressurised into talking?'

'No. In fact, he seemed to be hurting. There was something about pain.'

'Okay. Keep going, Gil.'

'He was shocked to learn about stars. They don't seem to have any astronomy. There's a permanent cloud cover – Felleth has it mixed up in his mind with the idea of a roof. He didn't know the relationship between planets and suns.'

'Are you certain? Surely they could have devised an astronomy.'

'How?' Snook felt oddly defensive.

'It wouldn't be too easy, I know, but there are lots of clues. The cycles of day and night, seasons ...'

'They don't think that way. Felleth didn't know that his world rotates. He thinks of night and day as being like black and white marks on a straight thread. They don't have seasons. They don't have years. For them, time ... everything else ... is linear. They don't have dates or calendars, as we know them. They count time forwards and backwards from the present.'

'The system would be too cumbersome,' Ambrose stated. 'You need fixed points of reference.'

'How the hell would you know?' Snook, still shaken, was unable to curb his annoyance at the other man's presumption. 'How would you know what way they think? Do you even know how other human beings think?'

'I'm sorry, Gil, but don't get side-tracked – what else can you remember?' Ambrose was unperturbed.

'Well, about the only thing that didn't surprise him was the explanation of the two universes I picked up from you. He said, "Particles. Anti-particles. Correct. Our relationship almost precisely defined".'

'This is interesting – nuclear physics, but no astronomy. And he qualified the thing a little? He said it was *almost* precisely defined?'

'Yes. Then there was something about time. And Thornton's Planet came into it ...' Snook's voice faltered.

'What's wrong?'

'I've just remembered ... this is where he seemed to get really worked up ... he said that something had happened a thousand days ago. I remember the figure because of the way it came through. I get the feeling he didn't mean exactly a thousand days – it was like the way we talk about something happening a year ago when we mean eleven or twelve or thirteen months.'

'What happened, Gil? Did he mention tides?'

'You knew!' Through his confusion, Snook was yet again aware of having to revise his opinions about Ambrose.

'Tell me what was said.' Ambrose had become gentle and persuasive, yet demanding.

'One thousand days ago the weight of our oceans decreased. The waters rose into the sky, until they touched the cloud-roof. Then they swept away the People. And the houses of the People.'

'This confirms all of my claims,' Ambrose said peacefully. 'I'll be known. From now on, I'll be known.'

'Who's talking about you?' Snook was baffled and angry as strange fears began to stir within him. 'What happened on Avernus?'

'It's quite straightforward. Thornton's Planet is of like material to Avernus, and therefore was able to drag it out of its orbit. The tidal effects would have been severe, of course, and we've already learned that Avernus is a watery world ...'

Snook pressed his hands to his temples. 'Most of them were drowned.'

'Naturally.'

'But they're real *people*! You don't seem to care.'

'It isn't that I don't care, Gil,' Ambrose said in a neutral voice. 'It's just that there's nothing we can do about it. There's nothing anybody can do to help them.'

Something in the way Ambrose spoke intensified the turmoil in Snook's mind. He lurched forward and grabbed the material of Ambrose's jacket. 'There's more, isn't there?'

'You're under a strain, Gil.' Ambrose did not move or try to break Snook's grip. 'Perhaps this isn't a good time to discuss it.'

'I want to discuss it. Now.'

'All right – we hadn't completed the de-briefing anyway. What happened after the Avernian learned about Thornton's Planet?'

'I don't ... There was something about predictions, I think. The last thing I remember is Felleth screaming, "No". Screaming isn't the right word – there wasn't any sound – but he seemed to be in pain.'

'This is fascinating,' Ambrose said. 'The adaptability and speed of your friend Felleth's brain is ... well, there's no other word for it ... super-human. And there's the efficiency of his telepathic communication. We've opened whole new fields of study.'

'Why did Felleth scream?'

Ambrose gently disengaged himself from Snook's grip. 'I'm trying to tell you, Gil. I'm only guessing, but it's a question of how much he was able to pull out of your mind. You're not interested in astronomy, are you?'

'No.'

'But you remember something of what you heard or read about Thornton's Planet being captured by our sun? And about the orbit it took up?'

'I don't know.' Snook tried to calm his mind. 'There was something about a precessing orbit … and about the planet coming back. In ninety-eight years, wasn't it?'

'Go on. It's important for us to find out if you really do know, at a conscious level, what's going to happen.'

Snook thought for a moment, the neural connections were made, and a great sadness descended over him. 'The next time Thornton's Planet comes,' he said in a dull voice, 'they reckon it will pass through the Earth.'

'That's correct, Gil. You did have the knowledge.'

'But Avernus should be separated from the Earth by that time.'

'By a short distance, and that's only if it keeps on separating at its present rate. In any case, it won't make any difference – the miss distance will be so small that the catastrophe will be just as complete as if there was a head-on collision.' Ambrose glanced around the silent, watchful group. 'The Earth won't be affected, of course.'

'Do you think Felleth got all that?' Snook was unable to escape from the lethal fugue which was resounding inside his head. 'Do you think that was why he screamed?'

'I'd say that's what happened,' Ambrose said, his gaze steady on Snook's face. 'You told the Avernian that his world, and everybody on it, will be destroyed in less than a century from now.'

CHAPTER NINE

As before, emerging from below ground into the pure pastel light of a new day had the effect of easing the pressure on Snook's mind, enabling him to put a distance between himself and the Avernians.

He filled his lungs with sun-seeded air and felt his body recover from the curious loss of muscle tone, post-coital in its essence, which had followed his encounter with the alien being. The world, his world, looked hearteningly secure and unchangeable, and it was almost possible to dismiss the notion that – within a matter of hours – another world would begin emerging into the light.

It was wrong, he told himself, to think of Avernus and its people breaking through into the light – because, for them, Earth's yellow sun would not exist. On Avernus there would continue to be the same low cloud-roof, so thick that day brought only a general lessening of the overhead darkness. It was a watery, misty world – a blind world – with its steep-roofed dwellings of russet stone clinging like molluscs to the chain of equatorial islands …

The Turner-like vision appeared in Snook's consciousness with such clarity that he knew, on the instant, it had come to him from Felleth. It was an after-image, a residue of the strange mind-to-mind communion which had briefly spanned two universes, two realities. He paused, wondering how much knowledge of Avernus had been implanted within him during the moment of supreme intimacy, and how much information he had yielded in return.

'All right, Gil?' Ambrose said, eyeing Snook with proprietary concern.

'I'm fine.' The desire to escape being used like a laboratory animal prompted Snook to remain quiet about his new discovery.

'You were looking slightly … ah … pensive.'

'I was wondering about the Avernian universe. You've proved there's an anti-neutrino sun inside our own sun – does that mean it's the same with the other stars in the galaxy?'

'There isn't enough evidence available to support even an educated guess. There's a thing called the Principle of Mediocrity which states that the local conditions in our Solar System must be regarded as being universal, and that – because there's an anti-neutrino sun congruent with Sol – the other stars in the galaxy are likely to have them as well. It's only a principle, though, and I've no idea what the average density of matter in the Avernian universe might be. For all we know, there might be only a handful of their suns scattered around our galaxy.'

'Barely enough to make a wreath.'

'A wreath?' Ambrose looked puzzled.

'The Avernians are going to die, aren't they?'

Ambrose lowered his voice in warning. 'Don't get personally involved, Gil – it's asking for trouble.'

The irony of hearing his own life-long creed from the lips of a stranger – and in circumstances which had so fully demonstrated its value – appealed to Snook. He gave a dry laugh, pretended not to notice Ambrose's worried stare, and walked towards the gate. As he had expected, two jeeps were parked in the lee of the gatehouse, but there had been a change of crews and the group passed without any reaction. They were almost out of sight, around a corner of the building, when an empty bottle shattered on the ground behind them, sending transparent fragments scuttling through the dust like glassy insects. A soldier in one of the jeeps gave a derisive hyena call.

'Don't worry – I'm making a note of all these incidents,' Ambrose said. 'A few of these gorillas are going to feel sorry for themselves.'

They went out through the gates, Murphy doing the obligatory talking with the security guards, and turned left up the slight incline which led to Snook's bungalow. The wooden dwellings and stores of the small mining community were deceptively quiet, but there were too many men standing at the street corners. Some of them called greetings to Snook and Murphy as the group went by, but their very cheerfulness was an indication of the tension which was gathering in the air.

Snook moved in beside Murphy and said, 'I'm surprised so many people are still here.'

'They haven't much choice,' Murphy replied. 'The Leopards are patrolling all the exit roads.'

At the bungalow Snook went ahead, key in hand, but the front door was opened before he could reach it and Prudence came out, looking cool, stylish and inhumanly perfect. She was wearing an abbreviated blouse held together by a single knot in the material, and murmured past Snook – in a flurry of silk-slung breasts, blonde hair and expensive perfume – to meet Ambrose. Snook watched jealously as they kissed, keeping his face impassive, and decided not to pass any comment.

'Touching reunion,' he heard himself saying, intellectual strategies thrown to the winds. 'We must have been away all of two hours.' The only discernible effect of his words was that Prudence seemed to press herself more closely to Ambrose's tall frame.

'I've been lonely,' she whispered to Ambrose, 'and I'm hungry. Let's have breakfast at the hotel.'

Ambrose looked uncomfortable. 'I was planning to stay here, Prue. There's so much work to be done.'

'Can't you do it at the hotel?'

'Not unless Gil goes as well. He's the star of the show now.'

'Really?' Prudence looked disbelievingly at Snook. 'Well, perhaps ...'

'I wouldn't dream of going into Kisumu looking like this,' he said, touching the black bristles of his crew-cut. Murphy, Quig and Culver exchanged smiles.

'We can eat later,' Ambrose said hastily, drawing Prudence into the house. 'In fact, a celebration is called for – we made scientific history a little while ago. Just wait till you *hear* this ...' Still talking enthusiastically he led Prudence into the living room.

Snook went into the kitchen, switched on the coffee machine and splashed his face with cold water at the sink. The homely domesticity of the place made the hopeless grey world of Avernus retreat a little further from his thoughts. He carried a cup of black coffee into the room where the others were discussing the success of the experiment. Culver and Quig were draped across armchairs, in extravagant postures of relaxation, talking about methods of analysing the few Avernian-originated sounds they had recorded. Murphy was standing at a window, chewing thoughtfully and looking out towards the mine.

'We've got coffee or gin,' Snook announced. 'Help yourselves.'

'Nothing for me,' Ambrose said. 'There's so much to do here that I don't know where to start, but let's try running over Gil's tape.' He took off his wrist recorder, adjusted its controls and set the tiny machine inside its amplifier unit.

'Now, Gil, listen carefully and see if this triggers off any other memories. We're dealing with a new form of communication here and we don't know yet how to make the best use of it. I still think pulse code modulation is the best avenue of approach for general communication with the Avernians, but with your help we may be able to learn their language in days instead of weeks or months.' He set the machine going and Snook's recorded voice filled the room.

'Deep peace of the running wave.'

Prudence, who was sitting on the arm of Ambrose's chair, burst out laughing. 'I'm sorry,' she said, 'but this is ridiculous. It's just too much.'

Ambrose silenced the machine and looked up at her in startled reproach. 'Please, Prue – this is important.'

She shook her head and dabbed her eyes. 'I know, and I'm sorry, but all you seem to have proved is that the Avernians are Celts. And it's so silly.'

'What do you mean?'

'"Deep peace of the running wave" – it's the first line of a traditional Celtic blessing.'

'Are you certain?'

'Positive. My room-mate at college had it pinned to her wardrobe door. "Deep peace of the running wave to you; Deep peace of the flowing air to you; Deep peace of …" I used to know the whole thing by heart.' Prudence gave Snook a confident, challenging smile.

'I never heard it before,' he said.

'I can't understand this.' Ambrose narrowed his eyes at Snook. 'Though I suppose it's possible you did hear those words somewhere, long ago, and that they were lying in your subconscious.'

'So what? I told you Felleth and I didn't have a conversation. I got ideas from him – and that's the way the first one came over to me.'

'It's odd, the coincidence of wording, but there must be an explanation.'

'I'll give you one,' Prudence said. 'Mister Snook found himself with no job, and – being a resourceful sort of a person – he created another one.'

Ambrose shook his head. 'That isn't fair, Prue.'

'Perhaps not, but you're a scientist, Boyce. What real evidence have you got that this wonderful telepathic experience was genuine?'

'There's enough internal evidence in Gil's story to satisfy me.'

'I don't give a damn whether anybody believes me or not,' Snook cut in, 'but I repeat that I didn't have an ordinary conversation with Felleth. Some of it came through in words, otherwise I wouldn't have a name for him, but a lot of it was in ideas and feelings and pictures. Avernus is mostly water. There's water right round it, and there's a steady wind, and the Avernians seem to like the idea of waves going continuously round the planet. It seems to signify contentment, or peace, or something like that for them.'

Ambrose made a note on a pad. 'You didn't mention that before. Not in so much detail, anyway.'

'That's the way it works. I might talk for a month and still be remembering extra bits at the end of that time. A while ago I just remembered what their houses look like – not the house we saw a part of, but a general impression of all their houses.'

'Go on, Gil.'

'They're made of brown stone, and they have long slanted roofs ...'

'They sound remarkably like ordinary houses to me,' Prudence said, smiling again, the slight inward slope of her teeth contriving to make her appear more scornful and aristocratic than ever.

'Why don't you go and ...' Snook broke off as his mind was flooded with a vivid image of a chain of low islands, each virtually covered with one complex multi-use building rising to a single roof peak in the centre. The images of the island-dwellings were reflected in calm grey seas, creating a series of diamond-shapes, elongated horizontally. One in particular was distinguished by a curious double-span arch, too large to be entirely functional, which perhaps united two natural summits. For a moment the vision was so clear that he could see the darker rectangles of windows, the doors whose sills were lapped by a tideless ocean, the small boats nodding gently at anchor ...

'This is getting us nowhere.' A note of impatience was appearing in Ambrose's voice.

'My feelings precisely.' Prudence rose to her feet and directed an imperious stare at Murphy. 'I suppose there's an eating place in the village?'

Murphy looked doubtful. 'The only place open at this time would be Cullinan House, but I don't think you should go there.'

'I'm quite capable of making that sort of decision for myself.'

Murphy shrugged and turned away as Snook joined in. 'George is right – you shouldn't go there alone.'

'Thank you for the show of concern, but I'm also capable of looking after myself.' Prudence spun on her heel and left the room. A moment later they heard the front door slamming.

Snook turned to Ambrose. 'Boyce, I think you should stop her.'

'What's it got to do with me?' Ambrose demanded irritably. 'I didn't ask her to attach herself to this group.'

'No, but you ...' Snook decided that a reference to the couple having shared the one bed would reveal too much about his own feelings. 'You didn't turn her away.'

'Gil, in case you haven't noticed it, Prudence Devonald is an extremely tough, emancipated young woman, and I quite believe her when she says she can look after herself in any company. *For Christ's sake!*' Exasperation pushed Ambrose's voice into the higher ranges. 'We've some of the most important scientific work of the century in front of us and all we can do is argue about chaperoning a piece of skirt who wasn't even supposed to be here. Do you think we could at least go through this tape a couple of times? Huh?'

'I've got quite a good shot of the Avernian roof structure here,' Quig said placatingly.

Ambrose took the photograph and examined it with determined interest. 'Thank you – this will be extremely useful. Now, let's play the tape again and make notes of any questions that occur to us.' He activated the tiny machine and sat with one ear turned to it in an exaggerated show of concentration.

Snook prowled around the room, drinking coffee and trying to focus his attention on the strange-sounding tones of his own voice issuing from the recorder. Finally, after about ten minutes, he set his cup down.

'I'm hungry,' he said. 'I'm going to eat.'

Ambrose blinked at him in surprise. 'We can have a meal later, Gil.'

'I'm hungry now.'

Murphy turned away from the window. 'I haven't much to do here – I think I'll join you.'

'*Bon appetit,*' Ambrose said sarcastically, returning his attention to his notes.

Snook nodded and went outside. He and Murphy walked slowly down the hill, ostensibly enjoying the moderate warmth of the air and the flaming colours of the bougainvillaeas, neither man talking very much. They turned into the main street, with its dwindling series of product and agency signs. The quietness and lack of people created a Sunday morning atmosphere. They walked to the corner of the side street in which Cullinan House was situated. As Snook had almost expected, there was a jeep parked outside the building. He exchanged glances with Murphy and, trying not to shed their air of casualness, they began to walk faster. They reached the dusty shade of the entrance and found a young Asian, who was wearing a barman's white apron, sitting on a beer keg and smoking a cheroot.

'Where's the girl?' Snook said.

'In there.' The youth spoke nervously, indicating a doorway on the left. 'But you better not go in.'

Snook pushed the door open and there was an instant of heightened perception in which his eyes took in every detail of the scene inside. The square room had a bar along the innermost wall and the rest of the floor area was taken up by small circular tables and cane chairs. Two soldiers were leaning on the counter holding beer glasses, their Uzi submachine guns beside them on bar stools. One of the tables had been laid for breakfast and Prudence was standing at it, her arms pinned behind her by a third soldier, a corporal. Lieutenant Curt Freeborn was standing close to the girl, and he froze for a moment – in the act of opening the central knot which held her blouse together – as Snook walked into the room with Murphy close behind him.

'Prudence!' Snook's voice was gently reproachful. 'You've started without us.'

He kept walking towards the table, aware that the soldiers at the bar were picking up their weapons, but relying on the mildness of his manner to prevent them from taking any hasty action. Freeborn glanced at the door and windows, and his face relaxed into a smile as he realised Snook and Murphy were alone. He returned his attention to Prudence and, with deliberate slowness, finished undoing the silken knot. The material slid aside to reveal her breasts, cupped in chocolate-coloured lace. Prudence's face was pale, immobile.

'Your friend and I have met before,' Freeborn said to Prudence. 'He likes the funny remarks.' His voice was abstracted, like that of a dentist who is making conversation to soothe a patient. He put his hands to Prudence's shoulders and began stripping the blouse downwards, his eyes intent, cool and professional.

Snook examined the breakfast table and saw that nothing on it even remotely resembled a weapon – even the knives and forks were plastic. He moved closer to the table, wishing Prudence could have been spared the degradation she was undergoing.

'Lieutenant,' he said unemotionally, 'I won't allow you to do this.'

'The remarks get funnier.' Freeborn took a brassiere strap between forefinger and thumb and drew it down over the curve of Prudence's shoulder. The corporal holding her smiled in anticipation.

Murphy took a step forward. 'Your uncle won't see anything funny in this.'

Freeborn's gaze flicked sideways at him. 'I'll deal with you later, trash.'

During the moment of distraction Snook leapt forward, driving himself high into the air, looped his left arm around Freeborn's neck, and when he hit the floor again he had the Lieutenant doubled over in a secure headlock. The soldiers at the bar started forward, both priming their guns. Snook reached sideways with his right hand, took a fork from the table and rammed its blunt tines into the side of Freeborn's startled, upturned eye. He pushed it

232

far enough into the eye socket to cause pain without inflicting severe injury. Freeborn gave a powerful upward surge, trying to lift him off the floor.

'Don't struggle, Lieutenant,' Snook warned, 'or I'll take your eye out like a scoop of ice cream.'

Freeborn gave a cry of mingled pain and outrage as Snook reinforced his words with extra pressure on the fork. The corporal pushed Prudence to one side and the soldiers began kicking tables out of their way as they advanced.

'And tell your gooks to lay down their guns and back off,' Snook commanded.

One of the soldiers, his eyes bulging whitely, raised his gun and carefully sighted at Snook's head. Snook twisted the fork a little and felt the warmth of blood on his fingers.

'Stay back, you fools!' Freeborn's voice was hysterical with panic. 'Do as he says!'

The two soldiers set the stubby weapons on the floor and backed away, the corporal joining them. Freeborn's hands fluttered imploringly against the backs of Snook's legs, like huge anxious moths.

'Lie down behind the bar,' Snook said to the retreating men.

Murphy picked up one of the discarded guns. 'Gil, there's a liquor store-room behind the bar.'

'That's even better. We'll need the keys to the jeep, as well.' Snook turned to Prudence who was re-tying her blouse with trembling hands. 'If you'd like to go outside, we'll be with you in a minute.'

She nodded without speaking and ran towards the exit. Still maintaining the fierce grip of his arm on Freeborn's neck, and keeping the fork in place, Snook led the lieutenant to the storeroom. Murphy had just finished bundling the three soldiers into the cramped space. He was carrying the machine gun with an unconscious ease which suggested he had experience with similar weapons. Freeborn was forced to shamble like an ape as Snook brought him behind the bar and backed him into the store with his men.

'We'd better have this, Gil.' Murphy opened the flap of Freeborn's holster and took the automatic pistol from it. Freeborn was swearing under his breath in a kind of rhythmic chant as Snook gave him a final shove and slammed the heavy door. Murphy turned the key, flipped it into a far corner of the room, ran out from behind the counter and gathered up the two remaining submachine guns.

'Do we want those?' Snook said doubtfully.

'We need them.'

Snook clambered over the bar and joined Murphy. 'Won't it change things if we steal Army weapons? I mean, up to now all we've done is defend Prudence from gang rape.'

'It wouldn't matter if we'd been defending the Virgin Mary.' Murphy smiled briefly over his shoulder as he led the way out to the jeep, past the watchful barman. 'I thought you knew this country, Gil. The only thing which will keep us safe – for a little while, anyway – is that Junior Freeborn daren't go to his uncle and report that he and three Leopards were tackled and disarmed in a public place by one unarmed white man. The loss of the weapons makes the humiliation complete, because it's the most shameful thing a Leopard can do.'

Murphy threw the guns into the jeep's rear seat and climbed in after them. Snook squirmed into the driving seat, beside Prudence, and got the vehicle into motion.

'Another thing is that the colonel is a black racialist. He's even been known to criticise the President for occasionally preferring a white girl – so young Curt will be treading on eggs for a while.'

Snook swung the jeep into the main street. 'You mean he won't take any action over this?'

'Grow up! All I mean is that the action won't be official.' Murphy looked around him with the air of a general considering tactics. 'We should leave the jeep here, so there'll be no reason for any of the military to go near your house. I'll put the guns under the back seat.'

'Right.' Snook brought the vehicle to a halt and they got out, ignoring the curious stares of the few passers-by.

Prudence, who had not spoken once during the whole encounter, was still pale, though she seemed to have recovered her composure. Snook tried to think of something to say to her, but was unable to find a sufficiently neutral form of words. As they were crossing the main street a sports car sliced past them, being driven too fast, and Snook instinctively caught Prudence's arm. He expected her to snatch it away, but to his surprise she sagged against him until he was supporting most of her weight. They crossed the road in that manner and he steered her into the entrance of an empty store, where she leaned against the wall and began to sob. The sound was painful to Snook.

'Come on,' he said awkwardly, 'I thought you were supposed to be a tough character.'

'It was horrible.' She tilted her head back against the postered wood, rolling it from side to side, and he saw the clear lacquer of tears on her cheeks. 'That lieutenant ... he was only a boy ... but he left me with *nothing* ...'

Snook gazed helplessly at Murphy. 'I think we all need a drink.'

'I was being dissected,' she whimpered. 'Pinned out and dissected.'

'I've got coffee or gin,' Snook said in a matter-of-fact voice. 'In your case I would recommend the gin. What do you say, George?'

'The gin is very good,' Murphy responded in similar tones. 'Gil should know – he practically lives on it.'

Prudence opened her eyes and looked at both men as though seeing them for the first time. 'I thought you were going to be killed. You *could* have been killed.'

'Nonsense!' Murphy's brown face was incredulous. 'What nobody back there realised was that plastic forks are only a part of Gil's armament.'

'Really?'

Murphy lowered his voice. 'He carries a stainless steel fork as well – in a special shoulder holster.'

Snook nodded. 'It used to be the jawbone of an ass, but I couldn't stand the smell.'

Prudence began to chuckle, Murphy joined in, Snook gave a shaky laugh, and within seconds they were reeling in the doorway like a trio of drunks, weeping with cathartic laughter as the tension left their bodies. On the way up the hill to the bungalow, still intoxicated with relief and the heady joy that comes with the finding of friends, they made dozens of jokes which had only to contain certain key words like 'fork' or 'jawbone' to be regarded as wildly hilarious. There were fleeting moments during the walk when Snook felt a sense of dismay over the unnaturalness of their behaviour, but he was determined to remain high for as long as possible.

'I've got to say something before we go in,' Prudence said when they reached the bungalow's front steps. 'If I don't thank you now it'll get more and more difficult for me. I'm not the easiest of people to ...'

'Forget it,' Snook said. 'Let's have that drink.'

Prudence shook her head. 'Please. I haven't laughed so much in years – and I know why you made me laugh – but it wouldn't have been at all funny if Boyce hadn't sent you after me.'

Murphy opened his mouth to speak, but Snook silenced him with a barely perceptible shake of his head.

'We'd better go inside,' he said. 'Boyce will be glad to see you.'

At noon a reduced party – consisting of Snook, Ambrose, Prudence and Quig – drove to the Commodore Hotel in Kisumu for a meal. Ambrose also needed to make some telephone calls there, because it had been discovered that the line to Snook's house had developed a fault. Prudence was sitting beside him in the front seat, occasionally leaning her head on his shoulder. Bright-hued shrubs and trees, many with great trusses of flowers, streamed past the car's windows like a continuous light show. Snook, who was in the rear seat with Quig, allowed the varicoloured display to hypnotise him into a mood of sleepy carelessness in which he was not required to think too deeply about his situation. Barandi had become a dangerous place for him and yet, instead of cutting the bonds and slipping away, he was allowing himself to become even more deeply enmeshed.

'I don't like the way things are working out here,' Ambrose said, echoing Snook's thoughts. 'Even without what you've told me, I can feel a definite hostility in the air. If we hadn't been so lucky in other respects I'd be tempted to pull up stakes and go to one of the other countries where the Avernians have been sighted.'

'Is it really worth hanging on here?' Snook said, sitting upright as his interest kindled. 'Why not move on?'

'It's mainly a question of geometry. Avernus is like a wheel rolling within a wheel at this time, and the point of contact is constantly moving around its equator. It means that the Avernians who were sighted in Brazil are a different lot to the Avernians who appear here – and we've had this fantastic stroke of luck in getting you together with Felleth. That's the big attraction in Barandi. That's what has given me the lead on all the others.'

Quig stirred out of his own reveries. 'How much more do you want to find out from him, Boyce?'

'Hah!' Ambrose hunched over the steering wheel and shook his head in despair. 'At the moment all I'm doing is unlearning.'

'I don't get you.'

'Well, I haven't discussed this because we've had so many immediate practical problems to deal with, but the descriptions of Avernus that Gil has given me – even the pictures we got of the Avernian roof structure – have upset a lot of our ideas about the nature of matter. According to our physics the Avernian universe should be very weakly bound compared to the one we know. If I'd been asked to describe it a week ago, I'd have said it could exist only because antineutrinos have different masses, depending on their energy, and that all objects in that universe would consist of heavy particles surrounded by clouds of lighter particles.' Ambrose began to speak faster as he got into his subject.

'This indicates that their compounds wouldn't be formed by electronic forces like electro-valency or covalency. The weakness of the interactions would mean that all bodies in that universe – even the Avernian people themselves – would be a lot more ... ah ... statistical than we are.'

'Hey!' Quig began to sound excited. 'You mean one Avernian should be able to walk right through another Avernian? Or through a wall?'

Ambrose nodded. 'That was the old picture, but we've learned that it's all wrong. Gil talked about stone buildings and islands and oceans ... the rest of us saw those Earth-like roof beams ... so it appears that an Avernian's world is just as real and hard and solid to him as ours is to us. There's one hell of a lot we have to learn, and Felleth seems to be the best source of information. Felleth teamed up with Gil, that is. That's why I hate the idea of quitting this place.'

Snook, who had been listening to the conversation with growing bafflement, suddenly felt that the relationship between Ambrose's world of nuclear theory and his own world of turbines and gearboxes was just as tenuous as that between Earth and Avernus. He had often been surprised at the sorts of things people needed to know in order to function in their jobs, but Ambrose's field of expertise – in which people were treated as mobile clouds of atoms – was cold and inimical to him. Memories began to stir in his mind, half-recollections of something gleaned during his last encounter with Felleth.

He tapped Boyce on the shoulder. 'Remember I told you Felleth said, "Particle, anti-particle – our relationship almost precisely defined"?'

'Yes?'

'I think something else has just come out of it.'

'What sort of thing?'

'Well, I don't understand this, but I've got a kind of a picture of the phrase "particle, anti-particle" representing one edge of a cube, only the cube isn't an ordinary cube. It seems to go off in a lot more directions … or maybe each edge of it is a cube in its own right. Does that make any kind of sense?'

'It sounds as though you're wrestling with the concept of multi-dimensional space, Gil.'

'What's the point of it?'

'I think,' Ambrose said gloomily, 'Felleth knows that the relationship be-tween our universe and his is only one of a whole spectrum of such relation-ships. There may be universe upon universe – and we haven't got the right sort of mathematics to let us even begin thinking about them. Hell, *I've got* to stay in Barandi as long as I can.'

Snook's thoughts reverted to the human aspects of the situation. 'Okay, but if we're going back to the mine in the morning, I think you should call the Press Association office and round up Gene Helig and force him to go with us. He's the nearest thing we've got to a guarantee of safe conduct.'

CHAPTER TEN

They reached the mine head without incident, largely because Murphy had seen Cartier in the afternoon and obtained a special permit to bring a car inside the enclosure. Two jeeps were parked in the lee of the gatehouse, as usual, and they switched on their spotlights as Ambrose's car swept by, but neither of them followed. Snook wondered if the crews had been tipped off about Gene Helig's presence. In any case, he was glad Prudence had decided to remain at the hotel.

When he stepped out into the pre-dawn blackness he discovered he had become intensely aware of the stars. The constellations were glittering like cities in the sky, the colours of their individual stars easily distinguished, and Snook found himself grateful for their presence. He decided it was an unconscious reaction against his earlier vision of life on a blind planet, from which – even if the cloud cover were to vanish – it might not be possible to see the glowing stellar hearths of other civilisations. As he stood looking upwards, he vowed that when he got clear of Barandi he would take a positive interest in astronomy.

'There's nothing to see up there, old boy,' Helig said jovially. 'I'm told it's all below ground these days.'

'That's right.' Snook shivered in a river of cold air, shoved his hands deep into his jacket pockets and followed the rest of the group into descending cages. Ambrose had calculated that top dead centre for the Avernians would occur just above one of the worked-out pipes on Level Two. It was not an ideal location, because the Avernians would rise up into the rock ceiling for a few minutes, but the relative movement would be fairly slow, and there would be two good opportunities for what Ambrose, in a resurgence of good spirits, had described as an 'inter-universal *téte-à-téte.*'

When he stepped on to the circular gallery of Level Two, Snook was relieved to find that his apprehension of the previous day had faded. The first instant of union with Felleth had been shocking, but not so much for its strangeness but its effectiveness. He had entered a mind, an intelligence which was the product of an unknown continuum, and yet it had been less alien to him than the minds of many human beings he had met. There had been in it, Snook believed, no capacity for murder or greed; and his certainty on this point made him marvel, yet again, that such a strange mode of communication should have been possible at all.

Ambrose had been emphatic in denying the possibility of previous long-range telepathic links between Avernians and humans – but, at the same time, Ambrose had confessed in the car that day that his knowledge of his specialist subject, nuclear physics, was faulty. He, Gilbert Snook, had suddenly become the world's foremost expert on mind-to-mind data transfer – admittedly without intending to do so – and it satisfied his sense of the fitness of things to postulate that Avernians and human beings, living on concentric biospheres for millions of years, had telepathically influenced each other's mental processes. The theory would account, perhaps, for the odd coincidence of words which Prudence had discovered, and for the widespread belief among primitive societies that another world existed below the surface of the Earth. Above all, and most important in Snook's opinion, it accounted for the compatibility of thought modes which made communication possible in the first place.

As he walked around the gallery to the pipe where the other men had gathered, Snook wondered if he could play the role of scientific researcher and take his theory one experimental step further. Having made the initial mental contact with Felleth – could he now, by conscious effort, reach him over a distance? The range would not be all that great, because at that moment Felleth would be somewhere below him and rising up through the rock strata, but the principle could be proved. He stopped walking, took off his Amplites, closed his eyes and tried to screen his brain from all sensory inputs. Feeling self-conscious, and aware that he was probably guilty of monstrous clumsiness in Avernian terms, he strove to form a mental picture of Felleth and to project the Avernian's name across the gulf which separated two universes.

In his mind there was nothing. Against the screen of his eyelids there was nothing, save the slow drifting of afterimages conjured by his retinas. The random patterns of pseudo-light continued to merge and mingle, then – very gradually – Snook began to feel he could see something behind them. A pale green wall which was not a wall because it was possessed of movement, and endless rising and overturning and falling of its elements; there was translucency coupled with strength; a sense of solidity and liquidity; a changeless state of eternal changing ...

Deep peace of the running ...

'Come on, Gil,' Ambrose called. 'We're nearly all set up. Getting it down to a fine art.'

Helig was standing beside Snook, the collar of his roll neck sweater pulled up over his chin. 'Yes, come and join us – there's no show without Punch, is there?'

Snook blinked at the two men and fought to hide his annoyance. Had he been working a confidence trick on himself? Had the words begun to form in his mind because he had been expecting them? How could a telepath distinguish between his own thoughts and those of another?

'Snap out of it, old boy,' Helig said, amiably impatient. 'Have you been at the mother's ruin again?'

'What the hell's the rush?' Snook demanded. 'We can't do anything until the Avernians get up to this level.'

'Oh!' Helig raised his eyebrows. 'Listen to our prima bloody donna!' He punched Snook playfully on the shoulder.

Snook fended off a second blow and forced himself to relax as they walked along the hollowed-out pipe to the area which Ambrose and Murphy, using drawings of the mine and a surveyor's tape, had marked off as the scene of operations. He was going to have his fill of telepathic experimentation in a matter of minutes, assuming that Felleth kept the implicit rendezvous. Ambrose, satisfied now that he had got his little team together, went on ahead to supervise Quig and Culver.

'Gene, you know this country better than most,' Snook said in a quiet voice. 'How long do you think Ogilvie will tolerate this mine being shut down?'

'Strangely enough, the President is taking it quite well. He's been flattered by the publicity Barandi has got out of it – these things are important to him – and I think he might be in two minds about what he ought to do. Tommy Freeborn is getting restless, though.' Helig's face was unreadable behind the dark lenses of his Amplites. 'Very restless.'

'Think he's getting ready to answer the call of destiny?'

'I don't know what you mean.'

'Come on, Gene – everybody knows Freeborn would like to give the two fingers to the United Nations, seal up the borders and get rid of all the whites and Asians.'

'All right, but I didn't tell you this.' Helig glanced around him, as if expecting to see microphones projecting from the stone. 'The smart money has started to flow out of the country. I can't see Tommy Freeborn letting that go on for more than a week.'

'I see. Are you leaving?'

Helig looked surprised. 'Just when I'll have some real work to do?'

'Your Press card won't mean anything to the Colonel.'

'It means something to me, old boy.'

'I admire your principles,' Snook said, 'but I won't be around to see them put into practice.'

They reached the other members of the group and Snook stood apart, trying to get his thoughts in order. The time had come for him to move on. All the signs were there, all the warnings had been sounded loud and clear, and although he had allowed himself to become involved in other people's problems, it was a mistake which could be rectified. It now seemed inevitable that there would be a Sharpeville-type slaughter of miners, but there was nothing he could do about that, and his worrying about it would have a negative result. Nature had yet to design a nervous system which was capable of sustaining the guilt of others.

Ambrose and Prudence represented a separate issue. They were sophisticated, well-educated adults – and the fact that he saw them as innocents abroad did not make him responsible for their welfare. Prudence Devonald, in particular, would resent it if he tried to offer advice, and if she wanted to hitch her wagon to Ambrose ...

The trend of his thinking filled Snook with sudden self-doubt. Would he have been coolly planning to cut and run if Prudence had fallen into his arms after the incident in the Cullinan? The storybooks all agreed that was the appropriate reward for a knight who rescued a damsel in distress, but was it possible that he – Gilbert Snook, the human neutrino

– had seriously expected her to translate romance to reality? And was it equally possible that he was preparing to abandon her in a fit of adolescent pique?

Disturbed at having blundered into emotional quicksands, Snook was almost relieved to see Ambrose studying his watch and giving the fluttering hand signals which indicated that top dead centre was imminent. Ambrose made some final adjustments to the boson field generator, and began explaining the entire procedure for Helig's benefit. There was less room than in the tunnels where the previous contacts had been made, and the members of the group were standing quite close together when the now-familiar glowing blue line appeared on the rock floor.

'Lateral displacement less than one metre,' Ambrose murmured into his wrist recorder. Quig's camera began clicking in the background.

Snook moved forward, eager and reluctant at the same time, and stood perfectly still as the line rose upward to become the apex of a triangular prism of luminosity. The prism expanded upwards and outwards until its peak was above Snook's head and he could see the ghostly geometries of roof structure all about him. The horizontal plane of a ceiling came next, rising over his ankles and knees like the surface of an insubstantial lake. Snook knelt to bring his head down into the volume of the Avernian room. The three translucent figures were waiting for him, Felleth in the centre, growing upwards from the solid rock like sculpted columns of bluish smoke.

Felleth moved closer to Snook, on legs that were as yet invisible, and his arms were outstretched. Again the mistpools of his eyes grew large. Snook inclined his head forward and, even before the contact was made, he could see the shimmering movement of the sea-green wall ...

Deep peace of the running wave.

I ask your forgiveness, Equal Gil. I was at fault for not understanding that you are not accustomed to the congruency of self which you refer to as telepathy. A few unfortunate members of our race are afflicted with the silence that separates and, in my egotism, I presumed that you were similarly flawed because you issued no greeting. I was glad to feel you trying to make contact with me a short while ago, because it showed that you had come to no harm as a result of my mistake. During this meeting I am using purely sequential thought structures to avoid overloading your neural pathways. This technique, which we use in the teaching of our children, reduces the rate of information transfer, but there will be again in effectiveness because your mind will be able to function in an approximation of its normal manner.

I ask your forgiveness, too, because in my blind pride I dared reject your stone house of proven knowledge in favour of my reed hut of conjecture. My only excuse is that I was shocked and in considerable pain – in one second I was given more new knowledge than has been accumulated by the People in the last million days, and much of the knowledge was of a kind I would have been happier not to have. I confess that I was also confused and alarmed by the nature of your arrival. The People have many myths about strange beings who live in the clouds, and when you descended from the sky it seemed to me – for an instant – that all the old superstitions had been proved true. This, of course, is a feeble excuse for my reaction, because the nature of your arrival was in itself a proof of all your claims. A moment of logical consideration would have shown that the vertical displacement of your body relative to mine was generated by a hypocycloid of planetary scale. Once that elementary step had been taken, all the other deductions were inevitable, including the final one concerning the fate of my world.

Snook: I'm sorry that I was the bringer of such news. *Do not distress yourself. The intellectual experience has been unique – and the end is not yet. Also, the knowledge you gave me has been put to good use. I have, for example, been able to explain to the satisfaction of the People certain disturbing phenomena which have occurred in distant lands, all of them near the equal-day line, which you refer to as the equator. Some individuals have been terrified by visions, and by intimations about the end of our world. Without knowing it, for there was nothing to see, they had come within self-congruency range of others of your race who live on or near your equator, and an accidental and partial communication was achieved,*

How is it that I am able to see you and your companions?

Please be at ease – it is not necessary for you to construct sentences, nor have we time for such laborious methods. You have a companion who has knowledge of nuclear physics and it was his idea to illuminate your body by placing it within what he calls an intermediate vector boson field. I wish to communicate with him, but he is surrounded by the silence which separates and I have no means of reaching him. It is a pity that the planetary motion gives us such a short time together, but there is something you can do to help, if you are willing.

Snook: I'll do anything I can.

I am grateful. When we are separated from each other, please obtain writing materials and have them in your hands when we are united again. I will then be able to communicate with Equal Boyce. In addition, I have a very important request to make of you and all the other members of your race. I have learned that yours is a troubled and divided world, and in order that my request be properly received I must teach you enough about the People to make it clear that the granting of the request will not add to your problems. In a few seconds we will separate, therefore – to achieve my purpose – I must resort to full congruency of self. Do not be alarmed, and do not at this stage attempt to impose language upon concept.

Simply receive …

... the People are mammalian, bisexual, vegetarian (images of many Avernians, idealised/transformed by Felleth's own vision; underwater farms; swimmers tending lines of tree-like plants)

... average life span is ninety-two of your/our years (unfamiliar method of reckoning)

... inter-personal communication is telepathic, complemented by vocal sound, expression and gesture (images of Avernian faces, idealised/transformed, made meaningful, fierce white light of truth)

... social organisation is paternal, flexible, informal – no equivalent term available in Earth languages (images of philosopher-statesmen holding congress in vast brown stone building covering two islands linked by a double-arched bridge)

... mass aggression and individual aggression unknown in recent history – corrective procedure for murder was voluntary cessation of breeding by all Avernians of same genetic strain (image of small wave losing momentum, subsiding into the unity of the ocean)

... planetary population is now 12,000,000 but was 47,000,000 before the weight of the oceans decreased (images of bodies of small children floating in water faces downward, numerous as autumn leaves on a forest floor, unmoving except for the slow jostling of the waves)

'Oh, God,' Snook whispered. 'It's too much. Too much.'

He became aware of the pressure of the uneven rock against his knees. His hands were holding the smooth plastic frame of his magniluct glasses, and a flashlight beam was dancing behind the silhouettes of human beings, shadows flailing and flickering in the confines of the tunnel.

'Well I'll be damned,' Helig said. 'I never saw anything like that.'

Murphy and Helig came forward and helped Snook to his feet. He looked around him and saw that Ambrose was close by, still wearing his Amplites, busy chalking marks on the tunnel wall, consulting his watch and talking into his recorder in a low voice, Quig was operating his camera, pointing it upwards, and Culver was doubled over the rectangular shape of the pulse code modulator. For an instant the scene was completely meaningless to Snook and he felt lost, then there was a shift of perception, and the strangers became known to him, their motivations familiar.

'How long did it last this time?' Snook's throat was dry, hoarsening his voice. 'How long was I in contact?'

'Your forehead was touching Felleth's for nearly a minute,' Murphy said. 'Was it Felleth, by the way?'

'Yes, that was Felleth.'

'They all look alike to me,' Murphy commented drily. 'Then he leaned forward and his head was right inside yours, the way it was yesterday, for about a second.'

'A second?' Snook pressed the back of a hand to his forehead. 'I can't go on like this. I spend my whole life avoiding people, because I just don't want to know, and now ...'

'They've gone,' Ambrose said in a firm voice. 'Everybody take their Amplites off – I'm turning on the big light.' A moment later the tunnel was filled with marble-white brilliance. There was a general shuffling of feet and flexing of shoulders. Snook felt in his pocket for his cigarettes.

'We can relax for ten minutes until the Avernians pass top dead centre and drop down again,' Ambrose continued.

'We drew a blank on the modulator,' Culver said. 'I don't think they were trying for light-sound communication this time – at least, I didn't see any equipment.'

'No, it looks as though they've decided to work through Gil.' Ambrose lit Snook's cigarette and his voice became unexpectedly sympathetic. 'How was it, Gil? Rough?'

Snook inhaled fragrant smoke. 'If anybody ever shoves an air hose in your ear and inflates your head to five times its normal size, you'll get some idea.'

'Can you give me a preliminary report?'

'Not now – I'll need a full morning with a recorder.' There was an abrupt stirring in Snook's memory. 'Felleth is going to send you a message, Boyce. I need a writing block and a pen before he comes back again.'

'A message? Have you any idea what it could be?'

'It's technical. And it's something big ...' Snook felt the coldness of prescience beginning to grow within him and he fought to quell it. 'Just give me the block and pen, will you?'

'Of course.'

Snook took the writing equipment, moved a short distance down the tunnel from the rest of the group and stood by himself. He lit a second cigarette and smoked it with quiet concentration, all the while wishing he was far away and above ground, in sunlight. The sunlight was important. There had to be clear skies, with views of infinity, a visual antidote to the blind grey skies of Avernus. There had to be an escape from the claustrophobic, doomed world, with its low islands reflecting as diamond-shapes in the tideless ocean, and the bodies of alien children drifting like sterile spawn ...

'Ready for you, Gil,' Ambrose called, and at the same moment the tunnel was returned to its former state of darkness. Snook put on his Amplites, creating a spurious blue radiance in which his cigarette end shone with magnified brilliance. He ground it out under his heel and walked back to the arena.

Deep peace of the running wave.

You will be interested to learn, Equal Gil, that although the People's transportation systems have largely been destroyed, our communications were not affected by the disaster a thousand days ago, The possibility of using electrical phenomena to transmit signals over great distances has been known to us for a long time – and we have demonstrated the method for purely scientific reasons – but for all general communications we rely on the congruency of self, which you know as telepathy.

In this way, the knowledge you brought me yesterday has already been dis-seminated to all of the People. The Responders have held communion and given their advice, and a decision has been made. It is contrary to our philos-ophy to surrender life to the forces of entropy, but we have agreed that we do not want our children's children to be born into a world which can offer them nothing but death. Accordingly, we will cease to fertilise our females.

It is not difficult for us – a logical consequence of our form of telepathy is voluntary control over the proto-minds of our seedlings. This has given us predetermination of the sex of our offspring, and it also permits us to choose sterility if we so desire.

We have been fortunate – some would say a greater power has ordained it – in that the time remaining to our world is slightly greater than the aver-age lifetime of our individual members. A small proportion of the People will therefore continue to produce children for another four hundred days. It will be the melancholy duty of this final generation to act as caretakers for the rest of us, to oversee our departure from life, and to organise our dwindling resources in such a way that in the last days there will be no starvation, no deprivation, no suffering, no loss of dignity. When the oceans rise again they will bring neither fear nor death – for we shall have gone.

Snook: How can you make a unanimous decision like that in such a short time?

The People are not like human beings. I am not claiming that we are supe-rior – it can be expected of any telepathic society that reason, which reinforces itself and grows stronger on the universality of truth, will prevail over unrea-son, which grows less coherent and weaker as its individual proponents are isolated in their own unrealities. The People will act in concert as one, in this final trial, as in the lesser ordeals of the past.

Snook: But how can they accept it so quickly when only two days ago you had no science of astronomy? How do they know that what I told you was true?

I do not know if you will be able to understand the difference in our phi-losophies, but the only reason we did not have a science of astronomy is that we had no requirement for it. It would have served no purpose. Our physics are not your physics. I have learned, from your store of knowledge, that you have a science of radio astronomy, with instruments which would tell you of the existence of other worlds and other stars even if Earth was permanently covered by cloud-but, although wave phenomena are similar in my universe, such instruments have not been constructed here because we could not have conceived a use for them. However, when we were presented with the evidence of your experience we were quite capable of using it as a foundation and building an appropriate logical edifice. The People were not persuaded by you, or by me. They were persuaded by truth.

Snook: But so quickly!

It is not the speed of acceptance which perplexes you, but the acceptance itself. But do not be deceived into thinking there is no grief. We are neither passive or submissive. The People are not content to bow out of existence. We accept that the vast majority of our race must cease to exist, but as long as a few of us survive our life-wave will be preserved and may grow strong again some day.

Snook: Is that possible? I've been told that your world will be totally destroyed – so how will it be possible for any of you to survive?

There is only one way in which we can survive, Equal Gil – and that is by entering your world.

On behalf of the People ... and in the name of Life ... I am asking your race to make room for us on Earth.

The bright light had been switched on again, transforming the tunnel into a pantomime setting, and the cast of strangers was assembled as before. Snook stared at each in turn, until they had assumed their identities. Murphy was looking at him with a slight frown, but the other men were standing near the light and their attention was focused on a flat rectangular object. It took Snook a few seconds to identify it as the writing pad which Ambrose had given him. Ambrose raised his eyes in a long, level stare.

'What is this, Gil?' he said. 'What's happening here?'

Snook flexed his fingers, trying to orient himself in his own body. 'I'm sorry. Felleth must have forgotten to give me the message, or perhaps there wasn't enough time.'

'I've got the message! Look at it!' Ambrose held the pad in front of Snook's face. The entire top sheet was covered with words and mathematical symbols, laid out in perfectly straight lines as if they had been typed.

Snook touched the block with his fingertips, feeling the faint indentations caused by the pen. 'Did I do that?'

'In about thirty seconds flat, old boy,' Helig said. 'I tell you, I've never seen anything like it. I've heard of automatic writing, but I never really believed in it till now. I tell you, this is ...'

'We can go into that later,' Ambrose cut in. 'Gil, do you know what this is?'

Snook swallowed with difficulty, playing for time in which to think. 'What does it look like to you?'

'These equations appear to outline a process, using inverse beta-decay, which would transmute anti-neutrino matter into protons and neutrons,'

Ambrose said in a sombre voice. 'At first glance it looks like a proposal for transferring objects from the Avernian universe into this one.'

'You've almost got it right,' Snook replied, reassured at hearing what might have been his own private fantasy voiced by another human being. 'But Felleth wasn't talking about transferring objects – he wants to send us some of his people.'

CHAPTER ELEVEN

They returned to the car in silence, each man in the lonely fortress of his own thoughts, and loaded it with the various items of equipment. On reaching the surface, Snook had not been surprised to note that the sky had clouded over in preparation for the grass rains which would last for approximately two weeks. It was as though the world was trying to model itself on his vision of Avernus, making ready for visitors. He shivered and nabbed his hands together, discovering as he did so that his right hand and forearm were curiously numb and tired. The group got into the car, with Ambrose taking the wheel, and the heavy silence continued until the vehicle had passed out through the gates of the mine enclosure.

'Gil's phone is out of action,' Ambrose said, turning to Helig. 'I suppose the first thing we should do is get you to another one.'

Helig smiled complacently and his eyelids drooped more than was usual. 'It isn't necessary, old boy. I'm accustomed to telephones mysteriously breaking down everywhere I go these days – so I brought a radio transmitter.' He tapped his jacket pocket. 'I'll file my story through a colleague in Matsa. All I need is somewhere to sit in peace for twenty minutes.'

'That's easily arranged. Are you going to write out your story for me to vet it?'

'Sorry – I don't work that way.'

'I thought you might want me to check the science.'

'I've done all the double-checking that's necessary.' Helig gave Ambrose a quizzical glance. 'Besides, the science isn't important – this is a news story.'

Ambrose shrugged and switched on the windscreen wipers as the first drops of rain began to shatter themselves on the dusty glass in front of him. The dust was momentarily smeared into two brownish sectors which disappeared as the rain grew heavier. There was another silence which lasted until they had stopped at the bungalow, at which point Ambrose turned right round in his seat and tapped Quig's knee. Quig, who had been sitting with nodding head and closed eyes, gave a start.

'Didn't you say you have a friend in the lab at the new power station?' Ambrose said.

'Yes, Jack Postlethwaite. He came out at the same time as Benny and myself.'

'Do you know for certain that they have a Moncaster machine in the laboratory?'

'I think so. Isn't it something like a signal generator, except that it gives you different kinds of radiation fields?'

'That's exactly what it is.' Ambrose took the ignition keys from the dash and dropped them into Quig's hand. 'Des, I want you and Benny to take my car, drive over to the power station right now and hire that machine from your friend.'

Quig's jaw sagged. 'But those things cost a fortune – and this one isn't even Jack's property.'

Ambrose opened his wallet, took out a thousand-dollar bill and dropped it in Quig's lap. 'That's for your friend, for a couple of days' hire of the machine. There'll be the same amount for you when you get back, to divide between you – provided you have the machine with you? Okay?'

'You bet it's okay.' While Culver nodded vigorously, Quig scrambled out of the car, sped round it to the driver's door and stood jigging in the rain while Ambrose got out.

'Not so fast,' Ambrose said to him. 'We still have to unship our gear.'

Snook, who had been watching the transaction with interest, kept an eye on Ambrose during the unloading operation. Overnight the scientist seemed to have grown a little older, a little harder around the eyes and mouth, and he was moving with the jerky energy of a man whose mind was on fire. As soon as the car had swished away down the hill with Quig at the wheel, Ambrose gave Snook a wry grin.

'Let's go inside,' he said. 'You've got one hell of a debriefing session in front of you.'

Snook remained leaning against a wooden upright of the veranda. 'Let's stay out here for a minute.'

'Why?'

'Because it's more private than in the house. You know, of course, that young Quig and Culver and their friend could get jail – or worse – if they're caught borrowing that machine. The power station is state property.'

'They won't get caught,' Ambrose said easily. He opened a pack of cigarettes and handed one to Snook.

'Do you need that machine to bring the Avernians through to Earth?'

'Yes. They couldn't do it if we didn't help by setting up the right local environment. I'll have to get a supply of hydrogen today, as well.'

'What's all the hurry?' Snook stared hard at Ambrose's face above the transparent blue shoot of his lighter flame. 'Why do you have to try this thing when the conditions are all wrong?'

'I disagree with you about the conditions, Gil – they'll never be as good again. You know that tomorrow top dead centre will occur just a couple of metres above ground level, but from then on Avernus will permanently be swelling out through the Earth's surface. It'll be like a flat dome which gets five hundred metres higher every day. That may not seem like much, but we're dealing with a tangent which is practically zero, which means that the edge of that dome will be spreading out in all directions at tremendous speed.

'True there'll be two lesser top dead centres, one north of the equator and one south of it, but they'll be running away from the equator all the time, and it will be difficult to set up equipment at one of them and hold station with respect to a corresponding point on Avernus. This time, right now, is the only time when we'll only have to deal with movement in one sense …' Ambrose halted the flow of words, meeting Snook's gaze.

'But those weren't the conditions you meant, were they?'

'No.'

'You were asking why I want to try it when we're stuck in the middle of nowhere, surrounded by trigger-happy storm-troopers who would shoot us as soon as look at us.'

'Something like that,' Snook said.

'Well, one reason is that nobody in the world today is going to like the idea of a race of alien supermen muscling in on what's left of our resources. The UN is likely to veto the whole thing on quarantine reasons alone, so it would be better to aim for a *fait accompli*. The chance is too good to miss.' Ambrose put his finger into a domed raindrop on the veranda railing and smeared it out flat.

'What's the other reason?'

'I got on to this thing first. I came here first. It's mine, Gil, and I *need* it. This is my one chance to be the person I set out to be a long time ago – can you understand that?'

'I think so, but does it mean so much that you don't care about people getting hurt?'

'I don't want anybody to get hurt – besides, I don't think I could drive Des and Benny off with a shotgun.'

'I was thinking more about Prudence,' Snook said. 'Why don't you use your influence with her and get her out of the country?'

'She's her own woman, Gil.' Ambrose sounded unconcerned as he turned to go indoors. 'What makes you think I've got any influence in that direction?'

'You've slept with her, haven't you?' Snook was unable to keep the bitterness out of his voice. 'Or doesn't that count any more?'

'That's *all* I've done – slept with her. I was too whacked for anything else that morning.' Ambrose looked at Snook with new interest. 'It's a good thing I was pole-axed – it probably spared me an embarrassing scene.'

'How?'

'Our Miss Devonald isn't as casual about sex as she likes people to believe. It's when you try to treat her like a woman that she begins acting like a man. And not just any man. General George S. Patton, I'd say.' Ambrose walked to the door of the house and then came back.

'How about you, Gil?' he said. 'Are you going to pull out on me?'

'No. I'll stay around.'

'Thanks – but why?'

Snook gave him a brief smile. 'Would you believe it's because I like Felleth?'

By the last decade of the twentieth century the standard of living in even the most advanced of the world's countries had become patchy. The Orwellian prediction that people would be able to afford nothing but luxuries had been amply fulfilled. It was, for example, difficult to obtain a safely edible fish, and the World Health Organisation had solemnly, and with every appearance of conviction, halved its mid-century estimate of the number of grammes of first-class protein that an adult needed each day to maintain good health.

On the other hand, communications were excellent – the synchronous satellite and the germanium diode ensured that practically everybody on the planet could be informed of an important event within minutes of its occurrence. It was, however, only possible to broadcast information – not understanding – and there were many who maintained that people in general would have been better off, certainly happier, without the ceaseless welter of news which bombarded them from the skies. The principal achievement of the telecommunications industry, they claimed, was that it was now possible to start in minutes the same riot that would have required days a few decades earlier.

Gene Helig's account of the events in Barandi National Mine No. 3 was in the hands of his colleague in the neighbouring statelet of Matsa before 8.00 a.m. local time, and in a further ten minutes had been relayed to the Press Association office in Salisbury, Rhodesia. Because both journalists concerned had the highest professional credentials, the story was accepted without question and beamed via satellite to several major centres, including London and New York. From there it was shared out among other

agencies with special ethnic, cultural, political or geographical interests. Up
to that point the original message had been analogous to the output grid
current in a thermionic valve, a puny trickle of electrons, but its character-
istics were suddenly amplified by the full power of the global news services
and it began to surge massively from pole to pole, swamping the various
media. Again as in the case of a thermionic valve, excessive amplification
led inevitably to distortion.

The reactions were almost immediate.

Tensions had been high in those equatorial countries in which the
Avernians had been sighted, and the news that the immaterial 'ghosts'
were planning to turn themselves into solid, substantial, material invaders
caused people to take to the streets. The terminator, the line which divided
night from day – and which also marked the emergence point of the alien
planet and its inhabitants – was proceeding westwards along the equator
at a leisurely rate of less than 1,700 kilometres an hour, and thus was far
outstripped by the rumours of the menace it was supposed to represent.
While morning sunlight was filtering down through the rain clouds which
covered Barandi, the darkness which still lay over Ecuador, Columbia and
three of the new countries which occupied northern Brazil was disturbed
here and there by the classical symptoms of panic. And far to the north,
in New York, members of several special United Nations committees were
summoned from their beds.

President Paul Ogilvie read carefully through the news summary
sheets and memoranda which had been left for his attention by his
personal secretary, then he pressed a switch on his communicator set
and said, 'I want Colonel Freeborn here immediately.'

He took a cigar from the silver box on his desk and busied himself with
the rituals of removing the band, cutting the sealed end and ensuring
that the tobacco was ignited evenly. His hands remained perfectly steady
throughout the entire operation, but he was not concealing from himself
the fact that he had been shocked by the news he had just read. His other
self, the one which obstinately clung to the old tribal name with which he
had begun life, felt a deep unease at the idea of ghosts stalking among the
lakeside trees, and the prospect of the ghosts materialising into solid flesh
smacked even more clearly of magic. The fact that the paraphernalia of nuclear physics was involved did not prevent the magic from being magic – the
knowledge that witch doctors used psychological techniques did nothing to
render them harmless.

At another level of consciousness, Ogilvie was disturbed by a conviction
that his present security and all his plans for the future were being threatened by the new developments at the mine. He enjoyed having fifty expensive suits and a fleet of prestige cars; he relished the superb food and wine,

and the exotic women which he imported like any other luxury commodity; and, above all, he savoured Barandi's growing acceptance among the other countries of the world, the imminence of its full membership of the United Nations. Barandi was his own personal creation, and official recognition by the UN would be history's seal of approval upon Paul Ogilvie, the man.

He had more to lose than any other man in the country, and his instincts were keener in proportion – it was becoming obvious to him that the affair at Three had been mishandled. Swift, stern measures at the outset might have quashed the whole thing, but it was too late for that now, and the danger was that Freeborn might go off the rails in full view of the world. Now that he thought of it, Colonel Freeborn was fast becoming an anachronism and a liability in a number of respects...

The communicator set buzzed softly and his secretary announced the Colonel's arrival. 'Send him in,' Ogilvie said, closing a mental file for the time being.

'Afternoon, Paul.' Freeborn strode into the big office with an air of barely controlled anger, his long-muscled galley slave's arms glistening beneath the half-sleeves of his drill shirt.

'Have you seen this stuff?' Ogilvie tapped the sheets on his blotter.

'I got my copies.'

'What do you think?'

'I think we've been pussy-footing around for far too long, and this is the outcome. It's time we went in there ...'

'I mean what do you think about these creatures from another world which are supposed to come through a machine?'

Freeborn looked surprised. 'I don't think anything of it – partly because I don't believe in fairy tales, but mainly because I'm going to kick those white *wabwa* out of the mine before they cost us any more time and money.'

'We can't do anything too hastily,' Ogilvie said, examining the ash of his cigar. 'I've just had word from New York that the United Nations is sending a team of investigators.'

'United Nations! United Nations! That's all I hear from you these days, Paul.' Freeborn clenched his fist around his gold-topped cane. 'What has happened to you? This is *our* country – we don't have to let anybody in if we don't want them.'

Ogilvie sighed, sending a flat cloud of grey smoke billowing on the polished wood of his desk. 'Everything can be handled diplomatically. The UN people want Doctor Ambrose to stop whatever it is he's doing, which suits us perfectly. As a matter of interest, did your friend Snook make any attempt to contact you and keep you informed as we arranged?'

'I've had no messages from him.'

'There you are! He ignored his brief, and that entitles me to tell him and

Doctor Ambrose to get out of the mine. And we'll be complying with the UN's wishes.'

Freeborn dropped into a chair and rested his forehead on one hand. 'I swear to you, Paul – this is making me ill. I don't care about Ambrose, but I've got to have this man, Snook. If I sent the Leopards back into …'

'Are you sure they could deal with him, Tommy? I've heard that when he's armed with a piece of cutlery he can overcome a platoon of Leopards.'

'I've just heard about that and haven't had time to investigate, but apparently there was an incident, a trivial incident, involving three of my men.'

'Three men and an officer, wasn't it?'

Freeborn did not raise his head, but a vein began to pulse on his shaven temple. 'What do you want me to do?'

'Get Snook's telephone line connected again,' Ogilvie said. 'I want to talk to him right now.' He sat back in his chair and watched as Freeborn took a small military communicator from his shirt pocket and spoke into it, noting with amusement that – even for such a minor detail – the Colonel used a prearranged code word. A minute later Freeborn nodded and put his radio away. Ogilvie instructed his secretary to get Snook on the line. He stared thoughtfully at the rain-streaming windows, deliberately presenting the appearance of a man in effortless control of his circumstances, until the connection was made.

'Good afternoon, Snook,' he said. 'Is Doctor Ambrose with you?'

'No, sir. He's down at the mine setting up some equipment.'

Freeborn stirred restlessly as Snook's voice reached him through the phone's loudspeaker attachment.

'In that case,' Ogilvie said, 'I'll have to deal with you, won't I?'

'Is there anything wrong, sir?' Snook sounded helpful, ready to please.

Ogilvie gave an appreciative laugh, recognising Snook's way of touching gloves with him. 'There appear to be quite a few things wrong. I don't like having to listen to the British Broadcasting Corporation to find out what's happening in my country. What happened to our arrangement that you would keep Colonel Freeborn informed of all developments at the mine?'

'I'm sorry, sir – but things have been happening so quickly, and my telephone has been out of order. In fact, yours is the first call to get through for days. I don't understand how it happened, because I've never had any trouble with the telephone before now. It might be something to do with the …'

'Snook! Don't overdo it. What's all this about a plan to make our so-called ghosts materialise into flesh and blood?'

'Is that what they said on the radio?'

'You know it is.'

'Well, that's Doctor Ambrose's department, sir. I don't even see how such a thing would be possible.'

'Neither do I,' Ogilvie said, 'but apparently some of the UN's science advisers think there could be something in it, and they don't like the idea any more than I do. They're sending a team of investigators with whom I'm going to cooperate to the fullest extent. In the meantime, Doctor Ambrose is to suspend all activities. Is that clear?'

'Very clear, sir. I'll contact Doctor Ambrose at once.'

'Do that.' Ogilvie replaced the phone and sat tapping it with a fingernail. 'Your friend Snook is as slippery as an eel – how many times did he address me as sir?'

Freeborn stood up, swinging his cane. 'I'd better get out to the mine and make sure they clear out of it.'

'No. I want the Leopards pulled right out and I want you to stay in Kisumu, Tommy – Snook gets under your skin too easily. I don't want any more trouble than I've already got.' Ogilvie gave Freeborn a moody, speculative stare.

'Besides, we both agree that the whole thing about visitors from another world is a ridiculous fairy tale.'

CHAPTER TWELVE

Snook had just set off down the hill to the mine when an unfamiliar car pulled up beside him, its wheel arches cascading yellowish muddy water. The passenger door opened and he saw Prudence leaning across the seat towards him.

'Where's Boyce?' she said. 'I don't see his car.'

'He's at the mine setting up some new equipment. I'm on my way to see him now.'

'Jump in and I'll take you – it's too wet for walking.' Prudence hesitated after Snook had got in. 'Will it be safe for me to go to the mine?'

'It's all right – my friends drove off in their jeeps about an hour ago.'

'They weren't your friends, Gil. I shouldn't have said anything like that.'

'I shouldn't have raked it up again. It's just ...' Snook held back the words which would make him vulnerable.

'Just what?' Prudence's eyes were steady on his own. She was still turned towards him, her skirt and blouse drawn tightly across her body in diagonal folds. Within the car, the dim afternoon light was reduced to a scented gloaming, the rain-fogged windows were screening off the rest of the world, and Prudence was smiling one of her rueful, perfect smiles.

'It's just,' Snook said, his heart assuming a slow, powerful rhythm, 'that I keep thinking about you all the time.'

'Dreaming up fresh insults?'

Snook shook his head. 'I'm jealous of you, and it's something that never happened to me before. When I walked into the Commodore, and saw you sitting with Boyce, I felt this pang of jealousy. It doesn't make any kind of sense, and yet I felt as if he'd robbed me. Since then ...' Snook stopped speaking, finding it genuinely difficult to form words.

'What is it, Gil?'

'Do you know what's happening now?' He smiled at her. 'I'm trying to make love to you without touching you – and it isn't easy.'

Prudence touched his hand and he saw in her face the beginnings of a special, unique softness. Her lips parted slowly, almost reluctantly, and he was leaning forward to claim fulfilment when a rear door of the car was thrown open and George Murphy exploded into their presence in a fluster of plastic clothing, rain splashes and mint-smelling breath. The car rocked on its suspension with the impact of his body.

'That was a bit of luck,' Murphy said breathlessly. 'I thought I'd have to walk all the way to the mine in that stuff. What a bloody day!'

'Hi, George.' Snook was oppressed by a sense of loss, of doors into the future closing with ponderous finality.

'You're going to the mine, aren't you?'

'Where else?' Prudence started the car moving down the hill and, in an immediate change of mood which filled Snook with an obscure pain, said, 'Gil wants to try out a new plastic pick axe.'

'It's bound to be better than the old-fashioned wood and steel jobs,' Murphy chuckled. 'Unless ... Unless ... How would it be if we tried making the *handles* out of wood and the blades out of steel?'

'Too revolutionary.' Prudence flashed him a smile over her shoulder. 'Everybody knows pick axes have to have wooden blades.'

Unable to match the levity, Snook said, 'I've just had a call from Ogilvie – he has ordered us out of the mine.'

'Why's that?'

'I suppose it's a reasonable demand, from his point of view.' Snook got a grim pleasure from stating the opposition case. 'Boyce was sent into the mine to lay ghosts, not to materialise them.'

They found Ambrose and Quig three hundred metres south of the mine head, working in a nondescript patch of flat ground which was used for the disposal of packing cases, scrap lumber and broken machine parts. Ambrose had calculated that the Avernians would attain an elevation of some two metres above ground at maximum, and he had constructed a makeshift platform of that height on which to place his equipment. He and Quig were soaked through, but were trudging about with a kind of water-logged cheerfulness which made Snook think of Great War soldiers giving thumbs-up signs for the benefit of correspondents' cameras. Already in place on the platform, and covered by a plastic sheet, was a bulky cube with Snook took to be the Moncaster machine. Ambrose came forward to meet the car, smiling uncertainly when he saw Prudence.

'What are you doing here?' he said, opening the driver's door.

Prudence took a handkerchief from her sleeve and dabbed the rain from his face. 'I've got a sense of history, *mon ami*. I've no intention of missing this show – provided there is a show, that is.'

Ambrose frowned. 'What does that mean?'

While Murphy got out of the car and distributed an armful of blue plastic raincoats, Snook gave Ambrose details of the telephone call from President Ogilvie. Ambrose accepted a raincoat, but made no move to put it on, and his mouth withered into a thin, hard line as he listened to Snook's report. He had begun shaking his head – slowly and steadily as an automaton – long before Snook had finished speaking.

'I'm not stopping,' he said in a harsh, unrecognisable voice. 'Not for President Paul Ogilvie. Not for anybody.'

Lieutenant Curt Freeborn listened to the words with a deep satisfaction which went a long way towards soothing the anguish which had been burning inside him for many hours.

He removed the headphones of the telebug system, being careful to avoid disturbing the patch of gauze over his right eye, and put them in the carrying case alongside the associated sighting scope. The foreigners were hundreds of paces away from him and completely wrapped up in their own affairs, but nevertheless he crawled on his hands and knees for quite a long distance to obviate the risk of being seen as he was leaving his observation post. When he had cleared the angular jungle of the dumping area, he got to his feet, brushed the clinging mud and grass from his slickers, and walked quickly to the entrance gate. None of the mine guards in the security building would have dared question his movements, but he waved to them in a friendly manner as he left the enclosure. He had evidence which would justify firm action against Snook and the others, and his spirits had improved at the prospect. More important, he had evidence of his own resourcefulness and value as an officer in the Leopard Regiment, evidence his uncle would have to accept.

Crossing the puddled surface of the street, he sheltered in a doorway and took his communicator from an inner pocket. There was a delay of only a few seconds while the local relay operator patched him through to his uncle's office in Kisumu.

'This is Curt,' he said tersely on hearing his uncle's identification. 'Are you free to speak?'

'I'm free to speak to you, Lieutenant, but I have no inclination to do so.' Colonel Freeborn replied with the voice of a stranger, and the fact that he was using the formal mode of address was a bad omen.

'I've just carried out a solo reconnoitre at the mine,' Curt said hurriedly. 'I got close enough to hear what Snook and the *daktari* were saying, and ...'

'How did you accomplish that?'

'Ah ... I used one of the K.80 remote listening sets.'

'I see – and did you bring it back with you?'

'Of course,' Curt said indignantly. 'Why do you ask?'

'I merely wondered if Mister Snook or his friend Murphy had decided to relieve you of it. From what I hear, you've been setting them up in the ex-army supplies business.'

Curt felt a needle spray of ice on his forehead. 'You've heard about ...'

'I think everybody in Barandi has heard – including the President.'

The sensation of stinging coldness began to spread over Curt's entire body, making him tremble. 'It wasn't my fault. My men were ...'

'Don't whine, Lieutenant. You went after a piece of white meat – regardless of my views on that sort of behaviour – and you let a couple of civilians disarm you in a public place.'

'I recovered the Uzis a few minutes later.' Curt did not mention that his automatic had not been found in the jeep.

'We can discuss the brilliance of your rearguard action at another time, when you're explaining why you didn't report the incident to me,' Colonel Freeborn snapped. 'Now get off the air and stop wasting my time.'

'Wait,' Curt said desperately, 'you haven't heard my report about the mine.'

'What about it?'

'They aren't leaving. They're planning to work on.'

'So?'

'But the President wants them to leave.' Curt was baffled by his uncle's reaction to his news. 'Wasn't it a firm order?'

'Firm orders have gone out of fashion in Barandi,' the Colonel said.

'With you, perhaps.' Curt could feel himself nearing a precipice, but he plunged onwards. 'But some of us haven't gone soft from sitting behind a desk all day.'

'You are hereby suspended from duty,' his uncle said in a cold, distant voice.

'You can't do this to me.'

'I'd have done it sooner if I'd known where you were hiding. I've already awarded floggings to the three soldiers you contaminated with your ineptness and reduced them to kitchen patrol. In your case, though, I think a court martial is called for.'

'No, uncle, no!'

'Do not address me in that manner.'

'But I can get them out of the mine for you,' Curt said, struggling against the wheedling note which was creeping into his voice. 'The President will be pleased, and that'll make everything ...'

'Wipe your nose, Lieutenant,' the Colonel ordered. 'And when you have finished wiping it, report to barracks. That is all.'

Curt Freeborn stared incredulously at his communicator for a moment, then he opened his fingers and let it fall to the concrete at his feet. Its pea-sized function indicator light continued to glow like a cigarette end in the gathering dimness. He smashed a metal-shod heel down on it, then stepped out into the rain, his smooth young face as impenetrable as that of an ebony carving.

At nightfall Ambrose called a temporary halt to the work and the group moved under the platform to drink coffee which he shared out from a huge flask. The rain had begun to ease off slightly and the presence of refreshments, coupled with the jostling comradeship, made the crude shelter seem cosy. They had been joined by Gene Helig, who added to the picnic atmosphere by producing a paper bag full of chocolate bars and a bottle of South African brandy. Culver and Quig became cheerfully intoxicated almost at once.

Twice during the amiable scrimmage Snook found himself standing next to Prudence. Self-consciously, like a schoolboy, he attempted to touch her hand – hoping to recreate something of the former moment of intimacy – but each time she moved away, seemingly oblivious to his presence, leaving him feeling thwarted and lonely.

Automatically, he countered with the defence measures which had served him without fail for many years in many countries. He threw the coffee from his cup, filled it to the brim with brandy, retreated to the outer edge of the shelter and lit a cigarette. The neat spirit kindled a fire inside him, but it was fighting a losing battle with the darkness which pressed in from the wilderness outside. Snook began to develop a gloomy conviction that Ambrose's enterprise was about to go disastrously wrong. He glanced around without interest as Ambrose came to stand beside him.

'Don't weaken,' Ambrose said. 'We'll be pulling out in the morning.'

'You're sure about that?'

'Positive. I had planned to follow later top dead centres up into the sky, but it's all becoming too difficult – I cancelled the helicopter today. I doubt if I would have been allowed to use it anyway.'

Snook swallowed more brandy. 'Boyce, what makes you so positive that

Felleth will be ready to attempt a transfer next time around?'

'He's a scientist. He knows as well as I do that tomorrow morning we'll have optimum conditions for the experiment.'

'Optimum, but not unique. I've been thinking about what you said, and I can see that when the surface of Avernus comes out through the Earth there'll be two top dead centres, one heading north and one heading south, but that only applies to this longitude, doesn't it? And what if they *are* moving? With a bit of time in hand, and international funding, you could beat that problem. And what about the poles? There must be very little movement there – just the sideslip.'

'You have been thinking, haven't you?' Ambrose raised his cup in a mock toast. 'Where would the international funding come from? It's the UN that's trying to block us right now.'

'But that's only their first reaction.'

'You want to bet?'

'All right – but what about the other points?'

'Can the Avernians travel round their equator at will? Have they got land in their temperate zones? Can they even reach their north and south poles?'

Snook delved into his fragmentary second memory. 'I don't think so, but ...'

'Believe me, Gil, tomorrow morning is the right time for this experiment.'

Snook was raising his cup to his lips when the significance of Ambrose's final word reached him. 'Wait a minute – that's the second time you've called it an experiment. Do you mean it isn't all cut and dried?'

'Hardly.' Ambrose gave Snook a strangely wan smile. 'That piece of paper you wrote on will advance our nuclear science by twenty years when I get it back to the States, but your friend Felleth is pushing his theoretical physics to the limit. I've looked at his equations and interactions, but – quite frankly – I'm not good enough to predict whether they'll work or not. They seem all right to me, but I'm not sure if Felleth will get through. There's also the possibility that he could make it and be dead on arrival.'

Snook was appalled by the new information. 'And you're still going to try it?'

'I thought you would understand, Gil,' Ambrose said. 'Felleth has to take this one ideal chance to prove that transfers are possible. His people need a ray of hope, and they need it fast. That's why we're committed.'

'Then ... you think that if you get proof the system works Earth will let them in later on?'

Ambrose grinned handsomely, tilting his cigarette with his lips like a matinee idol. 'Learn to think big, Gil. Times change – and there's almost a century to play with. Fifty years from now we might be ferrying Avernians down out of the sky in spaceships.'

'Well, I'll be …' Snook was impelled to grip the other man's hand. 'You know, I had you down as a self-centred bastard.'

'I am,' Ambrose assured him. 'It's just pure luck that this time I get a chance to disguise the fact.'

At that moment they were joined by George Murphy, who was nursing his bandaged right hand. 'I'm going over to the medical building to get myself a shot of something for this hand. I think I've toted too many bales with it, whatever that means.'

'I'll drive you there,' Ambrose said.

'No. I can do it on foot in a couple of minutes, and the rain has almost stopped.' Murphy set off into the blackness.

'I'll go with you,' Snook called after him, running to catch up. When they passed out of range of Ambrose's portable lights the going became treacherous and both men had to walk carefully, even with their Amplites on, until they reached the misty green radiance which surrounded the mine buildings. The medical building was as dark and lifeless as all the others in the vicinity.

'Here's the keys.' Murphy handed Snook a jingling cluster. 'Can you pick out number eight for me?'

'I expect so. If I can rebuild an aero engine I ought to be able …' Snook held still for a second, his senses probing the shadowed environment, then he lowered his voice. 'Don't look round, George – there's somebody behind you.'

'That's funny,' Murphy whispered, his left hand fumbling with the fastenings of his raincoat. 'I was going to say the same thing to you.'

'*Don't move!*' The command came from a tall young man who had stepped into view around a corner of the low building. He was wearing army slickers and a helmet with a lieutenant's bars on it, and there was a patch of white gauze over his right eye. A deep sadness welled up in Snook as he recognised Curt Freeborn. He glanced around him, assessing the chances of getting away, and saw three soldiers with drawn bush knives hemming them in. They were the same men he had encountered at the Cullinan, and they gave the impression of being determined that things would work out differently this time.

'What a stroke of luck!' Freeborn said. 'My two favourite people – the funny white man, and his Uncle Tom.'

Snook and Murphy looked at each other without speaking. 'No funny remarks, Mister Snook?' Freeborn began to smile. 'Aren't you feeling well?'

'What I'd like to know,' Murphy said, his left hand still working with the stiff, slippery plastic fastenings of his coat, 'is why four so-called Leopards are crawling around in the dark like rats.'

'I wasn't speaking to you, trash.'

'Take it easy, George,' Snook said anxiously.

'But this is an interesting point,' Murphy pressed on. 'The Colonel, for instance, would have come in with lights blazing. It seems to me that ...'

Freeborn gave a slight nod of his head, and almost immediately something struck Murphy in the back. The blow was so noisy, accompanied by a flapping crack of plastic, that Snook thought the corporal had slapped the big man down with the flat of his bush knife. Then he saw Murphy going down on his knees and, from a corner of his eye, the corporal pulling the blade back with difficulty. He caught hold of Murphy and felt the dreadful looseness of muscle and limb, a dead weight which pulled him inexorably downwards. Snook knelt, cradling Murphy in his left arm, and ripped open his coat. He slid his hand inside, feeling for a heartbeat, and was horrified to discover – even though the thrust had been at the back – that the whole chest region was bathed in a hot wetness. Murphy's mouth sagged open and, even in death, he smelled of mint.

'That was too quick,' Freeborn said to the corporal, his voice mildly reproachful, face impassive behind his Amplites. 'You let the Uncle Tom out too soon.'

'You ...' Snook tried to speak, but his throat closed on the words, the words which in any case would have failed to express his grief and hatred. He hugged Murphy's body to him and his right hand, sliding in blood, encountered a hard-edged, familiar shape. At that moment it was the most beautiful shape in the world, with a metallic perfection far beyond that of a priceless sculpture. Keeping his head lowered, Snook looked around him. He could see four pairs of legs, and – as he had prayed for them to be – they were all in the one quadrant of his vision. In one movement, he released Murphy's body and stood up with the automatic in his hand.

There was a long moment of throbbing, ringing silence as he faced the four men.

'We can come to an arrangement,' Lieutenant Freeborn said calmly. 'I know you're not going to pull that trigger, because you've waited too long. Your type needs to act on the spur of the moment, What happened just now was unfortunate, I'll admit, but there's no reason why we shouldn't fix up ...'

Snook shot him through the stomach, sending the doubled-up body hurtling against the wall, then wheeled on the three soldiers who had already begun to flee. Holding the automatic steady in a two-handed grip, he ranged on the corporal and squeezed the trigger again. The shot went through the corporal's shoulder, freakishly spinning him round so that he was facing the way he had come. Snook fired two more shots, each time seeing the plastic of the corporal's coat flap like a storm-caught sail, and he held the firing stance until his man had fallen, until he was certain that no further action was required of him. The two remaining soldiers disappeared from view.

All sound and movement ceased.

When humanity eventually returned to Snook, he took a deep quavering breath and dropped the automatic into his pocket. Without looking at Murphy again, he walked back to the area where he had left the group. When he got close they came forward to meet him, their faces watchful.

'What happened?' Ambrose said. 'Where's George?'

Snook kept walking until he was near enough to Quig to take the brandy bottle from his unresisting fingers. 'George is dead. We ran into Freeborn Junior and three of his men, and they killed George.'

'Oh, *no*,' Prudence murmured, and Snook wondered if she had guessed it had been the same group she had met.

'But this can't be.' Ambrose's face was grim and pale. 'Why should they shoot George?'

Snook took a drink from the bottle before he shook his head. 'They used a *panga* on George. I did the shooting – with this.' He took the automatic from his pocket and held it in the light where it could be seen. His hand was dark with blood.

'Did you hit anybody?' Helig said in a business-like voice.

Prudence looked at Snook's face. 'You did, didn't you?'

He nodded. 'I hit Freeborn Junior. And the man who killed George. I hit them square on.'

'I don't like the sound of this, old boy. Do you mind?' Helig retrieved his bottle, poured some brandy into a cup and gave the bottle back to Snook. 'This place will be swarming with troops in half an hour.'

'That's it then,' Ambrose said in a dull voice. 'It's all over.'

'Especially for George.'

'I know what you're thinking, Gil – but George Murphy wanted this project to go on.'

Snook thought about Murphy, the man with whom he had become friendly only a few days earlier, and was surprised by how little he knew about him. He had no idea where Murphy lived or even if he had any family. All he knew for certain was that Murphy had got himself killed because he was brave and honest, and because he cared about his friends and the miners who worked for him. George Murphy would have liked the transfer project to go on, and the more startling the end result the better, because the greater the world interest that was aroused the less opportunity there would be for force to be used on his miners.

'There might still be time,' Snook said. 'I don't think young Freeborn and his gang were acting under orders. If it was some kind of a private raid, they mightn't be missed until some time tomorrow.'

Helig frowned his doubt. 'I wouldn't count on it, old boy. The guards at the gate are bound to have heard the shooting. Anything could happen.'

'Anybody who wants to leave should go now,' Ambrose commented, 'but I'm staying as long as possible. We could be lucky.'

Lucky! Snook thought, wondering just how relative the meaning of a word could become. The brandy bottle was still one-third full and, laying tacit claim to it, he retreated to the same corner where he had stood with Ambrose only ten minutes earlier. Ten minutes was only a short span of time, and yet, because it separated him from a personal epoch in which Murphy had been alive, it could have been years or centuries. His own luck, he now realised, had begun to desert him that day in Malaq three years earlier when he had answered the emergency call to go to the airfield. Looking even more closely at the chain of circumstance, the emergency which had been sparked off by the passing of Thornton's Planet had not been an isolated event. He had quickly forgotten his single look at the livid globe in the sky, but the ancients and today's primitives were wise enough to regard such things as portents of calamities to come. Avernus had suffered at that time, been dragged out of her orbit, and he – without being aware of it – had been caught in the same gravitational maelstrom. Boyce Ambrose, Prudence, George Murphy, Felleth, Curt Freeborn, Helig, Culver, Quig – these were merely the names of asteroids which had been drawn into a deadly spiral, the motive forces of which emanated from another universe.

Looking out into the darkness, taking small regular sips from the bottle, Snook found it hard to credit that astronomy – that most remote and inhuman of the sciences – should have had such a devastating effect on his life. But he was, of course, wrong in thinking of the subject as being remote, especially now that – at points along the equator – the era of close-range astronomy was being ushered in. People could now look at another world from a distance of only a few metres. And in several years' time, when a large crescent of Avernus had emerged through the Earth, astronomy could even become a mass entertainment. It would be possible to stand on a hilltop on a dark night, wearing Amplites, and see the vast, luminous dome of the alien planet spanning the horizons and looming high into the sky. The rotation of the Earth would carry watchers closer and closer to the translucent enormity of the planet – revealing details of its land masses, the houses, the people – and finally plunge them under its surface, to emerge some time later on the daylight side, where Avernus would be rendered invisible.

Marshalling unfamiliar thoughts, Snook found, gave him some respite from the anguish he felt over Murphy's death. He tried to visualise the position some thirty-five years ahead when the two worlds were overlapping by only half a planetary diameter. Near the equatorial regions the two great spheres would be intersecting at right angles, in which case the spectators would see a vertical wall sweeping towards them at supersonic speed. On the face of that wall, fountaining upwards into the sky – also at supersonic speed – would be a steady procession of Avernian landmarks seen from directly above. It would require nerve not to close one's eyes at the moment of silent intersection; but a greater spectacle would come thirty-five years beyond that again when the two worlds fully separated from each other. The directions of rotational movement would be opposed to each other at the point of final contact. By that time magniluct glasses might have been improved to the point at: which they made Avernus appear completely solid. If so, there would come dizzy, mind-exploding minutes when it would be possible to see the surface of an upside-down world streaming past, just above one's head, at a combined speed of over three thousand kilometres an hour, bombarding the eyesight with inverted buildings and trees which – although insubstantial – would rip through a man's awareness like the teeth on a cosmic circular saw.

And following that, in the year of 2091, would come the ultimate spectacle, with the return of Thornton's Planet.

The separating gap would have increased to less than four thousand kilometres by that time, which meant that – for wearers of Amplites – Avernus would fill the entire sky. Earth would have a ringside seat for the destruction of a world …

Snook abruptly pulled back into the present, where he had enough problems of his own. He wondered if the rest of the group, Prudence in particular, understood that he was to die soon. If they did, if she did, no signs were being given to him. He could have done without a show of sympathy from the others, but it would have been good, very good, if Prudence had come to him with words of regret and love, and allowed him to cradle her neat golden head in the crook of his left arm. *Thy navel is like a round goblet, which wanteth not liquor*, the ancient words ran in his mind, *thy belly is like an heap of wheat set about with lilies.*

Thinking back on it, Snook found himself beginning to doubt that the moment of closeness in Prudence's car had actually occurred. Another possibility was that she had responded to him as momentarily and casually as if she had been patting a stray puppy on the head, and with no more meaning. The irony was that he was supposed to have a rare telepathic gift – yet he was less able to divine the workings of a girl's mind than any clumsy adolescent on his first date. Unless one was surrounded by like beings, he decided, telepathy would be an intensifier of loneliness. No apartment is as lonely as the one in which can be heard faint sounds of a party next door.

It occurred to Snook that he was rapidly becoming drunk, but he continued to sip the brandy. A certain degree of intoxication made it easier to accept the fact that there was no way he could get out of Barandi alive. It also made it easier to reach a relevant decision. When Colonel Freeborn came he would be looking for Gilbert Snook – not the other members of the group – and, once he had Snook, he was likely to devote all his attention to him for quite a long time, during which Ambrose might be able to complete the big experiment.

It was a perfectly logical decision, therefore, that – when the Leopards arrived at the mine – he should go forward and give himself up to them.

CHAPTER THIRTEEN

The soldier was so drunk that he would have been unable to stand but for the support of the two military policemen who gripped his arms. From the state of his uniform it was obvious that he had fallen more than once, and had been helplessly sick. In spite of his physical misery, he was terrified in the presence of Colonel Tommy Freeborn, and he told his story in disconnected groups of words – with frequent lapses into Swahili – which made sense only to someone who already had the general picture. When he had finished speaking, the Colonel stared at him with leaden-eyed contempt.

'You're positive,' Freeborn said, after a pause, 'that it was the white man, Snook, who had the weapon?'

'Yes, sir.' The soldier's head rolled from side to side as he spoke. 'And I only done what the Lieutenant told me.'

'Take this object away,' Freeborn ordered. As the redcaps bundled the soldier out of the office, the sergeant who accompanied them glanced back with an unspoken question. Freeborn nodded and mimed the action of pulling a hat down over his ears. The sergeant – who was a useful man, and knew that the invisible hat was a polythene bag – saluted correctly and left the office.

As soon as he was alone, Colonel Freeborn lowered his head and thought for a few moments about his brother's son, then he opened a communicator channel and gave a series of orders which would assemble a force of a hundred men at the entrance to National Mine No. 3. He picked up his cane, flicked a speck of dust from his half-sleeved shirt, and, walking with a firm and measured tread went outside to where his car was waiting. It was two hours before dawn and the night wind was cold, but he waved away the coat offered by his driver and got into the car's rear seat.

During the drive from Kisumu he sat without moving, bare arms folded, and in his mind apportioned the blame for his nephew's death. One part he allocated to himself – in his efforts to eradicate Curt's weaknesses he had pushed the boy too hard and threatened him with too much; a larger portion he laid at the door of Paul Ogilvie, without whose interference there would have been no unwanted foreigners meddling with the operation of the mine; but the greatest share of the guilt lay with the insolent trickster, Gilbert Snook, who should have been put down like a dog on the day he entered Barandi.

The hour was not yet ripe for Ogilvie to be brought to book, but within a short time – a very short time, Freeborn promised himself – Snook would regret that he had not been quietly suffocated three years earlier. Each thought of Snook was like the opening of a furnace door within Freeborn's head, and as he neared the mine he could feel himself being buoyed higher and higher on the searing blasts. It was like a plunge into black Arctic waters, therefore, when – on reaching the mine entrance – he saw one of the Presidential limousines parked outside the gates. Its gleaming waxy haunches looked incongruous against the backdrop of military trucks and watchful troops. He got out of his own car and, knowing what was required of him, went straight to the limousine and got into the rear seat beside Paul Ogilvie.

The President did not turn his head as he spoke. 'I want an explanation for this, Tommy.'

'The situation has changed since we ...' Uncharacteristically, Freeborn abandoned his officialese. 'Curt has been murdered by Snook.'

'I've heard about that. I'm still waiting for an explanation of why these men are here.'

'But ...' Freeborn felt his temples begin to throb. 'I've just told you – my nephew has been murdered.'

'Telling me that your nephew and other members of his regiment went into the mine against my orders does not explain why you have assembled this force of men here against my orders.' Ogilvie's voice was dry and cold. 'Are you challenging my authority?'

'I would never do that,' Freeborn said, flooding his voice with sincerity, while his mind weighed up the kind of factors which influence the history of nations. His service automatic was within reach of his right hand, but before he could use it he would have to open the leather flap of his holster. It was most unlikely that Ogilvie would have ventured out without protection, and yet he must have moved very quickly after being contacted by his informants. This moment, here in the darkness of the car, could be a pivotal point for the whole of Barandi – and Curt's death might have served a useful purpose ...

'A penny for them.' The note of complacency in Ogilvie's voice told Freeborn all he needed to know. The President was protected, and the *status quo* would have to remain for some time yet.

'Leaving personal issues aside,' Freeborn said, 'the Leopard Regiment is a keystone of our internal security. Those men out there don't know anything about international policies and diplomacies – what they *do* know is that two of their comrades have been shot down in cold blood by a white foreigner. They don't think very much about anything, but if they get the idea that such actions are not followed by swift punishment...'

'You don't need to spell it out for me, Tommy. But the UN people will be here tomorrow.'

'And will they be favourably impressed to learn that murderers go unpunished in Barandi?' Sensing he had found the right approach, Freeborn pressed home his argument. 'I'm not proposing a massacre of innocents, Paul. The only man I want is Snook, and he's probably an embarrassment to the others – they'll probably be glad to get rid of him.'

'What are you proposing?'

'Let me go in there with a couple of men and simply ask that he give himself up. I'd only have to hint that it would be for the benefit of the others. Including the girl.'

'You think it would be enough?'

'I think it would be enough,' Freeborn said. 'You see, Snook is that kind of a fool.'

Having disposed of the brandy, Snook climbed up on the platform and watched the others at work. Since hearing of Murphy's death they had gone about their tasks with a moody determination, only speaking when necessary. Ambrose, Culver and Quig spent most of their time kneeling at the complex control panel on the rear surface of the Moncaster machine. Even Helig and Prudence were busy with hammers and nails, erecting a makeshift handrail which Ambrose had decreed necessary for safety reasons. They had already completed another structure resembling a shower cubicle built of wood and clear plastic sheeting. Two cylinders of hydrogen stood inside the transparent box.

The concerted activity, in which he had no part, increased Snook's sense of not belonging, and it was almost with relief that he heard the distant growl of truck engines.

None of the others appeared to notice the sound, so he did not mention it. Minutes dragged by without any sign of military activity, and he began to wonder if his imagination had conjured with the irregular soughing of the night wind. The logical thing, bearing in mind the decision he had reached, would have been to stroll quietly towards the mine entrance, but he felt a powerful reluctance simply to fade away into the darkness. He was not of the group, and yet he did not want to face the alternative.

'That's it.' Ambrose stood up and rubbed his hands together. 'The mini-pile is delivering all the power we need. I think we're all set.' He glanced at his watch. 'Less than half an hour to go.'

'That's quite a machine,' Snook said, suddenly aware of the enormity of what was being attempted.

'It certainly is. Up until ten years ago you would have needed an accelerator about five kilometres long to produce the radiation fields we can make right in here.' Ambrose stroked the top of the machine as if it were a favourite pet.

'Isn't it dangerous?'

'It can be if you stand in front of it, but that applies to a bicycle as well. It's machines like this that have speeded up nuclear research so much in the last decade – and with what we're learning from Felleth ...'

'Watch out for the cubicle!' Ambrose shouted to Helig. 'We can't afford any rips in the plastic skin – it has to be airtight.'

Snook examined the flimsy structure with growing doubt. 'Is that where you're expecting Felleth to materialise?'

'That's the place.'

'But will he have to stay in there? How do you know he breathes hydrogen?'

'The hydrogen isn't for breathing, Gil. It's to provide the physical environment Felleth specified for his arrival, or part of it anyway. His knowledge is way beyond mine, but I think it's to provide a convenient supply of protons which he'll use to ...'

'Doctor Ambrose,' bellowed an amplified voice from the encircling blackness. 'This is Colonel Freeborn, Head of Barandian Internal Security. Can you hear me?'

Snook moved towards the ladder, but Ambrose gripped his arm with surprising strength. 'I can hear you, Colonel.'

'This afternoon President Ogilvie sent instructions that you were to stop working here. Did you receive the message?'

'I received it.'

'Then why are you disobeying?'

Ambrose hesitated. 'I'm not disobeying, Colonel. One of these machines has a miniature nuclear reactor inside it, and the controls aren't working properly. We've spent the last six hours trying to close it down.'

'That sounds like a very convenient story, Doctor Ambrose.'

'If you'd like to come up here I'll show you what I mean.'

'I'm prepared to let it pass for the time being,' Freeborn's voice boomed. 'I see that you have Snook with you.'

'Yes – Mister Snook is here.'

'I have come to place him under arrest for the murder of two members of the Barandian Armed Forces.'

'For *what*?' Ambrose's voice was hoarse with the effort of shouting.

'I think you heard me, Doctor.'

'Yes, but it was so unexpected that I ... We did hear some shooting, but I had no idea what was happening. This is terrible.' Ambrose released Snook's arm and backed away from him.

'The reason I'm keeping my distance is that Snook is armed. It will not prevent his arrest, of course, but I would prefer that he be taken without any shooting. I have no wish for the innocent members of your party to be hurt, and that can be avoided if Snook will give himself up.'

'Thank you, Colonel.' Ambrose's shadowed face was unreadable as he stared at Snook. 'You'll appreciate that this has come as a great shock to me and the other members of my party who, as you say, are innocent and had no idea of what was going on. May we have a little time to talk things over?'

'Fifteen minutes – no more.'

A lengthy silence ensued, showing that Freeborn considered the dialogue to have ended.

'Nice work, Boyce,' Snook said, keeping his voice low in case remote listening devices were trained on him. He recognised that Ambrose had acted with superb common sense in dissociating himself and the others, but the knowledge did not ease his irrational sense of betrayal. He nodded to Prudence and the three other men, and turned to leave.

'Gil,' Ambrose whispered fiercely, 'where in hell do you think you're going?'

'In hell? Any old place will do.'

'Stay right there. I'm going to get you out of this.'

Snook gave a humourless laugh. 'There's no way out. Besides, the little diversion could give you enough time to complete the experiment. That's the main item on the agenda, isn't it?'

Ambrose shook his head. 'We agreed earlier tonight that I'm a self-centred bastard, but I have to draw the line somewhere. I don't mind admitting I was hoping to be left alone long enough to go ahead as planned, but now the situation has changed.'

'Look ...' Snook tapped himself on the chest. 'I don't want to sound melodramatic, but I'm as good as dead already. There's nothing you can do about it.'

'I know you're as good as dead, Gil,' Ambrose said, his voice resonant. 'Otherwise I wouldn't risk offering you the one escape that's available.'

'Escape?' Snook felt the same old chill of premonition as he glanced at the cubical machine. 'Where to?'

'There's nowhere else for you to go,' Ambrose replied. 'Nowhere except ... Avernus.'

Snook took an involuntary step backwards, then looked around the rest of the group standing close by. Their faces were solemn and wide-eyed, like those of children, attention directed towards Ambrose.

'There's a risk involved,' Ambrose said. 'I can only do this with your consent and co-operation, and I wouldn't try it at all if you had any other hope of getting out of here.'

Snook swallowed painfully. 'What would you do?'

'There just isn't time to give you a course in nuclear physics, Gil. Basically it involves reversing Felleth's processes, making you neutron-rich – but you'll just have to trust me. Are you willing?'

'I'm willing,' Snook said. He glimpsed in his mind's eye the elongated diamond-shapes of Avernian islands. 'But it isn't what you came here to do.'

'That doesn't matter. In this situation I couldn't risk transferring Felleth, or any other Avernian, into our universe – somebody would probably shoot him.' Ambrose paused to light a cigarette, his gaze locked on Snook's face. 'But we can still prove the principle of operation, for Felleth's benefit.'

'All right.' Snook discovered he was more afraid than he had been at the prospect of merely being killed. 'What do you want me to do?'

'Well, the first thing you have to do is get in touch with Felleth and tell him about the change of plan.'

'Boyce, you make it sound … Have you got his phone number?'

'He'll need reaction time, Gil. He has a lot of expertise, but even so he'll need some warning so that he can make ready to receive you.' Ambrose's face was impassive, but Snook sensed that his brain was racing, evaluating probabilities like a world-class card player.

'Do you think he can do it in time?' Snook knew the question demanded resources of knowledge which did not exist on Earth, but was unable to hold it back.

'Felleth is way ahead of us in this field, and the energy relationships favour a transfer from this universe into his. I think that with him doing a lot of pulling, and us doing a bit of pushing, it should work out all right.'

Snook suddenly realised he had lost all human contact with Ambrose – it was impossible to tell whether he was giving reassurance as a friend, or taking the appropriate action to protect his experiment. It made no practical difference either way – his own choice was between the certainty of death on Earth and the possibility of life on Avernus. He turned towards Prudence, but she looked away from him immediately, and he knew at once that she was afraid. A fresh worry appeared in his mind.

'Boyce, supposing everything works out right and I sort of … disappear,' he said, 'what's going to happen here afterwards? Freeborn isn't going to like it very much.'

Ambrose was unperturbed. 'That problem will take care of itself – but you're not even going to have a chance to transfer unless you do something about contacting Felleth right now.' He examined his watch, clicking its display buttons. 'He'll be coming up through the station we marked on Level Two in just over four minutes.'

'I'll go,' Snook said quietly, aware that the time for talking had passed.

They went down the ladder and assembled in a tight group beneath the platform, giving cover for Snook as he slipped away towards the mine head. He ran as quickly as possible, depending on the blue lenses of his Amplites to keep him from falling over obstacles, and praying that Freeborn had not taken the precaution of saturating the area with his men. It came to him that Freeborn had been strangely gentle in his handling of the situation, but there was not time for analysis of his motives.

Nearing the entrance of the shaft, he remained as long as possible in the lee of the vacuum pipes which curved away from it like the tentacles of a huge octopus. By repeating the moves that Murphy had always made, he started the elevator machinery and was grateful for the silence of its operation. He stepped into a descending cage, rode it downwards to Level Two and leaped out on to the circular gallery. For a panicky moment he was unable to identify the opening of the south pipe, then he was inside it and running with the cold air sighing in his ears.

When he reached the area marked out by Ambrose he found that Felleth and several other Avernians were already present, visible from the waist up above the rock floor, and coming more fully into view with every second, their unnaturally wide mouths pouting and pursing. The bluish translucent figures were interspersed with what seemed to be machines and tall rectangular cabinets.

None of the Avernians reacted to his arrival, and Snook recalled that on this occasion he was not being illuminated for them by Ambrose's special equipment. He fixed his gaze on Felleth – one part of his mind wondering how he had made the identification – and went forward. Felleth suddenly raised his web-fingered hands to his head, and Snook saw the glint of the living green wall superimposed on his vision. He inclined his head towards Felleth's, once more seeing the mist-pools of the eyes grow larger and larger until they swamped his mind.

Deep peace of the running wave.

I understand you, Equal Gil. You may come.

Deep peace of the running wave.

Snook found himself kneeling on the uneven wet stone of the tunnel floor, his Amplites showing – apart from a view of his normal surroundings – only a vague general radiance. That meant, he remembered, that the surface of Avernus had already risen above his head. He looked up at the curving hewn roof, wondering how much time he had lost. If he was to have any chance of life he had to rendezvous with Felleth and Ambrose at a point directly above his present position. Felleth was already on his way, straight up through geological strata which, for him, were non-existent – but for Snook there was no option other than retracing his steps.

He got to his feet, trying to throw off the now-familiar weakness which followed telepathic union, and ran towards the shaft. Reaching the gallery, he climbed into an ascending cage and clung to its mesh sides until he had been carried up to ground level. He lowered his head and ran towards the platform, heedless now of anyone trying to stop him. The portable lights surrounding the platform came into view in the starless black, and with the sight there returned his appreciation of the need to avoid blundering into possible enemies. He slowed his pace, crouched low and silently made his way to the base of the platform. Ambrose and Helig were waiting for him at the foot of the ladder.

'I got to Felleth,' Snook blurted, fighting to control his breathing. 'It's all right.'

'Good work,' Ambrose said. 'We'd better go up and get started. There isn't much time.'

They climbed the ladder and found Prudence and the other three men standing in a silent group. Snook got the impression they had been holding a whispered conversation and had broken it off on his arrival. There was a strong feeling of embarrassment, none of them wanting to meet his gaze, and he knew that barriers had fallen into place in the same way as when it is learned that a member of a family or group is going to die. No matter how hard they may try, he realised, people who know they have a continuing future cannot help being alienated by the aura surrounding a person who is making ready to die. In theory, Snook's life was being saved by nuclear magic – but his world-line was about to be terminated with a finality equal to that of the grave, and the fact had to be subconsciously resented by all others present.

'We don't need this,' Ambrose said, pushing the plastic hydrogen tent out of the way. He upended a small wooden crate where the tent had been. 'You'd better sit on this, Gil.'

'Right.' Snook tried to appear stolid and unmoved, but a deathly chill had gathered inside him, and his knees felt weak as he crossed the platform and shook hands with Helig, Culver and Quig. He had no idea why the formality suddenly seemed necessary to him. Prudence took his hand in both of hers, but her face was the mask of a high priestess as he kissed her once, very lightly and very briefly. He was turning away when she spoke his name.

He said, 'What is it, Prudence?' There flickered in him the hope that she would give him something, a gift of words, to take to another world.

'I ...' her voice was almost inaudible. 'I'm sorry I laughed at your name.'

He nodded his head, strangely gratified and unable to speak, then went and sat down on the crate. The only occasion on which Prudence had shown amusement over his name had been at their very first meeting, and in his state of abject craving for human comfort it seemed to him that the odd apology had been her way of wiping clean the slate of subsequent events. *That's as good as you're going to get,* he thought. *Perhaps it was more than you could have expected, under the circumstances.* He looked all around him, taking in the sight which – barring some grotesque anti-climax – was to be his last view of Earth.

The five people on the platform stared back at him, but their blue-lenses Amplite glasses – which enabled them to see in darkness – made them look like blind people. Surrounding the crude wooden stage was a curtain of night which was now beginning to abate slightly, and he knew that dawn was near. Only the thick covering of low cloud, similar to that of Avernus, was keeping the level of light so low. Ambrose had moved in behind the Moncaster machine and was intent on its controls when Freeborn's voice crashed from out of the blackness.

'The fifteen minutes is up, Doctor,' it said, 'and I'm tired of waiting.'

'We haven't finished our discussion,' Ambrose shouted, his hands still busy.

'What is there to discuss?'

'You must understand that it's asking a lot for us to hand over a man when we have no evidence of his crime.'

'You've been playing games with me, Doctor.' The amplification and echoes made Freeborn's voice come from all sides at once. 'You'll be sorry you did that. If Snook doesn't give himself up immediately I'm coming to take him.'

The words brought it home to Snook that, regardless of what might have lain in store for him, he was still an inhabitant of Earth and retained all his responsibilities. 'I have to go down there, Boyce,' he said. 'We've run out of time.'

'Stay where you are,' Ambrose commanded. 'Kill the lights, Des.' Quig stooped and pulled a cable connection apart, and the faint light reflecting upwards from the ring of ground lights abruptly vanished.

'What good will that do?' Snook half-rose, then sank back on to his improvised seat. With the onset of full darkness, ghostly blue figures could be seen beyond the edge of the platform. The inhabitants of Avernus – silent, translucent and awesome – moved among and through the piles of dank lumber, their eyes turning without seeing, their wide mouths moving without speech. In a few seconds there came the cries of frightened men. A gun was fired time after time, but the shots were not directed at human targets, and eventually there was a return to silence. The Avernians continued their strolling, unaware of anything outside their own universe.

'I was sure we could buy some time that way,' Ambrose said, secure in his role of master magician as the faint outlines of a building became visible about him. 'Now, Gil, this is it. Felleth will be up level with us in a couple of minutes, and I've got to get you ready for him.'

With the removal of one danger, Snook's former fears returned to him and he sought the comfort of words again. 'What are you going to do to me, Boyce?' An instinct prompted him to take the automatic from his pocket and slide it away from him across the uneven timber.

'I'm surrounding you with a flux of neutrons, that's all.' Ambrose sounded calm. 'I'm making you neutron-rich.'

Incredibly, Snook found he was still capable of thought. 'But parts of a nuclear plant are bombarded with neutrons for years, and they just stay put. Don't they?'

'It isn't the same thing, Gil. In a power plant the neutrons don't exist long enough, or else they're manifested in other reactions.' Ambrose went on speaking in the same reassuring monotone as the figures of Felleth and other Avernians and their equipment rose up around him. 'This is mainly Felleth's show, of course – he's got all the work of synthesising your body with his elements. All we know is that the free neutrons to which you're being converted will decay into protons, electrons and anti-neutrons. And Felleth will ensure that the anti-neutrons are preserved ...'

Snook ceased listening to the incantation as the insubstantial framework of a cabinet was manoeuvred into place around him by Avernians who had luminous mist-pools for eyes. He looked for Prudence, but she had covered her face with her hands. There was just enough time for him to hope that she was crying for his sake ...

Then he journeyed beyond the stars.

CHAPTER FOURTEEN

The room was about ten metres square, but seemed smaller because of the amount of equipment it contained – and because of the presence of the Avernians.

Snook looked at them in silence, without trying to move, while his body recovered from the sensation of having been *jolted*. He was breathing normally, and his physical functions seemed to be continuing as they always did, but his nerves felt as though they were vibrating in the aftermath of a paralysing shock, like tunnels in which there lingered the echoes of a scream.

The Avernians stared back at him with brooding concentration, also in silence, their eyes watchful. Snook discovered that his growing familiarity with their general appearance as seen from Earth, the sketches in luminous mist, had not prepared him for the solid, three-dimensional reality. In previous encounters he had been impressed by their similarity to human beings; now he was in a room with them, breathing the same air, and his overwhelming impression was one of alienation.

One part of his mind felt a numb gratitude over the fact that he was alive, but with each passing second that consideration seemed less and less important, or even relevant. The only truth which retained any significance was that he was alone in a world peopled by unknown and unknowable beings whose eyes and noses were clustered too close to the tops of their heads, and whose mouths twitched and pursed and flowed with frightening mobility. The skin of the Avernians shaded from a pale yellow around the eyes and mouths to a coppery brown at the hands and feet, and had a waxy sheen to it. They were surrounded by an unnameable odour, suggestive of formaldehyde and perhaps cardamom, which added to their strangeness and caused an upward lift of Snook's stomach muscles.

Five seconds gone – thirty years to go, he thought, and with the thought came claustrophobic panic. *Why doesn't Felleth speak? Why doesn't he help me?*

'I have been ... talking to you, Equal Gil,' Felleth said in a laboured, husking voice. 'We have an unfortunate situation ... we have access to your mind ... but we are screened from yours ... and you would not wish for me ... to come closer.'

'No!' Snook jumped to his feet and stood swaying. His shoulder struck an open-fronted cabinet which had been enclosing him on three sides and it rolled backwards on castors. He looked down and saw that the wooden box on which he had been sitting was itself resting on an irregularly shaped section of wet timber which contrasted with the polished white floor beneath it. The words, JENNINGS ALES, stencilled on the side of the box might have been chosen for their homeliness, as a reminder that everything he knew had been left on the far side of infinity.

'I have to go back,' he said. 'Send me back Felleth. Anywhere on Earth.'

'That is not possible ... energy relationships not favourable ... no receiving station for you.' Felleth's chest heaved, apparently from the strain of reproducing human speech. 'You need time ... to adjust.'

'I can't adjust. You don't know ...'

'We do know ... we have access ... we know that we are ... repellent to you.'

'I can't help that.'

'Try to remember ... you impose greater strain on us ... we have access ... and you have killed.'

Snook looked at the robed figures of the Avernians, and there came a glimmer of understanding of the fact that they had needed courage to remain in the same room with him. The Avernians, he recalled, were a gentle, pacific race, and this particular group were bound to feel that they had conjured up a dangerous primitive. He glanced instinctively at his right hand and saw that it still bore traces of George Murphy's blood. His xeno-phobia began to be swept aside by a sense of shame.

'I'm sorry,' Snook said.

'I think it is important that you should rest ... to recover from the mental and physical effects ... of the transfer.' The breath whistled and sighed in Felleth's throat as he vocalised the words being taken from Snook's mind. 'This is not a dwelling place ... but we have prepared a bed ... in the adjoining apartment ... follow me.' Felleth walked with a stately gliding movement to a doorless opening which was narrower at the top than at the floor level.

Snook gazed after him for a few seconds without stirring. The notion of falling asleep was ludicrous, then he understood he was being given the chance to be alone. He started after Felleth, then turned, picked up the beer crate and took it with him. Felleth led the way along a short corridor which, at the far end, had a window giving a view of grey sky and grey ocean growing lighter with dawn. Snook followed his guide into a small room containing nothing but a simple couch. The room had a single window and the walls were decorated with horizontal strips of neutral colour, seemingly in a random pattern.

'We will meet again,' Felleth said. 'And you will feel better.'

Snook nodded, still holding the crate, and waited until Felleth withdrew. The doorway was of the same trapezoid shape as the first, but vertical leaves slid from recesses in the wall to seal it. Snook went to the window and looked out at the world which was to be his home. There was a descending vista of brown-tiled roofs, with occasional views of alleys and squares in which the People could be seen going about their unhurried, enigmatic affairs. They wore flowing, draped garments of white or blue, and from a distance they resembled citizens of ancient Greece. There were no vehicles in sight, no light standards or telephone poles, no antennae.

The ocean began without intervention of open land, stretching to the horizon, and a hundred islands were ranged across it like ships at anchor. Most of the islands rose to central low peaks, creating – with their reflections – elongated diamond-shapes, but in the middle distance a pair were made into one by a massive double-spanned arch. Snook had seen it before, in a vision implanted by Felleth.

He turned away from the window, his mind sated with strangeness, and went to the couch. He placed the orange-dyed wooden crate beside it, then took off his wrist watch and set it on top, establishing his own little island of the commonplace. Next, he removed his blue raincoat – which was still spattered with the moisture of Earth – rolled it up and placed it beside the crate. When he lay down he discovered an unutterable weariness coiling through his limbs, but it was a long time before he escaped into sleep.

Snook had a dream that he was with Prudence Devonald, and that they were shopping for coffee and cheese in a small-town store. Beyond the gold-lettered store windows was a busy high street, with red buses, a church spire and leaves scattering in an October breeze. The gem-like clarity of the dream made it very real, the simple happiness he felt was very real, and when it began to slip away he fought to hold on, because the tiny part of him which was not deceived told him the awakening would be bad.

It was.

He sat on the edge of the couch, with head lowered, then the mental habits of a lifetime began to reassert themselves. *Boy meets girl, boy loses girl,* he thought. *Boy has to find out if there's any plumbing in this place.*

He stood up, looked around the bare room and picked up his watch, which told him it was past noon. The increased brightness from the single window confirmed what he already knew, that Avernian time kept pace with that of Earth. He went to the door and tried to slide the two leaves apart, but they refused to move, and the central crack was too narrow to give his fingers any purchase. The idea that he had been locked in did not cross his mind – he was certain the door could be opened easily by anyone who knew what to do, and therefore he was reluctant to call for help. He tried moving around on the floor near the threshold, testing for pressure switches, then a tentative solution occurred to him. Blanking everything else from his thoughts, he walked steadily and confidently towards the door, *expecting* it to open.

The leaves parted at once and, before he had time to think about what was happening, he was outside in the corridor. He looked back at the opening in appreciative wonderment, revising his ideas about Avernian technology. Remarks passed by Ambrose had told him that Felleth and his co-workers were ahead of Earth in their understanding of nuclear physics, but Snook had formed an opinion that on Avernus advanced knowledge was stored rather than applied. His one view of the island he was on had reinforced his notion of a non-technical culture, but his judgements as a newcomer obviously were not valid, his eyes not adequate. Perhaps a patch of colour on a wall could be the equivalent of a heating system; perhaps a wall stone that was rounded instead of squared was a power receiver and distributor.

Snook walked to the end of the corridor and went down a short flight of stairs which had awkward proportions and sloping treads which gave him the feeling he was going to pitch forward. At the bottom was a much larger room than any he had been in, though – like the one in which he had slept – it was devoid of furnishings. The windows along two walls were of obscured glass, but the movement of shrub-like vegetation beyond them told him he was at ground level. There were patches of lighter colour on the greenish stone floor which suggested that objects had recently been removed and he recalled Felleth's statement that the building was not a dwelling. Questions began to well up in Snook's mind. Was it a store? A library? What had the Avernian upstairs thought when he had first seen Snook appear in the little room a week earlier?

A door opened in one of the end walls and Felleth entered the room, his large pale eyes fixed on Snook. For an instant, superimposed on his normal vision, Snook seemed to glimpse the rise and sparkling fall of a translucent green wave, and – without speaking – he tried to coax the image into sharp focus, thinking of the ocean as a symbol of tranquillity and endless power.

'I believe you will learn to hear and speak,' Felleth said in his laboured whisper.

'Thank you.' Snook felt gratified, then realised his acceptance of his new situation must be growing if he could respond with positive emotion to-wards a vaguely saurian biped in classical Mediterranean dress.

'Toilet facilities have been prepared for you.' Felleth indicated a second door with a gesture of a webbed hand. 'They are self-enclosed ... and there-fore not of the highest standard ... but it is only for a short period.'

Snook was baffled for a moment, then understanding came. 'Of course,' he said, 'I'm in quarantine.'

'Only for a short period.'

It dawned on Snook that, in his urgent need to get out of Barandi alive, he had unthinkingly accepted a great many things about conditions on Avernus. The atmosphere, for instance, could have been of a mix which was totally unacceptable for human beings, and its micro-organisms could al-ready be setting up deadly colonies in his lungs. Presumably, he could repre-sent a medical risk to the Avernians, which might explain why the building he was in had a scoured-out feel to it.

'I would not have brought you here ... if I had not been satisfied you would live,' Felleth responded to his thought. 'In any case, I could have provided ... breathing gases and a mask.'

'You think of everything.' Snook was reminded of the fact that Felleth was the Avernian equivalent of a leading philosopher/scientist.

'Not everything. There are important matters we must discuss ... while you are eating.'

After Snook had made use of the receptacles and water supply provided for him within a polished metal cubicle, he joined Felleth in another room containing a table and a simple stool which seemed to have been newly made from close-grained wood. On the table were ceramic platters of vegetables, cereals and fruit, plus a flask of water. Snook sat down at once, suddenly conscious that he had not eaten for a long time, and tried the food. The flavours were strange, though not unpleasant, his main criticism being that everything – even the fruit and green vegetables – had a tang of iodine and salt.

'I have to advise you, Equal Gil,' Felleth began, 'that in bringing you here I miscalculated in certain matters … and failed to consider others at all.'

'That doesn't sound like you, Felleth.' Snook had considered simply thinking his replies to the Avernian's remarks, but he found that speaking aloud called for less mental effort.

'At present I am not in good standing … with my fellow Responders … nor with the People … because I gave them advice in an important matter … without investigating all the evidence available to me.'

'I don't understand.'

'For example … I accepted, uncritically, everything I learned about astronomy … from your mind.'

Snook looked up at the enigmatic, robed figure. 'That doesn't seem like a blunder to me. After all, you'd only just heard of the subject, and on Earth they've had astronomy for thousands of years.'

'On Earth – that is precisely the point … your astronomers study a different universe.'

'I still don't get it.' Snook pushed his food aside, sensing that something important was coming.

'The picture they presented of my universe … contained only those elements of which they had become aware … a sun, this world … and the rogue world you call Thornton's Planet.'

'So?'

'The orbit they calculated for Thornton's Planet … was based on this simplistic universe-picture.'

'I'm sorry, Felleth – I'm not an astronomer and I still don't see what you are getting at.'

Felleth came closer to the table. 'You are not an astronomer … but you understand that all bodies in a planetary system … are influenced in their movements … by all other bodies in that system.'

'That's elementary,' Snook said. 'But if there aren't any other bodies in the …' He stopped speaking as the full implications of Felleth's words dawned on him. 'Have they begun to look?'

'A radio telescope has been designed … and at least twenty will be built.'

'But this is *good*.' Snook stood up to face Felleth. 'This gives you hope, doesn't it? I mean, if you can find just one other planet prowling around out there, it could pull Thornton's Planet off the collision course …'

'That is what I should have appreciated … at once.'

'How could you?'

'The People demand the highest standards of a Responder ... it is their right.'

'But ...'

'Equal Gil, your memory is imperfect by our standards ... but it may contain information which would enable me to make restitution to the People ... for my failure ... please permit me to touch you.'

Snook hesitated only briefly before stepping closer to Felleth. He inclined his head forward, and kept his eyes open while Felleth closed with him and their foreheads touched. The contact lasted only a second, then Felleth stepped back.

'Thank you,' Felleth said. 'The evidence is valuable.'

'I didn't feel anything – what evidence?'

'When you first heard of Thornton's Planet ... it was expected to pass through your world ... but it missed by many planetary diameters ... and the divergence from the predicted course ... was attributed to observational error.'

'I do seem to remember something about ...' Snook's excitement increased. 'That's evidence, isn't it? It shows there are other planets in your own system.'

'Not conclusive evidence.'

'It seems conclusive to me.'

'The only positive conclusion,' Felleth said, 'is that I am unworthy of the People's trust.'

'That's ridiculous,' Snook almost shouted. 'They owe you everything.'

The long slit of Felleth's mouth rippled in an emotional signal which Snook could not interpret. 'The People have different mental attributes to those of your race ... but they are not superior, as you believe ... we have successfully rid ourselves of the great destructive passions ... but it is more difficult to eradicate the trivial and the petty ... the fact that I am using the words indicates that I, too ...' Felleth broke off from the painful manufacture of speech sounds, his pale eyes locked on Snook's in an oddly human display of helplessness. Snook stared at him in silence, then ideas began to crystallise and dissolve far back in his consciousness.

'Felleth,' he said, 'is there something you have to tell me?'

Each day passed like a month; each month like a year.

Snook found that the small island allocated to him was sufficient for his needs, provided he worked hard with the simple agricultural tools which had been supplied, and regularly culled the shallows for edible sea plants. He had no tobacco or alcohol – the processes of fermentation were not used on Avernus outside science laboratories – but he had learned to live without them. The Avernians themselves, he knew, sometimes inhaled the vapours released from the pods of certain marine plants, claiming they had the power to elevate the spirit and enrich the vision. In the beginning, Snook had experimented with the pods, but always with negative results, and had concluded that his metabolism was wrong. 'It may be a universal law,' he had written on a scrap of paper, 'that you can only get high at home.'

When he was not busy with the growing of food, Snook had enough work of other kinds with which to occupy his time. The island's only house had to be kept in repair – especially the roof – and he also had to mend his own clothes and shoes. Heating was no problem, because the stone slabs of the floor grew warm at night, apparently spontaneously. Snook almost wished that the heating was of a more primitive nature – a log fire would have given him companionship of a kind. It would have been especially appreciated in the dark evenings when he had been incautious enough to start thinking of Prudence, and the lights of the other islands reminded him that the life of the planet was continuing without his aid.

There is no apartment so lonely, he recalled his own thought, *as the one in which can be heard faint sounds of a party next door.*

Being a prisoner on a small uninhabited island added little to the tribulations of being a prisoner in an alien universe, Snook had learned, even though the People had proved themselves much more human than he had expected. With Felleth as his sole model, he formed an idealised impression of the Avernians – the super-intelligent beings who were rebuilding their civilisation after one planet-wide disaster, and were stoically preparing themselves for the ultimate calamity.

It had come as a shock to him to discover that the race of reason-guided beings resented his presence on their world as a representative of a sister planet which was refusing them a helping hand. And he had been both saddened and angered to learn that Felleth had been permanently censured for having failed, as the Avernians saw it, in his duty as a Responder. They had also criticised Felleth for his unilateral action in transferring Snook into their world.

'It is more difficult,' Felleth had said, on the first day, 'to eradicate the trivial and the petty.'

These were things which Snook tried not to think about as he struggled with his own burden – that of enduring from one day to the next, then repeating the process over and over again. Living in a world where nobody wanted to kill him was one thing; but the reverse of the coin was that he existed in a universe in which nobody had given him life and where there was no prospect of his passing life on to others. The thoughts were painful for a man with his particular history, for a human neutrino, but then he had realised his mistake the day he had walked into a hotel in Kisumu and had seen ...

At that point in the evening Snook always went through the ritual of taking off his wrist watch and placing it on the orange-dyed crate beside his bed. And – if he had worked hard enough that day – he was blessed with sleep, sometimes with dreams.

Each day passed like a month; each month like a year.

CHAPTER FIFTEEN

Twelve months had passed, by Snook's reckoning, on the morning he received the wordless message that the Avernians had confirmed the existence of other worlds in their own planetary system.

His early experiences on Avernus had shown that his facility for mind-to-mind communication was not much greater than it had been when he had lived on Earth and occasionally had snared the thoughts of other men. Ironically, he had been able to achieve full congruency of self with Felleth only when they had inhabited different universes and had been able to merge their brains in the same volume of space. During Felleth's regular visits to the island he had tried to extend his ability to receive data, but progress had been uncertain if it existed at all.

On this special day, however, he could not fail to be aware of the mood of the People. The emotions of joy and triumph, amplified millions of times, were spangled across the islands like the gold of the sunsets they never saw.

'Not bad,' Snook said aloud, looking up from his digging. 'From complete ignorance of the skies to fully-fledged radio astronomy in one year. Not bad.'

He returned his attention to the work in hand, but kept scanning the waterways in the hope that Felleth would pay him a special visit to bring details of the new knowledge. The masses and orbital elements of the other worlds would determine the distance by which Thornton's Planet would miss Avernus on its next pass, and Snook felt a proprietary interest in the information. He was incapable of understanding the relevant sets of equations, but they had affected the whole course of his life, and he wanted to know whether Avernus was destined for another disaster, of greater or lesser proportions, or if it had been granted a total reprieve. It also occurred to him that the People might regard his presence among them less distasteful were they assured of their futures once more.

Should that prove to be the case, he would ask for the right to travel as freely as he had once done on Earth. Felleth had told him there were larger land masses to the west and east, and exploring them – perhaps circumnavigating the watery globe – might give his life a semblance of purpose.

No boat came near him that day, but when darkness fell he saw a profusion of coloured lights on the other islands which told him that celebrations were in progress. He watched the moving specks of brilliance for several hours before going to bed, wondering if it was another universal law that at times of happiness and victory sentient beings would express their feelings with pyrotechnics, the symbols of cosmic birth.

On the following morning a fleet of four boats passed the island at high speed, heading north-east. Snook, who could not recall seeing craft go in that direction before, watched them with some puzzlement. They were of a type powered by sophisticated batteries – in which the sea itself served as an electrolyte – and therefore had virtually unlimited range, but he had no knowledge of land on that particular bearing.

When the little fleet was at its nearest to him, a white-clad figure waved to Snook from the leading boat. He waved back, pleased for a moment by the simple act of communication, then began to wonder if the anonymous figure had been Felleth, and why he should be speeding off into an empty ocean. Within minutes the four boats had dwindled to invisibility on the flat grey waters.

In spite of several rain showers, Snook remained outside all that day, but did not see the boats return. By the following day the incident was fading from his mind, and he remained indoors concentrating on the task of constructing an earthenware oven from local clay. The Avernians were not only strictly vegetarian – they ate all their food in its natural state, and Felleth had not felt obliged to provide Snook with cooking facilities. He had adapted reasonably well to living on raw food, but lately had become obsessed with the idea of making hot soups. A doubly cherished ambition was that of grinding cereal, baking it into bread and serving it to himself with fruit jam. He was shaping the oven liner on an armature of dried twigs when there came the whine of a boat's engine running at low speed.

He went to the door and saw an Avernian craft nuzzling up to his landing stage, with Felleth standing at its prow. Three other boats were wheeling across the smooth grey waters, passing the island on their way south. Snook walked down to meet Felleth, and saw that the Avernian seemed to be holding a green-and-white object in one hand. He stared hard at Felleth, projecting the customary greeting and received fleeting image of the eternal running wave.

'I was hoping you would come,' he said as the Avernian stepped on to the aged planks of the landing stage. 'Is there good news?'

'I think that is how you would describe it,' Felleth said. With a year of practice behind him he could speak with some fluency, although his voice remained low and reedy.

'You've found another planet.'

'Yes.' Felleth's mouth rippled with an expression Snook had not seen before and could not interpret. 'Although we had some assistance.'

Snook shook his head. 'I don't understand you, Felleth.'

'Perhaps this will make things clear.'

Felleth brought the object he was holding into clear view and Snook saw, with a lurch of his heart, that it was a green bottle which – had he been on Earth – he would instantly have identified as containing gin. Attached to it, in place of a label, was a piece of paper covered with handwriting. Felleth offered the bottle to Snook, and he took it with trembling hands. It was full of clear liquid.

'Felleth,' he said in a faint voice, 'what is this?'

'I do not know,' Felleth replied. 'The message is written in English, or another human language, and therefore I cannot read it. I presume it is intended for you.'

'But ...' Snook gazed at Felleth in perplexity for a moment, then directed his attention to the closely written message. He read:

'Dear Gil, this is yet another of my famous long shots – but you know I'm prepared to try anything in the cause of science. We have discovered two more anti-neutrino planets, one inside Pluto and one inside Uranus, and they are massive enough to modify the orbit of Thornton's Planet considerably. Avernus is going to have some very high tides in 2091 – but, with proper precautions, there should be no loss of life. I have put all the relevant information into diagram form, which Felleth should be able to decipher, and it is going into a buoy which is fitted with a radio beacon. I know the Avernians do not need to use electro-magnetic phenomena for communications, but I am hoping they will detect the buoy by some means – if we get it through to Avernus safely. We have made a lot of progress in nuclear physics and in inter-universal physics in the past year, and are now in a good position to attempt a unilateral transfer on a modest scale. I am writing this on a ship in the Arabian Sea, which is as near to you as I can get on the circle of emergence, and am almost certain we can hold station with the northern top dead centre long enough to effect the transfer. If you are reading this, you will know that the experiment has been successful, and I hereby order you to celebrate by drinking the contents of the bottle. You may be interested to hear that we all got out of Barandi safely, just before there was a full-scale workers' revolution in which Ogilvie and Freeborn disappeared. Prudence has gone back to her job with UNESCO, but I know she would want me to send you her regards. Des Quig is working with me full time, and he sends his regards as well. You may also be interested to hear that I am now married – to a lovely girl called Jody, who talks a lot but keeps me from getting too puffed up with all the publicity I get these days. There is a tremendous amount of interest in the whole concept of inter-universal transfer, and a lot of research money is going into it. There is even talk of a full-scale, manned scientific expedition to Avernus some year, and if I'm not eclipsed in the field I'll have to consider going on it – coward though I am. I don't want to promise too much, Gil, but if you get this bottle safely, make a candle-holder out of it. And put the candle in your window. Yours. Boyce.'

Snook finished reading and raised his eyes to Felleth, whose slight figure was outlined on a backdrop of misty islands. He opened his mouth to say what he had read, then remembered that the Avernian would have absorbed the information directly from his mind. They looked at each other in silence, while an ocean breeze whispered past them on its journey around the world.

'It looks as though the future could be different to what I expected,' Snook said.

'The present has changed as well,' Felleth replied. 'If you would like to live among the People, and to travel among the larger islands, it can be arranged. I can take you to my home now.'

'I would like that, but I don't want to leave this island until tomorrow.' Snook hefted the gin bottle. 'I've got an old friend to keep me company tonight.'

He said goodbye to Felleth and began walking back to his solitary house, picking his way with care on the steep and stony path.

THE RAGGED ASTRONAUTS

PART I

Shadow at Noon

CHAPTER ONE

It had become obvious to Toller Maraquine and some others watching on the ground that the airship was heading into danger, but – incredibly – its captain appeared not to notice.

'What does the fool think he's doing?' Toller said, speaking aloud although there was nobody within earshot. He shaded his eyes from the sun to harden his perception of what was happening. The background was a familiar one to anybody who lived in those longitudes of Land – flawless indigo sea, a sky of pale blue feathered with white, and the misty vastness of the sister world, Overland, hanging motionless near the zenith, its disk crossed again and again by swathes of cloud. In spite of the foreday glare a number of stars were visible, including the nine brightest which made up the constellation of the Tree.

Against that backdrop the airship was drifting in on a light sea breeze, the commander conserving power crystals. The vessel was heading directly towards the shore, its blue-and-grey envelope foreshortened to a circle, a tiny visual echo of Overland. It was making steady progress, but what its captain had apparently failed to appreciate was that the onshore breeze in which he was travelling was very shallow, with a depth of not more than three hundred feet. Above it and moving in the opposite direction was a westerly wind streaming down from the Haffanger Plateau.

Toller could trace the flow and counter flow of air with precision because the columns of vapour from the pikon reduction pans along the shore were drifting inland only a short distance before rising and being wafted back out to sea. Among those man-made bands of mist were ribbons of cloud from the roof of the plateau – therein lay the danger to the airship.

Toller took from his pocket the stubby telescope he had carried since childhood and used it to scan the cloud layers. As he had half expected, he was able within seconds to pick out several blurry specks of blue and magenta suspended in the matrix of white vapour. A casual observer might have failed to notice them at all, or have dismissed the vague motes as an optical effect, but Toller's sense of alarm grew more intense. The fact that he had been able to spot some ptertha so quickly meant that the entire cloud must be heavily seeded with them, invisibly bearing hundreds of the creatures towards the airship.

'Use a sunwriter,' he bellowed with the full power of his lungs. 'Tell the fool to veer off, or go up or down, or ...'

Rendered incoherent by urgency, Toller looked all about him as he tried to decide on a course of action. The only people visible among the rectangular pans and fuel bins were semi-naked stokers and rakers. It appeared that all of the overseers and clerks were inside the wide-eaved buildings of the station proper, escaping the day's increasing heat. The low structures were of traditional Kolcorronian design – orange and yellow brick laid in complex diamond patterns, dressed with red sandstone at all corners and edges – and had something of the look of snakes drowsing in the intense sunlight. Toller could not even see any officials at the narrow vertical windows. Pressing a hand to his sword to hold it steady, he ran towards the supervisors' building.

Toller was unusually tall and muscular for a member of one of the philosophy orders, and workers tending the pikon pans hastily moved aside to avoid impeding his progress. Just as he was reaching the single-storey building a junior recorder, Comdac Gurra, emerged from it carrying a sunwriter. On seeing Toller bearing down on him, Gurra flinched and made as if to hand the instrument over. Toller waved it away.

'You do it,' he said impatiently, covering up the fact that he would have been too slow at stringing the words of a message together. 'You've got the thing in your hands – what are you waiting for?'

'I'm sorry, Toller.' Gurra aimed the sunwriter at the approaching airship and the glass slats inside it clacked as he began to operate the trigger.

Toller hopped from one foot to the other as he watched for some evidence that the pilot was receiving and heeding the beamed warning. The ship drifted onwards, blind and serene. Toller raised his telescope and concentrated his gaze on the blue-painted gondola, noting with some surprise that it bore the plume-and-sword symbol which proclaimed the vessel to be a royal messenger. What possible reason could the King have for communicating with one of the Lord Philosopher's most remote experimental stations?

After what seemed an age, his enhanced vision enabled him to discern hurried movements behind the ship's foredeck rails. A few seconds later there were puffs of grey smoke along the gondola's left side, indicating that its lateral drive tubes were being fired. The airship's envelope rippled and the whole assemblage tilted as the craft slewed to the right. It was rapidly shedding height during the manoeuvre, but by then it was actually grazing the cloud, being lost to view now and again as it was engulfed by vaporous tendrils. A wail of terror, fine-drawn by distance and flowing air, reached the hushed watchers along the shore, causing some of the men to shift uneasily.

Toller guessed that somebody on board the airship had encountered a ptertha and he felt a thrill of dread. It was a fate which had overtaken him many times in bad dreams. The essence of the nightmare was not in visions of dying, but in the sense of utter hopelessness, the futility of trying to resist once a ptertha had come within its killing radius. Faced by assassins or ferocious animals, a man could – no matter how overwhelming the odds – go down fighting and in that way aspire to a strange reconciliation with death, but when the livid globes came questing and quivering, there was *nothing* that could be done.

'What's going on here?' The speaker was Vorndal Sisstt, chief of the station, who had appeared in the main entrance of the supervisors' building. He was middle-aged, with a round balding head and the severely upright posture of a man who was self-conscious about being below average in height. His neat sun-tanned features bore an expression of mingled annoyance and apprehension.

Toller pointed at the descending airship. 'Some idiot has travelled all this distance to commit suicide.'

'Have we sent a warning?'

'Yes, but I think it was too late,' Toller said. 'There were ptertha all round the ship a minute ago.'

'This is terrible,' Sisstt quavered, pressing the back of a hand to his forehead. 'I'll give word for the screens to be hoisted.'

'There's no need – the cloud base isn't getting any lower and the globes won't come at us across open ground in broad daylight.'

'I'm not going to take the risk. Who knows what the ...?' Sisstt broke off and glared up at Toller, grateful for a safe outlet for his emotions. 'Exactly when did you become empowered to make executive decisions here? In what I believe to be my station? Has Lord Glo elevated you without informing me?'

'Nobody needs elevation where you're concerned,' Toller said, reacting badly to the chief's sarcasm, his gaze fixed on the airship which was now dipping towards the shore.

Sisstt's jaw sagged and his eyes narrowed as he tried to decide whether the comment had referred to his physical stature or abilities. 'That was insolence,' he accused. 'Insolence and insubordination, and I'm going to see that certain people get to hear about it.'

'Don't bleat,' Toller said, turning away.

He ran down the shallow slope of the beach to where a group of workers had gathered to assist in the landing. The ship's multiple anchors trailed through the surf and up on to the sand, raking dark lines in the white surface. Men grabbed at the ropes and added their weight to counter the craft's skittish attempts to rise on vagrant breezes. Toller could see the captain leaning over the forward rail of the gondola, directing operations. There appeared to be some kind of commotion going on amidships, with several crewmen struggling among themselves. It was possible that some-body who had been unlucky enough to get too close to a ptertha had gone berserk, as occasionally happened, and was being forcibly subdued by his shipmates.

Toller went forward, caught a dripping rope and kept tension on it to help guide the airship to the tethering stakes which lined the shore. At last the gondola's keel crunched into the sand and yellow-shirted men vaulted over the side to secure it. The brush with danger had evidently rattled them. They were swearing fiercely as they pushed the pikon workers aside, using unnecessary force, and began tying the ship down. Toller could appreciate their feelings, and he smiled sympathetically as he offered his line to an approaching airman, a bottle-shouldered man with silt-coloured skin.

'What are you grinning at, dung-eater?' the man growled, reaching for the rope.

Toller withdrew the rope and in the same movement threw it into a loop and snapped it tight around the airman's thumb. 'Apologise for that!'

'What the ...!' The airman made as if to hurl Teller aside with his free arm and his eyes widened as he made the discovery that he was not dealing with a typical science technician. He turned his head to summon help from other airmen, but Toller diverted him by jerking the rope tighter.

'This is between you and me,' Toller said quietly, using the power of his upper arms to increase the strain on the line. 'Are you going to apologise, or would you like your thumb to wear on a necklet?'

'You're going to be sorry for ...' The airman's voice faded and he sagged, white-faced and gasping, as a joint in his thumb made a clearly audible pop-ping sound. 'I apologise. Let me go! I apologise.'

'That's better,' Toller said, releasing the rope. 'Now we can all be friends together.'

He smiled in mock geniality, giving no hint of the dismay he could feel gathering inside him. It had happened yet again! The sensible response to a ritual insult was to ignore it or reply in kind, but his temper had taken con-trol of his body on the instant, reducing him to the level of a primitive crea-ture governed by reflex. He had made no conscious decision to clash with the airman, and yet would have been prepared to maim him had the apol-ogy not been forthcoming. And what made matters worse was the know-ledge that he was unable to back down, that the trivial incident might still escalate into something very dangerous for all concerned.

'*Friends,' the* airman breathed, clutching his injured hand to his stomach, his face contorted with pain and hatred. 'As soon as I can hold a sword again I'll ...'

He left the threat unfinished as a bearded man in the heavily embroidered jupon of an aircaptain strode towards him. The captain, who was about forty, was breathing noisily and the saffron material of his jupon had damp brown stains below his armpits.

'What's the matter with you, Kaprin?' he said, staring angrily at the airman.

Kaprin's eyes gave one baleful flicker in Toller's direction, then he lowered his head. 'I snared my hand in a line, sir. Dislocated my thumb, sir.'

'Work twice as hard with the other hand,' the captain said, dismissing the airman with a wave and turning to face Toller. 'I'm Aircaptain Hlawnvert. You're not Sisstt. Where is Sisstt?'

'There.' Toller pointed at the station chief, who was uncertainly advancing down the slope of the shore, the hem of his grey robe gathered clear of the rock pools.

'So that's the maniac who's responsible.'

'Responsible for what?' Toller said, frowning.

'For blinding me with smoke from those accursed stewpots.' Hlawnvert's voice was charged with anger and contempt as he swung his gaze to encompass the array of pikon pans and the columns of vapour they were releasing into the sky. 'I've been told they're actually trying to make power crystals here. Is that true, or is it just a joke?'

Toller, barely clear of one potentially disastrous scrape, was nonetheless affronted by Hlawnvert's tone. It was the principal regret of his life that he had been born into a philosophy family instead of the military caste, and he spent much of his time reviling his lot, but he disliked outsiders doing the same. He eyed the captain coolly for a few seconds, extending the pause until it was just short of open disrespect, then spoke as though addressing a child.

'Nobody can make crystals,' he said. 'They can only be grown – if the solution is pure enough.'

'Then what's the point of all this?'

'There are good pikon deposits in this area. We are extracting it from the soil and trying to find a way to refine it until it's pure enough to produce a reaction.'

'A waste of time,' Hlawnvert said with casual assurance, dismissing the subject as he turned away to confront Vorndal Sisstt.

'Good foreday, Captain,' Sisstt said. 'I'm so glad you have landed safely. I've given orders for our ptertha screens to be run out immediately.'

Hlawnvert shook his head. 'There's no need for them. Besides, you have already done the damage.'

'I …' Sisstt's blue eyes shuttled anxiously. 'I don't understand you, Captain.'

'The stinking fumes and fog you're spewing into the sky disguised the natural cloud. There are going to be deaths among my crew – and I deem you to be personally responsible.'

'But …' Sisstt glanced in indignation at the receding line of cliffs from which, for a distance of many miles, streamer after streamer of cloud could be seen snaking out towards the sea. 'But that kind of cloud is a general feature of this coast. I fail to see how you can blame me for …'

'Silence!' Hlawnvert dropped one hand to his sword, stepped forward and drove the flat of his other hand against Sisstt's chest, sending the station chief sprawling on his back, legs wide apart. 'Are you questioning my competence? Are you saying I was careless?'

'Of course not.' Sisstt scrambled to his feet and brushed sand from his robes. 'Forgive me, Captain. Now that you bring the matter to my attention, I can see that the vapour from our pans could be a hazard to airmen in certain circumstances.'

'You should set up warning beacons.'

'I'll see that it's done at once,' Sisstt said. 'We should have thought of it ourselves long ago.'

Toller could feel a tingling warmth in his face as he viewed the scene. Captain Hlawnvert was a big man, as was normal for one of a military background, but he was also soft and burdened with fat, and even someone of Sisstt's size could have vanquished him with the aid of speed and hate-hardened muscles. In addition, Hlawnvert had been criminally incompetent in his handling of the airship, a fact he was trying to obscure with his bluster, so going against him could have been justified before a tribunal. But none of that mattered to Sisstt. In keeping with his own nature the station chief was fawning over the hand which abused him. Later he would excuse his cowardice with jokes and try to compensate for it by mistreating his most junior subordinates.

In spite of his curiosity about the reason for Hlawnvert's visit, Toller felt obliged to move away, to dissociate himself from Sisstt's abject behaviour. He was on the point of leaving when a crop-haired airman wearing the white insignia of a lieutenant brushed by him and saluted Hlawnvert.

'The crew are ready for your inspection, sir,' he said in a business-like voice.

Hlawnvert nodded and glanced at the line of yellow-shirted men who were waiting by the ship. 'How many took the dust?'

'Only two, sir. We were lucky.'

'Lucky?'

'What I mean, sir, is that but for your superb airmanship our losses would have been much higher.'

Hlawnvert nodded again. 'Which two are we losing?'

'Pouksale and Lague, sir,' the lieutenant said. 'But Lague won't admit it.'

'Was the contact confirmed?'

'I saw it myself, sir. The ptertha got within a single pace of him before it burst. He took the dust.'

'Then why can't he own up to it like a man?' Hlawnvert said irritably. 'A single wheyface like that can unsettle a whole crew.' He scowled in the direction of the waiting men, then turned to Sisstt. 'I have a message for you from Lord Glo, but there are certain formalities I must attend to first. You will wait here.'

The colour drained from Sisstt's face. 'Captain, it would be better if I received you in my chambers. Besides, I have urgent ...'

'You will wait *here*,' Hlawnvert interrupted, stabbing Sisstt's chest with one finger and doing it with such force that he caused the smaller man to stagger. 'It will do you good to see what mischief your polluting of the skies has brought about.'

In spite of his contempt for Sisstt's behaviour, Toller began to wish he could intervene in some way to end the little man's humiliation, but there was a strict protocol governing such matters in Kolcorronian society. To take a man's side in a confrontation without being invited was to add fresh insult by implying that he was a coward. Going as far as was permissible, Toller stood squarely in Hlawnvert's way when the captain turned to walk to the ship, but the implicit challenge went unnoticed. Hlawnvert side-stepped him, his face turned towards the sky, where the sun was drawing close to Overland.

'Let's get this business over and done with before littlenight,' Hlawnvert said to his lieutenant. 'We have wasted too much time here already.'

'Yes, sir.' The lieutenant marched ahead of him to the men who were ranked in the lee of the restlessly stirring airship and raised his voice. 'Stand forward all airmen who have reason to believe they will soon be unable to discharge their duties.'

After a moment's hesitation a dark-haired young man took two paces forward. His triangular face was so pale as to be almost luminous, but his posture was erect and he appeared to be well in control of himself. Captain Hlawnvert approached him and placed a hand on each shoulder.

'Airman Pouksale,' he said quietly, 'you have taken the dust?'

'I have, sir.' Pouksale's voice was lifeless, resigned.

'You have served your country bravely and well, and your name will go before the King. Now, do you wish to take the Bright Road or the Dull Road?'

'The Bright Road, sir.'

'Good man. Your pay will be made up to the end of the voyage and will be sent to your next-of-kin. You may retire.'

'Thank you, sir.'

Pouksale saluted and walked around the prow of the airship's gondola to its far side. He was thus screened from the view of his former crewmates, in accordance with custom, but the executioner who moved to meet him became visible to Toller, Sisstt and many of the pikon workers ranged along the shore. The executioner's sword was wide and heavy, and its brakka wood blade was pure black, unrelieved by the enamel inlays with which Kolcorronian weapons were normally decorated.

Pouksale knelt submissively. His knees had barely touched the sand before the executioner, acting with merciful swiftness, had dispatched him along the Bright Road. The scene before Toller – all yellows and ochres and hazy shades of blue – now had a focal point of vivid red.

At the sound of the death blow a ripple of unease passed through the line of airmen. Several of them raised their eyes to gaze at Overland and the silent movement of their lips showed they were bidding their dead crewmate's soul a late journey to the sister planet. For the most part, however, the men stared unhappily at the ground. They had been recruited from the crowded cities of the empire, where there was considerable scepticism about the Church's teaching that men's souls were immortal and alternated endlessly between Land and Overland. For them death meant death – not a pleasant stroll along the mystical High Path linking the two worlds. Toller heard a faint choking sound to his left and turned to see that Sisstt was covering his mouth with both hands. The station chief was trembling and looked as though he could faint at any second.

'If you go down we'll be branded as old women,' Toller whispered fiercely. 'What's the matter with you?'

'The barbarism.' Sisstt's words were indistinct. 'The terrible barbarism ... What hope is there for us?'

'The airman had a free choice – and he behaved well.'

'You're no better than ...' Sisstt stopped speaking as a commotion broke out by the airship. Two airmen had gripped a third by the arms and in spite of his struggles were holding him in front of Hlawnvert. The captive was tall and spindly, with an incongruously round belly.

'... couldn't have seen me, sir,' he was shouting. 'And I was upwind of the ptertha, so the dust couldn't have come anywhere near me. I swear to you, sir – I haven't taken the dust.'

Hlawnvert placed his hands on his broad hips and looked up at the sky for a moment, signifying his disbelief, before he spoke. 'Airman Lague, the regulations require me to accept your statement. But let me make your position clear. You won't be offered the Bright Road again. At the very first signs of fever or paralysis you will go over the side. Alive. Your pay for the entire voyage will be withheld and your name will be struck from the royal record. Do you understand these terms?'

'Yes, sir. Thank you, sir.' Lague tried to fall at Hlawnvert's feet, but the men at his side tugged him upright. 'There is nothing to worry about, sir – I haven't taken the dust.'

At an order from the lieutenant the two men released Lague and he walked slowly back to re-join the rank. The line of airmen parted to make room for him, leaving a larger gap than was necessary, creating an intangible barrier. Toller guessed that Lague would find little consolation during the next two days, which was the time it took for the first effects of ptertha poison to become apparent.

Captain Hlawnvert saluted his lieutenant, turning the assembly over to him, and walked back up the slope to Sisstt and Toller. Patches of high colour showed above the curls of his beard and the sweat stains upon his jupon had grown larger. He looked up at the high dome of the sky, where the eastern rim of Overland had begun to brighten as the sun moved behind it, and made an impatient gesture as though commanding the sun to disappear more quickly.

'It's too hot for this kind of vexation,' he growled. 'I have a long way to go, and the crew are going to be useless until that coward Lague goes over the side. The service regulations will have to be changed if these new rumours aren't quashed soon.'

'Ah …' Sisstt strained upright, fighting to regain his composure. 'New rumours, Captain?'

'There's a story that some line soldiers down in Sorka died after handling ptertha casualties.'

'But pterthacosis isn't transmissible.'

'I know that,' Hlawnvert said. 'Only a spineless cretin would think twice about it, but that's what we get for aircrew these days. Pouksale was one of my few steady men – and I've lost him to that damned fog of yours.'

Toller, who had been watching a burial detail gather up Pouksale's remains, felt a fresh annoyance at the repetition of the indictment and his chief's complaisance. 'You don't have to keep on blaming our fog, Captain,' he said, giving Sisstt a significant glance. 'Nobody in authority is disputing the facts.'

Hlawnvert rounded on him at once. 'What do you mean by that?'

Toller produced a slow, amiable smile. 'I mean we all got a clear view of what happened.'

'What's your name, soldier?'

'Toller Maraquine – and I'm not a soldier.'

'You're not a …' Hlawnvert's look of anger gave way to one of sly amusement. 'What's this? What have we here?'

Toller remained impassive as the captain's gaze took in the anomalous aspects of his appearance – the long hair and grey robes of a philosopher combined with the height and blocky musculature of a warrior. His wearing of a sword also set him apart from the rest of his kin. Only the fact that he was free of scars and campaign tattoos distinguished him in physique from a full-blooded member of the military.

He studied Hlawnvert in return, and his antagonism increased as he followed the thought processes so clearly mirrored on the captain's florid face. Hlawnvert had not been able to disguise his alarm over a possible accusation of negligence, and now he was relieved to find that he was quite secure. A few coarse innuendoes about his challenger's pedigree were all the defence he needed in the lineage-conscious hierarchy of Kolcorron. His lips twitched as he tried to choose from the wealth of taunts available to him.

Go ahead, Toller thought, projecting the silent message with all the force of his being. *Say the words which will end your life.*

Hlawnvert hesitated, as though sensing the danger, and again the interplay of his thoughts was clearly visible. He wanted to humiliate and discredit the upstart of dubious ancestry who had dared impugn him, but not if there was serious risk involved. And calling for assistance would be a step towards turning a triviality into a major incident, one which would highlight the very issue he wanted to obscure. At length, having decided on his tactics, he forced a chuckle.

'If you're not a soldier you should be careful about wearing that sword,' he said jovially. 'You might sit on it and do yourself a mischief.'

Toller refused to make things easy for the captain. 'The weapon is no threat to me.'

'I'll remember your name, Maraquine,' Hlawnvert said in a low voice. At that moment the station's timekeeper sounded the littlenight horn – tonguing the double note which was used when ptertha activity was high – and there was a general movement of pikon workers towards the safety of the buildings. Hlawnvert turned away from Toller, clapped one arm around Sisstt's shoulders and drew him in direction of the tethered airship.

'You're coming aboard for a drink in my cabin,' he said. 'You'll find it nice and snug in there with the hatch closed, and you'll be able to receive Lord Glo's orders in privacy.'

Toller shrugged and shook his head as he watched the two men depart. The captain's excessive familiarity was a breach of the behavioural code in itself, and his blatant insincerity in embracing a man he had just thrown to the ground was nothing short of an insult. It accorded Sisstt the status of a dog which could be whipped or petted at the whim of its owner. But, true to his colours, the station chief appeared not to mind. A sudden bellowing laugh from Hlawnvert showed that Sisstt had already begun to make his little jokes, laying the groundwork for the version of the encounter he would later pass on to his staff and expect them to believe. *The captain loves people to think he's a real ogre – but when you get to know him as well as I do ...*

Again Toller found himself wondering about the nature of Hlawnvert's mission. What new orders could be so urgent and important that Lord Glo had considered it worth sending them by special carrier instead of waiting for a routine transport? Was it possible that something was going to happen to break the deadly monotony of life at the remote station? Or was that too much to hope for?

As darkness swept out of the west Toller looked up at the sky and saw the last fierce sliver of the sun vanish behind the looming immensity of Overland. As the light abruptly faded the cloudless areas of the sky thronged with stars, comets and whorls of misty radiance. Littlenight was beginning, and under its cover the silent globes of the ptertha would soon leave the clouds and come drifting down to ground level in search of their natural prey.

Glancing about him, Toller realised he was the last man out in the open. All personnel connected with the station had retreated indoors and the crew of the airship were safely enclosed in its lower deck. He could be accused of foolhardiness in lingering outside for so long, but it was something he quite often did. The flirtations with danger added spice to his humdrum existence and were a way of demonstrating the essential difference between himself and a typical member of one of the philosophy families. On this occasion his gait was slower and more casual than ever as he walked up the gentle incline to the supervisors' building. It was possible that he was being watched, and his private code dictated that the greater the risk of a ptertha strike the less afraid he should appear to be. On reaching the door he paused and stood quite still for a moment, despite the crawling sensation on his back, before lifting the latch and going inside.

Behind him, dominating the southern sky, the nine brilliant stars of the Tree tilted down towards the horizon.

CHAPTER TWO

Prince Leddravohr Neldeever was indulging himself in the one pursuit which could make him feel young again.

As the elder son of the King, and as head of all of Kolcorron's military forces, he was expected to address himself mainly to matters of policy and broad strategy in warfare. As far as individual battles were concerned, his proper place was far to the rear in a heavily protected command post from which he could direct operations in safety. But he had little or no taste for hanging back and allowing deputies, in whose competence he rarely had faith anyway, to enjoy the real work of soldiering. Practically every junior officer and foot soldier had a winestory about how the prince had suddenly appeared at his side in the thick of battle and helped him hew his way to safety. Leddravohr encouraged the growth of the legends in the interests of discipline and morale.

He had been supervising the Third Army's push into the Loongl Peninsula, on the eastern edge of the Kolcorronian possessions, when word had been received of unexpectedly strong resistance in one hilly region. The additional intelligence that brakka trees were plentiful in the area had been enough to lure Leddravohr into the front line. He had exchanged his regal white cuirass for one moulded from boiled leather and had taken personal control of part of an expeditionary force.

It was shortly after dawn when, accompanied by an experienced high-sergeant called Reeff, he bellied his way through forest undergrowth to the edge of a large clearing. This far to the east foreday was much longer than aftday, and Leddravohr knew he had ample reserves of light in which to mount an attack and carry out a thorough mopping-up operation afterwards. It was a good feeling, knowing that yet more enemies of Kolcorron were soon to go down weltering in blood before his own sword. He carefully parted the last leafy screen and studied what was happening ahead.

A circular area some four-hundred yards in diameter had been totally cleared of tall vegetation except for a stand of brakka trees at the centre. About a hundred Gethan tribesmen and women were clustered around the trees, their attention concentrated on an object at the tip of one of the slim, straight trunks. Leddravohr counted the trees and found there were nine – a number which had magical and religious links with the heavenly constellation of the Tree.

He raised his field glasses and saw, as he had expected, that the object surmounting one of the trees was a naked woman. She was doubled over the tip of the trunk, her stomach pressed into the central orifice, and was held immovably in place by cords around her limbs.

'The savages are making one of their stupid sacrifices,' Leddravohr whispered, passing his glasses to Reeff.

The sergeant examined the scene for a long moment before returning the glasses. 'My men could put the bitch to better uses than that,' he said, 'but at least it makes things easier for us.'

He pointed at the thin glass tube attached to his wrist. Inside it was part of a cane shoot which had been marked with black pigment at regular intervals. A pacebeetle was devouring the shoot from one end, moving at the unchanging rate common to its kind.

'It is past the fifth division,' Reef said. 'The other cohorts will be in position by now. We should go in while the savages are distracted.'

'Not yet.' Leddravohr continued watching the tribesmen through his glasses. 'I can see two look-outs who are still facing outwards. These people are becoming a bit more wary, and don't forget they have copied the idea of cannon from somewhere. Unless we take them completely by surprise they will have time to fire at us. I don't know about you, but I don't want to breakfast on flying rock. I find it quite indigestible.'

Reeff grinned appreciatively. 'We'll wait till the tree blows.'

'It won't be long – the top leaves are folding.' Leddravohr watched with interest as the uppermost of the tree's four pairs of gigantic leaves rose from their normal horizontal position and furled themselves around the trunk. The phenomenon occurred about twice a year throughout a brakka tree's span of maturity in the wild state, but it was one which as a native of Kolcorron he had rarely seen. In his country it was regarded as a waste of power crystals to permit a brakka to discharge itself.

There was a short delay after the top leaves had closed against the trunk, then the second pair quivered and slowly swung upwards. Leddravohr knew that, well below the ground, the partition which divided the tree's combustion chamber was beginning to dissolve. Soon the green pikon crystals which had been extracted from the soil by the upper root system would mingle with the purple halvell gathered by the lower network of roots. The heat and gas thus generated would be contained for a brief period of time – then the tree would blast its pollen into the sky in an explosion which would be heard for miles.

Lying prone on the bed of soft vegetation, Leddravohr felt a pulsing warmth in his groin and realised he was becoming sexually excited. He focused his glasses on the woman lashed to the top of the tree, trying to pick out details of breast or buttock. Until that moment she had been so passive that he had believed her to *be* unconscious, perhaps drugged, but the movement of the huge leaves farther down the trunk appeared to have alerted her to the fact that her life was about to end, although her limbs were too well bound to permit any real struggle. She had begun twisting her head from side to side, swinging the long black hair which hid her face.

'Stupid bitch,' Leddravohr whispered. He had limited his study of the Gethan tribes to an assessment of their military capabilities, but he guessed their religion was the uninspired mishmash of superstitions found in most of the backward countries of Land. In all probability the woman had actually volunteered for her role in the fertility rite, believing that her sacrifice would guarantee her reincarnation as a princess on Overland. Generous dosages of wine and dried mushroom could render such ideas temporarily persuasive, but there was nothing like the imminence of death to induce a more rational mode of thought.

'Stupid bitch she may be, but I wish I had her under me right now,' Reeff growled. 'I don't know which is going to blow first – that tree or mine.'

'I'll give her to you when we have finished our work,' Leddravohr said with a smile. 'Which half will you take first?'

Reeff produced a nauseated grimace, expressing his admiration for the way in which the prince could match the best of his men in any branch of soldiering, including that of devising obscenities. Leddravohr turned his attention to the Gethan look-outs. His field glasses showed that they were, as he had anticipated, casting frequent glances towards the sacrificial tree, upon which the third pair of leaves had begun to rise. He knew there was a straightforward botanical reason for the tree's behaviour – leaves in the horizontal attitude would have been snapped off by the recoil of the pollination discharge – but the sexual symbolism was potent and compelling. Leddravohr was confident that every one of the Gethan guards would be staring at the tree when the climactic moment arrived. He put his glasses away and took a firm grip on his sword as the leaves clasped the brakka's trunk and, almost without delay, the lowermost pair began to stir. The flailing of the woman's hair was frenetic now and her cries were thinly audible at the edge of the clearing, mingled with the chanting of a single male voice from somewhere near the centre of the tribal assembly.

'Ten nobles extra to the man who silences the priest,' Leddravohr said, reaffirming his dislike for all superstition-mongers, especially the variety who were too craven to do their own pointless butchery.

He raised a hand to his helmet and removed the cowl which had concealed its scarlet crest. The young lieutenants commanding the other three cohorts would be watching for the flash of colour as he emerged from the forest. Leddravohr tensed himself for action as the fourth pair of leaves lifted and closed around the brakka's trunk, gentle as a lover's hands. The woman trussed across the tip of the tree was suddenly quiescent, perhaps in a faint, perhaps petrified with dread. An intense pulsing silence descended over the clearing. Leddravohr knew that the partition in the tree's combustion chamber had already given way, that a measure of green and purple crystals had already been mixed, that the energy released by them could be pent up for only a few seconds ...

The sound of the explosion, although directed upwards, was appalling. The brakka's trunk whipped and shuddered as the pollinated discharge ripped into the sky, a vaporous column momentarily tinged with blood, concentrically ringed with smoke.

Leddravohr felt the ground lift beneath him as a shock wave raced out through the surrounding forest, then he was on his feet and running. Deafened by the awesome blast of sound, he had to rely on the evidence of his eyes to gauge the degree of surprise in the attack. To the left and right he could see the orange helmet crests of two of his lieutenants, with dozens of soldiers emerging from the trees behind them. Directly ahead of him the Gethans were gazing spellbound at the sacrificial tree, whose leaves were already beginning to unfurl, but they were bound to discover their peril at any second. He had covered almost half the distance to the nearest guard and unless the man turned soon he was going to die without even knowing what had hit him.

The man turned. His face contorted, the mouth curving downwards, as he shouted a warning. He stamped his right foot on something concealed in the grass. Leddravohr knew it was the Gethan version of a cannon – a brakka tube set on a shallow ramp and intended solely for anti-personnel use. The impact of the guard's foot had shattered a glass or ceramic capsule in the breech and mixed its charge of power crystals, but – and this was why Kolcorron had little regard for such weapons – there was an inevitable delay before the discharge. Brief though the period was, it enabled Leddravohr to take evasive action. Shouting a warning to the soldiers behind him, he veered to the right and came at the Gethan from the side just as the cannon exploded and sent its fan-shaped spray of pebbles and rock fragments crackling through the grass. The guard had managed to draw his sword, but his preoccupation with the sacrifice had rendered him untuned and unready for combat. Leddravohr, without even breaking his stride, cut him down with a single slash across the neck and plunged on into the confusion of human figures beyond.

Normal time ceased to exist for Leddravohr as he cut his way towards the centre of the clearing. He was only dimly aware of the sounds of struggle being punctuated by further cannon blasts. At least two of the Gethans he killed were young women, something his men might grumble about later, but he had seen otherwise good soldiers lose their lives through trying to differentiate between the sexes during a battle. Turning a killing stroke into one which merely stunned involved making a decision and losing combat efficiency – and it took only an eyeblink for an enemy blade to find its mark.

Some of the Gethans were trying to make their escape, only to be felled or turned back by the encircling Kolcorronians. Others were making a fight of it as best they could, but their preoccupation with the ceremony had been fatal and they were paying the full price for their lack of vigilance. A group of tribesmen, plait-haired and outlandish in skin mosaics, got among the nine brakka trees and used the trunks as a natural fortification. Leddravohr saw two of his men take serious wounds, but the Gethans' stand was short-lived. They were hampered by lack of room and made easy targets for spearmen from the second cohort.

All at once the battle was over.

With the fading of the crimson joy and the return of sanity Leddravohr's cooler instincts reasserted themselves. He scanned his surroundings to make sure he was in no personal danger, that the only people still on their feet were Kolcorronian soldiers and captured Gethan women, then he turned his gaze to the sky. While in the forest he and his men had been safe from ptertha, but now they were in the open and at some slight risk.

The celestial globe which presented itself to Leddravohr's scrutiny looked strange to a native of Kolcorron. He had grown up with the huge and misty sphere of Overland hanging directly overhead, but here in the Loongl Peninsula the sister world was displaced far to the west. Leddravohr could see clear sky straight above and it gave him an uncomfortable feeling, as though he had left an important flank exposed in a battle plan. No bluish specs were to be seen drifting against the patterns of daytime stars, however, and he decided it was safe to return his attention to the work at hand.

The scene all about him was a familiar one, filled with a medley of familiar sounds. Some of the Kolcorronians were shouting coarse jokes at each other as they moved about the clearing dispatching wounded Gethans and collecting battle trophies. The tribesmen had little that could be considered valuable, but their Y-shaped ptertha sticks would make interesting curios to be shown in the taverns of Ro-Atabri. Other soldiers were laughing and whooping as they stripped the dozen or so Gethan women who had been taken alive. That was a legitimate activity at this stage – men who had fought well were entitled to the prizes of war – and Leddravohr paid only enough attention to satisfy himself that no actual coupling had begun. In this kind of territory an enemy counterattack could be launched very quickly, and a soldier in rut was one of the most useless creatures in the universe.

Railo, Nothnalp and Chravell – the lieutenants who had led the other three cohorts – approached Leddravohr. The leather of Railo's circular shield was badly gashed and there was a reddening bandage on his left arm, but he was fit and in good spirits. Nothnalp and Chravell were cleaning their swords with rags, removing all traces of contamination from the enamel inlays on the black blades.

'A successful operation, if I'm not mistaken,' Railo said, giving Leddravohr the informal field salute.

Leddravohr nodded. 'What casualties?'

'Three dead and eleven wounded. Two of the wounded were hit by the cannon. They won't see littlenight.'

'Will they take the Bright Road?'

Railo looked offended. 'Of course.'

'I'll speak to them before they go,' Leddravohr said. As a pragmatic man with no religious beliefs he suspected his words might not mean much to the dying soldiers, but it was the sort of gesture which would be appreciated by their comrades. Like his practice of permitting even the lowliest line soldier to speak to him without using the proper forms of address, it was one of the ways in which he retained the affection and loyalty of his troops. He kept to himself the intelligence that his motives were entirely practical.

'Do we push straight on the Gethan village?' Chravell, the tallest of the lieutenants, returned his sword to its sheath. 'It's not much more than a mile to the north-east, and they probably heard the cannon fire.'

Leddravohr considered the question. 'How many adults remain in the village?'

'Practically none, according to the scouts. They all came here to see the show.' Chravell glanced briefly upwards at the dehumanised tatters of flesh and bone dangling from the tip of the sacrificial tree.

'In that case the village has ceased to be a military threat and has become an asset. Give me a map.' Leddravohr took the proffered sheet and went down on one knee to spread it on the ground. It had been drawn a short time previously by an aerial survey team and emphasised the local features of interest to the Kolcorronian commanders – the size and location of Gethan settlements, topography, rivers, and – most important from a strategic point of view – the distribution of brakka among the other types of forestation. Leddravohr studied it carefully, then outlined his plans.

Some twenty miles beyond the village was a much larger community, coded G31, capable of fielding an estimated three hundred fighting men. The intervening terrain was, to say the least of it, difficult. It was densely wooded and crisscrossed with steep ridges, crevasses and fast-flowing streams – all of which conspired to make it a nightmare for Kolcorronian soldiers whose natural taste was for plains warfare.

'The savages must come to us,' Leddravohr announced. 'A forced march across that type of ground will tire any man, so the faster they come the better for us. I take it this is a sacred place for them?'

'A holy of holies,' Railo said. 'It's very unusual to find nine brakka so close together.'

'Good! The first thing we do is bring the trees down. Instruct the sentinels to allow some villagers to get close enough to see what is happening, and to let them get away again. And just before littlenight send a detachment to burn the village – just to drive the message home. If we are lucky the savages will be so exhausted when they get here they'll barely have enough strength to run on to our swords.'

Leddravohr concluded his deliberately simplistic verbal sketch by laughing and tossing the map back to Chravell. His judgment was that the Gethans of G31, even if provoked into a hasty attack, would be more dangerous opponents than the lowland villagers. The forthcoming battle, as well as providing valuable experience for the three young officers, would let him demonstrate once again that in his forties *he* was a better soldier than men half his age. He stood up, breathing deeply and pleasurably, looking forward to the remainder of a day which had begun well.

In spite of his relaxed mood, ingrained habit prompted him to check the open sky. No ptertha were visible, but he was alerted by a suggestion of movement in one of the vertical panels of sky seen through the trees to the west. He took out his field glasses, trained them on the adjoining patch of brightness and a moment later caught a brief glimpse of a low-flying airship.

It was obviously heading for the area command centre, which was about five miles away on the western edge of the peninsula. The vessel had been too distant for Leddravohr to be certain, but he thought he had seen a plume-and-sword symbol on the side of the gondola. He frowned as he tried to imagine what circumstance was bringing one of his father's messengers to such an outlying region.

'The men are ready for breakfast,' Nothnalp said, removing his orange-crested helmet so that he could wipe perspiration from his neck. 'A couple of extra strips of salt pork wouldn't do any harm in this heat.'

Leddravohr nodded. 'I suppose they've earned that much.'

'They'd also like to start on the women.'

'Not until we secure the area. Make sure it is fully patrolled, and get the slimers brought forward immediately – I want those trees on the ground fast.' Leddravohr moved away from the lieutenants and began a circuit of the clearing. The predominant sound was now that of the Gethan women screaming abuse in their barbaric tongue, but cooking fires were beginning to crackle and he could hear Railo shouting orders at the platoon leaders who were going on patrol.

Near the base of one of the brakka trees was a low wooden platform heavily daubed in green and yellow with the matt pigments used by the Gethans. The naked body of a white-bearded man lay across the platform, his torso displaying several stab wounds. Leddravohr guessed the dead man was the priest who had been conducting the ceremony of sacrifice. His guess was confirmed when he noticed high-sergeant Reeff and a line soldier in conversation close to the primitive structure. The two men's voices were inaudible, but they were speaking with the peculiar intensity which soldiers reserved for the subject of money, and Leddravohr knew a bargain was being struck. He unstrapped his cuirass and sat down on a stump, waiting to see if Reeff was capable of any degree of subtlety. A moment later Reeff put his arm around the other man's shoulders and brought him forward.

'This is Soo Eggezo,' Reeff said. 'A good soldier. He's the one who silenced the priest.'

'Useful work, Eggezo.' Leddravohr gazed blandly at the young soldier, who was tongue-tied and obviously overawed by his presence, and made no other response. There was an awkward silence.

'Sir, you generously offered a reward of ten nobles for killing the priest.'

Reeff's voice assumed a throaty sincerity. 'Eggezo supports his mother and father in Ro-Atabri. The extra money would mean a great deal to them.'

'Of course.' Leddravohr opened his pouch and took out a ten-noble note and extended it to Eggezo. He waited until the soldier's fingers had almost closed on the blue square of woven glass, then he quickly returned it to his pouch. Eggezo glanced uneasily at the sergeant.

'On second thoughts,' Leddravohr said, 'these might be more ... convenient.' He replaced the first note with two green squares of the five-noble denomination and handed them to Eggezo. He pretended to lose interest as the two men thanked him and hurried away. They went barely twenty paces before stopping for another whispered conversation, and when they parted Reeff was tucking something into a pocket. Leddravohr smiled as he committed Reeff's name to long-term memory. The sergeant was the sort of man he occasionally had use for – greedy, stupid and highly predictable. A few seconds later his interest in Reeff was pushed into the hinterland of his consciousness as a howl of jovial protest from many Kolcorronian throats told him the slimers had arrived to deal with the stand of brakka trees.

Leddravohr rose to his feet, as anxious as anybody to avoid getting downwind of the slimers, and watched the four semi-nude men emerge from the surrounding forest. They were carrying large gourds slung from padded yokes and they also bore spades and other kinds of digging implements. Their limbs were streaked with the living slime which was the principal tool of their trade. Every artifact they carried was made from glass, stone or ceramic because the slime would quickly have devoured all other materials, especially brakka. Even their breech clouts were woven from soft glass.

'Out of the way, dung-eaters,' their round-bellied leader shouted as they marched straight across the clearing to the brakka. His words provoked a barrage of insults from the soldiers, to which the other slimers responded with obscene gestures. Leddravohr moved to keep upwind of the four men, partly to escape the stench they were exuding, but mainly to ensure that none of the slime's airborne spores settled on his person. The only way to rid one's self of even the slightest contamination was by thorough and painful abrasion of the skin.

On reaching the nearest brakka the slimers set down their equipment and began work immediately. As they dug to expose the upper root system, the one which extracted pikon, they kept up their verbal abuse of all soldiers who caught their gaze. They could do so with impunity because they knew themselves to be the cornerstone of the Kolcorronian economy, an outcast elite, and were accorded unique privileges. They were also highly paid for their services. After ten years as a slimer a man could retire to a life of ease – provided he survived the lengthy process of being cleansed of the virulent mucus.

Leddravohr watched with interest as the radial upper roots were uncovered. A slimer opened one of the glass gourds and, using a spatula, proceeded to daub the main roots with the pus-like goo. Cultured from the solvent the brakka themselves had evolved to dissolve their combustion chamber diaphragms, the slime gave out a choking odour like bile-laden vomit mingled, incongruously, with the sweetness of whitefern. The roots, which would have resisted the sharpest blade, swelled visibly as their cellular structure was attacked. Two other slimers hacked through them with slate axes and, working with showy energy for the benefit of their audience, dug further down to reveal the lower root system and the bulbous swelling of the combustion chamber at the base of the trunk. Inside it was a valuable harvest of power crystals which would have to be removed, taking the utmost care to keep the two varieties separated, before the tree could be felled.

'Stand back, dung-eaters,' the oldest slimer called out. 'Stand back and let ...' His voice faded as he raised his eyes and for the first time realised that Leddravohr was present. He bowed deeply, with a grace which went ill with his naked and filth-streaked belly, and said, 'I cannot apologise to you, Prince, because of course my remarks were not addressed to you.'

'Well put,' Leddravohr said, appreciating nimbleness of mind from such an unlikely source. 'I'm pleased to learn you don't suffer from suicidal tendencies. What's your name?'

'It is Owpope, Prince.'

'Proceed with your labours, Owpope – I never tire of seeing the wealth of our country being produced.'

'Gladly, Prince, but there is always a slight risk of a blowout through the side of the chamber when we broach a tree.'

'Just exercise your normal discretion,' Leddravohr said, folding his arms. His acute hearing picked up a ripple of admiring whispers going through the nearby soldiery, and he knew he had added to his reputation as the prince with the common touch. The word would spread fast – *Leddravohr loves his people so much that he will even converse with a slime.* The little episode was a calculated exercise in image-building, but in truth *he* did not feel he was demeaning himself by talking to a man like Owpope, whose work was of genuine importance to Kolcorron. It was the useless parasites – like the priests and philosophers – who earned his hatred and contempt. They would be the first to be purged out of existence when he eventually became King.

He was settling down to watch Owpope apply an elliptical pattern of slime to the curving base of the brakka trunk when his attention was again caught by a movement in the sky to the west. The airship had returned and was scudding through the narrow band of blue which separated Overland from the jagged wall of trees. Its appearance after such a short time meant that it had not landed at 01, the area command centre. The captain must have communicated with the base by sunwriter and then come directly to the forward zone – which made it almost certain that he was carrying an urgent message to Leddravohr from the King.

Mystified, Leddravohr shaded his eyes from the sun's glare as he watched the airship slow down and manoeuvre towards a landing in the forest clearing.

CHAPTER THREE

Lain Maraquine's domicile – known as the Square House – was positioned on Greenmount, a rounded hill in a northern suburb of Ro-Atabri, the Kolcorronian capital.

From the window of his study he had a panoramic view of the city's various districts – residential, commercial, industrial, administrative – as they sifted down to the Borann River and on the far bank gave way to the parklands surrounding the five palaces. The families headed by the Lord Philosopher had been granted a cluster of dwellings and other buildings on this choice site many centuries earlier, during the reign of Bytran IV, when their work was held in much higher regard.

The Lord Philosopher himself lived in a sprawling structure known as Greenmount Peel, and it was a sign of his former importance that all the houses in his bailiwick had been placed in line-of-sight with the Great Palace, thus facilitating communication by sunwriter. Now, however, such prestigious features only added to the jealousy and resentment felt by the heads of other orders. Lain Maraquine knew that the industrial supremo, Prince Chakkell, particularly wanted Greenmount as an adornment to his own empire and was doing everything in his power to have the philosophers deposed and moved to humbler accommodation.

It was the beginning of aftday, the region having just emerged from the shadow of Overland, and the city was looking beautiful as it returned to life after its two-hour sleep. The yellow, orange and red coloration of trees which were shedding their leaves contrasted with the pale and darker greens of trees with different cycles which were coming into bud or were in full foliage. Here and there the brightly glowing envelopes of airships created pastel circles and ellipses, and on the river could be seen the white sails of ocean-going ships which were bringing a thousand commodities from distant parts of Land.

Seated at his desk by the window, Lain was oblivious to the spectacular view. All that day he had been aware of a curious excitement and a sense of expectancy deep within himself. There was no way in which he could be certain, but his premonition was that the mental agitation was leading to something of rare importance.

For some time he had been intrigued by an underlying similarity he had observed in problems fed into his department from a variety of sources. The problems were as routine and mundane as a vintner wanting to know the most economical shape of jar in which to market a fixed quantity of wine, or a farmer trying to decide the best mix of crops for a certain area of land at different times of the year.

It was all a far cry from the days when his forebears had been charged with tasks like estimating the size of the cosmos, and yet Lain had begun to suspect that somewhere at the heart of the commonplace commercial riddles there lurked a concept whose implications were more universal than the enigmas of astronomy. In every case there was a quantity whose value was governed by changes in another quantity, and the problem was that of finding an optimum balance. Traditional solutions involved making numerous approximations or plotting vertices on a graph, but a tiny voice had begun to whisper to Lain and its message was the icily thrilling one that there might be a way of arriving at a *precise* solution algebraically, with a few strokes of the pen. It was something to do with the mathematical notion of limits, with the idea that ...

'You'll have to help with the guest list,' Gesalla said as she swept into the panelled study. 'I can't do any serious planning when I don't even know how many people we are going to have.'

A glimmering in the depths of Lain's mind was abruptly extinguished, leaving him with a sense of loss which quickly faded as he looked up at his black-haired solewife. The illness of early pregnancy had narrowed the oval of her face and given her a dark-eyed pallor which somehow emphasised her intelligence and strength of character. She had never looked more beautiful in Lain's eyes, but he still wished she had not insisted on starting the baby. That slender, slim-hipped body did not look to him as though it had been designed for motherhood and he had private fears about the outcome.

'Oh, I'm sorry, Lain,' she said, her face showing concern. 'Did I interrupt something important?'

He smiled and shook his head, once again impressed by her talent for divining other people's thoughts. 'Isn't it early to be planning for Yearsend?'

'Yes.' She met his gaze coolly – her way of challenging him to find anything wrong with being efficient. 'Now, about your guests ...'

'I promise to write out a list before the day is over. I suppose it will be much the same as usual, though I'm not sure if Toller will be home this year.'

'I hope he isn't,' Gesalla said, wrinkling her nose. 'I don't want him. It would be *so* pleasant to have a party without any arguments or fighting.'

'He *is* my brother,' Lain protested amiably.

'Half-brother would be more like it.'

Lain's good humour was threatened. 'I'm glad my mother isn't alive to hear that comment.'

Gesalla came to him immediately, sat on his lap and kissed him on the mouth, moulding his cheeks with both her hands to coax him into an ardent response. It was a familiar trick of hers, but nonetheless effective. Still feeling privileged even after two years of marriage, he slid his hand inside her blue camisole and caressed her small breasts. After a moment she sat upright and gave him a solemn stare.

'I didn't mean any disrespect to your mother,' she said. 'It's just that Toller *looks* more like a soldier than a member of this family.'

'Genetic flukes sometimes happen.'

'And there's the way he can't even read.'

'We've been through all this before,' Lain said patiently. 'When you get to know Toller better you'll see that he is as intelligent as any other member of the family. He *can* read, but he isn't fluent because of some problem with the way he perceives printed words. In any case, most of the military are literate – so your observation is lacking in relevance.'

'Well …' Gesalla looked dissatisfied. 'Well, why does he have to cause trouble everywhere he goes?'

'Lots of people have that habit – including one whose left nipple is tickling my palm at this moment.'

'Don't try to turn my mind to other things – especially at this time of day.'

'All right, but why does Toller bother you so much? I mean, we are pretty well surrounded by individualists and near-eccentrics on Greenmount.'

'Would you like it better if I were one of those faceless females who have no opinions about anything?' Gesalla was galvanised into springing to her feet, her light body scarcely reacting against his thighs, and an expression of dismay appeared on her face as she looked down into the walled precinct in front of the house. 'Were you expecting Lord Glo?'

'No.'

'Bad luck – you've got him.' Gesalla hurried to the door of the study. 'I'm going to vanish before he arrives. I can't afford to spend half the day listening to all that endless humming and hawing – not to mention the smutty innuendoes.' She gathered her ankle-length skirts and ran silently towards the rear stairs.

Lain took off his reading glasses and gazed after her, wishing she would not keep reviving the subject of his brother's parentage. Aytha Maraquine, his mother, had died in giving birth to Toller, so if there had been an adulterous liaison she had more than paid for it. Why could Gesalla not leave the matter at that? Lain bad been attracted to her for her intellectual independence as well as her beauty and physical grace, but he had not bargained for the antagonism towards his brother. He hoped it was not going to lead to years of domestic friction.

The sound of a carriage door slamming in the precinct drew his attention to the outside world. Lord Glo had just stepped down from the aging but resplendent phaeton which he always used for short journeys in the city. Its driver, holding the two bluehorns in check, nodded and fidgeted as he received a lengthy series of instructions from Glo. Lain guessed that the Lord Philosopher was using a hundred words where ten would have sufficed and he began to pray that the visit would not be too much of an endurance test. He went to the sideboard, poured out two glasses of black wine and wanted by the study door until Glo appeared.

'You're very kind,' Glo said, taking his glass as he entered and going straight to the nearest chair. Although in his late fifties, he looked much older thanks to his rotund figure and the fact that his teeth had been reduced to a few brownish pegs splayed behind his lower lip. He was breathing noisily after climbing the stairs, his stomach ballooning and collapsing under his informal grey-and-white robe.

'It's always a pleasure to see you, my lord,' Lain said, wondering if there was a special reason for the visit and knowing there was little point in his trying to elicit the information too soon.

Glo drank half his wine in one gulp. 'Mutual, my boy. Oh! I've got something … hmm … at least, I *think* I've got something to show you. You're going to like this.' He set his glass aside, groped in the folds of his clothing and eventually produced a square of paper which he handed to Lain. It was slightly sticky and mid-brown in colour except for a circular patch of mottled tan in the centre.

'Farland.' Lain identified the circle as being a light picture of the only other major planet in the local system, orbiting the sun at some twice the distance of the Land-Overland pair. 'The images are getting better.'

'Yes, but we still can't make them permanent. That one has faded … hmm … noticeably since last night. You can hardly see the polar caps now, but last night they were very clear. Pity. Pity.' Glo took the picture back and studied it closely, all the while shaking his head and sucking his teeth.

'The polar caps were as clear as daylight. Clear as daylight, I tell you. Young Enteth got a very good confirmation of the angle of … ah … inclination. Lain, have you ever tried to visualise what it would be like to live on a world whose axis was tilted? There would be a hot period of the year, with long days and short nights, and a cold … hmm … period, with long days … I mean *short* days … and long nights … all depending on where the planet was in its orbit. The colour changes on Farland show *that all* the vegetation is geared to a single ... hmm ... superimposed cycle.'

Lain concealed his impatience and boredom as Glo launched himself upon one of his most familiar set pieces. It was a cruel irony that the Lord Philosopher was becoming prematurely senile, and Lain – who had a genuine regard for the older man – saw it as a duty to give him maximum support, personally and professionally. He replenished his visitor's drink and made appropriate comments as Glo meandered on from elementary astronomy to botany and the differences between the ecology of a tilted world and that of Land.

On Land, where there were no seasons, the very first farmers must have had the task of separating the natural jumble of edible grasses into synchronous batches which matured at chosen times. Six harvests a year was the norm in most parts of the world. Thereafter it had simply been a matter of planting and reaping six adjacent strips to maintain supplies of grain, with no long-term storage problems. In modern times the advanced countries had found it more efficacious to devote whole farms to single-cycle crops and to work in six-farm combines or multiples thereof, but the principle was the same.

As a boy, Lain Maraquine had enjoyed speculating about life on distant planets – assuming they existed in other parts of the universe and were peopled by intelligent beings – but he had quickly found that mathematics offered him greater scope for intellectual adventure. Now all he could wish for was that Lord Glo would either go away and let him get on with his work or proceed to explain his visit. Tuning his thoughts back into the rambling discourse he found that Glo had switched back to the experiments with photography and the difficulties of producing emulsions of light-sensitive vegetable cells which would hold an image for more than a few days.

'Why is it so important to you?' Lain put in. 'Anybody in your observatory staff could draw a much better picture by hand.'

'Astronomy is only a tiny bit of it, my boy – the aim is to be able to produce totally ... hmm ... accurate pictures of buildings, landscapes, people.'

'Yes, but we already have draughtsmen and artists who can do that.'

Glo shook his head and smiled, showing the ruins of his teeth, and spoke with unusual fluency. 'Artists only paint what they or their patrons believe to be important. We lose so much. The times slip through our fingers. I want every man to be his own artist – then we'll discover our history.'

'Do you think it will be possible?'

'Undoubtedly. I foresee the day when everybody will carry light-sensitive material and will be able to make a picture of *anything in* the blink of an eye.'

'You can still outfly any of us,' Lain said, impressed, feeling he had momentarily been in the presence of the Lord Glo who used to be. 'And by flying higher you see farther.'

Glo looked gratified. 'Never mind that – give me more ... hmm ... wine.' He watched his glass closely while it was being refilled, then settled back in his chair. 'You will never guess what has happened.'

'You've impregnated some innocent young female.'

'Try again.'

'Some innocent young female has impregnated you.'

'This is a serious matter, Lain.' Glo made a damping movement with his hand to show that levity was out of place. 'The King and Prince Chakkell have suddenly wakened up to the fact that we are running short of brakka.'

Lain froze in the act of raising his own glass to his lips. 'I can't believe this, as you predicted. How many reports and studies have we sent them in the last ten years?'

'I've lost count, but it looks as though they have finally taken some effect. The King has called a meeting of the high ... hmm ... council.'

'I never thought he'd do it,' Lain said. 'Have you just come from the palace?'

'Ah ... no. I've known about the meeting for some days, but I couldn't pass the news on to you because the King sent me off to Sorka – of all places! – on another ... hmm ... matter. I just got back this foreday.'

'I could use an extra holiday.'

'It was no holiday, my boy.' Glo shook his large head and looked solemn. 'I was with Tunsfo – and I had to watch one of his surgeons perform an autopsy on a soldier. I don't mind admitting I have no stomach for that kind of thing.'

'Please! Don't even talk about it,' Lain said, feeling a gentle upward pressure on his diaphragm at the thought of knives going through pallid skin and disturbing the cold obscenities beneath. 'Why did the King want you there?'

Glo tapped himself on the chest. 'Lord Philosopher, that's me. My word still carries a lot of weight with the King. Apparently our soldiers and airmen are becoming ... hmm ... demoralised over rumours that it isn't safe to go near ptertha casualties.'

'Not safe? In what way?'

'The story is that several line soldiers contracted pterthacosis through handling victims.'

'But that's nonsense,' Lain said, taking a first sip of his wine. 'What did Tunsfo find?'

'It was pterthacosis, all right. No doubt about it. Spleen like a football. Our official conclusion was that the soldier encountered a globe at dead of night and took the dust without knowing it – or that he was telling ... hmm

... lies. That happens, you know. Some men can't face up to it. They even manage to convince *themselves* that they're all right.'

'I can understand that.' Lain drew in his shoulders as though feeling cold. 'The temptation must be there. After all, the slightest air current can make all the difference. Between life and death.'

'I would prefer to talk about our own concerns.' Glo stood up and began to pace the room. 'This meeting is very important to us, my boy. A chance for the philosophy order to win the recognition it deserves, to regain its former status. Now, I want you to prepare the graphs in person – make them big and colourful and ... hmm ... simple – showing how much pikon and halvell Kolcorron can expect to manufacture in the next fifty years. Five year increments might be appropriate – I leave that to you. We also need to show how, as the requirement for natural crystals decreases, our reserves of home-grown brakka will increase until we ...'

'My lord, slow down a little,' Lain protested, dismayed to see Glo's visionary rhetoric waft him so far from the realities of the situation. 'I hate to appear pessimistic, but there is no guarantee that we will produce *any* usable crystals in the next fifty years. Our best pikon to date has a purity of only one third, and the halvell is not much better.'

Glo gave an excited laugh. 'That's only because we haven't had the full backing of the King. With proper resources we can solve all the purification problems in a few years. I'm sure of it! Why the King even permitted me to use his messengers to recall Sisstt and Duthoon. They can give up-to-date reports on their progress at the meeting. Hard facts – that what impress the King. Practicalities. I tell you, my boy, the times are changing. I feel sick.' Glo dropped back into his chair with a thud which disturbed the decorative ceramics on the nearest wall.

Lain knew he should go forward to offer comfort, but he found himself shrinking back. Glo looked as though he could vomit at any moment, and the thought of being close to him when it happened was too distasteful. Even worse, the meandering veins on Glo's temples seemed in danger of rupturing. What if there actually were a fountaining of red? Lain tried to visualise how he would cope if some of the other man's blood got on to his own person and again his stomach gave a preliminary heave.

'Shall I go and fetch something?' he said anxiously. 'Some water?'

'More wine,' Glo husked, holding out his glass.

'Do you think you should?'

'Don't be such a prune, my boy – it's the best tonic there is. If you drank a little more wine it might put some flesh on your ... hmm ... bones.' Glo studied his glass while it was being refilled, making sure he received full measure, and the colour began returning to his face. 'Now, what was I talking about?'

'Wasn't it something to do with the impending rebirth of our civilisation?'
Glo looked reproachful. 'Sarcasm? Is that sarcasm?'

'I'm sorry, my lord,' Lain said. 'It's just that brakka conservation has
always been a passion with me – a subject upon which I can easily become
intemperate.'

'I remember.' Glo's gaze travelled the room, noting the use of ceramics
and glass for fitments which in almost any other house would have been
carved from the black wood. 'You don't think you ... hmm ... overdo it?'

'It's the way I feel.' Lain held up his left hand and indicated the black ring
he wore on the sixth finger. 'The only reason I have this much is that it was
a wedding token from Gesalla.'

'Ah yes – Gesalla.' Glo bared his divergent teeth in a parody of lecherous-
ness. 'One of these nights, I swear, you'll have some extra company in bed.'

'My bed is your bed,' Lain said easily, aware that Lord Glo never claimed
his nobleman's right to take any woman in the social group of which he was
dynastic head. It was an ancient custom in Kolcorron, still observed in the
major families, and Glo's occasional jests on the subject were merely his way
of emphasising the philosophy order's cultural superiority in having left the
practice behind.

'Bearing in mind your extreme views,' Glo went on, returning to his original subject, 'couldn't you bring yourself to adopt a more positive attitude to
the meeting? Aren't you pleased about it?'

'Yes, I'm pleased. It's a step in the right direction, but it has come so *late*.
You know it takes fifty or sixty years for a brakka to reach maturity and
enter the pollinating phase. We'd still be facing that time lag even if we had
the capability to grow pure crystals right now – and it's frighteningly large.'

'All the more reason to plan ahead, my boy.'

'True – but the greater the need for a plan the less chance it has of being
accepted.'

'That was very profound,' Glo said. 'Now tell me what it ... hmm ...
means.'

'There was a time, perhaps fifty years ago, when Kolcorron could have
balanced supply and demand by implementing just a few common sense
conservation measures, but even then the princes wouldn't listen. Now
we're in a situation which calls for really drastic measures. Can you imagine
how Leddravohr would react to the proposal that all armament production
should be suspended for twenty or thirty years?'

'It doesn't bear thinking about,' Glo said. 'But aren't you exaggerating the
difficulties?'

'Have a look at these graphs.' Lain went to a chest of shallow drawers, took
out a large sheet and spread it on his desk where it could be seen by Glo. He
explained the various coloured diagrams, avoiding abstruse mathematics as

much as possible, analysing how the country's growing demands for power crystals and brakka were interacting with other factors such an increasing scarcity and transport delays. Once or twice as he spoke it came to him that here, yet again, were problems in the same general class as those he had been thinking about earlier. Then he had been tantalised by the idea that he was about to conceive of an entirely new way of dealing with them, something to do with the mathematical concept of limits, but now material and human considerations were dominating his thoughts.

Among them was the fact that Lord Glo, who would be the principal philosophy spokesman, had become incapable of following complex arguments. And in addition to his natural disability, Glo was now in the habit of fuddling himself with wine every day. He was nodding a great deal and sucking his teeth, trying to exhibit concerned interest, but the fleshy wattles of his eyelids were descending with increasing frequency.

'So that's the extent of the problem, my lord,' Lain said, speaking with extra fervour to get Glo's attention. 'Would you like to hear my department's views on the kind of measures needed to keep the crisis within manageable proportions?'

'Stability, yes, stability – that's the thing.' Glo abruptly raised his head and for a moment he seemed utterly lost, his pale blue eyes scanning Lain's face as though seeing it for the first time. 'Where were we?'

Lain felt depressed and oddly afraid. 'Perhaps it would be best if I sent a written summary to you at the Peel, one you could go over at your leisure. When is the council going to meet?'

'On the morning of two-hundred. Yes, the King definitely said two-hundred. What day is this?'

'One-nine-four.'

'There isn't much time,' Glo said sadly. 'I promised the King I'd have a significant ... hmm ... contribution.'

'You will.'

'That's not what I ...' Glo stood up, swaying a little, and faced Lain with an odd tremulous smile. 'Did you really mean what you said?'

Lain blinked at him, unable to place the question in context properly. 'My lord?'

'About my ... about my flying higher ... seeing farther?'

'Of course,' Lain said, beginning to feel embarrassed. 'I couldn't have been more sincere.'

'That's good. It means so ...' Glo straightened up and expanded his plump chest, suddenly recovering his normal joviality. 'We'll show them. We'll show *all* of them.' He went to the door, then paused with his hand on the porcelain knob. 'Let me have a summary as soon as ... hmm ... possible. Oh, by the way, I have instructed Sisstt to bring your brother home with him.'

'That's very kind of you, my lord,' Lain said, his pleasure at the prospect of seeing Toller again modified by thoughts of Gesalla's likely reaction to the news.

'Not at all. I think we were all a trifle hard on him. I mean, a year in a miserable place like Haffanger just for giving Ongmat a tap on the chin.'

'As a result of that tap Ongmat's jaw was broken in two places.'

'Well, it was a firm tap.' Glo gave a wheezing laugh. 'And we all felt the benefit of Ongmat being silenced for a while.' Still chuckling, he moved out of sight along the corridor, his sandals slapping on the mosaic floor.

Lain carried his hardly-touched glass of wine to his desk and sat down, swirling the black liquid to create light patterns on its surface. Glo's humorous endorsement of Toller's violence was quite typical of him, one of the little ways in which he reminded members of the philosophy order that he was of royal lineage and therefore had the blood of conquerors in his veins. It showed he was feeling better and had recovered his self-esteem, but it did nothing to ease Lain's worries about the older man's physical and mental fitness.

In the space of only a few years Glo had turned into a bumbling and absent-minded incompetent. His unsuitability for his post was tolerated by most department heads, some of whom appreciated the extra personal freedom they derived from it, but there was a general sense of demoralisation over the order's continuing loss of status. The aging King Prad still retained an indulgent fondness for Glo – and, so the whispers went, if philosophy had come to be regarded as a joke it was appropriate that it should be represented by a court jester.

But there was nothing funny about a meeting of the high council, Lain told himself. The person who presented the case for rigorous brakka conservation would need to do it with eloquence and force, marshalling complex arguments and backing them up with an unassailable command of the statistics involved. His stance would be generally unpopular, and would attract special hostility from the ambitious Prince Chakkell and the savage Leddravohr.

If Glo proved unable to master the brief in time for the meeting it was possible he would call on a deputy to speak on his behalf, and the thought of having to challenge Chakkell or Leddravohr – even verbally – produced in Lain a cold panic which threatened to affect his bladder. The wine in his glass was now reflecting a pattern of trembling concentric circles.

Lain set the glass down and began breathing deeply and steadily, waiting for the shaking of his hands to cease.

CHAPTER FOUR

Toller Maraquine awoke with the knowledge, which was both disturbing and comforting, that he was not alone in bed.

He could feel the body heat of the woman who was lying at his left side, one of her arms resting on his stomach, one of her legs drawn up across his thighs. The sensations were all the more pleasant for being unfamiliar. He lay quite still, staring at the-ceiling, as he tried to recall the exact circumstances which had brought female company to his austere apartment in the Square House.

He had celebrated his return to the capital with a round of the busy taverns in the Samlue district. The tour had begun early on the previous day and had been intended to last only until the end of littlenight, but the ale and wine had been persuasive and the acquaintances he met had eventually begun to seem like cherished friends. He had continued drinking right through aftday and well into the night, revelling in his escape from the smell of the pikon pans, and at a late stage had begun to notice the same woman close to him in the throng time after time, much more often than could be accounted for by chance.

She had been tawny-haired and tall, full-breasted, broad of shoulder and hip – the sort of woman Toller had dreamed about during his exile in Haffanger. She had also been brazenly chewing a sprig of maidenfriend. He had a clear memory of her face, which was round and open and uncomplicated, with wine-heightened colouring on the cheeks. Her smile had been very white and marred only by a tiny triangular chip missing from one front incisor. Toller had found her easy to talk to, easy to laugh with, and in the end it had seemed the most natural thing in the world for them to spend the night together ...

'I'm hungry,' she said abruptly, raising herself into a sitting position beside him. 'I want some breakfast.'

Toller ran an appreciative eye over her splendidly naked torso and smiled. 'Supposing I want something else first?'

She looked disappointed, but only for an instant, then returned his smile as she moved to bring her breasts into contact with his chest. 'If you're not careful I'll ride you to death.'

'Please try it,' Toller said, his smile developing into a gratified chuckle. He drew her down to him. A pleasurable warmth suffused his mind and body as they kissed, but within a moment he became aware of something being wrong, of a niggling sense of unease. He opened his eyes and immediately identified one source of his worry – the brightness of his bedchamber indicated that it was well past dawn. This was the morning of day two-hundred, and he had promised his brother that he would be up at first light to help move some charts and a display easel to the Great Palace. It was a menial task which anybody could have done, but Lain had seemed anxious for him to undertake it, possibly so that he would not be left alone in the house with Gesalla while the lengthy council meeting was in progress.

Gesalla!

Toller almost groaned aloud as he remembered that he had not even seen Gesalla on the previous day. He had arrived from Haffanger early in the morning and after a brief interview with his brother – during which Lain had been preoccupied with his charts – had gone straight out on the drinking spree. Gesalla, as Lain's solewife, was mistress of the household and as such would have expected Toller to pay his respects at the formal evening meal. Another woman might have overlooked his behavioural lapse, but the fastidious and unbending Gesalla was bound to have been furious. On the flight back to Ro-Atabri Toller had vowed that, to avoid causing any tensions in his brother's house, he would studiously keep on the right side of Gesalla – and he had led off by affronting her on the very first day. The flickering of a moist tongue against his own suddenly reminded Toller that his transgressions against domestic protocol had been greater than Gesalla knew.

'I'm sorry about this,' he said, twisting free of the embrace, 'but you have to go home now.'

The woman's jaw sagged. 'What?'

'Come on – hurry it up.' Toller stood up, swept her clothes into a wispy bundle and pushed them into her arms. He opened a wardrobe and began selecting fresh clothes for himself.

'But what about my breakfast?'

'There's no time – I have to get you out of here.'

'That's just great,' she said bitterly, beginning to sort through the binders and scraps of near-transparent fabric which were her sole attire.

'I told you I was sorry,' Toller said as he struggled into breeches which seemed determined to resist entry.

'A lot of good that ...' She paused in the act of gathering her breasts into a flimsy sling and scrutinised the room from ceiling to floor. 'Are you *sure* you live here?'

Toller was amused in spite of his agitation. 'Do you think I would just pick a house at random and sneak in to use a bed?'

'I thought it was a bit strange last night ... getting a coach all the way out here ... keeping so quiet ... This is Greenmount, isn't it?' Her frankly suspicious stare travelled his heavily muscled arms and shoulders. He guessed the direction in which her thoughts were going, but there was no hint of censure in her expression and he took no offence.

'It's a nice morning for a walk,' he said, raising her to an upright position and hastening her – clothing still partially unfastened – towards the room's single exit. He opened the door at the precise instant needed to bring him into confrontation with Gesalla Maraquine, who had been passing by in the corridor. Gesalla was pale and ill-looking, thinner than when he had last seen her, but her grey-eyed gaze had lost none of its force – and it was obvious she was angry.

'Good foreday,' she said, icily correct. 'I was *told* you had returned.'

'I apologise for last night,' Toller said. 'I ... I got detained.'

'Obviously.' Gesalla glanced at his companion with open distaste. 'Well?'

'Well what?'

'Aren't you going to introduce your ... friend?'

Toller swore inwardly as it came to him that there was no longer the slightest hope of salvaging anything from the situation. Even allowing for the fact that he had been adrift on a vinous sea when he met his bed partner, how could he have overlooked such a basic propriety as asking her name? Gesalla was the last person in the world to whom he could have explained the mood of the previous evening, and that being the case there was no point in trying to placate her. *I'm sorry about this, dear brother*, he thought. *I didn't plan it this way...*

'The frosty female is my sister-in-law, Gesalla Maraquine,' he said, putting an arm around his companion's shoulders as he kissed her on the forehead. 'She would like to know your name, and – considering the sport we had during the night – so would I.'

'Fera,' the woman said, making final adjustments to her garments. 'Fera Rivoo.'

'Isn't that nice?' Toller smiled broadly at Gesalla. 'Now we can all be friends together.'

'Please see that she leaves by one of the side gates,' Gesalla said. She turned and strode away, head thrown back, each foot descending directly in front of the other.

Toller shook his head. 'What do you think was the matter with her?'

'Some women are easily upset.' Fera straightened up and pushed Toller away from her. 'Show me the way out.'

'I thought you wanted breakfast.'

'I thought you wanted me to go home.'

'You must have misunderstood me,' Toller said. 'I'd like you to stay, for as long as *you* want. Have you a job to worry about?'

'Oh, I have a very important position in the Samlue market – gutting fish.' Fera held up her hands, which were reddened and marked by numerous small cuts. 'How do you think I got these?'

'Forget the job,' Toller urged, enclosing her hands with his own. 'Go back to bed and wait for me there. I'll have food sent to you. You can rest and eat and drink all day – and tonight we'll go on the pleasure barges.'

Fera smiled, filling the triangular gap in her teeth with the tip of her tongue. 'Your sister-in-law ...'

'Is only my sister-in-law. I was born in this house and grew up in it and have the right to invite guests. You are staying, aren't you?'

'Will there be spiced pork?'

'I assure you that entire piggeries are reduced to spiced pork on a daily basis in this house,' Toller said, leading Fera back into the room. 'Now, you stay here until I get back, then we'll take up where we left off.'

'All right.' She lay down on the bed, settled herself comfortably on the pillows and spread her legs. 'Just one thing before you go.'

'Yes?'

She gave him her full white smile. 'Perhaps you'd better tell *me your* name.'

Toller was still chuckling as he reached the stairs at the end of the corridor and went down towards the central section of the house, from which was emanating the sound of many voices. He found Fera's company refreshing, but her presence in the house might be just too much of an affront to Gesalla to be tolerated for very long. Two or three days would be sufficient to make the point that Gesalla had no right to insult him or his guests, that any effort she made to dominate him – as she did his brother – would be doomed to failure.

When Toller reached the bottom flight of the main staircase he found about a dozen people gathered in the entrance hall. Some were computational assistants; others were domestics and grooms who seemed to have gathered to watch their master set off for his appointment at the Great Palace. Lain Maraquine was wearing the antique-styled formal garment of a senior philosopher – a full-length robe of dove grey trimmed at the hem and cuff with black triangles. Its silky material emphasised the slightness of his build, but his posture was upright and dignified. His face, beneath the heavy sweeps of black hair, was very pale. Toller felt a surge of affection and concern as he crossed the hall – the council meeting was obviously an important occasion for his brother and he was already showing the strain.

'You're late,' Lain said, eyeing him critically. 'And you should be wearing your greys.'

'There was no time to get them ready. I had a rough night.'

'Gesalla has just told me what kind of night you had.' Lain's expression showed a blend of amusement and exasperation. 'Is it true you didn't even know the woman's name?'

Toller shrugged to disguise his embarrassment. 'What do names matter?'

'If you don't know that there isn't much point in my trying to enlighten you.'

'I don't need you to ...' Toller took a deep breath, determined for once not to add to his brother's problems by losing his temper. 'Where is the stuff you want me to carry?'

The official residence of King Prad Neldeever was notable more for its size than architectural merit. Successive generations of rulers had added wings, towers and cupolas to suit their individual whims, usually in the style of the day, with the result that the building had some resemblance to a coral or one of the accretive structures erected by certain kinds of insects. An early landscape gardener had attempted to impose a degree of order by planting stands of synchronous parble and rafter trees, but over the centuries they had been infiltrated by other varieties. The palace, itself variegated because of different masonry, was now screened by vegetation equally uneven in colour, and from a distance it could be difficult for the eye to separate one from the other.

Toller Maraquine, however, was untroubled by such aesthetic quibbles as he rode down from Greenmount at the rear of his brother's modest entourage. There had been rain before dawn and the morning air was clean and invigorating, charged with a sunlit spirit of new beginnings. The huge disk of Overland shone above him with a pure lustre and many stars decked the surrounding blueness of the sky. The city itself was an incredibly complex scattering of multi-hued flecks stretching down to the slate-blue ribbon of the Borann, where sails gleamed like lozenges of snow.

Toller's pleasure at being back in Ro-Atabri, at having escaped the desolation of Haffanger, had banished his customary dissatisfaction with his life as an unimportant member of the philosophy order. After the unfortunate start to the day the pendulum of his mood was on the upswing. His mind was teeming with half-formed plans to improve his reading ability, to seek out some interesting aspect of the order's work and devote all his energies to it, to make Lain proud of him. On reflection he could appreciate that Geniis had had every right to be furious over his behaviour. It would be no more than a normal courtesy were he to move Fera out of his apartment as soon as he returned home.

The sturdy bluehorn he had been allocated by the stable-master was a placid beast which seemed to know its own way to the palace. Leaving it to its own devices as it plodded the increasingly busy streets, Toller tried to create a more definite picture of his immediate future, one which might impress Lain. He had heard of one research group which was trying to develop a combination of ceramics and glass threads which would be tough enough to stand in for brakka in the manufacture of swords and armour. It was quite certain that they would never succeed, but the subject was nearer to his taste than chores like the measuring of rainfall, and it would please Lain to know that he was supporting the conservation movement. The next step was to think of a way of winning Gesalla's approval ...

By the time the philosophy delegation had passed through the heart of the city and had crossed the river at the Bytran Bridge the palace and its grounds were spanning the entire view ahead. The party negotiated the four concentric bloom-spangled moats, whose ornamentation disguised their function, and halted at the palace's main gate. Several guards, looking like huge black beetles in their heavy armour, came forward at a leisurely pace. While their commander was laboriously checking the visitors' names on his list one of his pikemen approached Toller and, without speaking, began roughly delving among the rolled-up charts in his panniers. When he had finished he paused to spit on the ground, then turned his attention to the collapsed easel which was strapped across the bluehorn's haunches. He tugged at the polished wooden struts so forcibly that the bluehorn side-stepped against him.

'What's the matter with you?' he growled, shooting Toller a venomous look. 'Can't you control that fleabag?'

I'm a new person, Toller assured himself, *and I can't be goaded into brawls*. He smiled and said, 'Can you blame her for wanting to get near you?'

The pikeman's lips moved silently, he came closer to Toller, but at that moment the guard commander gave the signal for the party to proceed on its way. Toller urged his mount forward and resumed his position behind Lain's carriage. The minor brush with the guard had left him slightly keyed-up but otherwise unaffected, and he felt pleased with the way he had comported himself. It had been a valuable exercise in avoiding unnecessary trouble, the art he intended to practise for the rest of his life. Sitting easily in the saddle, enjoying the rhythm of the bluehorn's stately gait, he turned his thoughts to the business ahead.

Toller had been to the Great Palace only once before, as a small child, and had only the vaguest recollection of the domed Rainbow Hall in which the council meeting was to be held. He doubted that it could be as vast and as awe-inspiring as he remembered, but it was a major function room in the palace and its use as a venue today was significant. King Prad obviously regarded the meeting as being important, a fact which Toller found some-what puzzling. All his life he had been listening to conservationists like his brother issuing sombre warnings about dwindling resources of brakka, but everyday life in Kolcorron had continued very much as before. It was true that in recent years there had been periods when power crystals and the black wood had been in short supply, and the cost kept rising, but new re-serves had always been found. Try as he might, Toller could not imagine the natural storehouse of an entire world failing to meet his people's needs.

As the philosophy delegation reached the elevated ground on which the palace itself was situated he saw that many carriages were gathered on the principal forecourt. Among them was the flamboyant red-and-orange phaeton of Lord Glo. Three men in philosophy greys were standing beside it, and when they noticed Lain's carriage they advanced to intercept it. Toller identified the stunted figure of Vorndal Sisstt first; then Duthoon, leader of the halvell section; and the angular outline of Borreat Hargeth, chief of weapons research. All three appeared nervous and unhappy, and they closed on Lain as soon as he had stepped down from his carriage.

'We're in trouble, Lain,' Hargeth said, nodding in the direction of Glo's phaeton. 'You'd better take a look at our esteemed leader.'

Lain frowned. 'Is he ill?'

'No, he isn't ill – I'd say he never felt better in his life.'

'Don't tell me he's been ...' Lain went to the phaeton and wrenched open the door. Lord Glo, who had been slumped with his head on his chest, jerked upright and looked about him with a startled expression. He brought his pale blue eyes to focus on Lain, then showed the pegs of his lower teeth in a smile.

'Good to see you, my boy,' he said. 'I tell you this is going to be our ... hmm ... day. We're going to carry all before us.'

Toller swung himself down from his mount and tethered it to the rear of the carriage, keeping his back to the others to conceal his amusement. He had seen Glo the worse for wine several times before, but never so obviously, so comically incapable. The contrast between Glo's ruddy-cheeked euphoria and the scandalised, ashen countenances of his aides made the situation even funnier. Any notions they had about making a good showing at the meeting were being swiftly and painfully revised. Toller could not help but enjoy another person attracting the kind of censure which so often was reserved for him, especially when the offender was the Lord Philosopher himself.

'My lord, the meeting is due to begin soon,' Lain said. 'But if you are indisposed perhaps we could ...'

'Indisposed! What manner of talk is that?' Glo ducked his head and emerged from his vehicle to stand with unnatural steadiness. 'What are we waiting for? Let's take our places.'

'Very well, my lord.' Lain came to Toller with a hag-ridden expression. 'Nate and Locranan will take the charts and easel. I want you to stay here by the carriage and keep an ... What do you find so amusing?'

'Nothing,' Toller said quickly. 'Nothing at all.'

'You have no idea of what's at stake today, have you?'

'Conservation is important to me, too,' Toller replied, making his voice as sincere as possible. 'I was only ...'

'Toller Maraquine!' Lord Glo came towards Toller with arms outstretched, his eyes bulging with pleasurable excitement. 'I didn't know you were here! How are you, my boy?'

Toller was mildly surprised at even being recognised by Glo, let alone being greeted so effusively. 'I'm in good health, my lord.'

'You look it.' Glo reached up and put an arm around Toller's shoulders and swung to face the others. 'Look at this fine figure of a man – he reminds me of myself when I was ... hmm ... young.'

'We should take our places right away,' Lain said. 'I don't want to hurry you, but ...'

'You're quite right – we shouldn't delay our moment of ... hmm ... glory.' Glo gave Toller an affectionate squeeze, exhaling the reek of wine as he did so. 'Come on, Toller – you can tell me what you've been doing with yourself out in Haffanger.'

Lain stepped forward, looking anxious. 'My brother isn't part of the delegation, my lord. He is supposed to wait here.'

'Nonsense! We're all together.'

'But he has no greys.'

'That doesn't matter if he's in my personal retinue,' Glo said with the kind of mildness that brooked no argument. 'We'll proceed.'

Toller met Lain's gaze and issued a silent disclaimer by momentarily raising his eyebrows as the group moved off in the direction of the palace's main entrance. He welcomed the unexpected turn of events, which had saved him from what had promised to be a spell of utter boredom, but he was still resolved to maintain a good relationship with his brother. It was vital for him to be as unobtrusive as possible during the meeting, and in particular to keep a straight face regardless of what kind of performance Lord Glo might put on. Ignoring the curious glances from passers-by, he walked into the palace with Glo hugging his arm and did his best to produce acceptable small-talk in response to the older man's questioning, even though all his attention was being absorbed by his surroundings.

The palace was also the seat of the Kolcorronian administration and it gave him the impression of being a city within a city. Its corridors and state-rooms were populated by sombre-faced men whose manner proclaimed that their concerns were not those of ordinary citizens. Toller was unable even to guess at their functions or the subjects of their low-voiced conversations. His senses were swamped by the sheer opulence of the carpets and hangings, the paintings and sculptures, the complexity of the vaulted ceilings. Even the least important doors appeared to have been carved from single slabs of perette, elvart or glasswood, each one representing perhaps a year's work for a master craftsman.

Lord Glo seemed oblivious to the atmosphere of the palace, but Lain and the rest of his party were noticeably subdued. They were moving in a tight group, like soldiers in hostile territory. After a lengthy walk they reached an enormous double door guarded by two black-armoured ostiaries. Glo led the way into the huge elliptical room beyond. Toller hung back to give his brother precedence, and almost gasped as he got his first adult glimpse of the famed Rainbow Hall. Its domed roof was made entirely of square glass panels supported on intricate lattices of brakka. Most of the panels were pale blue or white, to represent clear sky and clouds, but seven adjacent curving bands echoed the colours of the rainbow. The light blazing down from the canopy was a mingling, merging glory which made the furnishings of the hall glow with tinted fire.

At the far locus of the ellipse was a large but unadorned throne on the uppermost level of a dais. Three lesser thrones were ranged on the second level for the use of the princes who were expected to be present. In ancient times the princes would all have been sons of the ruler, but with the country's expansion and development it had become expedient to allow some government posts to be filled by collateral descendants. These were numerous, thanks to the sexual license accorded to the nobility, and it was usually possible to allocate important responsibilities to suitable men. Of the current monarchy, only Leddravohr and the colourless Pouche, controller of public finances, were acknowledged sons of the King.

Facing the thrones were seats which had been laid out in radial sections for the orders whose concerns ranged from the arts and medicine to religion and proletarian education. The philosophy delegation occupied the middle sector in accordance with the tradition dating back to Bytran IV, who had believed that scientific knowledge was the foundation upon which Kolcorron would build a future world empire. In subsequent centuries it had become apparent that science had already learned all that was worth learning about the workings of the universe, and the influence of Bytran's thinking had faded, but the philosophy order still retained many of the trappings of its former eminence, in spite of opposition from others of a more pragmatic turn of mind.

Toller felt an ungrudging admiration for Lord Glo as the pudgy little man, large head thrown back and stomach protruding, marched up the hall and took his position before the thrones. The remainder of the philosophy delegation quietly seated themselves behind him, exchanging tentative glances with their opposites in neighbouring sectors. There were more people than Toller had expected – perhaps a hundred in all – the other delegations being augmented by clerks and advisors. Toller, now profoundly grateful for his supernumerary status, slid into the row behind Lain's computational assistants and waited for the proceedings to begin.

There was a murmurous delay punctuated by coughs and occasional nervous laughs, then a ceremonial horn was sounded and King Prad and the three princes entered the hall by way of a private doorway beyond the dais.

At sixty-plus the ruler was tall and lean, carrying his years well in spite of one milk-white eye which he refused to cover. Although Prad was an imposing and regal figure in his blood-coloured robes as he ascended to the high throne, Toller's interest was captured by the powerful, slow-padding form of Prince Leddravohr. He was wearing a white cuirass made from multiple layers of sized linen moulded to the shape of a perfectly developed male torso, and it was evident from what could be seen of his arms and legs that the cuirass did not belie what it covered. Leddravohr's face was smooth and dark-browed, suggestive of brooding power, and it was obvious from his bearing that he had no wish to be present at the council meeting. Toller knew him to be the veteran of a hundred bloody conflicts and he felt a pang of envy as he noted the obvious disdain with which Leddravohr surveyed the assembly before lowering himself on to the central throne of the second tier. He could daydream about playing a similar role, that of the warrior prince, reluctantly recalled from dangerous frontiers to attend to trivialities of civilian existence.

An official beat on the floor three times with his staff to signal that the council meeting had begun. Prad, who was noted for the informality with which he held court, began to speak at once.

'I thank you for your attendance here today,' he said, using the inflections of high Kolcorronian. 'As you know, the subject for discussion is the increasing scarcity of brakka and energy crystals – but before I hear your submissions it is my will that another matter be dealt with, if only to establish its relative unimportance to the security of the empire.

'I do not refer to the reports from various sources that ptertha have sharply increased in number during the course of this year. It is my considered opinion that the *apparent* increases can be explained by the fact that our armies are, for the first time, operating in regions of Land where – because of the natural conditions – ptertha have always been more plentiful. I am instructing Lord Glo to instigate a thorough survey which will provide more reliable statistics, but in any case there is no cause for alarm. Prince Leddravohr assures me that the existing procedures and anti-ptertha weapons are more than adequate to deal with any exigency.

'Of more pressing concern to us are rumours that soldiers have died as a result of coming into contact with ptertha casualties. The rumours appear to have originated from units of the Second Army on the Sorka front, and they have spread quickly – as such harmful fictions do – as far as Loongl in the east and the Yalrofac theatre in the west.'

Prad paused and leaned forward, his blind eye gleaming. 'The demoralising effect of this kind of scaremongering is a greater threat to our national interests than a two-fold or three-fold increase in the ptertha population. All of us in this hall know that pterthacosis *cannot* be passed on by bodily contact or any other means. It is the duty of every man here to ensure that harmful stories claiming otherwise are stamped out with all possible speed and vigour. We must do everything in our power to promote a healthy scepticism in the minds of the proletariat – and I look particularly to teacher, poet and priest in this respect.'

Toller glanced to each side and saw the leaders of several delegations nodding as they made notes. It was surprising to him that the King should deal with such a minor issue in person, and for a moment he toyed with the startling idea that there might actually be some kernel of truth in the odd rumours. Common soldiers, sailors and airmen were a stolid lot as a rule – but on the other hand they tended to be ignorant and gullible. On balance, he could see no reason to believe there was anything more to fear from the ptertha than in any previous era in Kolcorron's long history.

'... principal subject for discussion,' King Prad was saying. 'The records of the Ports Authority show that in the year 2625 our imports of brakka from the six provinces amounted to only 118,426 tons. It is the twelfth year in succession that the total has fallen. The pikon and halvell yield was correspondingly down. No figures are available for the domestic harvest, but the preliminary estimates are less encouraging than usual.

'The situation is exacerbated by the fact that military and industrial consumption, particularly of crystals, continues to rise. It is becoming obvious that we are approaching a crucial period in our country's fortunes, and that far-reaching strategies will have to be devised to deal with the problem. I will now entertain your proposals.'

Prince Leddravohr, who had become restless during his father's summation, rose to his feet at once. 'Majesty, I intend no disrespect to you, but I confess to growing impatient with all this talk of scarcity and dwindling resources. The truth of the matter is that there is an abundance of brakka – sufficient to meet our needs for centuries to come. There are great forests of brakka as yet untouched. The *real* shortcoming lies within ourselves. We lack the resolution to turn our eyes towards the Land of the Long Days – to go forth and claim what is rightfully ours.'

In the assembly there was an immediate flurry of excitement which Prad stilled by raising one hand. Toller sat up straighter, suddenly alerted.

'I will not countenance any talk of moving against Chamteth,' Prad said, his voice harsher and louder than before.

Leddravohr spun to face him. 'It is destined to happen sooner or later – so why not sooner?'

'I repeat there will be no talk of a major war.'

'In that case, Majesty, I beg your permission to withdraw,' Leddravohr said, his manner taking him within a hair-breadth of insolence. 'I can make no contribution to a discussion from which plain logic is barred.'

Prad gave his head a single birdlike shake. 'Resume your seat and curb your impatience – your newfound regard for logic may yet prove useful.' He smiled at the rest of the gathering – his way of saying, *Even a king has problems with unruly offspring* – and invited Prince Chakkell to put forward ideas for reducing industrial consumption of power crystals.

Toller relaxed again while Chakkell was speaking, but he was unable to take his eyes off Leddravohr, who was now lounging in an exaggerated posture of boredom. He was intrigued, disturbed and strangely captivated by the discovery that the military prince regarded war with Chamteth as both desirable and inevitable. Little was known about the exotic land which, being on the far side of the world, was untouched by Overland's shadow and therefore had an uninterrupted day.

The available maps were very old and of doubtful accuracy, but they showed that Chamteth was as large as the Kolcorronian empire and equally populous. Few travellers had penetrated to its interior and returned, but their accounts had been unanimous in the descriptions of the vast brakka forests. The reserves had never been depleted because the Chamtethans regarded it as the ultimate sin to interrupt the life cycle of the brakka tree. They drew off limited quantities of crystals by drilling small holes into the combustion chambers, and restricted their use of the black wood to what could be obtained from trees which had died naturally.

The existence of such a fabulous treasurehouse had attracted the interest of Kolcorronian rulers in the past, but no real acquisitive action had ever been taken. One factor was the sheer remoteness of the country; the other was the Chamtethans' reputation as fierce, tenacious and gifted fighters. It was thought that their army was the sole user of the country's supply of crystals, and certainly the Chamtethans were well known for their extensive use of cannon – one of the most extravagant ways ever devised for the expending of crystals. They were also totally insular in their outlook, rejecting all commercial and cultural contact with other nations.

The cost, one way or another, of trying to exploit Chamteth had always been recognised as being too great, and Toller had taken it for granted that the situation was a permanent part of the natural order of things. But he had just heard talk of change – and he had a deep personal interest in that possibility.

The social divisions in Kolcorron were such that in normal circumstances a member of one of the great vocational family of families was not permitted to cross the barriers. Toller, restless and resentful over having been born into the philosophy order, had made many futile attempts to get himself accepted for military service. His lack of success had been made all the more galling by the knowledge that there would have been no obstacle to his join-ing the army had he been part of the proletarian masses. He would have been prepared to serve as a line soldier in the most inhospitable outpost of the empire, but one of his social rank could be accorded nothing less than officer status – an honour which was jealously guarded by the military caste.

All that, Toller now realised, was concomitant on the affairs of the coun-try following the familiar centuries-old course. A war with Chamteth would force profound changes on Kolcorron, however, and King Prad would not be on the throne for ever. He was likely to be succeeded by Leddravohr in the not-too-distant future – and when that happened the old order would be swept away. It looked to Toller as though his fortunes could be directly affected by those of Leddravohr, and the mere prospect was enough to pro-duce an undertow of dark excitement in his consciousness. The council meeting, which he had expected to be routine and dull, was proving to be one of the most significant occasions of his life.

On the dais the swarthy, balding and paunchy Prince Chakkell was con-cluding his opening remarks with a statement that he needed twice his pres-ent supply of pikon and halvell for quarrying purposes if essential building projects were to continue.

'You appear not to be in sympathy with the stated aims of this gathering,' Prad commented, beginning to show some exasperation. 'May I remind you that I was awaiting your thoughts on how to reduce requirements?'

'My apologies, Majesty,' Chakkell said, the stubbornness of his tone con-tradicting the words. The son of an obscure nobleman, he had earned his rank through a combination of energy, guile and driving ambition, and it was no secret in the upper echelons of Kolcorronian society that he nursed hopes of seeing a change in the rules of succession which would allow one of his children to ascend the throne. Those aspirations, coupled with the fact that he was Leddravohr's main competitor for brakka products, meant that there was a smouldering antagonism between them, but on this occasion both men were in accord. Chakkell sat down and folded his arms, making it clear that any thoughts he had on the subject of conservation would not be to the King's liking.

'There appears to be a lack of understanding of an extremely serious problem,' Prad said severely. 'I must emphasise that the country is facing several years of acute shortages of a vital commodity, and that I expect a more positive attitude from my administrators and advisors for the remain-der of this meeting. Perhaps the gravity of the situation will be borne home to you if I call upon Lord Glo to report on the progress which has been made thus far with the attempts to produce pikon and halvell by artificial means. Although our expectations are high in this regard, there is – as you will hear – a considerable way to go, and it behoves us to plan accordingly.

'Let us hear what you have to say, Lord Glo.'

There was an extended silence during which nothing happened, then Bo-reatt Hargeth – in the philosophy sector's second row – was seen to lean forward and tap Glo's shoulder. Glo jumped to his feet immediately, obviously startled, and somebody across the aisle on Toller's right gave a low chuckle.

'Pardon me, Majesty, I was collecting my thoughts,' Glo said, his voice unnecessarily loud. 'What was your ... hmm ... question?'

On the dais Prince Leddravohr covered his face with one splayed hand to mime embarrassment and the same man on Toller's right, encouraged, chuckled louder. Toller turned in his direction, scowling, and the man – an official in Lord Tunsfo's medical delegation – glanced at him and abruptly ceased looking amused.

The King gave a tolerant sigh. 'My question, if you will honour us by bringing your mind to bear on it, was a general one concerning the experiments with pikon and halvell. Where do we stand?'

'Ah! Yes, Majesty, the situation is indeed as I ... hmm ... reported to you at our last meeting. We have made great strides ... unprecedented strides ... in the extraction and purification of both the green and the purple. We have much to be proud of. All that remains for us to do at this ... hmm ... stage is to perfect a way of removing the contaminants which inhibit the crystals from reacting with each other. That is proving ... hmm ... difficult.'

'You're contradicting yourself, Glo. Are you making progress with purification or are you not?'

'Our progress has been excellent, Majesty. As far as it goes, that is. It's all a question of solvents and temperatures and ... um ... complex chemical reactions. We are handicapped by not having the proper solvent.'

'Perhaps the old fool drank it all,' Leddravohr said to Chakkell, making no attempt to modulate his voice. The laughter which followed his words was accompanied by a frisson of unease – most of those present had never seen a man of Glo's rank so directly insulted.

'Enough!' Prad's milk-white eye narrowed and widened several times, a warning beacon. 'Lord Glo, when I spoke to you ten days ago you gave me the impression that you could begin to produce pure crystals within two or three years. Are you now saying differently?'

'He doesn't know *what* he's saying,' Leddravohr put in, grinning, his contemptuous stare raking the philosophy sector. Toller, unable to react in any other way, spread his shoulders to make himself as conspicuous as possible and sought to hold Leddravohr's gaze, and all the while an inner voice was pleading with him to remember his new vows, to use his brains and stay out of trouble.

'Majesty, this is a matter of great ... hmm ... complexity,' Glo said, ignoring Leddravohr. 'We cannot consider the subject of power crystals in isolation. Even if we had an unlimited supply of crystals this very day ... There is the brakka tree itself, you see. Our plantations. It takes six centuries for the seedlings to mature and ...'

'You mean six decades, don't you?'

'I believe I said decades, Majesty, but I have another proposal which I beg leave to bring to your attention.' Glo's voice had developed a quaver and he was swaying slightly. 'I have the honour to present for your consideration a visionary scheme, one which will shape the ultimate future of this great nation of ours. A thousand years from now our descendants will look back on your reign with wonder and awe as they ...'

'Lord Glo!' Prad was incredulous and angry. 'Are you ill or drunk?'

'Neither, Majesty.'

'Then stop prating about visions and answer my question concerning the crystals.'

Glo seemed to be labouring for breath, his plump chest swelling to take up the slack in his grey robe. 'I fear I may be indisposed, after all.' He pressed a hand to his side and dropped into his chair with an audible thud. 'My senior mathematician, Lain Maraquine, will present the facts on my ... hmm ... behalf.'

Toller watched with growing trepidation as his brother stood up, bowed towards the dais, and signalled for his assistants, Quate and Locranan, to bring his easel and charts forward. They did so and erected the easel with a fumbling eagerness which prolonged what should have been the work of a moment. More time was taken up as the chart they unrolled and suspended had to be coaxed to remain flat. On the dais even the insipid Prince Pouche was beginning to look restless. Toller was concerned to see that Lain was trembling with nervousness.

'What is your intention, Maraquine?' the King said, not unkindly. 'Am I to revisit the classroom at my time of life?'

'The graphics are helpful, Majesty,' Lain said. 'They illustrate the factors governing the ...' The remainder of his reply drifted into inaudibility as he indicated key features on the vivid diagrams.

'Can't hear you,' Chakkell snapped irritably. 'Speak up!'

'Where are your manners?' Leddravohr said, turning to him. 'What way is that to address such a shy young maiden?' A number of men in the audience, taking their cue, guffawed loudly.

This shouldn't be happening, Toller thought as he rose to his feet, the blood roaring in his ears. The Kolcorronian code of conduct ruled that to step in and reply to a challenge – and an insult was always regarded as such – issued to a third party was to add to the original slur. The imputation was that the insulted man was too cowardly to defend his own honour. Lain had often claimed that it was his duty as a philosopher to soar above all such irrationalities, that the ancient code was more suited to quarrelsome animals than thinking men. Knowing that his brother would not and could not take up Leddravohr's challenge, knowing further that he was barred from active intervention, Toller was taking the only course open to him. He stood up straight, differentiating himself from the seated nonparticipants all around, waiting for Leddravohr to notice him and interpret his physical and mental stance.

'That's enough, Leddravohr.' The King slapped the arms of his throne. 'I want to hear what the wrangler has to say. Go ahead, Maraquine.'

'Majesty, I …' Lain was now quivering so violently that his robe was fluttering.

'Try to put yourself at ease, Maraquine. I don't want a lengthy discourse – it will suffice for you to tell me how many years will elapse, in your expert opinion, before we can produce pure pikon and halvell.'

Lain took a deep breath, fighting to control himself. 'It is impossible to make predictions in matters like this.'

'Give me your personal view. Would you say five years?'

'No, Majesty.' Lain shot a sideways glance at Lord Glo and managed to make his voice more resolute. 'If we increased our research expenditure ten-fold … and were fortunate … we might produce some usable crystals twenty years from now. But there is no guarantee that we will ever succeed. There is only one sane and logical course for the country as a whole to follow and that is to ban the felling of brakka entirely for the next twenty or thirty years. In that way …'

'I *refuse* to listen to any more of this!' Leddravohr was on his feet and stepping down from the dais. 'Did I say maiden? I was wrong – this is an old woman! Raise your skirts and flee from this place, old woman, and take your sticks and scraps with you.' Leddravohr strode to the easel and thrust the palm of his hand against it, sending it clattering to the floor.

During the clamour which followed, Toller left his place and walked for-wards on stiffened legs to stand close to his brother. On the dais the King was ordering Leddravohr back to his seat, but his voice was almost lost amid angry cries from Chakkell and in the general commotion in the hall. A court official was hammering on the floor with his staff, but the only effect was to increase the level of sound. Leddravohr looked straight at Toller with white-flaring eyes, but appeared not to see him as he wheeled round to face his father.

'I act on your behalf, Majesty,' he shouted in a voice which brought a ringing silence to the hall. 'Your ears shall not be defiled any further with the kind of spoutings we have just heard from the so-called thinkers among us.'

'I am quite capable of making such decisions for myself,' Prad replied sternly. 'I would remind you that this is a meeting of the high council – not some brawling ground for your muddied soldiery.'

Leddravohr was unrepentant as he glanced contemptuously at Lain. 'I hold the lowliest soldier in the service of Kolcorron in greater esteem than this whey-faced old woman.' His continued defiance of the King intensified the silence under the glass dome, and it was into that magnifying hush that Toller heard himself drop his own challenge. It would have been a crime akin to treason, and punishable by death, for one of his station to take the initiative and challenge a member of the monarchy, but the code permitted him to move indirectly within limits and seek to provoke a response.

'"Old woman" appears to be a favourite epithet of Prince Leddravohr's,' he said to Vorndal Sisstt, who was seated close to him. 'Does that mean he is always very prudent in his choice of opponents?'

Sisstt gaped up at him and shrank away, white-faced, anxiously dissociating himself as Leddravohr turned to find out who had spoken. Seeing Leddravohr at close quarters for the first time, Toller observed that his strong-jawed countenance was unlined, possessed of a curious statuesque smoothness, almost as if the muscles were nerveless and immobile. It was an inhuman face, untroubled by the ordinary range of expression, with only the eyes to signal what was going on behind the broad brow. In this case Leddravohr's eyes showed that he was more incredulous than angry as he scrutinised the younger man, taking in every detail of his physique and dress.

'Who are you?' Leddravohr said at last. 'Or should I say, what are you?'

'My name is Toller Maraquine, Prince – and I take pride in being a philosopher.'

Leddravohr glanced up at his father and smiled, as if to demonstrate that when he saw it as his filial duty he could endure extreme provocation. Toller did not like the smile, which was accomplished in an instant, effortless as the twitching back of a drape, affecting no other part of his face.

'Well, Toller Maraquine,' Leddravohr said, 'it is very fortunate that personal weapons are never worn in my father's household.'

Leave it at that, Toller urged himself. *You've made your point and – against all the odds – you're getting away with it.*

'Fortunate?' he said pleasantly. 'For whom?'

Leddravohr's smile did not waver, but his eyes became opaque, like polished brown pebbles. He took one step forward and Toller readied himself for the shock of physical combat, but in that moment the glass axis of the confrontation was snapped by pressure from an unexpected direction.

'Majesty,' Lord Glo called out, lurching to his feet, looking ghastly but speaking in surprisingly fluent and resonant tones. 'I beg you – for the sake of our beloved Kolcorron – to listen to the proposal of which I spoke earlier.

Please do not let my brief indisposition stand in the way of your hearing of a scheme whose implications go far beyond the present and near future, and in the long run will concern the very existence of our great nation.'

'Hold still, Glo.' King Prad also rose to his feet and pointed at Leddravohr with the index fingers of both hands, triangulating on him with all the force of his authority. 'Leddravohr, you will now resume your seat.'

Leddravohr eyed the King for a few seconds, his face impassive, then he turned away from Toller and walked slowly to the dais. Toller was startled as he felt his brother grip his arm.

'What are you trying to do?' Lain whispered, his frightened gaze hunting over Toller's face. 'Leddravohr has killed people for less.'

Toller shrugged his arm free. 'I'm still alive.'

'And you had no right to step in like that.'

'I apologise for the insult,' Toller said. 'I didn't think one more would make any difference.'

'You know what I think of your childish ...' Lain broke off as Lord Glo came to stand close beside him.

'The boy can't help being impetuous – I was the same at his age,' Glo said. The brilliance from above showed that every pore on his forehead was separately domed with sweat. Beneath the ample folds of his robe his chest swelled and contracted with disturbing rapidity, pumping out the smell of wine.

'My lord, I think you should sit down and compose yourself,' Lain said quietly. 'There is no need for you to be subjected to any more of ...'

'No! You're the one who must sit down.' Glo indicated two nearby seats and waited until Lain and Toller had sunk into them. 'You're a good man, Lain, but it was very wrong of me to burden you with a task for which you are constitutionally ... hmm ... unsuited. This is a time for boldness. Boldness of vision. That is what earned us the respect of the ancient kings.'

Toller, rendered morbidly sensitive to Leddravohr's every movement, noticed that on the dais the prince was concluding a whispered conversation with his father. Both men sat down, and Leddravohr immediately turned his brooding gaze in Toller's direction. At a barely perceptible nod from the King an official pounded the floor with his staff to quell the low-key murmurings throughout the hall.

'Lord Glo!' Prad's voice was now ominously calm. 'I apologise for the discourtesy shown to members of your delegation, but I also add that the council's time should not be wasted on frivolous suggestions. Now, if I grant you permission to lay before us the essentials of your grand scheme, will you undertake to do so quickly and succinctly, without adding to my tribulations on a day which has already seen too many?'

'Gladly!'

'Then proceed.'

'I am about to do so, Majesty.' Glo half turned to look at Lain, gave him a prolonged wink and began to whisper. 'Remember what you said about my flying higher and seeing farther? You're going to have cause to reflect on those words, my boy. Your graphs were telling a story that even you didn't understand, but I ...'

'Lord Glo,' Prad said, 'I am waiting.'

Glo gave him an elaborate bow, complete with the hand flourishes appropriate to the use of the high tongue. 'Majesty, the philosopher has many duties, many responsibilities. Not only must his mind encompass the past and the present, it must illuminate the multiple pathways of the future. The darker and more ... hmm ... hazardous those pathways may be, the higher ...'

'Get on with it, Glo!'

'Very well, Majesty. My analysis of the situation in which Kolcorron finds itself today shows that the difficulties of obtaining brakka and power crystals are going to increase until ... hmm ... only the most vigorous and far-sighted measures will avert national disaster.' Glo's voice shook with fervour.

'It is my considered opinion that, as the problems which beset us grow and multiply, we must expand our capabilities accordingly. If we are to maintain our premier position on Land we must turn our eyes – not towards the petty nations on our borders, with their meagre resources – but towards the sky!'

'The entire planet of Overland hangs above us, waiting, like a luscious fruit ready for the picking. It is within our powers to develop the means to go there and to ...' The rest of Glo's sentence was drowned in a swelling tide of laughter.

Toller, whose gaze had been locked with Leddravohr's, turned his head as he heard angry shouts from his right. He saw that, beyond Tunsfo's medical delegation, Lord Prelate Balountar had risen to his feet and was pointing at Glo in accusation, his small mouth distorted and dragged to one side with intensity of emotion.

Borreat Hargeth leaned over from the row behind Toller and gripped Lain's shoulder. 'Make the old fool sit down,' he urged in a scandalised whisper. 'Did you know he was going to do this?'

'Of course not!' Lain's narrow face was haggard. 'And how can I stop him?'

'You'd better do something before we're all made to look like idiots.'

'... long been known that Land and Overland share a common atmosphere,' Glo was declaiming, seemingly oblivious to the commotion he had caused. 'The Greenmount archives contain detailed drawings for hot air balloons capable of ascending to ...'

'In the name of the Church I command you to cease this blasphemy,' Lord Prelate Balountar shouted, leaving his place to advance on Glo, head thrust forward and tilting from side to side like that of a wading bird. Toller, who was irreligious by instinct, deduced from the violence of Balountar's reaction that the churchman was a strict Alternationist. Unlike many senior clerics, who paid lip service to their creed in order to collect large stipends, Balountar really did believe that after death the spirit migrated to Overland, was reincarnated as a newborn infant and eventually returned to Land in the same way, part of a never-ending cycle of existence.

Glo made a dismissive gesture in Balountar's direction. 'The main difficulty lies with the region of neutral ... hmm ... gravity at the midpoint of the flight where, of course, the density differential between hot and cold air can have no effect. That problem can be solved by fitting each craft with reaction tubes which ...'

Glo was abruptly silenced when Balountar closed the distance between them in a sudden rush, black vestments flapping, and clamped a hand over Glo's mouth. Toller, who had not expected the cleric to use force, sprang from his chair. He grabbed both of Balountar's bony wrists and brought his arms down to his sides. Glo clutched at his own throat, gagging. Balountar tried to break free, but Toller lifted him as easily as he would have moved a straw dummy and set him down several paces away, becoming aware as he did so that the King had again risen to his feet. The laughter in the hall died away to be replaced by a taut silence.

'*You!*' Balountar's mouth worked spasmodically as he glared up at Toller. 'You touched me!'

'I was acting in defence of my master,' Toller said, realising that his reflex action had been a major breach of protocol. He heard a muffled retching sound and turned to see that Glo was being sick with both hands cupped over his mouth. Black wine was gouting through his fingers, disfiguring his robe and spattering on the floor.

The King spoke loudly and clearly, each word like the snapping of a blade. 'Lord Glo, I don't know which I find more offensive – the contents of your stomach or the contents of your mind. You and your party will leave my presence immediately, and I warn you here and now that – as soon as more pressing matters have been dealt with – I am going to think long and hard about your future.'

Glo uncovered his mouth and tried to speak, the brown pegs of his teeth working up and down, but was able to produce nothing more than clicking sounds in his throat.

'Remove him from my sight,' Prad said, turning his hard eyes on the Lord Prelate. 'As for you, Balountar, you are to be rebuked for mounting a physical attack on one of my ministers, no matter how great the provocation. For that reason, you have no redress against the young man who restrained you, though he does appear somewhat lacking in discretion. You will return to your place and remain there without speaking until the Lord Philosopher and his cortege of buffoons have withdrawn.'

The King sat down and stared straight ahead while Lain and Borreat Hargeth closed upon Glo and led him away towards the hall's main entrance. Toller walked around Vorndal Sisstt, who had knelt to wipe the floor with the hem of his own robe, and helped Lain's two assistants to gather up the fallen easel and charts. As he stood up with the easel under his arm it occurred to him that Prince Leddravohr must have received an unusually powerful reprimand to induce him to remain so quiet. He glanced towards the dais and saw that Leddravohr, lounging in his throne, was staring at him with an intent unwavering gaze. Toller, oppressed by collective shame, looked elsewhere immediately, but not before he had seen Leddravohr's smile twitch into existence.

'What are you waiting for?' Sisstt mumbled. 'Get that stuff out of here before the King decides to have us flayed.'

The walk through the corridors and high chambers of the palace seemed twice as long as before. Even when Glo had recovered sufficiently to shake off helping hands, Toller felt that news of the philosophers' disgrace had magically flown ahead of them and was being discussed by every low-voiced group they passed. From the start he had felt that Lord Glo was going to be unable to function well at the meeting, but he had not anticipated being drawn into a débâcle of such magnitude. King Prad was famed for the informality and tolerance with which he conducted royal business, but Glo had managed to transgress to such an extent that the future of the entire order had been called into question. And furthermore, Toller's embryonic plan to enter the army by someday finding favour with Leddravohr was no longer tenable – the military prince had a reputation for never forgetting, never forgiving.

On reaching the principal courtyard Glo thrust out his stomach and marched jauntily to his phaeton. He paused beside it, turned to face the rest of the group and said, 'Well, that didn't go too badly, did it? I think I can truthfully say that I planted a seed in the King's ... hmm ... mind. What do you say?'

Lain, Hargeth and Duthoon exchanged stricken glances, but Sisstt spoke up at once. 'You're absolutely right, my lord.'

Glo nodded approval at him. 'That's the only way to advance a radical new idea, you know. Plant a seed. Let it ... hmm ... germinate.'

Toller turned away, suddenly in fresh danger of laughing aloud in spite of all that had happened to him, and carried the easel to his tethered bluehorn. He strapped the wooden framework across the beast's haunches, retrieved the rolled charts from Quate and Locranan, and prepared to depart. The sun was little more than halfway between the eastern rim of Overland – the ordeal by humiliation had been mercifully brief – and there was time for him to claim a late breakfast as the first step in salvaging the rest of the day. He had placed one foot in the stirrup when his brother appeared at his side.

'What is it that afflicts you?' Lain said. 'Your behaviour in the palace was appalling – even by your own standards.'

Toller was taken aback. '*My* behaviour!'

'Yes! Within the space of minutes you made enemies of two of the most dangerous men in the empire. How do you do it?'

'It's very simple,' Toller said stonily. 'I comport myself as a man.'

Lain sighed in exasperation. 'I'll speak to you further when we get back to Greenmount.'

'No doubt.' Toller mounted the bluehorn and urged it forward, not waiting for the coach. On the ride back to the Square House his annoyance with Lain gradually faded as he considered his brother's unenviable position. Lord Philosopher Glo was bringing the order in disrepute, but as a royal he could only be deposed by the King. Attempting to undermine him would be treated as sedition, and in any case Lain had too much personal loyalty to Glo even to criticise him in private. When it became common knowledge that Glo had proposed trying to send ships to Overland all those connected with him would become objects of derision – and Lain would suffer everything in silence, retreating further into his books and graphs while the philosophers' tenure at Greenmount grew steadily less secure.

By the time he had reached the multi-gabled house Toller's mind was tiring of abstracts and becoming preoccupied with the fact that he was hungry. Not only had he missed breakfast, he had eaten virtually nothing on the previous day, and now there was a raging emptiness in his stomach. He tethered the bluehorn in the precinct and, without bothering to unload it, walked quickly into the house with the intention of going straight to the kitchen.

For the second time that morning he found himself unexpectedly in the presence of Gesalla, who was crossing the entrance hall towards the west salon. She turned to him, dazzled by the light from the archway, and smiled. The smile lasted only a moment, as long as it took for her to identify him against the glare, but its effect on Toller was odd. He seemed to see Gesalla for the first time, as a goddess figure with sun-bright eyes, and in the instant he felt an inexplicable and poignant sense of waste, not of material possessions but of all the potential of life itself. The sensation faded as quickly as it had come, but it left him feeling sad and strangely chastened.

'Oh, it's you,' Gesalla said in a cold voice. 'I thought you were Lain.'

Toller smiled, wondering if he could begin a new and more constructive relationship with Gesalla. 'A trick of the light.'

'Why are you back so early?'

'Ah ... the meeting didn't go as planned. There was some trouble. Lain will tell you all about it – he's on his way home now.'

Gesalla tilted her head and moved until she had the advantage of the light. 'Why can't you tell me? Was it something to do with you?'

'With *me*?'

'Yes. I advised Lain not to let you go anywhere near the palace.'

'Well, perhaps he's getting as sick as I am of you and your endless torrents of advice.' Toller tried to stop speaking, but the word fever was upon him. 'Perhaps he has begun to regret marrying a withered twig instead of a real woman.'

'Thank you – I'll pass your comments on to Lain in full.' Gesalla's lips quirked, showing that – far from being wounded – she was pleased at having invoked the kind of intemperate response which could result in Toller being banished from the Square House. 'Do I take it that your concept of a real woman is embodied in the whore who is waiting in your bed at this moment?'

'You can take ...' Toller scowled, trying to conceal the fact that he had completely forgotten about his companion of the night. 'You should guard your tongue! Felise is no whore.'

Gesalla's eyes sparkled. 'Her name is Fera.'

'Felise or Fera – she isn't a whore.'

'I won't bandy definitions with you,' Gesalla said, her tones now light, cool and infuriating. 'The cook told me you left instructions for your ... guest to be provided with all the food she wished. And if the amounts she has already consumed this foreday are any yardstick, you should think yourself fortunate that you don't have to support her in marriage.'

'But I do!' Toller saw his chance to deliver the verbal thrust and took it on the reflex, with heady disregard for the consequences. 'I've been trying to tell you that I gave Fera gradewife status before I left here this morning. I'm sure you will soon learn to enjoy her company about the house, and then we can all be friends together. Now, if you will excuse me ...'

He smiled, savouring the shock and incredulity on Gesalla's face, then turned and sauntered towards the main stair, taking care to hide his own numb bemusement over what a few angry seconds could do to the course of his life. The last thing he wanted was the responsibility of a wife, even of the fourth grade, and he could only hope that Fera would refuse the offer he had committed himself to making.

CHAPTER FIVE

General Risdel Dalacott awoke at first light and, following the routine which had rarely varied in his sixty-eight years of life, left his bed immediately.

He walked around the room several times, his step growing firmer as the stiffness and pain gradually departed from his right leg. It was almost thirty years since the aftday, during the first Sorka campaign, when a heavy Merrillian throwing spear had smashed his thigh bone just above the knee. The injury had troubled him at intervals ever since, and the periods when he was free of discomfort were becoming shorter and quite infrequent.

As soon as he was satisfied with the leg's performance he went into the adjoining toilet chamber and threw the lever of enamelled brakka which was set in one wall. The water which sprayed down on him from the perforated ceiling was hot – a reminder that he was not in his own spartan quarters in Trompha. Putting aside irrational feelings of guilt, he took maximum enjoyment from the warmth as it penetrated and soothed his muscles.

After drying himself he paused at a wall-mounted mirror, which was made of two layers of clear glass with highly different refractive indices, and took stock of his image. Although age had had its inevitable effect on the once-powerful body, the austere discipline of his way of life had prevented fatty degeneration. His long, thoughtful face had become deeply lined, but the greyness which had entered his cropped hair scarcely showed against its fair coloration, and his overall appearance was one of durable health and fitness.

Still serviceable, he thought. *But I'll do only one more year. The army has taken too much from me already.*

While he was donning his informal blues he turned his thoughts to the day ahead. It was the twelfth birthday of his grandson, Hallie, and – as part of the ritual which proved he was ready to enter military academy – the boy was due to go alone against ptertha. The occasion was an important one, and Dalacott vividly remembered the pride he had felt on watching his own son, Oderan, pass the same test. Oderan's subsequent army career had been cut short by his death at the age of thirty-three – the result of an airship crash in Yalrofac – and it was Dalacott's painful duty to stand in for him during the day's celebrations. He finished dressing, left the bedroom and went downstairs to the dining room where, in spite of the earliness of the hour, he found Conna Dalacott seated at the round table. She was a tall, open-faced woman whose form was developing the solidity of early middle age.

'Good foreday, Conna,' he said, noting that she was alone. 'Is young Hallie still asleep?'

'On his twelfth?' She nodded towards the walled garden, part of which was visible through the floor-to-ceiling window. 'He's out there somewhere, practising. He wouldn't even look at his breakfast.'

'It's a big day for him. For us all.'

'Yes.' Something in the timbre of Conna's voice told Dalacott that she was under a strain. 'A wonderful day.'

'I know it's distressing for you,' he said gently, 'but Oderan would have wanted us to make the most of it, for Hallie's sake.'

Conna gave him a calm smile. 'Do you still take nothing but porridge for breakfast? Can't I tempt you with some whitefish? Sausage? A forcemeat cake?'

'I've lived too long on line soldier's rations,' he protested, tacitly agreeing to restrict himself to small-talk. Conna had maintained the villa and conducted her life ably enough without his assistance in the ten years since Oderan's death, and it would be presumptuous of him to offer her any advice at this juncture.

'Very well,' she said, beginning to serve him from one of the covered dishes on the table, 'but there'll be no soldier's rations for you at the little-night feast.'

'Agreed!' While Dalacott was eating the lightly salted porridge he exchanged pleasantries with his daughter-in-law, but the seething of his memories continued unabated and – as had been happening more often of late – thoughts of the son he had lost evoked others of the son he had never claimed. Looking back over his life he had, once again, to ponder the ways in which the major turning points were frequently unrecognisable as such, in which the inconsequential could lead to the momentous.

Had he not been caught off his guard during the course of a minor skirmish in Yalrofac all those years ago he would not have received the serious wound in his leg. The injury had led to a long convalescence in the quietness of Redant province; and it was there, while walking by the Bes-Undar river, he had chanced to find the strangest natural object he had ever seen, the one he still carried everywhere he went. The object had been in his possession for about a year when, on a rare visit to the capital, he had impulsively taken it to the science quarter on Greenmount to find out if its strange properties could be explained.

In the event, he had learned nothing about the object and a great deal about himself.

As a dedicated career soldier he had taken on a solewife almost as a duty to the state, to provide him with an heir and to minister to his needs between campaigns. His relationship with Toriane had been pleasant, even and warm; and he had regarded it as fulfilling – until the day he had ridden into the precinct of a square house on Greenmount and had seen Aytha Maraquine. His meeting with the slender young matron had been a blending of green and purple, producing a violent explosion of passion and ecstasy and, ultimately, an intensity of pain he had not believed possible ...

'The carriage is back, Grandad,' Hallie cried, tapping at the long window. 'We're ready to go to the hill.'

'I'm coming.' Dalacott waved to the fair-haired boy who was dancing with excitement on the patio. Hallie was tall and sturdy, well able to handle the full-size ptertha sticks which were clattering on his belt.

'You haven't finished your porridge,' Conna said as he stood up, her matter-of-fact tone not quite concealing the underlying emotion.

'You know, there is absolutely no need for you to worry,' he said. 'A ptertha drifting over open ground in clear daylight poses no threat to anybody. Dealing with it is child's play, and in any case I'll be staying close to Hallie at all times.'

'Thank you.' Conna remained seated, staring down at her untouched food, until Dalacott had left the room.

He went out to the garden which – as was standard in rural areas – had high walls surmounted by ptertha screens which could be closed together overhead at night and in foggy conditions. Hallie came running to him, recreating the image of his father at the same age, and took his hand. They walked out to the carriage, in which waited three men, local friends of the family, who were required as witnesses to the boy's coming-of-age. Dalacott, who had renewed their acquaintanceship on the previous evening, exchanged greetings with them as he and Hallie took their places on the padded benches inside the big coach. The driver cracked his whip over his team of four bluehorns and the vehicle moved off.

'Oho! Have we a seasoned campaigner here?' said Gehate, a retired merchant, leaning forward to tap a Y-shaped ptertha stick he had noticed among the normal Kolcorronian cruciforms in Hallie's armoury.

'It's Ballinnian,' Hallie said proudly, stroking the polished and highly decorated wood of the weapon, which Dalacott had given him a year earlier. 'It flies farther than the others. Effective at thirty yards. The Gethans use them as well. The Gethans and the Cissorians.'

Dalacott returned the indulgent smiles the boy's show of knowledge elicited from the other men. Throwing sticks of one form or another had been in use since ancient times by almost every nation on Land as a defence against ptertha, and had been chosen for their effectiveness. The enigmatic globes burst as easily as soap bubbles once they got to within their killing radius of a man, but before that they showed a surprising degree of resilience. A bullet, an arrow or even a spear could pass through a ptertha without causing it any harm – the globe would only quiver momentarily as it repaired the punctures in its transparent skin. It took a rotating, flailing missile to disrupt a ptertha's structure and disperse its toxic dust into the air.

The bolas made a good ptertha killer, but it was hard to master and had the disadvantage of being too heavy to be carried in quantity, whereas a multi-bladed throwing stick was flat, comparatively light and easily portable. It was a source of wonder to Dalacott that even the most primitive tribesmen had learned that giving each blade one rounded edge and one sharp edge produced a weapon which sustained itself in the air like a bird, flying much farther than an ordinary projectile. No doubt it was that seemingly magical property which induced people like the Ballinnians to lavish such care on the carving and embellishment of their ptertha sticks. By contrast, the pragmatic Kolcorronians favoured a plain expendable weapon of the four-bladed pattern which was suitable for mass production because it was made of two straight sections glued together at the centre.

The carriage gradually left the grain fields and orchards of Klinterden behind and began climbing the foothills of Mount Pharote. Eventually it reached a place where the road petered out on a grassy table, beyond which the ground ascended steeply into mists which had not yet been boiled off by the sun.

'Here we are,' Gehate said jovially to Hallie as the vehicle creaked to a halt. 'I can't wait to see what sport that fancy stick of yours will produce. Thirty yards, you say?'

Thessaro, a florid-faced banker, frowned and shook his head. 'Don't egg the boy into showing off. It isn't good to throw too soon.'

'I think you'll find he knows what to do,' Dalacott said as he got out of the carriage with Hallie and looked around. The sky was a dome of pearly brilliance shading off into pale blue overhead. No stars could be seen and even the great disk of Overland, only part of which was visible, appeared pale and insubstantial. Dalacott had travelled to the south of Kail province to visit his son's family, and in these latitudes Overland was noticeably displaced to the north. The climate was more temperate than that of equatorial Kolcorron, a factor which – combined with a much shorter littlenight – made the region one of the best food producers in the empire.

'Plenty of ptertha,' Gehate said, pointing upwards to where purple motes could be seen drifting high in the air currents rolling down from the mountain.

'There's always plenty of ptertha these days,' commented Ondobirtre, the third witness. 'I'll swear they are on the increase – no matter what anybody says to the contrary. I heard that several of them even penetrated the centre of Ro-Baccanta a few days ago.'

Gehate shook his head impatiently. 'They don't go into cities.'

'I'm only telling what I heard.'

'You're too credulous, my friend. You listen to too many tall stories.'

'This is no time for bickering,' Thessaro put in. 'This is an important occasion.' He opened the linen sack he was carrying and began counting out six pertha sticks each to Dalacott and the other men.

'You won't need those, Grandad,' Hallie said, looking offended. 'I'm not going to miss.'

'I know that, Hallie, but it's the custom. Besides, some of the rest of us might be in need of a little practice.' Dalacott put an arm around the boy's shoulders and walked with him to the mouth of an alley created by two high nets. They were strung on parallel lines of poles which crossed the table and went up the slope beyond to disappear into the mist ceiling. The system was a traditional one which served to guide pertha down from the mountain in small numbers. It would have been easy for the globes to escape by floating upwards, but a few always followed such an alley to its lower end as though they were sentient creatures motivated by curiosity. Quirks of behaviour like that were the main reason for the belief, held by many, that the globes possessed some degree of intelligence, although Dalacott had always remained unconvinced in view of their complete lack of internal structure.

'You can leave me now, Grandad,' Hallie said. 'I'm ready.'

'Very well, young man.' Dalacott moved back a dozen paces to stand line abreast with the other men. It was the first time he had ever thought of his grandson as being anything more than a boy, but Hallie was entering his trial with courage and dignity, and would never again be quite the same person as the child who had played in the garden only that morning. It came to Dalacott that at breakfast he had given Conna the wrong assurances – she had known only too well that her child was never coming back to her. The insight was something Dalacott would have to note in his diary at nightfall. Soldiers' wives were required to undergo their own trials, and the adversary was time itself.

'I knew we wouldn't have to wait very long,' Ondobirtre whispered.

Dalacott transferred his attention from his grandson to the wall of mist at the far end of the netted enclosure. In spite of his confidence in Hallie, he felt a spasm of alarm as he saw that two pertha had appeared simultaneously. The livid globes, each a full two yards in diameter, came drifting low and weaving, becoming harder to see clearly as they moved down the slope to where the background was grass. Hallie, who had a four-bladed stick in his hand, altered his stance slightly and made ready to throw.

Not yet, Dalacott commanded in his thoughts, knowing that the presence of a second pertha would increase the temptation to try destroying one at maximum range. The dust released by a bursting ptertha lost its toxicity almost as soon as it was exposed to air, so the minimum safe range for a kill could be as little as six paces, depending on wind conditions. At that distance it was virtually impossible to miss, which meant that the ptertha was no match at all for a man with a cool head, but Dalacott had seen novices suddenly lose their judgment and coordination. For some there was a strange mesmeric and unmanning quality about the trembling spheres, especially when on nearing their prey they ceased their random drifting and closed in with silent, deadly purpose.

The two floating towards Hallie were now less than thirty paces away from him, sailing just above the grass, blindly questing from one net to the other. Hallie brought his right arm back, making tentative wrist movements, but refrained from throwing. Watching the solitary, straight-backed figure holding his ground as the ptertha drew ever closer, Dalacott experienced a mixture of pride, love and pure fear. He held one of his own sticks at the ready and prepared to dart forward. Hallie moved closer to the net on his left, still withholding his first strike.

'Do you see what the little devil is up to?' Gehate breathed. 'I do believe he's ...'

At that moment the aimless meanderings of the ptertha brought them together, one behind the other, and Hallie made his throw. The blades of the cruciform weapon blurred as it flew straight and true, and an instant later the purple globes no longer existed.

Hallie became a boy again, just long enough to make one exultant leap into the air, then he resumed his watchful stance as a third ptertha emerged from the mist. He unclipped another stick from his belt, and Dalacott saw that it was the Y-shaped Ballinnian weapon.

Gehate nudged Dalacott. 'The first throw was for you, but I think this one is going to be for my benefit – to teach me to keep my mouth shut.'

Hallie allowed the globe to get no closer than thirty paces before he made his second throw. The weapon flitted along the alley like a brilliantly coloured bird, almost without sinking, and was just beginning to lose stability when it sliced into the ptertha and annihilated it. Hallie was grinning as he turned to the watching men and gave them an elaborate bow. He had claimed the necessary three kills and was now officially entering the adult phase of his life.

'The boy had some luck that time, but he deserved it,' Gehate said ungrudgingly. 'Oderan should have been here.'

'Yes.' Dalacott, racked by bitter-sweet emotions, contented himself with the monosyllabic response, and was relieved when the others moved away – Gehate and Thessaro to embrace Hallie, Ondobirtre to fetch the ritual flask of brandy from the carriage. The group of six, including the hired driver, came together again when Ondobirtre distributed tiny hemispherical glasses whose rims had been fashioned unevenly to represent vanquished ptertha. Dalacott kept an eye on his grandson while he had his first sip of ardent spirits, and was amused when the boy, who had just overcome a mortal enemy, pulled a grotesque face.

'I trust,' Ondobirtre said as he refilled the adults' glasses, 'that all present have noticed the unusual feature of this morning's outing?'

Gehate snorted. 'Yes – I'm glad you didn't attack the brandy before the rest of us got near it.'

'That's not it,' Ondobirtre said gravely, refusing to be goaded. 'Everybody thinks I'm an idiot, but in all the years we've been watching this kind of thing has anybody seen a day when three globes showed up before the blue-horns had stopped farting after the climb? I'm telling you, my short-sighted friends, that the ptertha are on the increase. In fact, unless I'm getting winedreams, we have a couple more visitors.'

The company turned to look at the space between the nets and saw that two more ptertha had drifted down from the obscurity of the cloud ceiling and were nuzzling their way along the corded barriers.

'They're mine,' Gehate called as he ran forward. He halted, steadied him-self and threw two sticks in quick succession, destroying both the globes with ease. Their dust briefly smudged the air.

'There you are!' Gehate cried. 'You don't need to be built like a soldier to be able to defend yourself. I can still teach you a thing or two, young Hallie.'

Hallie handed his glass back to Ondobirtre and ran to join Gehate, eager to compete with him. After the second brandy Dalacott and Thessaro also went forward and they made a sporting contest of the destruction of every globe which appeared, only giving up when the mist rose clear of the top end of the alley and the ptertha retreated with it to higher altitudes. Dalacott was impressed by the fact that almost forty had come down the alley in the space of an hour, considerably more than he normally would have expected. While the others were retrieving their sticks in preparation for leaving, he commented on the matter to Ondobirtre.

'It's what I've been saying all along,' said Ondobirtre, who had been stead-ily drinking brandy all the while and was growing pale and morose. 'But everybody thinks I'm an idiot.'

By the time the carriage had completed the journey back to Klinterden the sun was nearing the eastern rim of Overland, and the littlenight celebra-tion in honour of Hallie was about to begin.

The vehicles and animals belonging to the guests were gathered in the villa's forecourt, and a number of children were at play in the walled garden. Hallie, first to jump down from the carriage, sprinted into the house to find his mother. Dalacott followed him at a more sedate pace, the pain in his leg having returned during the long spell in the carriage. He had little enthusiasm for large parties and was not looking forward to the remainder of the day, but it would have been discourteous of him not to stay the night. It was arranged that a military airship would pick him up on the following day for the flight back to the Fifth Army's headquarters in Trompha.

Conna greeted him with a warm embrace as he entered the villa. 'Thank you for taking care of Hallie,' she said. 'Was he as superb as he claims?'

'Absolutely! He made a splendid showing.' Dalacott was pleased to see that Conna was now looking cheerful and self-possessed. 'He made Gehate sit up and take notice, I can tell you.'

'I'm glad. Now, remember what you promised me at breakfast. I want to see you *eating* – not just picking at your food.'

'The fresh air and exercise have made me ravenous,' Dalacott lied. He left Conna as she was welcoming the three witnesses and went into the central part of the house, which was thronged with men and women who were conversing animatedly in small groups. Grateful that nobody appeared to have noticed his arrival, he quietly took a glass of fruit juice from the table set out for the children and went to stand by a window. From the vantage point he could see quite a long way to the west, over vistas of agricultural land which at the limits of vision shaded off into a low range of blue-green hills. The strip fields clearly showed progressions of six colours, from the pale green of the freshly planted to the deep yellow of mature crops ready for harvesting.

As he was watching, the hills and most distant fields blinked with prismatic colour and abruptly dimmed. The penumbral band of Overland's shadow was racing across the landscape at orbital speed, closely followed by the blackness of the umbra itself. It took only a fraction of a minute for the rushing wall of darkness to reach and envelop the house – then littlenight had begun. It was a phenomenon Dalacott had never tired of watching. As his eyes adjusted to the new conditions the sky seemed to blossom with stars, hazy spirals and comets, and he found himself wondering if there could be – as some claimed – other inhabited worlds circling far-off suns. In the old days the army had absorbed too much of his mental energy for him to think deeply on such matters, but of late he had found a spare comfort in the notion that there might be an infinity of worlds, and that on one of them there might be another Kolcorron identical to the one he knew in every respect save one. Was it possible that there was another Land on which his lost loved ones were still alive?

The evocative smell of freshly-lit oil lanterns and candles took his thoughts back to the few treasured nights he had spent with Aytha Maraquine. During the heady hours of passion Dalacott had known with total certainty that they would overcome all difficulties, surmount all the obstacles that lay in the way of their eventual marriage. Aytha, who had solewife status, would have had to endure the twin disgraces of divorcing a sickly husband and of marrying across the greatest of all social divisions, the one which separated the military from all other classes. He had been faced with similar impediments, with an added problem in that by divorcing Toriane – daughter of a military governor – he would have been placing his own career in jeopardy.

None of that had mattered to Dalacott in his fevered monomania. Then had come the Padalian campaign, which should have been brief but which in the event had entailed his being separated from Aytha for almost a year. Next had come the news that she had died in giving birth to a male child. Dalacott's first tortured impulse had been to claim the boy as his own, and in that way keep faith with Aytha, but the cool voices of logic and self-interest had intervened. What was the point in posthumously smirching Aytha's good name and at the same time prejudicing his career and bringing unhappiness to his family? It would not even benefit the boy, Toller, who would be best left to grow up in the comfortable circumstances of his maternal kith and kin.

In the end Dalacott had committed himself to the course of rationality, not even trying to see his son, and the years had slipped by and his abilities had brought him the deserved rank of general. Now, at this late stage of his life, the entire episode had many of the qualities of a dream and might have lost its power to engender pain – except that other questions and doubts had begun to trouble his hours of solitude. All his protestations notwithstanding, had he really intended to marry Aytha? Had he not, in some buried level of his consciousness, been relieved when her death had made it unnecessary for him to make a decision one way or the other? In short, was he – General Risdel Dalacott – the man he had always believed himself to be? Or was he a ...?

'*There* you are!' Conna said, approaching him with a glass of wheat wine which she placed firmly in his free hand while depriving him of the fruit juice. 'You'll simply have to mingle with the guests, you know. Otherwise it will look as though you consider yourself too famous and important to acknowledge my friends.'

'I'm sorry.' He gave her a wry smile. 'The older I get the more I look into the past.'

'Were you thinking about Oderan?'

'I was thinking about many things.' Dalacott sipped his wine and went with his daughter-in-law to make smalltalk with a succession of men and women. He noticed that very few of them had army backgrounds, possibly an indication of Conna's true feelings about the organisation which had taken her husband and was now turning its attention to her only child. The strain of manufacturing conversation with virtual strangers was considerable, and it was almost with relief that he heard the summons to go to the table. It was his duty now to make a short formal speech about his grandson's coming-of-age; then he would be free to fade into the background to the best of his ability. He walked around the table to the single high-backed chair which had been decked with blue spearflowers in Hallie's honour and realised he had not seen the boy for some time.

'Where's our hero?' a man called out. 'Bring on the hero!'

'He must have gone to his room,' Conna said. 'I'll fetch him.'

She smiled apologetically and slipped away from the company. There was delay of perhaps a minute before she reappeared in the doorway, and when she did so her face was strangely passive, frozen. She pointed at Dalacott and turned away again without speaking. He went after her, telling himself that the icy sensation in his stomach meant nothing, and walked along the corridor to Hallie's bedroom. The boy was lying on his back on his narrow couch. His face was flushed and gleaming with sweat, and his limbs were making small uncoordinated movements.

It can't be, Dalacott thought, appalled, as he went to the couch. He looked down at Hallie, saw the terror in his eyes, and knew at once that the twitching of his arms and legs represented strenuous attempts to move normally. Paralysis and fever! *I won't allow this*, Dalacott shouted inwardly as he dropped to his knees. *It isn't permitted!*

He placed his hand on Hallie's slim body, just below the ribcage, immediately found the tell-tale swelling of the spleen, and a moan of pure grief escaped his lips.

'You promised to look after him,' Conna said in a lifeless voice. 'He's only a baby!'

Dalacott stood up and gripped her shoulders. 'Is there a doctor here?'

'What's the use?'

'I know what this looks like, Conna, but at no time was Hallie within twenty paces of a globe and there was no wind to speak of.' Listening to his own voice, a stranger's voice, Dalacott tried to be persuaded by the stated facts. 'Besides, it takes two days for pterthacosis to develop. It simply can't happen like this. Now, is there a doctor?'

'Visigann,' she whispered, brimming eyes scanning his face in search of hope. 'I'll get him.' She turned and ran from the bedroom.

'You're going to be all right, Hallie,' Dalacott said as he knelt again by the couch. He used the edge of a coverlet to dab perspiration from the boy's face and was dismayed to find that he could actually feel heat radiating from the beaded skin. Hallie gazed up at him mutely, and his lips quivered as he tried to smile. Dalacott noticed that the Ballinnian ptertha stick was lying on the couch. He picked it up and pressed it into Hallie's hand, closing the boy's nerveless fingers around the polished wood, then kissed him on the forehead. He prolonged the kiss, as though trying to siphon the consuming pyrexia into his own body, and only slowly became aware of two odd facts – that Conna was taking too long to return with the doctor, and that a woman was screaming in another part of the house.

'I'll come back to you in just a moment, soldier,' he said. He stood up, tranced, made his way back to the dining room and saw that the guests were gathered around a man who was lying on the floor.

The man was Gehate – and from his fevered complexion and the feeble pawing of his hands it was evident that he was in an advanced stage of pterthacosis.

While he was waiting for the airship to be untethered, Dalacott slipped his hand into a pocket and located the curious nameless object he had found decades earlier on the banks of the Bes-Undar. His thumb worked in a circular pattern over the nugget's reflective surface, polished smooth by many years of similar frictions, as he tried to come to terms with the enormity of what had happened in the past nine days. The bare statistics conveyed little of the anguish which was withering his spirit.

Hallie had died before the end of the littlenight of his coming of age. Gehate and Ondobirtre had succumbed to the terrifying new form of pterthacosis by the end of that day, and on the following morning he had found Hallie's mother dead of the same cause in her room. That had been his first indication that the disease was contagious, and the implications had still been reverberating in his head when news had come of the fate of those who had been present at the celebration.

Of some forty men, women and children who had been in the villa, no fewer than thirty-two – including all the children – had been swept away during the same night. And still the tide of death had not expended its fell energies. The population of the hamlet of Klinterden and surrounding district had been reduced from approximately three-hundred to a mere sixty within three days. At that point the invisible killer had appeared to lose its virulence, and the burials had begun.

The airship's gondola lurched and swayed a little as it was freed from its constraints. Dalacott moved closer to a port hole and, for what he knew would be the last time, looked down on the familiar pattern of red-roofed dwellings, orchards and striated fields of grain. Its placid appearance masked the profound changes which had taken place, just as his own unaltered physical aspect disguised the fact that in nine days he had grown old.

The feeling – the drear apathy, the failure of optimism – was new to him, but he had no difficulty in identifying it because, for the first time ever, he could see cause to envy the dead.

PART II

The Proving Flight

CHAPTER SIX

The Weapons Research Station was in the south-western outskirts of Ro-Atabri, in the old manufacturing district of Mardavan Quays. The area was low-lying, drained by a hesitant and polluted watercourse which discharged into the Borann below the city. Centuries of industrial usage had rendered the soil of Mardavan Quays sterile in some places, while in others there were great stands of wrongly-coloured vegetation nourished by unknown seepings and secretions, products of ancient cesspools and spoilheaps. Factories and storage buildings were copiously scattered on the landscape, linked by deep-rutted tracks, and half-hidden among them were groups of shabby dwellings from whose windows light rarely shone.

The Research Station did not look out of place in its surroundings, being a collection of nondescript workshops, sheds and shabby single-storey offices. Even the station chief's office was so grimy that the typical Kolcorronian diamond patterns of its brickwork were almost totally obscured.

Toller Maraquine found the station a deeply depressing place in which to work. Looking back to the time of his appointment, he could see that he had been childishly naive in his visualisation of a weapons research establishment. He had anticipated perhaps a breezy sward with swordsmen busy testing new types of blades, or archers meticulously assessing the performance of laminated bows and novel patterns of arrowheads.

On arrival at the Quays it had taken him only a few hours to learn that there was very little genuine research on weapons being carried out under Borreat Hargeth. The name of the section disguised the fact that most of its funds were spent on trying to develop materials which could be substituted for brakka in the manufacture of gears and other machine components. Toller's work mainly consisted of mixing various fibres and powders with various types of resin and using the composite to cast various shapes of test specimens. He disliked the choking smell of the resins and the repetitious nature of the task, especially as his instincts told him the project was a waste of time. None of the composite materials the station produced compared well with brakka, the hardest and most durable substance on the planet – and if nature had been obliging enough to supply an ideal material what was the point in searching for another?

Apart from the occasional grumble to Hargeth, however, Toller worked steadily and conscientiously, determined to prove to his brother that he was

a responsible member of the family. His marriage to Fera also had something to do with his newfound steadiness, which was an unexpected benefit
from an arrangement he had plunged into for the sole purpose of confound-
ing his brother's wife. He had offered Fera the fourth grade – temporary,
non-exclusive, terminable by the man at any time – but she had had the
nerve to hold out for third grade status, which was binding on him for six
years.

That had been more than fifty days ago, and Toller had hoped that by this
time Gesalla would have softened in her attitude to both him and Fera, but if
anything the triangular relationship had deteriorated. Irritant factors were
Fera's monumental appetite and her capacity for indolence, both of which
were an affront to the primly sedulous Gesalla, but Toller was unable to
chastise his wife for refusing to amend her ways. She was claiming her right
to be the person she had always been, regardless of whom she displeased,
just as he was claiming the right to reside in the Maraquine family home.
Gesalla was ever on the look-out for a pretext on which to have him dismissed from the Square House, and it was sheer stubbornness on his part
which kept him from finding accommodation elsewhere.

Toller was pondering on his domestic situation one foreday, wondering
how long the uneasy balance could be maintained, when he saw Hargeth
coming into the shed where he was weighing out chopped glass fibres. Hargeth was a lean fidgety man in his early fifties and everything about him –
nose, chin, ears, elbows, shoulders – seemed to be sharp-cornered. Today he
appeared more restless than usual.

'Come with me, Toller,' he said. 'We have need of those muscles of yours.'

Toller put his scoop aside. 'What do you want me to do?'

'You're always complaining about not being able to work on engines of
war – and now is your opportunity.' Hargeth led the way to a small portable
crane which had been erected on a patch of ground between two workshops.
It was of conventional rafter wood construction except that the gear wheels,
which would have been brakka in an ordinary crane, had been cast in a
greyish composite produced by the research station.

'Lord Glo is arriving soon,' Hargeth said. 'He wants to demonstrate these
gears to one of Prince Pouche's financial inspectors, and today we are going
to have a preliminary test. I want you to check the cables, grease the gears
carefully and fill the load basket with rocks.'

'You spoke of a war engine,' Toller said. 'This is just a crane.'

'Army engineers have to build fortifications and raise heavy equipment –
so this is a war engine. The Prince's accountants must be kept happy, otherwise we lose funding. Now go to work – Glo will be here within the hour.'

Toller nodded and began preparing the crane. The sun was only halfway
to its daily occlusion by Overland, but there was no wind to scoop the heat

out of the low-lying river basin and the temperature was climbing steadily. A nearby tannery was adding its stenches to the already fume-laden air of the station. Toller found himself longing for a pot of cool ale, but the Quays district boasted of only one tavern and it had such a verminous aspect that he would not consider sending an apprentice for a sample of its wares.

This is a miserly reward for a life of virtue, he thought disconsolately. *At least at Haffanger the air was fit to breathe.*

He had barely finished putting rocks into the crane's load basket when there came the sounds of harness and hoofbeats. Lord Glo's jaunty red-and-orange phaeton rolled through the station's gates and came to a halt outside Hargeth's office, looking incongruous amid the begrimed surroundings. Glo stepped down from the vehicle and had a long discussion with his driver before turning to greet Hargeth, who had ventured out to meet him. The two men conversed quietly for a minute, then came towards the crane.

Glo was holding a kerchief close to his nose, and it was obvious from his heightened colouring and a certain stateliness of his gait that he had already partaken generously of wine. Toller shook his head in a kind of amused respect for the single-mindedness with which the Lord Philosopher continued to render himself unfit for office. He stopped smiling when he noticed that several passing workers were whispering behind their hands. Why could Glo not place a higher value on his own dignity?

'There you are, my boy!' Glo called out on seeing Toller. 'Do you know that, more than ever, you remind me of myself as a ... hmm ... young man?' He nudged Hargeth. 'How is that for a splendid figure of a man, Borreat? That's how I used to look.'

'Very good, my lord,' Hargeth replied, noticeably unimpressed. 'These wheels are the old Compound 18, but we have tried low-temperature curing on them and the results are quite encouraging, even though this crane is more-or-less a scale model. I'm sure it's a step in the right direction.'

'I'm sure you're right, but let me see the thing at ... hmm ... work.'

'Of course.' Hargeth nodded to Toller, who began putting the crane through its paces. It was designed for operation by two men, but he was able to hoist the load on his own without undue effort, and directed by Hargeth he spent a few minutes rotating the jib and demonstrating the machine's load-placing accuracy. He was careful to make the operation as smooth as possible, to avoid feeding shocks into the gear teeth, and the display ended with the crane's moving parts in apparently excellent condition. The group of computational assistants and labourers who had gathered to watch the proceedings began to drift away.

Toller was lowering the load to its original resting when, without warning, the pawl with which he was controlling the descent sheared through several teeth on the main ratchet in a burst of staccato sound. The laden basket dropped a short distance before the cable drum locked, and the crane – with Toller still at the controls – tilted dangerously on its base. It was saved from toppling when some of the watching labourers threw their weight on to the rising leg and brought it to the ground.

'My congratulations,' Hargeth said scathingly as Toller stepped clear of the creaking structure. 'How did you manage to do that?'

'If only you could invent a material stronger than stale porridge there'd be no …' Toller broke off as he looked beyond Hargeth and saw that Lord Glo had fallen to the ground. He was lying with his face pressed against a ridge of dried clay, seemingly unable to move. Fearful that Glo might have been struck by a flying gear tooth, Toller ran and knelt beside him. Glo's pale blue eye turned in his direction, but still the rotund body remained inert.

'I'm not drunk,' Glo mumbled, speaking from one side of his mouth. 'Get me away from here, my boy – I think I'm halfway to being dead.'

Fera Rivoo had adapted well to her new style of life in Greenmount Peel, but no amount of coaxing on Toller's part had ever persuaded her to sit astride a bluehorn or even one of the smaller whitehorns which were often favoured by women. Consequently, when Toller wanted to get away from the Peel with his wife for fresh air or simply a change of surroundings he was forced to go on foot. Walking was a form of exercise and travel for which he cared little because it was too tame and dictated too leisurely a pace of events, but Fera regarded it as the only way of getting about the city districts when no carriage was available to her.

'I'm hungry,' she announced as they reached the Plaza of the Navigators, close to the centre of Ro-Atabri.

'Of course you are,' Toller said. 'Why, it must be almost an hour since your second breakfast.'

She dug an elbow into his ribs and gave him a meaningful smile. 'You want me to keep my strength up, don't you?'

'Has it occurred to you that there might be more to life than sex and food?'

'Yes – wine.' She shaded her eyes from the early foreday sun and surveyed the nearest of the pastry vendors' stalls which were dotted along the square's perimeter. 'I think I'll have some honeycake and perhaps some Kailian white to wash it down with.'

Still uttering token protests, Toller made the necessary purchases and they sat on one of the benches which faced the statues of illustrious seafarers of the empire's past. The plaza was bounded by a mix of public and commercial buildings, most of which exhibited – in various shades of masonry and brick – the traditional Kolcorronian pattern of interlocked diamonds. Trees in contrasting stages of their maturation cycle and the colourful dress of passers-by added to the sunlit chiaroscuro. A westerly breeze was keeping the air pleasant and lively.

'I have to admit,' Toller said, sipping some cool light wine, 'that this is much better than working for Hargeth. I've never understood why scientific research work always seems to involve evil smells.'

'You poor delicate creature!' Fera brushed a crumb from her chin. 'If you want to know what a *real* stink is like you should try working in the fish market.'

'No, thanks – I prefer to stay where I am,' Toller replied. It was about twenty days since the sudden onset of Lord Glo's illness, but Toller was still appreciative of the resultant change in his own circumstances and employment. Glo had been stricken with a paralysis which affected the left side of his body and had found himself in need of a personal attendant, preferably one with an abundance of physical strength. When Toller had been offered the position he had accepted at once, and had moved with Fera to Glo's spacious residence on the western slope of Greenmount. The new arrangement, as well as providing a welcome relief from Mardavan Quays, had resolved the difficult situation in the Maraquine household, and Toller was making a conscientious effort to be content. A restless gloominess sometimes came upon him when he compared his menial existence to the kind of life he would have preferred, but it was something he always kept to himself. On the positive side, Glo had proved a considerate employer and as soon as he had regained a measure of his strength and mobility had made as few demands as possible on Toller's time.

'Lord Glo seemed busy this morning,' Fera said. 'I could hear that sunwriter of his clicking and clacking no matter where I went.'

Toller nodded. 'He's been talking a great deal with Tunsfo lately. I think he's worried about the reports from the provinces.'

'There isn't really going to be a plague, is there, Toller?' Fera drew her shoulders forward in distaste, deepening the cleft in her bosom. 'I can't bear having sick people around me.'

'Don't worry! From what I hear they wouldn't be around you very long – about two hours seems to be the average.'

'*Toller!*' Fera gazed at him in open-mouthed reproach, her tongue coated with a fine slurry of honeycake.

'There's nothing for you to fret about,' Toller said reassuringly, even though – as he had gathered from Glo – something akin to a plague had begun simultaneously in eight widely separated places. Outbreaks had first been reported from the palatine provinces of Kail and Middac; then from the less important and more remote regions of Sorka, Merrill, Padale, Ballin, Yalrofac and Loongl. Since then there had been a lull of a few days, and Toller knew the authorities were hoping against hope that the calamity had been of a transient nature, that the disease had burned itself out, that the mother country of Kolcorron and the capital city would remain unaffected. Toller could understand their feelings, but he saw little grounds for optimism. If the ptertha had increased their killing range and potency to the awesome extent suggested by the dispatches, they were in his opinion bound to make maximum use of their new powers. The respite that mankind was enjoying could mean that the ptertha were behaving like an intelligent and ruthless enemy who, having successfully tested a new weapon, had retired only to regroup and prepare for a major onslaught.

'We should think about returning to the Peel soon.' Toller drained his porcelain cup of wine and placed it under the bench for retrieval by the vendor. 'Glo wants to bathe before little-night.'

'I'm glad I won't have to help.'

'He has his own kind of courage, you know. I don't think I could endure the life of a cripple, but I have yet to hear him utter a single word of complaint.'

'Why do you keep talking about sickness when you know I don't like it?' Fera stood up and smoothed the wispy plumage of her clothing. 'We have time to walk by the White Fountains, haven't we?'

'Only for a few minutes.' Toller linked arms with his wife and they crossed the Plaza of the Navigators and walked along the busy avenue which led to the municipal gardens. The fountains sculpted in snowy Padalian marble were seeding the air with a refreshing coolness. Groups of people, some of them accompanied by children, were strolling amid the islands of bright foliage and their occasional laughter added to the idyllic tranquillity of the scene.

'I suppose this could be regarded as the epitome of civilised life,' Toller said. 'The only thing wrong with it – and this is strictly my own point of view – is that it is much too ...' He stopped speaking as the braying note of a heavy horn sounded from a nearby rooftop and was quickly echoed by others in more distant parts of the city.

'Ptertha!' Toller swung his gaze upwards to the sky.

Fera moved closer to him. 'It's a mistake, isn't it, Toller? They don't come into the city.'

'We'd better get out of the open just the same,' Toller said, urging her towards the buildings on the north side of the gardens. People all about him were scanning the heavens, but – such was the power of conviction and habit – only a few were hurrying to take cover. The ptertha were an implacable natural enemy, but a balance had been struck long ago and the very existence of civilisation was predicated on the ptertha's behaviour patterns remaining constant and foreseeable. It was quite unthinkable that the blindly malevolent globes could make a sudden radical change in their habits – in that respect Toller was at one with the people around him – but the news from the provinces had implanted the seeds of unease deep in his consciousness. If the ptertha could change in one way – why not in another?

A woman screamed some distance to Toller's left, and the single inarticulate pulse of sound framed the real world's answer to his abstract musings. He looked in the direction of the scream and saw a single ptertha descend from the sun's cone of brilliance. The blue-and-purple globe sank into a crowded area at the centre of the gardens, and now men were screaming too, counterpointing the continuing blare of the alarm horns. Fera's body went rigid with shock as she glimpsed the ptertha in the last second of its existence.

'Come on!' Toller gripped her hand and sprinted towards the peristyled guildhalls to the north. In his pounding progress across the open ground he had scant time in which to look out for other ptertha, but it was no longer necessary to search for the globes. They could be readily seen now, drifting among the rooftops and domes and chimneys in placid sunlight.

There could only have been few citizens of the Kolcorronian empire who had never had a nightmare about being caught on exposed ground amid a swarm of ptertha, and in the next hour Toller not only experienced the nightmare to the full but went beyond it into new realms of dread. Displaying their terrifying new boldness, the ptertha were descending to street level all over the city – silent and shimmering – invading gardens and precincts, bounding slowly across public squares, lurking in archways and colonnades. They were being annihilated by the panic-stricken populace, and it was here that the terms of the ancient nightmare became inadequate for the actuality – because Toller knew, with a bleak and wordless certainty, that the invaders represented the new breed of ptertha.

They were the plague-carriers.

In the long-running debate about the nature of the ptertha, those who spoke in support of the idea that the globes possessed some qualities of mind had always pointed to the fact that they judiciously avoided cities and large towns. Even in sizable swarms the ptertha would have been swiftly destroyed on venturing into an urban environment, especially in conditions of good visibility. The argument had been that they were less concerned with self-preservation than with avoiding wasting their numbers in futile attacks – clear evidence of mentation – and the theory had had some validity when the ptertha's killing range was limited to a few paces.

But, as Toller had intuited at once, the livid globes drifting down in Ro-Atabri were plague-carriers.

For every one of them destroyed, many citizens would be lost to the new kind of poisonous dust which killed at great range, and the horror did not stop there – because the grim new rules of conflict decreed that each direct victim of a ptertha encounter would, in the brief time remaining to them, contaminate and carry off to the grave perhaps dozens of others.

An hour elapsed before the wind conditions changed and brought the first attack on Ro-Atabri to an end, but – in a city where every man, woman and child was suddenly a potential mortal enemy and had to be treated as such – Toller's nightmare was able to continue for much, much longer …

A rare band of rain had swept over the region during the night and now, in the first quiet minutes after sunrise, Toller Maraquine found himself looking down from Greenmount on an unfamiliar world. Patches and streamers of ground-hugging mist garlanded the vistas below, in places obscuring Ro-Atabri more effectively than the blanket of ptertha screens which had been thrown over the city since the first attack, almost two years earlier. The triangular outline of Mount Opelmer rose out of an aureate haze to the east, its upper slopes tinted by the reddish sun which had just climbed into view.

Toller had awakened early and, driven by the restlessness which recently had been troubling him more and more, had decided to get up and walk alone in the grounds of the Peel.

He began by pacing along the inner defensive screen and checking that the nets were securely in place. Until the onslaught of the plague only rural habitations had needed ptertha barriers, and in those days simple nets and trellises had been adequate – but all at once, in town and country alike, it had become necessary to erect more elaborate screens which created a thirty-yard buffer zone around protected areas. A single layer of netting still sufficed for the roofs of most enclosures, because the ptertha toxins were borne away horizontally in the wind, but it was vital that the perimeters should be double screens, widely separated and supported by strong scaffolding.

Lord Glo had gratified Toller by giving him, in addition to his normal duties, the responsible and sometimes dangerous task of overseeing the construction of the screens for the Peel and some other philosophy buildings. The feeling that he was at last doing something important and useful had made him less unruly, and the risks of working in the open had provided satisfactions of a different kind. Borreat Hargeth's only significant contribution to the anti-ptertha armoury had been the development of an odd-looking L-shaped throwing stick which flew faster and farther than the standard Kolcorronian cruciform, and in which in the hands of a good man could destroy globes at more than forty yards. While supervising screen construction Toller had perfected his skill with the new weapon, and prided himself on having lost no workers directly to the ptertha.

That phase of his life had drawn to its ordained close, however, and now – in spite of all his efforts – he was burdened with a sense of having been caught like a fish in the very nets he had helped to construct. Considering that more than two thirds of the empire's population had been swept away by the virulent new form of pterthacosis, he should have been counting himself fortunate to be alive and healthy, with food, shelter and a lusty woman to share his bed – but none of those considerations could offset the gnawing conviction that his life was going to waste. He instinctively rejected the Church's teaching that he had an endless succession of incarnations ahead of him, alternating between Land and Overland; he had been granted only one life, one precious span of existence, and the prospect of squandering what remained of it was intolerable.

Despite the buoyant freshness of the morning air, Toller felt his chest begin to heave and his lungs to labour as though with suffocation. Close to sudden irrational panic, desperate for a physical outlet for his emotions, he reacted as he had not done since his time of exile on the Loongl peninsula. He opened a gate in the Peel's inner screen, crossed the buffer zone and went through the outer screen to stand on the unprotected slope of Greenmount. A strip of pasture – deeded to the philosophy order long ago – stretched before him for several furlongs, its lower end slanting down into trees and mist. The air was almost completely still, so there was little chance of encountering a stray globe, but the symbolic act of defiance had an easing effect on the psychological pressure which had been building within him.

He unhooked a pertha stick from his belt and was preparing to walk farther down the hill when his attention was caught by a movement at the bottom edge of the pasture. A lone rider was emerging from the swath of woodland which separated the philosophers' demesne from the adjacent city district of Silarbri. Toller brought out his telescope, treasured possession, and with its aid determined that the rider was in the King's service and that he bore on his chest the blue-and-white plume-and-sword symbol of a courier.

His interest aroused, Toller sat down on a natural bench of rock to observe the newcomer's progress. He was reminded of a previous time when the arrival of a royal messenger had heralded his escape from the miseries of the Loongl research station, but on this occasion the circumstances were vastly different. Lord Glo had been virtually ignored by the Great Palace since the débâcle in the Rainbow Hall. In the old days the delivery of a message by hand could have implied that it was privy, not to be entrusted to a sunwriter, but now it was difficult to imagine King Prad wanting to communicate with the Lord Philosopher about anything at all.

The rider was approaching slowly and nonchalantly. By taking a slightly more circuitous route he could have made the entire journey to Glo's residence under the smothering nets of the city's pertha screens, but it looked as though he was enjoying the short stretch of open sky in spite of the slight risk of having a pertha descend on him. Toller wondered if the messenger had a spirit similar to his own, one which chafed under the stringent anti-ptertha precautions which enabled what was left of the population to continue with their beleaguered existences.

The great census of 2622, taken only four years earlier, had established that the empire's population consisted of almost two million with full Kol-corronian citizenship and some four million with tributary status. By the end of the first two plague years the total remaining was estimated at rather less than two million. A minute proportion of those who survived did so because, inexplicably, they had some degree of immunity to the second-ary infection, but the vast majority went in continual fear for their lives, emulating the lowliest vermin in their burrows. Unscreened dwellings had been fitted with airtight seals which were clamped over doors, windows and chimney openings during ptertha alerts, and outside the cities and town-ships the ordinary people had deserted their farms and taken to living in woodlands and forests, the natural fortresses which the globes were unable to penetrate.

As a result agricultural output had fallen to a level which was insufficient even for the greatly reduced needs of a depleted population, but Toller – with the unconscious egocentricity of the young – had little thought to spare for the statistics which told of calamities on a national scale. To him they amounted to little more than a shadow play, a vaguely shifting background to the central drama of his own affairs, and it was in the hope of learning something to his personal advantage that he stood up to greet the arriving king's messenger.

'Good foreday,' he said, smiling. 'What brings you to Greenmount Peel?'

The courier was a gaunt man with a world-weary look to him, but he nodded pleasantly enough as he reined his bluehorn to a halt. 'The message I bear is for Lord Glo's eyes only.'

'Lord Glo is still asleep. I am Toller Maraquine, Lord Glo's personal at-tendant and a hereditary member of the philosophy order. I have no wish to pry, but my lord is not a well man and he would be displeased were I to awaken him at this hour except for a matter of considerable urgency. Let me have the gist of your message so that I may decide what should be done.'

'The message tube is sealed.' The courier produced a mock-rueful smile. 'And I'm not supposed to be aware of its contents.'

Toller shrugged, playing a familiar game. 'That's a pity – I was hoping that you and I could have made our lives a little easier.'

'Fine grazing land,' the courier said, turning in the saddle to appraise the pasture he had just ridden through. 'I imagine his lordship's household has not been greatly affected by the food shortages ...'

'You must be hungry after riding all the way out here,' Toller said. 'I would be happy to set you down to a hero's breakfast, but perhaps there is no time. Perhaps I have to go immediately and rouse Lord Glo.'

'Perhaps it would be more considerate to allow his lordship to enjoy his rest.' The courier swung himself down to stand beside Toller. 'The King is summoning him to a special meeting in the Great Palace, but the appointment is four days hence. It scarcely seems to be a matter of great urgency.'

'Perhaps,' Toller said, frowning as he tried to evaluate the surprising new information. 'Perhaps not.'

CHAPTER SEVEN

'I'm not at all sure that I'm doing the right thing,' Lord Glo said as Toller Maraquine finished strapping him into his walking frame. 'I think it would be much more prudent – not to mention being more fair to you – if I were to take one of the servants to the Great Palace with me and ... hmm ... leave you here. There is enough work to be done around the place, work which would keep you out of trouble.'

'It has been two years,' Toller replied, determined not to be excluded. 'And Leddravohr has had so much on his mind that he has probably forgotten all about me.'

'I wouldn't count on it, my boy – the prince has a certain reputation in these matters. Besides, if I know you, you're quite likely to give him a reminder.'

'Why would I do something so unwise?'

'I've been watching you lately. You're like a brakka tree which is overdue for a blow-out.'

'I don't do that sort of thing any more.' Toller made the protest automatically, as he had often done in the past, but it came to him that he had in fact changed considerably since his first encounter with the military prince. His occasional periods of restlessness and dissatisfaction were proof of the change, because of the way in which he dealt with them. Instead of working himself up to a state in which the slightest annoyance was liable to trigger an outburst, he had learned – like other men – to divert or sublimate his emotional energies. He had schooled himself to accept an accretion of minor joys and satisfactions in place of that single great fulfilment which was yearned for by so many and destined for so few.

'Very well, young man,' Glo said as he adjusted a buckle. 'I'm going to trust you, but please remember that this is a uniquely important occasion and conduct yourself accordingly. I will hold you to your word on this point. You realise, of course, why the King has seen fit to ... hmm ... summon me?'

'Is it a return to the days when we were consulted on the great imponderables of life? Does the King want to know why men have nipples but can't suckle?'

Glo sniffed. 'Your brother has the same unfortunate tendency towards coarse sarcasm.'

'I'm sorry.'

'You're not, but I'll enlighten you just the same. The idea I planted in the King's mind two years ago has finally borne fruit. Remember what you said about my flying higher and seeing …? No, that was Lain. But here's something for you to … hmm … think about, young Toller. I'm getting on in years and haven't much longer to go – but I'll wager you a thousand nobles that I will set foot on Overland before I die.'

'I would never challenge your word on any subject,' Toller said diplomatically, marvelling at the older man's talent for self-deception. Anybody else, with the possible exception of Vorndal Sisstt, would have remembered the council meeting with shame. So great was the philosophers' disgrace that they would surely have been deposed from Greenmount had the monarchy not been preoccupied with the plague and its consequences – yet Glo still nurtured his belief that he was highly regarded by the King and that his fantasising about the colonisation of Overland could be taken seriously. Since the onset of his illness Glo had shunned alcohol, and was able to comport himself better as a result, but his senility remained to distort his view of reality. Toller's private guess was that Glo had been summoned to the palace to account for the continuing failure to produce the efficacious long-range anti-ptertha weapon which was vital if normal agriculture were to resume.

'We've got to make haste,' Glo said. 'Can't risk being late on our day of triumph.' With Toller's help he donned his formal grey robe, working it down over the cane framework which enabled him to stand on his own. His formerly rotund body had shrunk to a loose-skinned slightness, but he had left his clothing unaltered to accommodate and hide the frame, hoping to disguise the extent of his disability. It was one of the human foibles which had earned him Toller's sympathy.

'We'll get you there in good time,' Toller said reassuringly, wondering if he should be trying to prepare Glo for the possible ordeal that lay ahead.

The drive to the Great Palace took place in silence, with Glo nodding ruminatively to himself now and then as he rehearsed his intended address.

It was a moist grey morning, the gloom of which was deepened by the anti-ptertha screens overhead. The level of illumination had not been reduced a great deal in those streets where it had been sufficient to put up a roof of netting or lattices supported on canes which ran horizontally from eave to eave. But where there were roofs and parapets of different heights in proximity to each other it had been necessary to erect heavy and complicated structures, many of which were clad with varnished textiles to prevent air currents and downdraughts from carrying ptertha dust through countless apertures in buildings which were designed for an equatorial climate. Many of the once-glittering avenues in the heart of Ro-Atabri now had a cavernous dimness to them, the city's architecture having been clogged and obscured and rendered claustrophobic by the defensive shroud.

The Bytran Bridge, the main river crossing on the way south, had been completely sheathed with timber, giving it something of the appearance of a giant warehouse, and from there a tunnel-like covered way crossed the moats and led to the Great Palace, which was now draped and tented. Toller's first intimation that the meeting was going to be different from that of two years earlier came when he noticed the lack of carriages in the principal courtyard. Apart from a handful of official equippages, only his brother's lightweight brougham – acquired after the banning of team-drawn vehicles – waited near the entrance. Lain was standing alone by the brougham with a slim roll of paper under his arm. His narrow face looked pale and tired under the sweeps of black hair. Toller jumped down and assisted Glo to leave his carriage, discreetly taking his full weight until he had steadied himself.

'You didn't tell me this was going to be a private audience,' Toller said.

Glo gave him a look of humorous disdain, momentarily appearing his old self. 'I can't be expected to tell you everything, young man – it's important for the Lord Philosopher to be aloof and ... hmm ... enigmatic now and again.' Leaning heavily on Toller's arm, he limped towards the carved arch of the entrance, where they were joined by Lain.

During the exchange of greetings Toller, who had not seen his brother for some forty days, was concerned at Lain's obvious debility. He said, 'Lain, I hope you're not working too hard.'

Lain made a wry grimace. 'Working too hard and sleeping too little. Gesalla is pregnant again and it's affecting her more than the last time.'

'I'm sorry.' Toller was surprised to hear that, after her miscarriage of almost two years ago, Gesalla was still determined on motherhood. It indicated a maternal instinct which he had trouble in reconciling with the rest of her character. Apart from the single curious shift in his perception of Gesalla on his return from the disastrous council meeting, he had always seen her as being too dry, too well-ordered and too fond of her personal autonomy to enjoy rearing children.

'By the way, she sends her regards,' Lain added.

Toller smiled broadly to signal his disbelief as the three men proceeded into the palace. Glo directed them through the muted activity of the corridors to a glasswood door which was well away from the administrative areas. The black-armoured ostiaries on duty were a sign that the King was within. Toller felt Glo's body stiffen with exertion as he strove to present a good appearance, and he in turn tried to look as though he was giving Glo only minimal assistance as they entered the audience chamber.

The apartment was hexagonal and quite small, lighted by a single window, and the only furnishings were a single hexagonal table and six chairs. King Prad was already seated opposite the window and by his side were the princes Leddravohr and Chakkell, all of them informally attired in loose silks. Prad's sole mark of distinction was a large blue jewel which was suspended from his neck by a glass chain. Toller, who had a strong desire for the occasion to pass off smoothly for the sake of his brother and Lord Glo, avoided looking in Leddravohr's direction. He kept his eyes down until the King signalled for Glo and Lain to be seated, then he gave all his attention to getting Glo into a chair with a minimum of creaking from his frame.

'I apologise for this delay, Majesty,' Glo said when finally at ease, speaking in high Kolcorronian. 'Do you wish my attendant to retire?'

Prad shook his head. 'He may remain for your comfort, Lord Glo – I had not appreciated the extent of your incapacity.'

'A certain recalcitrance of the … hmm … limbs, that is all,' Glo replied stoically.

'Nevertheless, I am grateful for the effort you made to be here. As you can see, I am dispensing with all formality so that we may have an unimpeded exchange of ideas. The circumstances of our last meeting were hardly conducive to free discussion, were they?'

Toller, who had positioned himself behind Glo's chair, was surprised by the King's amiable and reasonable tones. It seemed as though his own pessimism had been ill-founded and that Glo was to be spared fresh humiliation. He looked directly across the table for the first time and saw that Prad's expression was indeed as reassuring as it could be on features that were dominated by one inhuman, marble-white eye. Toller's gaze, without his conscious bidding, swung towards Leddravohr and he experienced a keen psychic shock as he realised that the prince's eyes had been drilling into him all the while, projecting unmistakable malice and contempt.

I'm a different person, Toller told himself, checking the reflexive defiant spreading of his shoulders. *Glo and Lain are not going to be harmed in any way by association with* me.

He lowered his head, but not before he had glimpsed Leddravohr's smile flick into being, the effortless snake-fast twitch of his upper lip. Toller was unable to decide on a course of action or inaction. It appeared that all the things they whispered about Leddravohr were true, that he had an excellent memory for faces and an even better one for insults. The immediate difficulty for Toller lay in that, determined though he was not to cross Leddravohr, it was out of the question for him to stand with his head lowered for perhaps the whole foreday. Could he find a pretext to leave the room, perhaps something to do with ...?

'I want to talk about flying to Overland,' the King said, his words a conceptual bomb-blast which blew everything else out of Toller's consciousness. 'Are you, in your official capacity as Lord Philosopher, stating that it can be done?'

'I am, Majesty.' Glo glanced at Leddravohr and the dark-jowled Chakkell as though daring them to object. 'We can fly to Overland.'

'How?'

'By means of very large hot air balloons, Majesty.'

'Go on.'

'Their lifting power would have to be augmented by gas jets – but it is providential that in the region where the balloons would practically cease to function the jets would be their most effective.' Glo was speaking strongly and without hesitations, as he could sometimes do when inspired. 'The jets would also serve to turn the balloons over at the midpoint of the flight, thus enabling them to descend in the normal manner.

'I repeat, Majesty – we can fly to Overland.'

Glo's words were followed by an air-whispering silence during which Toller, bemused with wonder, looked down at his brother to see if – as before – the talk of flying to Overland had come as a shock to him. Lain appeared nervous and ill at ease, but not at all surprised. He and Glo must have been in collaboration, and if Lain believed that the flight could be made – then it could be made! Toller felt a stealthy coolness spread down his spine to the accompaniment of what for him was a totally new intellectual and emotional experience. *I have a future*, he thought. *I have discovered why I am here* ...

'Tell us more, Lord Glo,' the King said. 'This hot air balloon you speak of – has it been designed?'

'Not only has it been designed, Majesty – the archives show that an example was actually fabricated in the year 2187. It was successfully flown several times that year by a philosopher called Usader, and it is believed – although the records are ... hmm ... vague on this point – that in 2188 he actually attempted the Overland flight.'

'What happened to him?'

'He was never heard of again.'

'That hardly inspires confidence,' Chakkell put in, speaking for the first time. 'It's hardly a record of achievement.'

'That depends on one's viewpoint.' Glo refused to be discouraged. 'Had Usader returned a few days later one might be entitled to describe his flight as a failure. The fact that he did *not* return could indicate that he had succeeded.'

Chakkell snorted. 'More likely that he died!'

'I'm not claiming that such an ascent would be easy or without its share of ... hmm ... risks. My contention is that our increased scientific knowledge could reduce the risks to an acceptable level. Given sufficient determination – and the proper financial and material resources – we can produce ships capable of flying to Overland.'

Prince Leddravohr sighed audibly and shifted in his chair, but refrained from speaking. Toller guessed that the King had placed powerful restraints on him before the meeting began.

'You make it all sound rather like an aftday jaunt,' King Prad said. 'But isn't it a fact that Land and Overland are almost five thousand miles apart?'

'The best triangulations give a figure of 4,650 miles, Majesty. Surface to surface, that is.'

'How long would it take to fly that distance?'

'I regret I cannot give a definite answer to that question at this stage.'

'It's an important question, isn't it?'

'Undoubtedly! The speed of ascent of the balloon is of fundamental importance, Majesty, but there are many variables to be ... hmm ... considered.' Glo signalled for Lain to open his roll of paper. 'My chief scientist, who is a better mathematician than I, has been working on the preliminary calculations. With your consent, he will explain the problem.'

Lain spread out a chart with trembling hands, and Toller was relieved to see that he had had the foresight to draw it on a limp cloth-based paper which quickly lay flat. Part of it was taken up by a scale diagram which illustrated the sister worlds and their spatial relationships; the remainder was given over to detailed sketches of pear-shaped balloons and complicated gondolas. Lain swallowed with difficulty a couple of times and Toller grew tense, fearing that his brother was unable to speak.

'This circle represents our own world ... with its diameter of 4,100 miles,' Lain finally articulated. 'The other, smaller circle represents Overland, whose diameter is generally accepted as being 3,220 miles, at its fixed point above our equator on the zero meridian, which passed through Ro-Atabri.'

'I think we all learned that much basic astronomy in our infancy,' Prad said. 'Why can't you say how long the journey from the one to the other will take?'

Lain swallowed again. 'Majesty, the size of the balloon and the weight of the load we attach to it will influence the free ascent speed. The difference in temperature between the gases inside the balloon and the surrounding atmosphere is another factor, but the most important governing factor is the amount of crystals available to power the jets.

'Greater fuel economy would be achieved by allowing the balloon to rise to its maximum height – slowing down all the while – and not using the jets until the gravitational pull of Land had grown weak. That, of course, would entail lengthening the transit time and therefore increasing the weight of food and water to be carried, which in turn would ...'

'Enough, enough! My head swims!' The King held out both his hand, fingers slightly crooked as though cradling an invisible balloon. 'Settle your mind on a ship which will carry, say, twenty people. Imagine that crystals are reasonably plentiful. Now, how long will it take that ship to reach Overland? I don't expect you to be precise – simply give me a figure which I can lodge in my cranium.'

Lain, paler than ever, but with growing assurance, ran a fingertip down some columns of figures at the side of his chart. 'Twelve days, Majesty.'

'At last!' Prad glanced significantly at Leddravohr and Chakkell. 'Now – for the same ship – how much of the green and purple will be required?'

Lain raised his head and stared at the King with troubled eyes. The King gazed back at him, calmly and intently, as he waited for his answer. Toller sensed that wordless communication was taking place, that something beyond his understanding was happening. His brother seemed to have transcended all his nervousness and irresolution, to have acquired a strange authority which – for the moment, at least – placed him on a level with the ruler. Toller felt a surge of family pride as he saw that the King appeared to acknowledge Lain's new stature and was prepared to give him all the time he needed to formulate his reply.

'May I take it, Majesty,' Lain said at length, 'that we are talking about a one-way flight?'

The King's white eye narrowed. 'You may.'

'In that case, Majesty, the ship would require approximately thirty pounds each of pikon and halvell.'

'Thank you. You're not going to quibble over the fact that a higher proportion of halvell gives the best result in sustained burning?'

Lain shook his head. 'Under the circumstances – no.'

'You are a valuable man, Lain Maraquine.'

'Majesty, I don't understand this,' Glo protested, echoing Toller's own puzzlement. 'There is no conceivable reason for providing a ship with only enough fuel for one transit.'

'A single ship, no,' the King said. 'A small fleet, no. But when we are talking about ...' He turned his attention back to Lain. 'How many ships would you say?'

Lain produced a bleak smile. 'A thousand seems a good round figure, Majesty.'

'A *thousand!*' There was a creaking sound from Glo's cane frame as he made an abortive attempt to stand up, and when he spoke again an aggrieved note had crept into his voice. 'Am I the only person here who is to be kept in ignorance of the subject under discussion?'

The King made a placating gesture. 'There is no conspiracy, Lord Glo – it's merely that your chief scientist appears to have the ability to read minds. It would please me to learn how he divined what was in my thoughts.'

Lain stared down at his hands and spoke almost abstractedly, almost as though musing aloud. 'For more than two hundred days I have been unable to obtain any statistics on agricultural output or ptertha casualties. The official explanation was that the provincial administrators were too severely overworked to prepare their returns – and I have been trying to persuade myself that such was the case – but the indicators were already there, Majesty. In a way it is a relief to have my worst fears confirmed. The only way to deal with a crisis is to face up to it.'

'I agree with you,' Prad said, 'but I was concerned with avoiding a general panic, hence the secrecy. I had to be certain.'

'Certain?' Glo's large head turned from side to side. 'Certain? Certain?'

'Yes, Lord Glo,' the King said gravely. 'I had to be certain that our world was coming to an end.'

On hearing the bland statement Toller felt a unique emotional pang. Any fear which might have been part of it fled at once before curiosity and an overwhelming, selfish and gloating sense of privilege. The most momentous events in history were being staged for his personal benefit. For the first time in his life, he was in love with the future.

'. . . as though the ptertha were encouraged by the events of the past two years, in the manner of a warrior who sees that his foe is weakening,' the King was saying. 'Their numbers are increasing – and who is to say that their foul emissions will not become even more deadly? It has happened once, and it can happen again.

'We in Ro-Atabri have been comparatively fortunate thus far, but throughout the empire the people are dying from the insidious new form of pterthacosis in spite of all our efforts to fend the globes off. And the newborn, upon whom our future depends, are the most vulnerable. We might be facing the prospect of slowly dwindling into a pitiful, doomed handful of sterile old men and women – were it not for the looming spectre of famine. The agricultural regions are becoming incapable of producing food in the quantities which are necessary for the upkeep of our cities, even allowing for our vastly reduced urban populations.'

The King paused to give his audience a thin sad smile. 'There are some among us who maintain that there is still room for hope, that fate may yet relent and wheel against the ptertha – but Kolcorron did not become great by supinely trusting to chance. That attitude is foreign to our national character. When forced to yield ground in a battle, we withdraw to a secure redoubt where we can gather our strength and determination to surge forth again and overwhelm our enemies.

'In the present case, as befits the ultimate conflict, there is the ultimate redoubt – and its name is Overland.

'It is my royal decree that we shall prepare to withdraw to Overland – not in order to cower away from our enemy, but to grow numerous and power-ful again, to gain time in which to devise means of destroying the ptertha in their loathsome entirety, and finally – regardless of how long it may take – to return to our home world of Land as a glorious and invincible army which will triumphantly lay claim to all that is naturally and rightfully ours.'

The King's oratory, enhanced by the formalism of the high tongue, had carried Toller along with it, opening up new perspectives in his mind, and it was with some surprise that he realised no response was forthcoming from either his brother or Glo. The latter was so immobile that he might have been dead, and Lain continued to stare down at his hands as he twisted the brakka ring on his sixth finger. Toller wondered, with a twinge of guilt, if Lain was thinking of Gesalla and the baby which would be born into tur-bulent times.

Prad ended the silence by choosing, oddly in Toller's view, to address himself to Lain. 'Well, wrangler? Have you another demonstration of mind reading for us?'

Lain raised his head and eyed the King steadily. 'Majesty, even when our armies were at their most powerful, we avoided going against Chamteth.'

'I resent the implications of that remark,' Prince Leddravohr snapped. 'I demand that . . .'

'Your *promise*, Leddravohr!' The King rounded angrily on his son. 'I would remind you of your promise to me. Be patient! Your time is at hand.'

Leddravohr raised both hands in a gesture of resignation as he settled back in his chair, and now his brooding gaze was fixed on Lain. The spasm of alarm Toller felt over his brother's welfare was almost lost in the silent clamour of his reaction to the mention of Chamteth. Why had he been so slow to appreciate that an interplanetary migration fleet, if it were ever con-structed, would require power crystals on such a vast scale that its needs could be met from only one source? If the King's awesome plans also in-cluded going to war against the enigmatic and insular Chamtethans, then the near future was going to be even more turbulent than Toller could read-ily visualise.

Chamteth was a country so huge that it could be reached just as readily by travelling east or west into the Land of the Long Days, that hemisphere of the world which was not swept by Overland's shadow and where there was no littlenight to punctuate the sun's progress across the sky. In the distant past several ambitious rulers had tried probing into Chamteth and the outcome had been so convincing, so disastrous that Chamteth had virtually been erased from the national consciousness. It existed, but – as with Overland – its existence had no relevance to the quotidian affairs of the empire.

Until now, Toller thought, striving to rebuild his picture of the universe. *Chamteth and Overland are linked ... bonded ... to take one is to take the other ...*

'War against Chamteth has become inevitable,' the King said. 'Some are of the opinion that it always has been inevitable. What do you say, Lord Glo?'

'Majesty, I ...' Glo cleared his throat and sat up straighter. 'Majesty, I have always regarded myself as a creative thinker, but I freely admit that the grandeur and scope of your vision have taken my ... hmm ... breath away. When I originally proposed flying to Overland I envisaged despatching a small number of pathfinders, followed by the gradual establishment of a small colony. I had not dreamed of migration on the scale you are contemplating, but I can assure you that I am equal to the responsibilities involved. The designing of a suitable ship and the planning of all the necessary ...' Glo stopped speaking as he saw that Prad was shaking his head.

'My dear Lord Glo, you are not a well man,' the King said, 'and I would be less than fair to you if I permitted you to expend what remains of your strength on a task of such magnitude.'

'But, Majesty ...'

The King's face hardened. 'Do not interrupt! The extremity of our situation demands equally extreme measures. The entire resources of Kolcorron must be reorganised and mobilised, and therefore I am dissolving all the old dynastic family structures. In their place – as of this moment – is a single pyramid of authority. Its executive head is my son, Prince Leddravohr, who will control and coordinate every aspect – military and civil – of our national affairs. He is seconded by Prince Chakkell, who will be responsible to him for the construction of the migration fleet.'

The King paused, and when he spoke again his voice had none of the attributes of humanity. 'Be it understood that Prince Leddravohr's authority is absolute, that his power is unlimited, and that to go counter to his wishes in any respect is a crime equivalent to high treason.'

Toller closed his eyes, knowing that when he opened them again the world of his childhood and youth would have passed into history, and that in its place would be a dangerous new cosmos in which his tenure might be all too brief.

CHAPTER EIGHT

Leddravohr was mentally tired after the meeting and had been hoping to relax during dinner, but his father – with the abundant cerebral energy which characterises some elderly men – talked all the way through the meal. He switched rapidly and effortlessly from military strategy to food rationing schemes to the technicalities of interworld flight, displaying his fascination with detail, trying to explore mutually incompatible probabilities. Leddravohr, who had no taste for juggling with abstracts, was relieved when the meal was finished and his father moved out to the balcony for a final cup of wine before retiring to his private quarters.

'Damn this glass,' Prad said, tapping the transparent cupola which enclosed the balcony. 'I used to enjoy taking the air here at night. Now I can scarcely breathe.'

'Without the glass you wouldn't be breathing at all.' Leddravohr flicked his thumb, indicating a group of three ptertha drifting overhead across the glowing face of Overland. The sun had gone down and now the sister world was entering the gibbous phases of its illumination, casting its mellow light over the southern reaches of the city, Arle Bay and the deep indigo expanses of the Gulf of Tronom. The light was good enough to read by and would steadily increase in strength as Overland, keeping pace with the rotation of Land, swung towards its point of opposition with the sun. Although the sky had darkened only to a rich mid-blue the stars, some of which were bright enough to be visible in full daylight, formed blazing patterns from Overland's rim down to the horizon.

'Damn the ptertha, too,' Prad said. 'You know, son, one of the greatest tragedies of our past is that we never learned *where* the globes come from. Even if they are spawned somewhere in the upper atmosphere, it might have been possible at one time to track them down and destroy them at source. It's too late now, though.'

'What about your triumphant return from Overland? Attacking the ptertha from above?'

'Too late for me, I mean. History will remember me for the outward flight only.'

'Ah, yes – history,' Leddravohr said, once again wondering at his father's preoccupation with the pale and spurious immortality offered by books and graven monuments. Life was a transient thing, impossible to extend beyond its natural term, and time spent in trying to do so was a squandering of the very commodity one was seeking to preserve. Leddravohr's own belief was that the only way to cheat death, or at least reconcile oneself to it, was to achieve every ambition and sate every appetite, so that when the time came the relinquishing of life was little more than discarding an empty gourd.

His single overriding ambition had been to extend his future kingship to every quarter of Land – including Chamteth – but that was now denied him by a connivance of fate. In its place was the prospect of a hazardous and *unnatural* flight into the sky, followed by little more than a tribal existence on an unknown world. He was angry about that, filled with a gnawing canker of rage unlike anything he had ever known, and somebody would have to pay ...

Prad sipped pensively at his wine. 'Have you prepared all your dispatches?'

'Yes – the messengers leave at first light.' Leddravohr had spent all his free time after the meeting personally writing orders to the five generals he wanted for his staff. 'I instructed them to use continuous thrust, so we should have distinguished company quite soon.'

'I take it you have chosen Dalacott.'

'He's still the best tactician we have.'

'Aren't you afraid that his edge might be blunted?' Prad said. 'He must be seventy now, and being down in Kail when the plague broke out there can't have done him much good. Didn't he lose a daughter and a grandchild on the very first day?'

'Something like that,' Leddravohr replied carelessly. '*He* is still healthy, though. Still of value.'

'He must have the immunity.' Prad's face became more animated as he fastened on to yet another of his talking points. 'You know, Glo sent me some very interesting statistics at the beginning of the year. They were collated by Maraquine. They showed that the incidence of plague deaths among military personnel – which you would expect to be high because of their exposure – is actually somewhat lower than for the population in general. And, significantly, long-serving soldiers and airmen are the least likely to succumb. Maraquine suggested that years of being near ptertha kills and absorbing minute traces of the dust might train the body to resist ptertha-cosis. It's an intriguing thought.'

'Father, it's a totally useless thought.'

'I wouldn't say that. If the offspring of immune men and women were also immune, from birth, then you could breed a new race for whom the globes were no threat.'

'And what good would that be to you and me?' Leddravohr said, disposing of the argument to his own satisfaction. 'No, as far as I'm concerned Glo and Maraquine and their ilk are ornaments we can well do without. I look forward to the day when ...'

'*Enough!*' His father was suddenly King Prad Neldeever, ruler of the empire of Kolcorron, tall and rigid, with one terrible blind eye and one equally fearsome all-seeing eye which knew everything Leddravohr would have wished to keep secret. 'Ours will not be the house which is remembered for turning its back on learning. You will give me your word that you will not harm Glo or Maraquine.'

Leddravohr shrugged. 'You have my word.'

'That came easily.' His father stared at him for a moment, dissatisfied, then said, 'Neither will you touch Maraquine's brother, the one who now attends to Glo.'

'That oaf! I have more important things with which to occupy my mind.'

'I know. I have given you unprecedented powers because you have the qualities necessary to bring a great endeavour to a successful conclusion, and that power is not to be abused.'

'Spare me all this, father,' Leddravohr protested, laughing to conceal his resentment at being admonished like a wilful child. 'I intend to treat our philosophers with all the consideration they deserve. Tomorrow I'm going to Greenmount for two or three days – to learn all I need to know about their skyships – and if you care to make enquiries you'll hear that I am emanating nothing but courtesy and love.'

'Don't overdo it.' Prad drained his cup with a flourish, set it down on the wide stone balustrade and prepared to leave. 'Good night, son. And remember – the future watches.'

As soon as the King had departed Leddravohr exchanged his wine for a glass of fiery Padalian brandy and returned to the balcony. He sat down on a leather couch and gazed moodily at the southern sky where three great comets plumed the star fields. *The future watches!* His father was still cherishing the notion of going down in history as another King Bytran, blinding himself to the probability that there would be no historians to record his achievements. The story of Kolcorron was drawing to a bizarre and ignominious end just when it should have been entering the most glorious era of all.

And I'm the one who is losing most, Leddravohr thought. *I'm never going to be a real King.*

As he continued drinking brandy, and the night grew steadily brighter, it came to Leddravohr that there was an anomaly in the contrast between his attitude and that of his father. Optimism was the prerogative of the young, and yet the King was looking to the future with confidence; pessimism was a trait of the old, and yet it was Leddravohr who was gloomy and prey to grim forebodings. Why?

Was it that his father was too wrapped up in his enthusiasm for all things scientific to concede that the migration was impossible? Leddravohr took stock of his thoughts and was forced to discard the theory. At some stage in the day-long meeting he had been persuaded by the drawings, the graphs and the chains of figures, and now he believed that a skyship could reach the sister world. What, then, was the underlying cause of the malaise which had entered his soul? The future was not completely black, after all – there was the final war with Chamteth to anticipate.

As Leddravohr tilted his head back to finish a glass of brandy his gaze drifted towards the zenith – and suddenly he had his answer. The great disk of Overland was now almost fully illuminated and its face was just starting to show the prismatic changes which heralded its nightly plunge into the shadow of Land. Deepnight – that period when the world experienced real darkness – was beginning, and it had its counterpart in Leddravohr's mind.

He was a soldier, professionally immune to fear, and that was why he had been so slow to acknowledge or even identify the emotion which had lurked in his consciousness for most of the day.

He was afraid of the Overland flight!

What he felt was not straightforward apprehension over the undeniable risks involved – it was pure, primitive and unmanning terror at the very idea of ascending thousands of miles into the unforgiving blueness of the sky. The force of his dread was such that when the awful moment for embarkation arrived he might be unable to control himself. He, Prince Leddravohr Neldeever, might break down and cower away like a frightened child, possibly having to be carried bodily on to the skyship in full view of thousands …

Leddravohr jumped to his feet and hurled his glass away, smashing it on the balcony's stone floor. There was a hideous irony in the fact that his introduction to fear should have taken place not on the field of battle, but in the quietness of a small room, at the hands of stammering nonentities, with their scribbles and scratchings and their casual visions of the unthinkable.

Breathing deeply and steadily as an aid to regaining mastery of his emotions, Leddravohr watched the blackness of deepnight envelope the world, and when he finally retired to bed his face had regained its sculpted composure.

CHAPTER NINE

'It's getting late,' Toller said. 'Perhaps Leddravohr isn't coming.'

'We'll just have to wait and see.' Lain smiled briefly and returned his attention to the papers and mathematical instruments on his desk.

'Yes.' Toller studied the ceiling for a moment. 'This isn't a sparkling conversation, is it?'

'It isn't any kind of conversation,' Lain said. 'What's happening is that I'm trying to work and you keep interrupting.'

'Sorry.' Toller knew he should leave the room, but he was reluctant to do so. It was a long time since he had been in the family home, and some of his clearest boyhood memories were of coming into this familiar room – with its perette wood panels and glowing ceramics – and of seeing Lain at the same desk, going about the incomprehensible business of being a mathematician. Toller's instincts told him that he and his brother were reaching a watershed in their lives, and he had a longing for them to share an hour of companionship while it was still possible. He had been vaguely embarrassed about his feelings and had not tried putting them into words, with the negative result that Lain was ill at ease and puzzled by his continuing presence.

Resolving to be quiet, Toller went to one of the stacks of ancient manuscripts which had been brought from the Greenmount archives. He picked up a leather-bound folio and glanced at its title. As usual the words appeared as linear trains of letters with elusive content until he used a trick which Lain had once devised for him. He covered the title with his palm and slowly slid his hand to the right so that the letters were revealed to him in sequence. This time the printed symbols yielded up their meaning: *Aerostatic Flights to the Far North*, by Muel Webrey, 2136.

That was as far as Toller's interest in a book normally went, but balloon ascents had not been far from his mind since the momentous meeting of the previous day, and his curiosity was further stirred by the realisation that the book was five centuries old. What had it been like to fly across the world in the days before Kolcorron had arisen to unify a dozen warring nations? He sat down and opened the book near the middle, hoping Lain would be impressed, and began to read. Some unfamiliar spellings and grammatical constructions made the text more oblique than he would have liked, but he persevered, sliding his hand across paragraph after paragraph which, disappointingly, had more to do with ancient politics than aviation. He was beginning to lose momentum when his attention was caught by a reference to ptertha: '... *and far to our left the pink globes of the ptertha were rising*'.

Toller frowned and ran his finger across the adjective several times before raising his head. 'Lain, it says here that ptertha are pink.'

Lain did not look up. 'You must have misread it. The word is "purple".'

Toller studied the adjective again. 'No, it says pink.'

'You have to allow a certain amount of leeway in subjective descriptions. Besides, the meanings of words can shift over a long period of time.'

'Yes, but ...' Toller felt dissatisfied. 'So you don't think the ptertha used to be a diff—'

'Toller!' Lain threw down his pen. 'Toller, don't think I'm not glad to see you – but why have you taken up residence in my office?'

'We never talk,' Toller said uncomfortably.

'All right, what do you want to talk about?'

'Anything. There may not be much … time.' Toller sought inspiration. 'You could tell me what you're working on.'

'There wouldn't *be* much point. You wouldn't understand it.'

'Still we'd have been talking,' Toller said, rising to his feet and returning the old book to the stacks. He was walking to the door when his brother spoke.

'I'm sorry, Toller – you're quite right.' Lain smiled an apology. 'You see, I started this essay more than a year ago, and I want to finish it before I get diverted to other matters. But perhaps it isn't all that important.'

'It must be important if you've been working on it all that time. I'll leave you in peace.'

'Please don't go,' Lain said quickly. 'Would you like to see something truly wonderful? Watch this!' He picked up a small wooden disk, laid it flat on a sheet of paper and traced a circle around it. He slid the disk sideways, drew another circle which kissed the first and then repeated the process, ending with three circles in a line. Placing a finger at each end of the row, he said, 'From here to here is exactly three diameters, right?'

'That's right,' Toller said uneasily, wondering if he had missed something.

'Now we come to the amazing part.' Lain made an ink mark on the edge of the disk and placed it vertically on the paper, carefully ensuring that the mark was at an outermost edge of the three circles. After glancing up at Toller to make sure he was paying proper attention, Lain slowly rolled the disk straight across the row. The mark on its rim described a lazy curve and came down precisely on the outermost edge of the last circle.

'Demonstration ended,' Lain announced. 'And that's part of what I'm writing about.'

Toller blinked at him. 'The circumference of a wheel being equal to three diameters?'

'The fact that it is *exactly* equal to three diameters. That demonstration was quite crude, but even when we go to the limits of measurement the ratio is exactly three. Does that not strike you as being rather astonishing?'

'Why should it?' Toller said, his puzzlement growing. 'If that's the way it is, that's the way it is.'

'Yes, but why should it be *exactly* three? That and things like the fact that we have twelve fingers make whole areas of calculation absurdly easy. It's almost like an unwarranted gift from nature.'

'But … But that's the way it *is*. What else could it be?'

'Now you're approaching the theme of the essay. There may be some other

...*place*... where the ratio is three-and-a-quarter, or perhaps only two-and-a-half. In fact, there's no reason why it shouldn't be some completely irrational number which would give mathematicians headaches.'

'Some other place,' Toller said. 'You mean another world? Like Farland?'

'No.' Lain gave him a look which was both frank and enigmatic. 'I mean another totality – where physical laws and constants differ from those we know.'

Toller stared back at his brother as he strove to penetrate the barrier which had slid into place between them. 'It is all very interesting,' he said. 'I can see why the essay has taken you so long.'

Lain laughed aloud and came round the desk to embrace Toller. 'I love you, little brother.'

'I love you.'

'Good! I want you to keep that in mind when Leddravohr arrives. I'm a committed pacifist, Toller, and I eschew all violence. The fact that I am no match for Leddravohr is an irrelevance – I would behave towards him in exactly the same way were our social status and physiques transposed. Leddravohr and his kind are part of the past, whereas we represent the future. So I want you to swear that no matter what insult Leddravohr offers me, you will stay apart and leave the conduct of my affairs strictly to me.'

'I'm a different person now,' Toller said, stepping back. 'Besides, Leddravohr might be in a good mood.'

'I want your word, Toller.'

'You have it. Besides, it's in my own interests to keep on the right side of Leddravohr if I want to be a skyship pilot.' Toller was belatedly shocked by the content of his own words. 'Lain, why are we taking all this so calmly? We have just been told that the world as we know it is coming to an end ... and that some of us have to try reaching another planet ... yet we're all going about our ordinary business as though everything was normal. It doesn't make sense.'

'It's a more natural reaction than you might think. And don't forget the migration flight is only a contingency at this stage – it might never happen.'

'The war with Chamteth is going to happen.'

'That is the King's responsibility,' Lain said, his voice suddenly brusque. 'It can't be laid at my door. I have to get on with my work now.'

'I should see how my lord is faring.' As Toller walked along the corridor to the main stair he again wondered why Leddravohr had chosen to come to the Square House instead of visiting Glo at the much larger Greenmount Peel. The sunwriter message from the palace had baldly stated that the Princes Leddravohr and Chakkell would arrive at the house before little-night for initial technical briefings, and the infirm Glo had been obliged to journey out to meet them. It was now well into aftday and Glo would be growing tired, his strength further sapped by the effort of trying to hide his disability.

Toller descended to the entrance hall and turned left into the dayroom where he had left Glo in the temporary care of Fera. The two had a very comfortable relationship because of – Toller suspected – rather than in spite of her lowly origin and unpolished manner. It was another of Glo's little affectations, a way of reminding those around him that there was more to him than the cloistered philosopher. He was seated at a table reading a small book, and Fera was standing by a window gazing out at the mesh-mosaic of the sky. She was wearing a simple one piece garment of pale green cambric which showed off her statuesque form.

She turned on hearing Toller enter the room and said, 'This is boring. I want to go home.'

'I thought you wanted to see a real live prince at close quarters.'

'I've changed my mind.'

'They're bound to be here soon,' Toller said. 'Why don't you be like my lord and pass the time by reading?'

Fera mouthed silently, carefully forming the swear words so that there would be no doubt about what she thought of the idea. 'It wouldn't be so bad if there was even some food.'

'But you ate less than an hour ago!' Toller ran a humorously critical eye over his gradewife's figure. 'No wonder you're getting fat.'

'I'm not!' Fera slapped her belly inwards and contracted her stomach, an action which caused a voluptuous ballooning of her breasts. Toller viewed the display with affectionate appreciation. It was a frequent source of wonder to him that Fera, in spite of her appetite and habit of spending entire days lolling in bed, looked almost exactly as she had done two years earlier. The only noticeable change was that her chipped tooth had begun to turn grey. She devoted much time to rubbing it with white powders, supposed to contain crushed pearls, which she obtained from the Samlue market.

Lord Glo looked up from his book, his clapped-in face momentarily enlivened. 'Take the woman upstairs,' he said to Toller. 'That's what I'd do were I five years younger.'

Fera correctly assessed his mood and produced the expected ribaldry. '*I* wish you were five years younger, my lord – merely mounting the stairs would be enough to finish my husband.'

Glo gave a gratified whinny.

'In that case, we'll do it right here,' Toller said. He darted forward, put his arms around Fera and drew her close to him, half-seriously simulating passion. There was an undeniable element of providing sexual titillation for Glo in what he and Fera were doing, but such was the relationship the three had built up that the overriding motif was one of companionship and friendly clowning. After a few seconds of intimate contact, however, Toller felt Fera move against him with a hint of genuine purpose.

'Do you still have the use of your old bedroom?' she whispered, pressing her lips to his ear. 'I'm beginning to feel like …' She stopped speaking and although she remained in his arms he knew that somebody had entered the room.

He turned and saw Gesalla Maraquine regarding him with cool disdain, the familiar expression she seemed to reserve just for him. Her dark filmy clothing emphasised her slimness. It was the first time they had met in almost two years and he was struck by the fact that, as with Fera, her appearance had not altered in any significant way. The sickness associated with her second pregnancy – which had caused her to miss the littlenight meal – had invested her pale features with a near-numinous dignity which somehow made him feel that he was a stranger to all that was important in life.

'Good aftday, Gesalla,' he said. 'I see you haven't lost your knack of materialising at precisely the wrong moment.' Fera slipped away from him. He smiled and looked down at Glo, expecting his moral support, but Glo indulged in playful treachery by gazing fixedly at his book, pretending to be so lost in it that he had been unaware of what Toller and Fera were doing.

Gesalla's grey eyes considered Toller briefly while she decided if he merited a reply, then she turned her attention to Glo. 'My lord, Prince Chakkell's equerry is in the precinct. He reports that the Princes Chakkell and Leddravohr are on their way up the hill.'

'Thank you, my dear.' Glo closed his book and waited until Gesalla had left the room before baring the ruins of his lower teeth at Toller. 'I thought you weren't … hmm … afraid of that one.'

Toller was indignant. 'Afraid? Why should I be afraid?'

'Huh!' Fera had returned to her position by the window. 'What was wrong with it?'

'What are you talking about?'

'You said she came in at the wrong moment. What was wrong with it?'

Toller was staring at her, exasperated and speechless, when Glo tugged his sleeve to signal that he wanted to get to his feet. In the entrance hall there were footfalls and the sound of a man's voice. Toller helped Glo to stand up and lock the verticals of his cane frame. They walked together into the hall, with Toller inconspicuously taking much of Glo's weight. Lain and Gesalla were being addressed by the equerry, who was aged about forty and had tallowy skin and out-turned liver-coloured lips. His dark green tunic and breeches were foppishly decorated with lines of tiny crystal beads and he wore the narrow sword of a duellist.

'I am Canrell Zotiern, representing Prince Chakkell,' he announced with an imperiousness which would have been better suited to his master. 'Lord Glo and members of the Maraquine family – no others – will stand here in line facing the door and will await the arrival of the prince.'

Toller, who was shocked by Zotiern's arrogance, assisted Glo to the indicated place beside Lain and Gesalla. He glanced at Glo, expecting him to issue the proper reprimand, but the older man seemed too preoccupied with the laboured mechanics of walking to have noticed anything amiss. Several of the household servants watched silently from the door leading to the kitchens. Beyond the archway of the main entrance the mounted soldiers of Chakkell's personal guard disturbed the flow of light into the hall. Toller became aware that the equerry was looking at him.

'You! The body servant!' Zotiern called out. 'Are you deaf? Get back to your quarters.'

'My personal attendant is a Maraquine, and he remains with me,' Glo said steadily.

Toller heard the exchange as across a tumultuous distance. The crimson drumming was something he had not experienced in a long time, and he was dismayed to find that his cultivated immunity to it was proved illusory. *I'm a different person*, he told himself, while a prickly chill moved across his brow. *I AM a different person.*

'And I have a warning for you,' Glo went on, speaking in high Kolcorronian and dredging up something of his old authority as he confronted Zotiern. 'The unprecedented powers the King has accorded Leddravohr and Chakkell do not, as you appear to think, extend to their lackeys. I will tolerate no further violations of protocol from you.'

'A thousand apologies, my lord,' Zotiern said, insincere and unperturbed, consulting a list he had taken from his pocket. 'Ah, yes – Toller Maraquine … and a spouse named Fera.' He swaggered closer to Toller. 'While the subject of protocol is in the air, Toller Maraquine, where is this spouse of yours? Don't you know that all female members of the household should be presented?'

'My wife is at hand,' Toller said coldly. 'I will …' He broke off as Fera, who must have been listening, appeared at the door of the dayroom. Moving with uncharacteristic demureness and timidity, she came towards Toller.

'Yes, I can see why you wanted to keep this one hidden,' Zotiern said. 'I must make a closer inspection on behalf of the prince.'

As Fera was passing him he halted her by the expedient of grasping a handful of her hair. The drumming in Toller's brain crashed into silence. He thrust out his left hand and hit Zotiern on the shoulder, knocking him off-balance. Zotiern went down sideways, landing on his hands and knees, and immediately sprang up again. His right hand was going for his sword and Toller knew that by the time he fully regained his feet the blade would be unsheathed. Propelled by instinct, rage and alarm, Toller went in on his opponent and struck him on the side of the neck with all the power of his right arm. Zotiern spun away, limbs flailing the air like the blades of a ptertha stick, crashed to the floor and slid several yards on the polished surface. He ended up lying on his back, unmoving, his head angled close to one shoulder. Gesalla gave a clear, high scream.

'What happens here?' The angry shout came from Prince Chakkell, who had just come through the entrance closely followed by four of his guard. He strode to Zotiern, bent over him briefly – his sparsely covered scalp glistening – and raised his eyes towards Toller, who was frozen in the attitude of combat.

'You! *Again!*' Chakkell's swarthy countenance grew even darker. 'What's the meaning of this?'

'He insulted Lord Glo,' Toller said, meeting the prince's gaze directly. 'He also insulted me and molested my wife.'

'That is correct,' Glo put in. 'Your man's behaviour was quite inexcus—'

'Silence! I've had my fill of this doltish upstart!' Chakkell swung his arm, signalling his guards to move in on Toller. 'Kill him!'

The soldiers came forward, drawing their black swords. Toller backed away, thinking of his own blade which he had left at home, until his heel touched the wall. The soldiers formed a semicircle and closed in on him, eyes slitted and intent beneath the rims of their brakka helmets. Beyond them Toller could see Gesalla hiding in Lain's embrace; the grey-robed Glo rooted to the spot, his hand raised in ineffectual protest; and Fera watching him through latticed fingers. Until that moment the guards had remained equally distant from him, but now the one on the right was taking the initiative and the point of his sword was describing eager little circles as he prepared for the first thrust.

Toller braced himself against the wall and made ready to launch himself forward beneath the thrust when it came, determined to inflict some degree of injury on his executioners rather than simply be cut down by them. The hovering sword tip steadied, purposefully, and its message for Toller was that time was at an end. Heightened perception of everything in his surroundings brought him the awareness that another man was entering the hall, and even in the desperate extremity he was able to feel a pang of regret that the newcomer was Prince Leddravohr, arriving just in time to savour his death ...

'Stand away from that man!' Leddravohr commanded. His voice was not unduly loud, but the four guards responded at once by stepping back from Toller.

'What the ...!' Chakkell wheeled on Leddravohr. 'Those men are in my personal guard and they take orders only from me.'

'Is that so?' Leddravohr said calmly. He aimed a finger at the soldiers and slowly swung it to indicate the opposite side of the hall. The soldiers went with the line of it, as though controlled by invisible rods, and took up new positions.

'But you don't understand,' Chakkell protested. 'The Maraquine lout has killed Zotiern.'

'It shouldn't have been possible – Zotiern was armed and the Maraquine lout wasn't. This is part of the price you pay, my dear Chakkell, for surrounding yourself with strutting incompetents.' Leddravohr went closer to Zotiern, looked down at him and gave a low chuckle. 'Besides, he isn't dead. He is damaged beyond repair, mind you, but he isn't quite dead. Isn't that so, Zotiern?' Leddravohr augmented the question by nudging the fallen man with his toe.

Zotiern's mouth emitted a faint bubbling sound and Toller saw that his eyes were still open, frantic and staring, although his body remained inert.

Leddravohr flicked his smile into existence for Chakkell's benefit. 'As you think so highly of Zotiern, we'll do him the honour of sending him off along the Bright Road. Perhaps he would even have chosen it himself were he still able to speak.' Leddravohr glanced at the four watchful soldiers. 'Take him outside and see to it.'

The soldiers, obviously relieved at being able to escape Leddravohr's presence, saluted hastily before swooping on Zotiern and carrying him outside to the precinct. Chakkell made as if to follow, then turned back. Leddravohr gave him a mock-affectionate slap on the shoulder, dropped a hand to his sword and padded across the hall to stand before Toller.

'You seem obsessed with placing your life in danger,' he said. 'Why did you do it?'

'Prince, he insulted Lord Glo. He insulted me. And he molested my wife.'

'Your wife?' Leddravohr turned and looked at Fera. 'Ah, yes. And *how* did you overcome Zotiern?'

Toller was puzzled by Leddravohr's tone. 'I punched him.'

'Once?'

'There was no need to do it again.'

'I see.' Leddravohr's inhumanly smooth face was enigmatic. 'Is it true that you have made several attempts to enter military service?'

'It is true, Prince.'

'In that case I have good news for you, Maraquine,' Leddravohr said. 'You are now in the army. I promise you that you will have many opportunities to satisfy your troublesome warlike urges in Chamteth. Report to the Mithold Barracks at dawn.'

Leddravohr turned away without waiting for a reply and began a murmured conversation with Chakkell. Toller remained as he was, his back still pressed to the wall, as he tried to control the seething of his thoughts. Despite his ungovernable temper he had taken human life only once before, when he had been set upon by thieves in a dark street in the Flylien district of Ro-Atabri and had left two of them dead. He had not even seen their faces and the incident had left him unaffected, but in the case of Zotiern he could still feel the appalling crunch of vertebrae and still could see the terrified eyes. The fact that he had not killed the man outright only made the event more traumatic – Zotiern had had a subjective eternity, helpless as a broken insect, in which to anticipate the final sword thrust. Toller had been floundering, trying to come to terms with his emotions, when Leddravohr had delivered his verbal bombshell, and now the universe was a chaos of tumbling fragments.

'Prince Chakkell and I will retire to a separate room with Lain Maraquine,' Leddravohr announced. 'We are not to be disturbed.'

Glo signalled for Toller to come to his side. 'We have everything ready for you, Prince. May I suggest that ...?'

'Suggest nothing, Lord Cripple – your presence is not required at this stage.' Leddravohr's face was expressionless as he looked at Glo, as though he were not even worthy of contempt. 'You will remain here in case I have reason to summon you later – though I confess I find it difficult to imagine your ever being of any value to anybody.' Leddravohr directed his cold gaze at Lain. 'Where?'

'This way, Prince.' Lain spoke in a low voice and he was visibly quaking as he moved towards the stair. He was followed by Leddravohr and Chakkell. As soon as they had passed out of sight on the upper floor Gesalla fled from the hall, leaving Toller alone with Glo and Fera. Only a few minutes had passed since they had been together in the dayroom, and yet they now breathed different air, inhabited a different world. Toller sensed he would not feel the full impact of the change until later.

'Help me back to my ... hmm ... seat, my boy,' Glo said. He remained silent until installed in the same chair in the dayroom, then looked up at Toller with a shamefaced smile. 'Life never ceases to be interesting, does it?'

'I'm sorry, my lord.' Toller tried to find appropriate words. 'There was nothing I could do.'

'Don't fret. You came out of it well – though I fear it wasn't in Leddravohr's mind to do you a favour when he inducted you into his service.'

'I don't understand it. When he was walking towards me I thought he was going to kill me himself.'

'I'll be sorry to lose you.'

'What about me?' Fera said. 'Has anybody thought about what's going to happen to me?'

Toller recalled his earlier exasperation with her. 'You may not have noticed, but we have all been given other things to think about.'

'There is no need for you to worry,' Glo said to her. 'You may remain at the Peel for as long as you ... hmm ... wish.'

'Thank you, my lord. I wish I could go there now.'

'So do I, my dear, but I'm afraid it's out of the question. None of us is free to leave until dismissed by the prince. That is the custom.'

'Custom!' Fera's dissatisfied gaze travelled the room before settling on Toller. 'Wrong moment!'

He turned his back on her, unwilling to confront the enigma of the feminine mind, and went to stand at a window. *The man I killed needed to be killed*, he told himself, *so I'm not going to brood about it*. He turned his thoughts to the mystery of Leddravohr's behaviour. Glo was quite right – the prince had not acted out of benignancy when summarily making him a soldier. There was little doubt that he hoped for Toller to be killed in battle, but why had he not seized the opportunity to take revenge in person? He could easily have sided with Chakkell over the death of the equerry and that would have been the end of the matter. Leddravohr was capable of spinning out the destruction of someone who had crossed him so that he could derive maximum satisfaction from it, but surely that would be placing too much importance on an obscure member of a philosophy family.

The thought of his own background reminded Toller of the astonishing fact that he was now in the army, and the realisation struck him with as much or more force than Leddravohr's original pronouncement. It was ironic that the ambition he had cherished for much of his life should have been achieved in such a bizarre fashion and just at a time when he was beginning to put such ideas behind him. What was going to happen to him after he reported to the Mithold Barracks in the morning? It was disconcerting to find that he had no coherent vision of his future, that beyond the coming night the pattern broke up into shards ... bitty reflections ... Leddravohr ... the army ... Chamteth ... the migration flight ... Overland ... the unknown swirling into the unknown ...

A gentle snore from behind him told Toller that Glo had gone to sleep. He left it to Fera to ensure that Glo was comfortable and continued staring through the window. The enveloping ptertha screens interfered with the view of Overland, but he could see the progression of the terminator across the great disk. When it reached the halfway mark, dividing the sister world into hemispheres of equal size but unequal brightness, the sun would be on the horizon.

A short time before that point was reached Prince Chakkell emerged from the lengthy conference and departed for his residence in the Tannoffern Palace, which lay to the east of the Great Palace. Now that the main streets of Ro-Atabri were virtually tunnels it would have been possible for him to stay longer in the Square House, but Chakkell was known for his devotion to his wife and children. After he and his retinue had left there was complete silence in the precinct, a reminder that Leddravohr had come to the meeting unaccompanied. The military prince was noted for travelling everywhere alone – partly, it was said, because of his impatience with attendants, but mainly because he scorned the use of guards. He was confident in his belief that his reputation and his own battle sword were all the protection he needed in any city of the empire.

Toller had hoped that Leddravohr would leave soon after Chakkell, but hour after hour went by with no sign of the discussion coming to an end. It appeared that Leddravohr was determined to absorb as much aeronautical knowledge as was possible in a very short time.

The weight-driven glasswood clock on the wall was showing the hour of ten when a servant arrived with platters of simple food, mainly fishcakes and bread. There was also a note of apology from Gesalla, who was too ill to perform the normal duties of hostess. Fera had been waiting for a substantial spread and was theatrically shocked when Glo explained that no formal meal could be served unless Leddravohr chose to go to table. She ate most of what was available single-handed, then dropped into a chair in a corner and pretended to sleep. Glo alternated between trying to read in the unsatisfactory light from the sconces and staring grimly into the distance. Toller received the impression that his self-esteem had been irreparably damaged by Leddravohr's casual cruelty.

It was almost the eleventh hour when Lain walked into the room. He said, 'Please return to the hall, my lord.'

Glo raised his head with a start. 'So the prince has finally decided to leave.'

'No.' Lain seemed slightly bewildered. 'I think the prince is going to do me the honour of staying the night in my home. We must present ourselves now. You and your wife as well, Toller.'

Toller was at a loss to explain Leddravohr's unusual decision as he raised Glo to his feet and helped him to leave the room. In normal times and circumstances it would indeed have been a great honour for a royal to sleep in the Square House, especially as the palaces were within easy reach, but Leddravohr hardly wanted to be gracious. Gesalla was already waiting near the foot of the stair, holding herself tall and straight in spite of her obvious weakness. The others formed a line with her – Glo at the centre, flanked by Lain and Toller – and waited for Leddravohr to appear.

There was a delay of several minutes before the military prince came to the head of the stair. He was eating the leg of a roast quickfowl, and added to the discourtesy by continuing to gnaw at the bone in silence until it was stripped of all flesh. Toller began to get sombre premonitions. Leddravohr threw the bone to the floor, wiped his lips with the back of a hand and slowly came down the stairs. He was still wearing his sword – another incivility – and his smooth face showed no sign of tiredness.

'Well, Lord Glo, it appears I have needlessly kept you here all day.' Leddravohr's tone made it clear that he was not apologising. 'I have learned most of what I need to know and will be able to finish here in the morning. Many other matters demand my attention, so to avoid wasting time in travelling back and forth to the palace I will sleep here tonight. You will be in attendance at the sixth hour. I take it you *can* bestir yourself by that time?'

'I shall be here at the sixth hour, Prince,' Glo said.

'That is good to know,' Leddravohr replied, jovially sarcastic. He strolled along the line, paused when he reached Toller and Fera, and produced the instantaneous smile which had nothing to do with humour. Toller faced him as woodenly as possible, his foreboding turning into a certainty that a day which had begun badly was going to end badly. Leddravohr turned off his smile, walked back to the stair and began to ascend. Toller was beginning to wonder if his premonitions could have been groundless when Leddravohr halted on the third step.

'What is this?' he mused, keeping his back to the attentive group. 'My brain is weary, and yet my body craves activity. There is a decision to be made here – shall I have a woman, or shall I not?'

Toller, already knowing the answer to Leddravohr's rhetorical question, brought his mouth close to Fera's ear. 'This is my fault,' he whispered. 'Leddravohr hates better than I knew. He wants to use you as a weapon against me, and there is nothing we can do about it. You'll just have to go with him.'

'We'll see,' Fera said, her composure unaffected.

Leddravohr drummed his fingers on the balustrade, prolonging the moment, then turned to face the hall. 'You,' he said, pointing at Gesalla. 'Come with me.'

'But ...!' Toller took one step forward, breaking the line, his body a pounding column of blood. He gazed in helpless outrage at Gesalla as she touched Lain's hand and walked towards the stair with a strange floating movement as though tranced and not really aware of what was happening. Her beautiful face was almost luminescent in its pallor. Leddravohr went ahead of her and the two were lost in the flickering dimness of the upper floor.

Toller wheeled on his brother. 'That's your wife – and she's pregnant!'

'Thank you for that information,' Lain said in a dead voice, regarding Lain with dead eyes.

'But this is all *wrong!*'

'It's the Kolcorronian way.' Incredibly, Lain was able to fashion his lips into a smile. 'It is part of the reason we are despised by every other nation in the world.'

'Who cares about the other ...?' Toller became aware that Fera, hands on hips, was staring at him with undisguised fury. 'What's the matter with you?'

'Perhaps if you had stripped me naked and thrown me at the prince things would have worked out more to your liking,' Fera said in a low hard voice.

'What do you mean?'

'I mean you couldn't wait to see me go with him.'

'You don't understand,' Toller protested. 'I thought Leddravohr wanted to punish *me.*'

'That's exactly what he ...' Fera broke off to glance at Lain, then returned her attention to Toller. 'You're a fool, Toller Maraquine. I wish I had never met you.' She spun on her heel, suddenly haughty in a way he had never seen before, walked quickly back into the dayroom and slammed the door.

Toller gaped after her for a moment, baffled, then paced an urgent circle around the hall and came back to Lain and Glo. The latter, looking more exhausted and frail than ever, had clasped Lain's hand.

'What would you like me to do, my boy?' he said gently. 'I could return to the Peel if you want the privacy.'

Lain shook his head. 'No, my lord. It is very late. If you will do me the honour of staying here I will have a suite prepared for you.'

'Very well.' As Lain left to instruct the servants Glo turned his large head in Toller's direction. 'You're not helping your brother with all your running about like a caged animal.'

'I don't understand him,' Toller muttered. 'Somebody should *do* something.'

'What would you ... hmm ... suggest?'

'I don't know. *Something.*'

'Would it improve Gesalla's lot if Lain were to get himself killed?'

'Perhaps,' Toller said, refusing to entertain logic. 'She could at least be proud of him.'

Glo sighed. 'Help me to a chair, and then fetch me a glass of something with heat in it. Kailian black.'

'Wine?' Toller was surprised despite his mental turmoil. 'You want wine?'

'You said somebody should do something, and that's what I'm going to do,' Glo said evenly. 'You will have to dance to your own music.'

Toller help Glo to a high-backed chair at the side of the hall and went to obtain a beaker of wine, his mind oppressed with the problem of how to reconcile himself to the intolerable. The mode of thought was unnatural for him and it seemed a long time before inspiration came. *Leddravohr is only playing with us,* he decided, seizing the thread of hope. *Gesalla can't be to the taste of one who is accustomed to trained courtesans. Leddravohr is only detaining her in his room, laughing at us. In fact, he can express his contempt all the better by scorning to touch any of our women ...*

In the hour that followed Glo drank four large bumpers of wine, rendering himself crimson of face and almost totally helpless. Lain had retired to the solitude of his study, still betraying no trace of emotion, and Toller was dejected when Glo announced his desire to go to bed. He knew he would not sleep and had no desire to be alone with his thoughts. He half carried Glo to the assigned suite and helped him through all the tedious procedures of toilet and getting to bed, then came into the long transverse corridor which linked the principal sleeping quarters. There was a whisper of sound to his left.

He turned and saw Gesalla walking towards him on the way to her own rooms. Her black garments, long and drifting, and blanched face gave her a spectral appearance, but her bearing was erect and dignified. She was the same Gesalla Maraquine he had always known – cool, private and indomitable – and at the sight of her he experienced a pang of mingled concern and relief.

'Gesalla,' he said, moving towards her, 'are you ...?'

'Don't come near me,' she snapped with a look of slit-eyed venom and walked past him without altering her step. Dismayed by the sheer loathing in her voice, he watched until she had passed out of view, then his gaze was drawn to the pale mosaic floor. The trail of bloody footprints told a story more dreadful than any he had tried to banish from his mind.

Leddravohr, oh Leddravohr, oh Leddravohr, he chanted inwardly. *We are wedded now, you and I. You have given yourself to me ... and only a death will set us apart.*

CHAPTER TEN

The decision to attack Chamteth from the west was taken for geographical reasons.

At the western limits of the Kolcorronian empire, somewhat north of the equator, was a chain of volcanic islets which ended in a low-lying triangle of land about eight miles on a side. Known as Oldock, the uninhabited island had several features which were of strategic importance to Kolcorron. One was that it was close enough to Chamteth to form an excellent jumping-off point for a sea-borne invasion force; another was that it was thickly covered with rafter and tallon trees, two species which grew to a great height and offered good protection against ptertha.

The fact that Oldock and the whole Fairondes chain lay in a prevailing westerly air stream was also advantageous to Kolcorron's five armies. Although the troop ships were slowed down and airships forced to make extensive use of their jets, the steady wind blowing across open seas had a greater effect on the ptertha, making it almost impossible for them to get within range of their prey. Telescopes showed the livid globes swarming in high-altitude contraflows but they were for the most part swept away to the east when they tried to penetrate lower levels of the atmosphere. When planning the invasion the Kolcorronian high command had allowed for up to one sixth of their personnel being lost to ptertha, whereas the actual casualties were negligible.

As the armies progressed westward there was a gradual but perceptible change in the patterns of night and day. Foreday grew shorter and aftday longer as Overland drifted away from the zenith and approached the eastern horizon. Eventually foreday was reduced to a brief dazzle of prismatics as the sun crossed the narrow gap between the horizon and Overland's disk, and soon after that the sister world was nesting on Land's eastern rim. Littlenight became a short extension of night, and there was a heightened sense of expectancy among the invaders as the celestial evidence told them they were entering the Land of the Long Days.

The establishment of a beachhead on Chamteth itself was another phase of the operation in which considerable losses had been expected, and the Kolcorronian commanders could scarcely believe their good fortune when they found the tree-covered strands unwatched and undefended.

The three widely separated invasion prongs met no resistance whatsoever, converging and consolidating without a single casualty apart from the accidental fatalities and injuries which are inevitable when large masses of men and matériel enter an alien territory. Almost at once brakka groves were found among the other types of forestation, and within a day bands of naked slimers were at work behind the advancing military. The sacks of green and purple crystals gutted from the brakka were loaded on to separate cargo ships – large quantities of pikon and halvell were never transported together – and in an incredibly short time the first steps had been taken to initiate a supply chain reaching all the way back to Ro-Atabri.

Aerial reconnaissance was ruled out for the time being, because airships were too conspicuous, but with ancient maps to guide them the invaders were able to push westwards at a steady pace. The terrain was swampy in places, infested with poisonous snakes, but presented no serious obstacles to well-trained soldiers whose morale and physical condition were at a high level.

It was on the twelfth day that a scout patrol noticed an airship of unfamiliar design scudding silently across the sky ahead of them.

By that time the vanguard of the Third Army was emerging from the waterlogged littoral and was reaching higher ground characterised by a series of drumlins running from north to south. Trees and other kinds of vegetation were more sparse here. It was the type of ground on which an unopposed army could have made excellent progress – but the first of the Chamtethan defenders were lying in wait.

They were swarthy men, long-muscled and black-bearded, wearing flexible armour made from small flakes of brakka sewn together like fish scales, and they fell on the invaders with a ferocity which even the most seasoned Kolcorronians had never encountered before. Some of them appeared to be suicide groups, sent in to cause maximum damage and disarray, creating diversions which enabled others to set up attacks using a variety of long-range weapons – cannon, mortars and mechanical catapults which hurled pikon-halvell bombs.

The Kolcorronian crack troops, veterans of many frontier engagements, destroyed the Chamtethans in the course of a diffuse, multi-centred battle which lasted almost the entire day. It was found that fewer than a hundred men had died, compared with more than twice that number of the enemy, and when the following day had passed without further incident the spirits of the invaders were again at a peak.

From that stage onwards, with secrecy no longer possible, the line soldiers were preceded by an air cover of bombers and surveillance ships, and the men on the ground were reassured by the sight of the elliptical craft patterning the sky ahead.

Their commanders were less complacent, however, knowing they had encountered only a local defence force, that intelligence concerning the invasion had been flashed to the heart of Chamteth, and that the might of a huge continent was being drawn up against them.

CHAPTER ELEVEN

General Risdel Dalacott uncorked the tiny poison bottle and smelled its contents.

The clear fluid had a curious aroma, honeyed and peppery at the same time. It was a distillation of extracts of maidenfriend, the herb which when chewed regularly by women prevented them from conceiving children. In its concentrated form it was even more inimical to life, providing a gentle, painless and absolutely certain escape from all the troubles of the flesh. It was greatly treasured among those of the Kolcorronian aristocracy who had no taste for the more honourable but very bloody traditional methods of committing suicide.

Dalacott emptied the bottle into his cup of wine and, after only the slightest hesitation, took a tentative sip. The poison was scarcely detectable and might even have been said to have improved the rough wine, adding a hint of spicy sweetness to it. He took another sip and set the cup aside, not wishing to slip away too quickly. There was a final self-imposed duty he had yet to perform.

He looked around his tent, which was furnished with only a narrow bed, a trunk, his portable desk and some folding chairs on straw matting. Other officers of staff rank liked to surround themselves with luxury to ease the rigours of campaign, but that had never been Dalacott's way. He had always been a soldier and had lived as a soldier should, and the reason he was choosing to die by poison instead of the blade was that he no longer regarded himself as worthy of a soldier's death.

It was dim inside the tent, the only light coming from a single military field lantern of the type which fuelled itself by attracting oilbugs. He lit a second lantern and placed it on his desk, still finding it a little strange that such measures should be necessary for reading at night. This far west in Chamteth, across the Orange River, Overland was out of sight beneath the horizon and the diurnal cycle consisted of twelve hours of uninterrupted daylight followed by twelve hours of unrelieved darkness. Had Kolcorron been in this hemisphere its scientists would probably have devised an efficient lighting system long ago.

Dalacott raised the lid of his desk and took out the last volume of his diary, the one for the year 2629. It was bound in limp green leather and had a separate sheet for each day of the year. He opened the book and slowly turned its pages, compacting the entire Chamteth campaign into a matter of minutes, picking out the key events which – insensibly at first – had led to his personal disintegration as a soldier and as a man ...

DAY 84. *Prince Leddravohr was in a strange mood at the staff conference today. I sensed that he was keyed-up and elated, in spite of the news of heavy losses on the southern front. Time and time again he made reference to the fact that ptertha appear to be so few in this part of Land. He is not given to confiding his innermost thoughts, but by piecing together fragmentary and oblique remarks I received the impression that he entertained visions of persuading the King to abandon the whole idea of migrating to Overland.*

His rationale seemed to be that such desperate measures would be unnecessary if it were established that, for some unguessable reason, conditions in the Land of the Long Days were unfavourable to ptertha. That being the case, it would only be necessary for Kolcorron to subjugate Chamteth and transfer the seat of power and the remaining population to this continent – a much more logical and natural process than trying to reach another planet...

DAY 93. *The war is going badly. These people are determined, brave and gifted fighters. I cannot bring myself to contemplate the possibility of our eventual defeat, but the truth is that we would have been severely tested in going against Chamteth even in the days when we could have fielded close on a million fully trained men. Today we have only a third of that number, an uncomfortably high proportion of them raw conscripts, and we are going to need luck in addition to all our skill and courage if the war is to be successfully prosecuted.*

An important factor in our favour is that this country is so rich in resources, particularly in brakka and edible crops. The sound of brakka pollination discharges is constantly being mistaken by my men for enemy cannon fire or bombs, and we have an abundance of power crystals for our heavy weaponry. There is no difficulty in keeping the armies well fed, in spite of the Chamtethans' efforts to burn the crops they are forced to abandon.

The Chamtethan women, and even quite small children, will indulge in that form of destruction if left to their own devices. With our manpower stretched to the limit, we are unable to divert combat troops into guard duties and for that reason Leddravohr has decreed that we take no prisoners, regardless of age or sex.

It is sound military thinking, but I have been sickened by the amount of butchery I have witnessed of late. Even the most hardened of the soldiery go about their business with set grey faces, and in the encampments at night there is a contrived and unnatural quality to the little merriment that one overhears.

This is a seditious thought, one I would not express anywhere except in the privacy of these pages, but it is one thing to spread the benefits of the empire to unenlightened and squabbling tribes – and quite another to undertake the annihilation of a great nation whose sole offence was to husband its resources of brakka.

I have never had time for religion, but now – for the first time – I am beginning to comprehend the meaning of the word 'sin'...

Dalacott paused in his reading and picked up the enamelled cup of wine. He stared into its beaded depths for a moment, resisting the urge to drink deeply, then took a controlled sip. So many people seemed to be calling to him from the far side of that barrier which separated the living from the dead – his wife Toriane, Aytha Maraquine, his son Oderan, Conna Dalacott and little Hallie...

Why had he been chosen to go on and on for more than seventy years, with the false blessing of the immunity, when others could have made much better use of the gift of life?

Without any conscious thought on his part, Dalacott's right hand slipped into a pocket and located the curious object he had found on the banks of the Bes-Undar all those years ago. He stroked his thumb in a circular motion over its mirrorlike surface as he again began to turn the pages of his diary.

DAY 102. *How does one account for the machinations of fate?*

This morning, after having put off doing so for many days, I began signing the sheaf of award citations on my desk and discovered that my own son – Toller Maraquine – is serving as an ordinary soldier in one of the regiments directly under my control!

It appears that he has been recommended for valour disks no less than three times in spite of the brevity of his service and lack of formal training. In theory a conscript, as he must be, should not be spending so much time in the front line, but perhaps the Maraquine family has used its intimate connections with the court to enable Toller to advance his belated military career. This is something I must enquire into if I ever have some freedom from the pressures of my command.

Truly these are changed times, when the military caste not only calls upon outsiders to swell its ranks, but catapults them into the utmost danger and what passes for glory.

I will do my best to see my son, if it can be arranged without exciting suspicion in him and comment from others. A meeting with Toller would be the one gleam of brightness in the deepnight of this criminal war.

DAY 103. *A company of the 8th Battalion was completely overrun in a surprise attack today in sector C11. Only a handful of men escaped the slaughter and many of those were so severely wounded that there was no option for them but the Bright Road. Disasters like that are becoming almost commonplace, so much so that I find myself more preoccupied with the reports which arrived this morning suggesting that our respite from the ptertha will soon come to an end.*

Telescopic observations from airships as far east from here as the Loongl Peninsula revealed some days ago that large numbers of ptertha were drifting south across the equator. The sightings have been patchy, because we have few ships in the Fyallon Ocean at present, but the opinion of scientists seems to be that the ptertha were moving south to take advantage of a 'wind cell' which would carry them west for a great distance and then north again into Chamteth.

I have never subscribed to the theory that the globes possess a rudimentary intelligence, but if they really are capable of such behaviour – i.e. making use of global weather patterns – the conclusion that they have a malign purpose is almost inescapable. Perhaps, like ants and some similar creatures, their kind as a whole has some form of composite mind, although individuals are quite incapable of mentation.

DAY 106. *Leddravohr's dream of a Kolcorron free from the scourge of the ptertha has come to an abrupt end. The globes have been sighted by fleet auxiliaries of the First Army. They are approaching the south coast in the Adrian region.*

There has also been a curious report, as yet unconfirmed, from my own theatre.

Two line soldiers in a forward area claim that they saw a ptertha which was pale pink. According to their story the globe came to within forty or so paces of their position, but showed no inclination to draw nearer and eventually rose and drifted away to the west. What is one to make of such strange accounts? Could it be that two battle-weary soldiers are conniving to obtain a few days of interrogation in the safety of the base camp?

DAY 107. *Today – although I take little pride or pleasure in the accomplishment – I justified Prince Leddravohr's confidence in my abilities as a tactician.*

The splendid achievement, perhaps the culmination of my military career, began with my making the kind of mistake which would have been avoided by a green lieutenant straight out of academy.

It all began in the eighth hour when I became impatient with Captain Kadal over his tardiness in taking a stretch of open ground in sector D14. His reason for hanging back in the security of the forest was that his hastily prepared aerial map showed the territory to be traversed by several streams, and he believed them to be deep gullies capable of concealing sizable numbers of the enemy. Kadal is a competent officer, and I should have left him to scout the ground in his own way, but I feared that numerous setbacks were making him timorous, and I was overcome by a foolhardy desire to set an example to him and the men.

Accordingly, I took a sergeant and a dozen mounted soldiers and rode forward with them in person. The terrain was well suited to the bluehorns and we covered the ground quickly. Too quickly!

At a distance of perhaps a mile from our lines the sergeant became visibly uneasy, but I was too puffed up with success to pay him any heed. We had crossed two streams which were, as indicated on the map, too shallow to provide any kind of cover, and I became inflamed with a vision of myself casually presenting the whole area to Kadal as a prize I had won on his behalf with my boldness.

Before I knew it we had advanced close on two miles and even in my fit of megalomania I was beginning to hear the nagging voice of common sense warning me that enough was enough, especially as we had crossed a vestigial ridge and were no longer in sight of our own lines.

That was when the Chamtethans made their appearance.

They sprang up from the ground on both sides as if by magic, though of course there was no sorcery involved – they had been hiding in the very gullies whose existence I had blithely set out to disprove. There were at least two hundred, looking like black reptiles in their brakka armour. Had their force been composed solely of infantry we could have outrun them, but a good quarter of their number were mounted and were already racing to block off our retreat.

I became aware of my men staring at me expectantly, and the fact that there was no sign of reproach in their eyes made my personal position all the worse. I had thrown away their lives with my overweening pride and stupidity, and all they asked of me in that terrible moment was a decision as to where and how they should die!

I looked all about and saw a tree-covered mound several furlongs ahead of us. It would afford some protection and there was a possibility that from high up in one of the trees we would be able to get a sunwriter message back to Kadal and call for help.

I gave the necessary order and we rode with all speed to the mound, fortuitously surprising the Chamtethans, who had expected us to flee in the opposite direction. We reached the trees well ahead of our pursuers, who in any case were in no particular hurry. Time was on their side, and it was all too clear to me that even if we did succeed in communicating with Kadal it would be to no avail.

While one of the men was beginning to climb a tree with the sunwriter slung on his belt I used my field glasses in an attempt to locate the Chamtethan commander, to see if I could divine his intention. If he was cognisant of my rank he might try to take me alive – and that was something I could not have permitted. It was while sweeping the line of Chamtethan soldiers with the powerful glasses that I saw something which, even at that time of high peril, produced in me a spasm of dread.

Ptertha!

Four of the purple-tinted globes were approaching from the south, borne on the light breeze, skimming over the grass. They were plainly visible to the enemy – I saw several men point at them – but to my surprise no defensive action was taken. I saw the globes come closer and closer to the Chamtethans and – such is the power of reflex – I had to stifle the urge to shout a warning. The foremost of the globes reached the line of soldiers and abruptly ceased to exist, having burst among them.

Still no defensive or evasive action was taken. I even saw one soldier casually slash at a ptertha with his sword. In a matter of seconds the four globes had disintegrated, shedding their charges of deadly dust among the enemy, who appeared to be quite uncaring.

If what had happened up to that point was surprising, the aftermath was even more so.

The Chamtethans were in the process of spreading out to form a circle around our inadequate little fortress when I saw the beginnings of a commotion among their ranks. My glasses showed that some of the black-armoured soldiers had fallen. Already! Their comrades were kneeling beside them to render aid and – within the space of several breaths – they too were sprawling and writhing on the ground!

The sergeant came to my side and said, 'Sir, the corporal says he can see our lines. What message do you want to send?'

'Wait!' I elevated my glasses slightly to take in the middle distance and after a moment picked out other ptertha weaving and wavering above the grasslands. 'Instruct him to inform Captain Kadal that we have encountered a large detachment of the enemy, but that he is to remain where he is. He is not to advance until I send a further command.'

The sergeant was too well disciplined to venture a protest, but his perplexity was evident as he hurried away to transmit my orders. I resumed my surveillance of the Chamtethans. By that time there was a general awareness that something was terribly amiss, evidenced by the manner in which the soldiers were running here and there in panic and confusion. Men who had begun to advance on our position turned and – not understanding that their sole hope of survival lay in fleeing the scene – re-joined the main body of their force. I watched with a clammy coldness in my gut as they too began to stagger and fall.

There were gasps of wonderment from behind me as my own men, even with unaided vision, took in the fact that the Chamtethans were swiftly being destroyed by some awesome and invisible agency. In a frighteningly short space of time every last one of the enemy had gone down, and nothing was moving on the plain save groups of bluehorns which had begun to graze unconcernedly among the bodies of their masters. (Why is it that all members of the animal kingdom, apart from types of simian, are immune to ptertha poison?)

When I had taken my fill of the dread scene I turned and almost laughed aloud as I saw that my men were gazing at me with a mixture of relief, respect and adoration. They had believed themselves doomed, and now – such are the workings of the common soldier's mind – their gratitude for being spared was being focussed on me, as though their deliverance had been won through some masterly strategy on my part. They seemed to have no thought at all for the wider implications of what had occurred.

Three years earlier Kolcorron had been brought to its knees by a sudden malevolent change in the nature of our age-old foe, the ptertha, and now it appeared that there had been another and greater escalation of the globes' evil powers. The new form of pterthacosis – for nothing else could have struck down the Chamtethans – which killed a man in seconds instead of hours was a grim portent of dark days ahead of us.

I relayed a message to Kadal, warning him to keep within the forest and to be on the alert for ptertha, then returned to my vigil. The glasses showed some ptertha in groups of two or three drifting on the southerly breeze. We were reasonably safe from them, thanks to the protection of the trees, but I waited for some time and made sure the sky was absolutely clear before giving the order to retrieve our bluehorns and to return to our own lines at maximum speed.

DAY 109. It transpires that I was quite wrong about a new and intensified threat from the ptertha.

Leddravohr has arrived at the truth by a characteristically direct method. He had a group of Chamtethan men and women tied to stakes on a patch of open ground, and beside them he placed a group of our own wounded, men who had little hope of recovery. Eventually they were found by drifting ptertha, and the outcome was witnessed through telescopes. The Kolcorronians, in spite of their weakened condition, took two hours to succumb to pterthacosis – but the hapless Chamtethans died almost immediately.

Why does this strange anomaly exist?

One theory I have heard is that the Chamtethans as a race have a certain inherited weakness which renders them highly vulnerable to pterthacosis, but I believe that the real explanation is the much more complicated one advanced by our medical advisors. It depends on there being two distinct varieties of ptertha – the blackish-purple type known of old to Kolcorron, which is highly venomous; and a pink type indigenous to Chamteth, which is harmless or relatively so. (The sighting of a pink globe in this area turns out to have been duplicated many times elsewhere.)

The theory further states that in centuries of warfare against the ptertha, in which millions of the globes have been destroyed, the entire population of Kolcorron has been exposed to microscopic quantities of the toxic dust. This has given us some slight degree of tolerance for the poison, increased our resistance to it, by a mechanism similar to the one which ensures that some diseases can be contracted only once. The Chamtethans, on the other hand, have no resistance whatsoever, and an encounter with a poisonous ptertha is even more catastrophic for them than it is for us.

One experiment which would go a long way towards proving the second theory would be to expose groups of Kolcorronians and Chamtethans to pink ptertha. No doubt Leddravohr will duly arrange for the experiment to be carried out if we enter a region where the pink globes are plentiful.

Dalacott broke off from his reading and glanced at the time-piece strapped to his wrist. It was of the type based on a toughened glass tube, preferred by the military in the absence of a compact and reliable chronometer. The pace beetle inside it was nearing the eighth division of the graduated cane shoot. The time of his final appointment was almost at hand.

He took a further measured sip of his wine and turned to the last entry in the diary. It had been made many days earlier, and after its completion he had abandoned the habit of a lifetime by ceasing to record each day's activities and thoughts.

In a way that had been a symbolic suicide, preparing him for tonight's actuality ...

DAY 114. *The war is over.*

The ptertha plague has done our work for us.

In the space of only six days since the purple ptertha made their appearance in Chamteth the plague has raged the length and breadth of the continent, sweeping away its inhabitants in their millions. A swift and casual genocide!

We no longer have to progress on foot, fighting our way yard by yard against a dedicated enemy. Instead, we advance by airship, with our jets on continuous thrust. Travelling in that manner uses up large quantities of power crystals – both in the propulsion tubes and the anti-ptertha cannon – but such considerations are no longer important.

We are the proud possessors of an entire continent of mature brakka and veritable mountains of the green and purple. We share our riches with none. Leddravohr has not rescinded his order to take no prisoners, and the isolated handfuls of bewildered and demoralised Chamtethans we encounter are put to the sword.

I have flown over cities, towns and villages and farmlands where nothing lives except for wandering domestic animals. The architecture is impressive – clean, well-proportioned, dignified – but one has to admire it from afar. The stench of rotting corpses reaches high into the sky.

> *We are soldiers no longer.*
> *We are the carriers of pestilence.*
> *We ARE pestilence.*
> *I have nothing more to say.*

CHAPTER TWELVE

The night sky, although it had much less overall brightness than in Kolcorron, was spanned by a huge spiral of misty light, the arms of which sparkled with brilliant stars of white, blue and yellow. That wheel was flanked by two large elliptical spirals, and the rest of the celestial canopy was generously dappled with small whirlpools, wisps and patches of radiance, plus the glowing plumes of a number of comets. Although the Tree was not visible, the sky was overlaid with a field of major stars whose intensity made them seem closer than all the other heavenly objects, imparting a sense of depth to the display.

Toller was only accustomed to seeing those configurations when Land was at the opposite side of its path around the sun, at which time they were dominated and dimmed by the great disk of Overland. He stood unmoving in the dusk, watching starry reflections tremble on the broad quiet waters of the Orange River. All about him the myriad subdued lights of the Third Army's headquarters glowed through the tree lanes of the forest, the days of open encampments having passed with the advent of the ptertha plague.

One question had been on his mind all day: *Why should General Dalacott want a private interview with me?*

He had spent several days of idleness at a transit camp twenty miles to the west – part of an army which, suddenly, had no work to do – and had been trying to adapt to the new pace of life when the battalion commander had ordered him to report to headquarters. On arrival he had been examined briefly by several officers, one of whom he thought might be Vorict, the adjutant-general. He had been told that General Dalacott wished to present him with valour disks in person. The various officers had plainly been puzzled by the unusual arrangement, and had discreetly pumped Toller for information before accepting that he was as unenlightened about the matter as they.

A young captain emerged from the nearby administrative enclosure, approached Toller through the spangled dimness and said, 'Lieutenant Maraquine, the general will see you now.'

Toller saluted and went with the officer to a tent which, unexpectedly, was quite small and unadorned. The captain ushered him in and quickly departed. Toller stood at attention before a lean, austere-looking man who was seated at a portable desk. In the weak light from two field lanterns the general's cropped hair could either have been white or blond, and he looked surprisingly young for a man with fifty years of distinguished service. Only his eyes seemed old, eyes which had seen more than was compatible with the ability to dream.

'Sit down, son,' he said. 'This is a purely informal meeting.'

'Thank you, sir.' Toller took the indicated chair, his mystification growing.

'I see from your records that you entered the army less than a year ago as an ordinary line soldier. I know these are changed times, but wasn't that unusual for a man of your social status?'

'It was specially arranged by Prince Leddravohr.'

'Is Leddravohr a friend of yours?'

Encouraged by the general's forthright but amiable manner, Toller ventured a wry smile. 'I cannot claim that honour, sir.'

'Good!' Dalacott smiled in return. 'So you achieved the rank of lieutenant in less than a year through your own efforts.'

'It was a field commission, sir. It may not be given full endorsement.'

'It will.' Dalacott paused to sip from an enamelled cup. 'Forgive me for not offering you refreshment – this is an exotic brew and I doubt if it would be to your taste.'

'I'm not thirsty, sir.'

'Perhaps you would like these instead.' Dalacott opened a compartment in his desk and took out three valour disks. They were circular flakes of brakka inlaid with white and red glass. He handed them to Toller and sat back to view his reactions.

'Thank you.' Toller fingered the disks and put them away in a pocket. 'I'm honoured.'

'You disguise the fact quite well.'

Toller was embarrassed and disconcerted. 'Sir, I didn't intend any ...'

'It's all right, son,' Dalacott said. 'Tell me, is army life not what you expected?'

'Since I was a child I have dreamed of being a warrior, but ...'

'You were prepared to wipe an opponent's blood from your sword, but you didn't realise there would be smears of his dinner as well.'

Toller met the general's gaze squarely. 'Sir, I don't understand why you brought me here.'

'I think it was to give you this.' Dalacott opened his right hand to reveal a small object which he dropped on to Toller's palm.

Toller was surprised by its weight, by the massy impact of it on his hand. He held the object closer to the light and was intrigued by the colour and lustre of its polished surface. The colour was unlike any he had seen before, white but somehow more than white, resembling the sea when the sun's rays were obliquely reflected from it at dawn. The object was rounded like a pebble, but might almost have been a miniature carving of a skull whose details had been worn away by time.

'What is it?' Toller said.

Dalacott shook his head. 'I don't know. Nobody knows. I found it in Redant province many years ago, on the banks of the Bes-Undar, and nobody has ever been able to tell me what it is.'

Toller closed his fingers around the warm object and found his thumb beginning to move in circles on the slick surface. 'One question leads to another, sir. Why do you want *me* to have this?'

'Because—' Dalacott gave him a strange smile – 'you might say it brought your mother and I together.'

'I see,' Toller said, speaking mechanically but not untruthfully as the general's words washed through his mind and, like a strong clear wave altering the aspect of a beach, rearranged memory fragments into new designs. The patterns were unfamiliar and yet not totally strange, because they had been inherent in the old order, needing only a single rippling disturbance to make them apparent. There was a long silence broken only by a faint popping sound as an oilbug blundered against a lamp's flame tube and slid down into the reservoir. Toller gazed solemnly at his father, trying to conjure up some appropriate emotion, but inside him there was only numbness.

'I don't know what to say to you,' he admitted finally. 'This has come so ... late.'

'Later than you think.' Again, Dalacott's expression was unreadable as he raised the cup of wine to his lips. 'I had many reasons – some of them not altogether selfish – for not acknowledging you, Toller. Do you bear me any ill will?'

'None, sir.'

'I'm glad.' Dalacott rose to his feet. 'We will not meet again, Toller. Will you embrace me ... once ... as a man embraces his father?'

'Father.' Toller stood up and clasped his arms around the sword-straight, elderly figure. During the brief period of contact he detected a curious hint of spices on his father's breath. He glanced down at the cup waiting on the desk, made a half-intuitive mental leap, and when they parted to resume their seats there was a prickling in his eyes.

Dalacott seemed calm, fully composed. 'Now, son, what comes next for you? Kolcorron and its new ally – the ptertha – have achieved their glorious victory. The soldiers' work is all but done, so what have you planned for your future?'

'I think I wasn't intended to have a future,' Toller said. 'There was a time when Leddravohr would have slain me in person, but something happened, something I don't understand. He placed me in the army and I believe it was his intention that the Chamtethans would do his work at a remove.'

'He has a great deal to occupy his thoughts and absorb his energies, you know,' the general said. 'An entire continent now has to be looted, merely as a preliminary to the building of Prad's migration fleet. Perhaps Leddravohr has forgotten you.'

'I haven't forgotten him.'

'Is it to the death?'

'I used to think so.' Toller thought of bloody footprints on pale mosaic, but the vision had become obscured, overlaid by hundreds of images of carnage. 'Now I doubt if the sword is the answer to anything.'

'I'm relieved to hear you say that. Even though Leddravohr's heart is not really in the migration plan, he is probably the best man to see it through to a successful conclusion. It is possible that the future of our race rests on his shoulders.'

'I'm aware of that possibility, father.'

'And you also feel you can solve your own problems perfectly well without my advice.' There was a wry twist to the general's lips. 'I think I would have enjoyed having you by me. Now, what about my original question? Have you no thought at all for your future?'

'I would like to pilot a ship to Overland,' Toller said. 'But I think it is a vain ambition.'

'Why? Your family must have influence.'

'My brother is the chief advisor on the design of the skyships, but he is almost as unpopular with Prince Leddravohr as I am.'

'Is it something you genuinely desire to do, this piloting of a skyship? Do you actually *want* to ascend thousands of miles into the heavens? With only a balloon and a few cords and scraps of wood to support you?'

Toller was surprised by the questions. 'Why not?'

'Truly, a new age brings forth new men,' Dalacott said softly, apparently speaking to himself, then his manner became brisk. 'You must go now – I have letters to write. I have some influence with Leddravohr, and a great deal of influence with Carranald, the head of Army Air Services. If you have the necessary aptitudes you will pilot a skyship.'

'Again, father, I don't know what to say.' Toller stood up, but was reluctant to leave. So much had happened in the space of only a few minutes and his inability to respond was filling him with a guilty sense of failure. How could he meet and say goodbye to his father in almost the same breath?

'You are not required to say anything, son. Only accept that I loved your mother, and ...' Dalacott broke off, looking surprised, and scanned the interior of the tent as though suspecting the presence of an intruder.

Toller was alarmed. 'Are you ill?'

'It's nothing. The night is too long and dark in this part of the world.'

'Perhaps if you lay down,' Toller said, starting forward.

General Risdel Dalacott halted him with a look. 'Leave me now, lieutenant.'

Toller saluted correctly and left the tent. As he was closing the entrance flap he saw that his father had picked up his pen and had already begun to write. Toller allowed the flap to fall and the triangle of wan illumination – an image seeping through the gauzy folds of probability, of lives unlived and of stories never to be told – swiftly vanished. He began to weep as he moved away through the star-canopied dimness. Deep wells of emotion were at last being tapped, and his tears were all the more copious for having come too late.

CHAPTER THIRTEEN

Night, as always, was the time of the ptertha.

Marnn Ibbler had been in the army since he was fifteen years old, and – like many long-serving soldiers – had developed a superb personal alarm system which told him when one of the globes was near. He was rarely conscious of maintaining vigilance, but at all times he had a full-circle awareness of his surroundings, and even when exhausted or drunk he knew as if by instinct when ptertha were drifting in his vicinity.

Thus it was that he became the first man to receive any inkling of yet another change in the nature and ways of his people's ancient enemy.

He was on night guard at the Third Army's great permanent base camp at Trompha in southern Middac. The duty was undemanding. Only a few ancillary units had been left behind when Kolcorron had invaded Chamteth; the base was close to the secure heartland of the empire, and nobody but a fool ventured abroad at night in open countryside.

Ibbler was standing with two young sentries who were complaining bitterly and at great length about food and pay. He secretly agreed with them about the former – never in his experience had army rations been so meagre and hard to stomach – but, as old soldiers do, he persistently capped every grievance of theirs with hardship stories from early campaigns. They were close to the inner screen, beyond which was a thirty-yard buffer zone and an outer screen. The fertile plains of Middac were visible through the open meshworks, stretching away to the western horizon, illuminated by a gibbous Overland.

There was supposed to be no movement in the outer gloaming – discounting the near-continuous flickering of shooting stars – so when Ibbler's finely attuned senses detected a subtle shifting of shade upon shade he knew at once that it was a ptertha. He did not even mention the sighting to his companions – they were safe behind the double barrier – and he continued the conversation as before, but a part of his consciousness was now engaged elsewhere.

A moment later he noticed a second ptertha, then a third, and within a minute he had picked out eight of the globes, all forming a single cluster. They were riding out on a gentle north-west breeze, and they faded from his vision some distance to his right where parallax merged the vertical strands of the mesh into a seemingly close-woven fabric.

Ibbler, watchful but still unconcerned, waited for the ptertha, to reappear in his field of view. On encountering the outer screen the globes, obeying the dictates of the air current, would nuzzle their way southwards along the camp's perimeter and eventually, having found no prey, would break free and float off towards the south-west coast and the Otollan Sea.

On this occasion, however, they seemed to be behaving unpredictably.

When minutes had passed without the globes becoming visible, Ibbler's young companions noticed that he had dropped out of the conversation. They were amused when he explained what was in his thoughts, deciding that the ptertha – assuming they had existed outside Ibbler's imagination – must have entered a rising air stream and gone over the camp's netted roofs. Anxious to avoid being classed as a nervous old woman, Ibbler allowed the matter to rest, even though it was rare for the ptertha to fly high when they were near humans.

On the following morning five diggers were found dead of pterthacosis in their hut. The soldier who blundered in on them also died, as did two others he ran to in his panic before the isolation drills were brought into force and all those thought to be contaminated were despatched along the Bright Road by archers.

It was Ibbler who noticed that the diggers' hut was close to and downwind of the point where the group of ptertha would have reached the perimeter on the night before. He secured an interview with his commanding officer and put forward the theory that the ptertha had destroyed themselves against the outer screen as a group, producing a cloud of toxic dust so concentrated that it was effective beyond the standard thirty-yard safety margin. His words were noted with considerable scepticism, but within days the phenomenon they described had actually been witnessed at several locations.

None of the subsequent outbreaks of the ptertha plague was as well-contained as at Trompha, and many hundreds had died before the authorities realised that the war between the people of Kolcorron and the ptertha had entered a new phase.

The general population of the empire felt the effect in two ways. Buffer zones were doubled in size, but there was no longer any guarantee of their efficacy. A light, steady breeze was the weather condition most feared, because it could carry invisible wisps of the ptertha toxin a long way into a community before the concentration fell below lethal levels. But even in gusty and variable wind a large enough cluster of ptertha could lay the stealthy hand of death on a sleeping child, and by morning an entire family or group household would be affected.

The second factor which accelerated the shrinkage of population was the further drop in agricultural output. Regions which had known food shortages began to experience outright famine. The traditional system of continuous harvesting now worked against the Kolcorronians because they had never developed any great expertise in the long-term storage of grain and other edible crops. Meagre reserves of food rotted or became pest-ridden in hastily improvised granaries, and diseases unconnected with the ptertha took their toll of human life.

The work of transferring huge quantities of power crystals from Chamteth to Ro-Atabri continued throughout the worsening crisis, but the military organisations did not go unscathed. Not only were the five armies stood down in Chamteth – they were denied transportation to Kolcorron and the home provinces, and were ordered to take up permanent residence in the Land of the Long Days, where the ptertha – as though sensing their vulner-ability – swarmed in ever-increasing numbers. Only those units concerned with gutting the brakka forests and shipping out the cargoes of green and purple crystals remained under the protective umbrella of Leddravohr's high command.

And Prince Leddravohr himself changed.

In the beginning he had accepted the responsibility for the Overland migration almost solely because of loyalty to his father, offsetting his pri-vate reservations against the opportunity to conduct an all-out war against Chamteth. Throughout all his preparation for the building of the fleet of skyships he had nourished deep within him the belief that the unappealing venture would never come to fruition, that some less radical solution to Kol-corron's problems would be found, one which was more in keeping with the established patterns of human history.

But above all else he was a realist, a man who understood the vital impor-tance of balancing ambition and ability, and when he foresaw the inevitable outcome of the war against the ptertha he shifted his ground.

The migration to Overland was now part of his personal future and those about him, sensing his new attitude, understood that nothing would be al-lowed to stand in its way.

CHAPTER FOURTEEN

'But today of all days!' Colonel Kartkang said forcibly. 'I suppose you realise your take-off is scheduled for the tenth hour?'

He was lightly-built for a member of the military caste, with a round face and a mouth so wide that there was a visible gap between each of his small-ish teeth. A talent for administration and an unfailing eye for detail had brought him his appointment as head of Skyship Experimental Squadron, and he clearly disliked the idea of permitting a test pilot to leave the base shortly before the most important proving flight in his programme.

'I'll be back long before that time, sir,' Toller said. 'You know I wouldn't take the slightest risk in this matter.'

'Yes, but … Do you know that Prince Leddravohr plans to watch the ascent in person?'

'All the more reason for me to be back in good time, sir. I don't want to risk high treason.'

Kartkang, still not easy in his mind, squared a sheaf of papers on his desk. 'Was Lord Glo important to you?'

'I was prepared to risk my life in his service.'

'In that case I suppose you had better pay your last respects,' Kartkang said. 'But keep it in mind about the prince.'

'Thank you, sir.' Toller saluted and left the office, his mind a battleground for incompatible emotions. It seemed cruelly ironic, almost proof of the existence of a malign deity, that Glo was to be buried on the very day that a skyship was setting out to prove the feasibility of flying to Overland. The project had been conceived in Glo's brain and had brought him ridicule and disgrace at first, followed by ignominious retirement, and just as he was about to receive personal vindication his beleaguered body had failed him. There would be no plump-bellied statue in the grounds of the Great Palace, and it was doubtful if Glo's name would even be remembered by the nation he had helped to establish on another world. Everything should have been very different.

Visions of the migration fleet touching down on Overland brought a resurgence of the icy excitement which Toller had been living with for days. He had been in the grip of his monomania for so long, working with total commitment towards selection for the first interplanetary mission, that he had somehow lost sight of its astonishing realities. His impatience had slowed the passage of time so much that he had unconsciously begun to believe his goal would forever remain ahead of him, flickering beyond reach like a mirage, and now – with shocking suddenness – the present had collided with the future.

The time of the great voyage was at hand, and during it many things would be learned, not all of them to do with the technicalities of interplanetary flight.

Toller left the S.E.S. administration complex and climbed a wooden stair to the surface of the plain which extended north of Ro-Atabri as far as the foothills of the Slaskitan Mountains. He requisitioned a bluehorn from the stablemaster and set off on the two-mile ride to Greenmount. The varnished linen of the tunnel-like covered way glowed in the foreday sunlight, surrounding him with a yellowish directionless light, and the trapped air was muggy, heavy with the smell of animal droppings. Most of the traffic was heading out from the city, flatbed carts laden with gondola sections and jet cylinders of brakka.

Toller made good time to the eastern junction, entered the tube leading towards Greenmount and soon reached an area protected by the older open-mesh screens of the Ro-Atabri suburbs. He rode through a moraine of abandoned dwellings on the exposed flank of the hill, eventually reaching the small private cemetery adjoining the colonnaded west wing of Greenmount Peel.

Several groups of mourners were already in attendance, and among them he saw his brother and the slender grey-clad figure of Gesalla Maraquine. It was the first time he had seen her since the night she had been abused by Leddravohr, more than a year earlier, and his heart jolted uncomfortably as he realised he was at a loss as to how to conduct himself with her.

He dismounted, straightened the embroidered blue jupon of his sky-captain's uniform and walked towards his brother and his wife, still feeling oddly nervous and self-conscious. On seeing him approach Lain gave him the calm half-smile, indicative of family pride tinged with incredulity, which he had used of late when they met at technical briefings. Toller took pleasure in having surprised and impressed his older brother with his single-minded assault on every obstacle, including reading difficulties, on his way to becoming a skyship pilot.

'This is a sad day,' he said to Lain.

Gesalla, who had not been aware of his approach, spun round, one hand flying to her throat. He nodded courteously to her and withheld a verbal greeting, leaving it to her to accept or decline the conversational initiative. She returned his nod, silently but with no visible evidence of her old antipathy and he felt slightly reassured. In his memory her face had been pared by pregnancy sickness, but now her cheeks were more fully curved and touched with pink. She actually looked younger than before and the sight of her filled his eyes.

He became aware of the pressure of Lain's gaze and said, 'Why couldn't Glo have had more time?'

Lain shrugged, an unexpectedly casual gesture for one who had been so close to the Lord Philosopher. 'Have you had confirmation about the ascent?'

'Yes. It's at the tenth hour.'

'I know that. I mean, are you definitely going?'

'Of course!' Toller glanced up at the netted sky and the nacreous morning crescent of Overland. 'I'm all set to tackle Glo's invisible mountains.'

Gesalla looked amused and interested. 'What does that mean?'

'We know the atmosphere thins out between the two worlds,' Toller said. 'The rate of attenuation has been roughly measured by sending up gas balloons and observing their expansion through calibrated telescopes. It is something which has to be verified by the proving flight, of course, but we believe the air is plenteous enough to sustain life, even at the midpoint.'

'Listen to the newly-fledged expert,' Lain said.

'I've had the best teachers,' Toller replied, unoffended, turning his attention back to Gesalla. 'Lord Glo said the flight was comparable to climbing to the peak of one invisible mountain and descending from another.'

'I never gave him credit for being a poet,' Gesalla said.

'There are many things for which he will never receive credit.'

'Yes – like taking in that gradewife of yours when you went off to play soldiers,' Lain put in. 'Whatever became of her, anyway?'

Toller gazed at his brother for a moment, puzzled and saddened by the hint of malice in his tone. Lain had asked him the same question some time ago, and now it seemed he was bringing up the subject of Fera for no other reason than that it had always been a sore point with Gesalla. Was it possible that Lain was jealous of his 'little brother' having earned a place on the proving flight, the greatest scientific experiment of the age?

'Fera soon got bored with life in the Peel and went back into the city to live,' Toller said. 'I presume she is in good circumstances – I *hope* she is – but I haven't tried to find out. Why do you ask?'

'Ummm ... Idle curiosity.'

'Well, if your curiosity extends as far as my term in the army I can assure you that the word "play" is highly inappropriate. I ...'

'Be quiet, you two,' Gesalla said, placing a hand on each man's arm. 'The ceremony begins.'

Toller fell silent in a fresh confusion of emotions as the burial party arrived from the direction of the house. In his will Glo had stated his preference for the shortest and simplest ceremony that could be accorded a Kolcorronian aristocrat. His cortege consisted only of Lord Prelate Balountar, followed by four dark-robed suffragens bearing the cylindrical block of white gypsum in which Glo's body had already been encased. Balountar, with head thrust forward and black vestments draping a bony figure, resembled a raven as he slow-marched to the circular hole which had been bored into the bedrock of the cemetery.

He intoned a short prayer, consigning Lord Glo's discarded shell to the parent body of the planet for reabsorption, and calling for his spirit to be given a safe passage to Overland, followed by a fortuitous rebirth and a long and prosperous life on the sister world.

Toller was troubled by guilt as he watched the lowering of the cylinder and the sealing of the hole with cement poured from a decorated urn. He wanted to be torn by sadness and grief on parting with Glo for ever, but his wayward consciousness was dominated by the fact that Gesalla – who had never touched him before – had allowed her hand to remain resting on his arm. Did it signal a change in her attitude towards him, or was it incidental to some twist in her relationship with Lain, who in turn had been acting strangely? And underlying everything else in Toller's mind was the pounding realisation that he was soon to ascend so far into the sky's blue dome that he would pass beyond the reach of even the most powerful telescopes.

He was relieved, therefore, when the brief ceremony drew to a close and the knots of mourners – most of them blood relatives – began to disperse.

'I must return to the base now,' he said. 'There are many things yet to be …' He left the sentence unfinished as he noticed that the Lord Prelate had separated himself from his entourage and was approaching the trio. Assuming that Balountar's business had to be with Lain, Toller took a discreet step backwards. He was surprised when Balountar came straight to him, close-set eyes intent and furious, and flicked him on the chest with loosely dangling fingers.

'I remember you,' he said. 'Maraquine! You're the one who laid hands on me in the Rainbow Hall, before the King.' He flicked Toller again, clearly intending the gesture to be offensive.

'Well, now that you have evened the score,' Toller said easily, 'may I be of service to you, my lord?'

'Yes, you can rid yourself of that uniform – it is an offence to the Church in general and to me in particular.'

'In what way does it offend?'

'In *every* way! The very colour symbolises the heavens, does it not? It flaunts your intention to defile the High Path, does it not? Even though your evil ambition will be thwarted, Maraquine, those blue rags are an affront to every right-thinking citizen of this country.'

'I wear this uniform in the service of Kolcorron, my lord. Any objections you have to that should be presented directly to the King. Or to Prince Leddravohr.'

'Huh!' Balountar stared venomously for a moment, his face working with frustrated rage. 'You won't get away with it, you know. Even though the likes of you and your brother turn your backs on the Church, in all your sophistry and arrogance, you will learn to your cost that the people will stand for just so much. You'll see! The great blasphemy, the great *evil*, will not go unpunished.' He spun and strode away to the cemetery gate, where the four suffragens were waiting.

Toller watched him depart and turned to the others with raised eyebrows. 'The Lord Prelate appears to be unhappy.'

'There was a time when you would have crushed his hand for doing that.' Lain imitated Balountar's gesture, flicking limp fingers against Toller's chest. 'Do you no longer see red so easily?'

'Perhaps I have seen too much red.'

'Oh, yes. How could I have forgotten?' The mockery in Lain's voice was now unmistakable. 'This is your new role, isn't it? The man who has drunk too deeply from the cup of experience.'

'Lain, I have no inkling of what I have done to earn your displeasure, and even though I'm saddened by it I have no time now to enquire into the matter.' Toller nodded to his brother and bowed to Gesalla, whose concerned gaze was switching between the two. He was about to leave when Lain, eyes deepening with tears, abruptly spread his arms in an embrace which brought his brother and wife together.

'Don't take any foolish risks up there in the sky, little brother,' Lain whispered. 'It's your family duty to come back safely, so that when the time of the migration arrives we can all fly to Overland together. I won't entrust Gesalla to any but the very best pilot. Do you understand?'

Toller nodded, not attempting to speak. The feel of Gesalla's gracile body against his own was asexual, as it had to be, but there was a *rightness* to it, and with his brother completing the psychic circuit there was a sense of comfort and healing, of vital energies being augmented rather than dissipated.

When Toller broke free of the embrace he felt light and strong, fully capable of soaring, to another world.

CHAPTER FIFTEEN

'We have sunwriter reports from as far away as fifty miles upwind,' said Vato Armduran, the S.E.S. chief engineer. 'The look-outs say there is very little ptertha activity – so you should be all right on that score – but the wind speed is rather higher than I would have wished.'

'If we wait for perfect conditions we'll *never* go.' Toller shaded his eyes from the sun and scanned the blue-white dome of the sky. Wisps of high cloud had overpainted the brighter stars without screening them from view, and the broad crescent of illumination on Overland's disk established the time as midforeday.

'I suppose that's true, but you're going to have trouble with false lift when you clear the enclosure. You'll need to watch out for it.'

Toller grinned. 'Isn't it a little late for lessons in aerodynamics?'

'It's all very well for you – I'm the one who's going to have to do all the explaining if you kill yourself,' Armduran said drily. He was a spiky haired man whose flattened nose and sword-scarred chin gave him something of the appearance of a retired soldier, but his practical engineering genius had led to his personal appointment by Prince Chakkell. Toller liked him for his caustic humour and lack of condescension towards less gifted subordinates.

'For your sake, I'll try not to get killed.' Toller had to raise his voice to overcome the noise in the enclosure. Members of the inflation crew were busily cranking a large fan whose gears and wooden blades emitted a continuous clacking sound as they forced unheated air into the skyship's balloon, which had been laid out downwind of the gondola. They were creating a cavity within the envelope so that hot gas from the power crystal burner could later be introduced without it having to impinge directly on the lightweight material. The technique had been developed to avoid burn damage, especially to the base panels around the balloon mouth. Overseers were bellowing orders to the men who were holding up the sides of the gradually swelling balloon and paying out attachment lines.

The square, room-sized gondola was lying on its side, already provisioned for the flight. In addition to food, drink and fuel it contained sandbags equivalent to the weight of sixteen people which, when taken with the weight of the test crew, brought the load up to the operational maximum. The three men who were to fly with Toller were standing by the gondola, ready to leap on board on command. He knew the ascent had to begin within a matter of minutes, and the emotional turmoil connected with Lain and Gesalla and Glo's burial was steadily fading to a murmur in lower levels of his consciousness. In his mind he was already voyaging in the ice-blue unknown, like a migrating soul, and his preoccupations were no longer those of an ordinary Land-bound mortal.

There was a sound of hoofbeats nearby and he turned to see Prince Leddravohr riding into the enclosure, followed by an open carriage in which sat Prince Chakkell, his wife Daseene and their three children. Leddravohr was dressed as for a military ceremony, wearing a white cuirass. The inevitable battle sword was at his side and a long throwing knife was sheathed on his left forearm. He dismounted from his tall bluehorn, head turning as he took in every detail of the surrounding activity, and padded towards Toller and Armduran.

Toller had not seen him at all during his time in the army and only at a distance since returning to Ro-Atabri, and he noted that the prince's glossy black hair was now tinged with grey at the temples. He was also a little heavier, but the weight appeared to have been added in an even subcutaneous layer all over his body, doing little more than blur the muscle definition and render the statuesque face smoother than ever. Toller and Armduran saluted as he approached.

Leddravohr nodded in acknowledgement. 'Well, Maraquine, you have become an important man since last we met. I trust it has made you somewhat easier to live with.'

'I don't class myself as important, Prince,' Toller said in a carefully neutral voice, trying to gauge Leddravohr's attitude.

'But you *are!* The first man to take a ship to Overland! It's a great honour, Maraquine, and you have worked hard for it. You know, there were some who felt that you were too young and inexperienced for this mission, that it should have been entrusted to an officer with a long Air Service career behind him, but I overruled them. You obtained the best results in the training courses, and you're not encumbered with an aircaptain's obsolete skills and habits, and you are a man of undoubted courage – so I decreed that the captaincy of the proving flight should be yours.

'What do you think of that?'

'I'm deeply grateful to you, Prince,' Toller said.

'Gratitude isn't called for.' Leddravohr's old smile, the smile which had nothing to do with amity, flickered on his face for an instant and was gone. 'It is only just that you should receive the fruits of your labours.'

Toller understood at once that nothing had changed, that Leddravohr was still the deadly enemy who never forgot or forgave. There was a mystery surrounding the prince's apparent forbearance of the last year, but no doubt at all that he still hungered for Toller's life. *He hopes the flight will fail! He hopes he is sending me to my death!*

The intuition gave Toller a sudden new insight into Leddravohr's mind. Analysing his own feelings towards the prince he now found nothing but a cool indifference, with perhaps the beginnings of pity for a creature so imprisoned by negative emotion, awash and drowning in its own venom.

'I'm grateful nevertheless,' Toller said, relishing the private double meaning of his words. He had been apprehensive about coming face to face with Leddravohr again, but the encounter had proved that he had transcended his old self, truly, once and for all. From now on his spirit would soar as far above Leddravohr and his kind as the skyship was soon to do over the continents and oceans of Land, and that was genuine cause for rejoicing.

Leddravohr scanned his face for a moment, searchingly, then transferred his attention to the skyship. The inflation crew had progressed to the stage of raising the balloon up on the four acceleration struts which constituted the principal difference between it and a craft designed for normal atmospheric flight. Now three-quarters full, the balloon sagged among the struts like some grotesque leviathan deprived of the support of its natural medium. The varnished linen skin flapped feebly in the mild air currents coming through the perforations in the enclosure wall.

'If I'm not mistaken,' Leddravohr said, 'it is time for you to join your ship, Maraquine.'

Toller saluted him, squeezed Armduran's shoulder and ran to the gondola.

He gave a signal and Zavotle, co-pilot and recorder for the flight, swung himself on board. He was closely followed by Rillomyner, the mechanic, and the diminutive figure of Flenn, the rigger. Toller went in after them, taking his position at the burner. The gondola was still on its side, so he had to lie on his back against a woven cane partition to operate the burner's controls.

The trunk of a very young brakka tree had been used in its entirety to form the main component of the burner. On the left side of the bulbous base was a small hopper filled with pikon, plus a valve which admitted the crystals to the combustion chamber under pneumatic pressure. On the opposite side a similar device controlled the flow of halvell, and both valves were operated by a single lever. The passageways in the right-hand valve were slightly enlarged, automatically providing the greater proportion of halvell which had been found best for providing sustained thrust.

Toller pumped the pneumatic reservoir by hand, then signalled to the inflation supervisor that he was ready to begin burning. The noise level in the enclosure dropped as the fan crew ceased cranking and pulled their cumbersome machine and its nozzle aside.

Toller advanced the control lever for about a second. There was a hissing roar as the power crystals combined, firing a burst of hot miglign gas into the balloon's gaping mouth. Satisfied with the burner's performance, he instigated a series of blasts – keeping them brief to reduce the risk of heat damage to the balloon fabric – and the great envelope began to distend and lift clear of the ground. As it gradually rose to the vertical position the crew holding the balloon's crown lines came walking in and attached them to the gondola's load frame, while others rotated the gondola until it was in the normal attitude. All at once the skyship was ready to fly, only held down by its central anchor.

Mindful of Armduran's warning about false lift, Toller continued burning for another full minute, and as the hot gas displaced more and more unheated air through the balloon mouth the entire assemblage began to strain upwards. Finally, too intent on his work to feel any sense of occasion, he pulled the anchor link and the skyship left the ground.

It rose quickly at first, then the curved crown of the balloon entered the wind above the enclosure walls, generating such a fierce extra lift that Rillomyner gasped aloud as the ship accelerated skywards. Toller, undeceived by the phenomenon, fired a long blast from the burner. In a few seconds the balloon had fully entered the airstream and was travelling with it, and as the relative airflow across the top dropped to zero the extra lift also disappeared.

At the same time, a rippling distortion caused by the initial impact of the wind expelled some gas back out through the mouth of the balloon, and now the ship was actually losing height as it was borne away to the east at some ten miles an hour. The speed was not great compared to what other forms of transport could achieve, but the airship was designed for vertical travel only and any contact with the ground at that stage was likely to be disastrous.

Toller fought the unintentional descent with prolonged burns. For a tense minute the gondola headed straight for the line of elvart trees at the eastern edge of the airfield as though attached to an invisible rail, then the balloon's buoyancy began to reassert itself. The ground slowly sank away and Toller was able to rest the burner. Looking back towards the line of enclosures, some of which were still under construction, he was able to pick out the white gleam of Leddravohr's cuirass among the hundreds of spectators, but – already – the prince seemed to be part of his past, his psychological importance diminishing with perspective.

'Would you like to make a note?' Toller said to Ilven Zavotle. 'It appears that the maximum wind speed for take-off with full load is in the region of ten miles an hour. Also, those trees should go.'

Zavotle glanced up briefly from the wicker table at his station. 'I'm already doing it, captain.' He was a narrow-headed youngster with tiny clenched ears and a permanent frown, as fussy and fastidious in his ways as a very old man, but already a veteran of several test flights.

Toller glanced around the square gondola, checking that all was well. Mechanic Rillomyner had slumped down on the sandbags in one of the passenger compartments, looking pale of face and distinctly sorry for himself. Ree Flenn, the rigger, was perched like some arboreal animal on the gondola's rail, busily shortening the tether on one of the free-hanging acceleration struts. Toller's stomach produced a chill spasm as he saw that Flenn had not secured his personal line to the rail.

'What do you think you're doing, Flenn?' he said. 'Get your line attached.'

'I can work better without it, captain.' A grin split the rigger's bead-eyed, button-nosed face. 'I'm not afraid of heights.'

'Would you *like* something to be afraid of?' Toller spoke mildly, almost courteously, but Flenn's grin faded at once and he snapped his karabiner on to the brakka rail. Toller turned away to hide his amusement. Capitalising on his dwarfish stature and comic appearance, Flenn habitually breached discipline in ways which would have earned the lash for other men, but he was highly expert at his work and Toller had been glad to accept him for the flight. His own background inclined him to be sympathetic towards rebels and misfits.

By now the ship was climbing steadily above the western suburbs of Ro-Atabri. The city's familiar configurations were blurred and dulled by the blanket of anti-ptertha screens which had spread over it like some threaded mould, but the vistas of Arle Bay and the Gulf were as Toller remembered them from childhood aerial excursions. Their nostalgic blue faded into a purple haze near the horizon above which, subdued by sunlight, shone the nine stars of the Tree.

Looking down, Toller was able to see the Great Palace, on the south bank of the Borann, and he wondered if King Prad could be at a window at that very moment, gazing up at the fragile assemblage of fabric and wood which represented his stake in posterity. Since appointing his son to the position of absolute power the King had become a virtual recluse. Some said that his health had deteriorated, others that he had no heart for skulking like a furtive animal in the shrouded streets of his own capital city.

Surveying the complex and variegated scene beneath him, Toller was surprised to discover that he felt little emotion. He seemed to have severed his bonds with the past by taking the first step along the five-thousand-mile high road to Overland. Whether he would in fact reach the sister planet on a later flight and begin a new life there was a matter for the future – and his present was bounded by the tiny world of the skyship. The microcosm of the gondola, only four good paces on a side, was destined to be his whole universe for more than twenty days, and he could have no other commitments ...

Toller's meditation came to an abrupt end when he noticed a purplish mote drifting against the white-feathered sky some distance to the north-west.

'On your feet, Rillomyner,' he called out. 'It's time you started earning your pay on this trip.'

The mechanic stood up and came out of the passenger compartment. 'I'm sorry, captain – the way we took off did something to my gut.'

'Get on to the cannon if you don't want to be really sick,' Toller said. 'We might be having a visitor soon.'

Rillomyner swore and lurched towards the nearest cannon. Zavotle and Flenn followed suit without needing to be ordered. There were two of the anti-ptertha guns mounted on each side of the gondola, their barrels made of thin strips of brakka bonded into tubes by glass cords and resin. Below each weapon was a magazine containing glass power capsules and a supply of the latest type of projectile – hinged bundles of wooden rods which opened radially in flight. They demanded better accuracy than the older scattering weapons, but compensated with improved range.

Toller remained at the pilot's station and fired intermittent bursts of heat into the balloon to maintain the rate of climb. He was not unduly concerned about the lone ptertha and had issued his warning as much to rouse Rillomyner as anything else. As far as was known, the globes depended on air currents to transport them over long distances, and only moved horizontally of their own volition when close to their prey. How they obtained impulsion over the final few yards was still a mystery, but one theory was that a ptertha had already begun the process of self-destruction at that stage by creating a small orifice in its surface at the point most distant from the victim. Expulsion of internal gases would propel the globe to within the killing radius before the entire structure disintegrated and released its charge of toxic dust. The process remained a matter for conjecture because of the impossibility of studying ptertha at close range.

In the present case the globe was about four hundred yards from the ship and was likely to stay at that distance because the positions of both were governed by the same air-flow. Toller knew, however, that the one component of their motion over which the ptertha had good control was in the vertical dimension. Observation through calibrated telescopes showed that a ptertha could govern its attitude by increasing or decreasing its size, thus altering its density, and Toller was interested in carrying out a double experiment which might be of value to the migration fleet.

'Keep your eye on the globe,' he said to Zavotle. 'It seems to be keeping on a level with us, and if it is that proves it can sense our presence over that distance. I also want to find out how high it will go before giving up.'

'Very good, captain.' Zavotle raised his binoculars and settled down to studying the ptertha.

Toller glanced around his circumscribed domain, trying to imagine how much more cramped its dimensions would seem with a full complement of twenty people on board. The passenger accommodation consisted of two narrow compartments, at opposite sides of the gondola for balance, bounded by chest-high partitions. Nine or so people would be crammed into each, unable either to lie down properly or move around, and by the end of the long voyage their physical condition was likely to be poor.

One corner of the gondola was taken up by the galley, and the diagonally opposite one by the primitive toilet, which was basically a hole in the floor plus some sanitation aids. The centre of the floor was occupied by the four crew stations surrounding the burner unit and the downward facing drive jet. Most of the remaining space was filled by the pikon and halvell magazines, which were also at opposite sides of the gondola, with the food and drink stores and various equipment lockers.

Toller could foresee the interplanetary crossing, like so many other historic and glorious adventures, being conducted in squalor and degradation, becoming a test of physical and mental endurance which not all would survive.

In contrast to the meanness and compression of the gondola, the upper element of the skyship was awesomely spacious, rarified, a giant form almost without substance. The linen panels of the envelope had been dyed dark brown to absorb the sun's heat and thereby gain extra lift, but when Toller looked up into it through the open mouth he could see light glowing through the material. The seams and horizontal and vertical load tapes appeared as a geometric web of black lines, emphasising the vastness of the balloon's curvatures. Up there was the gossamer dome of a cloud-borne cathedral. impossible to associate with the handiwork of mere weavers and stitchers.

Satisfied that the ship was stable and ascending steadily, Toller gave the order for the four acceleration struts to be drawn in and attached by their lower ends to the corners of the gondola. Flenn completed the task within a few minutes, imparting to the balloon/gondola assemblage the slight degree of structural stiffness needed to cope with the modest forces which would act on it when the drive or attitude jets were in use.

Attached to a lashing hook at the pilot's station was the rip line, dyed red, which ran up through the balloon to a crown panel which could be torn out for rapid deflation. As well as being a safety device it served as a rudimentary climb speed indicator, becoming slack when the crown was depressed by a strong vertical air flow. Toller fingered the line and estimated that they were ascending at about twelve miles an hour, aided by the fact that the miglign gas was slightly lighter than air even when unheated. Later he would almost double that speed by using the drive jet when the ship entered the regions of low gravity and attenuated air.

Thirty minutes into the flight the ship was high above the summit of Mount Opelmer and had ceased its eastward drift. The garden province of Kail stretched to the southern horizon, its strip farms registering as a shimmering mosaic, with each tessera striated in six different shades varying from yellow to green. To the west was the Otollan Sea and to the east was the Mirlgiver Ocean, their curving blue reaches flecked here and there by sailing ships. The ochraceous mountains of Upper Kolcorron filled the view to the north, their ranges and folds compacted by perspective. A few airships gleamed like tiny elliptical jewels as they plied the trade lanes far below.

From an altitude of some six miles the face of Land looked placid and achingly beautiful. Only the relative scarcity of airships and sailing craft indicated that the entire prospect, apparently drowsing in benign sunlight, was actually a battleground, an arena in which mankind had fought and lost a deadly duel.

Toller, as had become his habit when deep in thought, located the curiously massive object given to him by his father and rubbed his thumb over its gleaming surface. In the normal course of history, he wondered, how many centuries would men have waited before essaying the voyage to Overland? Indeed, would they ever have done so had they not been fleeing from the ptertha?

The thought of the ancient and implacable enemy prompted him to cast around and check on the position of the solitary globe he had detected earlier. Its lateral separation from the ship had not changed and, more significantly, it was still matching the rate of climb. Was that proof of sentience and purpose? If so, why had the ptertha as a species singled out man as the focus of its hostility? Why was it that every other creature on Land, with the exception of the Sorka gibbon, was immune to pterthacosis?

As though sensing Toller's renewed interest in the globe, Zavotle lowered his binoculars and said, 'Does it look bigger to you, captain?'

Toller picked up his own glasses and studied the purple-black smudge, finding that its transparency defied his attempts to define its boundaries. 'Hard to say.'

'Littlenight will be here soon,' Zavotle commented. 'I don't relish the idea of having that thing hanging around us in the dark.'

'I don't think it can close in – the ship is almost the same shape as a ptertha, and our response to a crosswind will be roughly similar.'

'I hope you're right,' Zavotle said gloomily.

Rillomyner looked round from his post at a cannon and said, 'We haven't eated since dawn, captain.' He was a pale and pudgy young man with an enormous appetite for even the vilest food, and it was said that he had actually gained weight since the beginning of the shortages by scavenging all the substandard food rejected by his workmates. In spite of a show of diffidence, he was a good mechanic and intensely proud of his skills.

'I'm glad to hear your gut is back to its normal condition,' Toller said. 'I would hate to think I had done it some permanent mischief with my handling of the ship.'

'I didn't mean to criticise the take-off, captain – it's just that I have always been cursed with this weak stomach.'

Toller clicked his tongue in mock sympathy and glanced at Flenn. 'You'd better feed this man before he becomes faint.'

'Right away, captain.' As Flenn was getting to his feet his shirt parted at the chest and the green-striped head of a carble peered out. Flenn hastily covered the furry creature with his hand and pushed it back into concealment.

'What have you got there?' Toller snapped.

'Her name is Tinny, captain.' Flenn brought the carble out and cradled it in his arms. 'There was nobody I could leave her with.'

Toller sighed his exasperation. 'This is a scientific mission, not a ... Do you realise that most commanders would put that animal over the side?'

'I swear she won't be any trouble, captain.'

'She'd better not. Now get the food.'

Flenn grinned and, agile as a monkey, disappeared into the galley to prepare the first meal of the voyage. He was small enough to be completely hidden by the woven partition which was chest high to the rest of the crew. Toller settled down to refining his control over the ship's ascent.

Deciding to increase speed, he lengthened the burns from three to four seconds and watched for the time-lagged response of the balloon overhead. Several minutes went by before the extra lift he was generating overcame the inertia of the many tons of gas inside the envelope and the rip line became noticeably slacker. Satisfied with a new rate of climb of around eighteen miles an hour, he concentrated on making the burner rhythm – four seconds on and twenty off – part of his awareness, something to be paced by the internal clocks of his heart and lungs. He needed to be able to detect the slightest variation in it even when he was asleep and being spelled at the controls by Zavotle.

The food served up by Flenn was from the limited fresh supplies and was better than Toller had expected – strips of reasonably lean beef in gravy, pulse, fried grain-cakes and beakers of hot green tea. Toller stopped operating the burner while he ate, allowing the ship to coast upwards in silence on stored lift. The heat emanating from the black combustion chamber mingled with the aromatic vapours issuing from the galley, turning the gondola into a homely oasis in a universe of azure emptiness.

Partway through the meal littlenight came sweeping from the west, a brief flash of rainbow colours preceding a sudden darkness, and as the crew's eyes adjusted the heavens blazed into life all around them. They reacted to the unearthliness of their situation by generating an intense camaraderie. There was an unspoken conviction that lifelong friendships were being formed, and in that atmosphere every anecdote was interesting, every boast believable, every joke profoundly funny. And even when the talk eventually died away, stilled by strangeness, communication continued on another plane.

Toller was set apart to some extent by the responsibilities of command, but he was warmed nonetheless. From his seated position the rim of the gondola was at eye level, which meant there was nothing to be seen beyond it but enigmatic whirlpools of radiance, the splayed mist-fans of comets, and stars and stars and ever more stars. The only sound was the occasional creak of a rope, and the only sensible movement was where the meteors scribed their swift-fading messages on the blackboard of night.

Toller could easily imagine himself adrift in the beaconed depths of the universe, and all at once, unexpectedly, there came the longing to have a woman at his side, a female presence which would somehow make the voyage meaningful. It would have been good to be with Fera at that moment, but her essential carnality would scarcely have been in accord with his mood. The right woman would have been one who was capable of enhancing the mystical qualities of the experience. Somebody like ...

Toller reached out with his imagination, blindly, wistfully. For an instant the feel of Gesalla Maraquine's slim body against his own was shockingly real. He leapt to his feet, guilty and confused, disturbing the equilibrium of the gondola.

'Is anything wrong, captain?' Zavotle said, barely visible in the darkness.

'Nothing. A touch of cramp, that's all. You take over the burner for a while. Four-twenty is what we want.'

Toller went to the side of the gondola and leaned on the rail. *What is happening to me now?* he thought. *Lain said I was playing a role – but how did he know? The new cool and imperturbable Toller Maraquine … the man who has drunk too deeply from the cup of experience … who looks down on princes … who is undaunted by the chasm between the worlds … and who, because his brother's solewife does no more than touch his arm, is immediately smitten with adolescent fantasies about her! Was Lain, with that frightening perception of his, able to see me for the betrayer that I am? Is that why he seemed to turn against* me?

The darkness below the skyship was absolute, as though Land had already been deserted by all of humanity, but as Toller gazed down into it a thin line of red, green and violet fire appeared on the western horizon. It widened, growing increasingly brilliant, and suddenly a tide of pure light was sweeping across the world at heart-stopping speed, recreating oceans and land masses in all their colour and intricate detail. Toller almost flinched in expectation of a palpable blow as the speeding terminator reached the ship, engulfing it in fierce sunlight, and rushed on to the eastern horizon. The columnar shadow of Overland had completed its daily transit of Kolcorron, and Toller felt that *he* had emerged from yet another occultation, a littlenight of the mind.

Don't worry, beloved brother, he thought. *Even in my thoughts I'll never betray you. Not ever!*

Ilven Zavotle stood up at the burner and looked out to the north-west. 'What do you think of the globe now, captain? Is it bigger or closer? Or both?'

'It might be a little closer,' Toller said, glad to have an external focus for this thoughts, as he trained his binoculars on the ptertha. 'Can you feel the ship dancing a little? There could be some churning of warmer and cooler air as littlenight passes, and it might have worked out to the globe's advantage.'

'It's still on a level with us – even though we changed our speed.'

'Yes. I think it wants us.'

'I know what I want,' Flenn announced as he slipped by Toller on his way to the toilet. 'I'm going to have the honour of being the first to try out the long drop – and I hope it all lands right on old Puehilter.' He had nominated an overseer whose petty tyrannies had made him unpopular with the S.E.S. flight technicians.

Rillomyner snorted in approval. 'That'll give him something worth complaining about, for once.'

'It'll be worse when you go – they're going to have to evacuate the whole of Ro-Atabri when you start bombing them.'

'Just take care you don't fall down the hole,' Rillomyner growled, not appreciating the reference to his dietary foibles. 'It wasn't designed for midgets.'

Toller made no comment about the exchange. He knew the two were testing him to see what style of command he was going to favour on the voyage. A strict interpretation of flight regulations would have precluded any badinage at all among his crew, let alone grossness, but he was solely concerned with their qualities of efficiency, loyalty and courage. In a couple of hours the ship would be higher than any had gone before – if one discounted the semi-mythical Usader of five centuries earlier – entering a region of strangeness, and he could foresee the little group of adventurers needing every human support available to them.

Besides, the same subject had given rise to a thousand equally coarse jokes in the officers' quarters, ever since the utilitarian design of the skyship gondola had become common knowledge. He himself had derived a certain amusement from the frequency with which ground-based personnel had reminded him that the toilet was not to be used until the prevailing westerlies had carried the ship well clear of the base ...

The bursting of the ptertha took Toller by surprise.

He was gazing at the globe's magnified image when it simply ceased to exist, and in the absence of a contrasting background there was not even a dissipating smudge of dust to mark its location. In spite of his confidence in their ability to deal with the threat, he nodded in satisfaction. Sleep was going to be difficult enough during the first night aloft without having to worry about capricious air currents bringing the silent enemy to within its killing radius.

'Make a note that the ptertha has just popped itself out of existence,' he said to Zavotle, and – expressing his relief – added a personal comment. 'Put down that it happened about four hours into the flight ... just as Flenn was using the toilet ... but that there is probably no connection between the two events.'

Toller awoke shortly after dawn to the sound of an animated discussion taking place at the centre of the gondola. He raised himself to a kneeling position on the sandbags and rubbed his arms, uncertain as to whether the coolness he could feel was external or an aftermath of sleep. The intermittent roar of the burner had been so intrusive that he had achieved only light dozes, and now he felt little more refreshed than if he had been on duty all night. He walked on his knees to the opening in the passenger compartment's partition and looked out at the rest of the crew.

'You should have a look at this, captain,' Zavotle said, raising his narrow head. 'The height gauge actually does work!'

Toller insinuated his legs into the cramped central floorspace and went to the pilot's station, where Flenn and Rillomyner were standing beside Zavotle. At the station was a lightweight table, attached to which was the height gauge. The latter consisted of nothing more than a vertical scale, from the top of which a small weight was suspended by a delicate coiled spring made from a hair-like shaving of brakka. On the previous morning, at the beginning of the flight, the weight had been opposite to the lowest mark on the scale – but now it was several divisions higher.

Toller stared hard at the gauge. 'Has anybody interfered with it?'

'Nobody has touched it,' Zavotle assured him. 'It means that everything they told us must be true. Everything is getting lighter as we go higher! We're getting lighter!'

'That's to be expected,' Toller said, unwilling to admit that in his heart he had never quite accepted the notion, even when Lain had taken time to impress the theory on him in private tutorials.

'Yes, but it means that in three or four days from now we won't weigh anything at all. We'll be able to float around in the air like ... like ... ptertha! It's all *true*, captain!'

'How high does it say we are?'

'About three hundred and fifty miles – and that agrees well with our computations.'

'I don't feel any different,' Rillomyner put in. 'I say the spring has tightened up.'

Flenn nodded. 'Me too.'

Toller wished for time in which to arrange his thoughts. He went to the side of the gondola and experienced a whirling moment of vertigo as he saw Land as he had never seen it before – an immense circular convexity, one half in near darkness, the other a brilliant sparkling of blue ocean and subtly shaded continents and islands.

Things would be quite different if you were lifting off from the centre of Chamteth and heading out into open space, Lain's voice echoed in his mind. *But when travelling between the two worlds you will soon reach a middle zone – slightly closer to Overland than to Land, in fact – where the gravitational pull of each planet cancels out the other. In normal conditions, with the gondola being heavier than the balloon, the ship has pendulum stability – but where neither has any weight the ship will be unstable and you will have to use the lateral jets to control its attitude.*

Lain had already completed the entire journey in his mind, Toller realised, and everything he had predicted would come to pass. Truly, they were entering a region of strangeness, but the intellects of Lain Maraquine and other men like him had already marked the way, and they had to be trusted ...

'Don't get so excited that you lose the burn rhythm,' Toller said calmly, turning to Zavotle. 'And don't forget to check the height gauge readings by measuring the apparent diameter of Land four times a day.'

He directed his gaze at Rillomyner and Flenn. 'And as for you two – why did the Squadron take the trouble to send you to special classes? The spring has *not* altered in strength. We're getting lighter as we get higher, and I will treat any disputing of that fact as insubordination. Is that clear?'

'Yes, captain.'

Both men spoke in unison, but Toller noticed a troubled look in Rillomyner's eyes, and he wondered if the mechanic was going to have difficulty in adjusting to his increasing weightlessness. *This is what the proving flight is for*, he reminded himself. *We are testing ourselves as much as the ship.*

By nightfall the weight on the height gauge had risen to near the half-way mark on the scale, and the effects of reduced gravity were apparent, no longer a matter for argument.

When a small object was allowed to drop it fell to the floor of the gondola with evident slowness, and all members of the crew reported curious sinking sensations in their stomachs. On two occasions Rillomyner awoke from sleep with a panicky shout, explaining afterwards that he had been convinced he was falling.

Toller noticed the dreamlike ease with which he could move about, and it came to him that it would soon be advisable for the crew to remain tethered at all times. The idea of an unnecessarily vigorous movement separating a man from the ship was one he did not like to contemplate.

He also observed that, in spite of its decreased weight, the ship was tending to rise more slowly. The effect had been accurately predicted – a result of the fading weight differential between the hot gas inside the envelope and the surrounding atmosphere. To maintain speed he altered the burn rhythm to four-eighteen, and then to four-sixteen. The pikon and halvell hoppers on the burner were being replenished with increasing frequency and, although there were ample reserves, Toller began to look forward to reaching the altitude of thirteen hundred miles. At that point the ship's weight, decreasing by squares, would be only a fourth of normal, and it would become more economical to change over to jet power until the zone of zero gravity had been passed.

The need to interpret every action and event in the dry languages of mathematics, engineering and science conflicted with Toller's natural response to his new environment. He found he could spend long periods leaning on the rim of the gondola, not moving a muscle, mesmerised, all physical energies annulled by pure awe. Overland was directly above him, but screened from view by the patient, untiring vastness of the balloon; and far below was the home world, gradually becoming a place of mystery as its familiar features were blurred by a thousand miles of intervening air.

By the third day of the ascent the sky, although retaining its normal coloration above and below, was shading on all sides of the ship into a deeper blue which glistered with ever-increasing numbers of stars.

When Toller was lost in his tranced vigils the conversation of the crew members and even the roar of the burner faded from his consciousness, and he was alone in the universe, sole possessor of all its scintillant hoards. Once during the hours of darkness, while he was standing at the pilot's station, he saw a meteor strike across the sky *below* the ship. It traced a line of fire from what seemed to be one edge of infinity to the other, and minutes after its passing there came a single pulse of low-frequency sound – blurred, dull and mournful – causing the ship to give a tentative heave which drew a murmur of protest from one of the sleeping men. Some instinct, a kind of spiritual acquisitiveness, prompted Toller to keep the knowledge of the event from the others.

As the ascent continued Zavotle was kept busy with his copious flight records, many of the entries concerned with physiological effects. Even at the summit of the highest mountain on Land there was no discernible drop in air pressure, but on previous high-altitude sorties by balloon some crew members had reported a hint of thinness to the air and the need to breathe more deeply. The effect had been slight and the best scientific estimate was that the atmosphere would continue to support life midway between the two planets, but it was vital that the predication should be verified.

Toller was almost comforted by the feel of his lungs working harder during the third day – more evidence that the problems of interworld flight had been correctly foreseen – and he was therefore less than happy when an unexpected phenomenon forced itself on his attention. For some time he had been aware of feeling cold, but had dismissed the matter from his thoughts. Now, however, the others in the gondola were complaining almost continuously and the conclusion was inescapable – as the ship gained altitude the surrounding air was growing colder.

The S.E.S. scientists, Lain Maraquine included, had been of the opinion that there would be an increase in temperature as the ship entered rarified air which would be less able to screen it from the sun's rays. As a native of equatorial Kolcorron, Toller had never experienced really severe coldness, and he had thought nothing of setting off on the interplanetary voyage clad in only a shirt, breeches and sleeveless jupon. Now, although not actually shivering, he was continuously aware of the increasing discomfort and a dismaying thought was beginning to lurk in his mind – that the entire flight might have to be abandoned for the lack of a bale of wool.

He gave permission for the crew to wear all their spare clothing under their uniforms, and for Flenn to brew tea on demand. The latter decision, far from improving the situation, led to a series of arguments. Time after time Rillomyner insisted that Flenn, acting out of malice or ineptitude, was either infusing the tea before the water had boiled properly or was allowing it to cool before serving it around. It was only when Zavotle, who had also been dissatisfied, kept a critical eye on the brewing process that the truth emerged – the water had begun to boil before it had reached the appropriate temperature. It was hot, but not 'boiling' hot.

'I'm worried about this finding, captain,' Zavotle said as he completed the relevant entry in the log. 'The only explanation I can think of is that as the water gets lighter it boils at a progressively lower temperature. And if that *is* the case, what is going to happen to us when the weight of everything fades away to nothing? Is the spit going to boil in our mouths? Are we going to piss steam?'

'We would be obliged to turn back before you had to suffer that indignity,' Toller said, showing his displeasure at the other man's negative attitude, 'but I don't think it will come to that. There must be some other reason – perhaps something to do with the air.'

Zavotle looked dubious. 'I don't see how air could affect water.'

'Neither do I – so I'm not wasting time on useless speculation,' Toller said curtly. 'If you want something to occupy your mind take a close look at the height gauge. It says we're eleven hundred miles up – and if that is correct we have been seriously underestimating our speed all day.'

Zavotle studied the gauge, fingered the rip line and looked up into the balloon, the interior of which was growing dim and mysterious with the onset of dusk. 'Now *that* could be something to do with the air,' he said. 'I think that what you have discovered is that thinner air would depress the crown of the envelope less at speed and make it seem that we're going slower than we actually are.'

Toller considered the proposition and smiled. 'You worked that out – and I didn't – so give yourself credit for it in the record. I'd say you're going to be the senior pilot on your next flight.'

'Thanks, captain,' Zavotle said, looking gratified.

'It's no more than you deserve.' Toller touched Zavotle on the shoulder, making tacit reparation for his irritability. 'At this rate we'll have passed the thirteen hundred mark by dawn – then we can take a rest from the burner and see how the ship handles on the jet.'

Later, while he was settling down on the sandbags to sleep, he went over the exchange in his mind and identified the true cause of the ill temper he had vented on Zavotle. It had been the accumulation of unforeseen phenomena – the increasing coldness, the odd behaviour of the water, the misleading indication of the balloon's speed. It had been the growing realisation that he had placed too much faith in the predictions of scientists. Lain, in particular, had been proved wrong in three different respects, and if his vaulting intellect had been defeated so soon – on the very edge of the region of strangeness – nobody could know what lay in store for those setting out along the perilous fractured glass bridge to another world.

Until that moment, Toller discovered, he had been naively optimistic about the future, convinced that the proving flight would lead to a successful migration and the foundation of a colony in which those he cared about would lead lives of endless fulfilment. It was chastening to realise that the vision had been largely based on his own egotism, that fate had no obligation to honour the safe conducts he had assigned to people like Lain and Gesalla, that events could come to pass regardless of his considering them unthinkable.

All at once the future had clouded over with uncertainty and danger.

And in the new order of things, Toller thought as he drifted into sleep, one had to learn to interpret a new kind of portent. Day-to-day trivia ... the degree of slackness in a cord ... bubbles in a pot of water ... These were niggardly omens ... whispered warnings, almost too faint to hear ...

By morning the height gauge was showing an altitude of fourteen-hundred miles, and its supplementary scale indicated that gravity was now less than a quarter of normal.

Toller, intrigued by the lightness of his body, tested the conditions by jumping, but it was an experiment he tried only once. He rose much higher than he had intended and for a moment as he seemed to hang in the air there was a terrible feeling of having parted from the ship for ever. The open gondola, with its chest-high walls, was revealed as a flimsy edifice whose pared-down struts and wicker panels were quite inadequate for their purpose. He had time to visualise what would happen if a floor section gave way when he landed on it, plunging him into the thin blue air fourteen hundred miles above the surface of the world.

It would take a long time to fall that distance, fully conscious, with nothing to do but watch the planet unfurl hungrily below him. Even the bravest man would eventually have to begin screaming ...

'We seem to have lost a good bit of speed during the night, captain,' Zavotle reported from the pilot's station. 'The rip line is getting quite taut – though, of course, you can't rely on it much any more.'

'It's time for the jet, anyway,' Toller said. 'From now on, until turn-over, we'll use the burner only enough to keep the balloon inflated. Where's Rillomyner?'

'Here, captain.' The mechanic emerged from the other passenger compartment. His pudgy figure was partially doubled over, he was clutching the partitions and his gaze was fixed on the floor.

'What's the matter with you, Rillomyner? Are you sick?'

'I'm not sick, captain. I ... I just don't want to look outside.'

'Why not?'

'I can't do it, captain. I can feel myself being drawn over the side. I think I'm going to float away.'

'You know that's nonsense, don't you?' Toller thought of his own moment of unmanning fear and was inclined towards sympathy. 'Is this going to affect your work?'

'No, captain. The work would help.'

'Good! Carry out a full inspection of the main jet and the laterals, and make *very* sure we have a smooth injection of crystals – we can't afford to have any surges at this stage.'

Rillomyner directed a salute towards the floor and slouched away to fetch his tools. There followed an hour of respite from the full burn rhythm while Rillomyner checked the controls, some of which were common to the downward-facing jet. Flenn prepared and served a breakfast of gruel studded with small cubes of salt pork, all the while complaining about the cold and the difficulty he was having in keeping the galley fire going. His spirits improved a little when he learned that Rillomyner was not going to eat, and as a change from lavatorial humour he subjected the mechanic to a barrage of jokes about the dangers of wasting away to a shadow.

True to his earlier boast, Flenn seemed quite unaffected by the soul-withering void which glimmered through chinks in the decking. At the end of the meal he actually chose to sit on the gondola wall, with one arm casually thrown around an acceleration strut, as he goaded the unhappy Rillomyner. Even though Flenn had tethered himself, the sight of him perched on the sky-backed rim produced such icy turmoil in Toller's gut that he bore the arrangement for only a few minutes before ordering the rigger to descend.

When Rillomyner had finished his work and retired to lie down on the sandbags, Toller took up his position at the pilot's station. He entered the new mode of propulsion by firing the jet in two-second bursts at wide intervals and studying the effects on the balloon. Each thrust brought creaks from the struts and rigging, but the envelope was affected much less than in experimental firings at low altitudes. Encouraged, Toller varied the timings and eventually settled on a two-four rhythm which acted in much the same manner as continuous impulsion without building up excessive speed. A short blast from the burner every second or third minute kept the balloon inflated and the crown from sagging too much as it nosed through the air.

'She handles well,' he said to Zavotle, who was industriously writing in the log. 'It looks as though you and I are going to have an easy run for the next day or two – until the instability sets in.'

Zavotle tilted his narrow head. 'It's easier on the ears, too.'

Toller nodded his agreement. Although the jet was firing for a greater proportion of every minute than the burner had been doing, its exhaust was not being directed into the great echo chamber of the balloon. The sound of it was flatter and less obtrusive, quickly absorbed by the surrounding oceans of stillness.

With the ship behaving so docilely and according to plan Toller began to feel that his forebodings of the night had been nothing more than a symptom of his growing tiredness. He was able to dwell on the incredible idea that in a mere seven or eight days, all being well, he was due to have a close look at another planet. The ship could not actually touch down on Overland, because doing so would involve pulling out the rip panel, and with no inflation facilities it would be unable to depart again. But it was to go within a few yards of the surface, dispelling the last traces of mystery about conditions on the sister planet.

The thousands of miles of air separating the two worlds had always made it difficult for astronomers to say much more than that there was an equatorial continent spanning the visible hemisphere. It had always been assumed, partly on religious grounds, that Overland closely resembled Land, but there remained the possibility that it was inhospitable, perhaps because of surface features beyond the resolving power of telescopes. And there was the further possibility – an article of faith for the Church, a moot case for philosophers – that Overland was already inhabited.

What would the Overlanders look like? Would they be builders of cities? And how would they react on seeing a fleet of strange ships float down from the sky?

Toller's musing was interrupted by the realisation that the coldness in the gondola had intensified in a matter of minutes. Simultaneously, he was approached by Flenn, who had the pet carble clutched to his chest and was visibly shivering. The little man's face was tinged with blue.

'This is killing me, captain,' he said, trying to force his customary grin. 'The cold has got worse all of a sudden.'

'You're right.' Toller felt a stirring of alarm at the idea of having crossed an invisible danger line in the atmosphere, then inspiration came to him. 'It's since we eased off on the burner. The blow-back of miglign was helping to keep us warm.'

'There was something else,' Zavotle added. 'The air streaming down over the hot envelope would have helped as well.'

'Damn!' Toller frowned up into the geometric traceries of the balloon. 'This means we'll have to put more heat in there. We have plenty of green and purple – so that's all right – but there's going to be a problem later on.'

Zavotle nodded, looking gloomy. 'The descent.'

Toller gnawed his lip as, yet again, difficulties unforeseen by the earthbound S.E.S. scientists confronted him. The only way for the hot-air craft to lose altitude was through shedding heat – suddenly a vital commodity as far as the crew were concerned – and to make matters worse the direction of the air flow would be reversed during the descent, carrying the reduced amount of warmth upwards and away from the gondola. The prospect was that they would have to endure days in conditions very much worse than those of the present – and there was a genuine possibility that death would intervene.

A dilemma had to be resolved.

Was the fact that so much depended on the outcome of the proving flight an argument for going on and on, even at the risk of passing an imperceptible point of no return? Or was there a higher obligation to be prudent and turn back with their hard-won store of knowledge?

'This is your lucky day,' Toller said to Rillomyner, who was watching him from his usual recumbent position in a passenger compartment. 'You wanted work to occupy your mind, and now you've got it. Find a way of diverting some heat from the burner exhaust back down into the gondola.'

The mechanic sat up with a startled expression. 'How could we do it, captain?'

'I don't know. It's your job to work out things like that. Rig up a scoop or something, and start right now – I'm tired of seeing you lie around like a pregnant gilt.'

Flenn's eyes gleamed. 'Is that any way to talk to our passenger, captain?'

'You've spent too much time on your backside, as well,' Toller told him. 'Have you needles and thread in your kit?'

'Yes, captain. Big needles, little needles, enough threads and twines to rig a sailing ship.'

'Then start emptying sandbags and making over-suits out of the sacking. We'll also need gloves.'

'Leave it to me, captain,' Flenn said. 'I'll fit us all out like kings.' Obviously pleased at having something constructive to do, Flenn tucked the carble into his clothing, went to his locker and began rummaging in its various compartments. He was whistling in shivery vibrato.

Toller watched him for a moment, then turned to Zavotle, who was blowing into his hands to keep them warm. 'Are you still worrying about relieving yourself in weightless conditions?'

Zavotle's eyes became wary. 'Why do you ask, captain?'

'You should be – it looks like a toss-up as to whether you produce steam or snow.'

Shortly before littlenight on the fifth day of the flight the gauge registered a height of 2,600 miles and a gravity value of zero.

The four members of the crew were tied into their wicker chairs around the power unit, their feet outstretched towards the warm base of the jet tube. They were muffled in crude garments of ragged brown sacking which disguised their human form and concealed the heaving of their chests as they laboured to deal with the thin and gelid air. Within the gondola the only signs of movement were the vapour featherings of the men's breath; and on the outside meteors flickered in deep blue infinities, briefly and randomly linking star to star.

'Well, here we are,' Toller said, breaking a lengthy silence. 'The hardest part of the flight is behind us, we have coped with every unpleasant surprise the heavens could throw at us, and we are still in good health. I'd say we are entitled to drink the brandy with the next meal.'

There was another protracted silence, as though thought itself had been chilled into sluggishness, and Zavotle said, 'I'm still worried about the descent, captain – even with the heater.'

'If we survived this far we can go on.' Toller glanced at the heating device which Rillomyner had designed and installed with some assistance from Zavotle. It consisted of nothing more than an elongated S-shape of brakka tubing sections jointed with glass cord and fireclay. Its top end curved over into the mouth of the burner and its bottom end was secured to the deck beside the pilot's station. A small proportion of each blast on the burner was channelled back down through the tube to send scorching miglign gas billowing through the gondola, making an appreciable difference to the temperature levels. Although the burner would necessarily be used less during the descent, Toller believed the heat drawn off from it would be sufficient for their needs in the two severest days.

'It's time for the medical report,' he said, signalling for Zavotle to make notes. 'How does everybody feel?'

'I still feel like we're falling, captain.' Rillomyner was gripping the sides of his chair. 'It's making me queasy.'

'How could we fall if we have no weight?' Toller said reasonably, ignoring the fluttering lightness in his own stomach. 'You'll have to get used to it. How about you, Flenn?'

'I'm all right, captain – heights don't bother me.' Flenn stroked the green-striped carble which was nestling on his chest with only its head protruding through a vent in his outer garment. 'Tinny is all right, as well. We help keep each other warm.'

'I suppose I'm in reasonable condition, considering.' Zavotle made an entry in the log, writing clumsily with gloved hand, and raised his reproachful gaze to Toller. 'Shall I put you down as being in fine fettle, captain? Best of health?'

'Yes, and all the sarcasm in the world won't get me to change my decision – I'm turning the ship over immediately after little-night.' Toller knew the co-pilot was still clinging to his opinion, voiced earlier, that they should delay turning the ship over for a full day or even longer after passing the zero gravity point. The reasoning was that doing so would get them through the region of greatest cold more quickly and with lost heat from the balloon protecting them from the chill. Toller could see some merit in the idea, but he would have exceeded his authority by putting it into practice.

As soon as you pass the midpoint Overland will begin attracting you towards it, Lain had impressed upon him. *The pull will be very slight at first, but it will quickly build up. If you augment that pull with the thrust from the drive jet you will soon exceed the design speed of the ship – and that must never be allowed to happen.*

Zavotle had argued that the S.E.S. scientists had not anticipated the life-threatening coldness, nor had they allowed for the fact that the thin air of the mid-passage exerted less force on the envelope, thus increasing the maximum safe speed. Toller had remained adamant. As captain of the ship he had considerable discretionary powers, but not when it was a case of challenging basic S.E.S. directives.

He had not admitted that his determination had been reinforced by an instinctive distaste for flying the ship upside down. Although during training he had been privately sceptical about the notion of weightlessness, he fully understood that as soon as the ship had passed the midpoint it would have entered the gravitational domain of Overland. In one sense the journey would have been completed, because – barring an act of human will translated into mechanical action – the destinies of the ship and its crew could no longer be affected by their home world. They would have been cast out, redefined as aliens by the terms of celestial physics.

Toller had decided that postponing the attitude reversal until littlenight had passed would use up all the leeway he had in the matter. Throughout the ascent Overland, though screened from view by the balloon, had steadily increased in apparent size and littlenight had grown longer accordingly. The approaching one would last more than three hours, and by the time it had ended the ship would have begun falling towards the sister planet. Toller found the progressive change in the patterns of night and day a powerful reminder of the magnitude of the voyage he had undertaken. There was no surprise as far as the intellect of the grown man was concerned, but the child in him was bemused and awed by what was happening. Night was becoming shorter as littlenight grew, and soon the natural order of things would be reversed. Land's night would have dwindled to become Overland's littlenight ...

While waiting for darkness to arrive, Toller and the others investigated the miracle of weightlessness. There was a rare fascination in suspending small objects in the air and watching them hold their positions, in defiance of all of life's teachings, until the next blast from the drive jet belatedly caused them to sink.

It is almost as if the jet somehow restores a fraction of their natural weight, ran Zavotle's entry in the log, *but of course that is a fanciful way of regarding the phenomenon. The real explanation is that they are invisibly fixed in place, and that the thrust from the jet enables the ship to overtake them.*

Littlenight came more suddenly than ever, wrapping the gondola in jewelled and fire-streaked blackness, and for its duration the four conversed in muted tones, recreating the mood of their first starlit communion of the flight. The talk ranged from gossip about life in the S.E.S. base to speculation about what strange things might be found on Overland, and once there was even an attempt to foresee the problems of flying to Farland, which could be observed hanging in the west like a green lantern. Nobody felt disposed, Toller noticed, to dwell on the fact that they were suspended between two worlds in a fragile open-topped box, with thousands of miles of emptiness lapping at the rim.

He also noticed that the crew had stopped addressing him as captain for the time being, and he was not displeased. He knew there was no lessening of his necessary authority – it was an unconscious acknowledgement of the fact that four ordinary men were venturing into the extraordinary, the region of strangeness, and that in their mutual need for each other they were equal …

One prismatic flash brought the daytime universe back into existence.

'Did you mention brandy, captain?' Rillomyner said. 'It has just occurred to me that some internal warmth might fortify this cursed delicate stomach of mine. The medicinal properties of brandy are well known.'

'We'll have the brandy with the next meal.' Toller blinked and looked about him, re-establishing connections with history. 'Before that the ship gets turned over.'

Earlier he had been pleased to discover that the ship's predicted instability in and close to the weightless zone was easy to overcome and control with the lateral jets. Occasional half-second bursts had been all that was necessary to keep the edge of the gondola in the desired relationship with the major stars. Now, however, the ship – or the universe – had to be stood on its head. He pumped the pneumatic reservoir to full pressure before feeding crystals to the east-facing jet for a full three seconds. The sound from the miniature orifice was devoured by infinity.

For a moment it seemed that its puny output would have no effect on the mass of the ship, then – for the first time since the beginning of the ascent – the great disk of Overland slid fully into view from behind the curvature of the balloon. It was lit by a crescent of fire along one rim, almost touching the sun.

At the same time Land rose above the rim of the gondola wall on the opposite side, and as air resistance overcame the impulsion from its jet the ship steadied in an attitude which presented the crew with a vision of two worlds.

By turning his head one way Toller could see Overland, mostly in black-ness because of its proximity to the sun; and in the other direction was the mind-swamping convexity of the home world, serene and eternal, bathed in sunshine except at its eastern rim, where a shrinking curved section still lay in little-night. He watched in rapt fascination as Overland's shadow swung clear of Land, feeling himself to be at the fulcrum of a lever of light, an in-tangible engine which had the power to move planets.

'For pity's sake, captain,' Rillomyner cried hoarsely, 'put the ship to rights.'

'You're in no danger.' Toller fired the lateral jet again and Land drifted majestically upwards to be occulted by the balloon as Overland sank below the edge of the gondola. The rigging creaked several times as he used the opposing lateral to balance the ship in its new attitude. Toller permitted himself a smile of satisfaction at having become the first man in history to turn a skyship over. The manoeuvre had been carried out quickly and with-out mishap – and from that point on the natural forces acting on the ship would do most of his work for him.

'Make a note,' he said to Zavotle. 'Midpoint successfully negotiated. I foresee no major obstacles in the descent to Overland.'

Zavotle freed his pencil from its restraining clip. 'We're still going to freeze, captain.'

'That isn't a major obstacle. If necessary we'll burn some green and purple right here on the deck.' Toller, suddenly exhilarated and optimistic, turned to Flenn. 'How do you feel? Can your head for heights cope with our present circumstances?'

Flenn grinned. 'If it's food you want, captain, I'm your man. I swear my arsehole has cobwebs over it.'

'In that case, see what you can do about a meal.' Toller knew the order would be particularly welcome because for more than a day the crew had opted to go without food or drink to obviate the indignity, discomfort and sheer unpleasantness of using the toilet facilities in virtual weightlessness.

He watched benignly as Flenn pushed the carble back into its warm sanc-tuary inside his clothing and untied himself from his chair. The little man was obviously struggling for breath as he swung his way into the galley, but the black cabochons of his eyes were glinting with good humour. He reappeared just long enough to hand Toller the single small flask of brandy which had been included in the ship's provisions, then there followed a long period during which he could be heard working with the cooking equip-ment, panting and swearing all the time. Toller took a sip of the brandy and had given the flask to Zavotle when it dawned on him that Flenn was trying to prepare a hot meal.

'You don't need to heat anything,' he called out. 'Cold jerky and bread will be enough.'

'It's all right, captain,' came Flenn's breathless reply. 'The charcoal is still lit … and it's only a matter of … fanning it hard enough. I'm going to serve you … a veritable banquet. A man needs a good … *Hell!*'

Concurrent with the last word there was a clattering sound. Toller turned towards the galley in time to see a burning piece of firewood rise vertically into the air from behind the partition. Lazily spinning, wrapped in pale yellow flame, it sailed upwards and glanced off a sloping lower panel of the balloon. Just when it seemed that it had been deflected harmlessly away into the blue it was caught by an air current which directed it into the narrowing gap between an acceleration strut and the envelope. It lodged in the juncture of the two, still burning.

'It's mine!' Flenn shouted. 'I'll get it!'

He appeared on the gondola wall at the corner, unhooking his tether, and went up the strut at speed, using only his hands in a curious weightless scramble. Toller's heart and mind froze over as he saw brownish smoke puff out from the varnished fabric of the balloon. Flenn reached the burning stick and grasped it with a gloved hand. He hurled the stick away with a lateral sweep of his arm and suddenly he too was separated from the ship, tumbling in thin air. Hands clawing vainly towards the strut, he floated slowly outwards.

Toller's consciousness was sundered by two focuses of terror. Fear of personal annihilation kept his gaze centred on the smoking patch of fabric until he saw that the flame had extinguished itself, but all the while he was filled with a silent-shrieking awareness of the bright void between Flenn and the balloon growing wider.

Flenn's initial impetus had not been great, but he had drifted outwards for some thirty yards before air resistance brought him to a halt. He hung in the blue emptiness, glowing in the sunlight which the balloon screened from the gondola, scarcely recognisable as a human being in his ragged swaddling of sackcloth.

Toller went to the side and cupped his hands around his mouth to aim a shout. 'Flenn! Are you all right?'

'Don't worry about me, captain.' Flenn waved an arm and, incredibly, he was able to sound almost cheerful. 'I can see the envelope well from here. There's a scorched area all around the strut attachment, but the fabric isn't holed.'

'We're going to bring you in.' Toller turned to Zavotle and Rillomyner. 'He isn't lost. We need to throw him a line.'

Rillomyner was doubled in his chair. 'Can't do it, captain,' he mumbled. 'I can't look out there.'

'You're going to look and you're going to work,' Toller assured him grimly.

'I can help,' Zavotle said, leaving his chair. He opened the rigger's locker and brought out several coils of rope. Toller, impatient to effect a rescue, snatched one of the ropes. He secured one end of it and flung the coil out towards Flenn, but as he did so his feet rose clear of the deck, and what he had intended as a powerful throw proved to be feeble and misdirected. The rope unfurled for only part of its length and froze uselessly, still retaining its undulations.

Toller drew the rope in and while he was coiling it again Zavotle threw his line with similar lack of success. Rillomyner, who was moaning faintly with every breath, hurled out a thinner line of glasscord. It extended fully in roughly the right direction, but stopped too short.

'Good for nothing!' Flenn jeered, seemingly undaunted by the thousands of miles of vacancy yawning below him. 'Your old grandmother could do better, Rillo.'

Toller removed his gloves and made a fresh attempt to bridge the void, but even though he had braced himself against a partition the cold-stiffened rope again failed to unwind properly. It was while he was retrieving it that he noticed an unnerving fact. At the beginning of the rescue effort Flenn had been considerably higher in relation to the ship, level with the upper end of the acceleration strut – but now he was only slightly above the rim of the gondola.

A moment's reflection told Toller that Flenn was falling. The ship was also falling, but as long as there was warmth inside the balloon it would retain some degree of buoyancy and would descend more slowly than a solid object. This close to the midpoint the relative speeds were negligible, but Flenn was nonetheless in the grip of Overland's gravity, and had begun the long plunge to the surface.

'Have you noticed what's happening?' Toller said to Zavotle in a low voice. 'We're running out of time.'

Zavotle assessed the situation. 'Is there any point in using the laterals?'

'We'd only start cartwheeling.'

'This is serious,' Zavotle said. 'First of all Flenn damages the balloon – then he puts himself in a position where he can't repair it.'

'I doubt if he did that on purpose.' Toller wheeled on Rillomyner. 'The cannon! Find a weight that will go into the cannon. Maybe we can fire a line.'

At that moment Flenn, who had been quiescent, appeared to notice his gradual change of position relative to the ship and to draw the appropriate conclusions. He began struggling and squirming, then made exaggerated swimming movements which in other circumstances might have been comic. Discovering that nothing was having any good effect he again became still, except for an involuntary movement of his hands when Zavotle's second throw of the rope failed to reach him.

'I'm getting scared, captain.' Although Flenn was shouting his voice seemed faint, its energies leaching away into the surrounding immensities. 'You've got to bring me home.'

'We'll bring you in. There's ...' Toller allowed the sentence to tail off. He had been going to assure Flenn there was plenty of time, but his voice would have lacked conviction. It was becoming apparent that not only was Flenn falling past the gondola, but that – in keeping with the immutable laws of physics – he was gaining speed. The acceleration was almost imperceptible, but its effects were cumulative. Cumulative and lethal ...

Rillomyner touched Toller's arm. 'There's nothing that will fit in the cannon, captain, but I joined two bits of glasscord and tied it to this.' He proffered a hammer with a large brakka head. 'I think it will reach him.'

'Good man,' Toller said, appreciative of the way the mechanic was overcoming his acrophobia in the emergency. He moved aside to let Rillomyner make the throw. The mechanic tied the free end of the glasscord to the rail, judged the distances and hurled the hammer out into space.

Toller saw at once that he had made the mistake of aiming high, compensating for a full-gravity drop that was not going to occur. The hammer dragged the cord out behind it and came to a halt in the air a tantalising few yards above Flenn, who was galvanised into windmilling his arms in a futile attempt to reach it. Rillomyner jiggled the cord in an effort to move the hammer downwards, but only succeeded in drawing it a short distance back towards the ship.

'That's no good,' Toller snapped. 'Pull it in fast and throw straight at him next time.' He was trying to suppress a growing sense of panic and despair. Flenn was now visibly sinking below the level of the gondola, and the hammer was less likely to reach him as the range increased and the angles became less conducive to accurate throwing. What Flenn desperately needed was a means of reducing the distance separating him from the gondola, and that was impossible unless ... unless ...

A familiar voice spoke inside Toller's head. *Action and reaction*, Lain was saying. *That's the universal principle ...*

'Flenn, you can bring yourself closer,' Toller shouted. 'Use the carble! Throw it straight away from the ship, as hard as you can. That will drift you in this direction.'

There was a pause before Flenn responded. 'I couldn't do that, captain.'

'This is an order,' Toller bellowed. 'Throw the carble, and throw it right *now!* We're running out of time.'

There was a further pounding delay, then Flenn was seen to be fumbling with the coverings on his chest. Sunlight flared on the lower surfaces of his body as he slowly produced the green-striped animal.

Toller swore in frustration. 'Hurry, *hurry!* We're going to lose you.'

'You've already lost me, captain.' Flenn's voice was resigned. 'But I want you to take Tinny home with you.'

There was a sudden sweeping movement of his arm and he went tumbling backwards as the carble sailed towards the ship. It was travelling too low. Toller watched numbly as the terrified animal, mewing and clawing at the air, passed out of sight below the gondola. Its yellow eyes had seemed to be boring into his own. Flenn receded a short distance before he stabilised himself by spreading his arms and legs. He came to rest in the attitude of a drowned man, floating face-down on an invisible ocean, his gaze directed towards Overland – thousands of miles below – which had taken him in its gravitational arms.

'You stupid little midget,' Rillomyner sobbed as he again sent the hammer snaking towards Flenn. It stopped short and a little to one side of its target. Flenn, body and limbs rigid, continued to sink with gathering speed.

'He'll be falling for maybe a day,' Zavotle whispered. 'Just think of it ... a whole day ... falling ... I wonder if he'll still be alive when he hits the ground.'

'I've got other things to think about,' Toller said harshly, turning away from the gondola wall, unable to watch Flenn dwindling out of sight.

His brief required him to abort the flight in the event of losing a crew member or sustaining some serious structural damage to the ship. Nobody could have foreseen both circumstances arising as a result of one trivial-seeming accident with the galley stove, but he felt no less responsible – and it remained to be seen if the S.E.S. administrators would also regard him as culpable.

'Switch us back to jet power,' he said to Rillomyner. 'We're going home.'

PART III

Region of Strangeness

CHAPTER SIXTEEN

The cave was in the side of a ragged hill, in an area of broken terrain where numerous gullies, rocky projections and a profusion of spiky scrub made the going difficult for man or beast.

Lain Maraquine was content to let the bluehorn pick its own way around the various obstacles, giving it only an occasional nudge to keep it heading for the orange flag which marked the cave's position. The four mounted soldiers of his personal guard, obligatory for any senior official of the S.E.S., followed a short distance behind, the murmur of their conversation blending with the heavy drone of insects. Littlenight was not long past and the high sun was baking the ground, clothing the horizon in tremulous purple-tinted blankets of hot air.

Lain felt unusually relaxed, appreciating the opportunity to get away from the skyship base and turn his mind to matters which had nothing to do with world crises and interplanetary travel. Toller's premature return from the proving flight, ten days earlier, had involved Lain in a harrowing round of meetings, consultations and protracted studies of the new scientific data obtained. One faction in the S.E.S. administration had wanted a second proving flight with a full descent to Overland and detailed mapping of the central continent. In normal circumstances Lain would have been in agreement, but the rapidly worsening situation in Kolcorron overrode all other consideration ...

The production target of one thousand skyships had been achieved with some to spare, thanks to the driving ruthlessness and Leddravohr and Chakkell.

Fifty of the ships had been set aside for the transportation of the country's royalty and aristocrats in small family groups who would travel in comparative luxury, though by no means all of the nobility had decided to take part in the migration. Another two hundred were designated as cargo vessels which would carry food, livestock, seeds, weapons and essential machinery and materials; and a further hundred were for the use of military personnel. That left six hundred and fifty ships which, with reduced two-man crews, had the capability of transporting almost twelve thousand of the general population to Overland.

At an early stage of the great undertaking King Prad had decreed that emigration would be on a purely voluntary basis, with equal numbers of males and females, and that fixed proportions of the available places would be allocated to men with key skills.

For a long time the hard-headed citizenry had declined to take the proposal seriously, regarding it as a diversion, a regal folly to be chuckled over in taverns. The small numbers who put their names forward were treated with derision, and it seemed that if the skyship fleet were ever to be filled it would only be at swordpoint.

Prad had chosen to bide his time, knowing in advance that greater forces than he could ever muster were on the move. The ptertha plague, famine and the abrupt crumbling of social order had exerted their powerful persuasions, and – in spite of condemnation from the Church – the roster of willing emigrants had swollen. But such was the conservatism of the Kolcorronians and so radical the solution to their problems that a certain degree of reserve still had to be overcome, a lingering feeling that any amount of deprivation and danger on Land was preferable to the near-inevitability of a highly unnatural death in the alien blue reaches of the sky.

Then had come the news that an S.E.S. ship had voyaged more than halfway to Overland and had returned intact.

Within hours every remaining place on the emigration flight had been allocated, and suddenly those who held the necessary warrants were objects of envy and resentment. There was a reversal of public opinion, swift and irrational, and many who had scorned the very notion of flying to the sister world began to see themselves as victims of discrimination.

Even the majority who were too apathetic to care much either way about the broad historical issues were disgruntled by stories of wagons loaded with scarce provisions disappearing through the gates of Skyship Quarter...

Against that background Lain had argued that the proving flight had achieved all its major objectives by successfully turning over and passing the midpoint. The descent to the surface of Overland would have been a passive and predictable business; and Zavotle's sketches of the central continent, viewed through binoculars, were good enough to show that it was remarkably free of mountains and other features which would have jeopardised safe landings.

Even the loss of a crew member had occurred in such a way as to provide a valuable lesson about the inadvisability of cooking in weightless conditions. The commander of the ship was to be congratulated on his conduct of a uniquely demanding mission, Lain had concluded, and the migration itself should begin in the very near future.

His arguments had been accepted.

The first squadron of forty skyships, mainly carrying soldiers and construction workers, was scheduled to depart on Day 80 of the year 2630.

That date was only six days in the future, and as Lain's steed picked its way up the hill to the cave it came to him that he was curiously unexcited by the prospect of flying to Overland. If all went according to plan he and Gesalla would be on a ship of the tenth squadron, which – allowing for delays caused by unsuitable weather or pertha activity – was due to leave the home world in perhaps only twenty days' time. Why was he so little moved by the imminence of what would be the greatest personal adventure of his life, the finest scientific opportunity he could ever conceive, the boldest undertaking in the entire history of mankind?

Was it that he was too timorous even to allow himself to think about the event? Was it that the growing rift with Gesalla – unacknowledged but ever present in his awareness – had severed a spiritual taproot, rendering him emotionally sere and sterile? Or was it a simple failure of the imagination on the part of one who prided himself on his superior qualities of mind?

The torrent of questions and doubts subsided as the bluehorn reached a rock-strewn shelf and Lain saw the entrance to the cave a short distance ahead. Grateful for the internal respite, he dismounted and waited for the soldiers to catch up on him. The four men's faces were beaded with sweat below their leather helmets, and they were obviously puzzled at having been brought to such a desolate spot.

'You will wait for me here,' Lain said to the burly sergeant. 'Where will you post your look-outs?'

The sergeant shaded his eyes from the near-vertical rays of the sun which were stabbing past the fire-limned disk of Overland. 'On top of the hill, sir. They should be able to see five or six observation posts from there.'

'Good! I'm going into this cave and I don't want to be disturbed. Only call me if there is a pertha warning.'

'Yes, sir.'

While the sergeant dismounted and deployed his men Lain opened the panniers strapped to his bluehorn and took out four oil lanterns. He ignited the wicks with a lens, picked the lanterns up by their glasscord slings and carried them into the cave. The entrance was quite low and as narrow as a single door. For a moment the air was even warmer than in the open, then he was in a region of dim coolness where the walls receded to form a spacious chamber. He set the lanterns on the dirt floor and waited for his eyes to adjust to the poor light.

The cave had been discovered earlier in the year by a surveyor investigating the hill as a possible site for an observation post. Perhaps through genuine enthusiasm, perhaps out of a desire to sample Lord Glo's noted hospitality, the surveyor had made his way to Greenmount and lodged a description of the cave's startling contents. The report had reached Lain a short time later and he had decided to view the find for himself as soon as he had time to spare from his work. Now, surrounded by a fading screen of after-images, he understood that his coming to the dark place was symbolic. He was turning towards Land's past and away from Overland's future, confessing that he wanted no part of the migration flight or what lay beyond it ...

The pictures on the cave walls were becoming visible.

There was no order to the scenes portrayed. It appeared that the largest and flattest areas had been used first, and that succeeding generations of artists had filled in the intervening spaces with fragmentary scenes, using their ingenuity to incorporate bosses, hollows and cracks as features of their designs.

The result was a labyrinthine montage in which the eye was compelled to wander unceasingly from semi-naked hunters to family groups to stylised brakka trees to strange and familiar animals, erotica, demons, cooking pots, flowers, human skeletons, weapons, suckling babes, geometrical abstracts, fish, snakes, unclassifiable artifacts and impenetrable symbols. In some cases cardinal lines had been graven into the rock and filled with pitch, causing the images to advance on the sight with relentless power; in others there was a spatial ambiguity by which a human or animal form might be defined by nothing more than the changing intensity of a patch of colour. For the most part the pigments were still vivid where they were meant to be vivid, and restrained where the artist had chosen to be subtle, but in some places time itself had contributed to the visual complexity with the stainings of moisture and fungal growths.

Lain was overwhelmed, as never before, by a sense of duration.

The basic thesis of the Kolcorronian religion was that Land and Overland had always existed and had always been very much as they were in modern times, twin poles for the continuous alternation of discarnate human spirits. Four centuries earlier a war had been fought to stamp out the Bithian Heresy, which claimed that a person would be rewarded for a life of virtue on one world by being given a higher station when reincarnated on the sister planet. The Church's main objection had been to the idea of a progression and therefore of change, which conflicted with the essential teaching that the present order was immutable and eternal. Lain found it easy to believe that the macrocosm had always been as it was, but on the small stage of human history there was evidence of change, and by extrapolating backwards one could arrive at ... *this!*

He had no way of estimating the age of the cave paintings, but his instinct was to think in millennia and not in centuries. Here was evidence that men had once existed in vastly different circumstances, that they had thought in different ways, and had shared the planet with animals which no longer existed. He experienced a pang of mingled intellectual stimulation and regret as he realised that here, in the confines of one rocky cavity, was the material for a lifetime of work. It would have been possible for him to complement the abstractions of mathematics with the study of his own kind, a course which seemed infinitely more natural and rewarding than fleeing to another world.

Could I still do it?

The thought, only half serious though it was, seemed to intensify the coolness of the cave and Lain raised his shoulders in the beginnings of a shudder. He found himself, as had happened several times recently, trying to analyse his commitment to flying to Overland.

Was it the logical thing to do – the coolly considered action of a philosopher – or did he feel that he owed it to Gesalla, and the children she was determined to have, to give them a divergent future? Until he had begun examining his own motives the issue had seemed clear cut – fly to Overland and embrace the future, or stay on Land and die with the past.

But the majority of the population had not had to make that decision. They would be following the very human course of refusing to lie down until they were dead, of simply ignoring the defeatist notion that the blind and mindless ptertha could triumph over mankind. Indeed, the migration flight could not even take place without the cooperation of those who were staying behind – the inflation crews, the men in the ptertha observation posts, the military who would defend Skyship Quarter and continue to impose order after the King and his entourage had departed.

Human life was not going to cease overnight on Land, Lain had realised. There could be many years, decades, of shrinkage and retrenchment, and perhaps the process would eventually produce a hard core of unkillables, few in number, living underground in conditions of unimaginable privation. Lain did not want to be part of that grim scenario, but the point was that he might be able to find a niche within it. The point was that, given sufficient will, he could probably live out his allotted span on the planet of his birth, where his existence had relevance and meaning.

But what about Gesalla?

She was too loyal to consider leaving without him. Such was her character that the very fact of their drifting apart mentally would cause her to cleave to him all the more in body, in obedience to her marriage vows. He doubted if she had even yet admitted to herself that she was ...

Lain's eyes, darting urgently over the time-deep panorama surrounding him, fastened on the image of a small child at play. It was a vignette, at the triangular juncture of three larger scenes, and showed a male infant absorbed with what appeared to be a doll which he was holding in one hand. His other hand was outstretched to the side, as though carelessly reaching for a familiar pet, and just beyond it was a featureless circle. The circle was devoid of coloration and could have represented several things – a large ball, a balloon, a whimsically placed Overland – but Lain was oddly tempted to see it as a ptertha.

He picked up a lantern and went closer to the picture. The intensified illumination confirmed that the circle had never contained any pigment, which was strange considering that the long-dead artists had shown great scrupulousness and subtlety in their rendering of other less significant subjects. That implied that his interpretation had been wrong, especially as the child in the fragmentary scene was obviously relaxed and unperturbed by the nearness of what would have been an object of terror.

Lain's deliberations were interrupted by the sound of someone entering the cave. Frowning with annoyance, he raised the lantern, then took an involuntary pace backwards as he saw that the newcomer was Leddravohr. The prince's smile flicked into existence for a moment as he emerged from the narrow passage, battle sword scraping the wall, and ran his gaze around the cave.

'Good aftday, Prince,' Lain said, dismayed to find that he was beginning to tremble. Many meetings with Leddravohr during the course of his work for the S.E.S. had taught him to retain most of his composure when they were with others and in the humdrum atmosphere of an office, but here in the constricted space of the cave Leddravohr was huge, inhumanly powerful and frightening. He was far enough removed from Lain in mind and outlook to have stepped out of one of the primitive scenes glowing in the surrounding half-light.

Leddravohr gave the entire display a cursory inspection before speaking. 'I was told there was something remarkable here, Maraquine. Was I misinformed?'

'I don't think so, Prince.' Lain hoped he had been able to keep a tremor out of his voice.

'You don't think so? Well, what is it that your fine brain appreciates and mine doesn't?'

Lain sought an answer which would not frame the insult Leddravohr had devised for him. 'I haven't had time to study the pictures, Prince – but I am interested in the fact that they are obviously very old.'

'How old?'

'Perhaps three or four thousand years.'

Leddravohr snorted in amusement. 'That's nonsense. You're saying these scrawls are far older than Ro-Atabri itself?'

'It was just my opinion, Prince.'

'You're wrong. The colours are too fresh. This place has been a bolt hole during one of the civil wars. Some insurgents have hidden out here and ...' Leddravohr paused to peer closely at a sketch depicting two men in a contorted sexual position. 'And you can see what they did to pass the time. Is this what intrigues you, Maraquine?'

'No, Prince.'

'Do you ever lose your temper, Maraquine?'

'I try not to, Prince.'

Leddravohr snorted again, padded around the cave and came back to Lain. 'All right, you can stop shaking – I'm not going to touch you. It may interest you to learn that I'm here because my father has heard about this spider hole. He wants the drawings accurately copied. How long will that take?'

Lain glanced around the walls. 'Four good draughtsmen could do it in a day, Prince.'

'You arrange it.' Leddravohr stared at him with an unreadable expression on his smooth face. 'Why does anybody give a fig about the likes of this place? My father is old and worn out; he has soon to face flying to Overland; most of our population has been wiped out by the plague, and the remainder are getting ready to riot; and even some units of the army are becoming unruly now that they are hungry and it has dawned on them that I soon won't be here to look after their welfare – and yet all my father is concerned about is seeing these miserable scrawls for himself. Why, Maraquine, *why?*'

Lain was unprepared for the question. 'King Prad appears to have the instincts of a philosopher, Prince.'

'You mean he's like you?'

'I didn't intend to elevate myself to ... '

'Never mind all that. Was that supposed to be your answer? He wants to know things because he wants to know things?'

'That's what "philosopher" means, Prince.'

'But ...' Leddravohr broke off as there was a clattering of equipment in the cave entrance and the sergeant of Lain's personal guard appeared. He saluted Leddravohr and, although agitated, waited for permission to speak.

'Go on, man,' Leddravohr said.

'The wind is rising in the west, Prince. We are warned of ptertha.'

Leddravohr waved the sergeant away. 'All right – we will leave soon.'

'The wind is rising quickly, Prince,' the sergeant said, obviously deeply unhappy at lingering beyond his dismissal.

'And a crafty old soldier like you sees no point in taking unnecessary risks.' Leddravohr placed a hand on the sergeant's shoulder and shook him playfully, an intimacy he would not have granted the loftiest aristocrat. 'Take your men and leave now, sergeant.'

The sergeant's eyes emitted a single flash of gratitude and adoration as he hurried away. Leddravohr watched him depart, then turned to Lain.

'You were explaining this passion for useless knowledge,' he said. 'Continue!'

'I ...' Lain tried to organise his thoughts. 'In my profession all knowledge is regarded as useful.'

'Why?'

'It's part of a whole ... a unified structure ... and when that structure is complete Man will be complete and will have total control of his destiny.'

'Fine words!' Leddravohr's discontented gaze steadied on the section of wall closest to where Lain was standing. 'Do you really believe the future of our race hinges on that picture of a brat playing ball?'

'That isn't what I said, Prince.'

'That isn't what I said, Prince,' Leddravohr mocked. 'You have told me nothing, philosopher.'

'I am sorry that you heard nothing,' Lain said quietly.

Leddravohr's smile appeared on the instant. 'That was meant to be an insult, wasn't it? Love of knowledge must *be* an ardent passion indeed if it begins to stiffen your backbone, Maraquine. We will continue this discussion on the ride back. Come!'

Leddravohr went to the entrance, turned sideways and negotiated the narrow passage. Lain blew out the four lanterns and, leaving them where they were, followed Leddravohr to the outside. A noticeable breeze was streaming over the uneven contours of the hill from the west. Leddravohr, already astride his bluehorn, watched in amusement as Lain gathered the skirts of his robe and inexpertly dragged himself up into his own saddle. After a searching look at the sky, Leddravohr led the way down the hill, controlling his mount with the straight-backed nonchalance of the born rider.

Lain, yielding to an impulse, urged his bluehorn forward on a roughly parallel track, determined to keep abreast of the prince. They were almost halfway down the hill when he discovered he was guiding his animal at speed into a patch of loose shale. He tried to pull the bluehorn to the right, but only succeeded in throwing it off balance. It gave a bark of alarm as it lost its footing on the treacherous surface and fell sideways. Lain heard its leg snap as he threw himself clear, aiming for a clump of yellow grass which had mercifully appeared in his view. He hit the ground, rolled over and jumped to his feet immediately, unharmed but appalled by the agonised howling of the bluehorn as it threshed on the clattering flakes of rock.

Leddravohr dismounted in a single swift movement and strode to the fallen animal, black sword in hand. He moved in quickly and drove the blade into the bluehorn's belly, angling the thrust forward to penetrate the chest cavity. The bluehorn gave a convulsive heave and emitted a slobbering, snoring sound as it died. Lain clapped a hand over his mouth as he fought to control the racking upsurges of his stomach.

'Here's another morsel of useful knowledge for you,' Leddravohr said calmly. 'When you're killing a bluehorn, never go straight into the heart or you'll get blood all over you. This way the heart discharges into the body cavities, and there is very little mess. See?' Leddravohr withdrew his sword, wiped it on the dead animal's mane and spread his arms, inviting inspection of his unmarked clothing. 'Don't you agree that it's all very ... philosophical?'

'I made it fall,' Lain mumbled.

'It was only a bluehorn.' Leddravohr sheathed his sword, returned to his mount and swung himself into the saddle. 'Come on, Maraquine – what are you waiting for?'

Lain looked at the prince, who had one hand outstretched in readiness to assist him on to the bluehorn, and felt a powerful aversion to making the physical contact. 'Thank you, Prince – but it would be improper for one of my station to ride with you.'

Leddravohr burst out laughing. 'What are you talking about, you fool? We're out in the real world now – the soldier's world – and the ptertha are on the move.'

The reference to the ptertha went through Lain like a dagger of ice. He took a hesitant step forward.

'Don't be so bashful,' Leddravohr said, his eyes amused and derisive. 'After all, it wouldn't be the first time you and I had shared a mount.'

Lain came to a standstill, his brow dewing over with cool perspiration, and he heard himself say, 'On consideration, I prefer to make my own way back to the Quarter on foot.'

'I'm losing patience with you, Maraquine.' Leddravohr shaded his eyes and scanned the western sky. 'I'm not going to plead with you to preserve your own life.'

'My life is my responsibility, Prince.'

'It must be something in the Maraquine blood,' Leddravohr said, shrugging as he addressed a notional third party.

He turned his bluehorn's head to the east and urged the beast into a canter. Within a few seconds he had passed out of sight behind a shoulder of rock, and Lain was alone in a harsh landscape which suddenly seemed as alien and unforgiving as a distant planet. He gave a shaky, incredulous laugh as he took stock of the predicament he had placed himself in with a single failure of reason.

Why now? he demanded of himself. *Why did I wait until now?*

There was a faint scraping sound from nearby. Lain wheeled in fright and saw that pallid multipedes were already writhing upwards out of their burrows, disturbing small pebbles in their eagerness to converge on the dead bluehorn. He lunged away from the spectacle. For a moment he considered returning to the cave, then realised it would offer only minimal protection during daylight – and after nightfall the entire hill was likely to be swarming with globes, patiently nuzzling and probing. The best plan was to head eastwards to Skyship Quarter with all possible speed and try to get there before the ptertha came riding down the wind.

The decision made, Lain began to run through the murmurous heat. Near the base of the hill he emerged on an open slope which gave him an unrestricted view to the east. A far-off plume of dust marked Leddravohr's course and a long way ahead of him, almost at the drab boundaries of the Quarter, a larger cloud showed how far the four soldiers had gone. He had not appreciated the difference in speed between a man on foot and one mounted on a galloping bluehorn. He would be able to make better progress when he reached the flat grassland, but even so it would probably be an hour before he reached safety.

An *hour!*

Is there any hope at all of my surviving for that length of time?

As a distraction from his growing physical distress, he tried to bring his professional skills to bear on the question. The statistics, when looked at dispassionately, were more encouraging than he might have expected.

Daylight and flat terrain were conditions which did not favour the ptertha. They had virtually no self-propulsive capability in the horizontal plane, depending on air currents to carry them across the face of the land, which meant that an active man had little to fear from ptertha while he was crossing open ground. Assuming they had not blanketed the area – something which rarely happened in daytime – all he had to do was observe the globes closely and be aware of the wind direction. When menaced by a ptertha, it was simply a matter of waiting until just before it came within the killing radius, then running crosswind for a short distance and allowing the globe to drift helplessly by.

Lain stumbled to a halt in a gully, his mouth filling with the salt froth of exhaustion, and leaned on a rock to recover his breath. It was vital that he should still have reserves of strength and be nimble on his feet when he reached the plain. As the tumult in his chest gradually subsided he indulged himself in a visualisation of his next encounter with Leddravohr, and – incredibly – he felt his gaping mouth trying to form a grin. This was the irony of ironies! While the renowned military prince had fled to seek refuge from the ptertha, the mild-mannered philosopher had strolled back to the city, in need of no armour but his intellect. This was proof indeed that he was no coward, proof for all to see, proof that even his wife would have to ...

I've gone mad! The thought caused Lain to moan aloud in sheer self-loathing. *I have truly lost what used to be my mind!*

I permitted a savage to breach my defences with all his crassness and malice, his celebration of stupidity and glorification of ignorance. I let him debase me

*until I was prepared to throw away life itself in a weltering of hatred and pride
– what laudable emotions! – and now I'm indulging in fantasies of childish
revenge, so gratified by my own superiority that I haven't even taken the basic
precaution of making sure there are no ptertha at hand!*

Lain straightened up and – sick with premonition – turned to look back
along the gully.

The ptertha was barely ten paces away, well within its killing radius,
and the breeze coursing along the gully was sweeping it closer to him with
mind-freezing swiftness.

It swelled to encompass his view, its glistening transparencies tinged with
purple and black. In one part of his mind Lain felt a perverse flicker of gratitude that the issue had been decided for him, so quickly and so finally. There
was no point in trying to run, no point in trying to fight. He saw the ptertha
as he had never seen one before, saw the livid swirlings of the toxic dust
inside it. Was there a hint of structure there? A globe within a globe? Was
a malign proto-intelligence knowingly sacrificing itself in order to destroy
him?

The ptertha filled Lain's universe.

It was everywhere – and then it was nowhere.

He took a deep breath and looked about him with the ruefully placid gaze
of the man who has only one further decision to make.

Not here, he thought. *Not in this blind and circumscribed place – it isn't at
all suitable.*

Recalling the higher slope which had afforded the good view to the east,
he retraced his steps along the bed of the ancient stream, walking slowly
now and emitting occasional sighs. When he reached the slope he sat on the
ground with his back to an agreeably shaped boulder and arranged his robe
in neat folds around his outstretched legs.

The world of his last day was laid out before him. The triangular outline
of Mount Opelmer floated low in the sky, seemingly detached from the horizontal ribbons and speckled bands which represented Ro-Atabri and the
derelict suburbs on the shores of Arle Bay. Closer and lower was the artificial
community of the Skyship Quarter, its dozens of balloon enclosures an illusory city of rectangular towers. The Tree glittered in the southern heavens,
its nine stars challenging the sun's brilliance, and at the zenith a broad crescent of mellow light was spreading insensibly across the disk of Overland.

The whole span of my life and work is in that scene, Lain mused. *I have
brought my writing materials and should try to make some kind of a summation ... not that the last thoughts of one who precipitated his own demise
in such a ludicrous fashion would be of much interest or value to others ...
at most I could record what is already known – that pterthacosis is not a bad
death ... as deaths go, that is ... nature can be merciful ... as the most horrific*

shark bites are often unaccompanied by pain, so the inhalation of ptertha dust can sometimes engender a strange mood of resignation, a chemical fatalism … in that respect at least, I appear to be fortunate … except that I am deprived of feelings which are mine by ancient right …

A burning sensation manifested itself below Lain's chest and spread radial tendrils into the rest of his torso. At the same time the air about him seemed to grow cold, as though the sun had lost its heat. He put a hand into a pocket of his robe, brought out a bag made of yellow linen and spread it on his lap. There was a final duty to be performed – but not yet.

I wish Gesalla were here … Gesalla and Toller … so that I could give them to each other, or ask them to accept each other … irony piles upon irony … Toller always wanted to be different, to be more like me … and when he became the new Toller, I was forced to become the old Toller … to the final extent of throwing down my life for the sake of honour, a gesture which should have been made before my beautiful solewife was ravaged and defiled by Leddravohr … Toller was right about that, and I – in my so-called wisdom – told him he was wrong … Gesalla knew in her head that he was wrong, and in her heart that he was right …

A stab of pain in Lain's chest was accompanied by a bout of shivering. The view before him was curiously flat. He could see more ptertha now. They were drifting down towards the plain in groups of two and three, but they had no relevance to what was left of his life. The dream-flow of his fragmentary thoughts was the new reality.

Poor Toller … he became what he aspired to be, and how did I reward him? … with resentment and envy … I hurt him on the day of Glo's interment, only able to do so because he loves me, but he responded to my childish spite with dignity and forbearance … brakka and ptertha go together … I love my 'little brother' and I wonder if Gesalla even yet realises that she too … these things can take such a long time … of course brakka and ptertha go together – it's a symbiotic partnership … only now do I understand why it was not in my heart to fly to Overland … the future is there, and the future belongs to Gesalla and Toller … could that be the underlying reason for my refusing to ride with Leddravohr, for choosing my own Bright Road? … was I making Toller's way clear? … was I excising an unbalancing factor from the equation? … equations used to mean so much to me …

The fire in Lain's chest was becoming hotter, expanding, causing him to struggle for breath. He was sweating profusely and yet his skin felt deathly cold, and the world was merely a scene painted on rippling cloth. It was time for the yellow hood.

Lain lifted it with clumsy fingers and drew it over his head – a warning to anyone who might come by that he had died of pterthacosis and that the body was not to be approached for at least five days. The eye slits were not in the right place, but he allowed his hands to fall to his side without adjusting them, content to remain in a private universe of formless and featureless yellow.

Time and space ran together in that undemanding microcosm.

Yes, I was right about the cave painting ... the circle represents a ptertha ... a colourless ptertha ... one which has not yet developed its specialised toxins ... who was it who once asked me if the ptertha used to be pink? ... and what was my reply? ... did I say the naked child is not afraid of the globe because he knows it will not harm him? ... I know I have always disappointed Toller in one respect, by my lack of physical courage ... my disregard for honour ... but now he can be proud of me ... I wish I could be there to see his face when he hears that I preferred to die rather than to ride with ... isn't it strange that the answer to the riddle of the ptertha has always been visible in the sky? ... the Tree and the circle of Overland, symbolising the ptertha, co-existing in harmony ... the brakka pollination discharges feed the ptertha with ... with what? ... pollen, green and purple, miglign? ... and in return the ptertha seek out and destroy the brakka's enemies ... Toller should be protected from Prince Leddravohr ... he believes himself to be equal to him, but I fear ... I FEAR I HAVE NOT TOLD ANYONE ABOUT THE BRAKKA AND THE PTERTHA! ... how long have I known? ... is this a dream? ... where is my lovely Gesalla? ... can I still move my hands? ... can I still? ...

CHAPTER SEVENTEEN

Prince Leddravohr picked up a looking glass and frowned at his reflection. Even when resident in the Great Palace he preferred not to be attended by body servants, and for his morning toilet he had spent a considerable time in honing a brakka razor to a perfect edge and softening his facial stubble with hot water. As a result, annoyingly, he had pared away too much skin at his throat. There were no real incisions, but droplets of blood were oozing through the skin, and no matter how often he dabbed them away more appeared in their place.

This what comes of living like a pampered maiden, he told himself, pressing a damp cloth to his throat and postponing the act of dressing until the bleeding had stopped. The mirror, made from two different kinds of glass bonded together, was almost totally reflective, but when he faced the window he could discern its brilliant rectangles through the glass sandwich, apparently occupying the same space as his own body.

It's only appropriate, he thought. *I'm becoming insubstantial, a ghost, in preparation for the ascent to Overland. My real life, the only life that has any significance, will be over and done with when ...* His thoughts were interrupted by the sound of running footsteps in the adjoining apartment. He turned and saw in the doorway of the toilet chamber the square-shouldered figure of Major Yachimalt, the adjutant responsible for communications between the palace and Skyship Quarter. Yachimalt's anxious eyes took in the fact that Leddravohr was naked and he made as if to back out of the room.

'Forgive me, Prince,' he said. 'I didn't realise ...'

'What's the matter with you, man?' Leddravohr snapped. 'If you have a message for me, spit it out.'

'It's a signal from Colonel Hippern, Prince. He says a mob is gathering at the main entrance to the Quarter.'

'He has a full regiment at his disposal, hasn't he? Why should I concern myself with the activities of a rabble?'

'The signal says that the Lord Prelate is inciting them, Prince,' Yachimalt replied. 'Colonel Hippern requests your authority to place him under arrest.'

'Balountar! That miserable sack of bones!' Leddravohr threw the looking glass aside and went to the rack which held his clothing. 'Tell Colonel Hippern that he is to hold his ground, but to make no move against Balountar until I arrive. I will deal with our Lord Scarecrow in person.'

Yachimalt saluted and vanished from the doorway. Leddravohr found himself actually smiling as he dressed quickly and strapped on his white cuirass. With only five days to go until the first squadron departed for Overland the preparations for the migration were virtually complete and he had not looked forward to a span of enforced idleness. When there was no work to be done his thoughts all too easily turned to the unnatural ordeal which lay ahead, and it was then that the pale maggots of fear and self-doubt began the insidious attack. Now he could almost feel grateful to the ranting Lord Prelate for presenting him with a diversion, the opportunity to be fully alive and functional once more.

Leddravohr buckled on his sword and the knife he wore on his left arm. He hurried out of his suite, heading for the principal forecourt, choosing a downward route on which there was little chance of encountering his father. The King maintained an excellent intelligence network and would almost certainly have heard about Lain Maraquine's suicidal behaviour of the previous aftday. Leddravohr had no wish to be quizzed about the absurd incident at that moment. He had given orders for a team of draughtsmen to go to the cave and copy the drawings, and he wanted to be able to present the transcription to his father at their next meeting. Instinct told him that the King would be angry and suspicious if, as was almost certainly the case,

Maraquine proved to be dead, but it was possible that the drawings would mollify him.

On reaching the forecourt Leddravohr signalled for an ostiary to bring forward the dappled bluehorn he normally rode and in a matter of seconds he was galloping towards the Skyship Quarter. Emerging from the double cocoon of netting which enveloped the palace he entered one of the tubular covered ways which crossed the four ornamental moats. The sheath of varnished linen was proof against ptertha dust and provided safe passage into Ro-Atabri itself, but the sense of being enclosed and herded was irksome to Leddravohr. He was glad when he reached the city, where the sky was at least visible through the overhead meshworks, and he could follow the embankments of the Borann to the west.

There were few citizens abroad and most of those he saw were making their way towards the Quarter, seemingly guided by an extra sense which told them of significant events taking place far ahead. It was a hot and windless morning, with no threat from ptertha. When he reached the western limit of the city he ignored the covered way which ran to the perimeter of the skyship base, riding south of it in the open air to where he could see a crowd gathered at the main entrance. The side panels of the flimsy tube had been furled, enabling the crowd to form a continuous obstruction across the security gate. On the far side of the gate he could see a line of pikes projecting into the air, indicating the presence of soldiers, and he nodded in approval – the pike was a good weapon for demonstrating to unruly civilians the error of their ways.

As he neared the mass of people Leddravohr slowed his bluehorn to a walking pace. When his approach was noticed the crowd parted respectfully to make way for him, and he was surprised to note how many were dressed in ragged garments. The plight of the ordinary citizens of Ro-Atabri was obviously worse than he had realised. Amid much whispering and jostling, the edge of the crowd flowed outwards to create a semi-circular space at the focus of which was the black-robed figure of Balountar.

The Lord Prelate, who had been haranguing an officer on the other side of the closed gate, turned to face Leddravohr. He started visibly at the sight of the military prince, but the expression of anger on his squeezed-in features did not change. Leddravohr rode to him at a leisurely pace, dismounted with a deliberate display of lazy confidence and signalled for the gate to be opened. Two soldiers drew the heavy gate inwards and now Leddravohr and Balountar were at the centre of a public arena.

'Well, priest,' Leddravohr said calmly, 'what brings you here?'

'I think you know why I am here.' Balountar waited a full three seconds before adding the royal form of address, thereby detaching it from his first remark and creating a deliberate insolence. 'Prince.'

Leddravohr smiled. 'If you have come to beg a migration warrant, you are too late – they have all been disbursed.'

'I beg for nothing,' Balountar said, raising his voice, addressing the crowd rather than Leddravohr. 'I come to make demands. Demands which must be met.'

'Demands!' Nobody had ever dared use that word to Leddravohr, and as he repeated it a strange thing happened to him. His body became two bodies – one physical and solid, anchored to the ground; the other weightless and ethereal, seemingly capable of drifting on the slightest breeze. The latter self severed the connection between the two by taking a step backwards. He felt as if he were no longer in contact with the surface of the plain, but poised at grass-top height, like a ptertha, with a comprehensive but detached view of all that was taking place. From that vantage point he watched, bemused, as his corporeal self played out an immature game ...

'Do not dare speak to me of demands!' the fleshly Leddravohr cried. 'Have you forgotten the authority invested in me by the King?'

'I speak with a higher authority,' Balountar insisted, yielding no ground. 'I speak for the Church, for the Great Permanence, and I command you to destroy the vehicles with which you plan to desecrate the High Path. Furthermore, all the food and crystals and other vital supplies which you have stolen from the people must be returned to them immediately. Those are my final words.'

'You speak truer than you know,' Leddravohr breathed. He unsheathed his battle sword, but some lingering vestige of regard for the processes of law dissuaded him from driving the black blade through the Lord Prelate's body. Instead, he moved away from Balountar, turned to the watchful army officers nearby and addressed himself to a stony-faced Colonel Hippern.

'Arrest the traitor,' he said sharply.

Hippern gave a low command and two soldiers ran forward, swords drawn. A curious growling, grumbling sound arose from the crowd as the soldiers took Balountar by the arms and marched him, in spite of his struggles, inside the line of the Quarter's perimeter. Hippern looked questioningly at Leddravohr.

'What are you waiting for?' Leddravohr stabbed a forefinger towards the ground, indicating that he wanted the Lord Prelate forced to his knees. 'You know the punishment for high treason. Get on with it!'

Hippern, face impassive beneath the rim of his ornate helmet, spoke again to the officers near him and a few seconds later a burly high-sergeant ran towards the two soldiers who were restraining Balountar. The Lord Prelate redoubled his efforts to break free, his black-swathed body undergoing inhuman contortions as his captors forced him to the ground. He raised his face to his executioner. His mouth opened wide as he tried to utter a prayer or a curse, creating a target which the sergeant chose unthinkingly on the murderous instant. The sergeant's blade drove into Balountar's mouth and emerged under the base of his skull, severing the spine, ending his life between heart-beats. The two soldiers released his body and stepped back from it as a moan of consternation went up from the crowd. A large pebble arched through the air and skittered through the dust near Leddravohr's feet.

For a moment the prince looked as though he would launch himself at the mob and attack them single-handed, then he wheeled on the high-sergeant. 'Get the priest's head off. Elevate it on a pike so that his followers can continue to look up to him.'

The sergeant nodded and went about his grisly work with the unruffled dexterity of a pork butcher, and within a minute Balountar's head had been raised on a pikestaff which was then lashed to a gatepost. Rivulets of blood spread swiftly down the staff.

There was a long moment of utter silence – a silence which burrowed into the ears – and it seemed that an impasse had been reached. Then it gradually became apparent to those watching from within the base that the situation was not truly static – the semi-circle of ground visible beyond the gate was slowly shrinking. Those on the edge of the mass of human beings appeared not to be moving their feet, but they were advancing nonetheless, like ranks of statues which were being inched forward by an inexorable pressure from behind. Evidence of the tremendous force being exerted came when a fence post to the right of the gate creaked and began to lean inwards.

'Close the gate,' Colonel Hippern shouted.

'Leave the gate!' Leddravohr faced the colonel. 'The army does not cower away from a civilian rabble. Order your men to clear the entire area.'

Hippern swallowed, showing his unease, but he met Leddravohr's gaze directly. 'The situation is difficult, Prince. This is a local regiment, mostly drawn from Ro-Atabri itself, and the men won't take to the idea of going against their own.'

'Do I hear you properly, colonel?' Leddravohr altered his grip on his sword and a worm of white light coiled in his eyes. 'Since when have common soldiers become arbiters in the affairs of Kolcorron?'

Hippern's throat worked again, but his courage did not desert him. 'Since they became hungry, Prince. It was ever the way.'

Unexpectedly, Leddravohr smiled. 'That's your professional judgment, is it, colonel? Now observe me closely – I am going to teach you something about the essential nature of command.' He turned, took several paces towards the triple row of waiting soldiers and raised his sword.

'Disperse the rabble!' he shouted, sweeping his sword downwards to indicate the direction of attack against the advancing crowd. Soldiers broke rank immediately and ran to engage the foremost of the intruders, and the comparative silence which had pervaded the scene was lost in a sudden uproar.

The crowd fell back, but instead of fleeing in complete disarray its members compacted again, having receded but a short distance, and it was then that a significant fact emerged – that only one third of the soldiers had obeyed Leddravohr's command. The others had scarcely moved and were gazing unhappily at their nearest junior officers. Even the soldiers who had confronted the mob appeared to have done so in a tame and half-hearted manner. They were allowing themselves to be overcome easily, losing their weapons with such rapidity that they had become an asset to the surging throng. Cheering was heard as a large section of the covered way was pulled to the ground and its framing broken up to provide even more weapons ...

The other Leddravohr – cool, ethereal and uninvolved – watched with a mild degree of interest as the body-locked, carnate Leddravohr ran to a fresh-faced lieutenant and ordered him to lead his men against the crowd. The lieutenant was seen to shake his head in argument and a second later he was dead, almost decapitated by a single stroke of the prince's blade. Leddravohr had lost his humanity, had ceased to register on the senses as a human being. Craned forward and shambling, black sword hurling a crimson spray, he went among his officers and men like a terrible demon, wreaking destruction.

How long can this go on? the other Leddravohr mused. *Is there no limit to what the men will stand?*

His attention was suddenly drawn to a new phenomenon. The sky in the east was growing dark as columns of smoke ascended from several districts of the city. It could only mean that the ptertha screens were burning, that some members of the community had been driven by anger and frustration to make the ultimate protest against the present order.

The message was clear – that all would go down together. Rich man and poor man alike. King and pauper alike.

At the thought of the King, alone and vulnerable in the Great Palace, the other Leddravohr's composure disintegrated. Vital and urgent work had to be done; he had responsibilities whose importance far outweighed that of a clash involving a few hundred citizens and soldiers.

He took a step towards his complementary self, and there came a swooping sensation, a blurring of time and space ...

Prince Leddravohr Neldeever opened his eyes to a flood of harsh sunlight. The haft of his sword was wet in his hand, and around him were the sounds of turmoil and the colours of carnage. He surveyed the scene for a moment, blinking as he sought to reorientate himself in a changed reality, then he sheathed his sword and ran towards his waiting bluehorn.

CHAPTER EIGHTEEN

Toller stared at the yellow-hooded body without moving for perhaps ten minutes, trying to understand how he was to deal with the pain of loss.

Leddravohr has done this, he thought. *This is the harvest I reap for allowing the monster to stay alive. He abandoned my brother to the ptertha!*

The foreday sun was still low in the east, but in the total absence of air movement the rocky hillside was already beginning to throw up heat. Toller was torn between passion and prudence – the desire to run to his brother's body and the need to remain at a safe distance. His blurred vision showed something white gleaming on the sunken chest, held in place by the waist-cord of the grey robe and one slim hand.

Paper? Could it be, Toller's heart speeded up at the thought, an *indictment of Leddravohr?*

He took out the stubby telescope he had carried since boyhood and directed it at the white rectangle. His tears conspired with the fierce brilliance of the image to make the scrawled words difficult to read, but at length he received Lain's final communication:

PTERTHA FRIENDS OF BRAK. KILL US BECAU WE KILL BRAK. BRAK FEED PTERTH. IN RETURN P PROTEC B. CLEAR → PINK → PURPLE P EVOLV TOXINS. WE MUS LIVE IN HARMONY WITH B. LOOK TO SKY

Toller lowered the telescope. Somewhere under the thundering turmoil of his grief was the realisation that Lain's message had a significance which reached far beyond the present circumstances, but for the present he was unable to relate to it. Instead he was overwhelmed by a baffled disappointment. Why had Lain not used the dregs of his mental and physical energy to accuse his murderer and thus pave a straight path for retribution? After a moment's thought the answer came to Toller, and he almost managed to smile with affection and respect. Lain, even in death, had been the true pacifist, far removed from thoughts of revenge. He had withdrawn his personal light from the world in a manner befitting his way of life – and Leddravohr still endured ...

Toller turned to walk across the slope to where the sergeant was waiting with the two bluehorns. He was fully in control of himself and there were no longer any tears to interfere with his vision, but now his thoughts were dominated by a new question which was raking his brain with the force and persistence of waves clawing at a beach.

How can I live without my brother? The heat reflected from slabs of stone pressed against his eyes, entered his mouth. *It's going to be a long hot day, and how am I going to live through it without my brother?*

'I grieve with you, captain,' Engluh said. 'Your brother was a good man.'

'Yes.' Toller stared at the sergeant, trying to suppress his feelings of dislike. This was the man who had been formally entrusted with Lain's safety, and who remained alive while Lain was dead. There was little the sergeant could have done against ptertha in this kind of terrain, and according to his story he had been dismissed by Leddravohr; and yet his presence among the living was an affront to the primitive in Toller's character.

'Do you want to go back now, captain?' Engluh showed no signs of being discomfited by Toller's scrutiny. He was a hard-looking veteran, undoubtedly skilled in the art of preserving his own skin, but Toller could not judge him as being untrustworthy.

'Not yet,' Toller said. 'I want to find the bluehorn.'

'Very good, captain.' A flickering in the depths of the sergeant's brown eyes showed his awareness of the fact that Toller had not fully accepted Prince Leddravohr's terse account of the previous day's events. 'I'll show you the path we took.'

Toller mounted his bluehorn and rode behind Engluh as they worked their way up the hill. About halfway to the top they came to an area of laminated rock bounded on its lower edge by an accumulation of flakes. The remains of the bluehorn lay on the loose material, already stripped to a skeleton by multipedes and other scavengers. Even the saddle and harness had been shredded and gnawed in places. Toller felt a coolness on his spine as he realised that Lain's body would have suffered a similar fate but for the ptertha poison in the tissues. His bluehorn had begun to toss its head and behave nervously, but he guided it closer to the skeleton and frowned as he saw the fractured shinbone. *My brother was living when that happened – and now he's dead.* As the pain raged through him with renewed force he closed his eyes and tried to think about the unthinkable.

According to what he had been told, Sergeant Engluh and the other three soldiers had ridden to the west entrance of Skyship Quarter after being dismissed by Leddravohr. They had waited there for Lain and had been astonished to see Leddravohr returning alone.

The prince had been in a strange mood, angry and jovial at once, and on seeing Engluh was reported to have said, 'Prepare yourself for a long wait, sergeant – your master disabled his mount and now he is playing hide-and-seek with the ptertha.' Thinking it was expected of him, Engluh had volunteered to gallop back to the hill with a spare bluehorn, but Leddravohr had said, 'Stay where you are! He chose to play a dangerous game with his own life – and that is no sport for a good soldier.'

Toller had made the sergeant repeat his account several times and the only interpretation he could place on it was that Lain had been offered transportation to safety, but had wilfully elected to flirt with death. Leddravohr was above the need to lie about any of his actions – and still Toller was unable to accept what he had been told. Lain Maraquine, who had been known to faint at the sight of blood, would have been the last man in the world to pit himself against the globes. Had he wanted to take his life he would have found a better way – but in any case there had been no reason for him to commit suicide. He had had too much to live for. No, there was a mystery central to what had happened on the barren hillside on the previous day, and Toller knew of only one man who could clear it up. Leddravohr may not have lied, but he knew more than ...

'Captain!' Engluh spoke in a startled whisper. 'Look over there!'

Toller followed the line of his pointing finger to the east and blinked as he saw the unmistakable dark brown shape of a balloon lifting into the sky above Ro-Atabri. A few seconds later it was joined by three others climbing in close formation, almost as though the mass ascent to Overland was beginning days ahead of schedule.

Something has gone wrong, Toller thought before he was stricken by a sense of personal outrage. The death of Lain would have been more than enough to contend with on its own, but to that had been added aggravating doubt and suspicion – and now skyships were rising from the Quarter in contravention of all the rigid planning that had gone into the migration flight. There was a limit to how much his mind could encompass at a single time, and the universe was unfairly choosing to disregard it.

'I have to go back now,' he said, urging his bluehorn into motion. They rode down the hill, rounded a briar-covered shoulder and reached the open slope where Lain's body lay. The unrestricted view to the east showed that more balloons were rising from the line of enclosures, but Toller's gaze was drawn to the dappled sweeps of the city beyond. Columns of dark smoke were rising from the central districts.

'It looks like a war, captain,' Engluh said in wonderment, rising in his stirrups.

'Perhaps that's what it is.' Toller glanced once towards the inert anonymous shape that had been his brother – You *will live in me, Lain* – then spurred his mount forward in the direction of the city.

He had been aware of the growing restlessness among Ro-Atabri's beleaguered population, but he found it hard to imagine how civil disturbances could have any real effect on the ordered course of events within the Quarter. Leddravohr had installed army units in a crescent between the skyship base and the edge of the city itself, and had seen to it that they were controlled by officers he could trust even in the unique circumstances of the migration. The commanders were men who had no personal wish to fly to

Overland and were stubbornly committed to preserving Ro-Atabri as an entity, come what may. Toller had believed the base to be secure, even in the event of full-scale riots, but the skyships were taking off long before their appointed time …

On reaching flat grassland he put the bluehorn into a full gallop and watched intently as the base's perimeter barrier expanded across his field of view. The west entrance was little used because it faced open countryside, but as he drew closer he saw there were large groups of mounted soldiers and infantry behind the gate, and supply wagons could be seen on the move beyond the double screens where they curved away to the north and south. More ships were drifting up into the morning sky, and the hollow roars of their burners were mingling with the clacking of the inflation fans and the background shouting of overseers.

The outer gates were swung open for Toller and the sergeant, then slammed shut again as soon as they had entered the buffer zone. Toller reined his bluehorn to a halt as he was approached by an army captain who was carrying his orange-crested helmet under his arm.

'Are you Skycaptain Toller Maraquine?' he said, mopping his glistening brow.

'Yes. What has happened?'

'Prince Leddravohr orders you to report to Enclosure 12 immediately.'

Toller nodded his assent. 'What has happened?'

'What makes you think anything has happened?' the captain said bitterly. He turned and strode away, issuing angry orders to the nearest soldiers, who had an overtly sullen look.

Toller considered going after him and extracting an informative reply, but at that moment he noticed a blue-uniformed figure beckoning to him from the inner gate. It was Ilven Zavotle, newly commissioned to the rank of pilot lieutenant. Toller rode to him and dismounted, noting as he did so that the young man looked pale and troubled.

'I'm glad you're back, Toller,' Zavotle said anxiously. 'I heard you had gone out to look for your brother, and I came to warn you about Prince Leddravohr.'

'Leddravohr?' Toller glanced upwards as a skyship briefly occulted the sun. 'What about Leddravohr?'

'He's insane,' Zavotle said, looking about him to ensure the treasonous statement had not been overheard. 'He's at the enclosures now … driving the loaders and inflation crews … sword in hand … I saw him cut a man down just for stopping to take a drink.'

'He …!' Toller's consternation and bafflement increased. 'What brought all this about?'

Zavotle looked up at him in surprise. 'You don't know? You must have left the Quarter before ... Everything happened in a couple of hours, Toller.'

'*What* happened? Speak up, Ilven, or there'll be more swordplay.'

'Lord Prelate Balountar led a citizens' march on the base. He demanded that all the ships be destroyed and the supplies distributed among the people. Leddravohr had him arrested and beheaded on the spot.'

Toller narrowed his eyes as he visualised the scene. 'That was a mistake.'

'A bad one,' Zavotle agreed, 'but that was only the beginning. Balountar had the crowds worked up with religion and promises of food and crystals. When they saw his head on a pole they started tearing down our screens. Leddravohr sent the army against them, but ... it was an amazing thing, Toller ... most of the soldiers refused to fight.'

'They defied Leddravohr?'

'They're local men – most of them drawn from Ro-Atabri itself – and they were being ordered to massacre their own people.' Zavotle paused as a skyship overhead produced a thunderous roar. 'The soldiers are hungry, too, and there's a feeling abroad that Leddravohr is turning his back on them.'

'Even so ...' Toller found it almost impossible to imagine ordinary soldiers rebelling against the military prince.

'That was when Leddravohr really became possessed. They say he killed more than a dozen officers and men. They wouldn't obey his orders ... but they wouldn't defend themselves against him either ... and he butchered them ...' Zavotle's voice faltered. 'Like pigs, Toller. Just like pigs.'

In spite of the enormity of what he was hearing, Toller developed an unaccountable feeling that he had another and more pressing cause for concern. 'How did it end?'

'The fires in the city. When Leddravohr saw the smoke ... realised the ptertha screens were burning ... he came to his senses. He pulled all the men who remained loyal to him back inside the perimeter, and now he's trying to get the whole skyship fleet off the ground before the rebels organise themselves and invade the base.' Zavotle studied the nearby soldiers from beneath lowered brows. 'This lot are supposed to defend the west gate, but if you ask me they aren't too sure which side they're on. Blue uniforms are no longer popular around here. We should get back to the enclosures as soon as ...'

The words faded from Toller's hearing as his mind made a rapid series of leaps, each one bringing him closer to the source of his subconscious alarm. *The fires in the city ... ptertha screens burning ... there has been no rain for many days ... when the screens go the city will be indefensible ... the migration MUST get under way at once ... and that means ...*

'Gesalla!' Toller blurted the name in a sudden accession of panic and self-recrimination. How could he have forgotten her for so long? She would be waiting at home in the Square House ... still without confirmation of

Lain's death ... and the flight to Overland had already begun ...

'Did you hear me?' Zavotle said. 'We should be ... '

'Never mind that,' Toller cut in. 'What's been done about notifying the migrants and bringing them in?'

'The King and Prince Chakkell are already at the enclosures. All the other royals and nobles have to get here under the protection of their own guards. It's a shambles, Toller. The ordinary migrants will have to get through by themselves, and the way things are out there I doubt if ... '

'I'm indebted to you for meeting me here, Ilven,' Toller said, turning to mount his bluehorn. 'I seem to remember you telling me when we were up there – freezing to death and with nothing to do but count the falling stars – that you have no family. Is that right?'

'Yes.'

'In that case you should get back to the enclosures and take the first ship that becomes available to you. I am not free to leave just yet.'

Zavotle came forward as Toller swung himself into the saddle. 'Leddra-vohr wants us both as royal pilots, Toller. You especially, because nobody else has turned a ship over.'

'Forget that you saw me,' Toller said. 'I'll be back as soon as I can.'

He rode into the base, taking a route which kept him well away from the balloon enclosures. The ptertha nets overhead were casting their patterns of shadow on a scene of confused and frenetic activity. It had been intended that the migration fleet would depart in an orderly manner over a period of between ten and twenty days, depending on weather conditions. Now there was a race to see how many ships could be despatched before the Quarter was overrun by dissenters, and the situation was made even more desperate by the fact that the vulnerable ptertha screens had been attacked. It was fortunate that there was no perceptible air movement – a circumstance which aided the skyship crews and kept ptertha activity to the minimum – but with the arrival of night the livid globes would come in force.

In their haste to load supply carts workers were tearing down the wooden storage huts with their bare hands. Soldiers belonging to the newly formed Overland Regiment – their loyalty guaranteed because they were due to fly with Leddravohr – roamed the area, noisily exhorting base personnel to make greater efforts and in some cases joining in the work. Here and there amid the chaos wandered small groups of men, women and children who had obtained migration warrants in the provinces and had arrived at the Quarter well in advance of their flights. Above and through everything drifted the racket of the inflation fans, the unnerving spasmodic roar of skyship burners and the marshy odour of free miglign gas.

Toller attracted scant attention from anybody as he rode through storage and workshop sections, but on reaching the covered way which ran east to the city he found its entrance guarded by a large detachment of soldiers. Officers with them were questioning everybody who passed through. Toller moved to one side and used his telescope to survey the distant exit. Compressed perspectives made the image hard to interpret, but he could see massed foot soldiers and some mounted groups, and beyond them crowds thronging the sloping streets where the city proper began. There was little evidence of movement, but it was obvious that a confrontation was still taking place and that the normal route to the city was impassable.

He was considering what to do when his attention was caught by shifting specks of colour in the scrubby land which stretched off to the south-east in the direction of the Greenmount suburb. The telescope revealed them to be civilians hurrying towards the centre of the base. From the high proportion of women and children Toller deduced they were emigrants who had breached the perimeter fence at a point remote from the main entrance. He turned away from the tunnel, located an auxiliary exit through the double ptertha meshes and rode out towards the advancing citizenry. When he got close to the leaders they brandished their blue-and-white migration warrants.

'Keep heading towards the balloon enclosures,' he shouted to them. 'We'll get you away.'

The anxious-faced men and women called out their thanks and hurried on, some carrying or dragging infants. Turning to look after them, Toller saw that their arrival had been noticed and mounted men were coming out to meet them. The sky behind the riders made a unique spectacle. Perhaps fifty ships were now in the air over the enclosures, dangerously crowded at the lower levels and straggling out as they receded into the zenith.

Not pausing to see what kind of reception the migrants would receive, Toller spurred his bluehorn on towards Greenmount. Far off to his right, in Ro-Atabri itself, the fires appeared to be spreading. The city was built of stone, but the timber and rope with which it had been cocooned to ward off the ptertha were highly flammable and the fires were becoming large enough to create their own convection systems, gaining ground with no assistance from the elements. It was only necessary, Toller knew, for a slight breeze to spring up and the whole city would be engulfed in a matter of minutes.

He urged the bluehorn into a gallop, judging his direction from the groups of refugees he met, and eventually espied a place where the perimeter barricade had been pulled to the ground. He rode through the gap, ignoring apprehensive stares from people who were clambering across the stakes, and chose a direct route up the hill towards the Square House. The streets he had roamed as a boy were littered and deserted, part of the alien territory of the past.

A minute after entering Greenmount district he rounded a corner and encountered a band of five civilians who had armed themselves with staves. Although obviously not migrants, they were hurrying towards the Quarter. Toller divined at once that it was their intention to harass and perhaps rob some of the migrant families he had seen earlier.

They spread out to block the narrow street and their leader, a slack-jawed hulk in a cloak thonged with dried pillar snakes, said, 'What do you think you're doing, bluecoat?'

Toller, who could easily have ridden the man down, reined to a halt. 'As you ask so politely, I don't mind telling you that I'm deciding whether or not I should kill you.'

'Kill *me*!' The man pounded the ground imperiously with his staff, apparently in the belief that all skymen went unarmed. 'And exactly how ...?'

Toller drew his sword with a horizontal sweep which lopped the staff just above the man's hand. 'That could just have easily been your wrist or your neck,' he said mildly. 'Do any or all of you wish to pursue the matter?'

The four others eyed each other and backed away.

'We have no quarrel with you, sir,' the cloaked man said, nursing the hand which had been jarred by the fierce impact on his staff. 'We'll go peaceably on our way.'

'You won't.' Toller used his brakka blade to point out an alley which led away from the skyship base. 'You will go that way, and back to your dens. I will be returning to the Quarter in a few minutes – and I swear that if I set eyes on any of you again it will be my sword that does all the talking. Now go!'

As soon as the men had passed out of sight he sheathed his sword and resumed the ascent of the hill. He doubted if his warning would have a lasting effect on the ruffians, but he had spared as much time as he could on behalf of the migrants, all of whom would have to learn to face many rigours in the coming days. A glance at the narrowing crescent of light on the disk of Overland told him there was not much more than an hour until littlenight, and it was imperative that he should take Gesalla to the base before then.

On reaching the crest of Greenmount he galloped through silent avenues to the Square House and dismounted in the walled precinct. He went into the entrance hall and was met by Sany, the rotund cook, and a balding man-servant who was unknown to him.

'Master Toller!' Sany cried. 'Have you news of your brother?'

Toller felt a renewed shock of bereavement – the pressure of events had suspended his normal emotional processes. 'My brother is dead,' he said. 'Where is your mistress?'

'In her bedchamber.' Sany pressed both hands to her throat. 'This is a terrible day for all of us.'

Toller ran to the main stair, but paused on the first flight. 'Sany, I'm returning to the Skyship Quarter in a few minutes. I strongly advise you and ...' He looked questioningly at the manservant.

'Harribend, sir.'

'... you and Harribend – and any other domestics who are still here – to come with me. The migration has started ahead of time in great confusion, and even though you don't have warrants I think I can get you places on a ship.'

Both servants backed away from him. 'I couldn't go into the sky before my time,' Sany said. 'It isn't natural. It isn't right.'

'There are riots in the city and the ptertha screens are burning.'

'Be that as it may, Master Toller – we'll take our chances here where we belong.'

'Think hard about it,' Toller said. He went up to the landing and through the familiar corridor which led to the south side of the house, unable to accept fully that this was the last occasion on which he would see the ceramic figurines glowing in their niches, or his blurred reflection ghosting along the polished glasswood panels. The door to the principal bedchamber was open.

Gesalla was standing at the window which framed a view of the city in which the dominant features were the seemingly motionless columns of grey and white smoke intersecting the natural blue and green horizontals of Arle Bay and the Gulf of Tronom. She was dressed as he had never seen her before, in a waistcoat and breeches of grey whipcord complemented by a lighter grey shirt – the whole being almost a muted echo of his own skyman's uniform. A sudden timidity made him refrain from speaking or tapping the door. How was one to impart the kind of news he bore?

Gesalla turned and looked at him with wise, sombre eyes. 'Thank you for coming, Toller.'

'It's about Lain,' he said, entering the room. 'I'm afraid I bring bad news.'

'I knew he had to be dead when there was no message by nightfall.' Her voice was cool, almost brisk. 'All that was needed was the confirmation.'

Toller was unprepared for her lack of emotion. 'Gesalla, I don't know how to tell you this ... at a time like this ... but you have seen the fires in the city. We have no choice but to ...'

'I'm ready to leave,' Gesalla said, picking up a tightly rolled bundle which had been on a chair. 'These are all the personal possessions I'll need. It isn't too much, is it?'

He stared at her beautiful unperturbed face for a moment, battling with an irrational resentment. 'Have you any idea where we're going?'

'Where else but to Overland? The skyships are leaving. According to what I could decipher of the sunwriter messages coming out of the Great Palace, civil war is breaking out in Ro-Atabri and the King has already fled. Do you think I'm stupid, Toller?'

'Stupid? No, you're very intelligent – very logical.'

'Did you expect me to be hysterical? Was I to be carried out of here screaming that I was afraid to go into the sky, where only the heroic Toller Maraquine has been? Was I to weep and plead for time to strew flowers around my husband's body?'

'No, I didn't expect you to weep.' Toller was dismayed by what he was saying, yet was unable to hold back. 'I don't expect you to feign grief.'

Gesalla struck him across the face, her hand moving so quickly that he was given no chance to avoid the blow. 'Never say anything like that to me again. *Never make* that kind of presumption about me! Now, are we leaving or are we going to stand here and talk all day?'

'The sooner we leave the better,' he said stonily, resisting the urge to finger the stinging patch on his cheek. 'I'll take your pack.'

Gesalla snatched the bundle away from him and slung it from her shoulders. 'I made it for *me* to carry – you have enough to do.' She slipped past him into the corridor, moving lightly and with deceptive speed, and had reached the main stair before he caught up with her.

'What about Sany and the other servants?' he said. 'Leaving them doesn't sit easy with me.'

She shook her head. 'Lain and I both tried to talk them into applying for warrants, and we failed. You can't force people to go, Toller.'

'I suppose you're right.' He walked with her to the entrance, taking a last nostalgic look around the hall, and went out to the precinct where his blue-horn was waiting. 'Where is your carriage?'

'I don't know – Lain took it yesterday.'

'Does that mean we have to ride together?'

Gesalla sighed. 'I have no intention of trotting along beside you.'

'Very well.' Feeling oddly self-conscious, Toller climbed into the saddle and extended a hand to Gesalla. He was surprised at how little effort it took to help her spring into place behind him, and even more so when she slipped her arms around his waist and pressed herself to his back. Some bodily contact was necessary, but it almost seemed as though she ... He dismissed the half-formed thought, appalled by his obscene readiness to think of Gesalla in a sexual context, and put the bluehorn into a fast trot.

On leaving the precinct and turning north-west he saw that many more ships were now in the sky above the Quarter, dwindling into specks as they were absorbed by the blue depths of the upper atmosphere. A slight east-ward drift was becoming apparent in their movement, which meant that the chaos of the departure might soon be made worse by the arrival of ptertha. Off to his left the towers of smoke rising from the city were being horizontally sheared and smeared where they reached high level air currents. Burning trees created occasional powdery explosions.

Toller rode down the hill as fast as was compatible with safety. The streets were as empty as before, but he was increasingly aware of the sounds of tumult coming from directly ahead. He emerged from the last screen of abandoned buildings and found that the scene at the Quarter's periphery had changed.

The break in the barricade had been enlarged and groups totalling perhaps a hundred had gathered there, denied entry to the base by ranks of infantry. Stones and pieces of timber were being hurled at the soldiers who, although armed with swords and javelins, were not retaliating. Several mounted officers were stationed behind the soldiers, and Toller knew by their sleeved swords and the green flashes on their shoulders that they were part of a Sorka regiment, men who were loyal to Leddravohr and had no particular affiliations with Ro-Atabri. It was a situation which could erupt into carnage at any moment, and if that happened rebel soldiers would probably be drawn to the spot to turn it into a miniature theatre of war.

'Hold on and keep your head down,' he said to Gesalla as he drew his sword. 'We have to go in hard.'

He spurred the bluehorn into a gallop. The powerful beast responded readily, covering the intervening ground in a few wind-rushing seconds. Toller had hoped to take the rioters completely unawares and burst through them before they could react, but the pounding of hooves on the hard clay attracted the attention of men who had turned to gather stones.

'There's a bluecoat,' the cry went up. 'Get the filthy bluecoat!'

The sight of the massive charging animal and of Toller's battle sword was enough to scatter all from his path, but there was no escaping the irregular volley of missiles. Toller was struck solidly on the upper arm and thigh, and a skimming piece of slate laid open the knuckles of his rein hand. He kept the bluehorn on course through the overturned timbers of the barricade and had almost reached the lines of soldiers when he heard a thud and felt an impact transmitted through Gesalla's body. She gasped and slackened her hold for an instant, then recovered her strength. The lines of soldiers parted to make way for him and he pulled the bluehorn to a halt.

'Is it bad?' he said to Gesalla, unable to turn in the saddle or dismount because of her grip on him.

'It isn't serious,' she replied in a voice he could scarcely hear. 'You must go on.'

A bearded lieutenant approached them, saluted and caught the bluehorn's bridle. 'Are you Skycaptain Toller Maraquine?'

'I am.'

'You are to report immediately to Prince Leddravohr at Enclosure 12.'

'That's what I'm trying to do, lieutenant,' Toller said. 'It would be easier if you stepped aside.'

'Sir, Prince Leddravohr's orders made no mention of a woman.'

Toller raised his eyebrows and met the lieutenant's gaze directly. 'What of it?'

'I ... Nothing, sir.' The lieutenant released the bridle and moved back.

Toller urged the bluehorn forward, heading for the row of balloon enclosures. It had been found, though nobody had explained the phenomenon, that perforated barriers protected balloons from air disturbances better than solid screens. The open western sky was shining through square apertures in the enclosures, making them look more than ever like a line of lofty towers, at the foot of which was the seething activity of thousands of workers, air crew and emigrants with all their paraphernalia and supplies.

It said much for the organising ability of Leddravohr, Chakkell and their appointees that the system was able to function at all in such extreme circumstances. Ships were still taking off in groups of two or three, and it occurred to Toller that it was almost a miracle that there had been no serious accidents.

At that moment, as if the thought had engendered the event, the gondola of a ship rising too quickly struck the rim of its enclosure. The ship was oscillating as it shot into clear air and at a height of two hundred feet overtook another which had departed some seconds earlier. At the limit of one of its pendulum swings the gondola of the uncontrolled ship drove sideways into the balloon of the slower craft. The latter's envelope split and lost its symmetry, flapping and rippling like some wounded creature of the deep, and the ship plunged to the ground, its acceleration struts trailing loosely. It landed squarely on a group of supply wagons. The impact must have severed its burner feed lines for there was an immediate gouting of flame and black smoke, and the barking of injured or terrified bluehorns was added to the general commotion.

Toller tried not to think about the fate of those on board. The other ship's appallingly bad take-off had looked like the work of a novice, making it seem that many of the one thousand qualified pilots assigned to the migration fleet were not available, possibly stranded by the disturbances in the city. New dangers had been added to the already daunting array of hazards facing the interworld voyagers.

He could feel Gesalla's head lolling against his back as they rode towards the enclosure, and his anxiety about her increased. Her lightweight frame was ill-equipped to withstand the sort of blow he had felt at a remove. As he neared the twelfth enclosure he saw that it and the three adjoining to the north were heavily ringed by foot soldiers and cavalry. In the protected zone there was an area of comparative calm. Four balloons were waiting in the enclosures, with the inflation teams to hand, and knots of richly dressed men and women were standing by heaps of ornamented cases and other belongings. Some of the men were sipping drinks as they craned to see the crashed ship, while small children darted around their legs as though at play on a family outing.

Toller scanned the area and was able to pick out a group at the core of which were Leddravohr, Chakkell and Pouche, all standing close to the seated figure of King Prad. The ruler, slumped on an ordinary chair, was staring at the ground, apparently oblivious to all that was happening. He looked old and dispirited, in marked contrast to the vigorous aspect which Toller remembered.

A youngish army captain came forward to meet Toller as he reined the bluehorn to a halt. He looked surprised when he saw Gesalla, but helped her to the ground readily enough and without any comment. Toller dismounted and saw that her face was totally without colour. She was swaying a little and her eyes had a distant, abstracted look which told him she was in severe pain.

'Perhaps I should carry you,' he said as the ranks of soldiers parted at a signal from the captain.

'I can walk, I can *walk*,' she whispered. 'Take your hands away, Toller – the beast is not to see me being assisted.'

Toller nodded, impressed by her courage, and walked ahead of her towards the royal group. Leddravohr turned to face him and for once did not produce his snake-strike of a smile. His eyes were smouldering in the marble-smooth face. There was a diagonal spattering of crimson on his white cuirass, and blood was congealing thickly around the top of his scabbard, but his manner was suggestive of controlled anger rather than the insane rage of which Zavotle had spoken.

'I sent for you hours ago, Maraquine,' he said icily. 'Where have you been?'

'Viewing the remains of my brother,' Toller said, deliberately omitting the required form of address. 'There is something highly suspicious about his death.'

'Do you know what you are saying?'

'Yes.'

'I see you have returned to your old ways.' Leddravohr moved closer and lowered his voice. 'My father once extracted a vow from me that I would not harm you, but I will regard myself as released from that vow when we reach Overland. Then, I promise you, I will give you what you have sought so long – but for now more important matters must engage my attention.'

Leddravohr turned and padded away, giving a signal to the launch supervisors. At once the balloon inflating crews went to work, cranking the big fans into noisy life. King Prad raised his head, startled, and looked about him with his single troubled eye. The spurious festive mood deserted the various noblemen as the clatter of the fans impressed on them that the unprecedented flight into the unknown was about to begin. Family groups drew together, the children ceased their play, and servants made ready to transfer their masters' belongings to the ships which would depart in the wake of the royal flight.

Beyond the protective lines of guards was a sea of apparently undirected activity as the work of despatching the migration fleet continued. Men were running everywhere, and supply wagons careered among the lumbering flatbed carts which were transporting skyships to the enclosures. Farther away across the open ground of the Quarter, taking advantage of the near-perfect weather conditions, the pilots of cargo ships were inflating their balloons and taking off without the aid of windbreaks. The sky was now thronged with ships, rising like a cloud of strange airborne spores towards the fiery crescent of Overland.

Toller was awed by the sheer drama of the spectacle, the proof that when driven to the limit his own kind had the courage and ability to stride like gods from one world to another, but he was also bemused by what he had just heard from Leddravohr.

The vow of which Leddravohr had spoken explained certain things – but why had he been asked to make it in the first place? What had prompted the King to single one of his subjects out of so many and place him under his personal protection? Intrigued by the new mystery, Toller glanced thoughtfully in the direction of the seated figure of the King and experienced a peculiar thrill when he saw that Prad was staring directly at him. A moment later the King pointed a finger at Toller, casting a line of psychic force through the groups of bystanders, and then beckoned to him. Ignoring the curious gazes of royal attendants, Toller approached the King and bowed.

'You have served me well, Toller Maraquine,' Prad said in a tired but firm voice. 'And now it is in my mind to charge you with one further responsibility.'

'You have but to name it, Majesty,' Toller replied, his sense of unreality increasing as Prad gestured for him to move closer and stoop to receive a private message.

'See to it,' the King whispered, 'that my name is remembered on Overland.'

'Majesty ...' Toller straightened up, beset with confusion. 'Majesty, I don't understand.'

'Understanding will come – now go to your post.'

Toller bowed and backed away, but before he had time to ponder on the brief exchange he was summoned by Colonel Kartkang, former chief administrator for the S.E.S. Following the dissolution of the Experimental Squadron the colonel had been given the responsibility for coordinating the departure of the royal flight, a task he could hardly have foreseen carrying out in such adverse conditions. His lips were moving silently as he directed Toller to a spot where Leddravohr was addressing three pilots. One of them was Ilven Zavotle, and another was Gollav Amber – an experienced man who had been short-listed for the proving flight. The third was a thick-bodied red-bearded man in his forties, who wore the uniform of a skycommander. After a moment's thought, Toller identified him as Halsen Kedalse, a former aircaptain and royal messenger.

'... decided that we will travel in separate ships,' Leddravohr was saying as his gaze flickered towards Toller. 'Maraquine – the one officer who has experience of taking a ship past the midpoint – will have the responsibility of piloting my father's ship. I will fly with Zavotle. Prince Chakkell will go with Kedalse, and Prince Pouche with Amber. Each of you will now go to his designated ship and prepare to ascend before littlenight is on us.'

The four pilots saluted and were about to walk to the enclosures when Leddravohr halted them by raising a hand. He studied them for what seemed a long time, looking uncharacteristically irresolute, before he spoke again. 'On reflection, Kedalse has flown my father many times during his long service as an aircaptain. He will fly the King's ship on this occasion, and Prince Chakkell will go with Maraquine. That is all.'

Toller saluted again and turned away, wondering what was signified by Leddravohr's change of mind. He had been quick to take the point when Toller had said he was suspicious about Lain's death. *My brother is dead!* Was that an indication of guilt? Had some grotesque twist of thought made Leddravohr unwilling to entrust his father's life to a man whose brother he had murdered, or at least caused to die?

The unmistakable sound of a heavy cannon being fired somewhere in the distance reminded Toller that he had no time to spare for speculation. He looked around for Gesalla. She was standing alone, isolated from the surrounding activity, and something about her posture told him she was still in extreme pain. He ran to the gondola where Prince Chakkell was waiting with his wife, daughter and two small sons. The pearl-coiffed Princess Daseene and the children gazed up at Toller with expressions of wary surmise, and even Chakkell seemed tentative in his manner. They were all deeply afraid, Toller realised, and one of the unknowns facing them was the nature of the relationship to be dictated by the man into whose hands chance had delivered their lives.

'Well, Maraquine,' Chakkell said, 'are we about to leave?'

Toller nodded. 'We could all be safely away from here in a few minutes, Prince – but there is a difficulty.'

'A difficulty? What difficulty?'

'My brother died yesterday.' Toller paused, taking advantage of the fresh anxiety he had glimpsed in Chakkell's eyes. 'My obligation to his widow can only be discharged by bringing her with me on this flight.'

'I'm sorry, Maraquine, but that is out of the question,' Chakkell said. 'This ship is for my use only.'

'I know that, Prince, but you are a man who understands family ties, and you can appreciate that it is impossible for me to abandon my brother's widow. If she can't travel on this ship, then I must decline the honour of being your pilot.'

'You're talking about treason,' Chakkell snapped, wiping perspiration from his bald brown scalp. 'I … Leddravohr would have you executed on the spot if you dared disobey his orders.'

'I know that too, Prince, and it would be a great pity for all concerned.' Toller directed a thin smile at the watchful children. 'If I weren't here an inexperienced pilot would have to take you and your family through that strange region between the worlds. I'm familiar with all the terrors and dangers of the middle passage, you see, and could have prepared you for them.'

The two boys continued to gaze up at him, but the girl hid her face in her mother's skirts. Chakkell stared at her with pain-filled eyes and shuffled his feet in an agony of frustration as, for the first time in his life, he had to consider subordinating himself to the will of an ordinary man. Toller smiled at him, falsely sympathetic, and thought, *If this is power, may I never need it again.*

'Your brother's widow may travel in my ship,' Chakkell finally said. 'And I won't forget about this, Maraquine.'

'I'll always remember you with gratitude too,' Toller said. As he was climbing into the pilot's station of the gondola he resigned himself to having hardened the enmity that Chakkell already felt for him, but he could feel no guilt or shame this time. He had acted with deliberation and logic to achieve what was necessary, unlike the Toller Maraquine of old, and had the further consolation of knowing he was in tune with the realities of the situation. Lain – *My brother is dead!* – had once said that Leddravohr and his kind belonged to the past, and Chakkell had just vindicated those words. In spite of all the catastrophic changes which had overwhelmed their world, men like Leddravohr and Chakkell acted as though Kolcorron would be created anew on Overland. Only the King seemed to have intuited that everything would be different.

Lying on his back against a partition, Toller signalled to the inflation crew that he was ready to start burning. They stopped cranking and hauled the fan aside, giving him a clear view of the balloon's interior. The envelope, partially filled with cool air, was sagging and rolling between the upraised acceleration struts. He fired a series of blasts into it, drowning out the sound of the other burners which were being operated all along the line of enclosures, and watched it distend and lift itself clear of the ground. As it reached the vertical position the men holding the crown lines closed in and fastened them to the gondola's load frame, and others rotated the light-weight structure until it was horizontal. The huge assemblage of balloon and gondola, now lighter than air, began to strain gently at its central anchor as though Overland was calling to it.

Toller leapt down from the gondola and nodded to Chakkell and the waiting attendants as a sign that the passengers and belongings could go aboard. He went to Gesalla and she made no objection as he unslung the bundle from her shoulder.

'We're ready to go,' he said. 'You'll be able to lie down and rest as soon as you're on board.'

'But that's a royal ship,' she replied, unexpectedly hanging back. 'I'm supposed to find a place on one of the others.'

'Gesalla, please forget all about what was *supposed* to happen. Many ships will fail to leave this place altogether, and it's likely that blood will be shed in the fight to get on to some of those that do. You must come now.'

'Has the Prince given his consent?'

'We talked it over, and he wouldn't even consider departing without you.' Toller took Gesalla by the arm and walked with her to the gondola. He went on board first and found that Chakkell, Daseene and the children had taken their places in one passenger compartment, tacitly assigning the other to him and Gesalla. She winced with pain as he helped her climb over the side, and as soon as he had shown her into the vacant compartment she lay down on the wool-filled quilts stored there.

He unbuckled his sword, placed it beside her and returned to the pilot's station. A heavy cannon again sounded in the distance as he reactivated the burner. The ship was lightly loaded compared to the one he had taken on the proving flight, and he waited less than a minute before pulling the anchor link. There was a gentle lurch and the walls of the enclosure began to slide vertically past him. The climb continued well even when the balloon had fully entered the open air, and in a few seconds Toller had a full-circle view of the Quarter. The three other ships of the royal flight – distinguished by white lateral stripes on their gondolas – had already cleared their enclo-sures and were slightly above him. All other launches had been temporarily halted, but he still felt the air to be uncomfortably crowded, and he kept a careful watch on the companion ships until the beginnings of a westerly breeze had brought about some dispersion.

In a mass flight there was always the risk of collision between two ships ascending or descending at different speeds. As it was impossible for a pilot to see anything directly above him, because of the balloon, the rule was that the uppermost of a pair had the responsibility of taking action to avoid the lower. The theory was sound as far as it went, but Toller had misgivings about it because almost the only option available in the climb phase was to climb faster and thus increase the risk of overtaking a third ship. That risk would have been minimal had the fleet been able to depart according to plan, but now he was uneasily aware of being part of a straggling vertical swarm.

As the ship gained height the scene on the ground below was revealed in all its astonishing complexity.

Balloons, inflated or laid out flat on the grass, were the dominant features in a matrix of paths and wagon tracks, supply dumps, carts, animals and thousands of people milling about in seemingly aimless activities. Toller could almost see them as communal insects labouring to save bloated queens from some imminent catastrophe. Off to the south, crowds formed a variegated mass at the main entrance to the base, but the foreshortened perspective made it impossible to tell if fighting was already breaking out between newly sundered military units.

Sketchy lines of people, presumably determined emigrants, were converging on the launch area from several points on the field's perimeter. And beyond them the fires were now spreading more quickly in Ro-Atabri, aided by the freshening breeze, stripping the city of its ptertha defences. In contrast to the seething turmoil engendered by human beings and their appurtenances, Arle Bay and the Gulf of Tronom formed a placid backdrop of turquoise and blue. A two-dimensional Mount Opelmer floated in the hazy distance, serene and undisturbed.

Toller, operating the burner by means of the extension lever, stood at the side of the gondola and tried to assimilate the fact that he was departing the scene for ever, but within him there was only a tremulous void, a near-subliminal agitation which told of suppressed emotions. Too much had happened in the space of a single foreday – *My brother is dead!* – and pain and regret had been laid in store for him, to be drawn upon when the first quiet hours came.

Chakkell was also looking outwards from his compartment, arms around Daseene and his daughter, who appeared to be aged about twelve. Toller, who had previously regarded him as a man motivated by nothing but ambition, wondered if he should revise his opinion. The ease with which he had been coerced in the matter of Gesalla indicated an overriding concern for his family.

Spectators could be seen at the rails of two other royal ships – King Prad and his personal attendants in one, the withdrawn Prince Pouche and retainers in another. Only Leddravohr, who seemed to have decided to travel unaccompanied, was not visible. Zavotle, a lonely figure at the controls of Leddravohr's ship, gave Toller a wave, then began drawing in and fastening his acceleration struts. As his ship was the least burdened of the four he could leave the burner for quite long periods and still match the others' rate of climb.

Toller, who had settled on a two-and-twenty rhythm, did not have the same latitude. As a result of what had been learned from the proving flight it had been decided that the migration ships could safely be operated by unaided pilots, thus freeing more lifting ability for passengers and cargo. During a pilot's rest periods he would entrust the burner or jet to a passenger, though always continuing to monitor the rhythm.

'Littlenight is almost here, Prince,' Toller said, speaking courteously to make amends for his earlier insubordination. 'I want to secure our struts before then, so I must request you to relieve me at the burner.'

'Very well.' Chakkell seemed almost pleased at having something useful to do as he took over the extension lever. His dark-haired boys, still shooting timid glances at Toller, came to his side and listened attentively while he explained the workings of the machinery to them. By the time Toller had hauled in and lashed the struts to the corners of the gondola, Chakkell had taught the boys to count the burner rhythm by making a chanting game of it.

Seeing that all three were engrossed for the time being, Toller went into the compartment where Gesalla was lying. Her eyes were alert and the strained expression had left her face. She extended a hand and offered him a rolled-up bandage which must have come from her bundle of possessions.

He knelt beside her on the bed of soft quilts, reviling himself for the flicker of sexual excitement the action brought, and took the bandage. 'How are you?' he said quietly.

'I don't think any of my ribs are actually broken, but they'll have to be bound if I'm to do my share of the work. Help me up.' With Toller's assistance she gingerly raised herself to a kneeling position, half-turned away from him and pulled up her grey shirt to expose a massive bruise at one side of her lower ribs. 'What do you think?'

'You should be bandaged,' he said, unsure of what was expected of him.

'Well, what are you waiting for?'

'Nothing.' He passed the bandage around her and began to lap it tight, but his actions were made awkward by the constrictions of her waistcoat and gathered shirt. Time after time, in spite of all his efforts to the contrary, his knuckles brushed against her breasts and the sensation darted through him like amber sparks, adding to his clumsiness.

Gesalla gave an audible sigh. 'You're useless, Toller. Wait!' She pulled open her shirt and removed both it and the waistcoat in a single movement, and now the slimness of her was naked from the waist up. 'Try it now.'

A vision of Lain's yellow-hooded body turned him into a senseless machine. He completed the bandage with the efficiency and briskness of a battlefield surgeon, and allowed his hands to fall to his sides. Gesalla remained as she was for a few protracted seconds, her gaze warm and solemn, before she picked up the shirt and put it on.

'Thank you,' she said, then put out her hand and lightly touched him on the lips.

There was a blaze of rainbow colours and suddenly the ship was in darkness. In the other passenger compartment Daseene or her daughter whimpered with alarm. Toller stood up and looked over the side. The fringed, curved shadow of Overland was speeding towards the eastern horizon, and almost directly below the ship Ro-Atabri was a tangle of orange-burning threads caught in a spreading pool of pitch.

When daylight returned the four ships of the royal flight had attained a height of some twenty miles – and were accompanied by a loose cluster of ptertha.

Toller scanned the sky all around and saw that one globe was only thirty yards away to the north. He went immediately to one of the two rail-mounted cannon on that side, took aim and released the pin which shattered the bilobed glass container in the gun's breech. There was a brief delay while the charges of pikon and halvell mixed, reacted and exploded. The projectile blurred along its trajectory, followed by a glitter of glass fragments, spreading its radial arms as it flew. It curved down through the ptertha and annihilated it, releasing a fast-fading smudge of purple dust.

'That was a good shot,' Chakkell said from behind Toller. 'Would you say we're safe from the poison at this range?'

Toller nodded. 'The ship goes with any wind there is, so the dust can't reach us. The ptertha are not much of a threat, really, but I destroyed that one because there can be some air turbulence at the edge of littlenight. I didn't want to risk the globe picking up a stray eddy and moving in on us.'

Chakkell's swarthy face bore an expression of concern as he stared at the remaining globes. 'How did they get so close?'

'Pure chance, it seems. If they are spread out over an area of sky and a ship happens to rise up through them, they match its rate of climb. The same thing happened on the …' Toller broke off on hearing two more cannon shots, some distance away, followed by faint screaming which seemed to come from below.

He leaned over the gondola wall and looked straight down. The convex immensity of Land provided an intricate blue-green background for a seemingly endless series of balloons, the nearest of which were only a few hundred yards away and looking very large. Many others were ranged out below them in irregular steps and random groupings, progressively shrinking in apparent size until they reached near-invisibility.

Ptertha could be seen mingling with the uppermost ships and, as Toller watched, another cannon fired and picked off a globe. The projectile quickly lost momentum and faded from sight in a dizzy plunge, losing itself in the cloud patterns far below. The screaming continued, regular as breathing, for some time before gradually fading away.

Toller moved back from the rail, wondering if the screams had been inspired by groundless panic, or if someone had actually seen one of the globes hovering close to a gondola wall – blind, malignant and utterly invincible – just before it darted in for the kill. He was experiencing relief tinged with guilt over having been spared such a fate when a new thought occurred to him. The ptertha had no need to wait for daylight before closing in. There was no guarantee that one or more of the globes had not driven itself against his own ship during the spell of darkness – and if that were the case neither he, Gesalla nor any of his passengers would live to set foot on Overland.

As he tried to come to terms with the notion he slipped a hand into his pocket, located the curious keepsake given to him by his father, and allowed his thumb to begin circling on the ice-smooth surface.

CHAPTER NINETEEN

By the tenth day of the flight the ship was only a thousand miles above the surface of Overland, and the ancient patterns of night and day had been reversed.

The period Toller still tended to think of as littlenight – when Overland was screening out the sun – had grown to be seven hours in length; whereas night – when they were in the shadow of the home world – now lasted less than half that time. He was sitting alone at the pilot's station, waiting for day-break and trying to foresee his people's future on the new world. It seemed to him that even native Kolcorronians, who had always been accustomed to living directly below the fixed sphere of Overland, might feel oppressed by the sight of a larger planet suspended directly above them and depriving them of a proportionately greater part of their day. Assuming Overland to be uninhabited, the migrants could be disposed towards building their new nation on the far side of the planet, in latitudes corresponding to those of Chamteth on Land. Perhaps a time would come when all memory of their origins had faded and ...

Toller's thoughts were interrupted by the appearance of Chakkell's seven-year-old son, Setwan, at the entrance to their compartment. The boy came to his side and leaned his head on Toller's shoulder.

'I can't sleep, Uncle Toller,' he whispered. 'May I stay here with you?'

Toller lifted the boy on to his knee, smiling to himself as he visualised Daseene's reaction if she heard one of her children address him as uncle.

Of the seven people confined to the punishing microcosm of the gondola, Daseene was the only one who had made no concessions to their situation. She had not spoken to Toller or Gesalla, still wore her pearl coif, and ventured out of the passenger compartment only when it was absolutely necessary. She had gone without food or drink for three whole days rather than submit to the ordeal of using the primitive toilet when near the midpoint of the voyage. Her features had become pale and pinched, and – although the ship had since descended to warmer levels of Overland's atmosphere – she remained huddled in the quilted garments which had been hastily manufactured for the migration flight. She answered in monosyllables when spoken to by her family.

Toller had a certain sympathy for Daseene, knowing that the traumas of recent days had been greater for her than for any of the others on board. The children – Corba, Oldo and Setwan – had not had enough years in the privileged dreamland of the Five Palaces to condition them irrevocably, and they had a natural sense of curiosity and adventure on their side. Chakkell's responsibilities and ambitions had always kept him fully in touch with the everyday realities of life in Kolcorron, and he had sufficient strength and resourcefulness to let him anticipate a key role in the founding of a new nation on Overland. Indeed Toller had been quite impressed by the way in which the prince, after the initial period of adjustment, had chosen to involve himself with the operation of the ship without shirking any task.

Chakkell had been particularly scrupulous as regards taking long spells at the microjets which gave the ship some control over its lateral position. It was expected and accepted that all other ships of the fleet would be dispersed by air currents over quite a large area of Overland after a journey of five thousand miles, but Leddravohr had decreed that the royal flight should be able to land in a tight group.

Different methods of tethering the four ships had been dismissed as impracticable, and in the end they had been fitted with miniature horizontal jets delivering only a small fraction of the thrust produced by the attitude control jets. When fired continuously for a long time they added a very slight lateral component to a ship's vertical motion, without causing it to rotate around its centre of gravity, and assiduous use of them had kept the four royal ships in close formation throughout the flight.

The proximity of the others had furnished Toller with one of the most memorable spectacles of his life, when the group had passed the midpoint and it came time to turn the ships over. Although he had been through the experience before, he found something awesome and ineffably beautiful in the sight of the sister planets majestically drifting in opposite directions, Overland gliding out from the occultation of the balloon and down the sky while Land, at the other end of an invisible beam, climbed above the gondola wall.

And with the transposition half complete a new dimension of wonder was added. A receding, dwindling series of ships seemed to reach all the way to each planet, visible as disks which progressively shrank to glowing points. Several of those going in the direction of Overland had delayed turning over and could be seen from underneath with their gondolas, attachments and jet pipes scribed in ever finer detail on the shrinking circles.

As if that were not enough to brim the eye and mind, there was also – against deep blue infinities seeded with swirls and braids and points of frozen brilliance – the sight of the three companion ships carrying out their own inversion manoeuvres. The structures, which were so fragile that they could be crumpled by a boisterous breeze, remained magically immune to distortion as they stood the universe on its head, proclaiming that this truly was the zone of strangeness. Their pilots, visible as enigmatic mounds of swaddling, surely had to be alien supermen gifted with knowledge and skills inaccessible to ordinary men.

Not all of the scenes witnessed by Toller had possessed such grandeur, but they were imprinted on his memory for different reasons. There was Gesalla's face in its varied moods and aspects – dubiously triumphant as she overcame the waywardness of the galley fire, wanly introspective after hours of 'falling' through the region of zero or negligible gravity ... the bursting of all the accompanying ptertha within minutes of each other, after a day of climbing ... the children's looks of astonishment and delight as their breath became visible in the surrounding chill ... the games they played during the brief period when they could suspend beads and trinkets in the air to sketch simplified faces and build three-dimensional designs ...

And there had been the other scenes, exterior to the ship, which told of distant tragedies and the kind of death which heretofore had belonged to the realms of purest nightmare.

The royal flight had taken off at quite an early stage in the evacuation of the Quarter, and Toller knew that by the time they were a day and more past the midpoint they had above them an attenuated linear cloud of ships perhaps a hundred miles high. Had they not already been screened from view by the sedate vastness of his own balloon most of them would have been rendered invisible by sheer distance, but he had received disturbing proof of their existence. It took the form of a sparse, spasmodic and dreadful rain. A rain whose droplets were solid and which varied in size, from entire skyships to human bodies.

On three separate occasions he had seen crumpled ships plunge down past him, the gondolas wrapped in the slow-flapping ruins of their balloons, bound on the day-long fall to Overland. It was his guess that all vestiges of order had disappeared during the latter hours of the escape from Ro-Atabri, and that in the chaos some ships had been taken up by inexperienced fliers or had even been commandeered by rebels with no aviation knowledge at all. It looked as though some of them had driven far past the midpoint without turning over, their velocity being augmented by the growing attraction of Overland until the stresses in the flimsy envelopes had torn them apart.

Once he had seen a gondola plummeting down without its balloon, maintaining its proper attitude because of the trailing lines and acceleration struts, and a dozen soldiers had been visible at its rails, mutely surveying the procession of still-airworthy ships which was to be their last tenuous link with humanity and with life.

But for the most part the falling objects had been smaller – cooking utensils, ornate boxes, sacks of provisions, human and animal forms – evidence of catastrophic accidents tens of miles higher in the wavering stack of ships.

Not very far past the midpoint, while Overland's pull was still weak and the fall speeds were low, a young man had dropped past the ships, so close that Toller could easily discern his features. Perhaps out of bravado, or a desperate craving for a last communion with another human being, the young man had called out to Toller, quite cheerfully, and had waved a hand. Toller had not responded in a way, feeling that to do so would have been to take part in some unspeakable parody of a jest, and had remained petrified at the rail, appalled and yet unable to avert his gaze from the doomed man for the many minutes that it took him to dwindle out of sight.

Hours later, when darkness was all about him and he was trying to sleep, Toller had kept thinking of the falling man – who by then might have been a thousand miles ahead of the migration fleet – and wondering how he was preparing himself for the final impact ...

Comforted by the drowsing presence of Setwan on his knee, Toller was operating the burner like an automaton, unconsciously timing the blasts with his heartbeats, when daylight abruptly returned. He blinked several times and saw at once that something was wrong, that only two ships of the royal flight were holding level with him, instead of three.

The missing skyship was the one in which the King was flying.

There was nothing very unusual about that – Kedalse was an ultra-cautious pilot who liked to slow his descent at night, preferring to keep the other ships a little below him where he could easily monitor their positions – but this time he was not even visible in the upper sweeps of the sky.

Toller swiftly lifted Setwan and had just placed him in the passenger compartment with his family when he heard frantic shouts from Zavotle and Amber. He glanced towards them and saw that they were pointing at something above his ship, and in the same moment a gust of hot miglign gas came belching down out of the balloon mouth, bringing a startled whimper from one of the children. Toller looked up into the glowing dome of the balloon and his heart quaked as he saw the square silhouette of a gondola impressed upon it, distorting the spider-web geometries of the load tapes.

The King's ship was directly above him and had come down hard on his own balloon.

Toller could see the circular imprint of the other ship's jet nozzle digging into the crown of the envelope, endangering the integrity of the rip panel. There was a chorus of creaks from the rigging and from the acceleration struts, and a rippling distortion of the balloon fabric expelled more choking gas down into the gondola.

'Kedalse,' he shouted, not knowing if his voice would be heard in the upper gondola. 'Lift your ship! Lift your ship!'

The faint voices of Zavotle and Amber joined with his own, and a sun-writer began to flash from one of their gondolas, but there was no response from above. The King's ship continued to bear down on the overloaded balloon, threatening to burst or collapse it.

Toller glanced helplessly at Gesalla and Chakkell, who had risen to their feet and were staring at him in open-mouthed dread. The best explanation he could think of for the crisis was that the King's pilot had been overcome by illness and was unconscious or dead at the controls. If that were the case somebody else in the upper gondola might begin firing the burner and separate the two craft, but it would need to be done very soon. And there was also the possibility – Toller's mouth went dry at the thought – that the burner had failed in some way and could not be fired.

He strove to force his brain into action as the deck swayed beneath his feet and the fabric of the balloon emitted sounds like the cracking of a whip. The pair of ships had already begun to lose height too quickly, as was evidenced by the fact that the other two visible ships had acquired a relative upward movement.

Leddravohr had appeared at the rail of his own gondola, for the first time since the take-off, and behind him Zavotle was still emitting futile blinks of brilliance from his sunwriter.

It was impossible for Toller to get away from the King's ship by increasing his own rate of descent. His craft had already lost gas and was coming perilously near the condition in which the air pressures of an excessive fall-speed could collapse the balloon, initiating a thousand-mile drop to the surface of Overland.

In fact, there was an urgent requirement to fire large quantities of hot gas into the balloon – but doing so, with the extra load imposed from above, was to risk increasing the internal pressure so much that the envelope would simply tear itself apart.

Toller locked eyes with Gesalla, and the imperative was born in his mind: I *choose to live!*

He twisted his way into the seat at the pilot's station and fired the burner in a long thunderous blast, engorging the hungry balloon with hot gas, and a few seconds later he pushed the lever of an attitude-control jet. The jet's exhaust was lost in the engulfing roar of the burner, but its effect was not diminished.

The other two members of the royal flight drifted downwards and out of sight as Toller's ship rotated around its centre of gravity. There came a series of low-pitched inhuman groans and shudders as the King's ship slid down the side of Toller's balloon and came into view above him. One of its acceleration struts tore free of its lower attachment point and began wandering and circling in the air like a duellist's sword.

As Toller watched, frozen into his own continuum, the sluggish movements so characteristic of skyships abruptly accelerated. The other gondola drew level with him and the free end of the strut came blindly stabbing down into the galley compartment of Toller's ship, imparting a dangerous tilt to the universe. The shock of the impact raced back along the strut and its upper end gouged into the other balloon.

A seam ripped apart – and the balloon *died*.

It collapsed inwards, writhing in a perfect simulation of agony, and now the King's ship was falling unchecked. The leverage it exerted through the strut turned Toller's gondola on its side and Overland flashed into view, eager and expectant. Gesalla screamed as she fell against the lowermost wall and the looking-glass she had been holding spun out into the blue emptiness. Toller threw himself into the galley, risking going over the side in the process, gripped the end of the strut and – summoning all the power of his warrior's physique – raised it and cast it free.

As the gondola righted itself he clung to the rail and watched the other ship begin its lethal plunge. At the height of a thousand miles gravity was at less than half strength and the tempo of events had again lapsed into dreamlike slow motion. He saw King Prad swim to the side of the falling gondola. The King, his blind eye shining like a star, raised one hand and pointed at Toller, then he was hidden from view by the swirls of his ship's ruined balloon. Gaining speed as it settled into the fall, still seeking a balance between gravitation and air resistance, the ship dwindled to become a fluttering speck at the limits of vision, and finally was lost in the fractal patterns of Overland.

Becoming aware of a fierce psychic pressure, Toller raised his head and looked at the two accompanying ships. Leddravohr was gazing at him from the nearer, and as their eyes met he extended both arms towards Toller, like a man calling a loved one to his embrace. He remained like that, mutely imploring, and even when Toller had returned to the burner he could almost feel the prince's hatred as an invisible blade knifing through his soul. A grey-faced Chakkell was gazing at him from the entrance to the passenger compartment, inside which Daseene and Corba were quietly sobbing.

'This is a bad day,' Chakkell said in a halting voice. 'The King is dead.'

Not yet, Toller thought. *He still has quite a few hours to go.* Aloud he said, 'You saw what happened. We're lucky to be here. I had no choice.'

'Leddravohr won't see it like that.'

'No,' Toller said pensively. 'Leddravohr won't see it like that.'

That night, while Toller was vainly trying to sleep, Gesalla came to his side, and in the loneliness of the hour it seemed perfectly natural for him to put his arm around her. She rested her head on his shoulder and brought her mouth close to his ear.

'Toller,' she whispered, 'what are you thinking about?'

He considered lying to her, then decided he had had enough of barriers. 'I'm thinking about Leddravohr. It all has to be settled between us.'

'Perhaps he will have thought the thing through by the time we reach Overland and will be of a different mind. I mean, it wasn't even as if sacrificing us would have saved the King. Leddravohr is bound to admit that you had no choice.'

'I may have felt I had no choice, but Leddravohr will say I acted too quickly in rolling us out from under his father's ship. Perhaps I would say the same thing if the positions were reversed. If I had waited a little longer Kedalse or somebody else might have got their burner going.'

'You mustn't think that way,' Gesalla said softly. 'You did what had to be done.'

'And Leddravohr is going to do what has to be done.'

'You can overcome him, can't you?'

'Perhaps – but I fear that he will have already given orders for me to be executed,' Toller said. 'I can't fight a regiment.'

'I see.' Gesalla raised herself on one elbow and looked down at him, and in the dimness her face was impossibly beautiful. 'Do you love me, Toller?'

He felt he had reached the end of a lifelong journey. 'Yes.'

'I'm glad.' She sat up straighter and began to remove her clothing. 'Because I want a child from you.'

He caught her wrist, smiling numbly in his disbelief. 'What do you think you're doing? Chakkell is on the burner just on the other side of this partition.'

'He can't see us.'

'But this isn't the way to …'

'I don't care about any of that,' Gesalla said, pressing her breast against the hand that was holding her wrist. 'I have chosen you to father my child, and there may be very little time for us.'

'It won't work, you know.' Toller relaxed back on the quilts. 'It's physically impossible for me to make love in these conditions.'

'That's what you think,' Gesalla said as she moved astride of him and brought her mouth down on his, moulding his cheeks with both her hands to coax him into an ardent response.

CHAPTER TWENTY

Overland's equatorial continent, seen from a height of two miles, looked essentially prehistoric.

Toller had been staring down at the outward-seeping landscape for some time before realising why that particular adjective kept coming to mind. It was not the total absence of cities and roads – first proof that the continent was uninhabited – but the uniform coloration of the grasslands.

Throughout his life every aerial view he had seen had been modified in some way by the six-harvest system which was universal on Land. The edible grasses and all other cultivated vegetation had been arranged in parallel strips in which the colours ranged from brown through several shades of green to harvest yellow, but here the plains were simply … *green*.

The sunlit expanses of the single colour shimmered in his eyes.

Our farmers will have to start the seed-sorting all over again, he thought. *And the mountains and seas and rivers all have to be given names. It really is a new beginning on a new world. And I don't think I'm going to be part of it …*

Reminded of his personal problems, he turned his attention to the artificial elements of the scene. The two other ships of the royal flight were slightly below him. Pouche's was the more distant, most of its passengers visible at the rail as they journeyed ahead in their imaginations to the unknown world.

Ilven Zavotle was the only person to be seen on Leddravohr's ship, sitting tiredly at the controls. Leddravohr himself must have been lying down in a passenger compartment, as he had done – except during the traumatic episode two days before – throughout the voyage. Toller had noted the prince's behaviour earlier and wondered if he could be phobic about the boundless emptiness surrounding the migration fleet. If that were the case, it would have been better for Toller if their inevitable duel could have been fought aboard one of the gondolas.

In the two miles of airspace below him he could see twelve other balloons forming an irregular line which increasingly flared off to the west, evidence of a moderate breeze in the lowest levels of the atmosphere. The general area into which they were drifting was sprinkled with the elongated shapes of collapsed balloons, which would later be used to build a temporary township of tents. As he had expected, Toller's binoculars showed that most of the grounded ships had military markings. Even in the turmoil of the escape from Ro-Atabri, Leddravohr had had the foresight to provide himself with a power base which would be effective from the instant he set foot on Overland.

Analysing the situation, Toller could see no prospect at all of his living for more than a matter of minutes if he put his ship down close to Leddravohr's. Even if he were to defeat Leddravohr in single combat, he would – as the man charged with the death of the King – be taken by the army. His single and desperately slim chance of survival, for a term to be measured in days at most, lay in hanging back during the touchdown and going aloft again as soon as Leddravohr's ship was committed to a landing. There were forested hills perhaps twenty miles west of the landing site, and if he could reach them with his balloon he might be able to avoid capture until the forces of the infant nations were properly organised in the cause of his destruction.

The weakest point of the plan was that it hinged on factors outside his own control, all of them concerned with the mind and character of Leddravohr's pilot.

He had no doubt at all that Zavotle would make the correct deductions when he saw Toller's ship being tardy during the landing, but would he be sympathetic with Toller's aims? And even if he were inclined to be loyal to a fellow skyman, would he take the personal risk of doing what Toller expected of him? He would have to be quick to pull the rip panel and collapse his balloon – just as it was becoming apparent to Leddravohr that his enemy was slipping out of his grasp – and there was no predicting how the prince might react in his anger. He had struck other men down for lesser offences.

Toller stared across the field of brightness at the solitary figure of Zavotle, knowing that his gaze was being returned, then he put his back against the gondola wall and eyed Chakkell, who was operating the burner at the one-and-twenty rhythm of the descent.

'Prince, there is a breeze at ground level and I fear the ship may be dragged,' he said, making his opening move. 'You and the princess and your children should be ready to go over the side even before we touch the ground. It might sound dangerous, but there's a good ledge all around the gondola for standing on, and our ground speed will be little more than a walking pace. Jumping off before touchdown is preferable to being in the gondola if it overturns.'

'I'm touched by your solicitude,' Chakkell said, giving Toller a tilt-headed look of surmise.

Wondering if he had blundered so early, Toller approached the pilot's station. 'We'll be landing very soon, Prince. You must be prepared.'

Chakkell nodded, vacated the seat and, unexpectedly, said, 'I still remember the first time I saw you, in the company of Glo. I never thought it would come to this.'

'Lord Glo had vision,' Toller replied. 'He should be here.'

'I suppose so.' Chakkell gave him another searching look and went into the compartment where Daseene and the children were making ready for the landing.

Toller sat down and took control of the burner, noting as he did so that the pointer on the altitude gauge had fully returned to the bottom mark. As Overland was smaller than Land he would have expected its surface gravity to be less, but Lain had said otherwise. *Overland has a higher density, and therefore everything there will weigh about the same as on Land.* Toller shook his head, half smiling in belated tribute to his brother. How had Lain known what to expect? Mathematics was one aspect of his brother's life which would forever remain a closed book to him, as looked like being the case with . . .

He glanced at Gesalla, who for an hour had been motionless at the outer wall of their compartment, her attention fully absorbed by the expanding vistas of the new world below. Her bundle of possessions was already slung on her shoulder, giving the impression that she was impatient to set foot on Overland and go about the business of carving out whatever future she had visualised for herself and the child which, possibly, he had seeded into her. The emotions aroused in him by the sight of her slim, straight and uncompromising form were the most complex he had ever known.

On the night she had come to him he had been quite certain he would be unable to fulfil the male role because of his tiredness, his guilt and the unnerving presence of Chakkell, who had been operating the burner only a few feet away. But Gesalla had known better. She had worked on him with fervour, skill and imagination, plying him with her mouth and gracile body until nothing else existed for him but the need to pulse his semen into her. She had remained on top of him until the climactic moment was near, then had insensibly engineered a change of position and had held it, with upthrust pelvis and legs locked around him, for minutes afterwards. Only later, when they had been talking, had he realised that she had been maximising the chances of conception.

And now, as well as loving her, he hated her for some of the things she had said to him during the remainder of that night while the meteors flickered in the dimness all around. There had been no direct statements, but there was revealed to him a Gesalla who, while displaying chilly anger over a fine point of etiquette, was at the same time prepared to defy any convention for the sake of a future child. In the milieu of the old Kolcorron it had seemed to her that the qualities offered by Lain Maraquine would be the most advantageous for her offspring, and so she had married him. She had loved Lain, but the thing which chafed Toller's sensibilities was that she had loved Lain for a reason.

And now that she was being projected into the vastly different frontier environment of Overland, it had been her considered judgment that attributes available through Toller Maraquine's seed were to be preferred, and so she had coupled with him.

In his confusion and pain, Toller was unable to identify the principal source of his resentment. Was it self-disgust at having been so easily seduced by his brother's widow? Was it lacerated pride over having his finest feelings made part of an exercise in eugenics? Or was he furious with Gesalla for not fitting in with his preconceptions, for not being what he wanted her to be? How was it possible for a woman to be a prude and a wanton at the same time, to be generous and selfish, hard and soft, accessible and remote, his and not his?

The questions were endless, Toller realised, and to dwell on them at this stage would be futile and dangerous. The only preoccupations he could afford were with staying alive.

He fitted the extension tube to the burner lever and moved to the side of the gondola to give himself maximum visibility for the descent. As the horizon began to rise level with him he gradually increased his burn ratio, allowing Zavotle's ship to move farther ahead. It was important to achieve the greatest vertical separation that was possible without arousing the suspicions of Leddravohr and Chakkell. He watched as the dozen ships still airborne ahead of the royal flight touched down one by one, the precise moment of each contact being signalled by the shocked contortion of the balloon, followed by the appearance of a triangular rent in the crown and the wilting collapse of the entire envelope.

The entire area was dotted with ships which had landed previously, and already some sort of order was beginning to be imposed on the scene. Supplies were being brought together and piled, and teams of men were running to each new ship as it touched down.

The sense of awe Toller had expected to accompany such a sight was missing, displaced by the urgency of his situation. He trained his binoculars on Zavotle's ship as it neared the ground and risked firing a long blast of miglign into his own balloon. On that instant, as though his ears had been attuned to the tell-tale sound, Leddravohr materialised at the gondola rail. His shadowed eyes were intent on Toller's ship, and even at that distance they could be seen flaring with coronas of white as he realised what was happening.

He turned to say something to his pilot, but Zavotle – without waiting for ground contact – pulled his rip line. The balloon above him went into the heaving convulsions of its death throes. The gondola skidded into the grass and was lost from view as the dark brown shroud of the envelope fluttered down around it. Groups of soldiers – among them one officer mounted on a bluehorn – ran to the ship and that of Pouche, which was making a more leisurely touchdown a furlong farther away.

Toller lowered his binoculars and faced Chakkell. 'Prince, for reasons which must be obvious to you, I am not going to land my ship at this time. I have no desire to take you or any other disinterested parties – ' he paused to glance at Gesalla – 'into an alien wilderness with me, therefore I'm going to go within grass level of the surface. At that point it will be very easy for you and your family to part company with the ship, but you must act quickly and with resolution. Is that understood?'

'No!' Chakkell left the passenger compartment and took a step towards Toller. 'You will land the ship in full accordance with normal procedure. That is my command, Maraquine. I have no intention of subjecting myself or my family to any unnecessary hazards.'

'Hazards!' Toller drew his lips into a smile. 'Prince, we are talking about a drop of a few inches. Compare that to the thousand-mile tumble they almost embarked upon two days ago.'

'Your meaning isn't lost on me.' Chakkell hesitated and glanced at his wife. 'But still I must insist on a landing.'

'And I insist otherwise,' Toller said, hardening his voice. The ship was still about thirty feet above the ground and with each passing moment the breeze bore it farther away from the spot where Leddravohr had come down, but the period of grace had to come to an end soon. Even as Toller was trying to guess how much time he had in hand he saw Leddravohr emerge from under the collapsed balloon. Simultaneously, Gesalla climbed over the gondola wall and positioned herself on the outer ledge, ready to jump free. Her eyes met Toller's only briefly, and there was no communication. He allowed the descent to continue until he could discern individual blades of grass.

'Prince, you must decide quickly,' he said. 'If you don't leave the ship soon, we all go aloft together.'

'Not necessarily.' Chakkell leaned closer to the pilot's station and snatched the red line which was connected to the balloon's rip panel. 'I think this restores my authority,' he said, and jabbed a pointing finger as he saw Toller instinctively tighten his grip on the extension lever. 'If you try to ascend I'll vent the balloon.'

'That would be dangerous at this height.'

'Not if I only do it partially,' Chakkell replied, displaying knowledge he had acquired while controlling production of the migration fleet. 'I can bring the ship down quite gently.'

Toller looked beyond him and in the distance saw Leddravohr in the act of commandeering the bluehorn of the officer who had rode to meet his ship. 'Any landing would be gentle,' he said, 'compared to the one your children would have made after falling a thousand miles.'

Chakkell shook his head. 'Repetition doesn't strengthen your case, Maraquine – it only brings to mind the fact that you were also saving your own skin. Leddravohr is now King, and my first duty is to him.'

There was a whispering sound from underfoot as the jet exhaust funnel brushed the tips of tall grass. Half-a-mile away to the east, Leddravohr was astride the bluehorn and was galloping towards the ship, followed by groups of soldiers on foot.

'And my first loyalty is towards my children,' the Princess Daseene announced unexpectedly, her head appearing above the partition of the passenger compartment. 'I've had enough of this – and of you, Chakkell.'

With surprising agility and lack of concern for her dignity she swarmed over the gondola wall and helped Corba to follow. Unbidden, Gesalla came swiftly around the gondola on the outside and aided in the lifting of the two boys on to the ledge.

Daseene, still wearing the incongruous pearl coif like a general's insignia, fixed her husband with an imperious stare. 'You are indebted to that man for my life,' she said angrily. 'If you refuse to honour the debt it can mean but one thing.'

'But ...' Chakkell clapped his brow in perplexity, then pointed at Leddravohr, who was rapidly gaining on the slow-drifting ship. 'What will I say to *him?*'

Toller reached down into the compartment he had shared with Gesalla and retrieved his sword. 'You could say I threatened you with this.'

'*Are* you threatening me with it?'

The sound of whipping grass became louder, and the gondola bucked slightly as the jet exhaust made a fleeting contact with the ground. Toller glanced at Leddravohr – now only two-hundred yards away and flailing the bluehorn into a wilder gallop – then shouted at Chakkell.

'For your own good leave the ship *now!*'

'Something else to remember you for,' Chakkell mumbled as he let go of the rip line. He went to the side, rolled himself over on to the ledge and immediately dropped away to the ground. Daseene and the children followed him at once, one of the boys whooping with pleasurable excitement, leaving only Gesalla holding on to the rail.

'Goodbye,' Toller said.

'Goodbye, Toller.' She continued to stand at the rail, staring at him in what looked like surprise. Leddravohr was now little more than a hundred yards away and the sound of his bluehorn's hoofbeats was growing louder by the second.

'What are you waiting for?' Toller heard his own voice cracking with urgency. 'Get off the ship!'

'No – I'm going with you.' In the time it took her to utter the words Gesalla had climbed back over the rail and dropped to the gondola floor.

'What are you *doing?*' Every nerve in Toller's body was screaming for him to fire the burner and try to lift the ship out of Leddravohr's reach, but his arm muscles and hands were locked. 'Have you gone crazy?'

'I think so,' Gesalla said strickenly. 'It's idiotic – but I'm going with you.'

'You're mine, Maraquine,' Leddravohr called out in a strange fervent chant as he drew his sword. 'Come to me, Maraquine.'

Almost mesmerised, Toller was tightening his grip on his own sword when Gesalla threw herself past him and dropped her full weight on to the extension lever. The burner roared at once, blasting gas into the waiting balloon. Toller silenced it by pulling the lever up, then he pushed Gesalla back against a partition.

'Thank you, but this is pointless,' he said. 'Leddravohr has to be faced at some stage, and this seems to be the ordained time.'

He kissed Gesalla lightly on the forehead, turned back to the rail and locked eyes with Leddravohr, who was on a level with him and now only a dozen yards away. Leddravohr, apparently sensing his change of heart, struck his smile into existence. Toller felt the first stirrings of a shameful excitement, a yearning to have everything settled with Leddravohr once and for all, regardless of the outcome, to know for certain if ...

His sequence of thought was broken as he saw an abrupt change of expression on Leddravohr's face. There was sudden alarm there, and the prince was no longer looking directly at him. Toller swung round and saw that Gesalla was holding the butt of one of the ship's ptertha cannon. She had already driven home the firing pin and was aiming the weapon at Leddravohr. Before Toller could react the cannon fired. The projectile was a central blur in a spray of glass fragments, spreading its arms as it flew.

Leddravohr twisted away from it successfully, pulling his mount off course, but shards of glass pocked his face with crimson. He gasped with shock and hauled the galloping bluehorn back into line, rapidly making up lost ground.

Staring frozenly at Leddravohr, knowing the rules of their private war had been changed, Toller fired the burner. The skyship had been made lighter by the departure of Chakkell and his family and had been disposed to rise ever since, but the inertia of the tons of gas inside the balloon made it nightmarishly slow to respond. Toller kept the burner roaring and the gondola began to lift clear of the grass, Leddravohr was now almost within reach and was raising himself in the stirrups. His eyes glared insanely at Toller from a mask of blood.

Is he mad enough to try leaping on to the gondola? Toller wondered. *Does he want to meet the point of my sword?*

In the next pounding second Toller became aware that Gesalla had darted around behind him and was at the other cannon on the windward side. Leddravohr saw her, drew back his arm and hurled his sword.

Toller gave a warning cry, but the sword had not been aimed at a human target. It arced high above him and sank to the hilt in a lower panel of the balloon. The fabric split and the sword fell clear, spinning down into the grass. Leddravohr reined his bluehorn to a halt, jumped down and retrieved the black blade. He remounted immediately and spurred the bluehorn forward, but he was no longer overtaking the ship, being content to pace it at a distance. Gesalla fired the second cannon, but the projectile plunged harmlessly into the grass well clear of Leddravohr, who responded with a courtly wave of his arm.

Still firing the burner, Toller looked up and saw that the rent in the varnished linen of the envelope had run the full length of the panel. The edges of it were pursed, invisibly spewing gas, but the ship had finally gained some upward momentum and was continuing its sluggish climb.

Toller was startled by the sound of hoarse shouting from close by. He spun round and discovered that, while all his attention had been concentrated on Leddravohr, the ship had been drifting directly towards a scattered band of soldiers. The gondola sailed over them with only a few feet to spare and they began to run along behind and below it, leaping in their efforts to grab hold of the ledge.

Their faces were anxious rather than hostile, and it came to Toller that they had only the vaguest idea of what had been happening. Praying he would not have to take action against any of them, he kept on blasting gas into the balloon and was rewarded by an agonisingly slow but steady gain in height.

'Can the ship fly?' Gesalla came to his side, straining to make herself heard above the roar of the burner. 'Are we safe?'

'The ship can fly – after a fashion,' Toller said, choosing to ignore her second question. 'Why did you do it, Gesalla?'

'Surely you know.'

'No.'

'Love came back to me.' She gave him a peaceful smile. 'After that I had no choice.'

The fulfilment Toller should have felt was lost in black territories of fear. 'But you attacked Leddravohr! And he has no mercy, even for women.'

'I don't need reminding.' Gesalla looked back at the slow-moving, attendant figure of Leddravohr, and for a moment scorn and hatred robbed her of beauty. 'You were right, Toller – we must not simply surrender to the butchers. Leddravohr destroyed the life in me once, and Lain and I compounded the crime by ceasing to love each other, ceasing to love ourselves. We gave too much.'

'Yes, but ...' Toller took a deep breath as he strove to accord Gesalla the rights he had always claimed for himself.

'But what?'

'We have to lighten the ship,' he said, passing the burner control lever to her. He went into the compartment vacated by Chakkell and began hurling trunks and boxes over the side.

The pursuing soldiers whooped and cheered until Leddravohr rode in among them, and his gestures showed that he was giving orders for the containers to be carried back to the main landing site. Within a minute the soldiers had turned back with their burdens, leaving Leddravohr to follow the ship alone. The wind speed was about six miles an hour and as a result the bluehorn was able to keep pace in a leisurely trot. Leddravohr was riding slightly beyond the cannons' effective reach, slouched in the saddle, expending little energy and waiting for the situation to turn to his advantage.

Toller checked the pikon and halvell magazines and found he had sufficient crystals for at least a day of continuous burning – the ships of the royal flight having been more generously provided than the others – but his principal concern was with the ship's lack of performance. The rip in the balloon was showing no sign of spreading past the upper and lower panel seams, but the amount of gas spilling through it was almost enough to deprive the ship of its buoyancy.

In spite of the continuous firing of the burner the gondola had gained no more than twenty feet, and Toller knew that the slightest adverse change in conditions would force a descent. A sudden gust of wind, for example, could flatten one side of the envelope and expel precious gas, delivering Gesalla and him into the hands of the patiently stalking enemy. Alone he would have been more than prepared to contend with Leddravohr, but now Gesalla's life also depended on the outcome ...

He went to the rail and gripped it with both hands, staring back at Leddravohr and longing for a weapon capable of striking the prince down at a distance. The arrival on Overland had been so different to all his imaginings. Here he was on the sister planet – *on Overland!* – but the malign

presence of Leddravohr, embodiment of all that was rank and evil in Kolcorron, had degraded the experience and made the new world an offshoot
of the old. Like the ptertha increasing their lethal powers, Leddravohr had
extended his own killing radius to encompass Overland. Toller should have
been enthralled by the spectacle of a pristine sky bisected by a zigzag line of
fragile ships which stretched down from the zenith, emerging from invisibility as they sank like windborne seeds in search of fertile ground – but
there was Leddravohr.

Always there was Leddravohr.

'Are you worried about the hills?' Gesalla said. She had sunk to a kneeling
position, out of Leddravohr's view, and had one hand raised to work the
burner's lever.

'We can lash that down,' Toller said. 'You won't need to keep on holding
it.'

'Toller, are you worried about the hills?'

'Yes.' He took a length of twine from a locker and used it to tie down the
lever. 'If we could get over the hills there'd be a chance of wearing Leddravohr's bluehorn out – but I don't know if we can gain enough height.'

'I'm not afraid, you know.' Gesalla touched his hand. 'If you would prefer
to go down and face him now, it's all right.'

'No, we'll stay aloft as long as possible. We have food and drink here and
can keep up our strength while Leddravohr is slowly losing his.' He gave
her what he hoped was a reassuring smile. 'Besides, littlenight will be here
soon, and that's to our advantage because the balloon will work better in the
cooler air. We may yet be able to set up our own little colony on Overland.'

Littlenight was longer than on Land, and by the time it had passed the
gondola was at an altitude of slightly more than two hundred feet – which
was a better gain than Toller had expected. The lower slopes of the nameless
hills were sliding by beneath the ship, and none of the ridges he could see
ahead seemed quite high enough to claw it out of the sky. He consulted the
map he had drawn while still on the skyship.

'There's a big lake about ten miles beyond the hills,' he said. 'If we can fly
over it we should be able to ...'

'Toller! I think I see a ptertha!' Gesalla caught his arm as she pointed to
the south. 'Look!'

Toller threw the map down, raised his binoculars and scanned the indicated section of sky. He was about to query Gesalla's remark when he picked
out a hint of sphericity, a near-invisible crescent of sunlight glinting on
something transparent.

'I think you're right,' he said. 'And it has no colour. That's what Lain
meant. It has no colour because ...' He passed the binoculars to Gesalla.
'Can you find any brakka trees?'

'I didn't realise you can see so much with glasses.' Gesalla, speaking with childish enthusiasm, might have been on a pleasure flight as she studied the hillside. 'Most of the trees aren't like anything I've ever seen before, but I think there are brakka among them. Yes, I'm sure. Brakka! How can that be, Toller?'

Guessing she was purposely distracting her mind from what was to come, he said, 'Lain wrote that brakka and ptertha go together. Perhaps the brakka discharges are so powerful that they shoot their seeds up into … No, that's only for pollen, isn't it? Perhaps brakka grow everywhere – on Farland and every other planet.'

Leaving Gesalla to her observations with the binoculars, Toller leaned on the rail and returned his attention to Leddravohr, the relentless pursuer.

For hours Leddravohr had been slumped in the saddle, giving the impression of being asleep, but now – as though concerned that his quarry could be on the point of eluding him – he was sitting upright. He had no helmet, but was shading his eyes with his hands as he chose the bluehorn's path through the trees and patches of scrub which dappled the slopes he was climbing. Off to the east the landing site and the line of descending balloons had been lost in blue-hazed distance, and it was as though Gesalla, Toller and Leddravohr had the entire planet to themselves. Overland had become a vast sunlit arena, held in readiness since the beginning of time …

His thoughts were interrupted by a sudden flapping sound from the balloon.

The noise was followed by a downward rush of heat from the balloon mouth which told him the ship had blundered into turbulent air flung up from a secondary ridge. The gondola abruptly began to yaw and sway. Toller fixed his gaze on the main crest, which was now only about two hundred yards away on the line of flight. He knew that if they could scrape over it there might be time for the balloon to recover, but in the instant of looking at the rocky barrier he realised the situation was hopeless. The ship, which had been so reluctant to take flight, was already abandoning the aerial element, sailing determinedly towards the hillside.

'Hold on to something,' Toller shouted. 'We're going down!'

He tore the extension lever free of its lashings and shut the burner off. A few seconds later the gondola began swishing through treetops. The sounds grew louder and the gondola bucked violently as it impacted with increasingly thicker branches and trunks. Above and behind Toller the collapsing balloon tore with a series of groans and snaps as it entangled itself with the trees, applying a brake to the ship's lateral movement.

The gondola dropped vertically as it took up the slack in its load cables, broke free at two corners and turned on its side, almost hurling its two occupants clear amid a shower of quilts and small objects. Incredibly, after the jolting and dangerous progression from treetop height, Toller found himself able to step down easily on to mossy ground. He turned and lifted Gesalla, who was clinging to a stanchion, and set her down beside him.

'You must get away from here,' he said quickly. 'Get to the other side of the hill and find a place to hide.'

Gesalla threw her arms around him. 'I should stay with you. I might be able to help.'

'Believe me, you won't be able to help. If our baby is growing in you, you must take this chance for it to live. If Leddravohr kills me he may not go after you – especially if he is wounded.'

'But ...' Gesalla's eyes widened as the bluehorn snorted a short distance away. 'But I won't know what has happened.'

'I'll fire one of the cannon if I win.' He spun Gesalla around and pushed her away with such force that she was obliged to break into a run to avoid falling. 'Only come back if you hear a cannon.'

He stood quite still and watched until Gesalla, with several backward glances, had disappeared into the cover of the trees. He had drawn his sword, and was looking about him for a clear space in which to fight, when it came to him that ingrained behaviour patterns were causing him to approach the clash with Leddravohr as though he were entering a formal duel.

How can you think that way when other lives are at stake? he asked himself, dismayed by the extent of his own naivety. *What was honour got to do with the plain task of excising a canker?*

He glanced at the slow-swinging gondola, decided on Leddravohr's most probable line of approach to it, and stepped back into the concealment of three trees which grew so closely that they might have sprung from the same root. The same excitement he had known before – shameful and inexplicably sexual – began to steal over him.

He quieted his breathing, ridding himself of his humanity, and a new thought occurred: *Leddravohr was nearby a minute ago – so why have I not seen him by now?*

Knowing the answer, he turned his head and saw Leddravohr about ten paces away. Leddravohr had already thrown his knife. The speed and distance were such that Toller had no time to duck or move aside. He flung up his left hand and took the knife in the centre of the palm. The full length of the black blade came through between the bones with so much force that his hand was driven back and the knife-point tore open his face just below the left eye.

A natural instinct would have been to look at the injured hand, but Toller ignored it and whipped his sword into the guard position just in time to deter Leddravohr, who had followed up on the throw with a running attack.

'You have learned a few things, Maraquine,' Leddravohr said, as he too went on guard. 'Most men would be dead twice over by this time.'

'The lesson was a simple one,' Toller replied. 'Always prepare for reptiles to behave as such.'

'I can't be goaded – so keep your insults.'

'I haven't offered any, except to reptiles.'

Leddravohr's smile twitched into existence, very white in a face made unrecognisable by traceries of dried blood. His hair was matted and his cuirass, which had been blood-stained before the migration flight began, was streaked with dirt and what looked like partially-digested food. Toller moved away from the constriction of the three trees, turning his mind to combat tactics.

Was it possible that Leddravohr was one of those men, fearless in all other respects, who were laid low by acrophobia? Was that why he had been seen so little throughout the flight? If so, Leddravohr could hardly be fit enough to embark on a prolonged struggle.

The Kolcorronian battle sword was a two-edged weapon whose weight precluded its use in formalised duelling. It was limited to basic cutting and thrusting strokes which could generally be blocked or deflected by an opponent with fast reactions and a good eye. All other things being equal, the victor in single combat tended to be the man with the most physical power and endurance. Toller had a natural advantage in that he was more than ten years younger than Leddravohr, but that had been offset by the disablement of his left hand. Now he had reason to suppose that the balance was restored in his favour – and yet Leddravohr, vastly experienced in such matters, had lost none of his arrogance ...

'Why so pensive, Maraquine?' Leddravohr was moving with Toller to maintain the line of engagement. 'Are you troubled by the ghost of my father?'

Toller shook his head. 'By the ghost of my brother. We never settled that issue.' To his surprise, he saw that his words had disturbed Leddravohr's composure.

'Why do you plague me with this?'

'I believe you are responsible for my brother's death.'

'I told you the fool was responsible for his own death.' Leddravohr made an angry stabbing movement with his sword and the two blades touched for the first time. 'Why should I lie about it, then or now? He broke his mount's leg and he refused a seat on mine.'

'Lain wouldn't have done that.'

'He did! I tell you he could have been at your side at this minute, and I wish he were – so that I could have the pleasure of cleaving both your skulls.'

While Leddravohr was speaking Toller took the opportunity to glance at his wounded hand. There was no great pain as yet, but blood was coursing steadily down the handle of the knife and beading off it to the ground. When he shook his hand the blade remained firmly in place, wedged to the hilt between the bones. The wound, though not a crippling one, would have a progressive effect on his strength and fighting capability. It behoved him to get the duel under way as soon as possible. He forced himself to disregard the lies Leddravohr was uttering about his brother, and to seek a reason for the noteworthy fact that a man whose potency must have been diminished by twelve days of dislocation and illness appeared overweeningly confident of victory.

Was there a significant clue he had overlooked?

He studied his opponent again – tenths of a second passing like minutes in his keyed-up state – and saw only that Leddravohr had sleeved his sword. Soldiers from some parts of the Kolcorronian empire, principally Sorka and Middac, had the practice of covering the base of a blade with leather so that on occasion one hand could be transposed ahead of the hilt and the sword used as a two-handed weapon. Toller had never seen much merit in the idea, but he resolved to be extra wary in the event of an unexpected variation in Leddravohr's attack.

All at once the preliminaries were over.

Each man had circled to a position which materially was no better than any other, but which satisfied him in some indefinable way as being the most propitious, the most suitable for his purpose. Toller went in first, surprised at being allowed that psychological advantage, starting on the backhand with a series of downward hacks alternating from left to right, and was immediately thrilled with the result. As was inevitable, Leddravohr blocked every stroke with ease, but the blade shocks were not quite what Toller had expected. It was as though Leddravohr's sword arm had given way a little at each blow, hinting at a serious lack of strength.

A few minutes could decide everything, Toller exulted as he allowed the sequence to come to a natural end, then his survivor's instinct reasserted itself. *Dangerous thinking! Would Leddravohr have pursued me this far – alone – knowing he was unequal to the struggle?*

Toller disengaged and shifted his ground, holding his dripping left hand clear of his body. Leddravohr closed in on him with startling speed, creating a low sweep triangle which almost forced Toller to defend his useless arm rather than his head and body. The flurry ended with a mighty backhand cross from Leddravohr which actually fanned cool air against the underside of Toller's chin. He leapt back, chastened, reminded that the prince in a debilitated condition was a match for an ordinary soldier in his prime.

Had that resurgence of power represented the trap he suspected Leddravohr of preparing for him? If so, it was vital not to allow Leddravohr breathing space and recovery time. Toller renewed his attack on the instant, initiating sequence after sequence with no perceptible interludes, using all his strength but at the same time modifying fury with intelligence, allowing the prince no mental or physical respite.

Leddravohr, breathing hard now, was forced to yield ground. Toller saw that he was backing into a cluster of low thorn bushes and forced himself closer, awaiting the moment when Leddravohr would be distracted, immobilised or caught off balance. But Leddravohr, displaying his genius for combat, appeared to sense the presence of the bushes without having to turn his head.

He saved himself by gathering Toller's blade in a circular counter parry worthy of a smallsword master, stepping inside his defences and turning both their bodies into a new line. For a second the two men were pressed together, chest to chest, their swords locked at the hilts overhead at the apex of the triangle formed by their straining right arms.

Toller felt the heat of Leddravohr's breath and smelled the foulness of vomit from him, then he broke the contact by forcing his sword arm down, making it into an irresistible lever which drove them apart.

Leddravohr aided the separation by jumping backwards and quickly sidestepping to bring the thorn bushes between them. His chest was heaving rapidly, evidence of his growing tiredness, but – strangely – he appeared to have been buoyed up rather than disconcerted by the narrowness of his escape from peril. He was leaning forward slightly in an attitude suggestive of a new eagerness, and his eyes were animated and derisive amid the filigrees of dried blood which covered his face.

Something has happened, Toller thought, his skin crawling with apprehension. *Leddravohr knows something!*

'By the way, Maraquine,' Leddravohr said, sounding almost genial, 'I heard what you said to your woman.'

'Yes?' In spite of his alarm, a part of Toller's consciousness was being taken up by the odd fact that the disgusting odour he had endured while in contact with Leddravohr was still strong in his nostrils. Was it really just the sourness of regurgitated food, or was there another smell there? Something strangely familiar and with a deadly significance?

Leddravohr smiled. 'It was a good idea. About firing the cannon, I mean. It will save me the trouble of going looking for her when I have disposed of you.'

Don't waste breath on a reply, Toller urged himself. *Leddravohr is putting on too much of a show. It means he isn't leading you into a trap – it has already been sprung!*

'Well, I don't think I'm going to need this,' Leddravohr said. He gripped the leather sleeve at the base of his sword, slid it off and dropped it to the ground. His eyes were fixed on Toller, amused and enigmatic.

Toller looked closely at the sleeve and saw that it seemed to have been made in two layers, with a thin outer skin which had been ruptured. Around the edges of the split were glistening traces of yellow slime.

Toller looked down at his own sword, belatedly identifying the stench which was emanating from it – the stench of whitefern – and saw more of the slime on the broadest part of the blade, close to the hilt. The black material of the blade was bubbling and vapouring as it dissolved under the attack of the brakka slime, which had been smeared there by Leddravohr's sword when the two were crossed at the hilts.

I accept my death, Toller mused, his thoughts blurring into frenzied battle tempo as he saw Leddravohr darting towards him, *on condition that I don't journey alone.*

He raised his head and lunged at Leddravohr's chest with his sword. Leddravohr struck across it and snapped the blade at the root, sending it tumbling away to one side, and in the same movement swept his sword round into a thrust aimed at Toller's body.

Toller took the thrust, throwing himself on to it as he knew he had to were he to achieve life's last ambition. He gasped as the blade passed all the way through him, allowing him to drive on until he was within reach of Leddravohr. He gripped the throwing knife and, with his left hand still impaled on it, ran the blade upwards into Leddravohr's stomach, circling and seeking with the tip. There was a gushing warmth on the back of his hand.

Leddravohr growled and pushed Toller away from him with desperate force, simultaneously withdrawing his sword. He stared at Toller, openmouthed, for several seconds, then he dropped the sword and sank to his knees. He pitched forward on to his hands and remained like that, head lowered, staring at the pool of blood gathering below his body.

Toller worked the knife free of the bones clamped around it, mentally remote from the pain he was inflicting on himself, then clutched his side in an effort to stem the sopping pulsations of the sword wound. The edges of his vision were in a ferment; the sunlit hillside was rushing towards him and retreating. He threw the knife away, approached Leddravohr on buckling legs and picked up the sword. Forcing all that remained of his strength into his right arm, he raised the sword high.

Leddravohr did not look up, but he moved his head a little, showing he was aware of Toller's actions. 'I have killed you, haven't I, Maraquine?' he said in a choking, blood-drowning voice. 'Give me that one consolation.'

'Sorry, but you hardly scratched me,' Toller said as he cleaved downwards with the black blade.

'And this is for my brother ... *Prince!*'

He turned away from Leddravohr's corpse and with difficulty steadied his gaze on the square shape of the gondola. Was it swinging in a breeze, or was it the one fixed point in a see-sawing, dissolving universe?

He set out to walk towards it, intrigued by the discovery that it was now very far away ... at a remove much greater than the distance from Land to Overland ...

CHAPTER TWENTY-ONE

The rear wall of the cave was partially hidden by a mound of large pebbles and rock fragments which over the centuries had washed down through a natural chimney. Toller enjoyed gazing at the mound because he knew the Overlanders lived inside it.

He had not actually seen them, and therefore did not know if they resembled miniature men or animals, but he was keenly aware of their presence – because they used lanterns.

The light from the lanterns shone out through chinks in the rock at intervals which were not attuned to the outside world's rhythm of night and day. Toller liked to think of Overlanders going about their own business in there, secure in their tumbledown fortress, with no concern for anything which might be happening in the universe at large.

It was the nature of his delirium that even in periods when he felt himself to be perfectly lucid one tiny lantern would sometimes continue to gleam from the heart of the pile. At those times he took no pleasure from the experience. Afraid for his sanity, he would stare at the point of light, willing it to vanish because it had no place in the rational world. Sometimes it would obey quickly, but there were occasions when it took hours to dim out of existence, and then he would cling to Gesalla, making her the lifeline which joined him to all that was familiar and normal ...

'Well, *I* don't think you're strong enough to travel,' Gesalla said firmly, 'so there is no point in carrying on with this discussion.'

'But I'm almost fully recovered,' Toller protested, waving his arms to prove the point.

'Your tongue is the only part of you which has recovered, and even that is getting too much exercise. Just be quiet for a while and allow me to get on with my work.' She turned her back on him and used a twig to stir the pot in which his dressings were being boiled.

After seven days the wounds on his face and left hand needed virtually no attention, but the twin punctures in his side were still discharging. Gesalla cleaned them and changed the dressings every few hours, a regimen which necessitated re-using the meagre stock of pads and bandages she had been able to make.

Toller had little doubt that he would have died but for her ministrations, but his gratitude was tinged with concern for her safety. He guessed that the initial confusion in the fleet's landing zone must have rivalled that of the departure, but it seemed little short of a miracle to him that he and Gesalla had since remained unmolested for so long. With each passing day, as the fever abated, his sense of urgency increased.

We are leaving here in the morning, my love, he thought. *Whether you agree or not.*

He leaned back on the bed of folded quilts, trying to curb his impatience, and allowed his gaze to roam the panoramic view which the cave mouth afforded. Grassy slopes, dotted here and there with unfamiliar trees, folded gently down for about a mile to the west, to the edge of a large lake whose water was a pure indigo seeded with sun-jewels. The northern and south-ern shores were banked forests, receding and narrowing bands of a colour which – as on Land – was a composite of a million speckles ranging from lime green to deep red, representing trees at different stages of their leaf cycles. The lake stretched all the way to a western horizon composed of the ethereal blue triangles of distant mountains, above which a pure sky soared up to encompass the disk of the Old World.

It was a scene which Toller found unutterably beautiful, and in the first days in the cave he had been unable to distinguish it with any certainty from other products of his delirium. His memory of those days was patchy. It had taken him some time to understand that he had not succeeded in firing a cannon, and that Gesalla had made an independent decision to go back for him. She had tried to make little of the matter, claiming that had Leddra-vohr been victorious he would soon have advertised the fact by coming in search of her. Toller had known otherwise.

Lying in the hushed peace of early morning, watching Gesalla go about the chores she had set for herself, he felt a surge of admiration for her cour-age and resourcefulness. He would never understand how she had managed to get him into the saddle of Leddravohr's bluehorn, load up with supplies from the gondola, and lead the beast on foot for many miles before finding the cave. It would have been a considerable feat for a man, but for a slightly-built woman facing an unknown planet and all its possible dangers on her own the achievement had been truly exceptional.

Gesalla is a truly exceptional woman, Toller thought. *So how long will it be before she realises I have no intention of taking her off into the wilderness?*

The sheer impracticability of his original plan had weighed heavily on Toller after his rationality had begun to return. Without a baby to consider it might have been possible for two adults to eke out some kind of fugitive existence in the forests of Overland – but if Gesalla was not already pregnant she would see to it that she became pregnant.

It had taken him some time to appreciate that the core of the problem also contained its solution. With Leddravohr dead Prince Pouche would have become King, and Toller knew him to be a dry, dispassionate man who would abide by Kolcorron's traditional leniency with pregnant women – especially as Leddravohr was the only one who could have testified about Gesalla's use of the cannon against him.

The task ahead, Toller had decided – while doing his best to ignore the gleam of the single, persistent Overlander's lantern in the mound of rubble – was to keep Gesalla alive until she was demonstrably with child. A hundred days seemed a reasonable target, but the very act of setting a term had somehow increased and aggravated his unease about the fleeting passage of time. How was he to strike the proper balance between leaving early and only being able to travel slowly, and leaving late – when the swiftness of a deer might prove insufficient?

'What are you brooding about?' Gesalla said, removing the boiling pot from the heat.

'About you – and about preparing to leave here in the morning.'

'I told you, you aren't ready.' She knelt beside him to inspect his dressings and the touch of her hands sent a pleasurable shock racing down to his groin.

'I think another part of me is starting to recover,' he said.

'That's something else you aren't ready for.' She smiled as she dabbed his forehead with a damp cloth. 'You can have some stew instead.'

'A fine substitute,' he grumbled, making an unsuccessful attempt to touch her breasts as she slid away from him. The sudden movement of his arm, slight though it was, produced a sharp pain in his side and made him wonder how he would fare trying to get astride the bluehorn in the morning.

He pushed the worry to the back of his thoughts and watched Gesalla as she prepared a simple breakfast. She had found a flattish, slightly concave stone to use as a hob. By mingling on it tiny pinches of pikon and halvell brought from the ship, she was able to create a smoke-free heat which would not betray their whereabouts to pursuers. When she had finished warming the stew – a thick mixture of grain, pulses and shreds of salt-beef – she passed a dish of it to him and allowed him to feed himself.

Toller had been amused to note – echo of the old Gesalla he thought he had known – that among the 'essentials' she had salvaged from the gondola were dishes and table utensils. There was a poignancy about eating in such conditions, with commonplace domestic items framed in the pervasive strangeness of a virgin world; with the romance which could have suffused the moment abnegated by uncertainties and danger.

Toller was not really hungry, but he ate steadily with a determination to win back his strength as quickly as possible. Apart from occasional snuffles from the tethered bluehorn the only sounds reaching the cave from elsewhere were the rolling reports of brakka pollination discharges. The frequency of the explosions indicated that brakka were plentiful throughout the region, and were a reminder of the question which had first been posed by Gesalla – if the other plant forms of Overland were unknown on Land, why did the two worlds have the brakka in common?

Gesalla had collected handfuls of grass, leaves, flowers and berries for joint scrutiny, and – with the possible exception of the grass, upon which only a botanist could have passed judgment – all had shared the common factor of strangeness. Toller had reiterated his idea that the brakka was a universal form, one which would be found on any planet, but although he was unused to pondering such matters he recognised that the notion had an unsatisfactory philosophical feel to it, one which made him wish he could turn to Lain for guidance.

'There's another ptertha,' Gesalla exclaimed. 'Look! I can see seven or eight of them going towards the water.'

Toller looked in the direction she was indicating and had to change the focus of his eyes several times before he picked out the bubble-glints of the colourless, near-invisible spheres. They were slowly drifting down the hillside on the air flow generated by the night-time cooling of the surface.

'You're better at spotting those things than I am,' he said ruefully. 'That one yesterday was almost in my lap before I saw it.'

The ptertha which had drifted in on them soon after littlenight on the previous day had come to within ten paces of Toller's bed, and in spite of what he had learned from Lain the nearness of it had inspired much of the dread he would have experienced on Land. Had he been mobile he would probably have been unable to prevent himself from hurling his sword through it. The globe had hovered nearby for a few seconds before sailing away down the hillside in a series of slow ruminative bounds.

'Your face was a picture!' Gesalla paused in her eating to parody an expression of fear.

'I've just thought of something,' Toller said. 'Have we any writing materials?'

'No. Why?'

'You and I are the only two people on the whole of Overland who know what Lain wrote about the ptertha. I wish I had thought of telling Chakkell. All those hours together on the ship – and I didn't even mention it!'

'You weren't to know there would be brakka trees and ptertha here. You thought you were leaving all that behind.'

Toller was gripped by a new and greater urgency which had nothing to do with his personal aspirations. 'Listen, Gesalla, this is the most important thing either of us will ever have the chance to do. You have got to make sure that Pouche and Chakkell hear and understand Lain's ideas.

'If we leave the brakka trees alone, to live out their time and die naturally, the ptertha here will never become our enemies. Even a modest amount of culling – the way they did it in Chamteth – is probably too much because the ptertha there had turned pink and that's a sign that ...' He stopped speaking as he saw that Gesalla was staring at him, her expression of odd blend of concern and accusation.

'Is there anything the matter?'

'You said *I* had to make sure that Pouche and ...' Gesalla set her dish down and came to kneel beside him. 'What's going to happen to us, Toller?'

He forced himself to laugh then exaggerated the effects of the pain it caused, playing for time in which to cover up his blunder. 'We're going to found our own dynasty, that's what is going to happen to us. Do you think I would let any harm come to you?'

'I know you wouldn't – and that's why you frightened me.'

'Gesalla, all I meant was that we must leave a message here ... or somewhere else where it will be found and taken to the King. I'm not able to move around much, so I have to turn the responsibility over to you. I'll show you how to make charcoal, and then we'll find something to ...'

Gesalla was slowly shaking her head and her eyes were magnified by the first tears he had ever seen there. 'It's all unreal, isn't it? It's all just a dream.'

'Flying to Overland was just a dream – once – but now we're here, and in spite of everything we're still alive.' He drew her down to lie beside him, her head cushioned on his shoulder. 'I don't know what's going to happen to us, Gesalla. All I can promise is that ... how did you put it? ... that we are not going to surrender life to the butchers. That has to be enough for us. Now, why don't you rest and let me watch over you, just for a change?'

'All right, Toller.' Gesalla made herself comfortable, fitting her body to his whilst being careful of his injuries, and in an amazingly short time she was asleep. Her transition from anxious wakefulness to the tranquillity of sleep was announced by the faintest of snores, and Toller smiled as he stored the event in his memory for use in future bantering. The only home they were likely to know on Overland would be built of such insubstantial timbers.

He tried to stay awake, to watch over her, but the vapours of an insidious weariness were coiling in his head – and the last Overlander's lantern was again glowing in the rock pile.

The only way to escape from it was to close his eyes ...

The soldier standing over him was holding a sword.

Toller tried to move, to take some defensive action in spite of his weakness and the encumbrance of Gesalla's body draped across his own, then he saw that the sword in the soldier's hand was Leddravohr's, and even in his befuddled state he was able to assess the situation correctly.

It was too late to do anything, anything at all – because his little domain had already been surrounded, conquered and overrun.

Further evidence came from the shifting of the light as other soldiers moved around beyond the immediate area of the cave mouth. There were the sounds of men beginning to talk as they realised that silence was no longer required, and from somewhere nearby came the snorting and slithering of a bluehorn as it made its way down the hill. Toller squeezed Gesalla's shoulder to bring her awake, and although she remained immobile he felt her spasm of alarm.

The soldier with the sword moved away and his place was taken by a slit-eyed major, whose head was in near-silhouette against the sky as he looked down at Toller. 'Can you stand up?'

'No – he's too ill,' Gesalla said, rising to a kneeling position.

'I can stand.' Toller caught her arm. 'Help me, Gesalla – I prefer to be on my feet at this time.' With her assistance he achieved a standing position and faced the major. He was dully surprised to find that, when he should have been oppressed by failure and prospects of death, he was discomfited by the trivial fact that he was naked.

'Well, major,' he said, 'what is it you want of me?'

The major's face was professionally impassive. 'The King will speak to you now.'

He moved aside and Toller saw the paunchy figure of Chakkell approaching. His dress was subdued and plain, suitable for cross-country riding, but suspended from his neck was a huge blue jewel which Toller had seen only once before, when it had been worn by Prad. Chakkell had retrieved Leddravohr's sword from the first soldier and was carrying it with the blade leaning on his right shoulder, a neutral position which could quickly become one of attack. His swarthy well-padded face and brown scalp were gleaming in the equatorial heat.

He came within two paces of Toller and surveyed him from head to toe. 'Well, Maraquine, I promised I would remember you.'

'Majesty, I daresay I have given you and your loved ones good cause to remember me.' Toller was aware of Gesalla drawing closer to him, and for her sake he went on to rid his words of any possible ambiguity. 'A fall of a thousand miles would have ...'

'Don't start rhyming at me again,' Chakkell cut in. 'And lie down, man, before you fall down!'

He nodded to Gesalla, ordering her to ease Toller down on to the quilts, and signalled for the major and the rest of his escort to withdraw. When they had retreated out of earshot he squatted in the dirt and, unexpectedly, lobbed the black sword over Toller and into the dimness of the cave.

'We are going to have a brief conversation,' he said, 'and not a word of it is to be repeated. Is that clear?'

Toller nodded uncertainly, wondering if he dared introduce hope to the confusion of his thoughts and emotions.

'There is a certain amount of ill-feeling towards you among the nobility and among the military who completed the crossing,' Chakkell said comfortably. 'After all, not many men have committed regicide twice in the space of three days. It can be dealt with, however. There is a great air of practicality in our new statelet – and the settlers appreciate that loyalty to one living king is more beneficial to the health than a similar regard for two dead kings. Are you wondering about Pouche?'

'Does he live?'

'He lives, but he was quick to see that the subtleties of his kind of statesmanship would be inappropriate to the situation we have here. He is more than happy to relinquish his claims to the throne – if a chair made from old gondola parts can be dignified with that name.'

It came to Toller that he was seeing Chakkell as he had never seen him before – cheerful, loquacious, at ease with his environment. Was it simply that he preferred supremacy for himself and his offspring in a seedling society to preordained secondary role in the long-established and static Kolcorron? Or was it that he possessed an adventurous spirit which had been liberated by the unique circumstances of the great migration? Looking closely at Chakkell, encouraged by his instincts, Toller experienced a sudden upwelling of relief and the purest kind of joy.

Gesalla and I are going to have children, he thought. *And it doesn't matter that she and I will have to die some day, because our children will have children, and the future stretches out before us … on and on … on and on, except that …*

One reality dissolved around Toller and he found himself standing on a rocky outcrop to the west of Ro-Atabri. He was gazing through his telescope at the sprawled body of his brother, reading that last communication which had nothing to do with revenge or personal regrets, but which – as befitted Lain's compassionate intellect – addressed itself to the welfare of millions as yet unborn.

'Prince … Majesty …' Toller raised himself on one elbow the better to confront Chakkell with the truth which had been placed in his keeping, but the incautious torsion of his body lanced him with an agony which stilled his voice and dropped him back into his bedding.

'Leddravohr came very near to killing you, didn't he?' Chakkell's voice had lost all of its lightness.

'That doesn't matter,' Toller said, smoothing Gesalla's hair as she bent over the renewed fire of the wounds in his side. 'You knew my brother and what he was?'

'Yes.'

'Very well. Forget all about me – my brother lives in my body, and he is speaking to you through my mouth ...' Toller went on, battling through riptides of nausea and weakness to paint a word-picture of the tortured triangular relationship involving humankind, the brakka tree and the ptertha. He described the symbiotic partnership between brakka and ptertha, using inspiration and informed imagination where real knowledge failed.

As in all cases of true symbiosis, both parties derived benefit from the association. The ptertha bred in high levels of the atmosphere, nourished – in all probability – by minute traces of pikon and halvell, or miglign gas, or brakka pollen, or by some derivation from the four. In return, the ptertha sought out all organisms who threatened the welfare of the brakka. Employing the blind forces of random mutation, they varied their internal composition until they chanced on an effective toxin, at which point – the path having been signposted – they concentrated and refined and *aimed* it to create a weapon capable of scourging the scourge, of removing from existence all traces of that which did not deserve to exist.

The way ahead for mankind on Overland lay in treating the brakka with the respect it deserved. Only dead trees should be used for their yield of super-hard materials and power crystals, and if the supply seemed insufficient it was incumbent on the immigrants to develop substitutes or to modify their way of life accordingly.

If they failed to do so, the history of humanity on Land would, inevitably, be repeated on Overland ...

'I admit to being impressed,' Chakkell said when Toller had finally finished speaking. 'There is no real proof that what you say is true, but it is worthy of serious consideration. Luckily for our generation, which has seen its full share of hardships, there is no need to make any hasty decisions. We have enough to worry about in the meantime.'

'You must not think that way,' Toller urged. 'You are the *ruler* ... and you have the unique opportunity ... the unique responsibility ...' He sighed and stopped speaking, yielding to a tiredness which seemed to dim the very heavens.

'Save your strength for another time,' Chakkell said gently. 'I should let you rest now, but before I leave I'd like to know one more thing. Between you and Leddravohr – was it a fair contest?'

'It was almost fair ... until he destroyed my sword with brakka slime.'

'But you overcame him just the same.'

'It was required of me.' Toller was experiencing the mysticism which can come with illness and utter weariness. 'I was born to overcome Leddravohr.'

'Perhaps he knew that.'

Toller forced his gaze to steady on Chakkell's face. 'I don't know what you
...'

'I wonder if Leddravohr had any heart for all of this, for our brave new
beginning,' Chakkell said. 'I wonder if he pursued you – alone – because he
divined that you were his Bright Road?'

'That idea,' Toller whispered, 'has little appeal for me.'

'You need to rest.' Chakkell stood up and addressed himself to Gesalla.
'Look after this man for my sake as well as your own – I have work for him.
I think it would be better not to move him for some days yet, but you seem
quite comfortable here. Do you need any supplies?'

'We could use more fresh water, Majesty,' Gesalla said. 'Apart from that
our wants are already satisfied.'

'Yes.' Chakkell studied her face for a moment. 'I'm going to take your
bluehorn because we have only seven all told, and the breeding must begin
as soon as possible, but I will post guards nearby. Call them when you deem
you are ready to leave here. Does that suit you?'

'Yes, Majesty – we are indebted.'

'I trust your patient will remember that when his health is recovered.'
Chakkell turned and strode away towards the waiting soldiers, moving with
the energetic assurance peculiar to those who feel themselves to be responding to the calls of destiny.

Later, when silence had again returned to the hillside, Toller awoke to see
that Gesalla was passing the time by sorting and arranging her collection of
leaves and flowers. She had spread them on the ground before her, and her
lips were moving silently as she thoughtfully placed each specimen in an
order of her own devising. Beyond her the vivid purity of Overland sparkled
and advanced on the eye.

Toller cautiously raised himself in the bed. He glanced at the mound of
rocky fragments in the rear of the cave, then turned his head away quickly,
unwilling to risk seeing the tiny lantern gleaming at him. Only when it had
ceased to shine altogether would he know for certain that the fever had
entirely left his system, and until then he had no wish to be reminded of
how close he had come to death and to losing all that Gesalla meant to
him.

She looked up from her emergent patterns. 'Did you see something back
there?'

'There's nothing,' he said, mustering a smile. 'Nothing at all.'

'But I've noticed you staring at those rocks before. What is your secret?'
Intrigued, and playing a game for his benefit, Gesalla came to him and knelt
to share his line of sight. The movement brought her face very close to his,
and he saw her eyes widen in surprise.

'Toller!' Her voice was that of a child, hushed with wonder. 'There's something shining in there!'

She rose to her feet with all the speed of which her weightless body was capable, stepped over him and ran into the cave.

Prey to a strange fear, Toller tried to call out a warning, but his throat was dry and the power of speech seemed to have deserted him. And Gesalla was already throwing the outermost stones aside. He watched numbly as she put her hands into the mound, lifted something heavy and bore it out to the brighter light at the entrance to the cave.

She knelt beside him, cradling the find on her thighs. It was a large flake of dark grey rock – but it was unlike any rock Toller had ever seen before. Running across and through it, integral to and yet differing from the stone, was a broad band of material which was white, but more than white, reflecting the sun like the waters of a distant lake at dawn.

'It's beautiful,' Gesalla breathed, 'but what is it?'

'I don't …' Grimacing with pain, Toller reached for his clothing, found a pocket and brought out the strange memento given to him by his father. He placed it against the gleaming stratum in the stone, confirming what he already knew – that they were identical in composition.

Gesalla took the nugget from him and ran a fingertip across its polished surface. 'Where did you get this?'

'My father … my real father … gave it to me in Chamteth just before he died. He told me he found it long ago. Before I was born. In the Redant province.'

'I feel strange.' Gesalla shivered as she looked up at the misty, enigmatic, watchful disk of the Old World. 'Was ours not the first migration, Toller? Has it all happened before?'

'I think so – perhaps many times – but the important thing for us is to ensure that it never …' His weariness forced Toller to leave the sentence unfinished.

He laid the back of his hand on the lustrous strip within the rock, captivated by its coolness and its strangeness – and by silent intimations that, somehow, he could make the future differ from the past.

If you've enjoyed these books and would like to read more, you'll find literally thousands of classic Science Fiction & Fantasy titles through the **SF Gateway**

✳

For the new home of
Science Fiction & Fantasy . . .

✳

For the most comprehensive collection
of classic SF on the internet . . .

✳

Visit the SF Gateway

www.sfgateway.com

Bob Shaw (1931–1996)

Bob Shaw was born in Belfast in 1931. After working in engineering, aircraft design and journalism he became a full time writer in 1975. Among his novels are *Orbitsville*, *A Wreath of Stars*, *The Ragged Astronauts* and his best-known work *Other Days, Other Eyes*, based on the Nebula Award-nominated 'Light of Other Days', the story that made his reputation. Although his SF novels and stories were for the most part serious, Shaw was well-known in fannish circles for his sense of humour, and his witty 'Serious Scientific Talks' were a favourite of attendees at Eastercons. Bob Shaw won two Hugos and three BSFA Awards. He died in 1996.